KT-555-408

Elizabeth George is the internationally bestselling author of highly acclaimed novels of psychological suspense in the Inspector Lynley series. Her work has been honoured with the Anthony and Agatha awards, the Grand Prix de Littérature Policière, and the MIMI, Germany's prestigious prize for suspense fiction. Her novels have been adapted for television by BBC TV. Elizabeth George lives on Whidbey Island, in the state of Washington. Visit her website at www.elizabethgeorgeonline.com

Praise for A BANQUET OF CONSEQUENCES and Elizabeth George:

'She's a designer of fastidious mosaics that never fail to intrigue.'                                                                 *Guardian*

'Ms George is the connoisseur's crime writer. Like fine wine, her words need to be savoured.'                        *Sunday Express*

'The author writes brilliantly and has an incredible ability to set a scene and create characters you want to know more about.' *Sun*

'Her crime novels combine Victorian craftsmanship, psychological observation and ingenious plotting. George's celebrated attention to detail keeps the reader totally immersed. Bliss.'
*Saga*

'Presses all the buttons to make us hoover her stuff up'
*Daily Telegraph*

'George's mystery unfolds with great psychological depth, finely drawn characters and gorgeous portraits of the English countryside.'                                                          *Washington Post*

'The most demanding and satisfying of the many detective novels by Elizabeth George featuring Havers and her New Scotland Yard partner, Inspector Thomas Lynley . . . The author combines an old-school aptitude for twist-riddled plots with modern psychological insights, ethical agonizing, realistic violence and sardonic humor.'                          *Wall Street Journal*

ELIZABETH GEORGE

# A BANQUET OF CONSEQUENCES

HODDER

First published in Great Britain in 2015 by Hodder & Stoughton
An Hachette UK company

First published in paperback in 2016

3

Copyright © Susan Elizabeth George 2015

The right of Elizabeth George to be identified as the Author of the Work has
been asserted by her in accordance with the Copyright, Designs and Patents
Act 1988.

A CIP catalogue record for this title is available from the British Library

B Format ISBN 978 1 444 78659 0
A Format ISBN 978 1 44 478665 1

Typeset in Plantin Light by
Palimpsest Book Production Limited, Falkirk, Stirlingshire

Printed and bound by CPI Group (UK) Ltd, Croydon, CRO 4YY

Hodder & Stoughton policy is to use papers that are natural, renewable and
recyclable products and made from wood grown in sustainable forests. The
logging and manufacturing processes are expected to conform to the
environmental regulations of the country of origin.

Hodder & Stoughton Ltd
Carmelite House
50 Victoria Embankment
London EC4Y ODZ

www.hodder.co.uk

In loving memory of Jesse Vallera:
every moment in his presence was
an absolute privilege.

'. . . the past is so hard to shift. It comes with us like a chaperone, standing between us and the newness of the present – the new chance.'
*Why Be Happy When You Could Be Normal?*
Jeannette Winterson

'Sooner or later, we all sit down to a banquet of consequences.'
*Under the Wide and Starry Sky*
Nancy Horan

# 8 December

★

THIRTY-NINE MONTHS BEFORE

Since it was only to be a weekend jaunt to Marrakesh, Lily Foster reckoned they could use one suitcase, and a carry-on at that. What did they need to take, really? It had been deadly cold, grey, and wet in London since the middle of November, but it wasn't going to be that way in North Africa. They would spend most of their time lounging round the pool, anyway, and when they weren't doing that, they'd be getting romantic in their room for which, obviously, they needed no clothes at all.

Packing took less than ten minutes. Sandals, summer trousers, a T-shirt for William. Sandals, a clingy frock, and a scarf for her. Swimming suits for them both and a few other essentials. That was it. Then began the wait which – confirmed by a glance at the plastic wall clock ticking away above the cooker – should have been less than thirty minutes. But it stretched instead into more than two hours during which time she texted him and she phoned him as well, only to receive no response. Just his pleasant voice saying 'This is Will. Tell me and I'll tell you back,' to which she said, 'Where are you, William? I thought the job was only in Shoreditch. And why're you still there in this rotten weather? Ring me soon as you get this, OK?'

Lily went to the window. The afternoon was spitting rain outside, the sky dark and angry with erupting clouds. In the best of weather, this particular housing estate was grim: a mixture of filthy brick blocks of flats tossed by the handful across a level plain, which was crisscrossed by cracked and heaving pavements that the residents ignored in favour of trudging across a dying patchwork of lawns. In weather like this, the place looked like a death trap and what was at risk of extermination was hope. They didn't belong here, and Lily knew it. It was bad for her; it was worse for William. But it was what they could afford for now and it was where they would remain until she built her business larger than what it was and William had his own on firmer footing.

That part was tricky: William's business. He regularly argued with his clients, and people didn't like that when they were paying someone to work for them.

'You *do* have to take on board what people think,' she kept telling him.

'People,' he countered, 'need to stay out of my way. I can't concentrate when they yammer at me. Why don't they get that? It's not like I don't tell them straightaway.'

Well, yes, right, Lily thought. Telling people was part of the problem. William needed to stop doing that.

Lily frowned down at the street. There was no one on the pavements below, certainly no William with his collar up, making a dash from his car to the narrow tower that contained their building's lift. Instead there was only a woman on a balcony of the block of flats sitting at an angle to theirs. She was gathering laundry in her arms, her bright yellow sari whipped by the wind. As for the rest of the buildings' balconies with their lines of dispirited laundry and their children's toys and their few haggard-looking plants and – always – their satellite dishes, whatever they contained was being left to fend for itself in the weather.

Through the window Lily could dimly hear the unrelenting city noise: the squeal of tyres on wet pavement as a car took a corner too swiftly, the metallic roar of a building site where yet something else was being redeveloped nearby but out of view, an ambulance siren on its way to hospital, and, much closer, the *thump thunka thump* of a too loud bass underscoring someone's musical preference.

She texted William again. After two minutes of no response, she rang him as well. She said, 'William, you *must* be getting my texts. Unless . . . Oh damn it, you haven't got your mobile on silent again, have you? You *know* I hate it when you do that. And this is important. I don't like to say but . . . Oh, hell, hell, hell. Look. I've a surprise planned for our anniversary. I know, I know. You'll say ten months can't be an anniversary but you know what I mean, so don't be difficult. Anyway, this surprise involves our *being* somewhere at a particular time, so if you're just not replying because you're playing silly buggers for some reason, please ring me back.'

And then there was nothing to do but to wait. She watched the minutes tick by and she tried to reassure herself that they had plenty of time to get to Stansted. All William had to do, really, was walk in the door because she had their passports in her bag, she had the tickets printed already, and every plan that needed to be made when one journeyed to another country even for a weekend had been made by her.

She realised that she should have told him that morning. But he'd been displeased with how the job in Shoreditch was shaping up, and she hadn't liked to break into his thoughts. Sometimes his clients took a bit of work on his part to bring on board, for even when William had a superb idea that he knew would work on their property, people liked to be in charge of things, even when they hired an expert, which was definitely what William Goldacre was. Expert, visionary, artist, and labourer. Give him your weed-choked garden and he worked magic.

When she finally saw his ancient Fiesta rounding the corner from Heneage Street, she had been waiting for him for four hours, and the Marrakesh plan was shot to hell. The money was wasted, they were stuck, and Lily was looking for someone to blame.

*Where* had he been? *What* had he been doing? *Why* hadn't he answered his bloody phone? Had he just done that early on – it was *one* simple thing, William – she could have told him about her plans and advised him to meet her at the airport. They could have even now been sitting happily shoulder to shoulder on that stupid plane as it winged them towards sunshine and a weekend of simple pleasure.

Lily was winding herself up as he got out of his car. She was choosing her words. *Inconsiderate* and *thoughtless* were at the top of her list. But then she caught sight of his face as he passed under one of the street lamps. She saw the set of his shoulders, and the way he walked towards the lift in the evening darkness. She thought, Oh no, and she knew what had occurred. He'd lost the Shoreditch client. That was two clients in three months, with both projects ending in acrimony, anger, and accusation. That would be on William's part. On the part of the clients would be a demand for the return of a rather hefty deposit, most of which would already have been spent on supplies.

Lily watched his progress from pool of light to pool of light till he disappeared from view. Then she took the carry-on through to the bedroom. She shoved it out of sight under the bed. By the time she'd got back to the sitting room, William's key was in the door lock, the door was opening, and she was sitting on the sagging sofa with her smartphone in her hand. She was checking her email. 'Pleasant trip, darling!' from her mum didn't do much to lift her spirits.

William saw her at once – he could hardly help it as the place was so small – and he averted his eyes. Then his gaze came back to her again, and she noticed that it shifted from her face to her phone. He said, 'Sorry.'

She said, 'I texted and rang you, William.'

'I know.'

'Why didn't you respond?'

'I broke the phone.'

He had a rucksack with him. As if to prove to her the truth of what he was saying, he unzipped the thing and dumped its contents. His mobile toppled to one side, and he handed it over. It was destroyed.

'Did you drive over it or something?' Lily asked him.

'I smashed it with a shovel.'

'But—'

'You kept . . . I don't know, Lily. I couldn't answer, but still you kept . . . It was the *ringing* and then the *buzzing* and every bloody thing was happening at once over there. My head felt like it was on the verge of exploding and the only thing I could do to make it all stop was to use a shovel on the phone.'

'What's going on?'

William left the contents of the rucksack where he'd strewn them. He crossed the room to a slingback chair. He flung himself into it, and she saw his face clearly. He was double-blinking in that way he had when things were moving from bad to what was going to be worse.

'It's no good,' he said.

'What?'

'Me. This. The whole bloody thing. I'm no good. It's no good. End of story.'

'Did you lose the Shoreditch clients, then?'

'What do you think? Losing things is what I do, isn't it? My car keys, my notebooks, my rucksack, my clients. You as well, Lily, and don't deny it. I'm losing you. Which is – let's face it – what you wanted to tell me, isn't it? You rang and you texted and it was all to get me to ring you back so you could do to me pretty much what everyone does. End things. Right?'

He was triple-blinking. He needed to be calm. Lily knew from experience there were very few ways to calm him if he got too far along in the direction he was taking, so she said, 'I was taking you to Marrakesh, actually. I'd found a hotel on the cheap, a pool and all the trimmings. It was supposed to be a surprise weekend and I should have told you this morning – at least that I had a surprise trip planned – but that would have meant . . . Oh, I don't know.' She ended rather lamely with, 'I thought it would be fun.'

'We've no money for that sort of thing.'

'My mum lent it me.'

'So now your parents know how bad things are? What a loser I am? What did you tell them?'

'Not him, her. Just my mum. I didn't tell her anything. And she didn't ask. She's not *like* that, William. She doesn't intrude.' *Not like your mum* was what she didn't add.

He heard it anyway because his look became sharp the way it always became when the subject of his mother came up between them. But he didn't go there and instead he said, 'I should have seen from the first they were bloody mad fools, but I didn't. Why do I never see what people are like? They say they want something special and I can give them something special and they *will* love it if they only let me get at it. But no, they want drawings and sketches and approval and control and daily receipts and I can't work like that.'

He stood. He walked to the same window at which she'd waited for so long for him. She didn't know what to tell him, exactly, but what she wanted to say was that *if* he couldn't work under the aegis of someone else, *if* he could only work alone, then he would have to learn how to deal with people because *if* he didn't learn that, then he would fail over and over and over again. She wanted to tell him that he wasn't being reasonable with people, that he couldn't expect them to hand over their gardens or even part of their gardens to his creative impulse. What if they don't like what you have in mind? she wanted to ask him. But she'd said it before and she'd asked it before and here they were again where they kept ending up.

'It's London,' he said abruptly, to the window glass.

'What's London?'

'This. It. Me. London's the reason. People here . . . They're different. They don't get me and I don't get them. I've got to get out of here. It's the only answer because I'm not going to freeload off you.'

He swung from the window then. The look on his face comprised, she knew, the very same expression he wore when his clients asked questions he deemed unreasonable. It signalled that he'd made his mind up about something. She reckoned she was seconds away from learning what that was.

He told her. 'Dorset.'

'Dorset?'

'I've got to go home.'

'This is your home.'

'You know what I mean. I've spent all day thinking and that's the answer. I'm going back to Dorset. I'm starting over.'

*Spitalfields*
*London*

She got him out of the flat, no matter the rain. She suggested the Pride of Spitalfields. It wasn't far, a bit gastro pub-ish with its creamy exterior and deep blue awnings dripping with rain, but inside there was still a decent cider to be had and usually a table or two tucked away in a corner. He was reluctant to go – 'I can't afford it, Lily, and I won't let you pay.'

She told him it was money from her mum to spend in Morocco and what did it matter as they were in things together, weren't they?

'It's . . . it's unseemly,' he said, and his use of that word suggested his mum was in one way or another behind every decision he'd made since falling out with his clients: from smashing his mobile into oblivion to declaring a need to return to Dorset.

Without doing what needed to be done to school herself to patience, she said to him, 'You've talked to her, haven't you? You told her about this before you told me. *Why* did you do that?'

'This isn't about my mum,' William said.

'Everything's about your mum,' she told him.

She entered the Pride of Spitalfields, and her annoyance with him was such that she found she didn't much care if he followed. But follow he did and they sat at the only table left, directly next to the door to the ladies', which shot a shaft of near blinding fluorescent light on their faces every time someone ducked in or out. Music was playing. An iPod or iPhone with a hookup to something of a satellite nature because it was a country and western mix of oldies only, Johnny Cash foremost with dashes of Willie Nelson, Patsy Cline, Garth Brooks, Randy Travis, and the Judds.

Lily said, 'You didn't answer me, William.'

He was looking round the pub but brought his gaze back to her. 'Untrue. I told you that—'

'You tried to misdirect me is what you did. So let's go back. You spoke to your mum. You told her what's happened before you told me.'

'I said this isn't about my mum.'

'Let me guess at the conversation. She told you to come home to Dorset. She told you that you can "start" again there. She promised help: hers, your stepdad's. When are you breaking *away* from them?'

'I'm not intending to live with Mum. At least not permanently. It's only till I can get established. It's for the best.'

'God, I can even hear her voice in you,' Lily fumed.

'I'm thinking of Sherborne,' he said. 'Or Somerset. Probably Yeovil because it's less costly but the business itself will do better in Sherborne. There's money there. Even Mum says—'

'I don't want to hear what "Mum" says.'

'It's London, Lily. It's attempting to have *any* kind of business in London.'

'I have a business. It's working out.'

'Tattoos, yes. Well, this is London after all. But what I'm trying to do . . . having my kind of business, what I'm *good* at, here . . . People don't connect the way I need to connect in London. You've said that yourself: the perfect place to be anonymous but if one wants anything more than anonymity, it's not going to happen. I've *heard* you say that. It's no go for me here. It's only because of you I've hacked it for this long.'

She looked towards the bar. She thought uselessly about how trendy Spitalfields was becoming as the City of London inched towards it one hideous glass tower block at a time. Even here – God, not that far from where Jack the Ripper haunted the narrow Whitechapel streets – there were young women wearing pencil skirts and young men in suits flirting with each other as they sipped white wine. White wine, for God's sake. Here. In the East End. They were only a sign that nothing ever stayed the same, that progress was relentless and that 'making progress' applied not only to society and economics and science and everything else but to people as well. She hated that: the very idea of constant change to which one had to become accustomed. But she also knew when fighting it was hopeless.

She said to him, 'I suppose that's it, isn't it?'

'What's it?'

'You and I. What else?'

He reached for her hand across the table. His palm was damp where it covered her balled fist. He said, 'You can come to Dorset as well. You can set up a shop there. I've already spoken to—'

'Yes. Right. To your mum. And she's assured you that there's plenty of scope for tattoos in a place like Dorset.'

'Well . . . yes, if it comes to that. You're reading her wrong, Lil. She wants you there as much as I do.'

14 December

*Spitalfields*
*London*

Will hadn't expected that Lily would be the first to move out of the flat. He'd more or less depended upon her to remain there – a constant presence in his life till he himself had packed up and departed. But two days later she was gone and this left him four days on his own till his mother and stepfather showed up with the bakery van to cart back to Dorset those of his belongings that didn't fit into the Fiesta.

Four days on his own put him where he didn't want to be and that was with his head as his only companion. Inside his head resided voices. They informed him of what he already knew: he'd wrecked his chances for a life with Lily; he'd proved once again what a loser he was; he'd been a wanking weirdo from the day of his birth and a look in the mirror'll show you that, Will. Which was what he did, of course. He walked into the bathroom and looked in the mirror and saw those things he hated about himself. His laughable height. *What are you, a dwarf?* A deformed right ear. *Your dad's a plastic surgeon and he wouldn't even bloody operate on you?* Thick eyebrows forming a peak over his eyes. *Got a gorilla in your make-up, laddie?* Cupid lips that looked like something off a doll.

*You are one arse-ugly bloke, my man. She didn't see past it. She couldn't. Who could? Gave her an out, and she took it mate and who can blame her? How long you think it took her, boyo, to spread 'em wide for someone else? And someone who can do it the*

*way it's meant to be done. No excuses no pills no fast and furious
and sorry but you just get me going, woman. The real thing instead,
which is what – let's face it – you were never up to.*

He rang his gran. He meant it to distract himself from what
was going on in his head. But when he told her he was returning
to Dorset, she said, 'Don't be a fool, Guillermo,' in her harsh,
smoker's Colombian voice. 'This plan of yours. You make a
mistake. You talk to Carlos about this, *si*? He tell you the
same.'

But there was no point in talking to Charlie. Will's brother
had a magical life, the polar opposite of Will's in every way.

'Dorset?' he would say. 'Fuck it, Will. Don't go to Dorset.
You're seeing her as the *solution*, you idiot, when she's been
your problem for twenty-five years.'

Charlie wouldn't believe what their grandmother didn't
believe what Lily couldn't believe and that was the imperman-
ency of this arrangement. Caroline Goldacre didn't want her
son home indefinitely any more than her son wanted it. She
herself had said, 'We're calling this a temporary arrangement,
Will. You do understand that, don't you?' and she hadn't allowed
any plans to be made until he agreed: a few weeks to sort
himself out and get reestablished somewhere. Sherborne, he
thought. It would have to be Sherborne.

She told him he would have to wait in London till she and
his stepfather could get away. The bakery didn't operate on
Sundays, so they would drive up to London on Sunday. He'd
be fine till then, wouldn't he? He said he would. But then Lily
left.

His mind had started roiling shortly thereafter and the voices
in his head were unrelenting. After twenty-four hours, he rang
his mum and said couldn't he come down in advance of Sunday?
He'd bring some of his gear in the Fiesta and then on Sunday
they could all return and pick up the rest.

'Darling, don't be silly,' his mother replied kindly. 'Surely
you can survive till Sunday. Can't you?' And then carefully,
'Will, you *are* taking your medications properly, aren't you?'

He said that he was. He didn't tell her that Lily had left. He didn't want her to associate the two: his meds and Lily. There was no point.

Four days stretched out like the creation of toffee. There was nothing to distract him from who he was. By the day on which his mother arrived, Will had taken to pacing the floor and hitting himself lightly on the forehead. When the hour of her appearance began its slow approach, he started waiting at the window like an abandoned dog.

Thus he saw the bakery van cruising into the street. He saw his mother get out, as usual, to direct his stepfather into a parking spot. She waved her arms and strode to the driver's window to have a word. More arm-waving ensued until poor old Alastair had managed to dock the vehicle without crashing it into another.

Will felt the bad rising within him as he watched. He tried to quell it. But his eyes began their double blinking and deep within him from a place he could not manage to harness, the words bubbled up. 'Cocksucking storm troop here it is.' He locked his hand over his mouth as his eyelids danced. 'Fucker fucker fucker bastard rain ice.' He backed off from the window and tried to strangle them off. But still they came forth like foul effluent emerging from a broken sewage pipe. 'Whore slag whoreson slough off pantering.'

The doorbell rang. He stumbled to the buzzer and released the lock that would allow them to ring for the lift. He slapped himself hard and could feel no pain. 'Fuckall merry men Robin Hood heap.'

He swung the door open but retreated across the room. He raised his wrist to his teeth and he bit down hard.

He heard their voices coming his way, his mother's soft and Alastair's gruff. He heard her say, 'It'll work out well,' and then they were coming into his flat.

She spoke first, a reference to his ringing them into the lift without a query as to who they were. 'Will, love,' she said, 'you really ought not to do that without seeing who's there. It could be anyone, and in this part of town . . .' Her words sank into silence as she took him in.

He was triple-blinking. He clutched his stomach to try to hold back what came out like a scourge intended for her alone. 'Hot cunt cold cunt doggy meat pork.'

She didn't react other than to say, 'Oh my dear.' Quickly, she came across the room to him. She took him into her arms. He clung to her, but the words continued to pour from within him, so he broke away and went to the wall. There he began to bang his head, but still they came on.

He heard his mother say, 'Darling, it's only a seizure. It's only words. You're quite fine behind them. But you must try—'

He laughed insanely. 'Bitch cock Broadmoor.'

'Not a bad idea,' he heard Alastair mutter.

'Let me handle this, Alastair,' his mother said sharply. 'If you could just begin to gather his things . . .? Perhaps take them out to the van . . . ?'

'Where's his gear, then?' Alastair said. 'Will, lad. Have you not packed? Did you not remember that your mum and I were coming?'

'Obviously, he hasn't been able . . . You'll have to . . . No. We'll just take some of his clothing for now and Lily can send the rest afterwards. I'll write her a note. God knows why she's not here. Will, where's Lily?'

'Lily cunt cock fuck the troubadour sings.'

The words were louder now. He pounded his fist on the wall. He felt his mother's hand close over his arm and try to draw him into the middle of the room, but he jerked away and made for the kitchen because if nothing else a knife was there and he could cut out his tongue or do something to pain himself deeply, for it seemed that only deeply felt pain was going to make the Wording cease.

'Stop this, William!' his mother cried. He heard her come after him. He felt her arms come round him. 'Please.'

'Caro,' Alastair said from the sitting room, 'p'rhaps the lad doesn't want to go.'

'He has to,' she replied. 'Look at the state of him. Will, listen to me. D'you want me to ring for an ambulance? Do you want to be taken to hospital? Elsewhere? I believe you don't want that, so you must sort yourself out at once.'

'I could ring Lily's mobile,' Alastair said. 'I could ask her to come. Isn't her shop nearby? Would she be working today?'

'Don't be foolish. It's Sunday. Look around. She's left. And Lily's the problem, not the solution. Just listen to him. You can hear it yourself.'

'But the words don't mean—'

'They mean what they mean.'

Will tore himself from his mother's grasp and clutched at his skull. 'Forks knives and spoons because rainfall torrent of floor to fuck. And you too both of you fucking like goats so I can shag is what shag shag shag cause that's how she wants it like Jesus and Mary did to each other cause what else was he doing for those first thirty years?'

'Holy God,' Alastair said.

'That's enough, William.' Caroline turned him to her and he knew that he was quadruple-blinking because he could barely see her. She said, 'You must stop this at once. If you aren't able, I'm going to have to ring nine-nine-nine and they'll take you God only knows where and you don't want that. Where are your medicines? Are they packed? Did you pack them? Will, answer me. *Now*.'

'And when he did from the cross and the fucking cow bitch put the bastard in a bun.'

Caroline said, 'This is no good. Alastair, will you wait below?'

'I hate to leave you, luv.'

'It's all right. You know I can handle him if it comes down to it. He won't hurt me. He just needs to get calm.'

'If you think . . .'

'I do.'

'Right, then. Ring me on my mobile. I'll be below.' The door closed as Alastair left the flat.

Then, 'Enough!' Caroline said sharply. 'I said *enough*. Do

you hear me, Will? You're acting like a two year old, and I won't have it. *How* did you let yourself get into this state when you know very well what to do to control it? God in heaven, can you *not* manage five minutes on your own?'

'Cunt in a bottle.'

She shook him hard, a teeth-rattling shake. She swung him round to face the sitting room. 'Get out of my sight,' she snapped. 'Get yourself in order, and do it now. You know what it takes, so do it. And do *not* make me tell you more than once.'

*Spitalfields*
*London*

Outside, Alastair MacKerron went directly to the bakery van. He was shaken more than usual by what was going on with Will. This was the worst he'd ever seen.

He'd had high hopes at first when Will had taken himself off to London. He'd found himself a girlfriend – bit edgy with all her piercings and those mad tattoos, but what did it matter at the end of the day? – and he'd managed to establish a business that did fairly well for a bit. He'd even made contact with his gran, and if he'd ignored his mum's advice to keep well clear of his dad and his dad's infant bride, what did that really matter either? He was setting off on his own at last, and the occasional upset surely wouldn't be enough to take him down. At least that was what Alastair had believed.

'Let him spread his wings, Caro,' had been Alastair's advice. 'You can't keep coddling the lad forever.'

Caroline didn't see it as coddling, of course. She saw it as being a proper mum. For being that to her boys was paramount to her, and she'd made this very clear to Alastair from the moment he'd realised – much to his chagrin – that he'd fallen hard for a married woman.

He'd felt lucky to have her for quite some time. From the moment he'd seen her at that Christmas panto, sipping a virtuous orange juice at the interval and observing, bright-eyed and smiling, the gaily garbed families surging through the bar and lined up for ice cream and purchasing souvenir programmes right and left, he'd wanted to know her. He'd been there with five of his nieces and nephews and she'd claimed the same: two nephews who were running about somewhere making trouble, no doubt, was how she put it. That the 'nephews' turned out to be her sons was something she admitted to only much later.

'I didn't know what you'd think,' she told him.

What she'd meant was that she didn't know what he'd think if she'd revealed she was married. Unhappily so. Tied to man who lacked sufficient interest in the act to bed her more than once each season. But married all the same.

He wouldn't have thought a thing, he told her. Only that she was slim and gorgeous with mounds of dark hair and staggeringly beautiful bosoms and great dark eyes and lips so full that he lost his breath merely looking upon her. And part of the breathlessness he felt took root in the fact that she actually wished to talk with him, him a toad to her fairy princess, short and plain and thin of hair, bespectacled, and not ever what he'd dreamed to be: SAS man, a killing machine, decorated soldier and all the rest. A chance of fate had taken care of that, a badly set leg in childhood rendering him a limping halting lump of a thing with one built-up shoe and no hope of the military life that would have made him the man he'd known he could be.

They'd talked happily that night at the panto: the coming holiday, the importance of family at Christmas, his parents in Scotland, her mum in London, what they would do, whom they would see. She'd revealed very little; he'd revealed much. Later when the bell sounded to call the audience back to their seats, he'd slipped her his card and said shyly that if she ever wished to meet for a drink or a coffee or if she would like to see his business . . .

'What sort of business?' was what she asked.

'Repurposing,' he said.

'What's that?'

'You must see.'

He'd hardly expected anything to come of their meeting, but she turned up at his shop in Whitecross Street not two weeks later. There he sold what he made of what he'd found in car boot sales, estate sales, junk shops, and tips. Huge factory gears fashioned into tables; polo mallets made into lamps; metal garden chairs where a decent coat of varnish formed a protective patina over an artistic display of rust and chipped paint; other people's lumber given new life.

She'd been charmed by it all because, truth to tell, he was very good at what he did, and she'd been filled with questions about how he decided what to make of what he found. He dipped a needy hand into her fount of admiration. There were people in the shop but he wanted to rid the place of them so that he could give Caro his full attention. He stammered and blushed and was determined to hide from her what his face was blazing: abject desire that could not be fulfilled.

She'd stayed till closing. They'd gone for a drink. They'd spent three hours talking of this and that and all he could remember of that evening was his heart pounding so hard that his eyeballs were pulsing and his bollocks were aching with desire.

At her car, she'd said how much she liked him, how he listened to her with interest, and how she felt completely safe with him. 'Which is very odd, as I barely know you,' she said. 'But I have a very good feeling about you and—'

He kissed her before he could stop himself. Animal lust or whatever it was, he simply had to feel her in his arms. To his surprise, she welcomed the kiss with her lips parting and her body fitting closely to his and not a murmur of protest when his hands slid from her waist to her soft, full bosoms that rested heavily in his two palms.

He felt he might actually black out with wanting her. He managed to get control of himself only because they were on a public street. He released her, wiping his mouth with the back of his hand over which he stared at this lovely creature and tried to think how to apologise, how to explain, how to go on with her as he wished to go on.

She was the one to speak. 'I shouldn't have . . . I shouldn't have . . .'

'No. It was me. It was the drink and you looking so bloody gorgeous standing there and—'

'It's that I'm married,' she said in a rush. 'The boys at the theatre with me . . . at the panto . . . They're my sons. And I feel . . . What's *wrong* with me that I would want to see you again when I have no right . . . And I wanted you to kiss me just now. I can't explain it except to say how different you are from . . . Oh Lord, I must go. Really, I must go.'

She struggled to unlock the door, and he saw how badly her hands were shaking, so he took the keys from her and unlocked it himself. She turned to him then and said only, 'How I wish . . .' but then she was gone.

He'd had no chance to say that it didn't matter a whit to him if she'd lied about nephews, if she'd not mentioned a husband, if she – in fact – had three legs and two heads. What mattered was the word *together*. He was in love before he even knew the names of her sons.

And now, seventeen years along, he loved her still. He stared up at the building where Will was suffering, and he recommitted himself to her, despite their occasional difficulties. He recommitted himself to the boy as well, for Will was a deeply troubled lad.

It was because of him that they had left London for Dorset, selling up everything they owned in order to purchase a business about which Alastair had known exactly nothing at the time. Baking, he'd thought, was the province of women, or so it had been in his childhood home. But this was a professional bakery, a thriving concern with a house on the property into which he could move Caroline and her boys. So he'd bought it, he'd employed its previous owner to teach him everything he could about working with flour and yeast and salt and sugar and all else that went into breads, rolls, yearly hot cross buns, cakes, and other confectionery. Years into it now, he had seven shops in the county and if the life of a baker was exhausting with its ungodly hours and its ruptured sleep, he'd been able to provide for his family.

Caroline had her hands full with the boys, especially with Will. Alastair only hoped that today in that flat with Will gone round the bend as badly as he'd ever witnessed, Caroline was able to wring a miracle out of the poor lad's madness. If she couldn't do that, they'd have to send for help or cart him off to hospital. Neither prospect made the promise of peace.

His mobile rang. He grabbed it from the console between the van's seats, and said, 'Is he in order now, luv?'

But it wasn't Caroline although he heard a woman's voice. She said, 'Alastair, are you quite all right? I've had a feeling all morning that you're in a bad way.'

He looked back at the building, at the windows of the sitting room that belonged to Will's flat. He felt a surprising pounding of his heart.

'I'm in London,' he said. 'But I'm that glad you rang.'

# 6 April

★

THIRTY-FIVE MONTHS BEFORE

*Bromley*
*London*

At first, Lily had not intended to see William again. She'd intended instead just to move on. She'd done so before, and she knew that she could do so another time because it was never as difficult as other women her age made it seem. She'd taken a cooking class where she'd quickly become part of a group of foodies who, like her, believed that eating on the cheap did not mean eating takeaway burgers from American fast food outlets, but rather, sussing out the best food stalls in every market from Spitalfields to Portobello Road. She'd taken a dancing class, where the Argentine instructor made it perfectly clear that he'd be only too delighted to share his smouldering looks and his smouldering body with just about anyone willing to have a go. She'd joined a crew of women who kept fit by rowing on the Thames early Saturday mornings. In short, she'd redeveloped the life she'd let go of during the ten months she'd been with William Goldacre, and she vowed she'd not get so entangled again. But then he rang her.

He sounded wonderful, like the William of old. He also turned out to be just as good as his word because he wasn't living with his mum at all. He was back on his feet, and he was living in the village of Yetminster. Did Lily know it? Not far from Sherborne?

Of course she didn't know it because what Lily knew about Dorset could fit into a teaspoon. But she told him that was brilliant news, and he went on to enthuse about his digs.

'Just a cottage in the village, not far from the high street. Well, nothing's far from the high street here, is it. It's not much more than two up and two down, but it's got the most amazing garden. You must see what I've done with it, Lil. *And* I've got my first client right here in the village. A bloke who stopped by and saw what I'd done and asked could I do the same for him. Surprise for his wife, he said, who's off in Australia visiting their daughter and the grandkids and he wants something special for her lest she decides she wants to emigrate. Best part is – and I *knew* this would happen if I got out of London – he's completely on board with the way I work. I told him what I'd put in but not how or the exact cost because – I said to him – I don't know the exact cost initially and that's how I work *but* I'll keep him in the picture every step of the way as costs come up and he says fine.'

'That's brilliant, William.'

'I knew you'd think so. Will you come down?'

Lily had known he was going to ask the moment she'd heard his voice on the phone. She'd been trying to prepare an answer as he spoke, but she didn't have one other than a hesitant, 'I don't know . . .'

He said, 'I want you to see the place. And its garden. And the other garden that I'm working on. It's not much, but I'm entirely on my own here. I knew it was London, Lily. The noise, the traffic, the herds of people. I can't cope with cities. Will you come? Listen, there's no tattoo here. I've checked.'

'There wouldn't be, would there, in a village?'

'I mean Sherborne, Lil. Yeovil. Shaftesbury. 'Course there might be something in Dorchester or Weymouth, but here there's not. You see what that means, don't you?'

Of course, she did. She could move house – to Dorset – and set up a shop, which was what he wanted. The problem was it wasn't what she wanted. There were far too many variables – who in the country wanted tattoos, after all? – and one of them was his mum.

She said, 'Your mum must be pleased you're doing so well.'

'Yes, of course she is. But don't let's go there. She helped me get back on my feet, and that's an end to the story. I hardly see her now. I *did* do her a garden, though. But that was when I was stopping with her and Alastair. She's been showing it off to people who come by the bakery for special orders and such, and there's been some interest there as well. She's supported me, Lily, but that's all. I'm on my own now, I'm fit, and I'm thriving. Will you come down and see for yourself? I swear I can make it so you don't regret it. We were good together, you and I. I know we can be good together again. I guess what I'm asking is will you try? Will you let *me* try?'

Lily considered. She was drawn to William when he was at his best. She was drawn to his joy and enthusiasm. But there was far more to him than that, as she'd discovered.

She said, 'I think it might be pointless, William. I'd never be able to support myself in Dorset and even if I could, we'd be setting ourselves up for enormous hurt.'

'Is there someone else, then?' he asked. 'I wouldn't blame you. After what I put you through . . . It was a rough patch for me. But I'm perfect now. I've a new medication to take care of the Wording. Not a single seizure since I've come home. See, it was the stress. I should have known that would happen in London. I should never have let myself get talked into giving London a try. I'm not like my brother. I can't even remember why I shipped myself there in the first place, to tell you the truth.'

Because you wanted to get away from your mum, Lily thought. And your brother, wanted the same for you. But Lily didn't say that because he did sound good and he had done what he said he would do. And she cared about him. There would always be that.

He seemed to sense in her hesitation a movement in his direction. He said, 'It's easy as anything, Lily. There's a station in the village. I'd have to wave down the train – dead quaint that, eh? – but if you tell me when your train's arriving, I'll be there to do it. And listen to this: after I show you the place, we'll go to Seatown. There's camping well in sight of the beach. I've even been on my own for a night, and it was brilliant. There're miles of walks. A pub. A shop. A village. We can do some walking up Golden Cap. The views, Lily! And with the weather being all right . . . still a bit cold but not raining . . .'

'Camping?' she said because she knew what that meant: a tent, close proximity, the suggestion of an intimacy she wasn't sure she wanted.

He said quickly, 'We'll do it just as friends. What I mean is that there'll be no expectations. We won't plan anything and we'll have an understanding about all that in advance. No worries on that score.'

His words were tumbling out of him, which was a little troubling, but every single one of them made perfect sense. It wasn't like when the Wording came upon him. It was normal, excited conversation.

She said to him, 'All right, then. But just as friends, William. I have to be honest with you about something anyway.'

'So you do have someone.'

'No, no. I've dated, but there's no one at present. What I was going to say is that I don't want to live in Dorset. I'm a London girl. Just so you know that. And if you want to with-draw the invitation now, I'll understand.'

'No way. You're going to change your mind when you see Dorset. You've never been, have you?'

'Sheep being not my thing.'

He laughed at this, his boyish appealing William laugh, absent during those final dreadful days in London. 'Just you wait,' he told her. 'You'll change your mind.'

# 14 April

It *was* more than sheep, as things turned out. Dorset was rolling chalk hills already green with spring, disrupted by copses of hardwood trees coming into leaf and woodlands thick with firs and chestnuts and birches and oaks. The open land consisted of wide vistas that dipped into huge bowl-shaped valleys, of magnificent slopes occasionally broken by the intriguing undulations in land: mediaeval strip lynchets long ago scalloped into the hillsides for farming. It was a country-side of hedgerows sheltering paddocks and fields, of brick and stone villages where flint-banded buildings nosed directly to the edge of the roads like suckling puppies, and of churches everywhere as if the people of Dorset knew something about the hereafter that the rest of the country was oblivious to.

As he'd promised, William met her at Yetminster station, where he waved down the train to stop. He hugged her hard, stood back, and looked at her with his face lively with a kind of health and happiness that, admittedly, she'd seen rarely on him in town. He squired her round Yetminster – a limestone village that popped up in the middle of farmland not far from the stately beauties of Sherborne with its castles and its distinguished school. He showed her his tiny cottage as if it were a structure in which every corner contained a jewel of architectural wonder. He took her into his garden so that she could admire – and she did admire – what he'd done to transform it with an artful potting shed on which the newly planted wisteria would someday climb, a stone path winding across lawn richly edged by herbaceous borders, a tiny two-level terrace with seating and pots in which his eye for colour and shape had led him to plants that would be showpieces as spring advanced to summer. She called it stunning, and it was.

He told her that he'd known she would love it and she would feel the same about Seatown, so off they went on their camping trip. No mention was made of anything else. No word about his mum, especially, and for this Lily was grateful. For obviously Caroline Goldacre – as she always had been called, never changing her name from the surname of her two boys to the surname of her husband Alastair MacKerron – had done a world of good for William, and Lily hated to admit this.

She wondered about the camping idea as they drove to Seatown, which was on the coast overlooking Lyme Bay. It was not just cold; it, had oddly become unseasonably bitter with the kind of frigid wind that blew its way occasionally from the Ural Mountains and swept across Europe, stunning everything in its path. She mentioned this to William but his response was, 'Not to worry. We'll have the tent, I've two duvets along with the sleeping bags, and once we start the walk up Golden Cap, we'll be warm enough. You've brought a hat, haven't you? Gloves as well? We'll be fine.'

Seatown comprised little more than a hamlet that was, wisely, tucked a good distance away from the bay in a fold of land that protected it from winter storms driving in from the English Channel. It was a small scattering of holiday cottages typical of many villages by the sea: nautical themes abounded on windowsills and in narrow gardens; upended fishing boats waited for their seasonal paint jobs; crab pots and floats and nets lay about, emitting the sharp scent of fish.

The camping area was just beyond the hamlet, facing directly onto the sea. The narrow lane they'd driven coursed past this area, dipping down a slope that ended abruptly at a shingle beach, where a stream bubbled across the pebbles, burying itself beneath them and reemerging near the salt water. The landscape, Lily saw, was as dramatic here as William had promised. For the beach was backed by tremendous cliffs looming over the shingle, and one was them was Golden Cap, the highest point in the county. It soared more than six hundred feet above Lyme Bay, providing – according to William – a stunning view not only of the water and of the town of Lyme Regis to the west of them, but also of Dorset itself which lay in splendour to the north. Walking here was where they would warm up, he told her, just as soon as they set up camp. And there was the Anchor pub down near the water – see it, Lil? – where they'd go for a hearty dinner after their climb.

The area for camping comprised two parts, both of which spread out on the east side of the lane to the beach, opposite to Golden Cap. Here, an area of caravans stood for hire on a shelf of land while slightly below and in front of these structures was the spot for tents. Perhaps a dozen of these mushroomed across grassland in rainbow colours, despite the cold.

Lily shook her head. 'We English,' she said.

William laughed, understanding. Nothing got in the way of the English when they intended a holiday. He swung into the camping area, parked, and dashed inside the little shop where he would pay for the privilege of a handkerchief square of land on which to set their tent. He was back in less than five minutes, and off they went. Another thirty minutes and their tent was set up, their sleeping bags and the duvets were inside, and all was ready for the strenuous walk up Golden Cap to see the view.

A sign posted the way. William led, with a rucksack on his back and confidence in his stride. They rested often, for there was no hurry. They paused to take pictures. They stopped to rustle through his rucksack, where she discovered he'd brought chocolate bars, nuts, fruit, water, and even a bottle of red wine and two glasses. They sat against a boulder and looked back across the magnificent sweep of Marshwood Vale, all the way to a hill fort that Will told her was called Pilsdon Pen. Another month and the gorse would be blooming on Golden Cap, he told her. Then it would be yellow explosions, floral bursts of sun on a mantle of green.

When they made it to the very top of the cliff, it was all that William had promised it would be. The wind was intense, so they did not remain long. But in the western distance the crescent of Lyme Regis winked in the afternoon light while to the east Dorset's Jurassic Coast introduced itself along the length of Chesil Beach, where boulders segued to rocks to stones to pea-sized pebbles as the strand travelled its incredible eighteen miles, backed by a glittering shield of water, an enormous lagoon that William identified as the Fleet.

The sea was grey on this day, but the sky was blue. Clouds scudded across it as if chased by the sun, but there were no birds, which Lily found odd. She'd expected gulls but not a bird was in sight. And the only sound was the relentless wind.

She said to William, 'You're dead mad, you are, bringing us up here. Even the birds can't cope.'

His response was a happy, 'Swim to France? I feel like I could.' He cast a look at her, and his face was boyish. He said spontaneously but a little shyly, which she found appealing, 'Lily, can I kiss you?'

'Odd question from a bloke I shared a tooth glass with.'

'Does that mean yes?'

'S'pose it does.'

He leaned to her and kissed her, a gentle kiss without expectation of anything more. This, too, she found appealing. She responded, and the kiss lingered. She felt the stirring within her, as she ever had.

*Seatown*
*Dorset*

On the way back down to their camping site, he kissed her again. This time he didn't ask permission. He merely stopped abruptly, and the expression on his face told her what was coming. She discovered that she wanted it to come, but there was danger in this.

She said, 'I've got my life back, William. I don't want to lose it again.'

'We're not going to talk about that,' he told her. 'Not yet. I won't say not ever because things have changed for me. I've moved on as well.'

'What's that mean? Is there someone . . . ?'

'I wouldn't have asked you to come down if there was someone and I bloody well hope you wouldn't have come if there was someone on your side as well.'

'I've said there isn't.'

'But has there been? In these last months? Because there hasn't for me and—'

'William . . .' She said his name like a gentle admonition.

'Never mind,' he said quickly. 'None of my business.' He resumed their walk.

They made love that night. Lily couldn't have said what was behind William's desire to be with her that way – aside from biology and the kind of animal lust that arises when a male and a female are thrust into intensely intimate quarters with each other after a pleasant day together – but on her part it was a half and half thing. Half lust, if she was honest with herself. Half curiosity, if she was more honest still. For their previous coupling had been an engagement of manic intensity where his release followed so hard on the heels of initiation that the end result had most often been abject apology, reassurance, and a promise to 'make things different next time'. They'd never been different, but she'd kept up her hopes. Now she was merely curious.

Thus she let him seduce her once she read the signs that he wanted to do so: the earnest looks, the warm hand on the back of her neck as they walked back from their meal at the pub, the fingers gently brushing her hair from her cheeks. When he said without the hesitant preamble she'd come to learn was his style, 'D'you want to make love with me, Lily?'

she admired that new courage in him that gave voice to desire instead of sidling into the act as if it was the expected thing between them. This made her consider that perhaps it had been her own lusty approach which had, all along, been the source of his troubles. So this time, she followed his lead and let him guide her as he wished. They lay together afterwards on their sides with their hands intertwined on her hip.

'I love you,' he said. 'Now and always.'

She smiled, but she didn't say the words he wanted to hear. She thought he might protest at this, asking for more as he'd done in the past, but he didn't. Instead he smiled back at her and said, 'So . . . How was it for you?'

'You know very well how it was for me. But, William . . .' She waited for him to steel himself but he didn't do so behind that open and generous expression on his face. She said, 'It doesn't change anything. It's lovely here. I recognise that. But I don't want to leave London.'

'Yet,' he said. 'Add yet. You know it's there, waiting to be said.'

'I don't know that.'

'Yet,' he said.

She saw the compromise he was offering her so she went along. 'I don't know that yet.'

He reached out then. His fingers brushed lightly against her nipple, and she felt what she was meant to feel, the answering rush of blood between her legs that said how quickly she could be ready for him.

'You're very naughty,' she told him.

'I can be naughtier still,' he replied.

# 15 April

Lily slept far better than she would have supposed possible in a tent, on the ground, in the axe-wielding cold. She slept dreamlessly and deeply, and when she awoke she could see the sun's halo on the canvas of the tent. She rolled onto her side to watch William in his sleep, but she found he was gone.

For a moment she felt like Juliet in the tomb but 'no friendly drop for me' related to her powerful thirst and not to a desire for oblivion. She was parched and she was also famished, the latter unusual as she normally did not wake with a need to eat. She stretched, yawned, and reached for whatever discarded clothing came to hand. She could see her breath from her nose like a snorting bull, and she had no intention of emerging from the warmth of the duvet and the bag till she was clothed.

No easy feat, she discovered, but she accomplished this with various grunts and groans. She called for William several times, but to no avail. She worked her way to the tent's zippered opening and stuck her head out into a brilliant morning. Not a cloud in the sky but still no birds. They'd taken off for Spain, she decided. She couldn't blame them.

She called William's name again and blinked in the morning light. No one was up and about near the other tents. It was either too cold or too early or both. A glance at her watch said half past seven. She grumbled and ducked back into the tent.

Her mouth and throat felt coated with a film of sand. There

had to be something to drink nearby, and she needed to get to it. She also needed to have a wee, but that could come later.

Will's rucksack was the answer for drink. Lily crawled over to it. Inside, was an orange left over from their snack on Golden Cap, some almonds, part of a chocolate bar, and – praise God – one quarter left of the bottle of water. She brought these treasures forth by dumping the rucksack's contents onto one of the sleeping bags. What tumbled out with them was a notebook as well.

Without a thought other than that William had begun putting his garden ideas onto paper prior to realising them, she opened the book. She uncapped the water, drank it all, and then glanced at the pages exposed before her. Several hasty sketches indicated a fountain here, a pond there, a rock course forming a dry stream bed. But then the use of the book altered. It became a journal in William's hand.

She would think later that what she should have done at once was carefully put the journal back, allowing William his private thoughts. But the same curiosity that had driven at least part of her willingness to be sexual with William on the previous night drove her now to read his words.

She could see that he had written in haste, feverish thoughts that effectively mirrored the Wording when it came upon him. But unlike the Wording, there was nothing of an execrable nature within the writing.

*recovering. a process. not something that happens in a day. process means movement and something changing. live through it and always hold on to better days coming.*

Lily frowned but she got it. Early days for him and he'd struggled. Who wouldn't have done? He'd lost his fledging business, and he'd also lost her. It had been bad for him. She flipped two pages, past another sketch, this a set of urns planted with gracious abundance. Then

*happened again. Talk over dinner like always but Lily comes up and then I go off and nothing stops it till what stops it stops it. then again later and if there isn't another way what do I do no fucking good bloody useless*

Lily felt the chill of warning. Then

*charlie rang. he says theres answers to everything come on Will he says you don't always have to be so afraid but it's not fear and he doesn't know that it's never been fear it's all inside where the twisting happens*

Outside in the distance, a dog barked. Closer by a car's engine turned over and someone stepped on the accelerator hard to rev it five times as someone else shouted to bloody well stop it as people were sleeping, you sodding fool. Lily dimly heard this as well as a child beginning to cry. Then

*so I looked close and it was there all along contempt like he said it would be and he must have always known only he doesn't know it all what I can't work out is how when I never saw it before only now I see it all the time and I want to die*

Lily felt the sure grip of fear when she reached those words. *I want to die* seemed to shimmer on the page. So she turned to the next one and she began her descent into the mind of a man she had never known at all.

*Seatown*
*Dorset*

William left the little shop with his breakfast purchases. He'd had to wait until eight for their opening time, but it had been no bother. He'd sat on the front step and he'd watched the morning sunlight striking the bay. He'd followed the progress of two early walkers who were crossing the emerald expanse of slope that rose to form the eastern cliff that hulked above the shingle beach. This one was far more friable than Golden Cap, signs posting its dangers. *Keep to the path. Dangerous cliff. Unstable ground.* The problem with it was that it looked so innocent: a steady upswing of cropped meadow grass leading towards a view and the azure sky. The occasional bench allowed for resting from one's exertions, but the wind-twisted hazels along the way offered no shelter from the weather.

Will breathed deeply of the morning air. He was completely back to himself. He hadn't had a seizure in weeks, and this wasn't entirely due to the religious taking of his medications. It was due to recovering from London, from the intrusion of people into his design process, from the pressure of being surrounded on all sides by individuals he didn't know and could not trust. It was also due, he knew this, to the fact that he'd established a residence away from his mum.

Lily had been correct about that. She'd also been incorrect about that. He'd had to get home to Dorset in order to recover, but he'd also had to strike out on his own and to prove to himself that he could be on his own. No living with Mum in Dorset. No living with Charlie and India in London. No clinging to Lily like a man going under and dragging her with him.

What he knew was that he needed the peace of the countryside, whether it be the rolling green downs with their patchwork farms, the shore with its magnificent cliffs and astounding geologic crumples, the deep pockets of woodland, the great distinguished overturned blue bowl of sky. He needed this place in order to live as a whole man and not as some blathering nincompoop afraid of his shadow and of everyone else's. There were no monsters in the cupboard or under the bed in the countryside. There was only the countryside itself.

His mum had known this. Lily would come to know it as well.

Lily, he thought. With her in this last day, he'd felt fully capable of winning her back. It would take time but they *did* have time, for they were young and the years stretched out ahead of them.

She could close up her shop in London. She could come to Dorset. He'd actually found her a place for her shop although he wouldn't tell her that yet. Given time and the gentle urging of which he now found himself so fully capable, Lily would see what was meant to be. He'd put her through a terrible time, but he knew that love didn't die so easily for a woman like Lily.

When the shop opened, he made his purchases. He had to linger a bit in order to get them each a freshly made coffee as well. He saw to this and added what he knew she liked – milk and no sugar – and he headed with his purchases back to their camp.

When he arrived, he saw that she still wasn't up. He set his bag of breakfast goodies on the ground, put the two coffees on a flat stone, and knelt to the tent. He thought of the ways in which he could awaken her: the caress, the kiss on the back of her neck.

But she was awake, he saw, when he opened the tent. She was also dressed. She was sitting cross-legged on her sleeping bag, with her sweet neck bent so that her ginger hair parted to reveal the soft white flesh.

He said, 'Ah, you're—' but her startled cry stopped his words. Her hands fell to her lap to try to cover what she'd been looking at. He saw it then. She said his name.

Then 'Oh my God,' came after that, and her expression broke as if a hammer had hit it.

He backed from the tent with a strangled cry. Where to go what to see what to do who to ask . . .

He began to run up the slope, towards the sea.

# 20 July

*

## TWO MONTHS BEFORE

*Victoria*
*London*

What took DI Thomas Lynley to the office of Detective Superintendent Isabelle Ardery had nothing to do with an investigation. Instead, it had to do with the very last thing he would ever have expected to bother him: Detective Sergeant Barbara Havers actually keeping herself in order for two months and counting. Forever had it been his most ardent wish that his longtime colleague would see the light of reason and begin to dress, talk, and otherwise comport herself in a manner designed to win the approval of those superior officers in control of her fate. But now he found that the version of Barbara Havers he'd been praying to see for years was simply no match for the Barbara Havers whose maddening company had always ended up inspiring the work they did together.

True, she'd been infuriating from the day she'd been assigned to him. But the fact of the matter was that even on her best days, with attitude seeping from her every pore, Barbara Havers was twice the officer of anyone else, with the possible exception of DS Winston Nkata who, admittedly, equalled her but in no way surpassed her except in dress sense. This new, putatively improved, toeing-the-line version of DS Barbara Havers, though . . . It didn't serve anyone's interests to have her keep her every thought to herself until she knew which way the wind was blowing. Least of all did it serve the interests of getting to the truth in an investigation. But so far she'd had absolutely no choice in the matter of her behaviour. For Isabelle Ardery held in her desk a transfer request that Barbara had signed, which could catapult her to the north of England. One wrong move and the date would be filled in, guaranteeing her a stunning new life in Berwick-upon-Tweed. No job was open up there, of course. But Isabelle Ardery knew people in high places, and a favour given was a favour owed. There were very few chief constables in the land who would turn away from the prospect of a favour owed them by a detective superintendent at the Met. Because of this, Lynley made the decision to have a word with the superintendent. He wanted to have a go at talking her into removing the sword of Damocles that was fixed above Barbara's head.

At Ardery's office, he asked politely if he could have a word, guv. Isabelle was dealing with some paperwork, but she set it aside. She gave him the eye at his tone of deference. She would, Lynley knew, be immediately suspicious.

She pushed back from her desk and rose. She went to a rather shabby credenza against the far wall and poured herself a glass of water from a jug that she held up in offer to him. He demurred. She said, 'Do sit, Tommy,' but she didn't do so herself.

Lynley saw that sitting at her command was going to please her. But he also understood that it would diminish him in both of their eyes. So he engaged in an eyelock moment with her as she waited for him to make up his mind. He did, saying, 'I'll stand if it's all the same,' to which she said, 'As you wish, of course.'

They were an identical height. His was by virtue of genetics. Hers was by virtue of wearing shoes with a modest two-inch heel. They brought her to six feet two, just like him, and when he stood in front of her desk with his fingertips on it, they were able to eyeball each other.

He knew he couldn't go at his subject directly. Still, there was no point to a quarter hour of social niceties, so he said, 'I've some concerns about Barbara Havers, guv.'

Isabelle's gaze on him narrowed. 'What's the exasperating woman done now?'

'Not a thing. I'm finding that a problem.'

'Because . . .'

'Because how she is just now – these last two months, actually – isn't how she does her best work.'

'She'll adjust.'

'That's what concerns me. Who she was and how she worked . . . That's disappearing a bit more every day. This new iteration of her—'

'I quite like this new iteration of her,' Ardery cut in. 'It's jolly good to know I can come into my office in the morning and not have someone storming along or ringing me up to demand my presence on high in order to discuss her latest misadventure.'

'But that's just it,' Lynley said. 'To do a decent job, one has to stumble now and again. If one becomes too cautious, too afraid of being disciplined or dragged into court or put through an internal investigation or . . .' He hesitated because if he said the rest, she would know instantly what he had in mind and he wasn't sure this was the route to go. Isabelle didn't take lightly to being offered advice.

'Or?' She lifted her glass and drank. Her gold button earrings caught the light as her blonde hair swept back briefly and then fell neatly into place.

'Or being forced to transfer,' he said, as finally there was simply nowhere else he could go.

'Ah.' She set her glass down on the desk. She herself sat and she gestured him to do likewise. He did so this time as she said, 'That's why you've come. Let's jump ahead and save ourselves five or ten minutes of potential metacommunicating with each other as I get enough of that when speaking to the father of my boys. You would like me to withdraw Sergeant Havers's transfer request.'

'I think it would help.'

'As before, Tommy, I like things as they are.'

He leaned towards the desk. In unconscious response, she leaned away from it. He said, 'It's that transfer request that you had her sign that's keeping her from doing her best work, and I'd think you would have known that would be the consequence when you had her sign it.'

'We define "her best work" differently, then, as I don't see her "best work" as becoming a filthy tabloid's snout—'

'Guv, she intended—'

'Don't take me for a fool. You know as well as I that Barbara provided *The Source* with information, that she used her rank as an officer of the Met to set up and pursue a completely unauthorised investigation of her own, that she defied orders and left without leave – left the bloody *country*, for God's sake – and involved herself in a foreign incident.'

'I don't deny she did all of that. But you of all people know what it's like to try to work while under constant scrutiny from the higher-ups. When you're under the magnifying glass, when you believe that the least little unguarded moment can result in your being taken to task or given the sack—'

'Sergeant Havers should have thought of that before she headed off to Italy without leave to do so, before she leaked details of an investigation to that loathsome journalist pal of hers, and before she forced me to transfer another DI simply because she and he could no longer coexist in the same department.'

'I think you know he's not her "pal."'

'Who?'

'The journalist. And as to your transferring John Stewart, wouldn't you agree that he hanged himself?'

'She's taken a baker's dozen of fully mad actions that have alienated me and every officer above me in rank. You *know* this.'

'A bit of an exaggeration, that, I daresay,' he pointed out.

'Do *not* go public school on me, Tommy. It's unbecoming.'

'Sorry,' he said.

'You'll have to be satisfied with the way things are and so

will she. If Barbara can't find it in herself to work not only as a member of a team but also as an individual whose responsibilities carry the weight of certain behavioural requirements, then she needs to find another line of employment. Frankly, I can come up with several but most of them have to do with sheep and the Falkland Islands and my guess is that lacks a certain appeal. Now.' She rose, and he knew what this meant. 'Are we finished here? I've work to do and so do you and so does Barbara who, I hope, has arrived on time, well dressed, and well adjusted.'

Lynley didn't know. He hadn't yet seen Havers that morning. But he blithely lied and told Ardery that well dressed and well adjusted appeared to be exactly Barbara Havers' state.

*Victoria*
*London*

He was in the corridor heading to his own office when he heard Dorothea Harriman behind him, her identity telegraphed by the snapping of her stiletto heels on the lino as well as her typical style of greeting anyone at the Met: by full title only, no initials allowed. She said, 'Detective Inspector Lynley?' When he turned, she was casting a glance back over her shoulder.

He waited for her to catch him up. That glance she'd tossed in the direction of Isabelle's office told him that Dorothea – the department's civilian secretary – had probably helped herself to an earful of what had gone on between the superintendent and him, a not unusual behaviour on her part. Information, Dee knew, was paramount when it came to police work, even at the secretarial level.

She said when she reached him, 'Could I have a word?' and she indicated one of the stairwells in the centre of the building, a frequent hideaway of Met smokers hoping to get away with a few drags to sustain them until they had time to duck outside and pace the requisite distance from the entrance. Lynley followed her through the door. Two uniformed constables were on the landing applying coins to a vending machine while having a conversation about 'the bloody bastard deserving what he got, you ask me.' Dorothea waited till they'd made their purchases and clomped down to the floor below. She didn't speak till she heard the door click shut behind them. Then she said, 'Not wishing to be the bearer of bad news, but going there anyway—'

'Christ. I haven't driven her to transfer Barbara at once, have I?'

'No, of course not. And rest assured she won't do that unless the detective sergeant forces her hand.'

'But Barbara being Barbara and hand-forcing being her primary forte, along with line crossing and going entirely off the rails . . .'

'You'd hoped to forestall what you see as the inevitable,' Dorothea said. 'That's what I reckoned you were up to. But really, there's not going to be a change in that direction, Detective Inspector.' Dorothea indicated the route she'd come from Isabelle's office as means of identifying the antecedent when she went on with, 'She thinks she's done the right thing and the only thing. She's not about to back off.'

'Not without a miracle the likes of which I've not yet encountered,' Lynley agreed.

'And truth to tell, the detective sergeant does look ever so *slightly* more put together these days, wouldn't you say?'

'Her physical appearance is hardly the point. As you no doubt overheard.'

Dorothea dropped her gaze and strove to look embarrassed although Lynley knew very well that the young woman experienced absolutely no shame when it came to her peerless skill at eavesdropping. 'Admittedly,' she said, 'things haven't been nearly as lively as they used to be now that Detective Sergeant Havers is being so . . . so not Detective Sergeant Havers. And things definitely have become less interesting.'

'You won't find me disagreeing, Dee. But aside from persuading the superintendent to be rid of that transfer request –'

'Which she will *never* do.'

– 'I've not the first idea how to put Barbara into the position where her brain is firing the way it once did without the additional problem of that same brain encouraging her to go her own way and ignore what she's been ordered to do.' Lynley sighed and looked down at his shoes which, he noted, wanted a decent polishing.

'That's what I wanted to talk to you about,' Dorothea said.

'How to bring Barbara's work up to snuff?'

'In a manner of speaking.'

'What does that mean?'

Dorothea smoothed a non-existent ruck in the seam of her frock. She was wearing a frothy summer dress of swirling, saturated colours, and she'd topped this with some sort of hot pink half-cardigan affair whose style Lynley's late wife would have been able to name without hesitation, but Lynley himself could not. It was far too dressy an ensemble for a day at the Met, but Dorothea as usual made it work.

She said, 'It's this. Obviously, she's desperately unhappy just now. She's being someone she isn't. She's like a pendulum that's swung too far one way and now is swinging too far the other.'

'That fairly well describes it,' Lynley said.

'Well, I think that there's *always* been a solution to the problems she has here at the Met although I'm fairly sure you aren't going to like it if I bring that solution to light. Shall I anyway?'

'Try me,' he said.

'Fine. Here it is. She's too focused. She always has been. She's been . . . let's call it hyper-focused. It's generally been on her work, an investigation, that sort of thing. But now the *only* focus she has is how to stay out of trouble with Detective Superintendent Ardery.'

'As Ardery's holding the transfer paperwork, I don't disagree with that assessment at all.'

'Well, that's due to *something*, don't you think?'

'What is?'

'Her problem with hyper-focus.'

'I daresay it's due to Barbara's not wanting to end up in Berwick-upon-Tweed. And I can hardly blame her.'

'Certainly, but that's only half of it, Detective Inspector. The rest of it is what she's *not* thinking about. And thinking about *that* would relieve her of the strain of thinking only about how not to get herself sent up north. Yes?'

'Agreed, more or less,' Lynley said cautiously. He did wonder where all this was heading. 'So tell me,' he went on. 'What is it that she's not thinking about that she actually ought to be thinking about?'

Dorothea looked patently startled at the question. 'Goodness, it's what everyone else is always thinking about, Detective Inspector.'

'I'm intrigued. Go on.'

'Sex,' she said.

'Sex.' He glanced round the stairwell to emphasise what he was about to say. 'Dorothea, ought we to be having this conversation?'

'Sexual harassment being all the rage, you mean? Detective Inspector Lynley, let's please set political correctness aside for a moment and just get down to facts.' Dorothea indicated the stairwell with a manicured hand, by which she also indicated the Met. 'Detective Sergeant Havers needs to think like the rest of humanity. She's always needed that. Which means she needs to think of something more than the Met, her job, and being transferred. Sex is just the ticket for that, and I suspect you know it as well as I do. Call it love, romance, making babies, finding a soul mate, settling down, or anything else you like, it all comes down to the same thing at the end of the day.

A mate. The detective sergeant needs an outlet. She needs someone special so that her whole entire world is *not* this place.'

Lynley eyed her. 'You're suggesting Barbara needs to find a man, aren't you.'

'I am. She needs a love life. We all need a love life. Have you ever known the detective sergeant to have one? You don't even need to answer. No. She hasn't had one and that's why she keeps falling afoul of—'

'Dee, has it occurred to you that not every woman on the planet wants – or even needs – a man?'

Dorothea took a step backwards, her smooth brow creased. 'Heavens, Detective Inspector, are you suggesting the detective sergeant is an asexual being? No? Then what? Not that she's . . . That's completely ridiculous. I don't believe it. Because she and that professor, her neighbour, the man with the lovely little daughter . . .' She paused, looking thoughtful. 'On the other hand, there *is* her hair. And the strange lack of interest in make-up. And her absolutely appalling dress sense. But still . . .'

'Have we gone down the rabbit hole?' Lynley asked. 'Or is this merely an intriguing illustration of random thinking?'

Dorothea looked flustered, which was entirely unlike her, but she gathered herself together heroically. 'No matter. All that's to be decided,' she said obscurely. 'But we'll use her professor friend as an example.'

'Taymullah Azhar,' Lynley told her. 'The daughter's called Hadiyyah. They were Barbara's neighbours. What are we using them as examples of?'

'What she needs,' she declared. 'What she might have had had they not left the country.'

'Barbara and Azhar,' Lynley clarified, just to be sure he was on the right track. 'What they might have had. Together.'

'Indeed.'

'Sex.'

'Yes. Sex, a relationship, a love affair, a romance. Had things gone that way, she'd be a different woman, you mark my words. And *being* a different woman is what she needs. And the way to get her there . . . ? The entire process of getting her there . . . ? I can be of help.'

Lynley felt his scepticism rise. 'You know, of course, that Azhar and his daughter are in Pakistan now. As far as I know, they're not coming back any time soon and Barbara certainly can't go to them. So what exactly are you suggesting? Surely not sending Barbara on a blind date? Pray not that.'

'Oh please. Detective Sergeant Havers is *not* about to step out on a blind date. No. This situation you and I are looking at? It must be gone at a bit more obliquely.' She straightened her shoulders and threw her head back. 'Detective Inspector, I'd like to offer to take the project in hand.'

'Towards what end?' Lynley enquired.

'To the obvious end,' she announced. 'The end that delivers her to love, of course, in any particular form it takes.'

'And you actually think this will make a difference?' Lynley asked her.

She smiled a smile replete with knowledge. 'Trust me,' she said.

# 23 July

As soon as she alighted at Liverpool Street station, Barbara Havers asked herself what on earth she'd been thinking in agreeing to any kind of jaunt with Dorothea Harriman. She and the departmental secretary had exactly one thing in common – the possession of two X chromosomes – and no amount of plumbing either the depths or the shallows of their personalities was going to change that immutable fact. Additionally, Dee had not clued Barbara in as to their destination. Just 'We'll start out at Liverpool Street station, Detective Sergeant Havers. The railway station, I mean. We'll meet and see what happens from there. I must pop by Wentworth Street first, though. Have you been . . . ?'

Barbara realised later that the innocence of that question should have told her a great deal, but at the moment she did not twig to anything other than Harriman's offer of a mercy outing during their off hours. Since she was doing nothing on the particular day and time of the proposed outing – when was she doing *anything* at this point in her life? she asked herself – Barbara shrugged and said Wentworth Street was fine by her and no, she'd never been. She had no clue what they would encounter in that part of London aside from the distinct possibility of urban renewal run amok, and being invited to engage in a Dorothea Harriman experience was a novelty anyway.

Barbara couldn't remember the last time she'd been in

Liverpool Street railway station, but as she emerged from the underground and wandered into the vast maw of the place, she did know it hadn't been then what it currently was: an enormous shopping mall cum railway station with loudspeakers blaring announcements, people rushing by with valises, briefcases, and rucksacks, uniformed police pacing round and giving the eye to potential terrorists – male, female, youth, adult, or aged grandparent behind explosive Zimmer frame – and adolescent girls with shopping bags the size of sandwich boards in one hand and smartphones in the other.

They'd agreed to meet at the flower vendor, which Dorothea had assured Barbara she would have no trouble finding, and this turned out to be the case. She sauntered up and interrupted the young woman in mid flirt with an antique gentleman who was attempting to press an armload of tuberoses upon her.

Barbara joined them with the excuse for her tardiness that every Londoner who used the underground had long ago expected to hear when someone was late for an appointment. 'Northern Line. There's going to be a riot on the platform one day.'

'Not a problem,' Dorothea told her. She waved goodbye to the gentleman, linked her arm to Barbara's and said confidentially, 'I've had a skinny latte, bought some new knickers, and practised turning down an indecent proposal from a seventy year old. Lord. Have you noticed how men *never* seem to take the fact of their ageing to heart while, as women, we're continually bombarded with reminders that middle age is out there, waiting to claim us with crow's feet?'

Barbara hadn't noticed. She'd never been the recipient of any sort of proposal, indecent or otherwise, and as for crow's feet, her attempts to avoid them had so far been limited to not looking into mirrors longer than it took to see if she had spinach between her teeth on the rare occasions when she actually ate spinach.

As they walked towards a glittering exit that loomed at the top of a set of escalators, Barbara cast an eye upon Harriman's day-out-in-east-London ensemble of slim navy trousers tapering down to slender ankles and ballerina shoes in tan and white. She'd topped the trousers with a red and white striped T-shirt, and she carried a tan and white handbag that matched the shoes. On her days off, Harriman managed to look as put together as she looked on her days on, Barbara thought.

In contrast, Barbara herself had taken directly to heart the word 'outing' that Dorothea had used to describe what they would be doing, and she had dressed accordingly. She wore drawstring trousers and a T-shirt with *Are you talking to yourself or just pretending that I'm listening?* emblazoned across it while on her feet she'd donned – in honour of the occasion – her new shoes. The fact that they were leopard-print high top trainers made a certain statement, she'd reckoned back in Chalk Farm when she'd put them on. Now, however, she decided that they might be a wee bit . . . well, 'out there' was probably the term of choice.

Right. Well. Too late to do anything about it, she decided. She followed Harriman onto the escalator. At the top, she decided a compliment was in order, and she told Dorothea that she looked – a word search was necessary – smashing. Harriman thanked her prettily and explained that Wentworth Street was largely responsible.

Barbara experienced an uh-oh moment. 'I hope you're not saying what I think you're saying.'

'Which is what?' Dorothea asked.

'Which is that you intend to make me over. I went that route once, Dee. It didn't take.'

'Heavens, no,' Dorothea said. 'I wouldn't presume. But I've a garden party to go to tomorrow afternoon and not a stitch to wear that everyone hasn't seen two thousand times. This will take five minutes.'

'And after that?'

'I think it's bric-a-brac day at Spitalfields Market. Are you interested in bric-a-brac, Detective Sergeant?'

'Do I look like someone who's interested in bric-a-brac?' Barbara enquired. 'Dee, what's this about?'

'Nothing at all.' Dorothea had stepped off the escalator and was heading towards the towering doors. She stopped, though, when Barbara said her name more insistently.

'You're not taking me in hand?' Barbara demanded. 'You're not following orders? Ardery says to you, "Do something with Sergeant Havers because she still isn't quite right," and you go along with it?'

'You're joking, of course. What on earth would I "do" with you? Come along and stop being so difficult,' Dorothea said, and she once again took Barbara's arm to make sure her directions were being followed.

They found themselves in Bishopsgate, where modern London of the City – in the form of looming glass tower blocks – was steadily creeping towards pre-Victorian London of Spitalfields. Here unrestrained capitalism was doing its best to destroy the history of the capital, and where there were not soaring buildings announcing themselves as multinational corporations, there were chain shops whose ownership by unknown multinational magnates fairly did the same.

The pavements were crowded. So was the street. But the congestion didn't deter Dorothea, who kept her arm linked with Barbara's and who carved an easy route through pedestrians, taxis, buses, and cars in order to cross over. Barbara expected her to pop inside one of the several shops they passed, but this did not happen. Instead, within five minutes, Harriman's sure pacing had taken them in a crisscross pattern of narrowing thoroughfares and back into a London of another century.

A hotchpotch of eighteenth- and nineteenth-century buildings sprang up in unwashed brick splendour, comprising questionable housing and forlorn places of business. There were colourful sari shops, dubious-looking hair studios with Mediterranean names, textile outlets, pubs announcing themselves as the Angel and the Pig and Whistle, and the kind of cafés where coffee came in either white or black via a kettle and a jar of powder. Within one hundred yards an open-air market sprang up, filled with stalls that offered a staggering array of products: from pin-striped business suits to ladies' crotchless underwear. There were also food vendors of every ilk, and accordingly the air was filled with the scents of curry, cumin, cooking oil, and cod.

Dorothea took everything in, sighed with evident pleasure, and said to Barbara, 'I know you've always wondered. I don't like to say because of what people might think.'

Barbara drew her eyebrows together. She hadn't the first clue what Harriman meant.

'This is how I dress myself,' Dorothea went on, with a gesture towards the dizzying number of clothing stalls that formed a colourful river spilling down the street in front of them. 'Twelve pounds for a frock, Detective Sergeant. Twenty pounds for a suit. Thirteen pounds for a pair of shoes. Wear it for a season, then toss it because it's probably falling part anyway.'

Barbara looked from the stalls to Dorothea. She shook her head. 'I don't believe you,' she said. 'Not what you wear, Dee.'

Dorothea said, 'Of course there's the occasional consignment piece. Well, there has to be, hasn't there? It's wise to have something decent *and* timeless now and then. But the rest is this. Cheaply made and cheaply sold but –' and here she held up a finger – 'it's utterly astonishing what a very good steam iron applied before wearing, the willingness to change the buttons, and the right accessories can do for a girl.'

*Spitalfields*
*London*

Barbara hardly expected to enjoy herself with a crawl through what she quickly discovered was Petticoat Lane market. But

Dorothea Harriman was having no interference from her in the quest for clothing. She repeated her need for a suitable frock for the following day's garden party, and she added the fact that a Certain Young Banker was going to be present at this affair. She firmly intended to catch his eye, she announced. *If* the detective sergeant wished to stand by mutely and watch the proceedings, she could certainly do that. On the other hand, if the detective sergeant wanted to do some browsing, Dorothea was only too happy to recommend her favourite stall where a Bangladeshi family of six supported themselves with knock-offs of garments worn by celebrities and the two or three sole fashionable members of the royal family. 'I don't know how they do it,' Dorothea explained, 'but I reckon it's with computer hacking. So if the right person wears it to a film opening or to Ascot or to visit the White House, they've got it here on sale within five days. It's brilliant. Will you browse or will you be difficult?'

'I'll browse, I'll browse,' Barbara told her. Dorothea's expression telegraphed delight until Barbara added, 'Over there,' and indicated the food stalls. At which point she sighed and said primly, 'I refuse to believe you're as hopeless as you wish me to think, Detective Sergeant Havers.'

'Think it,' Barbara told her. She took herself off to explore the edible offerings in Goulston Street, which were many, varied, and begging for purchase.

She was wandering along the pavement and digging into a second sumptuous offering from Tikka Express Indian Cuisine when she spied the display window of a shop that appeared to be directly up her alley. The place was called Death Kitty, the shop window exclusively given to T-shirts. Sagging paper plate in hand, she went to inspect them. Alas, she thought as she approached. All of the T-shirts were black and of a marginally obscene nature which made them unsuitable for anything other than wearing to visit her mum whose current mental state would preclude her comprehension of the finer points of double entendre.

Damn, blast, and oh well, Barbara thought airily. She was about to walk off when she spied a colourful poster mounted in the shop window as well. It was announcing the publication of a book and the local appearance of its author. *Looking for Mr Darcy: The Myth of Happily Ever After* was the first. Clare Abbott was the second. She would be reading and speaking at Bishopsgate Institute; women were encouraged to attend; men were dared to accompany them.

*Spitalfields*
*London*

Barbara made the decision to attend the reading at Bishopsgate Institute for two reasons, the first of which was a very late lunch with Dorothea at Spitalfields Market. There they tucked into speciality crêpes at a small café with artsy tables topped with stainless steel and chairs that looked like stretched-out colanders. Delicately unfolding her paper napkin, Dorothea blithely launched into the kind of conversation that Barbara had managed to avoid having with another human being for her entire adult life.

Dorothea speared a slice of chicken-and-asparagus crêpe, and she said to Barbara, 'Detective Sergeant, let me be blunt and ask you something: when was the last time you had a truly decent bonk? I mean a grabbing-the-bedposts-and-howling session orchestrated by a bloke who knows what he's about. This does, of course, eliminate any male who went to boarding school, but you know what I mean.' She chewed for a moment as Barbara attempted to ignore her by studying the mother and child at the next table who were engaged in a battle of wills over a miniature lorry that the child wished to plough across his plate of food. When Barbara didn't reply, Dorothea said, 'Do not make me drag the truth from you,' and tapped Barbara severely on the hand.

Barbara turned back to her. 'Never,' she said.

'Never as in you'll never answer me or never as in . . . you know.'

'As in you know.'

'Are you . . . You aren't saying you're a virgin, are you? Of course you're not.' She cocked her head and examined Barbara and a horrified expression upon her face indicated that a dawning thought had struck her. She said, 'You *are*. Oh my God. No wonder. How *stupid* of me. When Detective Inspector Lynley mentioned—'

'The *inspector*? Oh, that's brilliant, Dee. You and DI Lynley are discussing my sex life?'

'No, no, no. I mean, he's worried about you. With your friends being gone to Pakistan. We're *all* worried about you. And anyway, don't let's get off the subject.'

'Dee, this is cringe-worthy. I reckon you know that because you're not an idiot. So let's cut to the chase. I have a busy life, so when it comes to sex, I just don't have—'

'Do *not* say what you're about to say because no one on earth is too busy for sex,' Dorothea said. 'Good Lord, Detective Sergeant, how long does it take? Ten minutes? Twenty? Thirty if you want a shower as well?' She looked thoughtful and added, 'An hour, I suppose, if you require lengthy seduction. But the point is—'

'The point is changing the subject,' Barbara told her. 'Let's talk about films. Or the telly. Or books. Or celebrities. Or absolutely any member of the royal family, with or without prominent front teeth. You choose. I'm easy.'

'I have to ask, then. Do you *want* a man? Do you want a life beyond the Met?'

'Cops leave ruined marriages in their wake,' Barbara pointed out. 'Just look at our colleagues.' She picked up the menu and studied its possibilities. Another crêpe or possibly a dozen sounded good at this point.

But Dorothea plunged determinedly on. 'Good heavens, I'm not talking about marriage. Am I married? Do I look married? Do I look like someone desperate to *get* married?'

'To be honest? Yes. Aren't you the bird who said not an hour ago that there's some bloke you want to impress at a party?'

'Well . . . yes, of course. That's exactly what I said. But the point is: impress, date, bonk, whatever. And if that leads to something more at the end of the day, I'm on board with the idea. We all want marriage eventually.'

'We do?'

'Naturally. We're only lying to ourselves if we say we don't.'

'I don't.'

'Am I supposed to believe that?'

'Marriage isn't for everyone, Dee.'

'Stuff and nonsense and—'

Barbara got up from the table to approach the ordering counter. 'I'm having another crêpe,' she told her.

But when she returned to the table, she saw that her abrupt end to their conversation regarding her love life constituted only a pause in their minor conflict. The seat of her chair – so recently occupied by her substantial bum – now held a carrier bag. Barbara narrowed her eyes. Her gaze went from the bag to Dorothea, who said, 'I *had* to get it. I *know* it will suit you. You mustn't protest, Detective Sergeant Havers.'

'You said this wasn't going to be an attempt to make me over, Dee.'

'I know, I know. But when I saw these . . . and you did mention my own clothes today. I just wanted you to see that dressy casual *isn't* . . . Look. It's only trousers, a jacket, and a shirt. Just try them. The colour is going to be perfect, the jacket will hit you just where it needs to, the trousers—'

'Stop. Please. All right. If I say I'll try them, will you cease and desist?' And not waiting for an answer, Barbara pushed the bag onto the floor and dug her wallet from her shoulder bag. 'What did you pay?'

'Good heavens, no!' Dorothea protested. 'This is entirely on me, Detective Sergeant.'

That did put an end to their discussion, and Barbara drove

it out of her mind that evening by shoving the clothing under her day bed when she returned home. She might have forgotten everything about the excursion to Spitalfields save for Radio Four, which she tuned into prior to beginning the chore of weekly knickers-washing in the kitchen sink. She'd rigged up the drying line and she was dousing her under things with Fairy liquid when she heard the sonorous voice of the radio host say to his guest, 'That's all well and good, but you appear to be arguing against the natural order of things. So I must ask this: at what juncture does this all become either posturing for publicity's sake or a case-in-point of she "doth protest too much"?'

A woman's harsh voice answered. She seemed to bark rather than to talk, saying, 'Natural order of things? My good man, from the time of the troubadours, Western Civilisation has encouraged women to believe that "someday my prince will come", which is hardly natural and which more than anything has kept women subservient, uneducated, ill-informed generally, and willing to do everything from binding their feet to having ribs removed in order to produce the waistlines of five-year-old girls so as to please men. We're offered injections to keep our faces without wrinkles, garments as comfortable as being embraced by a boa constrictor to keep our flab in check, hair dyes to keep our flowing locks youthful, and the most uncomfortable footwear in history to facilitate very strange fantasies that have to do with ankle licking, toe sucking, and – depend upon it – schoolboy spanking.'

The radio host chuckled, saying, 'Yet women do go along with all this. No one forces them into it. They hand over their cash or their credit cards, all in the hope—'

'This isn't "hope". That's just my point. This is rote behaviour designed to produce a result they're schooled to believe they must have.'

'We're not talking about automatons, Ms Abbott. Can't it be argued that they're willing participants in their own . . . Would you call it enslavement? Surely not.'

'What choice do women have when they're bombarded with images that mould their thinking from the time they can pick up a magazine or use a telly remote? Women are told from infancy that they are nothing if they don't have a man, and they're even less if they don't have what is now *ridiculously* called "a baby bump" – God, where did that extremely stupid term come from? – within six months of capturing their man. And in order to end up with the requisite man and the requisite bump, they damn well better have perfect skin, white teeth, and eyelashes long enough, curled enough, and dark enough when they leave the house in the morning because God only knows their prince might be waiting on their doorstep with an armload of roses.'

'Yet you yourself have been married twice. Couldn't it be argued that the position you now take arises from bitterness at the failure of those marriages?'

'Of course that could be argued,' the woman agreed. 'It could also be argued that the position I take arises from having the veil lifted from my eyes after experiencing wifehood first hand and coming to realise that wifehood and motherhood chosen blindly in order to fulfil someone else's definition of a successful life or chosen without regard for other possibilities robs women of the very opportunities that have given men dominance over them from the Garden of Eden onward. My position is that women must be able to choose with their eyes wide open as to the consequences of their choices.'

'Which are not, as you say, "happily ever after".'

'Believe me, the very first time Cinderella heard the prince emit an explosive fart, the entire idea of happily ever after got itself flushed directly down the loo.'

The radio host laughed. 'And perhaps that says it all. We've been speaking with longtime feminist icon Clare Abbott about her controversial new book *Looking for Mr Darcy: The Myth of Happily Ever After*. She'll be appearing at Bishopsgate Institute tomorrow evening at half past seven. Get there early because I have a feeling there's going to be a crowd.'

# 24 July

India Elliott resumed using her maiden name eight months after she left her husband, which was two weeks after she accepted a second date with a man she'd met on her regular bus ride from the Wren Clinic at St Dunstan's Hill to her shabby little house in Camberwell. Prior to that, she'd been India Goldacre although she'd never much cared for the name and had only changed over to it because Charlie had insisted when they married. 'You're not actually married if you don't change your name, darling,' was how he'd put it, and only half in jest. 'I mean, obviously you're *married* but it's like you're hiding it from the world.' So she'd given in because when Charlie insisted on something, he never let up. And what, after all, did a little thing like a surname matter at the end of the day? It pleased Charlie for her to change it, and she wanted to please him.

Everything had been perfect at first in their relationship, and everything had remained close to perfect for quite a while. But she knew now – these months after she'd walked out on him – that she'd been far too compliant in her marriage. And she had to admit that she'd been completely seduced by Charlie's mother.

The first time she'd been introduced to Caroline Goldacre, India had felt admired, embraced, and welcomed. On that day in Dorset, while Charlie had been appreciatively inspecting the transformation of the heating element used to fire his stepfather's enormous bakery ovens, Caroline had declared to India confidentially over tea *à deux* how delighted she was that 'Charlie's found someone after all his dithering about with those piles of education he has.' Then within four days of being introduced, Caroline had sent her a scarf she'd found in Swan's Yard in Shaftesbury with a brief note declaring the gift 'a little something for you with great admiration from Charlie's mum.' The colours were perfect for India's complexion, as if Caroline had made a study of her so that she would know what suited her best.

'For lovely India' had been written next, on a card accompanying a silver bracelet that Caroline had found 'in of all places, one of our charity shops! With much affection, from Charlie's mum.' Then had followed a string of intriguing beads, a handbag, and a small piece of antique silver. Not all at once, of course. And not every day. Not even every week. But just dropped into the post now and then or sent back with Charlie when he went down to Shaftesbury as he regularly did to visit his mum and his stepdad.

And then quietly one Sunday when she and Charlie had both gone down to Dorset for a midday meal, Caroline had said to her, 'Thank you for humouring me, India. My entire life I've longed for a daughter – *please* don't tell either of the boys – and it gives me a great deal of pleasure to buy you the occasional little thing when I happen to see it. But don't feel you have to pretend to like everything! Something unsuitable? Just give it to a friend. I won't be at all offended.'

Caroline was so reasonable a woman, so chatty and filled with stories of her life 'with my boys', that India had relaxed her normal reserve, convinced that any caution she felt around Charlie's mum was the product of years spent as the only child of career diplomats who early on had inculcated in their daughter the message that a life spent moving from pillar to post suggested that her best interests lay in placing her trust largely if not solely in her parents when advancing through a foreign culture.

But Caroline Goldacre did not constitute a foreign culture, despite her Colombian birth. She'd lived since early childhood in England, and over time, India found herself charmed by her. So when she and Charlie married and Caroline asked her, 'Please, would you call me Mum?' despite India's having a mother who was alive and well and, frankly, the only person India truly wanted to call her mother, she had gone along.

She'd told herself that it didn't really matter. She had always called her own mother *Mama*, with the accent on the second syllable in the fashion of someone out of the more antique sections of the British upper classes, so it wasn't as if the term *Mum* meant much to her. But it had meant a great deal to Caroline, and her evident pleasure the first time India had referred to her as Mum had caused Charlie's face to glow with gratitude. He'd mouthed *thank you* when Caroline hadn't been looking, and his blue eyes shone with a loving fullness.

What they'd had together during the years of their marriage wasn't a diamond perfect thing, but India asked herself realistically what marriage *was* diamond perfect? She'd known from conversations with her own mother as well as with girlfriends that marriage meant compromise, as well as weathering sporadic storms with one's life's partner. But that was the point. One *had* a partner with whom one grew, and life without growth wasn't life at all.

She'd found it helped enormously that Charlie was a postgraduate student of psychology when they'd met, on an afternoon in the Wren Clinic with him on her acupuncture table and with her speaking in the gentle murmur she employed the first time she guided one of the thin needles into a nervous patient's skull. Because of his education, he knew how people and their relationships ticked, and that knowledge grew over the years once he opened his practice. By the time they married, he was a busy psychotherapist with a set of skills that he used to help India and himself through the occasional bad time that came up. And if it bothered her that he sometimes employed a therapist's technique when they were engaged in discussions that occasionally grew heated about this or that, she got past it because he always dropped it with a quick 'Sorry, darling', when she pointed out to him that he was 'doing it again'. When he did that – giving her that affable apology – it set them immediately to rights.

But all that ended when Charlie's brother Will had died in Dorset. A single hysterical phone call from Caroline became the first blow upon what India had slowly come to realise was the far too delicate structure of the relationship she had built with her husband. The how of Will's death, the why of it, the where of it . . . These had been mere details to accompany the devastating fact of it: running madly up the hillside to the top of the lesser of two cliffs in a place called Seatown, where the greater cliff was six hundred and fifty feet above a stony beach and the lesser cliff dropped a jumper five hundred feet to certain death below. Only one person knew for certain what had actually occurred to fire Will's act that terrible day, while everyone else believed what they chose to believe which was what they could bear to believe or could not bear or did not wish to face bearing, ever.

Charlie was in the latter group, and India found this diffi-cult to take in and more impossible to live with as the months wore on. The man was a psychotherapist, she told herself. He knew better than to avoid either his feelings or the truth. But avoid them he did, never mentioning his brother's name, exhib-iting a false sense of heartiness – hail fellow well met and all the trimmings – that she was supposed to take as real, offering ill-timed jokes that were not the least amusing, shooting out inappropriate remarks so totally unlike him that she began to wonder if she knew him at all. All of this was meant to carry him through days that were torture for him while every moment declared a terrible truth that he could neither look at nor live with: he had not been able to help his brother.

Will's death had not been a horrible accident in which someone had wandered too close to a cliff edge that comprised sands and clay and was thus frighteningly unstable. There had been no terrible incident of someone backing up to pose for a photo with the sea behind him, no drug-induced flight from the tent where Will had been camping with Lily Foster. There had been instead a deliberate storming up the slope to the cliff's top in broad daylight, with Will's erstwhile lover chasing after him.

Lily Foster had seen it all, bearing witness to the excruciating spectacle of a young man's throwing himself to his death. At the base of the cliff, Will's head had splattered on a boulder while part of the fragile landscape above him descended on his body in a mock burial.

How do you regain yourself when your only brother takes his own life? There was a way, of course. What India believed was that there *had* to be a way. But Charlie Goldacre had obdurately refused to seek it. India Elliott – as she was now again and as she ever would be – bore with this refusal and its burdens on her marriage as long as she could, which turned out to be only as long as twenty-nine months after William's death. At that point she came to understand that, difficult as it was to face, there were times when the only life you could save was your own.

Part of that saving had been leaving Charlie. Part of it, she felt, was accepting the second date with Nathaniel Thompson. He preferred to be called Nat. She preferred Nathaniel as she found it a lovely name, but she went along with his desire and said, 'All right then, Nat,' and when after seven bus rides from St Dunstan's Hill to Camberwell, he'd asked her if she wouldn't like to have a glass of wine near Camberwell Green, she said she would like that very much, thank you, although the walk from Camberwell Green to her house would be a long one if she disembarked there.

The glass of wine had become dinner had become coffee. The hour was late at the end of this, so Nat phoned for a minicab and he rode along with her and then on to his own place after a chaste kiss on the cheek and a 'See you tomorrow, then?' in reference to their regular bus ride together.

India found that the prospect of a real, planned date with Nat Thompson had an appeal to it that she hadn't expected, so when on the next day's bus ride he told her of a show at Tate Britain that he was thinking of looking at and was she interested if he managed two tickets, she said yes she was. She went back to calling herself India Elliott after that, something that Charlie discovered when he phoned the clinic. He'd been upset – 'Come along, India. What man *wouldn't* be?' – but she'd held firm.

That was before his mother showed up. Cleverly, Caroline had made an appointment at the clinic. More clever still, she'd made it under the surname MacKerron, which India glanced at but didn't twig to as she took the folder from the holder mounted on the treatment room's door, opening the first in prelude to opening the second. C.K. MacKerron was the patient's name. New, she saw. Married, she saw. Female, she saw. Forty-nine years old and a martyr to unspecified hip pain.

She said, 'Mrs MacKerron,' as she entered, and then she stopped on the threshold with the doorknob still in her hand.

Caroline's first words were, 'Please don't be angry, India. I thought you might not see me if I used Goldacre. I've had to come to London for an event with Clare, so I decided . . . Well, you see.' She was sitting on a straight-backed chair in the corner of the treatment room. The light was dim as it would be in a clinic built from what remained of the ruin that had been Sir Christopher Wren's re-building of an ancient Saxon church. Destroyed in the Blitz, what had been the church was a garden now defined by concentric circles, a fountain to dull the roar of traffic from Lower Thames Street, lush plantings, and ancient walls reaching upward, unroofed, to the sky. Only Wren's original tower remained and in this was the clinic. Small rooms and few windows defined the space.

India didn't know what to say, so she went with, 'I'm not at all angry,' which was the truth. She wasn't sure what she *did* feel at this unexpected sight of her mother-in-law, aside from surprise at the amount of weight Caroline was continuing to gain, but the heartbeat that tapped lightly behind her eardrums told her it was something and she would do herself a service to know.

She set the patient folder on a counter. She herself sat on the physician's stool. The treatment table stood between them.

Caroline said, 'You've done yourself up. Your hair, the new cut of it and the colour, the make-up as well . . . I don't quite know what to say about it. It's unexpected. You were always so natural.'

'Indeed. I was.' India didn't add what she could have. That her 'natural' look had been manufactured, at Charlie's insistence and to please his mother. Caroline Goldacre didn't like to see young women who – as he put it – felt the need to alter their 'native' looks. What Charlie had never been able to explain was why his mother felt like that when she herself was so thoroughly dyed and painted. But she'd cooperated with Charlie – had India – even to the extreme of going *au naturel* on her wedding day. What on earth had she been thinking, India asked herself now.

Caroline opened her handbag and for a moment India thought she was going to bring forth a gift, which she was going to have to refuse. But it was a packet of tissues, and Caroline took one, as if knowing it was going to be needed in the next few minutes. She said, 'She told me you're India Elliott now. Over the phone when I made the appointment and said Goldacre, they said it's Elliott now. What am I to take it that means? He's devastated already. This will probably kill him. No, don't say anything. Just listen for a moment, and I'll be gone.'

India knew where this meeting would head. She already felt wretched about leaving Charlie, as if she'd stamped on someone who was already lying wounded in the street. But she'd also done everything she knew to do in order to help him recover from his brother's death, and they'd reached a point where Charlie himself had to do something, which he would not.

Caroline seemed to read this response on India's face because she said, 'There's no timeline on grief. You can't say that someone must get over a death – not a death like Will's – the way you'd recover from the death of a friend or even a spouse. This was his brother.' Her chin began to quiver at that word *brother*, and India knew how difficult it was for Caroline to speak of the suicide of her younger son. But she forged on although tears began to make crooked pathways down her cheeks. 'There's not going to be another brother for him. He can't pick up the pieces and just soldier on. You have no siblings, so you probably can't understand how close they were, how Charlie stood in place of Will's father when he had no actual *interested* father and Charlie himself only ten years old and a thousand times he was there for Will when Will needed someone to be his mate, his protector, his . . . his everything when their own father wouldn't . . . India, I didn't mean to coddle either one of the boys, Will *or* Charlie, but when a child is troubled, then a parent has to do something or to face the worst. And now it's happened. And so to have him gone now, his only brother ripped out of his life, and on top of it, to lose you. You can't do this. You must see where it could lead and how afraid I am that—'

India went to her mother-in-law, who held her hands up in a pleading gesture. She quite understood Caroline's deep fear: that Charlie would also kill himself. She feared this as well. Her fear was what had kept her in place for more than two years till something had to happen to force Charlie to take action, and removing herself as his crutch and emotional whipping boy had been the only route she could take.

'He needs to get help, Mum,' India said. 'He knows that, but he won't do it. He says I'm his help—'

'You *are*.'

– 'but you and I know that isn't the truth. He's lost most of his clients. He's stopped leaving the flat. There're days when he doesn't even dress. He just lies on the sofa and stares at the ceiling. And when I ask him or try to talk to him or—'

'I know, I know.' Caroline wept, abject in her grief. 'You've a

right to a life that's not like this one. But can you not see . . . ?'
She had shredded her tissue, so she got another and pressed it
to her wet cheeks. This action seemed to calm her because when
she next spoke, her voice was altered, no longer pleading but
reasoned and gentle as well. 'Can you at least not file for divorce,
India?'

'I have no plans to do that.'

'Oh thank God. Because, you see, he's in pieces now that
you've begun to date, and to go from that to receiving papers
telling him you're . . .'

But India didn't attend to the rest because, in that moment,
she understood. She'd told not a soul she was dating. She'd
not yet said a word even to her own mother. So if Caroline
Goldacre knew that she was seeing someone, there was only
one way she could have found out.

Charlie had told her. He'd rung her and told her and, as
she'd done for years, Caroline had rushed in to do the work
meant for one of her boys.

But that wasn't the worst of it, actually. For India also had
never told Charlie that she was seeing someone. So if he knew,
he'd been following her.

*Spitalfields*
*London*

The only real clues that Charlie Goldacre had that he hadn't
been out of the flat in two weeks were the rubbish bags and
the fridge. The first were beginning to stack up in the entry
like spine-slumped debutantes hoping in vain for a dance
partner. The second was bare of everything but condiments,
some mouldy cheese, three eggs, and a carton of milk whose
odour suggested the way of wisdom would have been to pour
its contents straight down the drain. Other than that, there

was – at least to his eyes – nothing to suggest he'd been holed up inside what had once been his home with his wife since seeing her out with another man.

Prior to that, he'd had good days and bad days. While it was true that most of them had been bad, there had been mornings when he'd managed to muster enough energy to shove from his chest the hundredweight that seemed to flatten him to the mattress. On those days, he did go out. And while he found himself largely incapable of meeting with clients, he was able to walk the streets, to stare at his surroundings, and to try to make sense of stories he read in discarded broadsheets and tabloids on the occasions that he stopped for a coffee. But what he read, he quickly forgot, just as he also forgot where he had been and what he had seen.

Life continued around him. Traffic roared into the City in the morning and out of the City in the afternoon. Pavements were crowded with office workers, shop assistants, and skulking young men in black hoodies and jeans. The markets in Middlesex Street and Goulston Street continued to thrive despite the cold. All of this seemed so curious to Charlie. His own life had ground to a halt, so it was difficult to take in the reality that for everyone else, the struggle went on.

That's what it was, he'd decided. An eternal struggle to come to terms with realities that shifted from day to day. One day you were going about your business, secure in the illusion that you had arrived at the exact point for which you'd been aiming. The next day, you found yourself on a runaway train about to derail. He had known this was possible, of course, considering the years of study that had gone into his making as a psychotherapist. But the level at which he knew it was the level at which he applied it to other people and not to himself. Yet he should have understood all along how fragile was the ice on which he had established his life because every human being's life was a fragile thing. He should also have been prepared that at any moment his world would tilt on its axis in such a way that only by clinging desperately to a few familiar items within it would he keep himself from sliding off his personal planet and into oblivion.

After Will's death, he'd clung to India. Then, when she'd left him, he'd clung to his remaining clients. When those tortured souls had finally moved on to find someone who actually listened to their weekly tales of woe instead of observing them blankly, he'd begun to cling to his home.

Art Deco, India had called it. Charlie, Charlie, we must have it! The smallest flat they'd seen, it was perfect crown mouldings and stunning bookshelves. It was pristine railings and hardwood floors and glossy tiles. It was Egyptian revival and razzle-dazzle, and they should have walked out of the place the moment after they had walked in. But she'd been desperate for it, and he'd wanted to please her after the extremes she'd gone to just to please him. To please his mother, actually. For it had seemed so crucial at the time that Caroline Goldacre approve of India.

What anyone else thought of Charlie's choice of mate didn't matter to him. But Caroline's approval had been paramount. India had questioned this, but not enough. *Why* had she been so docile? he wondered. Why hadn't she tried to fight him?

But he more or less knew the answer to this. One always ended up living to please his mother. One didn't even see the change in oneself as pleasing her became a way of life.

He was thinking of this when he heard a key unlock the door to the flat. He was in the kitchen where on the wall he had mounted a small whiteboard on which he kept a record of his daily activities. Prior to Will's death there had been need for this, for Charlie was an inveterate volunteer on mornings or afternoons or evenings when he had no clients. He walked dogs from the Battersea home, he worked a suicide hotline – wasn't *that* a bloody good joke, he thought – he read to pensioners with failing vision in care homes, he helped a group of disadvantaged kids maintain an allotment south of the river. But these pursuits had become too overwhelming. One at a time, he'd given them up and when the flat door opened and he heard his mother's voice calling out a quiet hello, he was in the process of erasing the last of them from the whiteboard.

He heard Caroline's footsteps as she entered the sitting room. She would see that he'd been sleeping on the sofa and had he known she was coming, he would have hidden this evidence. She wouldn't understand why he couldn't bring himself to use the bed he'd shared with India. Indeed, until India had removed the last of her belongings from the flat, he could hardly bear to touch a single surface, so fraught with memories was everything for him.

He heard his mother sigh, and then she went towards the bedroom, calling his name. He didn't answer as the flat was so small it would be a matter of five seconds before she found him. He was applying the thick felt rubber to the word *Samaritans* when she spoke behind him. 'Why didn't you answer me, Charlie? Turn round and let me look at you, please.'

She drew in a slow breath when he did as she asked. She shook her head as if to say 'Do not utter a word' and she left him. But she was back soon enough, in her hand a mirror that she'd brought from the bathroom. She held it up before him and said, 'Do it, please,' and he gazed upon what he didn't wish to see.

He was hollow-faced, unshaven. His eyes – blue like his father's and his maternal grandfather's – were grimy with sleep and half-ringed with purple. His hair was uncombed. And the rest of him that the mirror didn't show was, he knew, not much better. For he couldn't recall the last time he had changed his clothes or even had a shower, and his shoulders slumped habitually now while his chest caved inward as it had done for years in order to disguise his height to spare the feelings of his younger brother.

His gaze went from his reflection to his mother's face. He saw love in her expression and he tried to reflect that back to her as he turned the mirror in her hand so that she could look on her own image. He said, 'What do they say? "Physician heal"—' but she cut him off.

'Don't,' she said. 'This has nothing to do with Will, and you know it.' *This* referred to the enormous amount of weight she'd gained since his brother's death, rendering her moon-faced now, a once-slender woman taken to disguising her bulk with flowing garments and copious amounts of ethnic jewellery. She wore today a piece that he recognised as having once belonged to India. Caroline had taken it from the back of the bathroom door one evening. India had seen it on her later – so had he in fact – but neither one of them had said a word. God, he thought now. What was *wrong* with them when it came to his mum?

'What does it have to do with, then?' he asked her, turning back to the whiteboard.

'Cortisone, Charlie. For my hip. You know that very well.'

'Ah,' he said. 'As you wish, of course. If fantasy cortisone injections "for your hip" help you to deal with Will, then you must have them. But the truth is generally better. You're eating your way through your grief, Mum.'

'And what are *you* doing?'

Charlie chuckled uselessly and set the felt rubber on the edge of the whiteboard. 'I haven't a clue.'

He heard her place the mirror down on the table. He turned. She said, 'Don't let's do this. It's difficult enough for both of us without picking away at each other.'

He nodded. 'Truce, then.'

She came to him and hugged him. 'Best boy,' she murmured. 'My second self, Charlie.'

That had been their secret. 'We share a soul,' she'd told him. 'I think that's what happens with one's first born.'

He'd allowed her to say this. He'd never pointed out that he knew the truth. And now, he didn't say a thing. But still he tensed in the presence of her lie, and she must have felt this. She released him from her embrace and said, 'Let's talk. There's much to say.'

She led him into the sitting room. There, before she said another word, she carefully folded the blanket and removed the sheets. Her nose wrinkled at the odour coming from them. She balled them up and did the same with the pillow case that she removed from the pillow. All of these things she took to the bedroom. She returned, sat, and gestured for him to do the same.

She looked round. She would, of course, see the differences in the room since the touches that India had supplied to make the flat their home were gone. When she'd removed the last of her belongings, she left only a photo in a frame, and it made a silent declaration of who she had once been. In the picture, they were on a rooftop terrace, drinks in hands and grins on faces. India wore a sundress, long earrings, and bright pink lipstick. He wore a striped shirt with the sleeves rolled up. He'd known her three weeks, and she'd not yet met his family, so they were idiotically happy. This is who I was before I changed myself for you, the photo announced.

No fool, Caroline saw this. She took up the picture and looked long at it. Then she carefully placed it back where it had been, on the table next to the sofa. She said, 'We were too close. That was the problem.'

He said nothing. He knew she wasn't referring to closeness to India but rather closeness to him.

'I should have done things differently. When you wanted me to have a key to this flat, for example, I should have said no. I should have said, "Your life's with India now, not with your mum." That would have made a difference. I know I'm not the first mother who wanted to maintain close ties with her children, but I carried things too far. I saw India as *one* of my children once you married. I wanted a tie with her, and I failed to see that she didn't need or want a tie with me.'

Still, he said nothing. She would have liked reassurance, he reckoned, a passionate statement from him that the breakdown of his marriage was not her fault. And it wasn't. But he couldn't muster the words to tell her this as doing so would open the door to confidences he didn't want to share and others that he didn't want to hear.

Caroline put her hand on his. 'I've been to see her, Charlie.

I had to be in town today anyway, so I went to the clinic. No, don't say anything yet. I knew you wouldn't want me to go. But once you told me she'd begun seeing someone . . . What else could I do? If there's the slightest chance that I can make her see reason . . . You do see that I had to take that chance, don't you?'

He knew he ought to be horrified: his mother going to see his wife in order to plead his case. But even beginning to carry their conversation in that direction felt enervating to him. So he did what he'd been doing with his clients before they left him. He merely stared.

Caroline's grasp tightened on his hand. 'She's not been intimate with him. I asked her directly. What else could I do? She said he's not even been inside her house, and she hasn't the first clue where he lives other than somewhere in Camberwell. That should tell you a great deal.'

At that Charlie was aware of something stirring within him. He couldn't put a name to it, but whatever it was, it gave him the energy to say, 'What's it supposed to tell me, Mum?'

'That nothing's been decided, that this is just a period in which India needs to think things through just as you need to think things through. This happens sometimes. It isn't the end of the world.'

'What it is is only a matter of time,' was his reply. 'India's lovely. This bloke will want her. She'll go along because that's what India always does – she just goes along – and that will be that.'

Caroline rose from the sofa to walk to the window that overlooked Leyden Street. Right fist to her mouth, she tapped her knuckles against her lips. She was keeping herself from shouting at him, Charlie knew. Impatient at heart for things to go her way, his mum had a temper but she rarely let it get the better of her.

She finally said to the window, 'Charlie, you must pull yourself back from the brink. You don't have Will's problems. You never once had Will's problems, but even Will—'

'Don't go to Will, Mum.'

– 'was on his way to winning that pierced and tattooed creature Lily Foster back. And believe me, I was staying completely out of it, just as I will stay out of your trials with India.'

He shot her a look. She turned from the window and caught it on his face. She said, 'Darling, I had to know where things stood between her and this chap she's met. That's all it was and now I'm finished. You have the information – it's a casual thing between them and nothing more – and now that you know it, it's time for you to step onto the pitch and get her back. You can't just sit here day after day in this flat and wait for—'

'I can't, Mum.'

'Of course you can.'

'Not India, but what happened. I can't come back from it. I've tried. I'm trying. But I can't shake it.'

She returned to the sofa. She sat close to him. She put her arm round his shoulders, and she smoothed his hair from his temple. She said quietly, 'Listen to me, my dear. What you can't shake isn't Will's death so much as the fact that you couldn't help him. And you help so many people, Charlie. You help your clients but beyond your clients, just look at all the people you've helped through the services you do them. But you couldn't help Will and neither could I and neither could any of the doctors he saw throughout his life because what was wrong at the heart of him went too deep. It was slowly killing him and nothing could stop it. He had his work, and that brought him a bit of joy, but in the end that wasn't enough. Nor was Lily enough. Nor was I or your stepfather.'

'I should have had the skills. I *have* the skills.'

She turned his head so he had to look at her. 'You spent your life being his most devoted brother. He took that from you when he . . .' She faltered then seemed to force herself to go. 'When he leaped from that cliff. But you must find something more to sustain you because if you don't . . . Please, Charlie, you simply must try.'

Then she stopped talking. But he could tell that something was working its way up from deep within her. She finally said with what looked like an enormous effort to control her emotions, 'I promised myself,' which broke her voice. But she held up her hand in a gesture that said she needed a moment to compose herself. He gave it to her. When she was ready, she went on. 'Please don't forget that I, too, loved him. He was so long at the centre of nearly every effort in motherhood that I made. I took him to specialists, to child psychologists, to counsellors, to psychiatrists. I found schools that I thought would work for him, and I got on my knees and begged your father to give me the money for those schools, which he would not do. For his own son, he wouldn't do this, Charlie. And he – your father with all his talents – would not even perform the basic surgery that would have at least made Will less self-conscious about his ear . . . the terrible deformity of it . . . the bullying that went with it. "For the love of God, Caroline," he said to me, "have you ever seen the *real* deformities out there? There's not a thing wrong with him that *you* don't emphasise to make certain he's aware of it to the point of being a social cripple and why the hell are you doing this to him?" I tried to pursue other sources but there were none and who was I anyway but a woman who needed to work just to keep food on our table. If Alastair hadn't come along, we all would have ended up in the street.'

Part fact and part fantasy, but once again Charlie allowed it. His mother had her own grief at Will's sudden death, and if it helped her to recreate the past in a way that painted a picture at odds with the memories he had of it, who was he – a bloody hermit in a flat he'd once shared with his wife – to deny her this? Besides, this tale she was telling got them off the subject of India and himself, so he wasn't about to stop her.

She wasn't derailed, however. 'This isn't about me: my troubles, my concerns, my feelings,' she said. 'This is about you. You are all I have now and I can't stand knowing you've isolated yourself inside this flat, and I can't bear thinking of you here alone. If I lose you on top of everything else . . .' She began to weep, then. 'I'm *sorry*. I don't mean to cry. But sometimes . . . Here's how it is and I know you understand: sometimes I want to die because how much more pain is one person supposed to deal with? What I'm saying is that I *know* what you're feeling. I feel it as well. And if I can't help you . . . *Let* me help you. For God's love, tell me you'll do something to pull yourself back together.'

Charlie felt his gaze lock onto hers, and he couldn't look away. Neither could he not recognise the agony that she was experiencing: a mother who had lost more than one child, and although she didn't know he'd discovered this about her, he couldn't tell her that now.

He said, 'I'll try.'

She embraced him. She said, 'One step at a time is all that I'm asking, Charlie. You can do that, can't you?'

'I'll try,' he said again.

*Thornford*
*Dorset*

On its surface, an invitation to dinner was completely innocent, so Alastair MacKerron accepted it. Despite their relative positions as employer and employee, he told himself that they were really colleagues who would merely share a meal together, and if that meal was going to be served in the home of the employee instead of in a public restaurant, that was not of particular import.

Sharon Halsey had worked for the bakery for years. Widowed far too young at twenty-four years old, she'd raised two children

in straitened circumstances and against all odds but with stead-
fast determination and tremendous success. One – the daughter
– was now a cancer specialist in San Francisco and the
other – a son – was a linguist in Strasbourg, and if their mum
badly missed them now, the pain of their absence actually made
her an outstanding part of Alastair's professional life. For she
liked to keep busy, did Sharon, and keeping busy meant growing
his business. Because of this, she was the real reason he owned
seven shops across the county, each one of them highly profitable.

She managed them, working a half day in each every week
to keep in the picture of how sales were going and what was
needed to supply their customers. She kept the books, she
ordered supplies, she managed the wages, she hired and sacked
employees. She allowed Alastair to do what he did best – the
baking – and in doing so she took the burden of business
ownership off his shoulders.

He admired her greatly although 'Such a mouse of a woman'
was how Caroline dismissively described her. But if Sharon's
self-effacing manner and her careworn looks made her seem
like a mouse, she was firm of purpose, with endless ideas and
equal energy. She'd worked for the bakery when Alastair
purchased it, and he'd taken the previous owner's advice to
heart: 'Whatever you do, mate, keep Sharon happy. A rise in
wages? A new car? A bloody flat in Paris? You see to all of it
and she won't fail you.' She had not.

She lived in Church Road in Thornford, a village some
eighteen miles from Shaftesbury. In what had once been the
ancient house of a thriving farm that spread out behind it, her
home now stood as part of a line of cottages, deceptive from
the outside since it appeared too tiny ever to have housed
more than a single individual. Inside, though, it stretched in
both directions from a small stone-floored entry, becoming a
quirky warren of rooms that, over time, had been transformed
into sitting room, dining room, office, kitchen, playroom for
children no longer there, and staircase leading to three bedrooms
above. It offered a low ceiling, comfortable furniture, prints

on the walls, lace curtains at the windows, and flowers from Sharon's garden although God only knew when the woman had time to grow them, so busy was she as she darted round Dorset making certain that MacKerron Baked Goods maintained its reputation for quality.

They met twice a month to discuss the affairs of the bakery, and today had been one of their meetings. During it, Alastair had mentioned that Caroline was off with Clare Abbott on business relating to Clare's new book, and Sharon responded with, 'Is she? Then why not come to dinner tonight? I've put a nice pork shoulder into the slow cooker this morning. I'll share it with you.'

He'd said, 'You'll be wanting it for leftovers, won't you?'

'But not *needing* it for that,' she said. 'Come along, Alastair. I'm used to eating alone but you're not. How long is she gone?'

'Caro?' He wasn't entirely sure. More and more since Will's death, they'd been going their own ways. They'd both taken his suicide like a brick to the head, but he'd been recovering from the grief more quickly. As would be the case, he told himself. He cared for Caro's boys – always had done – but they were not his and he would never feel as a proper dad would feel, with a chain broken irreparably. Caroline didn't understand this. She'd seen his recovery as a failure of his love for Will, and he'd not been able to persuade her otherwise. At the end of the day, it was becoming easier for them to avoid each other rather than look each other in the eye and weigh the value of what the other was feeling. He said, 'I expect a night or two. They're in London but Clare's got a home there as well.'

'Lucky Clare,' Sharon said, and she meant it truly, as he could tell. She didn't have a bone of jealousy in her, nor did she possess the need to cling to a past in which she'd lost someone she loved. She wasn't, he thought, a bit like Caro. But even to think such a thing was deeply disloyal and if he was to dine with Sharon, he needed to keep Caro in his thoughts in a most positive way.

Sharon admitted him into the house, where the entry was scented with a large vase bursting with the roses she grew. Pink, they were, and so were her cheeks. She'd either used a bit of make-up in honour of having a guest for a meal or she was blushing.

She'd dressed a bit for dinner as well, and Alastair felt that roughly hewn in her presence. She wore a sundress against the warmth of the summer, showing nicely browned shoulders with a handful of freckles speckling her chest and dipping into a modest shadow of cleavage. She had sandals on her feet, a thin gold chain round her left ankle – he'd never seen such a thing – and her legs were slimmer than he expected and a lovely toast colour with smooth firm skin. In contrast, he himself had merely risen from his usual afternoon nap and stepped into his regular bakery clothing of jeans so exposed to flour that their seams were permanently white and a shirt buttoned right to the throat as usual, although he'd rolled up the sleeves in a bow to the heat.

It occurred to him that he should have brought something along with him: flowers, wine, a cake. He hadn't thought to do so. He said as much, and she shook her head. 'Rubbish. We're old friends – me and you – so we're not about to stand on any ceremonies right from the start, eh?'

*Right from the start* should have made him question what he was doing in Thornford. But he took it as a mere chance of words meaning as little as he wished them to mean.

She offered him a drink. Summertime and she herself was having a Pimm's, she told him. But she had a good lager if he preferred, cider as well, and there was gin. They'd have wine with dinner so he should know that. 'I don't want you to end up blind drunk on the side of the road,' she said with a laugh.

He chose the Pimm's. He followed her to the kitchen to watch her make it, at her invitation. From there, they went to the garden behind the farmhouse. The fields of the original farm stretched out behind it, rich land onto which the village of Thornford had never intruded. They sat in lawn chairs next to a youthful laburnum tree, where long brown pods hung beanlike from glossy-leafed branches, a lovely feature of the garden that she'd not added till her children were adolescents.

'I was always scared they'd eat the pods as little ones,' she said. 'I'd have told them they're poison, but you know how kids are. And if I'd lost one of them after already losing their dad—' And then quickly, 'Pardon, Alastair. That was thoughtless of me to talk about losing a child. I'm that nervous is what it is. I don't have guests to dinner as a rule. I'm also a bit sloshed.'

'You're pink in the face, is what,' he said. Stupid, he thought immediately afterwards. Why had he never been able to speak easily to a woman?

'Am I?' she said. 'It's not the drink. I . . . well, I used some blusher, and I generally don't. I expect I look a dead scary sight if you've noticed it. Like a clown, eh?'

'You don't look like a clown,' he told her. He took a gulp of his Pimm's and then another and he hoped the spirit would loosen his tongue. When it did, all he managed was, 'How long's he been gone?'

She looked only momentarily surprised. She took a sip of her drink. 'Kev? More'n twenty years now.'

'You never said . . .'

'How he died? Gangrene.' And when she saw his expression of surprise and horror, 'It was his gut. He had a condition he didn't take care with, seeds and such getting trapped in these odd little sacs that formed in his gut. They got themselves infected. He was supposed to take care with what he ate and he never did and it killed him.'

'Christ,' he said.

'No one on God's green earth should have to die like that. It took months as they carted him in and out of operating theatres removing more and more of him but still it came back.'

'How old?'

'Twenty-seven when he died.'

'Leaving you—'

She reached for his arm to stop him going further. 'Alastair, it's no matter. I mean, it *is*, but we all face something. And then she added, 'How's Caroline coping? I've not seen her at the bakery in a good long time.'

Since Sharon was the one to introduce the subject, Alastair decided that no disloyalty was involved in revealing a few facts. More than three years since Will's death and she'd not come back from it, he said quietly. She eats, she reads, and she watches the telly, he said, full stop. His fear – one among many that he had – was that she'd eat herself straight into the grave. Her two diversions were the Women's League in Shaftesbury and her work for Clare Abbott. Praise God for that last as Alastair thought it was saving her life. It was, he admitted, saving his.

Sharon looked surprised. He realised that he'd said too much, his tongue too oiled by the drink. He looked away, out towards the fields where a flock of sheep grazed placidly, plump white clouds on a sky of green. Sharon said she was sorry to hear of his struggles and she added, 'Especially that last bit. You're a hard worker and . . . Well, I'm sorry for whatever it is that's going on between you and Caroline.'

'Nothing's going on, truth to tell,' he said with a rueful laugh. 'Not in some time.' He didn't add the rest: that long before Will had died had come a cooling in the relationship he had with his wife. The heady passion he'd felt for her and she for him was not, of course, something that could be sustained. But he'd reckoned on it altering to warmth, affectionate couplings in a marital bed blessed with more children, growing understanding, and loving commitment. He'd come to understand, however, that Caro had no interest in such things once the initial flames of her lust had cooled. He'd finally reckoned, in fact, that she'd never felt those initial flames at all.

He said nothing of this to Sharon and he swore that he wouldn't. Not so much because it constituted a betrayal of his troubled wife but because of what it said about him. Doubtless, her question to him would be 'But why do you stay?' to which he would have to admit that Caroline's need for him – sworn to in a thousand different ways – allowed him to feel what he'd never felt before: a person of significance in the eyes of someone else.

He felt that Sharon was looking at him, so he finally forced himself to meet her eyes. She didn't look pitying as he'd thought she might at what he'd revealed. Instead she looked puzzled and, perhaps, rather intrigued.

'Now that's a real shame,' were her words.

*Bishopsgate*
*London*

As luck would have it, Barbara was held up at work, and she didn't manage to reach Bishopsgate Institute until a quarter past eight. It wasn't too far along the street beyond a grimly institutional-looking police station, and a poster board just inside the door indicated the direction she was supposed to take to get to the event. This was being held on one of the upper floors of the building, along a corridor displaying a stunning array of Art Deco tiles in rich greens and mild yellows.

Barbara followed the noise: laughter, outcries of protest, and an amplified female voice whose scratchiness told Barbara she was hearing the well-known feminist herself. She saw double doors opened along the corridor, and she went towards them to find herself at the entry to a very large room with a parquet floor and bright white walls, not unlike a dance studio. Harsh fluorescent lights illuminated it, folding metal chairs provided seating that was mercifully padded in red upholstery, and at the far end of the room a dais elevated the speaker who was at that moment striding back and forth in front of a lectern, microphone in hand.

Barbara had never seen Clare Abbott in person. Now, she concluded that the woman was quite striking, but not for reasons that anyone might have considered congruent with the accepted image of femininity. Thus, Barbara liked her at once. Broad-shouldered, solid, and tall, she favoured head-to-toe tailored but decidedly crumpled black linen with a single stripe of cream offset from shoulder to hem of the shirt she wore. Its collar was half up and half down but not as a casual fashion statement. Rather it appeared to have been designed that way and it disappeared into dishevelled shoulder length hair of a grey that was as dull as a rainy November sky. She wore heavy framed spectacles that, as she spoke, she repeatedly pushed up the bridge of her nose or removed to wave in emphasis. From the sound she was producing as she tramped back and forth across the dais, Barbara reckoned she was also wearing military boots beneath her trousers.

The crowd was mostly women. They appeared largely to comprise office workers of middle age and younger, some of them accompanied by men who looked dazed, defiant, or dead uncomfortable. It was an SRO situation, so Barbara positioned herself at the back of the room. There, a flashily outfitted, overweight woman of an interesting, mixed ethnicity and too much jewellery was getting in the way of a harried bookseller and fussing with a display of books while not too far from her and leaning against the wall another woman in black appeared to be a relative of the author, so similar was she to Clare Abbott in build and appearance. She was, however, a far trendier version of the writer since her salt-and-pepper hair was styled short and carefully disarranged in an artful manner and her black and grey clothing did not appear to have been purchased in nearby Wentworth Street. She was holding in her arms what seemed to be a furry mixed-breed dog of tan and black, wearing – for some reason and despite the heat – a bright green vest. She was also watching the writer with a smile on her face while the other, flashier woman glanced up from her book-fussing with an expression that indicated the sooner they were finished with this business, the supremely better.

Barbara couldn't blame her. It was boiling hot in the room which, typical to London, had no air conditioning. There were also no windows. Laughably, a single fan had been provided. It stirred the tepid air near the book table, but that was it. Yet no one appeared to be in a hurry as Clare Abbott fielded their questions.

She answered the marriage-and-children questions first with yes and no. She *had* been married, but she'd never had children. Her first had been a starter marriage of nineteen months when she and the husband were twenty-one – 'Good God, we were babies!' – and her second had been a longer one ten years later. When someone enquired whether her new and controversial book might be the result of those failed marital relationships, she was as unoffended as she'd been on Radio Four. Her reply of, 'One *might* argue that if one considers the end of a marriage some sort of personal failure instead of the outcome of arriving at a mutual decision based upon an understanding of differences and an agreement about the future. My first husband and I awakened one morning and realised that aside from an Oxford education, we had nothing in common but a predilection for pizza. As for my second husband, he wished to take a posting in the Middle East. I did *not* wish to live in a land where women are forced to wear black bed sheets in the roaring heat. In both cases, we parted as friends.'

And if one party wishes to end a marriage while the other doesn't? someone asked.

If the marriage's end comes about as the result of an affair? someone else enquired.

And then in rapid succession from others:

Isn't our job on earth to raise our own awareness and to develop as spiritual beings in peaceful interaction with other spiritual beings?

Don't you believe there is a greater plan, one designed by God?

Why have males and females of a species at all if we're not intended to join together for procreation?

The writer took all the questions in her stride. She remained unruffled and clearly unrepentant of her philosophical positions. Finally, at a signal from the woman at the back who looked like her sister, Clare Abbott said in conclusion, 'I'm being told by my editor that it's time to sign books, but let me say this. I'm not telling any of you to leave your marriage or even to avoid marriage in the first place. I'm asking you to examine your beliefs and to determine which of them come not from your sense of who you are but instead from an urging from outside forces as to who you ought to be. Marriage itself is all well and good if you like that sort of thing – regular sex with the same partner and a familiar face at the breakfast table. But to depend upon it for anything at all *except* familiarity is lunacy. It's fine to want a home and traditions and establishing a history with someone. It's fine and normal to like regular sex and to wish to have it with one person only or at least serially. But these things cannot be relied upon to fulfil an individual, which is why silly books end with the happily ever after bit and honest books end with Anna Karenina depositing herself on the railway tracks. Let us not forget that Romeo and Juliet killed themselves, Guinevere and Lancelot destroyed Camelot, and Madame Butterfly went for seppuku. There's a reason for all of that and wise is the woman who works out what it is. Open your eyes because there is no happy ending unless you work like the devil to reach something you can label that way. Which is the point of *Looking for Mr Darcy*.' She smiled and added, 'Which I encourage you to buy in multiple copies. Now, let me sign some books so that we can decamp and have a cold cider at the nearest pub.'

With applause, people began to rise and collect their belongings. The sisterlike woman whom Clare Abbott had identified as her editor set her dog on the floor and called out, 'We'll form a queue along that wall. I promise you that, even if I have to muzzle her, Clare will not be allowed to do *anything* other than sign your books, so you'll be out of here in less than an hour,' while the jewellery-wearing woman behind the book table ripped open a package of Post-its as Clare Abbott worked her way through the crowd. She paused here and there to greet well- wishers, to laugh boisterously at something someone said, to shake hands with a stranger, or to accept someone's business card, which she slipped into the pocket of her trousers. She finally arrived at the signing table, where she threw herself into the chair provided as the crowd surged forward to purchase her book.

Had it not been for her uncomfortable discussion with Dorothea Harriman, Barbara might have left at that point. But that discussion, in combination with the Radio Four interview, in combination with what she'd heard of this presentation at Bishopsgate Institute, prompted Barbara to make her way into the queue. She had no intention of purchasing the book for herself. She wasn't much of a reader beyond dipping into the sort of romance novels that would likely make Clare Abbott's hair fall out. But it was clear to her that Dorothea Harriman's manner of thinking needed some serious adjustment, and *Looking for Mr Darcy* appeared to be just the ticket to make all the adjustments that were necessary.

The signing was a well-organised affair. The author took her place at the far end of the book table while the flashy woman handed over the Post-its to the editor who, dog at her side, moved along the queue and wrote on the Post-its the names that people wished to have inscribed in their purchased copies of *Looking for Mr Darcy*. The bookseller dealt efficiently with selling the books, but it soon appeared that the editor's promise to have them all out of there in less than an hour was not going to be fulfilled.

Too many members of the audience wanted to talk to Clare Abbott, yet no one seemed to mind this particularly as all round Barbara eager conversations appeared to indicate that the writer was well able to provoke discussion. So the queue of women and the rare, brave man inched forward. Books sold briskly. The room began to feel more and more like a sauna. The bookselling woman attempted to urge people along in as courteous a manner as she could, but it was evident that the writer was not about to be hurried.

Barbara was glad that she'd thought to bring a change of clothes to work that day. At least she wasn't sweltering in tights, skirt, and an Ardery-approved high-necked and long-sleeved blouse. She'd ducked into the ladies and switched her garments for the evening, going for her usual T-shirt, drawstring trousers, and comfortable trainers. So while it could not be said that she was pleasantly cool, at least she wasn't feeling the need to divest herself of heavier clothing in a manner that was likely to get her arrested.

It was her clothing that turned out to be the key to her conversation with the feminist. Fifty-four minutes after the signing had commenced, Barbara had managed to work her way to the book table and to purchase a copy of *Looking for Mr Darcy*. She'd fixed onto the volume the Post-it with Dorothea's name neatly printed on it when she heard 'On the eighth day God created bacon,' spoken in Clare Abbott's scratchy voice. This was followed by her raucous laugh, her question, '*Where* did it come from? I must have one,' which was followed by Barbara's realisation that the writer was reading the front of her T-shirt.

Clare Abbott's flashy companion glanced over and murmured something to the writer, which the writer ignored. She said instead to Barbara, 'You must tell me where you bought that because I intend to wear one next time I have to face my doctor for the yearly lecture about my cholesterol. My primary weakness is clotted cream, though. Can I get one with clotted cream instead of bacon? Where did it come from?'

'Camden Lock Market,' Barbara told the writer. 'I expect they'll do you clotted cream if they don't have it already. They did this one for me.'

'It was your creation?'

'What it says? Yes. For my sins,' Barbara told her.

'I do love it,' she said. 'Tell me where in the market. I'm absolutely serious. I must have one.'

'Well, it's nearer the Stables than the lock. But it's open only Sundays, so it takes two Sundays since they have to print it and—'

'Oh God. Camden Lock on Sunday. Oh well. There are times when one must prevail over one's loathing of shopping hordes and this could be one of those times. C'n you write down where I might find the stall so I don't actually have to battle my—'

'Clare, darling . . .' The flashy woman cast a hurry-along-please look at Barbara.

'I'll get one for you, if you like,' Barbara told the writer quickly. 'If you actually want one. It's not a problem as I live near the market.'

'That's more than kind, but I can't ask you—'

'Clare . . .'

The writer acknowledged her companion at the table, saying, 'Yes, yes, Caroline. I know you're doing your best to keep me on task. I'm about to obey. You've got one of my cards, haven't you? Will you hand me one?'

Caroline pulled a slim silver case from a pocket in the summery tunic she wore over her bulk, and from this she extricated a business card. She handed it to Clare. Clare passed it to Barbara, saying, 'It's got both London and Shaftesbury on it. Use either address. Caroline, what about twenty-five pounds as well as I've nothing on me and I can't have this kind woman . . . I'm terribly sorry. I haven't asked your name.' She looked at the book Barbara had handed over for signature. 'Dorothea, is it?' she said, reading the Post-it.

'Barbara Havers,' Barbara told her. 'That's a gift. The book, I mean. Here . . .' And Barbara rooted round in her shoulder bag to bring forth her own card, which she handed over.

Clare Abbott took it from her with thanks, sliding it among

the others that Barbara had seen people hand to her during the signing. For her part, she slid Clare Abbott's card into her trouser pocket and promised her that the T-shirt she wanted would soon be in the post. She demurred the twenty-five pounds from Caroline, saying, 'It'll be on me,' as she went on her way.

She didn't get far. She'd just reached the corridor and was heading towards the stairway when she heard, 'Excuse me . . . ?' behind her. She turned to see Caroline following her.

'Caroline Goldacre,' the woman said by way of introducing herself. 'I'm Ms Abbott's personal assistant.' She looked a bit hesitant as she said, 'I don't know how else to say this, but if I don't keep my eyes and ears open, she gets herself into all sorts of trouble.'

Barbara wasn't sure what to make of this, so she waited for more.

'I must get back to her, so just to be brief: may I ask you to return her card to me please? She's terribly impulsive when it comes to meeting people. She gets wound up and makes promises that she can't possibly keep and I'm the one who has to sweep up after here. I'm awfully sorry. I feel wretched about it, but it's my job.'

'Oh. The T-shirt thing . . .'

Caroline made a regretful face. 'You're not to take her at all seriously. And you're definitely not to go to the trouble. It's just her way. She loves meeting people and chatting to them but afterwards . . . ? She can't remember a thing and when the phone starts ringing or the front doorbell goes, she wants to know why I didn't stop her before she even got started. So if you wouldn't mind . . .'

Barbara shrugged. She dipped into her trousers and brought forth the business card. As she handed it over, she asked curiously, 'What d'you do with all the cards she collects from people, then, during one of these events?'

'She gives them to me to bin on the way out,' Caroline said frankly as she put Clare's card into her tunic pocket. 'It's just the way she is.'

From her position at one side of the room, Rory Statham had been keeping an eye on everything, so she saw Caroline Goldacre's manoeuvre. As was her wont, Caroline had been trying to hurry Clare along. This was something that Caroline saw as her job. 'Clare's minder,' she said in reference to herself. 'God only knows how she'd get anything done if I didn't keep her on task.'

Rory found this claim curious. She herself had been working with Clare Abbott from the time of her first book – a brilliant and brilliantly reviewed polemic called *The Uterine Dilemma* that had sold a discouraging three thousand five hundred and sixty one copies before it sank into permanent obscurity – and as Clare's editor she'd cajoled the writer over the creation of ten other volumes and countless articles for demanding publications to make her work more accessible to the ordinary reader. *Looking for Mr Darcy* was the result of that cajoling, and Rory was enjoying Clare's success as much as Clare was. She wasn't, however, entirely enjoying the presence of Caroline Goldacre in Clare's life and although she'd tried to question Clare more than once about employing the woman as her assistant, she'd not got far in learning what the attraction was. Clare had never seemed to need someone to sort her, monitor her, mind her, or otherwise keep her on track but for quite some time, Caroline Goldacre had been doing just that.

'I could *always* use a bit more organisation in my life,' was how Clare had explained it. Rather too breezily, Rory thought. Her own conclusion was that something more was going on.

*Jealous, Rory?* she asked herself.

She didn't *feel* jealous. But she certainly felt something.

So when she'd seen Clare in laughing conversation with the T-shirt woman, she'd watched their interaction, and she'd seen Caroline watching it as well. She knew what the outcome would be once Caroline followed the T-shirt woman out of the room.

So she waited until Caroline returned, her expression announcing that all had gone according to her wishes. At that point, Rory herself left the meeting room with Arlo trotting at her side. She headed in the direction of the stairway, and she caught the T-shirt woman up.

She said to her, 'I beg your pardon . . . ?' and she scooped Arlo up from the floor, tucking him beneath one arm so his weight was balanced on her hip. He settled against her. He was quite used to this procedure in which he became a canine shield. The shield allowed Rory to ignore her racing heart.

The woman turned. She was remarkably ill-dressed although Rory couldn't blame her. The heat inside the building was intolerable and had she not believed in looking professional when appearing with one of her authors, she might have dressed in a similar manner sans slogan printed across her chest. The woman slung a blob-like shoulder bag into position and used the back of her wrist to blot the perspiration on her upper lip.

Rory joined her at the head of the stairs. 'I couldn't help seeing that Ms Goldacre followed you out of the room.' She looked back at the doorway and shifted her topic to say, 'Well. Right. That's not quite true. I make it my business to keep an eye on things when it comes to Clare, so I was watching. I saw her give you her card, I saw you leave, I saw Caroline follow, and I have an idea what happened from there.' She set Arlo on the floor for a moment and worked her shoulder bag open. She dug within it to find her card case, from which she extricated one of Clare's cards and one of her own. As she did this, she said, 'Something tells me you're not a stalker.'

'I'm a cop,' the woman replied. 'Barbara Havers,' she added.

'Ah. Well, Ms Goldacre is sometimes too dedicated to keeping Clare safe from what she considers undesirable elements who might lure her from her assigned task of writing and lecturing. I, on the other hand, know that nothing and no one on earth can lure Clare Abbott from her work because she thrives upon it. She wanted you to have her card for some reason, so . . .' Rory extended it to Barbara. But before Barbara could reach for it, Rory said, 'You're not, right? I mean, a stalker. You're not just *claiming* to be a cop?'

Barbara Havers tucked her copy of *Looking for Mr Darcy* under her arm and fished inside her own shoulder bag. She brought forth a tattered wallet. From this she took her police warrant card as well as a business card printed with her name and all the relevant details that established her as part of the team 'working together for a safer London' from Victoria Block in New Scotland Yard. Rory looked at the one and took the other in hand. She saw that Barbara Havers was a detective sergeant attached to a homicide squad. She'd never met a detective before.

She said, 'Homicide. Goodness. Did . . . This is terribly odd of me to ask, but why is it that Clare gave you her card?'

Barbara Havers pointed to her T-shirt and said, 'Told her I'd fetch her one from Camden Lock Market and post it along. She said she wanted to wear it next time she saw her doctor.'

'That sounds exactly like her.' Rory extended Clare's card to the detective and added, 'Then here, please take it because Clare doesn't give out her business card if she isn't serious. The better course will be to send the T-shirt to her Shaftesbury address rather than her London address. She'll be heading there directly after her tour. If you can wait . . . say, perhaps six weeks?'

'Can do,' Barbara said. 'But I c'n also send it along to her publisher if it's going to cause a problem with her minder.'

'Caroline? Please don't give that a thought. Clare Abbott really has no minder but Clare Abbott. I'm her editor, by the way. Victoria Statham. Rory, actually. And this is Arlo,' she added as she reestablished the dog on her hip.

'I saw him earlier,' Barbara said. 'Bit hot for a vest, isn't it?' She indicated the canvas jacket on Arlo, green and PAD printed in large white letters on either side of it. 'What's PAD?'

'Psychological Assistance Dog,' Rory said.

The policewoman frowned. 'Psychological . . . what?'

'He makes it easier for me to go out in public.' Not wishing to explain further about how essential Arlo was to her, Rory hurried on with. 'Now, you *will* take Clare's request seriously, won't you?'

'Will do, of course,' Barbara Havers told her. 'I have to say it, though.'

'What's that?'

'Someone actually liking one of my T-shirts? It's more or less a first.'

*Camberwell*
*South London*

India Elliott was finding more of her old self every day. This was the self that had been confident and capable of making friends quickly, the self who also had learned early on and at the knee of her father to 'cut your losses when you realise you must'. He'd instructed her carefully on that aspect of life, saying, 'There's no shame in it, my girl. Better to end something than to carry on in a losing situation.'

She hadn't yet decided if cutting her losses applied to her marriage to Charlie, but she knew it was a possibility. Nat Thompson was part of the reason behind this. While she wasn't sure if Nat was going to be a fixture in her life, she enjoyed his company. Yet, the very last thing she wanted was to end up yet again the docile and agreeable mate of a man who cared for her.

She was frank about this. As a woman separated but not divorced from her husband, she thought it only fair that Nat knew the truth. So on their third date, she'd explained her situation. They'd gone to Somerset House and wandered through a Matisse exhibition, and afterwards over a shared slice of chocolate gateau, she'd told him about Charlie, about Will's death, and about herself.

She didn't begin with those topics. She wasn't the sort to offer mounds of personal information to anyone, a habit also learned at the knee of her father. He called it 'holding one's cards close, India'. He'd always loved gambling metaphors.

So she began with the logical questions about schooling and growing up and work. Ultimately, she asked about marriage. Had Nat ever been married? He was thirty-four, well of the age to have a failed starter marriage behind him. But he said no. 'I've always been a late bloomer. What about you?'

'Separated from my husband,' she told him. 'It was . . . I've been through a rather difficult time and so has he. There was a suicide in the family.'

He looked concerned. 'I'm sorry to hear that. Not your own immediate family, I hope.'

That seemed to give her entrée to speak about Will and his death. Nat, she discovered, had great sympathy for them all.

After that date, there had been another. On that one, he'd taken her to see his work. He was, she discovered, an expert in the preservation of old buildings, his last completed project a row of almshouses that had been under threat of being torn down. Tucked away near Streatham with the sounds of road-works rising from a brick wall behind them, they'd been ready for the earth mover when Nat had taken them in hand.

They were London's history, he explained. 'If someone doesn't take a stand against tearing things down merely because they're old and in disrepair, we lose part of who we are.' Then he added with an appealing shrug of his shoulders, 'Very old-fashioned of me, but there you have it.'

'I don't find you old-fashioned.'

'I'm glad of that,' he told her.

When he took her home later that evening, he kissed her goodnight. She'd begun wondering if he was even attracted to her, so the kiss was something of a relief. It lingered and then grew more intimate and she found that she liked this very much. When they broke off from each other, he said, 'I like you a great deal, India.'

'And I like you.'

To which he said, 'No. I mean I really like you. As in . . . I don't know. I'm not very good at this sort of thing. As I said, I'm a late bloomer.' He seemed to read the *oh no!* in her expression because he hastily added, 'Not in that way. It's just that I've never mastered the art of the chat so I guess what I'm saying is that . . .' Even in the faint illumination from the porch light she could see him blushing, 'I feel some quite serious desire when I'm around you. I don't feel it for every woman I meet. Of course, that could be because most of the women I meet are wearing twinsets and pearls and carrying large handbags filled with news articles about a building they wish to save. But I don't think so. It's just that—'

'Shush,' she said. 'I feel the same about you. Please kiss me again.'

He did. Then, as was his way, he left her after making sure she got safely inside and had locked the door behind her. He waited till she came to the window of the sitting room that she used as her surgery. After she waved an all's well, he turned and left her.

Less than thirty seconds later, her doorbell rang, so she assumed that he'd returned. She swung the door open with a ready smile. But on her front step was Charlie.

*Camberwell*
*South London*

Charlie knew she thought he was the other bloke ringing the bell. He saw this in her face, which was still aglow from kissing, and she'd believed he'd returned for what logically followed the kissing as the night the day.

He saw her expression immediately alter. She was at once alarmed. She looked at the street – for the other bloke, obviously

– then back at him. While her expression asked what on earth he was doing there, her words said something different.

'You look terrible, Charlie.'

That hardly mattered. It was no wonder to him that her first remark would refer to his appearance. He had, after all, just had a very good look at the bugger who'd a moment earlier had his tongue in her mouth, and he wasn't doing well by comparison.

'You're planning to sleep with him, aren't you?' were his first words although he hadn't intended them to be. They simply slipped from him nearly without his awareness, and he wanted to snatch them back the moment he said them. But since he couldn't do that, he went on instead. 'And it will be normal, won't it? It'll be excellent. It will actually be what you've—'

'I'm not planning anything, Charlie.'

'You're thinking about it, more each day. You're developing a fantasy about what it's going to be like to be *taken* instead of having to cajole your partner into it and then having to allow him to suckle in your arms like an infant while you—'

'Don't *do* this to yourself. You don't deserve it.'

That stopped him cold. He said bitterly, 'That's why.'

'What?'

'Why I won't let you go. You've understood me from the first. Even that first day at acupuncture, you knew.'

'You misconstrue. That first day at acupuncture I was no different with you than I am with any first time patient who's nervous. How are your headaches?'

'This isn't about my headaches. They're there, they're gone, they're back again. They don't make a difference. This makes a difference.' He gestured at the neighbourhood and then at the house. He gazed at her and after a moment he asked, 'Who is he? A patient?'

'He's just someone I met.'

'Where?'

'Charlie . . .'

God, it wasn't going according to his design at all. He'd meant to come only to make a start with her. But seeing her with him and watching her kiss him and knowing as he himself did the taste of her and the feel of her . . . It had done him in.

'No,' he said. 'He wouldn't be a patient. You've gone that route once and you're no fool. I expect you met him just as you say. A pub? The internet? Sharing a taxi in the rain?'

'We met on the bus,' she said.

'Which you wouldn't have done had you not left me because you wouldn't have been on the bus in the first place, having to trail up to the City from this . . . this neighbourhood. It's dangerous, India. You shouldn't be here alone.'

'That's not true. And anyway, it's what I can afford. I have a surgery here to make extra money at the weekend as well.' She indicated a sign in the sitting room's bay window. *Acupuncture*, it announced, along with the hours on Saturdays and Sundays when she was available.

He said to her, 'Money? I can give you money.'

She looked at him, said, 'Charlie, please don't,' because she knew there was no money that, at this point, did not come to him via his mother.

'Are you going to let me in?' he said.

He saw her swallow and imagined he heard it as well. She said, 'There isn't any point. This thing . . . with Nat . . .'

'That's his name, then. Nat. What sort of name is Nat? Is he a bug or something? Why not midge or fly or mosquito? Any of those would suit, wouldn't they?'

He saw that she was allowing this ridiculous line of interrogation because she could see how upset he was and, India being India, she felt sorry for that. But he reckoned she was also probably relieved that, at least, he'd got himself out of the flat in Spitalfields. But this visit of his, coming so hard on the heels of his mother's turning up at the Wren Clinic for that 'word' she wished to have with India, was going to tell her more than he wished her to know.

And so it did. India ignored the nonsense questions about Nat and said to him, 'What did your mum say to you this time? What did she threaten?'

'She wants me happy. She's terrified. Who wouldn't be? In her position. After Will.'

'You aren't Will. You never were. But you *must* pull yourself through this. You won't survive if you don't.'

'I won't survive without you.'

'You of all people know how stupid a thing that is to say,' she told him.

Unthinking, he reached for a sprig of holly that grew from an urn to the right of the doorstep. He jerked on it to break it from the plant, only to wince when the sharp point of one of the leaves pierced his thumb. India was watching but she didn't intervene to stop him from jerking on yet another sprig and meeting the same result.

He looked bleakly away from her, towards the street. No one was there. No one would see if he forced his way into her house and . . . did *what*? he wondered. Had his way with her like some Dark Ages lord and master who owned her body but wanted her soul as well? He said to the street and not to her, 'We're meant to be together, India.'

'No one is "meant" to be together.'

'Which goes for you and the midge. The mosquito. The gnat. All right, then. Nat.'

'I don't disagree.'

He turned back to her. 'Are you promising you won't . . . ? Saying that you won't . . . ? Saying that this whatever-it-is between you and him isn't going to end up in something more than what it is now?'

'I'm not saying that. And you must leave.' She took a step back and he knew she was going to close the door.

He made a move to stop her, his hand on the red surface of the smoothly painted wood. 'I want to come in. I want to see where you live. I want to understand why you left and why you're here and why you want to stay here.'

'You know all of that already. This is how it must be just now. You're worried and frightened and you're thinking that if you do something – the right thing – we can go back to being what we were. But we can't. Too much has happened. We can only go on and what we must wait to see is whether we're meant to go on separately or together.'

He felt as if the house tilted towards him, and he wanted to push back to keep it upright. The need to act was upon him. It felt as compelling as the struggle for air when a man knows he's drowning. He said, 'I want it to be together. I'll do anything to make it together. Anything.'

She looked at him with the sort of compassion that declared a seismic shift in their love that could not be repaired. She said, 'I know you'll do anything, Charlie. But don't you see? That's just the problem.'

*Spitalfields*
*London*

'Tell me honestly,' Rory Statham asked. 'Have you ever actually cooked a meal in this kitchen?' She and Clare Abbott were engaged in a postmortem of the evening's proceedings. They were at a recycled metal-topped table in the basement of Clare's ancient house in Elder Street. With Caroline Goldacre, they'd been picking through a typical Clare Abbott meal whose remains were spread out before them in containers, bags, bowls, boxes, and waxed wrapping paper: cheeses, grapes, savoury biscuits, olives, nuts, sliced peaches, a baguette, and a thoroughly hacked-at salami. Caroline had left the kitchen in order to stagger off to bed, but they had remained. Now they were finishing a second bottle of wine, alone in the room save for Arlo, who was snoozing on the floor with his moplike head resting on Rory's foot.

At the question, Clare looked round the room. Like the rest
of the house, she'd renovated it over the years. A wreck when
she'd bought it in the days when Spitalfields was considered
a backwater to which no respectable person would ever aspire,
it now stood along a terrace of similar residences in a narrow
cobbled street where once French Huguenot weavers had plied
their trade. They'd lived in abject conditions of damp, darkness,
and disease, the stench of their poverty a miasma not even the
rain could clear. Right into the middle of the twentieth century
the place had been a ghetto. Now, on the other hand and like
more and more of London, it was something of a coup to find
housing that was remotely affordable in this spot, so gentrified
had it become.

Cleverly, Clare had done little to change the exterior of
her home. Her front door was still spattered with yellow
graffiti, and the window boxes – where they existed and had
not fallen off the building entirely – offered up dead plants
and the occasional bird's nest. The windows were never
washed, and the ill-hung Venetian blinds behind them were
intended to suggest that nothing worthwhile could be found
within. This made sense to Rory in an area undergoing great
change. It also made sense when the house stood unoccupied
for weeks at a time while Clare was in Dorset or off lecturing
somewhere.

Inside the place, though, all was first rate. This included the
kitchen which, Clare admitted ruefully, she'd never used to
cook a full meal. She did her breakfast, of course. She made
the occasional sandwich as well. She heated up soup. And she
did bring in takeaway, if that counted for something. Rory
laughed and told her it didn't. To her question of Why go to
the expense of a kitchen like this, you mad woman?, Clare
offered the excuse of It's quite nice to look at, wouldn't you
say?

She poured herself the last of the wine, dividing it with
Rory. Above them on the street, they heard footsteps running
along the pavement. Someone shouted and someone else

replied. The smell of cigarette smoke came to them faintly through the open basement window.

'You were brilliant tonight,' Rory told Clare. 'I could tell something special set you off. What was it?' When Clare didn't reply at first, she added, 'Have you put a man in his place recently? A lover who began to have expectations of you?'

'It was the audience,' Clare said. 'There was a group of women right up front, some religious group, I daresay. They were positively firing eye bullets at me from the moment I picked up the microphone. Lord, how I love getting up people's noses.'

Rory smiled. 'This book's done it for you, Clare. D'you know we've gone back for a ninth printing?'

'That's down to the Darcy bit,' Clare declared. 'I'm not so stupid as to think the book took off on its own merits. It's the title. And the cover image, coming up with the visual that the name implies. Tight trousers, knee boots, some sort of delicious cutaway, frothy whatever at the neck of his shirt, tousled hair, burning eyes directed across the room at Elizabeth Bennet. Who wouldn't want Darcy? I bet even you want him. He could probably turn a heterosexual man.'

Rory laughed. 'You really are terrible. But, on the other hand, it's true.'

'Which part? That Darcy could make you like men or that you're a genius for coming up with the title and the image?'

'The latter,' Rory said. 'Those tight cream trousers—'

'Ah ha!' Clare pounced. 'So he's in there, isn't he? In the back of your mind. You're waiting for those burning eyes of his, Rory. Every woman is, no matter her inclination.'

'You included?'

Clare shot her a look. She did not, however, make a reply. Instead, she sawed off another chunk of salami, topped it with a large hunk of cheese, and took a huge and very Clarelike bite. 'Thank God for imported food,' she said, past her chewing. 'What about you?'

'Me and food? I adore imported food.'

'You and you-know-very-well. Anyone on the horizon yet?'

Rory bent and ran her fingers through Arlo's tousled fur. 'I don't think I want to go there again, Clare.'

Clare nodded thoughtfully in that way she had. It told one she was considering what she wanted to say. This was characteristic of her when she was with friends. Out in public, the woman was a cannon of witty or acerbic off-the-cuff remarks. But with those close to her, she was entirely different. She was careful, she knew her power to wound, and she never used it with those she cared for. She said, 'I'm not about to say to you that what happened was a lifetime ago, because it wasn't. But what is it now, Rory? Nine years?'

'Nearly.'

'And you've come a bloody long way in recovering. But for someone like you, there's a final step. Unlike me, you aren't meant to be alone. There's a woman out there who wants what you have to offer, and who's also ready to receive it.'

Rory felt that hardening inside of her, as if part of herself was undergoing a very quick freeze. It had always been thus when the truth wasn't quite being spoken as it needed to be, and that was especially the case just now. She reached for her wine glass, and said to Clare, 'You know this, do you?'

Clare tapped her temple and said, 'You need to listen to Auntie Clare. She knows what's what.'

'If that's the case . . . knowing what's what . . .' Rory glanced at the bottom of the stairway that led up to the living quarters in the house. It was an automatic move on her part to check for listeners. Clare followed her gaze and frowned. She was no conversational fool, so she would sense a coming change in topic. Rory said, 'Listen, Clare, something quite extraordinary happened this evening.' And she told her about Caroline removing Clare's business card from the woman to whom she'd given it. Rory referred to her as 'that T-shirt woman. She turned out to be a detective from the Met. I only mention it because this isn't the first time I've noted that Caroline tends to overstep. Now, don't say anything for a moment. I understand that part of her job is to keep you out of trouble when you're being too generous with people, but when I spoke to this woman – the Scotland Yard detective—'

'Scotland Yard detective?' Clare barked a laugh. 'I feel like Miss Marple!'

'Let me finish, Clare. When I spoke to this woman and found out why you'd given her your card – because of this T-shirt thing – it seemed to me that as she'd been standing right there, Caroline must have known fully well why you'd handed your card over: so the woman could post you something. Look, I know it's none of my business—'

'My life *is* your business.'

– 'but do you *want* her to do this sort of thing so arbitrarily? You might have given your card to someone who wishes you to speak, to be part of a conference or a seminar, to travel to Europe or even to America where, as we both know, the opportunities for your books are virtually untapped.'

'Always the businesswoman,' Clare said lightly.

'That's part of my job. But this situation . . . it's more than that. She really shouldn't be overstepping herself.'

Clare reached for her wine and a handful of olives. She began popping the latter into her mouth as she took in Rory's words. Rory thought at first she meant not to answer at all, but she finally said, 'Listen. I really couldn't do without her. I might be not competent at reining her in when she truly gets herself going, but she's only doing what you would do in the same position.'

'Fishing your business cards out of the pockets of people to whom you gave them? I hardly think so.'

'Attempting to keep me on course. That's all it is.'

Rory was unconvinced. There was something about Caroline Goldacre that worried her. She wanted to get to the heart of what it was, but she couldn't put a name to it, so she said, 'At least tell me why she's begun to travel with you. You've never before needed a minder on the road.' A thought suddenly struck her. She said, 'Clare, is something *wrong*? You're not ill,

are you? Has something happened that you can't manage on
your own any longer?'

Clare hooted. 'Darling, I'm strong as a horse. Unless . . .
D'you mean early dementia, or something? Absolutely not.
I'm fit as a mule. Pardon the equine references. I do note I
just gave you two. That's certainty not a good sign.'

'I'm not joking. You've always had me to manage things
when it comes to your book signings. You've had me as well
if you needed someone when you've gone on tour. So now to
have us both with you . . . I have to ask it. If there's nothing
gone wrong with you, with your health, is there something else
happening that I need to know about?'

Clare took more olives. She looked at Rory frankly. 'What
would that be?' she asked.

'I don't *know*. But I'm asking because I'm rather worried.
Look, I understand how you might want her in Shaftesbury:
dealing with your mail, managing your schedule, setting up
appointments and engagements, even keeping your house and
doing your cooking. But beyond that . . . Clare, I must be
frank. It seems as if she's rather too dug *into* your life.'

'Because I brought her with me to London? That's nothing.
She wanted to see her son. He lives not far from here. She
popped over there late this afternoon.' As Rory had done,
Clare glanced towards the stairway before going on. 'See here,
Rory. This is what it is: her younger boy died three years ago,
before she and I met. He killed himself, and there was no
mistaking it for an accident. She's had a rotten time of it since
then. The way I see it is that she lost someone quite precious
to her and when that happens, the survivor needs . . .' Clare
seemed to catch the expression Rory couldn't keep from her
face because she said, 'Oh Christ. I'm *so* bloody sorry.'

'It's all right. Fiona didn't kill herself.'

Clare nodded but her brow furrowed. From this, Rory knew
she believed she'd gone too far. It was the wine, she was thinking.
It made fools of them all. At her feet Arlo had begun to snore
lightly. She glanced down at him, feeling how her heart actu-

ally did swell – as they always declared in novels – with love for the little beast. She said, 'I'd be dead myself without this bloody little dog.'

'I don't believe that. You owe your life to your courage. But Caroline doesn't have that. She's not as strong as you are. She's not found a way to cope with her loss, aside from working for me.'

'Is that what she tells you?'

'It's what I see.'

'So are you trying to do for her what you did for me, then? Giving her time and a place just to . . . I don't know . . . just to recover?'

'I'm giving her employment.'

'And is she at least good at her employment?'

'Not particularly. Not all of it.'

'Then why not have her do something else? Be . . . merely a housekeeper for you?'

Clare rose from the table and began removing the items. She told Rory to stay where she was in order not to disturb her sleeping dog. She loved the little pooch, perhaps not as much as Rory, but with equal gratitude for how Arlo made it possible for Rory to go out again in the world. She said, 'I did try that, but she wouldn't have it. Oh, she did a bit of house-keeping for me at first, but she kept declaring herself capable of so much more. Research, ideas, a resource of individuals available for me to interview or study, editorial services, website designs and maintenance, Twitter feeds, blogs, the whole lot of what you at the publishing house would have me do and what I've been avoiding. She asked me for a chance just to show me how many ways she could be useful to me and – for my sins – I decided to give her that chance. Well heavens, darling, what else could I do? There was always the possibility that I'd stumbled on a gold mine of talent there in Shaftesbury.'

'So how has it worked out? Is she helping you with the next book? Has she blogged in your name? Is she maintaining a Twitter feed for you?'

Clare wrapped the salami, began to dump the olives and peaches and grapes into their separate containers. 'I expect you know the answer to that.'

'Then why not sack her? Or if not that, why not say "Afraid it has to be merely housekeeping full stop, old girl, as you're not up to the rest"?'

'It's simply not that easy.'

Rory frowned. There was something Clare wasn't telling her. She could feel it there, just out of reach, hovering like one of the Huguenot ghosts who walked the nighttime streets of Spitalfields. She said, 'Tell me why. Please.'

Clare seemed to think the request over as she stored their food in the fridge. She didn't answer till she'd finally returned to the table and sat. Then she said, 'As women, we have a responsibility to each other that men don't have. I've lived my life trying to follow that creed.'

'As you did with me. I know.'

'So when I first met Caroline – this was at the Women's League in Shaftesbury – and I heard her story, I thought how simple a thing it would be to extend my hand to her, if only to relieve one small part of the suffering she was going through. I've been enormously lucky in my own life and—'

'You grew up on a bloody sheep farm in the Shetland Islands. You had a brother who in the dark of night—'

'Yes. Right. Let's not go there please. My point is that I had parents who believed in me, a bloody good education, a chance to travel the world, a wonderful gap year in East Asia that opened my eyes to what women in male-dominated societies – not to mention in real poverty – have to endure. And on and on. While she had an early and very unhappy marriage to flee from her mum, and she never managed to find her own strength and purpose. She made her purpose her children, like so many women do, Rory. And then one of them killed himself. These are things I've never had to face. And when one's been lucky as I've been lucky . . .' She shrugged. 'I have no other way to explain it to you. Other than to say it's who I am.'

Rory took this in. Everything Clare had said was the truth. She did believe in a fellowship of women. She had spent most of her life acting upon that belief. So there was really *nothing* untoward in what she'd been doing for Caroline Goldacre. Yet Rory continued to feel unsettled.

She said, 'I suppose I have to accept it all then,' although she could hear the reluctance in her voice. 'But . . . She's not getting in the way of your next book, is she? How's it coming along? It's a brilliant idea as a follow-up to Darcy. I salivate each time I think of it, Clare.'

'The going's a bit slow at the moment with all the Darcy hoopla. *But*, dear editor, I shall make the deadline as I ever have.'

'If you can't, all you need to do is to let me know. Anything can be pulled from the catalogue.'

Clare waved off this idea. 'I'm entirely dedicated to striking while the iron is et cetera, as you well know,' she said. 'I fully intend to have it finished on time so that you and I can move into the future rich and fat and famous, my dear.'

31 July

As he approached her from the labyrinthine security area, Lynley didn't realise at first that the woman waiting for one of the lifts was Dorothea Harriman. He had never seen the departmental secretary reading a book and because of this, he didn't at first take note of the perfect ensemble and perfect blonde locks that marked her as forever Dorothea. It wasn't until she said his name that he recognised, from her habitual use of his full rank, Dorothea as the speaker.

'Why've you got paint on your hands, Detective Inspector Lynley?' she enquired. 'And are you aware there's also quite a streak of it in your hair above your right ear?'

'Is there indeed?' He felt for the latter and recognised from its unusual texture that she was correct. Of course, the colour alone would have indicated paint to her since fuchsia rather announced itself in ways that, perhaps, brown would not have done. 'Ah,' he said. 'Clearly, not enough shampoo this morning.' And to divert her from repeating her question, he asked one of his own, 'What are you reading? You looked fairly engrossed.'

She closed the book and handed it over. 'Rubbish,' she said.

He read the cover. *Looking for Mr Darcy: The Myth of Happily Ever After*. He took in the author's name and flipped, as was his habit, to see if there was a recent photo of the well-known feminist. There was. Over the years, Clare Abbott had become quite rakish in appearance, wildly grey-haired and looking fierce behind thick-framed spectacles of a style that had gone by the wayside at least seventy years earlier. He started to return the book to Dorothea who held up her hands in a gesture that told him she wanted no further part of the thing. The lift doors opened, and they entered together. She punched for their floor and settled back against the railing that ran along the wall.

'You're not enjoying it?' he asked politely.

'Stuff and nonsense written by a lesbian, a man-hater, or a general misotrist.'

Lynley didn't correct her on the final word. He got the point. 'So I suppose you're *not* reading in advance of taking the marital plunge?'

'Detective Sergeant Havers gave it to me.' She gazed up at the numbers that lit to show them the floors they were passing. She sighed and gestured to the book. 'This, I'm afraid, was the result of our first experience together in life beyond the walls of New Scotland Yard.'

'Are you saying you took her to a book shop, Dee?'

She levelled a look at him. 'Do you think I'm thick? I took her to Middlesex Street. I actually *revealed* to her the source of virtually my entire wardrobe. All right, not all of it. I mean, obviously, I do have some basic pieces – more or less foundations but not foundation *garments* in the strictest sense of the word, but building blocks on which anyone with any sense of fashion can begin to at least *structure* a wardrobe.'

Lynley felt all out at sea. Nonetheless, he tried to look encouraging. He said, 'Ah,' and waited for more.

The lift doors opened. They stepped into the corridor, where Dorothea went on. 'Essentially, I showed her everything. I explained how it's done. We went over accessories and the importance of owning a very good steam iron and purchasing buttons to alter the look in order to make the piece seem more expensive. *And* I even told her *where* because if one wants vintage, one has to know where it can be found.'

He went with one word, 'Vintage?'

'Vintage *buttons*, Detective Inspector. Leather-covered. Shell. Oyster. Even Bakelite. One takes a very simple suit that costs twenty pounds—'

He raised an eyebrow.

'Yes, yes, they exist. Obviously *you* wouldn't be seen dead in one, but—'

'That's hardly the case. I was about to ask where such bargains can be—'

'Middlesex Street. Like I said. So if you take the suit or the jacket or whatever and change its buttons to something . . . well, rather flash . . . then people concentrate on the buttons instead of on the suit and because the buttons are special, they naturally conclude that the suit is as well.'

'I see.' He held up the book. 'As to this?'

'She said she saw a poster advertising it. I have *no* idea where because within fifteen seconds of my getting her to the market, she'd disappeared in the direction of the food stalls.'

'Why am I not surprised?'

'She didn't find it in one of the food stalls, of course. She found several plates of pad Thai or something. At least that's what she told me. But when she gave me that –' a nod at the book – 'she said it was down to our jaunt to the clothing market and thank you very much, Dorothea. Don't ask me how she discovered it. P'rhaps someone handed it over to her in the hope that . . . whatever. I do *not* know.'

Lynley opened the book and saw the inscription. He said, 'It's signed to you.'

'It never is!' When Dorothea saw the title page, her blue eyes widened. Then they narrowed, as she apparently took in the barb behind being given such a book. 'She did it as a joke then, didn't she? She thinks I exist *merely* to capture a man because I think that's what life is all about. I find a man and he rescues me from this –' with a wave of her arm to encompass all of New Scotland Yard – 'and takes me to . . . to Surrey where we buy a twee little cottage and make babies together.'

'Surely not Surrey,' Lynley said gravely but with a smile.

She smiled as well, in spite of herself. 'Berkshire then. Perhaps Buckinghamshire.'

'Yes. Perhaps that,' he said.

'Well, I shall sort her, Detective Inspector Lynley. My first plan didn't work. Obviously.' She frowned for a moment and tapped her foot. She said, 'Gardening? Vegetable growing? One can meet all sorts of men these days in gardening centres . . .'

'Lord,' was Lynley's reply.

'DIY, then. Going into those shops where you have to ask questions of guys who're only too happy . . .' A sudden thought seemed to strike her. 'Which, by the way, brings us back to where we started, doesn't it? You never answered me. Why d'you have paint in your hair? You've never seemed the DIY type.'

'Dorothea,' he said, 'there are depths to me of which you are completely unaware.'

'Hmmm. But fuchsia, Detective Inspector Lynley?'

'Let it be our secret,' he replied.

*Belsize Park*
*London*

Fuchsia was merely the accent colour in the bathroom, a touch of it only in a horizontal stripe six inches above a wainscoting of white tiles set in, he'd learned, a pattern called subway. Otherwise, the room was a pale grey with darker grey towels and further touches of fuchsia in what Daidre called 'the extras'. These consisted of a vase, a rug on the floor that was polka dotted, and a vertical stripe rendered in special paint for fabric on the Roman blind that covered the new double-glazed window – 'energy efficient, Tommy' – that she'd had installed. That window, the electrical wiring, and the plumbing were the three

projects that Daidre Trahair had not taken on herself. The rest
of the room she'd done by inches and degrees on her free time
away from London Zoo, where she was the large animal veterinarian. When Lynley had time and when he wished to see
her, he was her Man Friday in the DIY renovation of a disas-
trous flat in Belsize Park which she'd purchased in order to
have a home near to the zoo. She could bicycle there, she'd
declared. And once the flat was made livable, she'd be in her
element.

He'd had his doubts about the project, but Daidre had
pooh-poohed them. She'd declared herself very handy, and
she'd proved that over the months she'd been in residence.
She'd done the bathroom as project number one, and the
accent paint had gone up last. He'd lent a hand, not because
he was particularly handy himself – he absolutely was not –
but because it was the only way to spend a few hours with
her at present.

Now with the key she'd given him, he let himself into the
flat that same evening. He'd come armed with yet another
pizza as their dinner, walking it down from the shops in Belsize
village and trying not to consider that he'd not eaten so much
pizza since his time at university. He set it under the bay
window where they took their makeshift meals when he called
upon her. Their seating consisted of two camping stools, their
table was the discarded window from the bathroom placed
over two rusty lobster pots that Daidre declared she'd found
among the rubble in her back garden when she'd had the filthy
cooker and the disreputable fridge hauled away from where
they'd been shoved by their previous owner.

There was no kitchen yet. There was barely a bedroom.
Daidre slept on a camp bed kitted out with a sleeping bag in
the larger of the two rooms designated for that purpose, but
like the kitchen, that room remained what it had been when
she'd made her purchase: a wreck with holes in the walls and
a window painted blue and painted shut. It wasn't high on her
priority list, she said. The kitchen, she'd told him, had to come

next. How are you with kitchens, Tommy? she'd asked. His skills there, he'd told her, were fairly comparable to those for bathrooms.

The nature of their relationship remained as she'd told him from the very first it would have to be. She held a large part of herself *to* herself, and Lynley understood that she believed she had to do this. But he continued to want to draw her out, and he'd begun to ask himself if this longing had to do with the challenge she presented or with something more than that. He had no answer yet. But she was, he thought, completely self-reliant and utterly self-sufficient, and this also made her profoundly intriguing.

He went to check on the kitchen. He saw that, according to plan, the new double-glazed window had been installed sometime today. The French windows for behind the room's eating area leaned against the far wall that, at present, featured only a narrow doorway to the garden. Those French windows would go in next, but only when the construction on the wall had been completed, which it had not. Nothing else had been done.

He returned to what would be the sitting room. He'd brought with him *Looking for Mr Darcy* and he reached in his jacket for his spectacles and dipped into the book as he waited for Daidre. It began, he saw, with the subject of Tristan and Iseult. This myth, declared the author, was where the entire wrong-headed modern idea of romantic love had begun, centuries ago within the tale of a knight, his lady, and the great impossibility of their passion for each other.

Lynley was deep into Tristan's half of the tale when he heard Daidre's key in the lock. He set the book aside, removed his glasses, and rose from the camping stool. She came in, rolling her bicycle into the flat and saying with a start, 'Tommy! I didn't see your car.' She looked back over her shoulder, apparently trying to work this out. 'Surely you didn't come by public transport.'

'You know me too well. It's parked up in the village. I walked from there. With dinner, as it happens,' and he indicated the pizza box.

'Is someone minding the Healey Elliott, then? Are you paying a twelve-year-old to keep the dust from its bonnet?'

He smiled at this. 'He's fifteen.'

'And happy to be of service, I expect. Are you letting him sit in it?'

'Good Lord. I'd hardly go that far.'

She leaned the bicycle against the wall and said as he took a step towards her to kiss her hello, 'Keep at a distance. I must have a shower. What have you brought?'

'They were having a special on goat at the Turkish restaurant.'

'Why do I see a pizza box, then?'

'A clever disguise. Had I walked out of the place with the appropriate takeaway carton, there's a very good chance I would have been mobbed.'

'Hmmm. Yes. Well, I hope the "goat" is olive, mushroom, and mozzarella.'

'Why else live I in our native land?'

She laughed. Once again, he began to cross the room to her. She held up her hand. 'Elephants, today. Truly. I must have a shower.' She dashed away from him, down the narrow corridor and to the bathroom, where she closed the door.

She liked her showers long, so Lynley knew she would be a while. He took out his spectacles again, went back to his camping stool, and picked up the book along with a glass of the wine they'd not finished three nights earlier. He continued his reading.

He moved on to Iseult's half of the tale, the Irish daughter of the sorceress Queen. She was the feminine ideal, he saw, the other half of a doomed courtly romance. He was on to the author's analysis of this when Daidre returned. She stood behind him, put her hand on his shoulder, and he caught the fresh scent of her as she said, '*Looking for Mr Darcy*? What on earth are you reading? Are you seeking some pointers in the area of masculine perfection? Or merely wondering why women are still smitten by someone so . . . so . . .'

'So?' he enquired, looking up at her.

'Well, he's a terrible snob, isn't he?'

'The marriage proposal *was* rather teeth grating,' Lynley said. 'But he was brought to his knees in the end by the love of a good woman. At least that's what we're led to believe, along with the assertion that despite having the most horrifying mother-in-law in literature, he and his wife managed to live happily ever after at Pemberley among the Van Dycks and Rembrandts and on the vast acreage inclusive, as I recall, of a very fine trout stream.'

'That was the ticket to their happiness, I expect. One does love fresh trout. So what is that, actually?' She nodded at the book.

He told her of the book's origins, ending with, 'Dorothea believes that Barbara must have a diversion from fixating on her work troubles. A sexual diversion, to be specific. For her part, Barbara apparently believes that Dorothea needs her thinking adjusted on the topic of men.'

'Sounds like a friendship made in heaven. And you?'

He set the book on the floor and rose. 'I was merely engaged in some light reading as I waited for you.'

'Has your thinking undergone an adjustment from your reading?'

'It's all so blasted difficult, isn't it?'

'Entanglements generally are. Which is why I avoid them, preferring animals instead.'

He gazed at her and she met that gaze directly. There was no challenge in her eyes, for that was not her way. Daidre always spoke the truth as she knew it. It was part of her appeal. He said, 'Right. But let's not drift in that direction just now. I've not said hello to you properly.'

'You're better off for it. Because of the elephants. I do think the shower's taken care of that, though.'

'I hope so, although it probably wouldn't have mattered much.'

'Have you ever smelled elephant?'

'On my bucket list.' He kissed her lightly and then again. He found the scent of her intoxicating, despite its being merely the scent of her soap and shampoo.

She ended the kiss but not all at once, and he found that gratifying. She gazed at him with unmistakable fondness. 'You've had wine,' she said. 'I haven't. It's hardly fair.'

'That can, of course, be immediately remedied.'

'A very good idea.' She went to their makeshift table and opened the pizza box. He watched her, noting the unselfconscious nature of her movements as she brushed her damp sandy hair off her face, securing it behind her ears, and then sat and dipped into the olive, mushroom, and mozzarella masterpiece. She took a bite and looked up at him. 'After a day with elephants, heaven,' she declared. She gestured with the pizza slice at his own camping stool and at the book that lay next to it on the floor. 'So tell me about *Looking for Mr Darcy* and living happily ever after,' she said. 'I note it has the word *myth* in its title.'

*Camberwell*
*South London*

It was half past seven when Charlie Goldacre rang the bell at India's small house in Benhill Road. There were no lights on, but he told himself that she could be in a back room of the place. She wasn't. When no one answered his ring, he stepped back from the tiny front porch to look above at the first floor windows. Nothing indicated a human presence.

He gazed round the neighbourhood. While it was true that he could have just as well phoned her with the message he wished to deliver, he'd thought it wiser to come in person. Now, however, what to do?

He decided upon a walk to Camberwell Church Street, just at the end of Benhill Road. If he could find a moderately decent pub there, he could while away an hour or so and then return in the hope that India would have arrived home.

He set off up the street. He didn't get far. He was opposite a nondescript yellow building with the look of a community centre when the sound of raucous, joyful singing burst forth from the open doors. He slowed.

It was gospel music, sung a cappella. The volume of it along with the lyrics arrested him, declaring that *Abel's blood for vengeance/Pleaded to the skies;/But the blood of Jesus/For our pardon cries.* As the song continued, Charlie crossed over curiously. Then he saw that the building in question wasn't a community centre at all, but rather Jesus Saviour Pentecostal Church of Camberwell, and what he was hearing was the church's choir in rehearsal. *Oft as it is sprinkled/On our guilty hearts,/Satan in confusion/Terror struck departs* they sang.

He peeked in the doorway from the vestibule. At least forty strong, the choir stood on risers in what served as the chancel, their director before them. As Charlie watched, he pointed out a soloist who stepped forward and belted out the next verse. It was a mixed bag of people in the choir, he saw, a real United Nations of church going. They wore their street clothes as did their director, but Charlie could imagine them as they would be on a Sunday, kitted out in red or blue or gold cassocks and moving rhythmically, as they were at the moment, to the uplifting beat of the song. He was thinking that having a listen to them would be far more enjoyable than whiling away an hour alone in a pub when he saw India.

She was, amazingly, in the choir. She was, as joyfully as the others, clapping and singing the back-up notes in accompaniment of the soloist.

To Charlie, it was an astounding sight: India, his self-effacing wife, in a mixed race choir, openly enjoying herself. He could not remember ever having seen her like this. He pulled back and looked round the vestibule. There was a window ledge with brochures fanned out on it. He went to this and leaned against it. He would wait for her here and listen.

There were four more songs to be rehearsed. He found they did much to buoy his spirits. When the rehearsal ended, he heard the choir director giving them instructions for Sunday's service. He concluded with, 'And you, Izzy Bolting, had better show up on time because there is no way I'm allowing you to slip into the choir late, fall on your bum, and make us all look like damn fools again.' Someone called out, 'Language, Pastor Perkins!' and laughter followed. Then came the sounds of the choir noisily disbanding. Footsteps trod up the aisle.

Before any of the choir members reached the vestibule, however, a man entered the church, and Charlie shrank back. He recognised him as India's new bloke Nat, obviously there to fetch her. The man wouldn't recognise Charlie, but still Charlie did not come forward. Thus, he saw the greeting between the two of them – India and her bloke – before either one of them knew he was there.

She came out with the last of the choir. She walked to Nat at once, saying, 'You're here. Lovely. I've just got to pop back to the house for five minutes,' and lifting her face to his for a kiss. She said, 'Hmm. You taste of chocolate.'

He said, 'On purpose. Would you like more?' and she laughed.

She stepped back from him, and that was when she saw Charlie by the window. Immediately all colour drained from her face. At that, Charlie knew that India had begun sleeping with the other man. He felt momentarily paralysed by his own agony.

India said, 'Charlie! What are you doing here? How did you know where to find me?'

He took from this that she thought he'd been stalking her again, and he wanted to protest, but at India's saying of his name, Nat put his arm protectively round her shoulders in a way that made Charlie wonder exactly what she'd said about him. Was it that he hadn't adjusted yet to the end of things between them? Was it that he'd been trying to reason with her, to explain that he was attempting to overcome those things about himself that she'd said he needed to overcome? Or was it more than that . . . such as what it was like to be with him when he was at his most pathetic, requiring her to be the Madonna and the Whore simultaneously for him so that he could reach one searing moment of forgetting? Charlie couldn't believe India would have told Nat about that. But it seemed to him that she'd revealed something because knowledge of a sort flashed across the man's face and with that knowledge a bone deep contempt.

India said again, 'Charlie, what are you doing here?'

He said stupidly albeit honestly, 'I was in the neighbourhood.'

'No one's "in the neighbourhood" who doesn't live here.'

Charlie said with a nod at Nat, 'What about him?'

'You know what I mean,' she said. 'You've been following me again, haven't you?'

Nat said, 'She hasn't rung the police yet, but if this doesn't stop, she will do. You know what stalking is, don't you?'

Charlie felt the first flush of anger. 'Shut up. This doesn't concern you.'

Nat took a step towards him. India put her hand on his arm. She said not to him but to Charlie, 'We're going out to dinner.'

'I don't expect you're inviting me along,' Charlie said. 'Third wheel and all that. Just the husband getting in the way of the wife and her fancy man.' And to Nat Thompson, 'She did tell you I'm the husband, didn't she?'

'For now,' Nat said.

At that, Charlie wanted to hurl himself at the bloke. He wanted to drag him over to one of the church's windows and drive his head straight through it. But he knew at the same time how utterly risible the image was. Although shorter than Charlie by an inch or more, Nat had the body of someone who took care to keep himself fit, and already Charlie could see that his hand – the one not firmly clasping India's shoulder – had curled into an anticipatory fist.

India said quickly, 'Nat, will you wait outside for a moment?'

The man didn't answer at once. Instead, he did an assessment of Charlie, and Charlie could see that in Nat's estimation, he was coming up very short. When India said his name quietly another time, though, he nodded. 'If you need me . . .' he told her.

'Thank you, darling.' As soon as she said the final word, India's face flooded crimson. When Nat walked out of the church, she said to Charlie, 'That wasn't deliberate. I'm sorry.'

Despite what he was feeling, an anguish intensified so greatly that his entire body was throbbing with it, Charlie said, 'I do know who you are, India.'

'Thank you,' she said. 'Now you need to tell me why you've come. If this is about Nat, it's simply not on that you—'

'There's a memorial meant for Will.' If she didn't talk about Nat, Charlie could pretend, if only for a moment, that he did not exist. 'I thought you might want to come.'

She frowned, looking perplexed. 'But before the cremation, we had a service.'

'It's not that sort of memorial. There's an actual memorial, a physical memorial and it's being dedicated. I hoped you . . .' He cleared his throat, for it had begun to tighten. 'It would mean a great deal to me if you came, India.'

'Where?'

'Shaftesbury.'

He saw her defences rise in the way her posture altered, her neck lengthening as her chin lifted. 'Not your mum's house.'

'That's not where it is. There's a spring on some land below Bimport Street—'

'Where?'

He waved off her question with, 'It's not important. It's below the property where Clare Abbott lives. Mum can walk to it – to the spring – on workdays when she wants to think about Will or meditate or something.' He coughed roughly, surprised by the sudden emotion that overcame him. He said, 'It's this thing Clare Abbott's done for her, just to be kind, I presume. Because of Will. She's brought in someone to do the design. I think it's a seating area at the spring along with a stone for Will's name and I don't know what else. Clare phoned me up as she's had it in the works for a while and now it's ready. She'll take her there on some sort of pretext and the rest of us will be waiting.'

'Your dad as well?'

Charlie snorted. 'That would be a real slap in Mum's face. No, he's not been invited. It'll be Clare, Alastair, me . . . I was hoping for you as well. I've been looking for Lily to tell her, but no luck there. I think women from the Shaftesbury Women's League will attend. I don't know exactly. I was just . . . I know it's a lot to ask India, what with Nat in the picture.'

He stopped his rambling discourse when he saw that she was softening. He hated the idea that she was softening because she probably felt sorry for him, but he decided he would take that if it meant she would go down to Shaftesbury with him. They could drive together and he'd be able to spend the day with her. He could prove to her . . . something . . . anything . . . whatever needed to be proved to make her consider returning to him.

She said, 'Of course I'll go.' She reached out her hand, but she'd kept her distance, so she did not touch him. 'I'm terribly sorry, Charlie. About everything. You know.'

'But not about him,' he said, inclining his head towards the door of the church and the man who waited for India outside.

'I can't be sorry about Nat.'

'So what does that mean?'

'I don't know exactly,' she said.

# 10 August

*

SIX WEEKS BEFORE

A Londoner from birth, Rory Statham always arrived in Shaftesbury with the very same feeling: that she was casting herself adrift from civilisation, entering a place where the wind that swept up the stone spur of greensand from the wide, marshy bowl of Blackmore Vale rendered the town bleak in winter and far too exposed to the vicissitudes of English weather the rest of the year. As far as she was concerned, Shaftesbury's one claim to fame was a picturesque cobbled lane called Gold Hill, and this brief, descending thoroughfare actually offered the casual visitor only two opportunities for delight. The first presented the chance to admire a row of admittedly lovely old cottages that tumbled down the hillside. The second tendered a heart-stopping climb back up to the town centre should one be foolish enough to descend the length of the lane to arrive at the neighbourhood of St James below. At the top of this climb, a panorama of Blackmore Vale presented itself on a clear day from a tarmac promenade called Park Walk. Here one could see as far as the emerald lumps of Hambledon and Bulbarrow Hills and in the distance the chalk ridges and lime-stone plateaus of the Isle of Purbeck some thirty-five miles away. But otherwise, as far as Rory could tell, there was nothing at all in the town to enchant.

Clare Abbott always claimed that this conclusion of Rory's was complete tosh as the town centre had a *quite* decent medi-eval church plopped down in the market place as well as a town hall that, while admittedly only pre-Victorian, was at least built to look like a companion of the ancient church next to it. And yes, yes, although there seemed to be a plethora of charity shops for so small a town, Shaftesbury also had the requisite pubs, tea shops, hotel, supermarket, clothing shops, and police station. All of life's requirements, she declared. To Rory's insistent queries about *how* Clare could possibly spend so much time in such a backwater when she had, after all, a home in London, Clare would go on with a dismissive, Because it *isn't* London, Rory. To which she would add that Shaftesbury's very lack of London's diversions or – 'let us face it' – its lack of even Sherborne's diversions, was precisely why Clare had chosen to live here. King Alfred, she'd declared more than once, had selected well when he established the town. It had excellent defensive properties since its exposed position allowed one to see the approach of the enemy for miles around. To Rory's pointed demand about enemies from whom Clare thought she needed to be kept safe, Clare laughed and said they were the enemies that shouted in her mind when she attempted to work. The wind out shouts them, she liked to say.

Rory couldn't disagree with that. There was wind aplenty. Clare's house in Bimport Street sat in the west part of the town, facing south-east, and while its spacious front garden offered a pleasant lawn from which one could enjoy the sun while lounging upon one of the several mossy deck chairs with the house itself as protection from buffeting, its rear garden suffered the same prospect as did Park Walk: gale force winds storming across the valley and sweeping like ceaseless tidal waves to beat against the back of Clare's house. Only in the finest weather could one actually use her back garden. The rest of the time, it was similar to the town itself, victimised by its position in the landscape.

Now Rory pulled up to Clare's house and opened the wrought iron gate that marked the property as private. Beyond this gate, a short drive led to a parking area for visitors and, beyond this, to the garage for Clare's ageing Jetta. High summer, and there was not a breeze stirring in the oak trees standing between the house and the street as Rory got out of her Fiat and went to the car's hatchback for Arlo's travel kennel. She let the dog out and he bounded happily across the lawn, sniffing and marking along the flower beds. It was a bright, warm day of perfect weather with more promised for the morrow, which Clare had chosen as the dedication day for the memorial she'd had built to honour the memory of Caroline Goldacre's younger son.

Rory and Arlo had come to Shaftesbury for 'the ceremony' as Clare was calling it. Rory had no clue what sort of ceremony was intended, and she would have vastly preferred to skip the entire dedication, for there were far too many unanswered questions in her mind about Caroline Goldacre, and she remained uneasy about all of them. But Clare had been insistent and when it came to Clare, Rory generally wavered first and caved in second.

'Let's just say I'd love to have you here as my friend,' was how Clare put it. 'Please say that you'll come, Rory. Afterwards, we can . . . I don't know . . . take a drive to Chesil Beach? Corfe Castle? A long walk for Arlo on Castle Hill? Name your price.'

Rory had told her that there was no price and that she would be there, and so she was. But when she walked along the limestone path to the front door and rang the bell, no one was at home. Rory fished in her bag for her coin purse in which she kept the keys she had to both of Clare's houses. She whistled for Arlo to cease his explorations among the shrubbery and she let herself in, calling Clare's name. No reply. She called Caroline's next. Same result. But it was no matter. Rory knew the house well, so she said, 'Come along, then' to her dog and took her overnight case up to the bedroom she always used. There she opened the window. She leaned out to look at the view as Arlo did his best to make sure the room was up to his sniff standards.

She could see from this spot the site that Clare had chosen for the memorial. Some fifty yards beyond her back garden, the landscape fell away to a narrow strip of paving called Breach Lane and on the north side of this little street and somewhat along the way of it, Rory could see a white canopy set up and within the canopy a stack of folding chairs waiting to form a seating area. Near those chairs, three people were talking. Rory recognised one of them as Clare. Her arms were crossed and her gaze was directed towards a spring just beyond the tent, where water bubbled into a pool set off by new shrubbery. There, benches of what looked like Purbeck limestone appeared to be a feature of the spot, as did something quite large and covered with sheeting, which was presumably the memorial.

Rory observed this thoughtfully. Why Clare wanted to honour a young man she'd never met was a mystery to her. All she'd been able to get from Clare on the subject was just that she thought it 'would please Caroline', and she'd not asked further questions, deciding it would be best to let this particular dog lie. Please Caroline? had been her thought, though. Why on *earth* did Clare wish to please Caroline?

Rory turned from the window and checked the bed. It wanted sheets and pillow cases, so she went to fetch them from the airing cupboard. Arlo trotted along at her side. She bent to pet him, told him what a good boy he was, and rooted for what she needed in the cupboard. When she had the room set up, she descended the stairs to the kitchen, where she made herself a cup of tea and offered Arlo a bowl of water. She searched out the bed she kept for him in Shaftesbury, found it on top of the washing machine, and got him established in the sitting room, along with her tea and a plate of three lemon biscuits. She'd just placed this on a table in the bay window that over-looked the front garden when she heard the door open and close and footsteps come into the flagstone-floored entry. She went to the sitting room door to see that Caroline Goldacre had arrived, bearing the day's post and a smallish parcel.

Caroline started with a cry when she saw Rory, although

Rory found this reaction odd since her car was in plain sight next to Clare's and, indeed, Caroline would have had to park behind her anyway. The woman also dropped a handful of letters and the parcel, saying, 'Rory! You gave me quite a start.' She ignored Arlo who came to greet her, tail wagging in doggy hello. She glanced at him and then away, saying to Rory, 'Clare didn't tell me you were coming down. I would have been here to meet you.'

'I've got the key,' Rory told her. 'Arlo . . .' to the dog who was busy sniffing Caroline's ankles, 'back to bed please.'

Caroline watched the dog as if to make sure he didn't take a pillow from the sofa with him in order to chew it to bits. She then said, 'Still and all . . . Well, no matter. Obviously, I've not seen to the spare room.'

'Not a problem,' Rory said. 'I saw to it myself.'

'Oh.' Caroline glanced at the stairs. 'It's very odd that Clare wasn't here to greet you.' And then after a moment she added carefully, 'Rory, forgive me. I must ask. Clare *does* know you're coming, doesn't she?' Caroline made the question casual but there was no masking its probing nature.

'She invited me,' Rory said.

'How strange that she didn't tell me.'

Rory wanted to ask why Caroline seemed to require knowledge about anyone's intended visit to Clare, but she merely said, 'She's been busy. I daresay it slipped her mind.'

'Setting off somewhere, just the two of you then?' Caroline asked. 'Or I suppose I should say the three of you as, of course, you will have your little dog, won't you.'

'I certainly will,' Rory replied pleasantly.

'Well, she didn't tell me that either, if you *are* setting off. Does she have an event she's forgotten to tell me about? You aren't heading to a conference, are you?'

Rory shook her head. 'This is just a visit.'

'In the midst of all her publicity work for the Darcy book? Extraordinary.' Caroline flashed her a smile. 'Ah well. As long as you're sure this isn't a surprise.'

'As I've said. She knows I'm coming.'

'Very odd that she wasn't here to greet you then.'

'As *you've* said,' Rory pointed out. 'Twice now.'

'It's just that . . .' Caroline blew out a breath and shoved her mass of dark hair off her shoulders. 'There's actually not enough food in the house, Rory. Of course, I'll go back into town for groceries when I have a moment. But if I'd known in advance . . .'

'I won't have you do that at all,' Rory told her. 'I've had a very long drive and it'll be good to have a walk into the town centre. I can pick up what I want. And Arlo needs a walk.'

'Now that *would* be a blessing,' Caroline said. 'And if you wouldn't mind doing it straightaway . . . ? So that I can sort out what needs to be prepared for dinner?'

'Actually, I was just about to have a cup of tea,' Rory said, as pleasantly as she could manage. 'And not to worry about tonight. I'm quite happy to take Clare out for a meal.'

That said, Rory turned and went back into the sitting room, leaving Caroline with the day's post and whatever sorting out she needed to do with it. She was enjoying her tea and her second lemon biscuit along with a copy of *Majesty* that Clare religiously bought for the unintended amusement value of its photo spreads and its breathlessly admiring reportage on obscure royal families round the globe when she heard Caroline at the door to the sitting room. She looked up.

Caroline was holding a T-shirt before her, still bearing the signs of having been folded. Its colour was black and across the front of it scrolled the words 'On the eighth day, God created clotted cream', beneath which was the depiction of a mound of that substance with a fanciful serving spoon sticking out of it.

Rory chuckled. 'That would be from the woman at the Bishopsgate signing. Was that in the parcel just now?'

Caroline didn't join in the amusement. She said, 'How did this come to be sent here? Clare was merely being polite. You *know* how she is: completely incapable of giving people the casual brush off. So what I'm employed to do is to brush them off for her. I took Clare's card back from that person because I knew she didn't actually want this ridiculous thing, Rory. She was merely offering someone one of those moments in which one human being thinks a connection is being made with another. A feel good moment, as Americans would call it. So how did this T-shirt end up being purchased and sent directly here to her home? Because I have to tell you what that suggests.'

'What?'

'That you went behind my back and gave whoever-she-was one of Clare's cards despite having seen me take it from her. Which, of course, you *had* to have seen or you wouldn't have given her another card in the first place.'

'If you know all this, what are your questions, Caroline?'

Caroline dropped the T-shirt over the back of an armchair as she came into the room. 'You hate that I work for her, don't you?' She positioned herself directly in front of Rory, who laid her magazine aside and said, 'Actually, no. I don't understand exactly what it is that you do for her that makes you so indispensable, but Clare can employ anyone she wishes to employ.'

'That's a rubbish answer. You hate that I do precisely what she's told me to do because it's generally something that *you* don't want her to do at all. So let me ask you this. D'you think I *want* to be her gatekeeper? Do you think I *enjoy* following her round and cleaning up her messes?'

Rory observed the other woman, noting the unmistakable fire in her eyes. She said, '"Messes"? What are you talking about?'

'I'm talking about the fact that, despite the however-many-it-is years of your alleged "friendship", you haven't yet twigged that Clare Abbott isn't at *all* who you think she is. How well do you actually know her at the end of the day?'

Rory could see this for what it was, an invitation to a very strange confrontation that she didn't wish to have. She said mildly, 'How well do we ever know another person?'

'Well enough in this case for me to be able to tell you that Clare isn't who you wish her to be and you can believe that as I live and breathe.'

Rory stood. She'd finished her cup of tea and although there was another biscuit left, she thought the course of wisdom might be to leave the other woman to do whatever stewing she felt she needed to do on the matter of who knew whom and what sort of difference that made anyway. She said, 'I'll walk to the town centre now. Come along, Arlo. Is there anything at all you'd like me to fetch you, Caroline?'

'You're the wedge,' was Caroline's reply.

'What?'

'You're not *trying* to drive a wedge between me and Clare. You're *being* the wedge.'

'This is only a T-shirt,' Rory said patiently. 'You're creating out of it—'

'I'm not a fool, Rory. Don't think I don't know that you've been reminding Clare every chance you have that you and she have history together while I am merely her employee. You see her as brilliant and clever, don't you? But you have *no* idea what really goes on or the efforts I go to in order to keep her on the straight and narrow instead of exposing herself to situations that could ruin her in an instant, which – let me be brutally honest here – she is probably doing at this precise moment.'

Rory blinked. She said quietly, 'I'm taking Arlo for a walk now. I'm going to fetch some groceries while I'm out. You're seeing to the day's post, I believe. What we're not doing is discussing Clare any further. Arlo, come.' She headed past her, out of the sitting room, to the front door, taking up Arlo's lead from the stool where she'd left it when she'd entered the house. She clipped it to his collar.

Behind her, Caroline said, 'As long as you know she's never going to give you what you really want from her. And as long as *she* knows that's why you keep hanging about.'

Rory stopped, hand on the doorknob, door partially open,

Arlo already outside. She said to Caroline, 'I hang about, as you say, because Clare Abbott and I have a friendship that goes back decades. Now, I suggest you do your job as you're paid to do while I go to the supermarket.'

*Shaftesbury*
*Dorset*

Clare waved off Rory's concerns about Caroline Goldacre that night. They'd had a surprisingly decent meal of takeaway Chinese brought in by Rory from a doubtful-looking shop in Bell Street, and they had decamped to the back garden to enjoy a rare windless evening afterwards. They were finishing up a bottle of white wine while Arlo dozed at Rory's feet.

Clare said, 'She's just a mother hen. That's all it is.'

'You've no idea how she went *on* about your not being here when I arrived,' Rory countered. 'As if it meant something dire that you had forgotten what time I planned to get here.'

'But I didn't forget.'

'I know that. And as I have my own key, what does it matter? Yet she kept banging on about it. Then she began making strange comments about who you "really" are beneath who you appear to be. Who you appear to be to *me*, at least. To her, you are apparently the genuine article, all your evils hidden when I'm around.'

Clare turned from Rory and appeared to examine the view. The evening was drawing on, and across Blackmore Vale where the occasional farmhouse and hamlet stood, lights were beginning to wink in the distance as above them the first stars did the same. She said dismissively, 'I put that sort of thing – the occasional bizarre outburst she has – down to what she's been through in the past few years. And now things are – as she tells me – rather difficult with her husband.'

'What could *any* of that have to do with what she said to me about you?'

'Nothing at all. But you and I know that people cope with their lives in all sorts of ways. Part of her coping is that she seems to think I'll go off course if she's not constantly ministering to me. And I've not been able to persuade her otherwise. Perhaps I should go on holiday . . .' Clare let the sentence drift, as if she was considering potential destinations.

'*Are* you going on holiday?'

'You know I hate holidays. I can barely cope with a weekend away from work. But I suppose I could pretend to go on one.'

'That's completely mad. To have to pretend to go on holiday just to get time away from someone that you employ? Clare, what on earth is—'

'I wouldn't be attempting to get away from her.' Clare got to her feet abruptly. Wineglass in hand, she went to the edge of the property where crevices in a waist-high stone retaining wall sprouted ferns, tall ox-eye daisies, and white campion with its bladdered sepals and rich green leaves. Her fingers felt for one of the daisies, which she twirled restlessly. 'I'd merely be giving her the chance to deal with whatever seems to be going on just now with Alastair. You really dislike her, don't you, Rory? She's not mentioned Fiona, has she?'

'Why do you ask that?'

'It's just that she seems to have a deeper curiosity about people than I've encountered before. I think she looks into anyone I associate with as a means of protecting me.'

'"Looks into"? How?'

'I'm not exactly sure. She certainly asks a lot of questions.'

'About me?'

'About everyone I know or meet. But it's always with my alleged safety in mind.'

'As if you need protecting. *Where* on earth would she get the idea you're wanting a watchdog?'

Clare shook her head, turning from the view to look at Rory once again. She said, 'I don't know. But she's not said anything to you about what happened, has she? She's not spoken about Fiona?'

Rory said that she had not.

Clare said, 'And you will tell me if she does?'

Rory wanted to say 'Why are you asking that? *What* does it mean?' But speaking of Fiona was always such a peril for her that instead she said, 'You're not to worry about me. She might surprise me at some point by coming out of nowhere with something she knows about me that I don't realise she knows, but she can't harm me with it. What happened, happened. It's not a secret.'

Clare returned to her chair, then. She plopped down in it, scooped up the wine bottle, poured them each another glass, which finished it off. She said, 'I want you to find someone, Rory. You're meant to be part of a couple.'

Rory made herself chuckle. She tilted the glass in a salute to the other woman, saying, 'As you've said before. But I can't believe you of all people are recommending it. Not after *Looking for Mr Darcy* or, in my case, *Ms Darcy*.'

'I'm not declaring you'd live happily ever after if you found someone,' Clare countered. 'Just that you would live more fully than you've been living these last few years.'

'What about you?'

'Me?' Clare looked out at the darkness once more. 'Good God,' she said quietly, 'the last thing on earth I want is a partner.'

11 August

India didn't give Nat Thompson the word that she was going down to Dorset with Charlie. She told herself there was no need. As she intended to drive in a separate car – all the better to depart more easily when the memorial's dedication was over – she wasn't exactly going *with* Charlie anyway.

They left town in a convoy of two cars, picking their way through south London to the M3. From there they made good time as there was little traffic, and they arrived in Shaftesbury just before lunch. As the dedication of Will's memorial wasn't set till three o'clock, they had far more time to kill together than India would have liked. But when Charlie suggested a meal at the Mitre, she could hardly say no without seeming unfriendly.

The Mitre stood not far from the fan of paving that indicated Shaftesbury's market square. It was just along the way from the grim visage of St Peter's Church and built from the same limestone, blackened from lichen and the damp. A sign in front of the inn told them that every Monday was quiz night and that everyone had a chance at the jackpot. It also declared that the specials of the day were cottage pie, fresh cod and chips, and roast with sprouts and new potatoes, although the sign was vague as to what was being roasted.

India followed Charlie inside. She wasn't hungry. She was instead, quite uneasy of stomach. Intent upon not giving Charlie the wrong idea about anything she said or did, she'd been finding herself at sea with him since he'd arrived in Camberwell, rung her bell, and said with too much false heartiness, 'Ready to set off into the wilds of Dorset?' when she answered. She could tell it was a new Charlie attempting unsuccessfully to channel the Charlie of old.

Now, they made their way into the pub, where Charlie fetched them menus from the bar. 'Absolutely starving,' he told her. 'What about you? Want the roast?'

'Oh, I don't think so. My weight, you know,' she said dismissively. 'I've got to watch it.'

'Why?' He asked the question lightly but then added to its significance by saying, 'Nat likes his women too rich and too thin?'

She looked up from her menu and he seemed to read her expression because he said, 'Sorry. None of my business. Only . . . it is, more or less.'

'We're not meant to talk about it, Charlie.'

'What? That you're my wife and you're sleeping with another man?'

'I'm not—'

'Which part, India? My wife or India having a new lover?'

She pushed back from the table. He said quickly, 'I'm sorry. I promised myself. Don't go. I won't . . .' He clutched the ubiquitous metal container of mustard that sat with the brown sauce, the salt, and the pepper on the table. 'I didn't mean . . . Look, it just slipped out. I'll be . . . What's the word I want? Good. Yes. I'll be good.'

She said, 'I wasn't leaving, just going to order.'

'Let me do that.'

'I prefer to pay on my own.'

She went to do this, and he followed her. But he stood back and let her place her order and pay for her food – a bowl of tomato soup, a bread roll, and a bottle of Perrier – and he did the same when she'd completed her transaction. He said nothing else till they were seated again, and then he kept the conversation light, a tale about a very rough night with the Samaritans and then another about a fellow volunteer at the Battersea home for dogs. Both were designed to illustrate Charlie Goldacre getting back to his old life.

India wanted to tell him not to try so hard. She wanted to explain to him that sometimes too much water passed beneath the bridge, and she was trying to learn if this was the case for them. She needed him to know that it was taking her time to understand herself, her reactions to him, the reasons she'd lost the self that she was when they were together and, above all, why she was finding Nat Thompson compelling in ways Charlie had never been. But she couldn't do that without taking them too near to the despair that he was attempting to hide from her. So she listened to as much as she could bear and she nodded and said, 'I'm so glad, Charlie,' and when it finally reached the point that she felt she could bear no more of his false good cheer without her heart cracking, she covered his hand with hers and said, 'Don't. It hurts me to see you like this, just as much as it hurt me to see you inert on the sofa week after week.'

This, of course, cut him dead. He was completely silent for a nearly unendurable forty-five seconds before he smiled briefly and said, 'Sometimes I come face to face with the fact that you don't know the first thing about me.'

India set her spoon down. 'What does that mean?'

'It means I'm fine.' And to her expression, which she knew was caught somewhere between compassion and exasperation, he said, 'All right. Perhaps not altogether fine but on my way back to *being* fine, which is something I'd think you'd support.'

'I'm trying to be supportive. Please let's not quarrel.'

He sat back in his chair, looking about as if he sought someone to whom he could make his next declaration. 'I don't know who you are any longer. Nat's woman, perhaps?'

'I'm not someone's appendage, Nat's *or* yours.'

'What you are is my wife. How did you put it? "I'm who and where I want to be today and into the future, beloved of you as you are of me." Weren't those your matrimonial words?'

'Please,' she repeated. 'Don't *do* this. Let's have this day and be at peace with each other.'

'And after today?'

'Why can't you allow me not to know just now?'

He thought about this. The pub door opened, letting in a welcome breath of fresh summer air, bringing with it a group of walkers with rucksacks on their backs and sticks in their hands. They were happy and noisy and 'bloody hungry enough to eat a sow *and* her litter, eh?' They glanced in the direction of India and Charlie and nodded their greetings as people do.

Charlie said, perhaps because of their presence, perhaps because he meant it, 'I apologise, India. Thank you for coming. It means a great deal to me and it'll mean the same to Mum.'

India accepted this at face value. 'Does she know yet?' She indicated the out-of-doors, by which she meant the memorial and the ceremony to come.

'She's not got a clue, if Clare Abbott's to be believed. I've no idea how Clare's managed to put everything together without Mum finding out, though. She's always been a champion when it comes to discovering things she's not meant to know.'

*Shaftesbury*
*Dorset*

When Charlie and India arrived at the site of the memorial for Will, something of a crowd had gathered. Charlie knew most of them as they worked for his stepfather, both in Alastair's bakery and in his seven shops across Dorset where he sold his baked goods. Among them was the middle-aged widow who managed these businesses for Alastair and arranged near her were the ladies of Shaftesbury's Women's League, always identifiable by the hats they wore to any occasion deemed remotely suitable for headgear.

Breach Lane was the location of the spring into which Clare Abbott had invested funds in exchange for being allowed to place a memorial to Will within the immediate area. She'd managed to create from the space something that Will would have loved, Charlie saw. Indeed, Will might have designed it himself. The spring now flowed into a rocky pool before spilling naturally over it and on its way down the hill, and paving stones of greensand carved with the markings of moving water made an area for simple limestone benches. A garden of grasses and shrubbery had been planted and in the midst of this a large boulder stood, covered by a green tarpaulin at the moment, but presumably the cenotaph for Charlie's brother.

The mayor of Shaftesbury was there, decked out in her mayoral chain. The town council was accounted for as well. So were Clare and a woman with a black and tan dog of indeterminate breed, both of whom stuck closely at Clare's side. Charlie went to greet them, first extending his arm to India. He was grateful when she took it. They crossed an area of summer-dead grass and were introduced to Rory Statham and Arlo, her dog.

He said to Clare, 'How'd you ever manage all this without Mum knowing? She *doesn't* know, does she?'

'Far as I can tell, she's still completely in the dark.' Clare, he saw, was wearing her habitual black. Rather unfortunately crumpled, it was all linen in answer to the day's warmth, and her grey hair was ponytailed haphazardly. 'She's not been into work today, which gave me a bit of a scare, but I phoned up Alastair and he assured me he'd get her here one way or another.'

'Not ill, is she?' Charlie asked.

'Honestly? I think they may have had some sort of set-to, she and Alastair. He was rather cagey about it all. "Not herself today" was how he put it.' Clare gave a glance to her companion as she said this. Rory Statham remained expressionless. 'Anyway, Alastair's bringing her on some pretext. Had she come to work, I could have walked her down from the house, but as it is . . . Ah. I think he's coming just now. Lovely to meet you, India. I've saved you two places in the front. If you'll excuse me . . .'

Charlie nodded. Clare strode off to meet his mother as she got out of the van, her friend Rory remaining behind, as silent as before. She picked up her dog and meditatively rubbed her fingers through the long hairlike fur on his tousled head. She watched the action of Caroline's arrival.

Once he'd parked the bakery van in which they'd arrived, Alastair hastened round the side of it to open the door for Charlie's mum. He extended his hand to her. She ignored it. As a result, she heaved herself gracelessly from the vehicle, which Charlie knew would embarrass her, particularly as people were watching expectantly.

At first, she seemed puzzled as she took in the scene: the white canopy stretching over a broken horseshoe of four rows of chairs with a central aisle, the people smiling and waiting in all their finery, the mayor at the very front of the crowd, and then the spring with its new surrounding garden. Finally, her gaze found Charlie and India and her expression altered. A light seemed to come into her face, and she quickened her pace past Clare, past the waiting people, past the mayor and the town council and the ladies of the Women's League in order to get to Charlie and his wife.

She said, 'Oh my dears . . . I'm *so* delighted . . .' as she looked from one of them to the other, her hand reaching out to grasp Charlie's arm. It came to him that she thought a ceremony was about to take place that would once again tie him and India together, perhaps a renewal of their wedding vows, although God only knew why they'd choose Shaftesbury for such a moment. Yet her conclusion wasn't entirely unthinkable, he realised, for the white canopy alone not to mention the arrangement of chairs certainly suggested something of a matrimonial nature.

Before he could disabuse his mother of any idea she might have in that regard, Clare rejoined them. She indicated the chairs with *reserved* printed on placards on their seats, and she asked everyone else to sit as well.

The ceremony began with words from the lady mayor that Charlie listened to only dimly. She spoke gratefully about Clare Abbott's project to enhance the natural beauty of the area, making it a spot from which the citizens of Shaftesbury could not only enjoy the view of Blackmore Vale but also find the peace that promotes contemplation. She went on a bit too long for Charlie's liking. He faded out and glanced down the row at his mother. She was watching serenely but beginning to appear a little confused. Obviously, this wasn't looking like anything close to Charlie and India's declaring their renewed devotion to each other.

Finally, the mayor turned the event over to Clare, who went to stand near the tarpaulin covered stone. She clasped her hands in front of her and said prefatorily, 'Caroline. Alastair. Charlie. India.' She exchanged a glance with her friend Rory and then went on. 'No matter how it comes, the loss of someone dearly loved is a devastating thing. This happened to all of you when your William died, and while I was not so fortunate to have ever known him, I *have* known and seen what the loss of William has done to you. Particularly to you, Caroline. I think that, when someone young dies, one of the fears a parent has is that, because his life was cut off prematurely, there's a chance that the very *fact* of his living at all will somehow be forgotten. Not by you, of course, but by other people and by all those people who never knew him in the first place, the sorts of people whose lives he might have been able to touch. I hope this place prevents that. I hope that it gives all of you some peace. It's long been a favourite spot of mine, and I've often thought as I passed it on my daily walks how lovely it would be to fashion it into what you see now. But with one addition that the town council has generously allowed to be placed here. Alastair . . . ?'

This was, Charlie saw, a cue. His stepfather rose and offered his arm to Caroline. He brought her to Clare who then unveiled the memorial stone and, upon it, the fine bronze plaque. As Caroline read it, Clare did so as well, aloud: 'In Loving Memory of William Francis Goldacre. "From the contagion of the world's slow stain/He is secure, and now can never mourn/A heart grown cold, a head grown grey in vain.'" Included were the dates of Will's birth and death, and beneath these, a depiction of some sort of wreath.

There was a moment of complete silence. Then, as if on some soundless cue, an enormous flock of starlings rose from the hillside beneath Breach Lane and soared in unison as starlings will do, patterning the sky above the ceremony with the black cloud of their rhythmic flying.

Caroline took a few steps towards the memorial stone. She said nothing. Alastair went to her side. For several moments in which the starlings soared and swooped, it seemed she might not speak at all. Then she said, 'He would have loved this spot. It would have given him so much joy just to . . .' She could go no further. Alastair put his arm round her shoulders, saying quietly, 'That he would.'

At that, Caroline reached out towards Clare Abbott, saying, 'Thank you. This means so much.'

Finally, as if to give the moment's emotion release to join the still rhythmically swooping starlings, those gathered beneath the canopy applauded. The mayor gestured them forward to enjoy the spring and its pool, to see the memorial stone. Charlie joined them, India at his side. People mingled and much was said about the stone and its handsome bronze plaque, about the now-pooled spring, about the benches and the garden.

An announcement was made of a reception to be held at Clare Abbott's home in Bimport Street, just above Breach Lane. All were invited for champagne, afternoon tea, and a chance to mingle and enjoy the summer sun.

People began to wander off, and that was the moment when India grasped Charlie by the arm and said, 'Oh my God, Charlie,' looking towards Breach Lane.

A young woman was standing there, draped in black like a banshee come to call. But after a very brief moment, she was not what Charlie took in at all. For beyond her and coming along the verge was his father Francis. With him was his second wife, Sumalee, bearing an armload of Asiatic lilies.

*Shaftesbury*
*Dorset*

India saw only the young woman. So altered was she that India didn't realise at first that Lily Foster had at some point arrived at the ceremony. It was only when Lily acknowledged India by raising her hand in a form of greeting that India understood that Will's lover – present at the moment of his death – had somehow got word that this event was going to take place. God only knew where she had come from.

India loosed herself from Charlie and, at that point, took note of Francis Goldacre and his much younger Thai-born wife. She and Charlie took separate paths then. He set off to speak to his father and, doubtless, to question why he'd been so callous as to bring the beautiful Thai sign of his familial desertion in tow. She went to Lily.

Lily came no nearer than four cars parked away from the site. As India drew close to her, Lily retreated to a bend in Breach Lane that effectively would keep her out of sight of anyone else at the memorial ceremony.

Lily could not have been more different from the person Will had brought to meet Charlie and her early on in London. India saw that the change in Lily went beyond dull black hair in place of her lovely ginger curls to include many more piercings and studs and now even a thick hoop through her septum. She wore some sort of body-shrouding black gown and floppy black hat from which her long hair limply hung. Only the Doc Martens showing themselves from beneath the gown remained the same from the Lily of old.

India didn't need to ask what on earth had happened to

Lily that she was so changed, for she knew the likely cause. Only in Lily's case this cause was so much more excruciating. In pursuit of Will when he'd flung himself over the cliff in Seatown, she'd scrambled to the body afterwards, not the first person to arrive since a few others had been below on the beach, but far in advance of anyone who would have known to keep her away from the sight on the stones of the brains and blood and tissue of her lover.

That Caroline Goldacre blamed Lily for Will's death was something that had come out just after the service that preceded the cremation of the body. There, grief-stricken beyond the capacity to consider the impact of her words, Will's mum had confronted Lily. Caroline hadn't known Lily was even in Dorset until after Will's death. She hadn't known that they'd gone to Seatown to camp. She hadn't known anything save that Will was trying to win Lily Foster back. And Caroline declared this to be the cause of his death: Lily's selfish rejection of him since 'he *never* fell apart till you came into his life, you self-consumed little bitch.' It had been a terrible scene between the two of them, and India had not seen Lily since.

Now she said to her, 'Lily, *Lily*,' and she held out her arms to the other woman. 'Please. Don't go. You've come to see the memorial, haven't you?'

Lily moved off no farther. India saw that she had a padded envelope in one hand and this she lifted to clutch to her chest. India dropped her arms and went to stand before her. Close, she could see that Lily was skeletally thin. Where her wrists emerged from the sleeves of her gown, they looked like a child's. Unlike a child's, however, they were now even more tattooed than they'd been at the time of Will's death although India could see nothing of the artwork that disappeared into the fabric of the sleeves. Her eyes were red rimmed as if with drug use or with weeping.

'What's happened to you?' India asked her. 'Where did you go? Where have you been?'

'Here,' Lily said.

'Dorset? Shaftesbury? Ever since Will . . . ? Why?'

'She knows. Ask her.' Lily inclined her head in the direction of the ceremony just down the lane.

'Who? Not Clare. Caroline, then?'

'Caroline, then.'

'Are you staying with them?' India realised how ridiculous the query was once she'd made it. Lily's having been blamed for Will's death by his mother made it unlikely that she'd take up residence with the woman. She said, 'Never mind. What a stupid thing to say. Where do you live now?'

'Here,' she said.

'Shaftesbury. Whyever . . . Lily, what are you *doing* here? This can't be . . .' It was somehow worse than Charlie, she thought. Charlie had been suffering extraordinarily. But this looked like self-punishment on Lily's part.

'Tattoos,' Lily said obscurely.

'On your arms. I see that you've got more than—'

'I'm *doing* tattoos, India. Just like in London. I saw a niche here. I stepped into fill it.'

'Tattoos in Shaftesbury? Is there actually business for you here?'

'Enough. And even if there wasn't, it doesn't matter. That's not why I'm here. She's why I'm here. Because until she's punished for William, there's no point to anything else.'

India felt a shudder quake through her at the word *punished*. She said, 'You can't mean . . . Lily, you can't *want* to be here. Not near them. Not after . . . I mean, not with what she thinks about you . . . and what she said at the cremation to you.'

'Oh, it's exactly what I want. To be close to the source.'

India was about to say 'The source of what,' when the sound of agitated voices reached her, coming from the direction of the spring and its memorial. She swung round but could see nothing as the lane's curve prevented her. But she recognised Caroline's cry and Alastair's angry voice. Something had happened and, since she'd caught sight of Francis Goldacre and his wife, she had a fairly good idea what it might be.

She turned back to Lily who also was looking in the direction of whatever was going on. She could see that Lily knew as well what the source of the disturbance was. She could also see that Lily was gratified, which spoke volumes about her part in whatever was going on.

India said, 'You invited them, didn't you? Lily, why? And how did you know in the first place?'

Lily looked back at her. 'I make it my business to know everything that's going on with Caroline.' She thrust the padded envelope at India. 'Charlie's meant to have this,' she told her. 'Will you see that he gets it?'

India didn't want to take it as everything about Lily felt wrong and bent on malevolence. She said, 'What is it, then?'

'Just *give* it to him, India.'

'Why don't you give it to him yourself?'

'Because I can't.'

Still India did not take the envelope, so Lily dropped it to the dead wild grasses of the verge. She turned then and walked away, in the direction of The Knapp and Tout Hill, which would take her back up to the town centre above them.

*Shaftesbury*
*Dorset*

Clare clocked the armful of Asiatic lilies first and the exquisite visage of the woman who carried them second. Then she took in the man accompanying her, and in that moment what she felt was horror that, on this day of all emotionally wrought days, Francis Goldacre would show his face and would bring along with that face the woman for whom – according to Caroline – he'd deserted home, hearth, and paternal responsibilities. Thankfully, many of the invited guests were already trekking up Breach Lane in the general direction of Bimport

Street, so they were unaware of Francis Goldacre's arrival or of what came next.

Caroline seemed to shrink back from the sight of her former husband and his current wife. She said her own husband's name and Alastair moved to stand in front of her, as if she needed protecting.

Clare heard Rory say next to her, 'Who on earth . . . ?'

'The ex and his current missus,' Clare said in an undertone.

'Heavens. Clare, you didn't invite them!'

''Course not. P'rhaps I can head them off in some way.' She went to do so as Rory retreated towards the invited guests.

Charlie Goldacre moved towards his father. Apparently clueless, both Francis Goldacre and his wife greeted Charlie with smiles. These faded when Francis put his hand fondly on Charlie's shoulder, and Charlie shook him off. His wife, not seeing this as she was searching the faces of the remaining people for someone, said, 'I have brought these for your mum, Charlie. Is she . . . ?'

'You damn well leave this instant,' Charlie hissed at his father. 'What the hell's the matter with you, coming here like this? *And* bringing Sumalee. D'you ever think of anyone besides yourself?'

Clare heard all of this, thanking God it was not loud enough to carry to the dispersing group. Behind her, she heard Rory say to those who remained beneath the canopy, 'We're beginning with champagne all round up at Clare's. Do follow me,' in a way that urged the rest of the guests to disband. As Clare approached the Goldacres, she passed Caroline and Alastair, still keeping their distance from the new arrivals. She heard Caroline say, 'But why would anyone . . . ?' and Alastair reply, 'Let me see to this, Caro.'

That was *all* they needed, Clare thought. She hastened to reach the others before Alastair could. Charlie was in the midst of telling his father to clear out and take his Thai slag with him, which Francis wasn't receiving in a particularly good light. His face had gone the colour of dried putty when Charlie had shaken the man's hand from his shoulder. At Charlie's words, though, fire washed up his neck and onto his cheeks.

Sumalee took a step backwards, her head lowered in what could have been either embarrassment or shame. Francis said hotly, 'You bloody well watch that tongue of yours or I'll have it out of your head,' and Clare thought Wonderful. She intervened.

'I'm Clare Abbott,' she said determinedly to the man and his wife. Then locking extremely meaningful eyes with Francis, she went on with, 'You're Will and Charlie's father.'

He took this up. 'Thank you for the invitation to come. I was hoping . . . Obviously, I was hoping for too much.'

Clare drew her eyebrows together as Charlie said, '*You*? Jesus, what is this, Clare? Some sort of sick joke?'

Clare had no chance to reply to this, for Alastair was with them, then, and it looked as if every hair on his bulky arms was standing on end in agitation. He said to Francis, 'Clear off. I don't want to tell you twice.'

Francis said, 'As this is a memorial for my son—'

'Oh *that's* rich,' Charlie cut in. 'Your son. Your *son*.'

– 'I think I have a place here, Alastair.'

'I was more a dad to Will than you ever thought long enough to be,' was Alastair's answer to this. 'Since he was a wee lad, I was his dad. Now are you going to clear out or am I going to have to do something to encourage you? And don't you take one step closer to her, or I swear to God, I'll rip your head off.'

The *her* was obvious to them all. Caroline had retreated to the memorial stone, and she stood by it protectively, as if she thought Francis and Sumalee Goldacre had come to deface it before it was one hour old.

'I'll see the memorial before I go,' Francis said coldly.

'You'll have to walk straight through me to get to it,' Alastair said. 'You who couldn't be bothered even to come when the lad was cremated. What the hell sort of father are you? What the hell sort of father were you *ever*? That poor lad with his monster ear that you never saw your precious way to fixing when you had the means and the talent and the—'

'You haven't the slightest clue what you're talking about,' Francis said. 'Darling,' to his wife as he extended his hand to her, 'we'll set the flowers by the stone and then we'll be off if that's fine with you?'

Sumalee looked up. She was many years younger than her husband. Her dark hair fell completely to her waist, and the sun glinted off it and off the smooth caramel of her unlined skin. She said, 'As you wish, Francis,' and she took his arm.

Alastair put his hand on Francis's chest as Francis took his first steps towards the memorial stone. He said hotly, 'Are you hard of hearing? I think I told you—'

'Get your hand off me.' Francis's words were icy. 'If you don't, the consequences—'

'You're half a man at the best of times and we both know it,' Alastair said. 'You really want me to take the rest of you down to nothing?'

'Please. Francis.' It was Sumalee speaking. She bent and placed her armful of fragrant lilies on the ground at Alastair's feet. She said, 'If you will place these by William's stone, we will go no closer.'

Francis said, 'Don't let this lout frighten you into—'

'Shut up,' Charlie said. 'Alastair's right. He's been more a dad to me than you ever were and he was the same to Will. So don't you *bloody* pretend you've the slightest interest in honouring anyone except yourself.'

'We'll put Sumalee's flowers near the stone,' his father said.

'Oh will you indeed?' Charlie stepped forward and began to trample them. His father surged towards him. Alastair burst towards Francis with a roar of, 'You touch that lad and I'll bloody kill you!'

'Stop it!' Sumalee cried.

Clare grabbed Alastair, who was many inches shorter than Francis, but stockier by far. She thought this would stop the action, but it only exacerbated it. Francis landed a blow squarely on Alastair's jaw and this knocked Clare off balance so that she released her grip upon him. Alastair launched himself at Francis and when Sumalee tried to intervene by stepping between them, Charlie went for her, dragging her off and then tossing her to the ground to give his stepfather access to his father.

Fights between men were shocking, ugly, silent things, having none of the drama or excitement of filmed depictions of them. This particular fight was over in less than two minutes when Alastair head-butted Francis, knocking him to the ground and then grabbing him and jerking him upwards by means of an arm locked round the other man's neck. When he tightened his grip, panting and red in the face, Clare attempted to pull him off but he was far too strong. He punched Francis's face repeatedly. Clare shouted, 'Charlie, *do* something,' only to hear Charlie say, 'He fucking deserves it and so do you, Clare.'

'He's going to kill him.'

'And I hope he does.'

'Francis!' Sumalee cried.

'Alastair! Stop it!' This was, at last, Caroline. She came at a run from the memorial stone. 'Stop it! Stop it!' she shrieked.

That was when Charlie's wife India arrived, running up the lane. She fell upon Alastair to help Clare drag him back from Francis. They achieved this, leaving Francis gasping for air among the weeds and the scrambled earth.

Sumalee crawled to Francis. He struggled to breathe. She was wide-eyed as she looked at all of them. 'What kind of people are you?' she asked.

That, Clare thought, was the question of the hour.

*Shaftesbury*
*Dorset*

Rory had, Clare saw, managed to get everyone out of the memorial site. They were either already in the back garden at the house above in Bimport Street or, at least, they were well on their way up the lane in that direction and consequently completely out of earshot. No one remained but herself and those involved in the confrontation.

Both Francis Goldacre and Alastair MacKerron were filthy, and bruises were blooming on Francis's face. Clare thought it amazing that so much damage could be done to the body in so little time. Alastair's own face was swelling from the blow it had taken, his trousers were ripped at one knee, and his shirt and jacket were streaked with what looked like dog excrement. Francis was also bruised round the neck, and his fine summer suit would need repair. But the worst appeared to be Sumalee, who cradled her wrist at her breast.

The first words were spoken by Francis and not to Alastair but rather to his son. 'I could kill you for that.' He got to his feet and raised his wife to hers. He said to Charlie, 'If you ever think to come within fifty yards of her again . . .'

'Francis,' Sumalee said, 'you must not.'

'He's hurt you and I'll have him in the dock for assault.'

'You leave that lad out of this,' Alastair said. 'This's between us. Be a man for once, you limp little—'

'Enough. *Please*, Alastair.' It was Caroline who spoke. She said to Francis, 'I don't know why you've come. I don't know why you brought her.' Her chin began to quiver. 'But you can see that—'

'We came because we were invited,' Francis snapped. 'We had a message by phone. We were stupid enough to take the invitation as a sign not only that you had finally come to your senses but also that you had apparently decided to begin living in the real world instead of one you invent as you go along.'

Caroline swiftly turned towards Clare as Alastair took a threatening step in Francis's direction to deal with the insult. This time Charlie stopped his stepfather as Caroline said to Clare, 'You! You phoned . . . But *why* . . . Did you actually *think* this would make me . . . Oh my God.' She covered her mouth with her hand.

This gave Clare opportunity to say to her, 'I had *no* idea. You can't possibly believe—'

'You planned it *all*, didn't you? This . . . and . . . and Francis and her showing up to humiliate me.'

'Caroline, that's absolutely *not* true.'

'Lily invited them.' It was India who spoke. 'I've only just talked to her. She more or less told me she'd invited them.'

Charlie said, 'Lily? Is she *here*?' and with the others he looked round among the cars on the verge.

'That bloody . . . If she's round here, I'll sort her,' Alastair said.

Caroline had gone quite pale. '*Lily's* come to the memorial?' And once again, 'Clare. Did you . . . Lily Foster as well?' And now she did finally weep. It was as if the name of Lily Foster had done her in.

'Where did you see her?' Charlie said.

'Just up the street,' India explained. 'But Charlie, she's very changed. And she gave me this for you.' And here she bent to retrieve a padded envelope that she'd thrown to one side when she'd come to assist Clare in the midst of the men's scuffle.

'Don't open it!' Caroline cried. 'It could be a bomb.'

Charlie cast his mother a look. 'I doubt Lily's taken up bomb making,' he said.

'You don't know what she's become,' Caroline said. 'She's gone straight round the bend. *Don't* open it. Alastair, tell him.'

Alastair was terse in his explanation. Lily Foster had turned up in Dorset some twenty months ago. She'd begun at first to haunt his shops, never buying but always lurking, talking to his customers and warning them off whatever she fancied he was putting into his baked goods to poison the populace. Then she'd installed herself on the grounds of the bakery, waiting for what no one knew, always watching his every move, taking notes and murmuring cryptically. When he'd phoned the police about her, she moved off to the road. But after a week, she was at the house itself. Then in the mornings, they began to find nasty bits on their doorstep. Animal excrement, a dead bird, a half-eaten rat, and finally the head of a cat.

'She's had an ASBO filed on her,' he concluded. 'We've not seen her since.'

'She told me she has a tattoo shop in town,' India said.

'How would she have known about this?' It was Francis who asked.

'She told me she knows everything,' India said. And then to Caroline directly, 'She said she makes it her business to know everything that's going on in your lives.'

'Whose lives?' Clare asked.

'Caroline's. Alastair's. She means to cause trouble,' India concluded, her gaze directed to her husband now. 'Your mum's right, Charlie. Don't open the envelope. Toss it in the rubbish. Burn it. Lily's completely changed. She doesn't mean you well.'

Charlie turned the envelope in his hands. It was stapled shut. All of them could see his name printed in large letters across the front of it. He said, 'She could just as easily have mailed it. She knows where I live. It's probably nothing.'

'Give it to the police, lad,' Alastair told Charlie.

'Please do, Charlie,' his mother begged. 'She's done terrible things to us. And now if something happens to you because of her . . . If it's awful – what's inside there – then the police will have another reason to file some kind of charges against her . . . Because something has to be done to force her to leave us in peace.'

Charlie nodded. He said he would take the envelope to the police station in town, where the name Lily Foster was, it seemed, well known.

# 29 September

*

## NOW

*Marylebone*
*London*

Rory Statham employed as much patience as she could muster as she gave her explanation once again to the literary agent seated opposite her: the advance offered her client could not possibly be increased. Why? Because the publishing house was sitting on ten thousand copies of the author's last book, all of which were going to have to be remaindered; because while the discovery of the body of Richard the Third in a Leicester car park did indeed shine a spotlight on that controversial king, it was not likely that yet another book on the disappearance of the Princes in the Tower—

In the midst of her explanation and through the interior windows of her office, Rory caught sight of Clare Abbott's arrival. She frowned when she saw Caroline Goldacre trailing her. She thought she'd talked Clare out of bringing Caroline along. Obviously, her argument for leaving the woman behind in Shaftesbury had accomplished nothing. Rory said to the agent, 'I *am* sorry. And I certainly understand if Professor Okerlund wishes to take his book to another publisher.' She stood and Arlo did the same, stretching and eyeing the literary agent's capacious shoulder bag from which a wrapped sandwich was protruding. He was too good a dog to go anywhere near it, but Rory could see how much he wanted to do so.

She bid the agent a friendly but firm farewell and went to greet Clare. She was there to affix her signature to one thousand copies of *Looking for Mr Darcy* prior to their being shipped into the European marketplace. Caroline was there to assist, Clare said, after which the two women were heading to Cambridge for an event at Lucy Cavendish College: what purported to be a lively debate between Clare and the very Reverend Marydonna Patches, a long-ago graduate of Lucy Cavendish and a well-known proponent of a-woman's-place-is-at-the-kitchen-sink, according to how Clare described her. She and Caroline would spend the night in the university city, and in the morning Clare would do a live radio programme, followed by a lecture in the afternoon.

With Arlo padding along at her side, Rory took Clare and Caroline to the conference room just along the corridor where her assistant had unpacked the cartons of books. They stood in neat stacks both on the floor and on the table, and Rory saw Caroline's lips press together when she took them in. She murmured to Clare, 'I'll do my very best.'

'Soldier on till you can't cope, and I'll manage from there,' Clare told her.

'It's just that . . .' Caroline cast a glance at Rory. Something unspoken passed between Caroline and Clare.

'I'll help as well,' Rory said. 'The books have been flapped, so it shouldn't take terribly long.'

Caroline said, 'But you probably have other business to attend to?'

'None so important that I can't help here. Are you unwell today, Caroline?'

'A bit.'

'Perhaps you should be at home?'

'I'm not that unwell. Clare? If you're ready . . . ?'

Rory said nothing more until a mere one tenth of the way through the signing of the books, Caroline suddenly declared that she needed the ladies' toilet at once. This took her quickly out of earshot. Then what Rory said was, 'If she's ill, why are you taking her with you to Cambridge, Clare?'

She was surprised when Clare's answer was, 'She needed to get away.' She glanced through the open door and down the corridor, where Caroline was rushing towards the ladies' toilet. 'It's Alastair. He's become involved with another woman. Seriously, it seems.'

'*Alastair*? You said they were having difficulties, but I thought he was devoted to Caroline. How did this come to light?'

'Photographs. Sent anonymously to Caroline at my address.'

'Who would have done such a thing?'

'I wager it was Lily Foster.' She explained to Rory who the young woman was, concluding with, 'It wouldn't be out of character for her to have dug up something to hurt Caroline as she holds her responsible for Will's death. And vice versa.'

'Do they know for certain?'

'That she sent the pictures? I doubt there's a way to prove it. Whoever sent them was wise enough to post them from Dorchester.'

'What about the woman? Alastair's paramour. God. Where do these antique terms come from? Who is she?'

'Sharon Halsey. She works for him. He's been grovelling at Caroline's feet since the Big Reveal, seeking for grace and vowing to be wise hereafter, but Caroline isn't ready to forgive unless Alastair gives the woman the sack. Well, who can blame her for that? But he doesn't want to sack her.'

'Whyever not?'

'Evidently, Sharon Halsey has been holding his business together for years. Without her, according to Alastair, the whole enterprise would go under in weeks. So he has no intention of sacking her, and he and Caroline have reached an impasse about it all. Thus –' She waved her hand round the conference room as Rory continued to place open books in front of her and she continued to sign them – 'this little outing. A brief break from the drama at home.'

'She's going to be useless to you in Cambridge if she's ill. She probably won't even be able manage her own luggage.'

'I can manage luggage for both of us. Really, Rory.' Clare looked up at her and blew a few wiry strands of grey hair off her forehead. 'The poor woman has had a trolley full of horse dung dropped into her lap. First Will's suicide, then Charlie's breakdown and his marriage falling into ruin, then Lily Foster tormenting her, and now this. She's reeling. She's not yet come close to recovering from Will and—'

'Oh for God's sake, Clare. Does she *want* to recover?'

Rory saw that Clare's surprise straightened her spine like a pole. She said, 'What a very odd thing to ask.'

Rory said, 'Sorry. I don't mean to be cruel. But it's just that one progresses through grief. It's a process, and if one wants to recover, one engages in the process. One joins a grief group. One gets involved in other aspects of life. One struggles to get through it. Has she done any of that?'

Clare set her pen to one side. She pulled a chair out from the table – as Rory had been standing – and patted its seat. Rory obliged her and Arlo did the same, jumping to take a place on Rory's lap. Clare said, 'You did, darling. You got through it. But what she endured is the loss of a child and, childless though you and I both are, I think we can agree there's nothing worse than that. The love a mother has for her child . . . It's different from the love you had for Fiona. I'm not saying it's stronger or better,' she added as Rory turned her head away, 'but merely different. It has to be simply because of the actual birthing of a child and then the raising of it . . . One *has* to be altered by that, don't you agree? So the loss and the recovery from the loss will be different from the loss of someone else dearly loved.'

'I don't think I've ever heard you sound so compassionate.' Rory was aware of the sadness in her own voice. She couldn't have kept it away.

'I'm not exactly devoid of compassion. I expect you know that.'

'Oh, I *do*.' Rory covered her friend's hand with her own. Impulsively, they leaned towards each other, each resting her forehead against the other's.

'Goodness! Am I disturbing a tender moment between you two?'

They started, moved away from each other. Caroline was back with them, standing in the doorway.

Rory got to her feet, sliding Arlo to the floor. She said to Clare, 'I've an appointment in a quarter hour. I'll check back afterwards to see how you're coping with all this.' She left her, then, Arlo trotting at her side.

She wasn't quick enough, though, to miss Caroline's question to Clare. 'Really, Clare, it's completely unseemly. Can't she keep her hands to herself?'

# 30 September

Rory finished her swim at her normal time, just after eight in the morning. She always arrived at the old leisure centre as early as she could drag herself there, which was generally at a quarter past six. Today had been different due to a late night phone call from Clare, reporting on the event at Lucy Cavendish College. She'd ultimately felt sorry for the very Reverend Marydonna Patches, Clare had admitted with a rueful laugh. It had not been the wisest venue for the clergywoman to have chosen for the debate. As Clare had put it, 'When one depends entirely upon the Bible for one's interpretation of what it is to be female . . . Well, you know how that sort of thing is likely to go down in circumstances in which you're surrounded by university women.'

'A crucifixion, if I might borrow from the Bible myself.'

'Hmmm, perhaps a stoning? But book sales were quite brisk at the end, I'm happy to tell you. And I daresay there wasn't a woman present who wanted even to picture poor Elizabeth Bennet's life post her marriage to the smouldering Fitzwilliam. When the curtain falls, the drudgery begins. Pemberley be damned.'

Rory laughed. 'You must have been in your element.'

'Darling, I *was*.'

'And Caroline?' Rory couldn't resist asking the question. 'How did she hold up?'

'I'm sorry to report we've only just now had a few too many

sharp words and she's gone to her room in a huff. I didn't make things easy for her tonight, I'm afraid. I'd sworn that we'd be finished up by ten but the event went on till half past eleven and she was rather put out by that. I can't actually blame her. It was the signing. It went on and on. Everyone wanted to have a word when they got to the table and Caroline's best laid plans to get the entire business over and done with simply fell apart. Absolutely no one who wanted to have a chat was to be moved along quickly, no matter what she tried.'

'Did she remove your business cards from whomever you might have given them to?'

Clare chuckled. 'Probably but I've actually no clue.' She yawned loudly and added, 'Good God. Look at the time.' At which point, they rang off.

Now, Rory lifted herself from the pool, muscles spent. All of the lanes were occupied at this point, and hers was taken over before she had a chance to remove her goggles and pick up her towel. The volume of noise had increased in the cavernous hall which housed the pool, and the air was heavily redolent of chlorine. Best to vacate the premises at once, Rory thought.

Arlo rose from the folded towel that was usually his post, stretched forelegs and hind legs languorously, and observed Rory as if questioning the sanity of her entire morning's routine. She patted his head and rolled up his towel. Next came the steam room, and he would wait without while she took her fifteen minutes in there on the slick white tiles that formed the benches along the walls of the room's two chambers. She was one of eight other women in various stages of undress, who sweated in the wet heat of the place. At the end of the quarter hour, she went off to the showers.

It was after her shower and while she was dressing that she saw there was a message on her mobile phone. It had come in at half past eight, and the number was Clare's. She finished dressing and dried her hair. It was just before nine when she returned Clare's call.

Caroline Goldacre answered. Rory felt a swell of what she knew was completely irrational irritation at the other woman's intrusion. *What* was Caroline doing with Clare's mobile? And what next? Access to her cashpoint card?

Rory said, 'Clare rang me, Caroline. Is she—'

'It *wasn't* Clare. It was me,' Caroline cried. 'Clare's dead! Rory, she's dead!'

*Thornford*
*Dorset*

Alastair took the phone call from Caroline while sitting at Sharon Halsey's breakfast table. He hadn't intended to spend the night. He had called it a fling – 'just a bit of fun, eh?' – when he'd first broken off relations with Sharon, deliberately trying to wipe himself out of her heart and herself out of his. He'd only had her five times before he'd been caught, anyway. One could hardly call that an affair, but one had to call it something in order to kill it off, yes? One couldn't just say, 'We best end this thing between us, girl, 'cause it's going nowhere with nowhere to go.' That wasn't true anyway. For he'd quickly discovered 'this thing between us' had a real body and soul to it.

But he couldn't admit that to himself. He couldn't even *think* it lest Sharon see the longing on his face and feel the pull inside him that kept dragging him towards her.

He hadn't taken her to bed that first night after dinner in her ancient farmhouse. He'd insisted on helping with the washing up, and he'd stayed far later than he'd intended. They'd talked themselves into exhaustion over six long hours in each other's company, discovering how much they had in common: from being the lost children in too-large families with careworn mums and put-upon dads to having secret dreams of an adulthood that had gone unfulfilled. Hers: to live for a time in New Zealand's Bay of Islands where she would take up a career that involved the resident dolphins and the sea. His: always the impossible wish to be a warrior, with weapons of destruction slung across his chest, using those weapons to bring death to those who terrorised the innocent. Both of them laughed at dreams that came from childhood but still maintained their hold.

'I c'n see you with them dolphins,' he told her.

'Well, I *can't* see you harming so much as a fly. Not you, Alastair. Not with your—'

'It's my leg that got broke,' he told her. 'And the bloke who set it . . . ? A dog's dinner, that was, what he made of it.'

'I was going to say not with your sense of decency,' she told him. 'As to your leg? See here, it's just a leg. Shorter than the other, yes? I've seen your shoe, how it's built up.'

'Army wouldn't take me nor would anyone else,' he said. 'Well, save Caro. I was man enough for her.'

'That's silly. You're man enough for anyone,' she replied.

She'd taken him to bed the third time they were alone together. It wasn't her bed. Nor was it his. She'd called him to Yeovil to have a talk with the staff at the bakery shop there. She'd called it 'good for business when the managing director himself comes to pay a call.'

Generally, he went directly to bed once the bakery vans set off with their morning deliveries to the shops across Dorset. He would have been at work since half past two and after five hours with little enough sleep preceding them, he was in need of a kip. But Sharon's recommendation made sense. What would it cost him to lose a few hours of sleep? Not much, he reckoned.

The meeting at the bakery shop went according to plan, but what he hadn't expected was the secondary plan. This one took them to a nearby inn for a morning coffee. The morning coffee took them upstairs to a room Sharon had already taken. How she put it was 'I've got you a room for your kip, Alastair.

I reckon you gave that up in order to speak to the staff and you must be dead on your feet. Would you be wanting to go up for a bit?'

He'd said, 'Aye.' And then he'd added – God have mercy – 'But not without you.' So it had begun, and the aftermath was not guilt at all but rather a kind of immense gratitude that God had given this woman to him.

Oddly, that was how it felt. She was his. To care for, to love, to cherish, to . . . What? he'd asked himself as they parted after that first time. What in God's name was he supposed to do?

As he had no answer, he set about finding one and his only course to that end was to have her again. He told himself that he needed to understand what they were to each other because if he had to make some sort of decision about her, then he had to be clear that what was going on between them was not the same mad lust that had fuelled his earliest days with his wife.

Indeed, Caroline was dominant in his thoughts most of the time. How could she not be? One didn't walk out on a woman who'd been through what Caroline had. It would be a death blow to her and he could not deal it. He couldn't begin to picture the moment when he faced her over dinner in the garden on a country drive as she did the laundry while she cooked him a meal, and he'd be there telling her that he'd fallen hard for someone else, harder even than he'd fallen for her and 'Let's look at it square, Caro, what've we really got, you and me? Not much, eh? Best we go our separate ways.'

As it turned out, he didn't have to play out that scenario, for Caroline had come by a stack of photos sent to her by God only knew who. He could only thank the almighty they'd been merely as graphic as photographing a long and open-mouthed kiss would make them, or depicting handholding, or catching him caressing Sharon's gorgeous bum. All of that had been bad enough, however. Caroline's reaction had terrified him. Not a bit of rage, no tears, and not a single accusation. Just an offer that she made when he looked up from the photos she'd placed on his plate instead of the sandwich he'd been expecting.

She would kill herself if that's what he wanted, she told him. I can see you love her. I can see you want her and who can blame you because look at what I've become. But it's because I can't get over him, Alastair. I try and I fail and I give you nothing. You're everything to me, but I've *never* managed to be everything to you. I won't divorce you because you'll lose too much when it comes to a settlement and you don't deserve that. But I'll kill myself if that's what you want.

God's mercy, he *didn't* want that! He jumped to his feet and begged her to forgive him for 'this bloody stupid fling with Sharon'. It just happened before he knew it was happening, was how he put it. One moment he was talking to her 'bout the shop in Dorchester the new building in Poundbury having to sack the shop assistant in Corfe the need for more freshly baked goods in Wareham . . . What did it matter? He babbled, he begged, he professed whatever he needed to profess in order to assure his wife that he felt nothing for Sharon Halsey.

He almost convinced himself. He steeled himself to tell Sharon that the nothing which they had equated to a nothing future. 'Bit 'f fun, eh?' was how he put it, and he made himself walk away from her sweet face as it collapsed upon itself as if from a blow.

He felt noble for two days and three sleepless nights. And then he'd rung her. He couldn't do it, he told her. 'You're the woman for me,' he told her.

When they lay together in her old iron bed, sated and staring into each other's eyes, it was easy to think how he would manage it all. Losing half of what he owned meant nothing to him if he could have Sharon. He'd give Caro the house. He'd give her half the shops. He'd give her – if he had to – his very soul. But when he finally broached the subject, Caro had made good on her offer. She'd cut herself, directly on the vein and deeply enough for him to see what the reality was and would always be.

So he was caught, but he could not give up Sharon. He would, he promised himself and her, find a way.

He didn't lie when his mobile rang, and Caroline said, 'Where are you, Alastair? I rang the house first, so don't tell me I've awakened you from your nap. You've spent the night with her, haven't you? You've decided that the best course is to take my heart in your mouth and chew it up.'

He glanced at Sharon, who was at the cooker in slippers and dressing gown with her baby fine hair a mess that needed a careful brushing to detangle it. She looked his way and registered his expression. She came to him where he sat at table, she stood behind his chair, and she put her arms round him. She rested her cheek on the top of his head.

He said into the mobile, 'You've not waked me.'

'As to the rest? You're with her, aren't you?' And then, 'Why don't you simply kill me yourself? Why don't *both* of you plan something to be rid of me because that's what you want, a clear path, isn't it? And who can blame you for wanting to be rid of me because look at what I've become. Look at *who* I've become. I have nothing in my life now and I've rung you to tell you it's over. What I touch turns to ash, who I am poisons the air. Will knew it and you do as well and now Clare . . . Oh my God *Clare* . . .'

Alastair frowned. 'What of Clare? Caro, what of Clare?'

'She's dead and I'm alone here with her and I've rung Charlie but he's not answering and I *need* you and that's why I've phoned. *Not* because I'm checking on you. Not because I'm half mad with wanting you and wanting to keep you. She died in the night and the police are coming and I *need* you. Alastair. If I have to talk to the police on my own, if I have to find my way home on my own . . . I don't know what to do or who to ring if I can't ring you . . . And you're with Sharon, aren't you, I know you're with her and you've spent the night and *why* would you want to come to me now but please, *please*.'

'Caro,' he said. 'Caro, get hold of yourself, luv. I'll be there soon.'

Sharon released him then. She went to the cooker. She saw to the eggs and the bacon. She slotted slices of toast in the holder.

He said to her, 'Shar, it's that Clare Abbott . . . Something's happened to her up in Cambridge and Caro's in a right state about it.'

She brought the toast to the table along with a plate of eggs and bacon. To this she'd added grilled tomatoes and mushrooms and a heaping portion of beans. A proper English breakfast it was, the sort of breakfast he'd not had at home in years.

'Eat your meal, then, Alastair,' she told him quietly. 'It's a long drive you've got before you.'

*River House Hotel*
*Cambridge*

Due to roadworks on the motorway, it was noon by the time Rory reached the hotel in Cambridge. She felt caught in a nightmare from which there was going to be no awakening. Her conversation with Caroline Goldacre had been interrupted by paroxysms of that woman's tears. From it, though, Rory had managed to piece together an outline of what had happened.

Although Clare's radio interview had not been scheduled till half past ten, Caroline knew that she was an extremely early, pre-dawn riser. But she also knew not to disturb her employer when she was working, which Clare would be doing as she had an article to finish for a magazine's deadline. Thus, Caroline hadn't knocked on Clare's door till eight a.m. When there was no answer, she wasn't concerned. Clare, she reckoned, would be downstairs in the hotel's restaurant, having her break-fast. That she normally ate earlier did not concern Caroline. It had been a late night, and there was always a possibility that Clare had not risen as early as she normally did.

But Clare wasn't in the restaurant and a question in the

lobby of the hotel gave Caroline the information that Ms Abbott hadn't been seen going out for a walk along the river or anywhere else. As far as anyone knew, she was still in her room.

When a second knock on Clare's door achieved nothing, Caroline returned to her own room. As they had adjoining rooms, she entered that way.

Why had she not done that from the first? was what Rory wanted to know.

Because she'd been told a thousand times not to bother Clare when she was at work! was Caroline's reply. She went on to say she didn't know what had happened to Clare. There she was on the floor and she was dead and she'd been dead for hours and Caroline raced to phone—

To Rory's question of how Caroline had known that Clare was dead at all, let alone dead for hours, Caroline shrieked, 'D'you *know* what it looks like when someone's been dead for hours? D'you *want* me to give you chapter and verse? I rang reception and they came on the run and they phoned emergency and there was nothing to be done. The paramedics didn't even *try* CPR because there was no point. D'you understand? Dead means dead and I don't know what happened. It's a heart attack or a stroke or something and I don't *know*.'

Now in Cambridge, Rory pulled into the car park of the hotel. The River House sat on the bank of the River Cam, walking distance from the city's great colleges, a modern affair of wood and glass but sympathetically designed to blend in with the great willows and sycamores that shaded it. She slipped Arlo into his vest, clipped him onto his lead, and hurried towards reception. She was opening the door as a heavy-set man came out, accompanied by a police officer in uniform. The heavy man's words to 'seal it off, then, until word comes round' told her he too was probably with the Cambridge police.

The presence of police on the scene made Rory feel faint. As he was trained to do, Arlo sensed this and bumped into her leg, nudging her towards a large planter box on which she could sit if she felt it necessary.

She said to the heavy man, 'Clare Abbott?' and he paused. He jerked his head at the uniformed officer with a get-about-your-business expression, and he said nothing to Rory until the man had done as ordered. Then he introduced himself as Detective Chief Superintendent Daniel Sheehan, standing in this morning as duty inspector, and who was she? She used the words *close friend* first and *colleague* second and only third did she tell him she was Clare Abbott's editor from London, here in Cambridge because Clare's assistant Caroline Goldacre had rung her. Where is Clare? she added. What happened? How is . . . ?

But Rory knew there was no point to *how is she*. There was no chance that Caroline had been mistaken, not once the paramedics had arrived. Prior to that, perhaps, but not afterwards. To her horror, she began to weep. Arlo stepped in, nudging her again. The detective took her arm and led her into the hotel, where he sat her on a sofa and joined her. Arlo lay at her feet. The detective bent and petted his tousled-haired head, saying to him, 'I expect you're a helper dog of some sort, aren't you?' before he spoke to Rory.

They were attempting to suss out the deceased woman's next of kin, he told her, but they weren't able to get much sense from the lady who'd discovered the body. She'd had to be given a mild sedative, so distraught was she. They'd insisted she ring for someone to come to her aid, as it didn't seem likely that it would be safe for her to take herself home when the time came for her to leave. Could Ms Statham give them the next of kin for the deceased? There was the formality of an identification of the body that would have to take place prior to the autopsy, which itself would occur once—

'Autopsy?' The idea of Clare being cut open . . . the thought of her skin being pulled back . . . the image of organs removed and weighed and a terrible incision in her chest sewn up . . . Rory pressed her fingers to her forehead. Arlo leaped onto the sofa and assumed the drop position, his chin in her lap.

'No cause for alarm,' Daniel Sheehan said sympathetically, putting his hand on her arm and squeezing it briefly. He called out to the receptionist. Could a pot of tea be brought? Some biscuits as well? A teacake would do if they had one. He turned back to Rory. 'It's procedure,' he told her. 'When an otherwise healthy individual dies suddenly? There'll be a coroner's inquest to determine what happened. But prior to that, a kinsman needs to do the formal identification. Has she a husband? Children? Siblings?'

'There's no one,' Rory said. 'Her parents are dead and she has no children. There's a brother but they've been estranged for years. Things are . . . were . . . difficult between them.' No need to say more than that, Rory thought. To use Clare's own words, her older brother was part of her past best forgotten. She had not continued to hate him for what he'd done to her childhood innocence in the dark of night, but two decades spent learning how to forgive him had not concluded with Clare's wanting him to be a presence in her life. Rory added to what she'd said about the estrangement. 'Clare wouldn't want him here. If it's allowed, I'll identify her.'

Sheehan said that he would see to the arrangements, then.

Rory said, 'C'n I ask . . . ?' The detective looked expectant but also kind and sympathetic, and she appreciated that. 'It's just that I don't quite understand the police being here.'

The pot of tea arrived. Everything was set out: a china pot – not one of those terrible tin ones – with matching cups, saucers, milk jug, and sugar bowl. Five ginger biscuits were arranged on a plate. Sheehan frowned at these. He lifted the teapot's lid and stirred its contents. He poured them each a cup. He broke a biscuit in half and asked if he could give it to Arlo. Rory liked him for this. He told her briefly that any call to 999 was always evaluated by a police official, the force incident manager. Any death was considered suspicious until proven otherwise, so a uniformed patrol officer would be dispatched. That officer made sure the victim was indeed deceased, sealed off the scene, and rang for the duty inspector. 'Me, in this case,' Sheehan said. 'We're short-handed at the moment.'

'So it doesn't mean that someone could someone have hurt her? It's just that I can't bear to think . . .' Rory opened her eyes as wide as she could, straining to keep herself from breaking down a second time.

Sheehan said, 'Let me say that there's no evidence at all of . . . well, of foul play. One drinking glass overturned on the bedside table, and that's it. Ease your mind on that score.'

But as to the rest? Rory asked herself. How could she ease her mind about anything until she knew for certain what had happened to Clare?

She said, 'It was her assistant who rang me. Can you tell me where she is?'

Resting in her own room was the detective's reply. She'd told the police that this unexpected death had reignited the anguish she'd experienced at the recent death of her own son. So she wasn't coping well.

'Who can blame the poor woman?' Sheehan concluded.

Who indeed, Rory thought.

*Spitalfields*
*London*

Charlie Goldacre heard it in Alastair's voice the moment the man said, 'Is that you, lad?' when he answered the phone. To Charlie's 'What's wrong?' Alastair said, 'I've got to go up to Cambridge. Lad, I need you to go with me. See, your mum and me . . . sorry to say we're still having our problems down here and—'

'What's going on?' Charlie's pulse had started beating in his fingertips. He could feel it from the way he was gripping the phone. He said, 'Cambridge? Alastair, has something happened to Mum?'

'No, no,' Alastair reassured him hastily. 'It's that Clare Abbott's died of a sudden. She and your mum—'

'Clare Abbott? Good Christ. What happened?'

'She and your mum were up there in Cambridge for some do. Clare wanted your mum to go along with her as per usual cause there were books to be sold and all that rubbish that goes with it. She died in the night and your poor mum found her just like that this morning. She rang, she's a wreck, and there's no way on God's green earth she c'n get herself back to Dorset on her own, so I've got to—'

'Died?' Charlie was still trying to get his mind round the fact that Clare Abbott, who to him always seemed much more than mere mortal, was actually dead. 'Was there an accident? God, she didn't *do* something to herself?'

'Don't know anything beyond her being dead. Only that your mum rang me and she can't get back here on her own in the state she's in and having to take the train and change in London and manage the luggage. She's not making a lot of sense on the phone, but the police have been and she's had to talk to them and that set her off in a bad way.'

'The *police*?' Charlie wanted to rattle his brains like a cartoon character to keep himself from playing the echo.

Alastair said, 'They've had your mum in for some questions, but they'd do that, wouldn't they? They've got to speak with who found the . . . well, her. Clare. With who found Clare and that was your mum. Wish it'd been the hotel maid or something but there you go. It's all unnerved her. What I know is the police have been and that Rory person – Clare's good friend who's a bit peculiar with that dog, you know? – she's there now. So what it is is this, lad. I need your help with your mum 'cause we're still in a bad way with each other and she's asked for you as well. Fact is, she'd rather have you from the word go and she only rang me as you weren't answering.'

'I've had clients all this morning. I've only just taken a break.'

'No need to explain. But will you go? I don't mean on your own. I'll come up there and we c'n set off. Will you do it, Charlie?'

'Of course,' Charlie said. 'But my God, Alastair, this might push her straight over the edge, after Will.'

'I know,' Alastair said.

They made the arrangements. As it happened, Alastair was already on his way, only phoning Charlie when he'd stopped for petrol at a Welcome Break along the motorway. They worked out where to meet so that Alastair could avoid having to trek through London, and after that Charlie made quick work of cancelling the remaining appointments he had that day.

It was a terrible irony, he thought. Clare Abbott, as far as he knew, had been the picture of absolute health while his mother was in the worst physical condition of her life, with uncontrolled weight gain taking her ever closer to a heart attack or stroke. How in God's name had Clare turned out to be the person to die unexpectedly?

*River House Hotel*
*Cambridge*

Rory watched the laughing tourists make a hash of trying to punt on the Cam. Obviously, they'd decided to go it alone on the river instead of having the pole wielded by one of the many straw-hatted young men available for the activity. As it was, they were merely floating in circles while boaters far wiser and in the hands of skilled punters sat back and enjoyed the smooth ride taking them in the direction of Grantchester. Behind her, at one of the tables set out on the lawn to enjoy the afternoon summer sun while it lasted, Caroline Goldacre was refusing the hotel's special afternoon tea being urged upon her by her husband and son. She didn't want to drink and she couldn't eat, she was telling them. What did they think she was? Clare had died, did they not understand? Yet another person had been ripped from her life—

'From his mother's womb untimely ripped' came to Rory. How odd it was, she thought numbly, that a single word could trigger a line from Shakespeare completely unrelated to the events at hand.

She couldn't blame Caroline for refusing the offer of finger sandwiches, scones, and sweets. She herself had eaten nothing all day. She'd found something for poor Arlo and he'd made short work of it, but as for herself the sight and the smell of food in any form closed off her throat. She could barely manage a cup of tea.

Caroline's son and her husband had taken her out of the hotel because she'd not been able to cope once they descended with her to the lobby. She couldn't breathe inside the place, she told them, and she couldn't muddle through the checkout procedure at all. Not with everyone staring at her and knowing that she'd found Clare's body and believing that she had some-thing to do with what had happened. It was the bloody police, she had hissed. It was that they had insisted upon questioning her away from her own room and at a distance from Clare's. People saw them escorting her to a conference room, and now they thought she had something to do with what had happened in the middle of the night.

They knew that much: Clare had died between midnight and three a.m. But even that was mere speculation on the part of the forensic pathologist. More would be forthcoming later: a more specific time of death and the cause.

While still at the tea table with them, Rory had asked Caroline why the police had wanted to question her. It had seemed an innocent enough question as she voiced it, but Caroline's icy reply of 'Why do you *think* they wanted to question me? Have you recently gone stupid?' prompted Rory to push back from the table, rise, and walk to the low wall separating the garden from the Cam. Caroline's voice followed her, '*Are* you stupid? Because it seems to me you'd have already worked out that she went to bed healthy and she dropped dead in the night and they want to know what happened to her. Did I see anything, did I hear anything, why didn't I go to her if she was in distress?'

Rory turned from the view. As there were others in the garden having their own afternoon tea, she walked back to the table and said in a lower voice, 'In distress? What do they mean?'

'They mean she was on the floor, Rory,' Caroline said. 'They mean the connecting door between our rooms – the door on her side – was open. *They* think that looks damn well suspicious . . . as if I'd hatched some nefarious plan to kill her in the night, God only knows how.'

Charlie extended his hand towards her. 'Mum, you're in a state and that's not a surprise, considering what's happened. But perhaps it's wiser to go inside – somewhere private? – if we want to talk about this.'

'Of course I'm in a state!' Caroline cried. Other tea takers looked in their direction, interest on their faces. Caroline ignored them as she went on. 'And *you* sit there . . . look at him just sitting there staring like I've come from Mars. *She* doesn't get herself into a state, does she? No, no, not our darling Sharon.' She was speaking about Alastair and his lover, Rory knew. She glanced at Charlie. He looked distinctly uncomfortable.

Rory sat again. Arlo whined. He could tell, of course, that things were heading in the direction of off the rails, but the situation was beyond his instincts for protecting Rory since she herself was angry but not afraid. She said to Caroline, 'Didn't you hear her?'

'Don't you dare talk to me like a cop! I was asleep. I didn't hear a damn thing! What was I supposed to hear? If she was having a heart attack or a stroke or *whatever*, she wouldn't exactly have been making any noise.'

'But if she was well enough to get to the doors between your rooms, why didn't she fetch you? She'd opened one of the doors, why not the other?'

'Because it was locked, all right?' Caroline cried. 'Because I locked it. Because I wanted a little privacy for once. I didn't even *want* to be here, d'you know that? I came for her sake, but you would think she was the one doing *me* a favour. So at the end of it all, I locked the door and I went to bed and if she needed me in the night, she could have bloody well rung me on the phone.'

A waiter approached the table, with the excuse of a water jug in his hand. He murmured to Alastair that, perhaps, their party might like to move indoors where a private room could be made available to them?

Alastair stood. Charlie did as well, looking enormously relieved that somehow his suggestion to his mother had been anticipated by the hotel staff. He went to the back of Caroline's chair and said, 'Mum, let's take our conversation—'

'Did she know you locked the door?' Rory cut in.

'Of course she knew it. We'd had a few words and I'd had enough of her for one night, so I shut the damn door and told her I was locking it. *And* I told her I wanted my own private room henceforth and who can blame me. No more of this adjoining rooms rubbish.'

'Clare told me about the words you two had,' Rory said. 'What she didn't tell me was what they were about.'

'*Stop* this!' Caroline shouted.

At that, the waiter said, 'I really must insist . . .'

'You're acting as if you think . . . What do you think? That I killed your precious goose? That I stopped her from laying any more gold eggs for you? Why the hell would I do that as, aside from *everything* else, it puts me straight out of a job?'

'What else?' In her peripheral vision, Rory saw a neatly attired man come bustling from the hotel into the garden. He was striding directly towards them, a fixed smile on his face, and she reckoned he was the manager. She felt desperate for information from Caroline and with the other woman's rising agitation, she felt also certain that she could prise from her details that she might otherwise keep to herself. She said, 'What else, Caroline?' and she didn't care a fig who heard her.

'What?' Caroline snapped.

'You said "aside from everything else". What else?'

'Is there anything I might help you with?' It was the hotel manager speaking, and he brushed at non-existent lint on the sleeves of his jacket and attempted to look pleasant. He nodded at a nearby table of camera-laden tourists who were listening, agog with the drama unfolding before them. The waiter took the opportunity to beat a hasty retreat, leaving the matter in the other man's hands. 'Anything at all?' the manager said meaningfully.

'I'm not putting up with this,' Caroline said, ignoring him. But she did at last rise from her chair. Rory did likewise.

The manager, apparently believing he'd effected the desired result of his appearance on the scene, smiled broadly at their party and said, 'Yes, yes, if you'll come this way . . .'

'I *said* I'm not putting up with any of this,' Caroline snapped. 'You stand there like a whimpering statue –' this to Alastair – 'while she accuses me of God knows what because her *friend* dropped dead in the night and we all know what you wanted from her, Rory, and how does it feel knowing you aren't ever going to get it now?'

'Pet, patience,' Alastair murmured.

She swung on him, 'Is that what you call *her* as well? Your little two-quid whore. "Pet, pet"?'

'For God's sake, Mum,' Charlie said.

She flung herself at him, but it was not to attack. Rather it was to seek the shelter of his filial arms. 'Take me home,' she cried out. 'Charlie, please. Take me home.'

*Camberwell*
*South London*

India wouldn't have admitted the fact to most people, but she'd taken largely to getting her news from the internet. It was in this way, late in the evening, that she learned of Clare Abbott's sudden death, a piece of unexpected information that appeared in one of those boxes of data that tried to entice the internet user away from whatever other reason they'd logged on in the first place. In this case, the facts given were limited to *Famed Feminist Dead at 55* with an accompanying picture of Clare. So startled was she to see this that India forgot for a moment what she'd been looking for.

Behind her, Nat said, 'Something wrong?' and she recalled what she'd meant to do: to find a romantic inn for them in Norfolk, if such a thing existed. Nat had suggested a weekend away from London and they'd settled on the Broads as the weather was still good and what could be more pleasant than bracing sea air, a tramp among the dunes, and a visit to Horsey Mere? They could stay in the village and set out from there.

India had welcomed the idea and she'd set about finding them a place to stay. Now Nat came to stand behind her, his hands on her shoulders. He kissed the top of her head.

'Clare Abbott,' she said and clicked on the story. The information was limited: Cambridge, the River House Hotel, in town for a debate with a conservative female priest. Clare had died sometime during the night. There was no cause given. 'She's the woman Charlie's mum works for,' India told Nat. 'How dreadful. Nat, she was only fifty-five. This will send Charlie's mum into a real state.'

India had already told Nat about the dedication of Will Goldacre's memorial stone, about the appearance of Will's erstwhile lover on the periphery of the event, about the additional appearance of Francis Goldacre and his young Thai wife. She hadn't intended to do so, but Nat had rung her twice during her absence that long day and his question of, 'Have you been out and about today?' was spoken in so friendly a fashion that she'd told him everything, including Charlie's wanting her to be there in Shaftesbury with him. That had caused a little wobble in their young relationship, but they'd got past it when she explained to Nat that had she not been there to talk to Lily Foster, no one would have believed that Clare had not invited Francis Goldacre to the event with the express purpose of tormenting his former wife. To Nat's question of why anyone would have thought that, she'd said, 'Because that's how they are. It's the oddest thing, Nat, but all of this chaos inside Charlie's family was starting to seem quite normal to me until I finally left them.'

Now Nat nodded at the computer's screen. 'As to our getaway on the Broads . . . ?'

'Definitely,' she said, but she hesitated all the same, staring at Clare Abbott's face looking out sternly at her, not the best photo in the circumstances. Odd, she thought, how difficult it was actually to capture the spirit of a person in a photograph. One had to have a level of skill that went far beyond—

'You're concerned,' Nat said. 'Is it the woman herself? Clare Abbott?'

'Not quite,' she said and thought about the entire idea of concern. She said, more like a meditation than a declaration, 'Perhaps I ought to ring her.'

'Who?' Nat drew an ottoman over to the desk and sat, which put his head lower than hers and slightly in shadow. He watched her, his eyes gone quite dark.

'Caroline,' she said. 'I could offer her sympathy. As I was her daughter-in-law for years . . . as I'm still her daughter-in-law technically . . .'

'Hmm. Yes. When are we going to talk about that?' He rubbed the back of his neck as he said this, making the question appear just a casual thought triggered by the term she'd used: daughter-in-law. To her question, 'About what?', he said, 'India,' in the disappointed voice of a father knowing his child is avoiding a necessary discussion of an infraction committed. 'About you and Charlie,' he told her, 'and what you're going to say to him and when you're going to say it.'

She felt her spine loosen when she sighed. 'I'm avoiding, obviously.'

'Obviously. It's been how many months now?'

'Since you and I . . . ?' She smiled at him fondly. She found that she wanted to take him straight to bed, to prove that he had nothing to worry about when it came to her marriage. 'I would expect you to know to the very minute, Nathaniel Thompson.'

'Two months, twenty days, four hours, and –' he glanced at his watch 'thirty-seven minutes. No, thirty-eight.'

'You're joking!' she laughed.

He reached for her hand and kissed her palm. 'As to the minutes and hours, yes. But as to the months and days, I do have them down. Have I told you what I first noticed about you on the bus?' And when she shook her head, he went on with, 'How intently you read. It was days before you even looked up from your book and gave me a glance.'

'Was it? How odd. I have no memory of a first glance at all.'

'You wouldn't have.' He laced his fingers with hers. 'I expect everything was all too fresh for you then.'

'What?'

'Leaving Charlie. How many months has it been?'

'Just over ten.'

'And when will you tell him that you're not going back?'

She drew her hand away from his. She looked back at the computer screen, at Clare Abbott's intelligent face. Clare, she knew, would have called India's present life a very good example of out of the frying pan and into the fire. Going from one man to another? After such a brief hiatus? Clare would not have approved, and who could blame her? What did she really know of Nathaniel Thompson, India asked herself. She said, 'I don't know.'

'You don't know when you're going to tell him or you don't know whether you're making this separation from him permanent?'

'Either,' she said.

He rose. They were in the second bedroom of her tiny house, which she used as a sitting room and office since the real sitting room was her weekend acupuncture clinic. The room was tiny, but Nat found enough space to pace its perimeter. He was a tall man, and he seemed to fill the area not only with his presence but also with his feelings. Odd, she thought, that she would end up with another man who lived so openly with his feelings, as Charlie had done prior to Will's death. What was the attraction? she wondered. Her determination *not* to end up with her father? But why would that be? She'd have been wise to choose a man like her father, diplomat that he long had been.

'So what are we, you and I?' Nat asked her. 'Merely a break from your normal routine?'

'You know that isn't the case.' She turned from the computer to watch him.

'I know that you haven't said a thing about how you feel. I've been forthcoming with you, the whole heart spread out on a boulder for the carrion eaters. What's stopping you if it isn't Charlie? What is it about him, India? Since when did neediness become so compelling?'

'Let's not quarrel. If I haven't said it, it's not because I doubt it but because . . .' She hesitated, searching for a way to explain what she herself only imperfectly understood.

'What?'

'I don't know,' she said. 'Truly, Nat, I don't. And no, neediness is not compelling. But I don't want to deal him a death blow.'

'So you'll do what instead? Keep both of us hanging?'

'I don't mean to do that.'

He resumed his pacing, but his steps took him only as far as the window which looked down at the street, through her tangle of a front garden barely the size of a steamer trunk. He said to this view rather than to her, 'I know he's not a proper man to you.' He turned then, perhaps to gauge her reaction.

India knew she looked startled, for she'd never said a word. It had seemed too disloyal to Charlie.

Nat said as if in answer to a question she didn't ask, 'It was the way you reacted. And what you said: "Such a long time."'

'I didn't say that.'

'You did, in fact. Before you fell asleep. Just on the edge of asleep and awake. You felt as you hadn't felt in years. We both know why.'

She felt the wound of his words although every one of them was the truth. She said again, 'Please. Let's not quarrel.'

He came back to her then. He raised her from her chair and took her into his arms. 'So we won't,' he told her. 'Not when it comes to the truth. We won't quarrel about that.'

# 1 October

I t was an escape from speed dating, of all bloody mad things, that revealed to Barbara Havers twenty-four hours after the fact that Clare Abbott had unexpectedly died. She'd arrived home, thoroughly knackered by what it was taking in the energy department for her to maintain the dispiriting air of panting cooperation personified, all for the pleasure of Detective Superintendent Isabelle Ardery. Jaw clenching, lip biting, teeth grinding, fingernails digging, and tongue holding were all taking their toll, and Barbara wasn't sure how much longer she could hold on to this new twist in her personality without the top of her head erupting. Berwick-upon-Tweed was starting to sound like paradise to her. So when she trudged up the driveway of the Edwardian villa behind which she lived – having been forced to park her Mini practically at the top of Haverstock Hill – the last activity she wished to engage in was speed dating.

It was all Dorothea Harriman's idea, and she'd proved herself unrelenting on the topic. Dee's outlook on life, unfortunately, had not been adjusted by *Looking for Mr Darcy* which, it turned out, she'd only glanced at before pressing it upon DI Lynley. After that, having apparently given up on the idea of making Barbara over, she'd decided upon another way to put an end to the sad state of affairs that was Barbara's love life. Speed dating, she announced, was going to get Barbara's feet wet in the waters in which hordes of available men were apparently swimming.

Barbara had attempted protest. She'd never been interested in pulling men.

To this, Dorothea had said, 'Everyone is interested in pulling men, Detective Sergeant Havers. So I'm not listening to no. And neither is anyone else.'

'What's that supposed to mean?'

Dorothea had been forced to confess, at that point, that 'everyone wants you *back*, Detective Sergeant. We're rather desperate to have you back, not to put too fine a point on things.'

To Barbara's hot, 'I haven't *gone* any-bloody-where,' Dorothea said, 'You know what I mean. This Berwick-upon-Tweed situation? And Detective Superintendent Ardery? And you being extra-extra special good? You see, while I think it's terribly heroic for Detective Inspector Lynley to have *tried* to pull the plug on all that—'

'*What?*' Barbara cried. 'What did he do?'

'Oh dear. I'm saying too much. I'm getting flustered. Look, let's just try this, shall we? Let's call it a new experience, something to tell your mum next time you see her . . . Please? And afterwards . . .' Dorothea paused, apparently to give the afterwards some thought. 'Afterwards, I'll take you to dinner. You name the restaurant. I'll pay the bill.'

'I'd rather have my toenails pulled out,' Barbara told her.

'No. You'd rather have something on your mind besides Berwick-upon-Tweed. I'm not taking no for an answer, by the way. You can't reject something you've never tried.'

Thus, the evening that lay before her. Dee had found the experience they were about to undergo by browsing through the ads at the back of *Time Out*. There it had been, tucked beneath an offer for Expert Thai Massages Given in Your Hotel Room. The event was scheduled to take place in Holloway, conveniently close – as things turned out – to HM's Prison for Women.

Wonderful, Barbara thought as she plodded towards the pub that was going to house the affair. Off duty screws looking for love. She should fit right in.

Dorothea was waiting just inside the door. To Barbara's greeting of, 'Are you half-mad, Dee? Do you actually reckon anyone decent is going to turn up *here*?', Dorothea said, 'We're going to shine, like pearls among the . . . whatever.' And she led the way into the function room before Barbara could point out to her that pearls generally didn't shine at all.

The function room was decorated . . . just. Twisted crepe paper crisscrossed the ceiling and above the reception table a clutch of helium balloons floated. Here sat three female greeters, who were collecting money and providing drinks tickets. In front of them, *Hello! I'm* nametags waited to be filled out in black marker pen, and once the arriving singles had accomplished this, they drifted to the sides of the room and milled about, surreptitiously examining the other singles.

Five rows of long tables indicated where the speed daters were supposed to sit. Each held a sign affixed to a metal pole. *25–30* said one. *31–40, 41–50, 51–60, 60+* said the others. Lined along each were chairs for the daters and in the centre of each table and spaced along its length were slim white vases holding plastic daisies.

A corpulent man with slicked-back black hair of a suspiciously youthful hue began to 'set up the rules' , which were simple enough. He said his name was Sunny Jack Domino and he was going 'to keep you lot in line, this evening.' Keeping them in line referred to a timer he held up and whose workings he demonstrated by having it sound and then following it with a hand-held bell of town-crier variety. Their 'dates' would be five minutes long, he told them. When they heard the timer, they had thirty seconds to finish up at which point, he would ring the bell. The gents would move to the chair on their right while the ladies remained seated. 'You c'n pass your details to whoever you take a fancy to,' he said. 'Only rule is to keep moving.'

The mention of details told Barbara she should have brought some business cards on the very remote chance that she actually made a connection with someone. She had a moment of concern about this, but that faded soon enough once Sunny Jack Domino explained the purpose of the signs on the tables. Those, he said, indicated the age groups. Daters were to sit in accordance with their years. 'And *no* cheating,' he warned them with a show of excessively white teeth.

It was all rather like being in school. The daters headed for their age-appropriate tables, with Sunny Jack chortling about the fun to come. With a 'Ready, steady, go!', he set the daters upon each other.

Soon enough Barbara discovered that while the women had taken themselves to the age-appropriate table, few of the men had done so, instead shaving a decade and in one case three off their ages. Thus she found herself conversing with blokes from forty-one to sixty-seven years of age.

She lasted three dates. Her first exposed her to a devotee of a diet that appeared to consist of laying into flapjacks and chip butties, a sort of nutritional Russian roulette that contributed to a girth which oozed over the chair he occupied. He gazed at Barbara and waited, apparently, for her to entertain him, which she was loath to do. Her next encounter proved to be a gentleman who admitted readily that he wasn't close to being in his 30s – this would be the sixty-seven year old – but 'I like 'em young an' bouncy, I do, and I got the stamina of a bull,' he said, with a wink and a meaningful gesture employing the index finger of his right hand and the circled index finger and thumb of his left. Her final meeting had her listening to a man who demanded 'what sort 'f music you listen to, eh? 'Cause what I've found is that if the music doesn't fit, nothing else is going to.'

It was at that point, that Barbara rose from the table and headed for the exit. She hadn't made good her escape before Dorothea was upon her, crying, 'Detective Sergeant Havers! You aren't—'

Barbara saw that only a lie would do. She held up her mobile. 'Just got a call, Dee. I'm on rota tonight, and you know how that is . . .' With a wave, she was gone, out onto the pavement.

She sought out a chippy. She'd not had dinner and after the speed dating folly she reckoned she was owed. She set off down the road. Fittingly, it seemed, it began to rain, not a gentle autumn shower to wash the summer's grime from the trees but a real downpour. And, of course, she had no umbrella.

She stumbled upon a newsagent within fifty yards, and she went inside to get out of the rain. A meaningful gaze from the hijab-wearing woman behind the counter indicated that Barbara ought to make a purchase, and she was happy to do so. Wrigley's spearmint, a packet of Players, a plastic lighter, and a copy of her favourite light reading material, a tabloid called *The Source*. She handed these over for payment and enquired the location of the nearest chippy. She discovered that it was close to where she was, a mere eight or ten doors farther along the way.

Inside, she placed her order for haddock and chips. There were no tables, only a Formica-topped eating counter that ran round the walls. Stools with greasy looking vinyl seats stood before this, which made sitting an unappealing prospect, but as eating chips in the rain was less appealing still, Barbara decided to be satisfied with the fact that the counter was wide enough to accommodate her reading material. And really, she reckoned, what more could one ask for on a rainy evening?

So it was that she uncovered the information telling her that well-known feminist author and lecturer Clare Abbott was dead at fifty-five years of age. This wasn't front page material, though. Instead the front page was given to the shocking revelation that a footballer previously said to be devoted to his wife – always a dead giveaway, Barbara thought sardonically – had been keeping a mistress on the coast of Spain for the last three years. 'I'm faithful to them both,' he was claiming, 'which is more than you can say for the rest of this lot.' It didn't seem to be a problem for him that his wife had recently given birth – she was pictured leaving their house, bundled baby in her arms, weeping inconsolably – and that the mistress was pregnant. 'I'm only a human being!' had been his protest at being discovered a perfect lout.

Barbara made the jump to page five where this sad tale continued. It was on her way to this page that she saw first Clare Abbott's picture and then the news about her death. Although the exact cause wasn't given, it appeared to be a heart attack, she read. That was a pity as she hadn't been old, Barbara thought. The idea of a heart attack caused her to look a bit askance at her fish and chips, though. She decided to douse them both with another round of malt vinegar. This, she reckoned, could stand in place of the vegetables that she should have been eating.

# 4 October

Rory Statham sat in silence as David Jenkins read and turned the pages. Arlo was with her, lying comfortingly at her feet. Jenkins hadn't looked up since bidding Rory to take one of the two seats on the far side of his desk, and she was glad of this. It suggested to her that he shared her concern, and why wouldn't he? He'd been Clare's physician for the better part of thirty years, and when Rory had phoned and asked for his last appointment of the day because his patient Clare Abbott had died unexpectedly five days earlier, he'd responded at once with, 'Good heavens. Yes. Of *course*. I'm afraid it won't be till half past six,' which was absolutely fine with her. She was hoping to go over the autopsy report with him, she confided.

Now she watched him, trying to gauge his reaction to what she herself had already read: a seizure caused by fatal cardiac arrhythmia. She wasn't sure what it meant other than something having gone badly wrong with Clare's heart.

How could it have happened? It seemed to Rory that if Clare's heart had failed her in some way, her physician would have known that this was a possibility and would have warned her of it. She waited in an agony of nerves and grief as the doctor read on.

Jenkins was the age of a pensioner, very avuncular in the way he'd welcomed Rory, very kind about the unexpected presence of an assistance dog. He was one of what Rory thought

of as the old-fashioned doctors of Harley Street vintage, despite
his surgery not being on Harley Street at all. He wore a three-
piece suit that was far too heavy for the time of year, and he
used half-moon spectacles perched on the end of his nose. He
sprouted ear hairs, nose hairs, and the chinstrap beard of
another century. Oddly enough, Rory thought, she found this
comforting.

At last he looked up. He removed the half-moon spectacles
and from his wallet he excavated a purpose-made square of
cloth on which he cleaned them. He drew rather impressive
eyebrows together and rolled his chair back from his desk.
He'd set a fan to blowing in an attempt to cool the room which
had benefited from the afternoon sun, and he made an adjustment to this before he said to her, 'Will you tell me exactly
how you fitted into Clare's life?'

Rory said, 'I'm her editor and her friend,' and to her morti-
fication, she felt the onset of tears. She pressed her fingers to
her upper lip in an effort not to weep. She'd been doing so
for days. She couldn't seem to get control of herself. She'd
been gently asked by the managing director of the publishing
house to take a few days off, but she hadn't been able to do
so. Being alone with her thoughts was so terrible an idea that
she would have done anything at all to escape such a fate. She
said, 'We've been very close, Clare and I. As she has no family
in England, I was long ago made the one who would take care
of matters should anything happen . . .' She lowered her head.
Arlo raised his, his brown eyes questioning.

'Yes, I see,' Jenkins said. 'And her body?'

'It's on its way . . . She's on her way to Shaftesbury. There'll
be a cremation but it's still to be arranged, so the mortuary
will keep her . . .' Talking about the disposal of the remains
felt so inhuman, not only like a desecration of who Clare had
been but also a desertion of the friendship they'd shared. She
changed course. 'It seems to me that there would have been
some indication, somewhere, somehow . . . How could she not
know that her heart was bad?'

Jenkins steepled his long fingers beneath his chin, elbows on his desk. 'It happens occasionally, this business with her heart. The accompanying seizure, however? I do find that rather troubling.'

Rory wanted to cling to that last bit. She wanted it to mean something, although she could not have said what.

Jenkins continued, meditatively. 'Children sometimes have seizures – we call them benign seizures – accompanying high fevers, but adults generally don't. So to have a seizure brought on by the arrhythmia . . . It's rather odd that there wasn't an indication of a tumour in the brain or even an old traumatic scar from a head injury. But there's no mention or even suggestion of that in the report. If you'll excuse me for a moment . . . ?' He left his office but he was not gone for long. He returned with a thick manila filing folder which turned out to be the history of Clare's health: all the years of her relationship with Jenkins. He spent a good few minutes looking through this, and when Rory was about to ask him what he was searching for, he told her that there was nothing in Clare's medical file to indicate she'd ever sustained a head injury. She had undergone a physical examination once a year – 'Commendably so,' he added – and at the age of fifty she'd insisted upon her first colonoscopy, an electrocardiogram, a bone density screening, and a stress test to measure her heart's endurance. She had all her yearly 'female tests' on schedule, he said, adding that he only wished the rest of his female patients were as attentive to their health.

'Her diet was rather wretched,' Rory said, with a fond smile. 'I doubt she'd eaten a balanced meal in a year. And she did like her wine. But, that was it. She wasn't even a smoker. So for this to happen to her . . . I still don't understand.'

The doctor said, 'As I said, it does happen. Even to people as fit as long distance runners.' He went on to say that when it came to the human body, really, anything could occur with or without an explanation. That was one of life's mysteries, he told her.

He ended with, 'I'm terribly sorry. I can see how much Clare meant to you. To other people as well, as I've been reading about her latest controversy.' He smiled in a fond and sad way. 'That book of hers. She was quite a lively thinker, wasn't she? It's a great loss for you and for everyone who knew her.'

# 5 October

Barbara Havers decided that her best course was to button-hole DI Lynley in the underground car park, so she arrived at New Scotland Yard forty minutes earlier than usual, and she was standing in his regular parking bay when he finally pulled in. She moved to one side. She'd smoked six cigarettes down to the nub during her wait for him, and their dog ends were lying crushed round her feet. He sighed when she hopped inside his pristine vehicle, undoubtedly in reaction to how redolent she was with smoke at seven fifty-two in the morning.

She didn't give him a chance to pull out the air freshener. She said at once, 'You're doing your best. I see that, sir. Mind you, I didn't at first. I was that cheesed off. But I've had a think, and now I see what you're about and I more or less appreciate the thought. But you've got to chuck it as it's just no good.'

He considered all this before saying, 'What are you talking about, Havers?'

'She's not going to rip up those transfer documents. Not in my lifetime and not in yours. Who can blame her? In her position, I wouldn't rip them up either. I've made my bed and all the rest, and I get that. I also don't regret it, so let it be.'

He looked away from her, but the only thing to see was what was directly in front of them: the stunning concrete wall of the underground car park, which in this particular location bore a disturbing wet patch resembling the silhouette of Queen

Victoria in her declining years. On so many levels it was not a pretty sight. Barbara was about to remark on this, when Lynley said, 'Frankly? You're not doing your best work. You haven't been for months. You and I and Isabelle all know that. So how is not doing your best work going to serve anyone in the long run?'

'I'm trying to find my way,' she told him. 'Or better said, I'm trying to find *a* way.'

'A way for what?'

'To navigate all this.'

'And might I ask what constitutes "all this"?'

Her chest developed a hard sore spot. She knew what that meant and what to do to fend it off: be brief and be gone. She said, 'The job, sir. So just let me do it,' and she put her hand on the door handle, ready to open it. 'But ta, anyway. I appreciate that—'

He stopped her with, 'I know what it is to miss someone, Barbara.'

That only made things worse. She *couldn't* leave him then, and he bloody well knew it. She sank back into her seat and looked straight ahead, at poor old widowed VR and her triple chin. She said, 'I know that, sir. In my own case, I also know how stupid it is. Helen was your wife, for God's sake, and she was murdered. These were my neighbours and they've only moved house.'

'Love is love,' was his reply. 'God knows that it doesn't require shared blood or legal documents or anything else to make it more intense. When someone's gone, they're gone, but what we've felt for them isn't. To cope with that – having no place to put those feelings any longer – it takes a monumental effort of will.'

She turned her head to look at him. He was watching her. Those dark brown eyes of his – always unexpected in a bloke whose hair went completely blond in summer – were fixed on her with what she knew he felt but what she also believed she didn't deserve: compassion. Their situations were different, no matter how he tried to paint them. Nothing would ever make them similar. But she owed him so much, and she felt a real need to tell him that in the only way possible, which was obliquely.

She said, 'Thank you for that.'

'For what?'

'What you just said. You're a decent bloke, for all your fine ways and your family silver and ancestral portraits.'

'Ah.'

They were silent together, both of them studying the Healey Elliott's fascia with its knobs and dials and mysterious indicators. Finally, Barbara said to him, 'On the other hand . . . D'you think you could get her to take a step away? Not the guv. I mean Dorothea. She had me speed dating the other night and she's been banging on about dancing lessons for the last two days. I've managed to hold her off by claiming fallen arches, but I don't think she intends to take that one on board permanently by a long chalk.'

He nodded but his lips twitched in an effort not to smile. 'On the other hand,' he said, 'a fine rumba is a beautiful thing, Barbara. It's not quite a tango, but it's a very close second.'

She smiled as well. 'Sod you,' she said. They chuckled together companionably.

They left the car park and rode up in the lift, separating when they reached their floor. Barbara worked her way to her desk. She was stopped by one of the younger DCs. Phone message, he told her, and he handed it over.

It was Rory Statham who'd rung her, she saw. The message was merely to ring her back on an urgent matter concerning Clare Abbott.

It was the notation about Clare Abbott that helped Barbara recall who Rory Statham was: the woman at the book signing in Bishopsgate Institute, the one who'd given Barbara one of Clare Abbott's cards after the feminist's minder had removed it from her. She dug out her mobile and placed a call to the number on the message.

'Thank God,' were Rory Statham's first words, followed at once by, 'I need to speak with you. Privately but in person. It's to do with Clare. She's died in Cambridge and—'

'I saw that in the paper,' Barbara said. 'I'm dead sorry about it. Heart attack?'

'That's just it. There was never anything wrong with her heart. I've the autopsy report and I've taken it to her doctor and he's said . . . Look, can you meet me? I'll come to you. Or I'll meet you anywhere at any time. It's dreadfully important.'

She sounded in a real state. Barbara couldn't blame her. When it came to loss, she was becoming something of an expert on how it felt. She said, 'I c'n do round eleven o'clock,' which was her break time. 'But you'll have to come to me. And I got to say that if something burning comes up here in the meantime, I'll have to cancel.' She hated to have to couch things in such terms, but if she knew nothing else, she knew she had to toe the line.

Eleven o'clock at New Scotland Yard was no problem at all, Rory Statham told her. She would be there.

*Victoria*
*London*

At precisely eleven, Barbara's phone rang. Rory Statham was phoning from below. She had Arlo with her, and the security team were giving her a very difficult time about the dog.

'I'll be down,' Barbara told you. 'They probably think you've fed him explosives with his morning brekkie.'

The reception area was its usual knot of police, civilian workers, and visitors. Barbara spied Rory Statham through the crowd. She was waiting directly next to one of the large ground floor windows, this one possessing a spectacular view of the vast array of concrete barriers that protected the centre of

London's policing from individuals driving lorries packed with Semtex.

Barbara worked her way over to the woman, extended her hand in greeting, and tilted her head towards the exterior of the building. It would be easier to talk outside, she told her. They couldn't go far as, unfortunately, she didn't have much time.

They got as far as the pavement just across the street. With a brisk autumn wind rattling to the ground the leaves of the London planes nearby, Rory handed over a manila envelope.

'I need your help,' she told Barbara. 'I'm not sure where to turn. They're saying she died of . . . It's more or less two causes, they're telling me. Heart arrhythmia and then a seizure. Only her doctor – Clare's doctor? – has seen the autopsy – that's what I've brought with me – and he's compared it to her medical history. He's been her physician for decades and he's told me that there's nothing from her history with him or from anything she indicated when he took her on as a patient that would explain why she had the seizure. No brain trauma. No tumour. Nothing.'

Barbara could see how agitated the woman was. So could, apparently, her dog. Arlo whined at her feet, and Rory scooped him up and held him childlike, with his paws against her chest. Barbara said to her, 'As to the heart?'

'Arrhythmia?' Rory licked her lips. She seemed hesitant. Barbara repeated her question. Rory finally said, 'He said it *could* happen. He said that sometimes it *does* happen unexpectedly. Rapid beating, slowed beating, misfiring, all of it. Only, you see, Clare'd been tested. All the heart tests you can imagine five years ago, so for this to occur . . .'

'What're you suspecting?' Barbara said.

'I don't *know*,' Rory said. 'Only, you see, she wasn't alone in Cambridge. Caroline Goldacre – d'you remember the woman from the Bishopsgate signing? the one who didn't want you to have Clare's card? – she was there. They had adjoining rooms, and Caroline had locked the door between them so that Clare wouldn't be able to . . .' She shifted Arlo from one shoulder to the other. It seemed an action designed to allow her a moment to get herself in order. She said, 'There are too many things that don't seem right, and I don't know where to turn.'

Barbara nodded. The fact that the door was locked between their rooms could have meant nothing and it probably did. Still, she opened the envelope and pulled out the report.

She scanned it quickly. Height, weight, marks on the body, examination and weight of individual organs, toxicology, contents of stomach, condition of brain. A cursory reading suggested to Barbara that the conclusion of a seizure caused by cardiac arrhythmia was probably correct.

She looked up. The expression on Rory Statham's face killed off Barbara's words before she could say them. Then Rory spoke. 'They've released the body to me and I've had it . . . I've had her sent to Shaftesbury. Her parents're long dead, you see, and her brother . . . The last thing Clare would have ever wanted was to give her brother access to her body. She has no other close relatives and she and I have been family to each other since . . .' She took a steadying breath. 'You see, I lost my partner some nine years ago? We were on holiday and—' Arlo gave a small yelp. Rory started. She'd been clutching at the dog and it seemed she'd inadvertently grabbed at him too tightly. Rory lowered him to the pavement with apologies, as if he could understand her words which, perhaps, he could. She stayed crouched next to him and looked up at Barbara, saying, 'Clare got me through it. And now to think that something might have happened to her . . .'

Barbara said, 'Of course.' She was at a loss, though. She wanted to help but she wasn't sure how. Bloody Christ, she thought, there was so much sodding pain in the world. How did anyone manage to live to old age?

She put the report back into the envelope. She said the only thing she could. 'C'n I hold on to this? I can't promise anything. It *looks* straightforward. Still, there might be a chance that something's been missed and as I'm not an expert . . . What I'm saying is not to make any arrangements about the body yet. I'll be in touch.'

The woman's gratitude came at her in a rush, like a wave that released energy too long held in. She said, 'Thank you, *thank* you,' and she buried her face in her small dog's wiry hair. She said to Barbara, 'Will you ring me, then?'

'I will,' Barbara promised.

*Victoria*
*London*

She'd reckoned on having to dig someone up from SO7 to look over the material that Rory Statham had handed to her. But that didn't turn out to be necessary. Instead, a brief conversation with DI Lynley resulted in her giving the autopsy report to him. He'd come by her desk with a 'Lunch, sergeant?' invitation to join him at Peeler's. He added, 'On me and in celebration,' to which she said, 'Of what?' His reply, 'Mission accomplished. At least on one front. It wasn't easy. It required all my reserves of diplomacy, so I daresay we're both owed a decent meal.'

In the Met's marginally decent restaurant, he revealed that he'd spoken at some length with Dorothea Harriman. The secretary had admitted that the speed dating had been a terrible idea. 'I'd no *idea* the men would all pretend to be younger,' she'd said. 'Isn't that what women are supposed to do? I myself ended up "dating" at least five blokes who – I swear to you – weren't a day under forty, Detective Inspector Lynley.'

When Barbara expressed her relief, Lynley held up a hand lest she think that Dorothea had thrown in the towel on all matters romantic when it came to Barbara. As he put it, Dorothea hadn't *quite* released into the void her hopes that she could still somehow persuade Detective Sergeant Havers to attend dancing lessons with her. 'I can only report that she promised to "give it a rest for now",' Lynley told Barbara frankly.

'Ta, sir,' Barbara said. 'I c'n fend off the dancing lessons. No worries there.'

'It might help if, in a week or two, you claim to be newly –' he seemed to search for a word – 'newly "involved" with someone. Or perhaps with something?'

'Some*thing*?' Barbara asked. 'Like romantically inclined towards a car, you mean? I'd need the Healey Elliott for that. I see how you look at that motor, sir.'

'Admittedly, it's love. But I meant a . . . perhaps a recently acquired hobby? Too busy to be called upon for dancing lessons and the like because you're now . . . what could it be?'

'Embroidering tea towels and pillow cases for my bottom drawer?' Barbara asked sardonically. She shook her head. 'I'll hold her off without sinking to lies. Meantime . . .' She opened the envelope with the autopsy materials inside. She said, 'I've had this given to me,' and she explained the rest: Clare Abbott, her death, Rory Statham, her promise to that woman, and all the relevant details. She said, 'I've had a look and it seems straightforward enough, but could you . . . ?'

Lynley brought his reading specs from his jacket pocket and slid them on. They'd placed their orders before Barbara had offered him the report, and it wasn't until their meal arrived that he looked up from his careful perusal of it. He said, 'You're right, Barbara. It does seem to be all here. There's only one area that might be worth pursuing. But it's a minor possibility at best.' He went on to talk about the toxicology report. A simple screening had been done, he told her, as she no doubt had noticed. This type of test looked for an array of common drugs, some legal and some not: drugs like amphetamines, barbiturates, benzodiazepines, narcotics, cannabis, and cocaine. The presence of any of them would trigger a more detailed and sophisticated test to determine exactly what form of the drug was present. Was it something for a congested head cold or crystal methamphetamine, for example. In the case of Clare Abbott, the simple toxicology screening had been done, no drugs were present, so no further toxicology test was performed.

'If there were no drugs present,' Barbara said, 'why would they go further? It all looks straightforward, doesn't it?'

'It does, unless you consider that the death might have been caused by something that a simple screening doesn't show but a more complex analysis would. That would involve blood, urine, and tissue samples. Gas chromatographs and mass spectrometers. It would also involve a large expense which can be avoided if the obvious conclusion is –' here he looked to the part of the report that indicated the forensic pathologist's conclusion – 'sudden heart arrhythmia causing a violent seizure causing death.'

'But that *is* what happened.'

He removed his spectacles, folded them, and returned them to his pocket. 'Yes. But if there's a question at all about the death, it should deal with what could have *caused* those two events. This –' he tapped his fingers on the autopsy report – 'depended upon the forensic pathologist's curiosity and – unfortunately – his funding. With no indication at the scene that anyone messed her about, there would be no cause for him to delve once he could assign a cause of death.'

'It would take a second autopsy then, wouldn't it?' Barbara said.

'It would,' he told her. 'Not a simple thing to arrange in these circumstances in which nothing at all seems untoward.'

Barbara considered this. She thought about the likelihood of a second autopsy being ordered merely at the request of Clare Abbott's friend. It would take the participation of solicitors and magistrates and coroners and God only knew who else. But perhaps with a nudge from the Metropolitan police . . . ? Surely something more efficient could be effected if the Met got involved.

She said thoughtfully, 'I think it's what we need.'

'The second autopsy? With not a single sign that anything was amiss at the scene, Barbara—'

'A locked door,' she said. 'Between adjoining rooms.'

'Hardly earth shaking.'

'I know. But this woman, sir? This Rory Statham? I get the impression Clare Abbott was like her only family or she was like Clare's only family or something like that but the point is . . . If it can set her mind at rest . . . I expect that Clare Abbott's estate would even pay for it, if it came to that. And then Rory wouldn't have to go through the rest of her life wondering why and how and who and what. She'd know. That's worth something, isn't it?'

She knew this last wasn't entirely fair, not the fact of it but the saying of it. The why of Lynley's own wife's death was shrouded in the silence of a young boy who would not name the individual who'd been with him in Eaton Terrace on the day of Helen's murder. Thus, Lynley did not know why the young boy had shot Helen. Chances were, he would never know.

He nodded without speaking. He took up the autopsy report and laid it on the floor next to his chair. They tucked into their meals.

'Thank you, Inspector,' Barbara said to him.

# 11 October

India didn't inform Nat that she was going to attend Clare Abbott's funeral. She assured herself that this was because she couldn't adequately explain to *herself* why she was going, so she wouldn't be able to explain it to him. The truth, however, was something different. During the last ten days, she and Nat had seen each other four times and on two occasions, he'd brought up Charlie. They hadn't quarrelled, but the mention of Charlie's name produced a tension between them that wasn't easily diffused.

Part of her understood that she was playing a game with herself, one in which if she made no decision, she wouldn't have to face consequences that were at present unknown. But another part of her knew very well that not to make a decision *was* in fact making a decision. And the consequence of that was going to be watching Nat Thompson eventually walk out of her life.

'He wants you back,' Nat had said. 'He wants your sympathy, and sometimes, India, people mistake sympathy for love.'

'I don't,' had been her reply. Yet what she didn't add was that Charlie's suffering had always touched her. When this happened, her father's lifelong advice about cutting her losses seemed not good sense but rather the easy way out of a relationship in which she'd had expectations that had gone unmet.

But that, Nat would have told her had she revealed to him what was causing her to temporise, was exactly what Charlie wanted her to feel. Yet India didn't see things that way. Instead she saw that, having lost her, Charlie was doing his best to recover from a blow that might have felled him. She couldn't ignore that, for they shared history together.

His request that she go to Clare Abbott's funeral with him hadn't been unreasonable. He felt duty-bound to go for his mum's sake as she'd been on a business trip with Clare when the feminist died, he explained. She'd been badly shaken by the discovery of Clare's dead body and by everything that had followed that discovery: the arrival of the police, the questions she'd had to answer, the loss of her friend and employer. Then there was also the not small matter of Alastair's having an affair with Sharon Halsey . . .

India hadn't known about that. An affair? *Alastair*, of all people?

'Who would have thought it, eh?' Charlie said. 'It's been going on for a while. Mum wants her sacked, but he won't do it. Calls her "essential to the business". I've been down a few times since Will's memorial trying to broker peace between them, but it's no go.'

He went on to explain that with all this piled on Caroline's head, it was likely that there would be drama either at the funeral or afterwards. It was that he wished to avoid, and with India as his companion needing to be back in London, he knew he could put in an appearance and then depart. He needed to be able to do that, anyway, he admitted. He had eight clients now and two of them had appointments the morning after the funeral. He didn't want to cancel them. India *did* know he was seeing clients again, didn't she?

She couldn't remember if he'd told her. She was, admittedly, too taken up with Nat to remember much at all. But Charlie sounded so like the Charlie of old, and she was drawn to him. Not in the old way, but still the pull was there.

Thus she found herself in St Peter's Church just off the market square in Shaftesbury. It was a disappointing place in which to hold a funeral, she decided, as a well meaning church committee with who-knew-what in mind had at some point in time decided to 'modernise' the interior of the medieval structure. So it was brightly lit, floored in hardwood instead of stones, and its vestibule looked more like a secondhand book shop than the entrance to an edifice of worship. There was none of the wonderful musty stone smell of old churches, either, although in this case whatever stony scent there might have been was overpowered by the flowers, which were everywhere.

If the flower arrangements were anything to go by, Clare Abbott had been much loved. It wasn't just her coffin that was draped with blooms. Enormous pedestal baskets stood intermittently along the central aisle of the nave and the chancel was fairly stuffed with them. There was also a great crowd of mourners: fellow feminists, along with individuals representing the dead woman's publishing and academic life, as well as her life here in Shaftsbury, including the well-hatted women from the Women's League whom India recognised from the dedication to Will's memorial in the summer.

Thinking of that event, she looked around. Lily Foster wasn't there. Any potential drama that might have developed from her presence would, India concluded with relief, be avoided.

This was good, for from the moment she and Charlie met up with his mum at her house outside of town, India had reckoned that the makings for some sort of commotion were roiling round Caroline's head. These, she learned, sprang from two sources. The first was the delay in cremating Clare Abbott, due to a second autopsy being ordered. This was unseemly and unnecessary, Caroline had declared, yet another desecration of a corpse brought about at the whimsy of *one* individual who couldn't come to grips with the fact of Clare's sudden death. 'It's that Rory Statham behind all of it,' Caroline had informed them. 'She's gone to someone and made an issue of things, and they jumped to do what she wanted.' To Charlie's careful 'I don't think it quite works that way, Mum,' Caroline snapped, 'What do *you* know about it?' And then quickly as she apparently clocked the expression on his face, 'I'm sorry. I didn't mean that, Charlie. I'm in bits, at the absolute breaking point.'

That breaking point was the second part of the makings for future commotion. It consisted of Rory Statham's having 'descended upon Clare's house like some sort of bloody avenging angel'. She'd changed the locks and announced that the house would remain off limits to everyone until, as literary executrix of Clare's estate, she had the opportunity to go through and catalogue every single item in it. Clare's papers – which she'd left to her college library at Oxford University – had to be sifted through, and as to everything else inside the place, it was all Rory Statham's now as Clare had left her the house and its contents in her will. Her London house would go to her college. Her fortune – 'whatever it is,' Caroline said – would go to Rory as well.

'Got what *she* wanted,' Caroline said. 'Aside from you-know-what from Clare.' As for Caroline herself, Clare had left her nothing. 'No shock to me,' Caroline added. 'There are things about Clare Abbott that most people don't know, and her stingy nature is only one of them.'

Whatever the other unknown areas were, Caroline didn't elaborate on prior to the funeral and, if India had her way, she wouldn't be in Shaftesbury to hear any of them once the funeral was finished, as it now was. There would be no grave-side service since Clare's body was soon to be consigned to the fires of the nearest crematorium and her ashes would be deposited according to her wishes, which Rory Statham had not revealed. A swelling of music – thankfully not some lugubrious pop song, which was becoming too prevalent in religious services these days – indicated the service had come to an end. Everyone stood as the coffin was wheeled back down the aisle.

India didn't see the representatives of Clare Abbott's family until this point. Then, they followed the coffin towards the exit. She recognised Clare's friend Rory who, accompanied by her ever-present dog, walked at the head of the group, and immediately behind her two men of similar age to Rory's, who followed each with a woman on his arm. India heard whispers of former husbands and their wives, and she thought this quite nice. Apparently there had been no bad blood between Clare Abbott and the men to whom she'd once been wed.

People mingled outside St Peter's Church. The wind had come up and word went round quickly that next door at the Mitre a reception was waiting with food, drink, and shelter from what looked to be a coming rainstorm.

'We'll just put in an appearance and be gone,' Charlie said to her. 'A sandwich or something so we needn't stop on the way back to town?'

This was reasonable, India reckoned. So they joined the group moving in the direction of the old inn just beyond the church, where Rory had arranged a buffet. When they got inside, a queue had already formed. Mourning was a hungry business.

Rory Statham stood just inside the entrance. With her were the two men who'd followed her out of the church. She introduced them as people passed and greeted her: Mr Weisberg was one. Mr Tart was the other. She gave no other elaboration.

Charlie's mum and Alastair were just behind them in the group entering the Mitre, so India heard the brief exchange between Rory and Caroline that followed the introduction to Messrs Weisberg and Tart. Since Clare's body was being cremated, Rory said to Caroline, she was wondering if a second plaque might be added to the large stone at the spring in Breach Lane where Will Goldacre's name had been placed.

Caroline raised a hand to her chest. She said politely, 'What d'you mean?'

Rory said, 'A second plaque, Caroline, on the memorial stone,' with an expression that indicated no elaboration could possibly be necessary since a plaque was a plaque after all.

'Something saying that Clare placed the stone for Will?' Caroline asked.

India glanced at her. It seemed she was being deliberately

obtuse. Charlie appeared to feel likewise, for he said, 'Mum, something for Clare herself.'

'*For* Clare?' Caroline said. 'D'you mean with her name and the dates and all the rest? On Will's stone?'

Her neck had taken on a ruby colour, which Alastair apparently took note of because he put his hand on her elbow as he began to urge her towards the buffet. Caroline shot him an irritated look. She said, 'That won't be possible, Rory. True, it's miles from my home, and I can't get there as often as I'd like but be that as it may, the stone belongs to Will.'

Rory's lips parted. But she said nothing, merely nodding. Caroline moved along, heading to the buffet. Alastair said, 'Sorry,' to Rory in reference either to Caroline or to Clare's death, God only knew which.

India and Charlie allowed several other mourners to make a barrier between themselves and Caroline in the queue at the buffet. India said to him quietly, 'What on earth was she thinking? What possible difference could it make? The stone's enormous. There's room for another plaque. And even to mention its distance from her house . . .'

Charlie cast a glance towards Caroline before saying, 'Will. A funeral. Mentioning his name. It brings it all back.'

'That's absurd. It's a *stone*.'

Charlie gave her a look. It wasn't at all like India to criticise anyone, let alone her mother-in-law. She was, after all, the woman who'd spent a good few years altering her appearance till she was mousy enough to please Caroline Goldacre. She repeated, 'It *is* absurd, and you know it. She's been using Will as an excuse for her behaviour for ages. Why do you put up with it? Why does Alastair?'

'She's my mum. I c'n hardly trade her in for another.'

'Well, that doesn't explain Alastair.'

'It does go a distance towards explaining Sharon Halsey, though. After Mum, she must be quite an enormous relief. Just a bloody good bonk. That's what most men want at the end of the day.'

'Is it?' she asked.

'I did say *most* men, darling.' The term of affection had slipped out, it seemed. They stared at each other. Charlie quickly went on. 'She's just not *aware*, India. She's like most people, more or less stumbling along without understanding the effect their words have on others.'

'Most people recognise that a funeral requires a certain awareness of others' grief,' India pointed out. 'Most people know that a funeral isn't the place for anything at all save sympathy and – if one must – diplomacy. Rory Statham's upset and she wants to do something to remember Clare and even if your mum *didn't* want Will's stone polluted or whatever, she could have said "Let's speak later, dear."'

'You'll get no argument from me.'

'Then . . .'

He raised an eyebrow. 'Then what?'

That was indeed the question. Not only for Charlie in his dealings with his mum but also for her. What came next?

A quick meal, apparently, which they took at a table to which Caroline waved them. India fixed a polite expression on her face. It wouldn't take long to down her ham and tomato sandwich, after all.

It turned out that whatever emotion had driven Caroline's words had receded. As they sat, she said, 'I was completely out of order. Please forgive me. I'll apologise to Rory before I leave. It was the mention of Will. And everything else that's happened.'

'Rough times, pet,' Alastair murmured.

'Will you stay for supper?' Caroline said to her son and India. 'Perhaps for the night? Tomorrow we can go to Will's stone. There's a gorgeous little tree nearby where people have begun hanging ribbons, Charlie. Remembrance ribbons, they're being called. Thin little strips of satin in blue or pink. People print the name of their loved one on them, and hang them on the tree. It's very sweet. I'd be so pleased if you'd stop so that we can go there tomorrow.'

India was the one to speak. 'It's down to me, I'm afraid. I've got to be back for early appointments tomorrow at the clinic. And I think Charlie's got . . . ?' She looked in his direction encouragingly, but she saw that he was gazing out of the window which faced onto the street. She followed the direction of his gaze. Lily Foster was just outside.

As before, she was all in black. She wore a hood over her hair against the rain, and it was part of a cape that draped to her ankles. But there was no mistaking her or her intentions. She could hardly be in violation of her ASBO if she happened to be on a public thoroughfare when Caroline Goldacre also happened to be there.

Charlie roused himself and said, 'Wish I could stay, Mum, but it's an early morning for me as well. Clients popping up everywhere. It feels bloody good to be back at work.' For good measure, he covered India's hand with his own.

At this, Caroline beamed. She reached across the table as if to make a threesome of their hands – a little pile akin to the Three Musketeers, India reckoned – but she and Charlie separated before she could do so.

'In fact,' Charlie said, 'we must be off at once.'

'You'll be back soon?' Caroline said. 'Both of you? Because I must say how lovely—'

'Soon,' Charlie told her.

They made their farewells, Alastair rising to embrace them both but Caroline remaining seated at the table. Her back was to the window, thank God, so she had no view either of the street or of Lily Foster lurking within shouting distance. Charlie and India had a final word with Rory and soon enough were outside the Mitre. Lily saw them. She crossed at once.

The last thing they needed was Lily's being seen from the window, so Charlie and India hurried off in the direction of the Bell Street car park, in the expectation that she would follow them, which she did. Once they were in front of the savings bank that formed one arm of the triangle that served as Shaftesbury's market square, they stopped.

'Why hasn't anything been done?' Lily demanded of Charlie. 'You told me . . . You promised me . . . But *nothing's* been done and she just goes on and on and on. And *you* have no intention of doing a thing. Did you even read it?'

Charlie said, 'Lily, you've got to stay clear of Mum. You'll get in more trouble and you can't want that.'

'What I want is her suffering.'

'You *must* leave this area before she comes out of the Mitre or there'll be a scene. You can't let that happen. Not with the ASBO already in place. All right?'

'I want her to die,' she told him.

Charlie's face, India saw, was all sympathy towards Lily, despite her words. He put his arm around her and he spoke firmly but not unkindly. 'You've got to stay in the here and now, Lil. If you can't manage that, what's going on in your head will take you down.'

'I want things to change.'

'Things can't help changing. Things always change. Now you've got to leave and so must we.'

Something about Charlie's voice seemed to convince Lily of the danger she was in, lurking about and waiting for a chance to have a go at Caroline Goldacre. For she nodded and with a tortured glance at India, she turned and set off up the street. They watched her till she disappeared round a corner.

'What's happened to her?' India said. 'What did she mean? "Did you even read it?"'

'She's talking about that envelope, I think,' he said. 'The one she handed over to you the day Will's stone was dedicated.'

'You said you were taking it to the police. Didn't you do that? Charlie, she's obviously going mad and she could be dangerous. *Tell* me you gave over that envelope to the police.'

'Of course I did,' he told her.

'What happened to it, then?'

'The cops recognised her name straight off when I told them where it came from. They had me wait for the officer who's been dealing with her. He was the one to open the envelope.'

'He *opened* it. With you there? It could have been a bomb. A letter bomb or something . . . something worse like whatever that stuff is that terrorists put inside letters to kill people off when they're exposed to it. What's it called? Anthrax, that's it. It could have been anthrax. Charlie, she's mad. She's like . . .' India couldn't even think of how to complete the thought, so disturbed was she by the entire idea of anything that might have harmed Charlie actually being opened in his presence.

His face softened at her tone. 'It was nothing. A collection of mad writings that she'd done since Will's death. A sort of "*J'accuse*". A catalogue of all the ways in which she holds Mum responsible for what happened to Will. The handwriting alone told the tale of how wild she is to have Mum suffer. The officer looked through it and said they'd add it to her file. I felt dead bad about that, as if I'd only made things worse for Lily, but what could I do at that point but let them keep it, so that's what I did. And there's an end to it.'

'But she said you told her—'

'What else could I do? You've seen her: the state she's in. She rang me and I told her I'd "handle things" but *only* if she keeps clear of Mum so she doesn't get arrested.'

He looked up the street in the direction that Lily Foster had taken. 'I've been trying to hold her off, India. There've been too many victims of my brother's death. I don't want Lily to be another one of them.'

13 October

*Fulham*
*London*

It was half past ten in the evening when Rory Statham arrived back in London. It had been a very long and difficult few days, culminating in a disturbing confrontation with Caroline Goldacre that had ended with Rory's ushering her out of Clare Abbott's house and then leaving Shaftesbury herself in something of a turmoil. It wasn't till she got halfway home and stopped for petrol that she saw she'd left her overnight case behind. Then she cursed herself that once again Caroline had invaded her peace of mind. Thus, back in Fulham, she felt drained and ready for only two occupations once she gave Arlo his last stroll of the day: bathing and sleeping.

The weather had permanently altered, bringing with it that melancholy time of year which seemed to Rory a fitting partner to Clare's unexpected death. Autumn was intensely upon them with its sudden rain showers and its gusts of wind attacking the leaves on the trees. The light had changed as well, golden in the late afternoon, departing more quickly and bringing darkness earlier every day. Rory wasn't looking forward to winter. She couldn't work her mind round the idea of getting through it without Clare.

At the end of Arlo's walk and back at her car, Rory grabbed the carrier bag of Clare's post and the other bag of Arlo's food, toys, and treats. She'd leave his travel kennel for the morning, she decided.

She carried the bags up the steps and as she did so, she

wondered if she was truly up to all the tasks that lay before her. In the last two days, she'd quickly assessed that the process of sorting through Clare's personal belongings – let alone her professional belongings – was going to take several months, and she didn't look forward to any of it, especially as the sorting was going to put her in Shaftesbury, which meant she would be in the sphere of Caroline Goldacre time and again. To make certain everything was secured in the Shaftesbury house over this period of time, she'd arranged to have an alarm system installed soon. In addition to changing all of the locks on the doors before she departed, this hadn't been a popular move with Clare's assistant. What had been even less popular was Rory's informing Caroline this very morning that her services would no longer be required. She would, of course, give her three months' wages to soften the blow of sudden unemployment.

To Caroline's 'But who's going to deal with the post? Who's going to care for the house? Who's going to see to it that Clare's work continues?', Rory lifted a questioning eyebrow. Since Clare had been writing and lecturing for thirty odd years, Rory could hardly name someone to carry the torch. There *was* no torch bearer unless another feminist was able to step forward with a reputation like Clare's. Even if there was such a woman, it would take years for her to acquire the kind of following that Clare had enjoyed. Surely Caroline Goldacre didn't see herself as a potential Clare Abbott. Did she?

Rory had told her that what needed to be dealt with would be dealt with by her as she was the executrix of Clare's literary estate. As she wished to take her time going through Clare's papers, the occupation required to put everything in order was going to extend over many months. During this period, Clare's post would be diverted to Rory in London, the house would be checked by a cleaning service once each week, the future security system would ensure that there were no break-ins – not that Shaftesbury was a hotbed of burglaries – and Clare's legacy to her fellow feminists would sort itself out in the way these things usually did. As for her newest book, Rory herself would deal with what was to happen to it. Perhaps she herself would complete it. Perhaps the publishing house would take on someone to do so.

'Newest book?' Caroline stared at her as if she'd begun speaking in tongues. 'What're you talking about? There *is* no newest book.'

'Of course there's a book,' Rory told her. She aimed for patience but recognised her tone was instead rather more snappish than was warranted. On the other hand, the woman was utterly exhausting to be around.

'That's simply not true,' Caroline insisted. 'I don't know what she told you – and I've tried to explain that she wasn't who you think she was, Rory – but I spent hours with Clare every day and I know she was working on nothing.'

'There are twenty-four hours in a day, Caroline,' Rory said. 'I seriously doubt you spent every one of them at Clare's side. Her work habits—'

'I know her work habits, and she *wasn't* writing a book. Did you find evidence of a book? You've been hours looking round her office in the last two days. If there was a book she was writing, I expect you'd've seen it.'

When Rory made no immediate reply to this, Caroline added, 'I don't know how to make this sound . . . well . . . other than speaking ill of her, but the truth is that Clare hadn't a *clue* what to write next. She didn't tell you that? What *did* she tell you?'

Rory didn't at all wish to go into Clare's writing, her intentions, or her work habits any further. If Clare had been writing in the dead of night, Caroline would hardly have known. And while it was true that an initial cursory culling through Clare's belongings had turned up nothing, Rory knew that so little evidence of Clare's lack of productivity was inconsequential. Clare had files everywhere. She had notes everywhere. It was going to take months to go through everything. So Rory ignored what seemed to be an inappropriate yet unmistakable note of triumph in Caroline's final remarks and she got herself out of Shaftesbury as soon as she could.

All things put into the balance, she considered it generous that she'd given Caroline three months' wages and fifteen minutes to clean out her desk. During that time, Rory remained in the same room with her, the better to make certain Caroline removed nothing from the house save what was hers.

At her own front door at last, Rory let herself and Arlo inside. She lived on the first floor of the building, and she unclipped Arlo's lead and told him to go ahead. She followed him up the stairs with her carrier bags. He waited at her flat, his tail swishing against the floor and once the door was unbolted, he trotted for the kitchen. She could hear him nosing his empty bowl along the floor. She chuckled and joined him, doing the appropriate business with his food and water. He set to, and wearily she put on the kettle.

On the worktop, she saw that her answer machine was blinking. She punched the button for messages as she took tea from the cupboard and rustled in the fridge for a pint of milk. She poured it into a jug, brought down her teapot, and took note of the messages that came off the answer machine. Her sister, her mum, her managing director, two hang-ups, and then, 'Called your mobile but couldn't get through,' a woman's voice said. Working class, Rory thought, west London by the sound of it. 'It's Barbara Havers here,' the voice then clarified. 'I've got the results of the second autopsy and I'd like to come round and have a chat. It's what you thought. They've sorted a different cause of death.' She went on to leave two numbers: her mobile and her work number at the Met. If Rory could ring her so they could set up a time to meet . . . ?

Yes! Rory thought. She knew it. She *knew* it.

She glanced at the time. Eleven twenty. It seemed rude to phone Barbara Havers on her mobile and wake her if she was asleep, so Rory rang the work number and left a recorded message. She would be at home all day tomorrow – 'or rather today by the time you get this,' she told the detective sergeant – so if Barbara came round, they could easily meet, and she was eager to do so.

That said, she made her tea and thought about the message the detective had left: a different cause of death altogether. She'd *known* Clare had the heart of an ox, Rory told herself. Thank God she'd not rested content when she'd been told about a fatal arrhythmia.

*Shaftesbury*
*Dorset*

Alastair rose at midnight. He'd slept only fitfully from nine p.m. He was due to rise at two, and after lying awake from half past ten onwards, he gave up entirely on the idea of sleep. He didn't want to be abed anyway, at least not in this bed, in this room, in this house.

The last twelve days had brought a complete sea change to Caroline. It was as if she'd been holding some disquieting form of herself in complete abeyance for years until the moment that Clare Abbott had died. Or perhaps it had been the appearance of Clare's friend Rory Statham first in Cambridge and then in Shaftesbury that had finally undone her. Alastair didn't know. All he was able to understand was that this version of Caroline was set to drive him off the edge.

*Just like Will*, came to him, a horrible thought. He pushed it from his mind and sat with his head in his hands on the edge of the bed where he'd slept alone for ages. And *alone* defined how life was going to be till the end of it, unless he took action.

Caro was taking action aplenty. First she'd cleaned every inch of the house, up at dawn and working madly through the day and into the night: using toothbrushes on the grout between the tiles, rags in her hands and knees on the hardwood as she did the floors, buckets and newspapers and sharp white vinegar on every window, the cooker and the fridge and every cupboard emptied and cleaned in the minutest detail with cotton wool swabs, rooms emptied of all their furniture and their furniture polished, rugs dragged outside and scrubbed and hosed, clothes cupboards divested of every scrap within them, curtains laundered, walls cleaned, ceilings and lighting fixtures scoured. During it all, she did not speak. When it was over, however, she began to talk.

Her childhood and the hurts she'd suffered at the hands of an unmarried Colombian mother who had not wanted her, who had been forced to keep her, who had taken her from the land she'd known the land of her birth the presence of the only person in her life who'd actually and truly loved her the wonderful nurturing grandmother who'd given her a beautiful kitten that had been left behind when she and mother had journeyed to London where she was as alone as she'd ever been . . .

The early marriage to escape only to escape do you understand the Colombian mother who'd long been deserted herself by the man who'd made her pregnant with Caro . . .

This marriage to a man a surgeon who'd not cared two figs about her once he'd got what he wanted off her, his two sons . . .

Whom he did not love do you hear me he could not love them because he only loved himself and one of those sons tormented from childhood with a ghastly misshapen deformed do you hear me *deformed* ear, a diminutive stature, an affliction of words that he could not control and that none of them ever understood and with *no* one to help her deal with this care for him help him serve him . . .

Till the husband left her that was what he did he left her long before she left him because he was there but he *wasn't* there unwilling even to touch her and did he know how that felt . . . have you any idea how that feels Alastair . . .

And what it did to her to be so rejected and how seeing him that night at the panto had made her feel whole again for the first time so that she could actually *feel* something beyond the despair that had been haunting her for years because of what she herself had been made to do that her own mother had forced her to do . . .

So *leave* me if you want to and dance on my grave when I kill myself because I see it in your eyes every day how you wish how you want how you compare me to her and curse the day that I phoned you and said I've left him darling come to me now because I'd slept with you and I thought I was meant to be with you after that because why else would I have slept with you it's not as if you're anything to write home about you know.

He shouted at her. He wanted to strike her, just to silence her. Nothing more than that. But then she shut herself up in her room for forty-eight hours and he'd begun to fear and he'd begun to hope and he asked himself what had happened to him that fear and hope were one and the same now. He'd rescued her, he thought. He'd rescued her, hadn't he, from the husband and the miserable life she had with him, but who was now there to rescue him?

He rose from the bed in the dark and went to the window. There was faint moonlight on the road outside. Across the street where a hedgerow marked a farmer's field, a dark shape waited and watched the house. Lily Foster, he thought. Who else would huddle like a ghoul in the darkness in the middle of the night, praying each day to bring ruin upon them?

The ASBO hadn't stopped her as Alastair had known it would not. She was too filled with hate. Until she extracted from them whatever it was that she believed needed to be extracted, she would continue to dog them. But now she was far cleverer than she'd been at first, when she'd shown up at the bakery, when she'd invaded their house, when she'd followed them, when she'd harangued them from near and from far, when she'd left her unsettling calling cards of faeces, dead birds, and worse on their front step. If he rang the police in this dead of night, he knew she'd be gone long before they arrived despite her not being able to see him moving towards the phone, punching in the number, murmuring She's back, she's just outside, she's a threatening presence who means us harm and you must stop her now. The police would come, but they'd not find her or any sign of her on the verge where the ground was soft and her footprints might have been left had she been less clever about where she stood. He was helpless in the face of her continued presence. It was as if she anticipated what every move inside the house would be, long before either he or Caro made it.

God, Alastair thought, what had happened to them all? Will dead, Charlie with a marriage in ruins, himself a discarded husband in his own house, and Caro . . . Who knew who she was any longer because Alastair did not recognise in her the woman he'd married with his heart full of hope.

That heart was Sharon's now. And sleepless as he was this night, he would go to her. So he took his shoes up from the floor and he descended the stairs. Out in the night, he made no effort to hide the sound of the bakery van roaring to life. Eighteen miles to drive, and they would pass as if he flew above them because at the end of them Sharon was waiting.

He had his own key, and he let himself in to her house. Quietly and in the darkness, he climbed the stairs.

She'd not closed the curtains in her bedroom. She never did, he'd learned. She liked the moonlight as it moved across her room, and she liked being able to see the stars, which she could do, for the window faced the back of the house and the paddock beyond it with no obstruction at all but a barbed wire fence and far in the distance the shadows of a wood.

He watched her sleep. He allowed himself to feel the strength of his longing for her. Everything seemed possible with Sharon, if they could be allowed to forge a path on their own.

The word *yes* came to him, and it was a *yes* in all possible ways, sweeping aside impossibility, duty, pledge, and promise.

He told himself that he could not live another day as he'd been living with Caro. He vowed that no matter the cost, he would not fail to bring an order to his life that was being defined by this lovely woman who lay sleeping before him.

Sharon's eyes opened. She did not start as someone else would have done, waking to see a man standing over her bed. She was instantly aware of who he was, for she pushed bedcovers from her body and she extended her hand to him.

She wore an insubstantial gown, and through it he could see the tempting brown aureoles on her breasts and the dark triangular thatch between her legs. When she said his name like a question, he told her he wanted just to look at her.

Do you not want to sleep? she asked him.

He told her there would be no sleeping for him tonight but that was really of no account as he had only two hours before he had to begin his work.

Shall we make love then? was what she asked next.

No. I just want to look at you, was his response.

She sat up then. Over her head she pulled the gown, which she dropped to the floor. She turned on her side and, in doing so, she put him in mind of a painting he'd seen long ago, in some museum where he'd gone to dodge a harsh winter rain up in London. In this painting, a woman lay naked on her side, with only a necklace of pearls hanging upon her voluptuous body. She had her arms extended over her head and in a corner a servant of some sort – she'd been a black woman, hadn't she? he asked himself – acted as the guard of her vulnerability. She'd presented herself as an offering to the painter, just as Sharon did for him now, with one arm curled beneath her head and the other resting along her thigh.

He drew the bedroom's only chair next to the bed. He asked her if she was cold like that, with every inch of her exposed.

She said no, for the room was warm and although the window was cracked open to the night, there was no draught. She asked him if he was certain he didn't want to come to bed. She murmured You've not slept this night, have you? And after a moment she added in a whisper he would have missed had he not been so acutely listening, What's she done?

He shook his head. He told her not to worry about him. For she was his waking and his sleeping, he said. She was the ground that he walked upon.

She said to him, Alastair, don't be mad. I'm mere flesh and blood.

Not to me, he told her.

# 14 October

Barbara had phoned Rory in advance, within minutes of arriving at New Scotland Yard where the other woman had left her message, but she'd got no answer. As it was early, she reckoned Rory was either in the shower or providing her dog with his morning walkies. So she left a message about her time of arrival in Fulham and didn't worry when her call wasn't returned. She had more important activities to consume her. Getting permission to sally forth from the Yard was directly on the top of that list.

She put some thought into it. DI Lynley's intercession had brought about the additional autopsy. He had two connections that he'd employed with his usual blue-blooded finesse: a forensics specialist he'd long ago been a pupil with at Eton and the Detective Chief Superintendent in Cambridge with whom he had worked – along with Barbara – when a university student had met her death by the river a few years earlier. The first of these two individuals undertook a study of the initial autopsy report, after which he'd made a formal written recommendation for another look into matters concerning Clare Abbott's death. The second had fielded the phone call from Lynley, which garnered the Cambridge cops' cooperation in the matter. What Barbara had thought was No skin off their noses, as it wasn't down to the Cambridge police that the initial autopsy hadn't been as thorough as it might have been. But Lynley liked to smooth the waters before sailing upon them, so she didn't argue with his plan. She was depending upon this water-smoothing quirk in his character when it came to getting herself into a position to go to Fulham.

Isabelle Ardery wouldn't want this. She liked Barbara Havers just where she could see her, monitor her, and jump upon her the moment she stepped out of order. In fact, it was likely she'd already bought Barbara an open-ended rail ticket to Berwick-upon-Tweed, so sure would she be that Barbara couldn't possibly keep her nose clean for long. So giving her the go-ahead to deliver information to Fulham wasn't an activity she was certain to embrace. She would instead tell Lynley to use a courier to do the job. Or she would instruct him to do it himself. Or she would say that a uniformed constable could take on the responsibility.

Lynley would counter by arguing that this simple act of providing information to the Fulham woman was *exactly* the sort of thing Isabelle could use to test Barbara's level of professionalism and the true depth of change in her character. He would say that Isabelle could not possibly intend to keep Barbara Havers on a short lead forever and the only manner in which she would learn if she could actually trust the detective sergeant was going to be to provide her with certain opportunities to bollocks things up.

He'd say *Isabelle*, as well, Barbara thought. She'd tell him to call her *ma'am* or *guv* or *boss* or even *superintendent* but he'd want her to remember those sweaty moments when he'd groaned or murmured or shouted her name as they'd writhed together on a lumpy mattress somewhere in London. That *could* work against him, of course, but Barbara reckoned it wouldn't. As former lovers, Ardery and Lynley had each other's back when it came down to it, whether they would ever admit it or not.

So when he came to her, handed her the report, and said, 'Do not step across a single line, Barbara,' after his meeting with the superintendent, she wasn't altogether surprised. She promised him six ways to Sunday that she would be a model of every possible facet of admirable police work, and at the time she actually meant it.

Barbara wasn't overly concerned when she rang the bell next to Rory's surname on the panel near the front door of her building but failed to rouse her. She was inconvenienced by the fact that it had begun to rain, but she had on her mack and there was shelter enough from the wind to allow her to light up and smoke a fag. When she'd topped up the nicotine in her bloodstream, she rang the bell again. Nothing. Its position on the panel suggested that Rory Statham lived on the building's first floor and it seemed to Barbara that behind a closed French window on that level, a dog yipped as she rang the bell another time.

This was moderately disconcerting. Barbara tried another of the bells on the panel. A man's voice answered and she told him who she was and why she was there. Could he release the door and allow her inside? she asked him. She explained that she was unable to rouse the tenant of flat 3 and as she could hear the dog barking—

'Bloody hell, I wish you'd shoot him. He's been going on for hours.' The man cut her off and released the lock on the door.

Barbara made for the stairs. There was only a single door on the first floor and behind it, she could hear the dog. Her knocking sent the animal into a frenzy. A door above opened and someone came powering down towards her.

By his voice, she recognised Mr Shoot-the-Dog. He was, he said, trying to work. Had been trying to work since dawn. He was trying to concentrate on what the worldwide markets were doing, and *this* wasn't helping matters. Was she going to do something? Because if the police weren't capable of responding for five hours when a call was made, what the hell were they good for?

This was Barbara's first clue that a phone call had been made to the local rozzers who, undoubtedly with more on their plates than settling a barking canine, had put the complaint directly to the bottom of their daily must-dos. She dug out her warrant card, allowed the seething gent to have his way with it, and told him she was not there because of the animal within the flat – clearly in *distress*, she informed him – but rather to have a word with the woman who lived there. Did he know where she was?

Of course he didn't bloody God damn know, he told her, and if she couldn't do something about that mongrel . . . Let her *call* it a sodding assistance dog if she would but he had no intention of putting up with—

With neighbours like this, Barbara thought, who needed vagrants accosting one in street corners and dope deals going down in the nearest park? She thanked the gentleman for his deep concern about the welfare of the woman inside the flat and suggested he take himself back to where he belonged. She had some serious thoughts on exactly where this was, but she didn't share them with him.

She went back outside the building, making sure to wedge the front door open by means of the autopsy report she'd brought with her, along with her shoulder bag. On her way out, she looked for a porter or a concierge – not very likely in a building this size but one could always hope – and failing that, she rang at one of the two ground floor flats to see if extra keys were perhaps kept somewhere? No such luck, hence her return to the street.

There were several possibilities. One was to ring the local rozzers herself and ask them to break down Rory Statham's door. Another was to ring 999 with the same request. Both of those could take hours and she didn't have hours before Isabelle Ardery would be climbing up her backside, so she went for option three.

A thick wisteria that looked to be about fifty years old grew on the front of the building, its substantial trunk twisting and turning in the habitual way of that plant as it forged a route towards the roof four floors above. It hadn't shed its leaves yet, so there would be a bit of interference from them – not to mention rainwater – but it grew close to the small balcony onto which the French windows of what had to be Rory Statham's flat opened. If Barbara was in luck, those windows might be unlocked.

She reckoned she could manage the climb as wisterias provided plenty of hand- and footholds and the French windows were, after all, only on the first floor. So she gave herself a mental pat on the back for having worn brogues instead of court shoes that would have made short work of plunging her off the vine and onto the ground.

Given, she wasn't much for the Tarzan aspects of life. Given, she was in wretched physical condition. But desperate times and all the rest set her upon the wisteria vine with determination. One false start toppled her back to the ground with a painful thud, but after that it was buttering a crumpet.

The front of her was soaked from residual rainwater on the wisteria leaves by the time she reached out for the railing of the balcony on the first floor. The back of her was soaked from the continuing rainfall. The railing of the balcony was stone, thank God, but Barbara tested it all the same to make certain it was securely in place.

It didn't give. So far, so good. Getting herself onto the balcony didn't require a leap, either, as it would have done in a television drama. Instead, it was an arm's length away from her. She wriggled a bit higher on the wisteria, felt it creak menacingly, hoped for the best, and flung herself at the balcony. She came to rest on her stomach across the stone railing, in something of a downward facing dog pose. Her legs flailed, she sent thanks heavenward that she was wearing pristine knickers, and with a grunt and a heave and a determined scissoring of legs, she tumbled onto the balcony.

She landed on her cheek and hit a puddle. She cursed and scrambled to her feet. The surface of the balcony comprised slick marble squares, which didn't make this an easy manoeuvre, and she nearly went over the side of the railing when she slid on what appeared to be moss – did moss even grow on marble, she wondered? – that formed miniature continents rising from the damp.

She glanced down at her clothes. Her mack now had a ruined zip and beneath it, her beige skirt was filthy. Her tights had ladders suitable for use by the fire brigade, her shoes were badly scuffed, and she could only imagine what the rest of her looked like.

Inside the flat, the barking had moved from the door to the French windows. Barbara heard Arlo frantically scratching at something just on the other side of the glass. The damn curtains were closed, so there was nothing to see. But Arlo's presence inside, his state, the absence of his owner all boded the worst.

She tried the French windows. Of course, they were locked. What else would they be? she asked herself. She looked round for something to ease her entry into the flat, but there was nothing at all. Not even a convenient flower pot with an azalea drooping in its soil.

As far as she could see, she had two choices. The first was her foot and the second was her elbow. She reckoned there might well be an artery in her foot and her luck being what it was, she knew she'd slice right into it and languish on the balcony bleeding to death before she could get inside the flat. That left her elbow.

She backed against the French windows. She gave thanks that the building did not have double glazing and with a mighty shriek that she'd seen employed in martial arts films, she drove her elbow into the glass.

It took three tries, but she managed it, all the time trying to settle the dog inside who'd gone berserk with the first blow she struck. When the pane finally broke, Barbara reckoned that someone somewhere surely must have phoned the local cops by now, but not a siren sounded anywhere.

She cleared the glass from the opening she'd made. Carefully, she stuck her hand inside. The windows hadn't been bolted at top and bottom as they could have been, so when she felt for a key and turned it, she managed to get herself inside.

She said, 'Arlo, Arlo. Good boy. Nice dog,' and was truly relieved that Rory's assistance dog was not an Alsatian who would have probably taken off her arm first and her face second. When she worked her way through the curtains, the dog came to her immediately. In fact, so pleased was he to see her that he low crawled across the room to her, whimpering. She extended her hand and he sniffed accordingly. She passed the dog test.

She looked round. The heavy curtains swathed the room in darkness, but they did nothing to cover the scent. Faeces, urine, and something more. Vomit? Vomit mixed with blood?

Barbara felt the hair on her arms stir. She pushed the curtains back to flood the room with the muted daylight outside. She was fairly certain what she was about to find inside the flat, and so she found it: Rory Statham was twisted into an agonised posture, somehow wedged between the sofa and the wall, on the sitting room floor.

*Chelsea*
*London*

In handing over the second autopsy report to Barbara Havers, Lynley had thought matters would be quickly resolved. Barbara's brief had been to share the information from the report with Rory Statham while he turned over a copy of it to the Cambridge police. For Clare Abbott's death had been either suicide or murder. A more detailed toxicology study had revealed the cause of her death but not the means through which a poisonous substance had found its way into her body.

'Sodium azide,' he'd said to Barbara when he handed the autopsy report to her.

She'd taken it from him and asked, logically, what sodium

azide was. He hadn't known himself, but he'd earlier phoned his longtime friend Simon St James for the information.

'Labs use it as a preservative so bacteria don't grow in reagents,' the forensic scientist told him in answer. 'It's deadly poison. Is that what killed the woman in Cambridge, Tommy?'

To Havers, Lynley said, 'If someone ingests it, it apparently works something like cyanide, just not quite as quickly.'

'So Rory Statham was spot on, wasn't she?'

'In that the cause wasn't natural, yes. In that it was murder, that remains to be seen.'

He'd pointed out to Havers that Clare Abbott could have taken her own life. Barbara scoffed at this. The woman had been at the top of her game, she said. He'd argued that celebrated figures at the top of their game *had* been known to do away with themselves, to which she'd countered that there was no way on earth *this* celebrated figure would have offed herself, not with her new book flying off the bookshop shelves. To Lynley's comment that they didn't really know the woman, did they?, Havers had said, 'We know a bit about human nature, sir. And let me tell you this: Clare Abbott did herself in the way I just gave up Pop Tarts for breakfast.'

Point taken, he'd said. But suicide or murder, Clare Abbott's death wasn't their remit. It belonged to Detective Chief Superintendent Daniel Sheehan. Their job was limited to passing along information to him. Or so things had been supposed to go.

When his phone rang, Lynley had hoped it would be Daidre Trahair. He hadn't seen her in days, and he missed her rather more than he wanted to consider. It turned out to be Havers, however, although it was difficult at first to tell because a dog was barking, it seemed, directly into the detective sergeant's mobile.

'She's been poisoned, sir,' Havers said, her voice rising with agitation. 'I swear to God she's been bloody *poisoned*. Someone got to her. I found her on the floor and she'd sicked up every-where and I think she's in a coma and—'

'Rory Statham?'

'Who bloody else?'

'She's still alive?'

'Barely breathing. Barely anything. I rang nine-nine-nine and they've taken her off to A and E.'

'Where are you, then? Christ, Barbara. Whose dog is barking?'

'Hers. I'm in her flat. He's an assistance dog or something, like blind people have. He's meant to stay with her and he's gone bonkers now they've taken her out of here.'

'Is there some place you can put him?'

'Hang on.' More barking ensued, growing progressively more panicked. Then it faded and Barbara returned. 'He's in her bedroom. Bloody hell. I have no clue about dogs but if he could talk, I wager he'd tell a real tale about all this.'

'Have you phoned the police?'

'I *am* the police. *We're* the police. Look, the means have to be the same, Inspector. Whatever got to Clare—'

'Sodium azide.'

– 'got to her. Rory.'

'Perhaps. But this isn't ours, Barbara. If anything, it's Fulham's.'

'The means are the *same*. Murder and now attempted murder. Of two women who were known to each other, connected to each other in more ways than one. Professionally. Personally.'

'Nonetheless—'

'You can make things happen, and I need you to do it. I *know* you understand why. What it can mean. For me. In everyone's eyes so I can finally . . .' She stopped herself. He could hear her ragged breathing. When she said, 'Inspector, I need you to help me,' he was as torn as he'd ever been.

Still he said, 'Barbara, you're on someone else's patch. Considering what you've got going on there, I'm surprised Fulham hasn't sent a uniform already.'

'They don't send uniforms when all they know is that someone was carted off to hospital. And as of now that's *all* they know and we can keep things that way. You can keep things that way.'

'Christ. Listen to yourself. It's *exactly* this sort of thinking—'

'All right. Understood. On board and all the rest. So meet me at Chelsea and Westminster Hospital. That's all I'll ask.'

'You can't possibly expect me to believe that. And even if I agreed to meet you, what would be the point?'

'The point would be talking to the casualty blokes. Talking to the doctors. Talking to whoever. Listen, the paramedics didn't even want to *touch* her when I said sodium azide. They actually put on hazmat suits. So they'll be looking for the poison straightaway at hospital and if we speak to them, we'll know what we're working with.'

'We're not "working with" anything.'

'You *know* that's bollocks. Someone took out Clare Abbott and then slithered over here to take care of Rory Statham. Meet me at the hospital, sir, so we can know for sure what happened to Rory. If I'm wrong, I swear to you I'll wipe my nose and get back to Victoria Street. But in the meantime—'

'All right. I'll meet you there. Don't make me regret this.'

'You won't. I swear it. Straight and narrow all the way.'

'That had better be the case, Sergeant Havers.'

It was a nightmare getting to Chelsea, the hospital's location in Fulham Road. With the traffic and the rain providing their usual patience-taxing combination, it was only through choosing some creative alternatives through the upmarket neighbourhoods of Belgravia and upper Chelsea that he was able to make it to the hospital's precincts in under three quarters of an hour, a drive that would have taken ten minutes in the dead of night.

The rain was unrelenting. Once he'd parked the Healey Elliott, he turned up the collar of his father's ancient trench coat, and he set back up the street. He found A and E a rain-sodden disaster area, as a car-lorry-and-multi-bicycle smash-up in the vicinity of Battersea Bridge had brought seven injured people into casualty moments before he arrived. They lay on trolleys, bleeding and groaning as medical personnel in scrubs dashed round them shouting orders at each other while an intercom belted out cries for various doctors to pick up phones, go to radiology, or proceed at once to the operating theatre.

None of this was what Lynley had hoped to encounter, and it didn't bode well for being able to gather any information about Rory Statham. He searched through the milling throng for Havers, hearing her before he found her when she called his name. She was crossing to him from a swinging door beyond which he could see only a corridor and a set of lifts. She looked as bedraggled as he'd ever seen her, and he could only pray that she managed to keep out of the way of Superintendent Ardery once she returned to Victoria Street. Which, he also prayed, would be very soon as he'd not put Isabelle in the picture as to what was going on.

He said, 'What happened?'

'They've got her—'

'I mean to you, Barbara. What on earth have you done to yourself?'

She grimaced, glancing down at her clothing. She looked like someone who'd dived headfirst into a bin of garden clippings. 'I fell. More or less.'

'Which part?'

'What?'

'The more or the less.'

'Less, I s'pose.' She looked round, as if for escape from what she knew was coming. 'Look. I had to break in, sir. There was a wisteria vine on the front of the building and—'

'Please Christ don't tell me anything else. Where is she?'

'In isolation till they know for sure. They've all suited up even to touch her. It's that deadly, this stuff, and she's lucky she didn't drop off the twig.'

'What are they doing for her?'

'Don't know for certain. It's been dead wild here –' with a gesture round the room with its teeming hordes – 'so I followed them as far as they'd let me. There're chairs and a coffee machine near isolation and I've been waiting . . .' She brushed at her hair with the flat of her hand. This didn't improve its overall appearance. She added, 'Arlo's in my car. He can't stay there f'rever, so I was also hoping—'

'Who's Arlo?'

'The dog. Her dog. I couldn't leave him in the flat, could I? If I'm to take on this case, he'll need to be taken care of and, see, I was thinking that you might also be willing . . . You know. Till she gets out of hospital?'

He stared at her for a good ten seconds before replying. 'Havers,' he said, 'does it ever occur to you that one day you might push things too far? With me, I mean.'

'It's only that I know you like animals, sir.'

'Is it indeed? May I ask how you arrived at this conclusion? As well as the conclusion that you're going to take on this case?'

'There's those horses at your pile in Cornwall,' she said, going for his first question and avoiding the second. 'I know you ride. You love to ride, don't you? And your mum has those nice dogs of hers. Retrievers, aren't they? Some sort of retrievers? Or maybe they were greyhounds?'

He took a deep breath. 'Take me to where they've put her.'

She headed back to the swinging doors and from there to the lift. On the second floor, he followed her down one corridor and then another till they were at a corner of the hospital, and it was here, behind closed doors accessed only through a release operated from within, that Rory Statham apparently occupied a hospital bed while procedures were set in place to save her life.

Mercifully, Havers said nothing more for the moment. In an evident attempt to wriggle back into his good graces, she went to the coffee machine and brought them both a cup of that beverage. They were drinking this in silence, when a woman in the process of removing official protective garb came out of the isolation area. Next to him, Barbara said, 'This is who . . .' and got to her feet. He did likewise.

Wisely, considering her appearance, Havers did not produce her warrant card. She let him do those honours, perhaps knowing that the doctor's credulity would be too far stretched should Havers have declared herself an officer of the Metropolitan police.

The doctor's name tag identified her as Mary Kay Bigelow. She was tall, thin, and she looked exhausted. Lynley wondered how long she'd been on duty. He explained that his companion Barbara Havers had been the one to come upon Rory Statham as she'd had an appointment with her that morning. Because Barbara had been aware of the cause of the recent death of Rory's friend Clare Abbott, she'd concluded that Rory had somehow come into contact with the same substance, sodium azide. He did not use the word *murder* at all, but he knew that his presence suggested it.

Bigelow said that they were certain of nothing yet, but that all precautions were being taken. They were treating the patient as they would for cyanide poisoning, which was the only protocol available when it came to sodium azide, if that was what they were actually dealing with. So at present, the patient was receiving sodium nitrite and sodium thiosulphate intravenously. The doctor also spoke of horizontal nystagmus, flapping tremor, and a high blood concentration of lactates and well as lower potassium than was normal. Shortly after admission to hospital, Bigelow revealed, the patient had gone into cardiac arrest, but she'd been brought back and, at the moment, she was stable but critical and comatose.

To Havers's question about when Rory Statham might be available for a brief conversation, the doctor shot her a withering look. 'If she lives through the next twenty-four hours, we can talk about miracles. As to conversations, that's not going to happen.'

'But it *is* sodium azide,' Havers said. 'What poisoned her, I mean.'

'It presents as sodium azide,' Bigelow admitted.

Havers's expression replied that was good enough. She turned to Lynley the moment that the doctor walked in the direction of the coffee machine. She said tersely, 'I *knew* the second I saw her on the floor . . . She's bloody lucky I showed up at her flat, Inspector. Someone was depending on her being alone long enough to bite it like Clare. These two women were connected in life and now they're connected in poisoning as well. We've got a death in Cambridge and a near death in Fulham and you know what that means. Or what it *could* mean if you take my part.'

He did indeed, but Lynley wasn't about to head in that direction. He said, 'Barbara, I can't ask Isabelle—'

'*Isabelle*,' she said pointedly. 'And you bloody well can.'

It was his own damn fault, Lynley thought. A strange form of madness had caused him to become involved with their guv, and despite the fact that this madness had arisen from his grief over Helen's murder, he couldn't use that to excuse himself. He'd never admitted openly to having been the superintendent's lover and God knew Isabelle would never speak of it, but Havers was no fool. She'd drawn a conclusion that was not incorrect. But what *was* incorrect was where she was allowing it to lead her.

Havers thought that their entanglement would prompt Isabelle Ardery to grant his wishes, either as a form of submitting to blackmail or perhaps from some kind of sentimental attachment to the time they'd spent in her bed. Lynley knew otherwise.

He said to Havers, 'The superintendent goes her own way, Sergeant.'

'Fine. Then we can work around her. You can work around her. Cambridge is going to need to know about this. You're going to need to tell them. You're going to need to supply them with the second autopsy on Clare—'

'Which I've already sent along to Sheehan. I've spoken to him about it as well. And I see where you're heading. But it's just not on. This –' He nodded to the isolation ward's door. 'Must be handed to the locals and handled by the locals and Clare Abbott's death must be handled by Cambridge. If they want help in coordinating, they can—'

'Shaftesbury,' Havers said. 'You're forgetting Shaftesbury.'

'What about Shaftesbury?'

'That's where Clare Abbott lived. That's also where Caroline Goldacre lives.'

'Who?'

'She was with Clare Abbott the night she died. *And* Rory Statham was recently in Shaftesbury, where she would have had contact with her as well.'

'Are you suggesting she murdered Clare Abbott? And then tried to murder this woman Rory?'

'I don't know *what* I'm suggesting, but I want to find out, and you can make that happen.' She shifted her feet. 'You want me back, yes?' she demanded shrewdly. 'You all want me back, don't you? So let me come back. But let me come back on my own terms. Let me get that transfer paperwork torn up by proving myself to her because that's the only way she's ever going to tear it up. I swear to you, sir. I'm begging you here. Please don't make me do it on my knees.'

God, she was the most infuriating woman, he thought. But what was the point of her keeping her job if she couldn't do the job as it was meant to be done?

*Chelsea*
*London*

Lynley did not return at once to Victoria Street, although he insisted Havers swear that she herself would do so. Instead, he dropped down to the King's Road, joined the eternal tail-back of cars, taxis, and buses heading in the direction of Sloane Square, and ultimately zigzagged towards the river. On the corner of Cheyne Row and Lordship Place stood the tall umber brick home of his longtime friend Simon St James. If, he decided, he was going to attempt battle with Isabelle Ardery, he might as well have all the necessary facts.

St James himself answered the door, accompanied by the household dog, a longhaired dachshund with the unlikely name of Peach. She inspected Lynley's shoe soles and ankles and deemed them acceptable before returning to her previous employment, which appeared to be begging morsels of toast from her master. This toast St James was at the moment munching. A very late elevenses, he revealed. Did Lynley wish to join him? They'd have to make do on their own with the toaster and the coffee press as he was alone in the house with neither his wife nor his father-in-law to call upon for assistance in matters culinary.

Lynley demurred. He followed St James into the room to the left of the house's entry. Here St James combined his study with a sitting room, but it wasn't a place for social gatherings as it was crammed floor to ceiling with books, a collection interrupted only by a small Victorian fireplace taking up a bit of space on part of one wall and a display of his wife's black and white photographs taking all the space on the other.

He'd been catching up on some reading, St James told Lynley, indicating his desk where his coffee cup and his plate of toast rested among piles of what looked like scientific monographs. What brought Lynley to Chelsea, he enquired, since it was apparently not in search of toast? St James took one of the two old leather wingback chairs that stood perpendicular to the fireplace and faced a sofa of antique vintage where, with no toast forthcoming, Peach had deposited herself and was currently creating dog circles upon, prefatory to settling in for a snooze. St James indicated the other chair and asked once again if Lynley was absolutely certain that he didn't want a coffee.

'Completely,' Lynley told him. 'I've only just indulged at Chelsea and Westminster Hospital. It was Barbara's peace offering. Not entirely undrinkable, which was something of a surprise. It put me in mind of that café in Windsor we used to haunt.'

St James laughed. 'Powdered coffee, powdered milk, hot

water from the tap, and sugar cubes that would not melt. May I assume that their coffee wasn't what took you to hospital?'

Lynley told his old friend about Rory Statham and Havers's discovery of the poor woman. St James set his coffee cup on the table between their chairs. He turned on the lamp to dispel the gloom brought on by the wet day outside. He said, 'You're assuming sodium azide again?'

'Havers is. But the fact that she's still alive . . . ? Is that even possible, Simon? When you and I spoke earlier, I had the impression that virtually any dose would be fatal.'

St James scrubbed his hands through his hair, always too long and mostly untamed, with curls falling well below his shirt collar. He yawned, said sorry, explained that it was the soporific nature of the bloody monographs, and answered Lynley's question. It would depend on the amount of sodium azide used, he said, and on the method of exposure to it. Mixed with water or an acid, for example, the compound would change to a toxic gas. Breathing the gas would quickly lead to a perilous drop in blood pressure, followed by respiratory failure and death. Ingesting it in some food source – once again depending on the amount – would sicken someone, inducing coughing, dizziness, headache, nausea, et cetera, but would not necessarily kill them should they get to treatment soon enough. The tricky bit here, though, St James said, was that, ingested, sodium azide mixed with stomach acids, rendering the person who ingested it consequently both toxic and explosive. 'Hydrazoic acid gets formed,' St James told him. 'Which would be why they're being so careful with this woman Barbara discovered. They've no idea how it got into her system, but that fact that she was still alive indicates she wasn't exposed to the gas it forms but rather through some other means, and ingesting it with food or drink is the most likely, I expect.'

Lynley thought about the likelihood of someone's being able to get into Rory Statham's flat and mix sodium azide with something she would eventually eat or drink. There could, of course, be an extra key to the place floating about, but it was more probable that she had unknowingly invited her poisoner into her home. It would, after all, only take a moment while she was out of the room for someone to put the chemical into . . . what? The sugar bowl? A container of milk? Her breakfast cereal?

'Of course,' St James said, his tone indicating he was thinking aloud, 'this stuff is so toxic that it could merely have been on the dead woman's clothing if she killed herself up in Cambridge. And if this second woman – what was her name, Tommy?'

'Rory Statham.'

'If Rory Statham came into contact with the sodium azide by touching her clothes—'

'Why would it be on her clothes?'

'If she poisoned herself. If she hadn't taken care when she mixed it with whatever she was going to down herself: water, tea, coffee, wine, a soft drink.'

'Barbara says no a thousand times to the idea that Clare Abbott killed herself, Simon. She was in the midst of quite a professional success.' He explained it all: Clare Abbott, her book, its sales, and the author's notoriety, which St James – an inveterate reader of newspapers – was already aware of. 'Barbara declares it improbable.'

'Sometimes suicides are,' St James said. 'All of that – this book business and Clare Abbott's success – constitutes the outer trappings. As to the inner woman . . . ? It could have been quite different.'

'Assuming for the moment that it was, that she did indeed take a dose of sodium azide to kill herself, where on God's earth would she have got her hands on it?'

St James said, 'Laboratories, hospitals, clinics. Any location where they'd have reagents.'

'As to handling the stuff once it was in one's hands . . . ?'

'If someone killed her, you mean?'

'Yes.'

'Whoever managed to get it would have known in advance, I assume, that exposure to it is absolutely deadly, especially if breathed as a gas or dust. But the risk of exposure could be minimised: a surgical mask or a painter's mask, latex gloves, a thorough scrub down and the laundering – or better yet, the disposal – of whatever one was wearing at the time of mixing the compound into whatever was going to be its carrier. That would probably take care of the risk.'

'And then afterwards? Assuming that all of the sodium azide wasn't used? Where would one dispose of it?'

'It's white, crystalline.' St James shrugged. 'One wouldn't need to dispose of it at all but merely to disguise it as something else never intended for use. Or one could put it – fully sealed – into the rubbish and allow it to be carted off to a landfill somewhere. The world's run amok with terrorists, but I suspect the government haven't yet begun requiring the dustmen to employ dogs to sniff the rubbish for sodium azide.'

Lynley nodded. It was a reasonable conclusion. Still, he said, 'It seems to me, though, that there are dozens if not hundreds of ways to poison someone without resorting to something so potentially dangerous to the person using it.'

'Of course. But consider that this substance had the forensic pathologist concluding the first woman had a seizure triggered by cardiac arrhythmia, Tommy. Had her friend not insisted otherwise, had she not had a passing acquaintance with Barbara, had you not asked me to look over the first autopsy, had I not strongly recommended a second, what was a murder would have gone down as natural if unexpected causes, and that would have been an end to it. That being the case, it was a brilliant choice of weapon. You merely have to find the person with a combination of native intelligence, wiliness, and the capacity to hate enough to do away with your victim.'

'And Rory Statham as well.'

'Indeed. Rory Statham as well. So you have your work cut out for you.'

'No, it'll be Barbara's work, if things go my way,' Lynley said.

*Victoria*
*London*

'How many different ways do I have to say no, Tommy?' Detective Superintendent Isabelle Ardery set her cutlery at the appropriate I've-finished-my-meal angle. She'd had the plaice. He'd had the beef. She'd pronounced her fish perfectly cooked and he'd wished he could have said the same.

He'd talked her into a late lunch at Peeler's instead of her usual, which was a sandwich either at her desk or taken on the run. She'd accepted and they'd had their meal *à deux* without being interrupted by anyone as there was no one else there at this hour. This allowed Lynley ample time to broach the subjects of one death, one poisoning, two investigations, and the completely sensible need for someone to see to it that the flow of information between the disparate investigations was well maintained. Since Shaftesbury was also part of the mix, there were many complications that could result in something vital to the uncovering of the truth being cast aside, ignored, or deliberately swept under the carpet. That could result in an internal investigation of the sort that went on for months, produced ill will everywhere, and cost a fortune. They didn't want that to happen, did they?

'None of that is our concern.' Ardery had spoken pleasantly enough, but Lynley could see the glint of warning in her eyes.

He'd continued, undaunted. As a case in point, he stressed, the detective superintendent needed to consider the source of the sodium azide. It had to have come from somewhere, and it had to have been carefully placed in a substance that had been ingested, breathed, or cutaneously applied. Thus, both victims' belongings were meant to be forensically studied. She would agree to that, wouldn't she?

'Of course, but it's not within our purview to orchestrate a forensic examination of anything, I'm afraid. Shall I ask for the bill? Let's make this Dutch as I've obviously not gone the route you'd hope and the guilt ensuing from allowing you to pay will doubtless give me indigestion.'

'Hear me out,' he said.

'When it will make no difference?' She sighed. She nodded at the waiter and ordered a coffee. She then said to him, 'All right. You've ten more minutes. Do go ahead.'

He explained that, upon the erroneous conclusion of the initial forensic pathologist that Clare Abbott had died of natural causes, those belongings that she'd had with her in Cambridge – previously in the possession of the Cambridge police – had been sent along to her friend and editor Rory Statham. Those belongings – wherever they were and one presumed in Shaftesbury – now needed to be returned to Cambridge for close examination. In the meantime, Rory Statham's flat and everything in it needed to be handled by SO7. Additionally, the contents of Clare Abbott's two homes would have to be considered, one by the Shaftesbury police and the other by the police out of the Bishopsgate station, which was nearest to her London home. The chance of all these different groups being consistently and continually willing to communicate with each other in order to share information that could be vital to sorting out exactly what happened to these two women was, they needed to face it, remote.

Isabelle had remained unmoved and she stayed unmoved as her coffee arrived along with milk and sugar, neither of which she used.

Lynley said to her, 'Someone got to both of these women. With an identical means of murder and of attempted murder in front of us—'

'We don't know the first is murder at all, Tommy. And – unless you've recently become prescient – we don't know if the second situation is even identical to the first.'

'Come along, Isabelle—'

She shot him a look.

'Guv, what else could they be when the condition of the women was identical?'

'Considering one is dead and one is alive—'

'She's in a coma. She's clinging to life.'

– 'I'd hardly call their condition identical. Nor can you, incidentally. Nor can Sergeant Havers, Tommy. Because this *is* about Barbara Havers, isn't it, at the end of the day? You can't have asked me to lunch because you're determined to talk me into handing yet another investigation over to *you*. Aren't you occupied enough?'

He decided to sidestep. He said, in reference to her earlier remark, 'I seriously doubt a rational person would choose sodium azide as a means of suicide, Isabelle.'

She looked up sharply once again at his use of her given name. She said nothing. He went on.

'Consider it: one woman in Cambridge and another in London and both of them technically alone when it happened. And both ingesting an identical deadly poison.'

'Yes, I see it's all suspicious or whatever you'd like to call it,' Isabelle said. '*If* the second woman was poisoned using the same means at all which, let me press this point as I seem not to be getting through to you, we do not know at present. But in any case, we're not about to go banging into someone else's investigation. It's just not on. As far as I can tell, an investigation into the Cambridge death will begin the moment that someone hands over the second autopsy report to the police there, which I assume is going to happen today or, pray God, has already happened. In the meantime, the locals in Fulham will handle whatever needs to be handled once they determine the situation of the second woman who – let's face it – might have been attempting suicide.'

'She'd rung Barbara Havers. She'd left a message to arrange a meeting. That hardly seems a prologue to suicide. You have to admit that her phone call to Barbara doesn't suggest the kind of despair that leads one to make an attempt on one's life.'

'She's lost her friend, Tommy. Someone she loves, let's presume. She hardly expected her to die so suddenly, so she's grief-stricken, bereft. She feels as if the world has ended because her own life now seems—' Isabelle clocked his expression and he saw her clock it. She said quickly, 'Good God. I'm sorry. That was unforgivable of me.'

Lynley wasn't about to go near the topic of Helen's death. He said, 'She wouldn't have killed herself or even made the attempt and left her dog just to remain in her flat. She would have made some sort of arrangement for him.'

'I never would have taken you for an animal lover. Where is it?'

'What?'

'What have you done with that dog? If you've not already taken it to Battersea—'

'This is a dog apparently trained to help her in some way,' he said. 'I'm not about to hand it over to a dog home while its owner is in hospital. Barbara took him from the flat.'

'And? Where is it then? Please don't tell me one of you has tied the creature up next to your desk.'

'I don't tie up dogs as a rule,' he said stiffly.

'Damn it, Tommy—'

'Underneath.'

'What?'

'The dog. He's lying underneath my desk. Untied, as it happens.'

'You're impossible. Do something with him at once. We're *not* running an animal shelter, for the love of God. Although truth is I sometimes think we're running a zoo.'

'Of course. A zoo,' he said, the solution to the problem of Arlo in front of him. 'It's for a brief time only. I have a place for him to go.'

'See to it, then.'

'As to the other . . . ? Guv, you made the arrangement for Berwick-upon-Tweed with a single phone call, and I know you can do the same for this. Beyond that . . . Barbara's intent upon proving herself to you. She'd like very much to allay your concerns about her.'

'She'd like very much me to shred the transfer request. And that, I must tell you, is not going to happen.'

He sighed. They were going round and round and ending up each time where they began. He reached for a roll that had been left on their table. He pocketed it as he nodded at the waiter for the bill.

'What are you doing with that roll?' Isabelle asked him sharply.

'I'm giving it to the dog,' he told her.

# 15 October

*Belsize Park*
*London*

He'd had to have Arlo with him on the following day at work, but he'd managed this with the help of his colleagues. Between enjoying walkies in the company of whoever was available, having surreptitious snacks beneath one desk or another, and being dashed off into the ladies or gents when the coast looked to become unclear, the dog had remained a secret from the detective superintendent. That additional day keeping Arlo at the Met was all that Lynley needed: he had an engagement with Daidre for dinner in the evening.

This particular night promised to be the unveiling of Daidre's new kitchen in which, she declared, she was going to prepare him a celebratory gourmet meal that matched the beauties she'd managed to bring about in the renovation of the room. He hadn't yet seen it as she'd not let him set a foot near it once she'd begun what she'd referred to as 'the serious part of the work', and because of this, he'd brought champagne along for a proper christening, in addition to Arlo.

She saw the dog at his side at once when she opened the door. She said, 'What have we here? How sweet! What a face! Have you a dog now, Tommy?' which he adroitly sidestepped by presenting the champagne, kissing her hello, and telling the truth: 'I've missed you.'

Daidre said, 'Have you? It's been only a week. Or is it ten days? No matter. I've missed you as well. It was this final push in the kitchen. I needed every free moment. And now it's completed. You must see it at once.'

He followed her, stood in the kitchen doorway, and simply admired. Aside from the electrical work and the plumbing, Daidre had as usual done everything. She was, he thought, a most remarkable woman. Everything about her kitchen was state-of-the-art. Stainless steel appliances, granite worktops, tiled splashbacks, sleek cupboards, modern lighting, six burner cooker, microwave, espresso maker . . . The flooring was hardwood, the windows were double glazed, the walls were replastered and perfectly painted, and the comfortable eating area looked out of the French windows and onto the garden-yet-to-be.

Lynley turned to her. 'I'm beginning to wonder if there's anything you can't do, Daidre. You never needed me to repair the glazing in that window in Cornwall, did you?'

'The one that you broke to get into the cottage?' She smiled. 'Actually? No. But it *did* give you employment and I saw you needed that.'

'Perhaps,' he said. 'But perhaps I needed you rather more.'

'That's the sort of remark that tends to lead men and women directly to the bedroom.'

'Does it indeed? Tell me you've completed it, then.'

'The bedroom? Not yet.'

He did wonder about that, whether she was putting off the bedroom for reasons having to do not with the logic of completing the more difficult projects first but rather with keeping him at a safe distance from her. He didn't mind so much that she was still insisting upon sleeping inside a sleeping bag on a camp bed. But it did prevent him spending the night, which he minded a great deal. He also minded that she was still refusing to spend a night beneath his own roof. She'd dine with him. She'd allow herself to be seduced into an hour or more in his bedroom, but that was it. It wasn't owing to Helen, she told him. It was rather the idea that she might actually become too comfortable spending time in his home.

'What's the problem with becoming comfortable?' he'd asked her.

'I think you know the answer to that.'

When she gestured round his Eaton Terrace townhouse, he forced himself to see it through her eyes. It was no matter that the antiques had been in his family since they weren't antiques, and it was no matter that the same applied to the paintings on the walls, the silver on the sideboard, and the porcelain in the cabinets. The very presence of these items marked the difference between them, a form of Rubicon that – in Daidre's mind – neither of them could cross.

Now she took the champagne from him and fetched two flutes for it. From the fridge, she brought forth a tray of various toppings meant, she told him, to give them something she called 'a bruschetta buffet'. She announced that she'd not had lunch that day, and she'd be cross if he wasn't famished. She poured the champagne, clicked glasses with him, put her hand to his cheek and said 'It *is* so lovely to see you, Tommy,' and then asked him about the dog.

'Ah. Arlo.' He made as quick a job of it as he could, telling her what little he knew of Arlo's purpose in the life of Rory Statham. He told her of Rory's condition in hospital and of the earlier death of her friend Clare Abbott. He explained how he himself had come to have Rory's dog in his possession, touching upon Barbara Havers's part in everything. Daidre already knew how tenuous was Barbara's position at New Scotland Yard, and Lynley had many weeks earlier put her into the picture of the potential transfer to the north of England that Barbara had ostensibly 'requested'. What he hadn't told her was his own part in the most recent knot in the skein that comprised the death in Cambridge and the poisoning in London, if such it was. This had involved a second and far less official telephone call to Detective Chief Superintendent Daniel Sheehan of the Cambridge police.

Isabelle, he'd assured himself before contacting Sheehan, had brought it all on. She was being as bloody-minded about Barbara

Havers as Barbara Havers was being bloody-minded about inserting herself into an investigation that did not belong to the Met. But between the two of them, Barbara's bloody-mindedness did at least seem to Lynley to have a potential positive outcome whereas Isabelle's obdurate refusal to allow Barbara enough slack to give her wiggle room seemed absolutely destined to take the detective sergeant once more afoul of her duty.

He'd been honest with Daniel Sheehan. Eschewing Oscar Wilde, he'd resorted to the plain and simple truth. Detective Sergeant Barbara Havers needed to work on the Clare Abbott death in some fashion in order to prove herself to Detective Superintendent Isabelle Ardery, he'd explained to Sheehan. She also needed to work on the Clare Abbott death in some fashion in order to prove herself to herself. This had to involve an exercise in police work in which she was able to operate within guidelines she'd been given by her superintendent: obeying orders as she was given them but at the same time following her own instincts, within the boundaries of regular police work, of course.

Sheehan had remembered Barbara Havers, which was no surprise to Lynley since he and Havers had spent several days on Sheehan's patch as intermediaries between the Cambridge Constabulary and the officials at St Stephen's College when one of their female students was murdered. Once Lynley explained to him the complexities of the case in hand – one death, an ostensible poisoning by means of the same substance, two locations, a third location which had housed the first victim – Sheehan had been willing to do what he could to get Barbara involved.

When this had been accomplished, Isabelle's fury had been, admittedly, somewhat unnerving. Her shout of, 'In*spec*tor Lynley, in my office. *Now*,' reminded him of his schooldays although he'd never been one to be hauled into the headmaster's domain for a proper dressing down, so cooperative a pupil had he always been. When Isabelle refused to allow him to shut her office door – the better to discipline him at a volume guaranteed to display her displeasure to his colleagues – he bore with their meeting as his just due.

'You've deliberately orchestrated this in defiance of my orders,' she hissed, 'and I God damn well ought to have paper-work drawn up for your transfer to the Hebrides.'

To his mild and completely spurious, 'Guv . . . I've not the least idea—' she picked up a holder for pens and pencils and threw it at him.

'Don't you say a bloody word,' she shouted. 'I've heard from Sheehan, he's made his request, he's paved the way, and the rest is history. But you hear me well, Detective Inspector. If you *ever* again defy me on a matter of personnel or anything else, I'll have you up before CIB2 so fast you won't know what hit you. How dare you go behind my back and make arrange-ments for *anyone* – let alone that infuriating undisciplined *excuse* of a police detective – to work a case that is not in our jurisdiction let alone—'

'Isabelle.' He'd walked towards the door to shut it.

'Stay where you are!' she shrieked. 'I did not give you leave to move a single inch and I don't intend to until I've finished with you. Is that clear?'

He shot her look and then took a breath to calm himself.

She evidently caught this and said, 'Not used to it, are you? His mighty lordship hasn't been dressed down in his entire career, has he? Well, you listen to me. The next time you take it upon yourself to machinate an assignment, it will be your last. I'm in charge here. You are not. This isn't a game, Inspector. No one is your chess piece. Now get the hell out of my sight and stay there.'

He walked to the door, having been given leave to do so, but instead of leaving he closed it.

She fairly howled, 'Get out!'

He said, 'Isabelle.'

'Guv!' she shouted. 'Boss. Ma'am. Superintendent. Do you ever do *anything* you prefer not to do?'

He walked over to her. She was behind her desk, but he

made no attempt to join her there, just stood in front of her and spoke quietly. 'You see me as wanting my way in things that don't concern me.'

'Bloody damn well right.'

'What you don't see is that she's useless at the moment.'

'She's *always* been useless.'

'That's not the case. That's never been the case. She's difficult. She requires a deft hand. She—'

'You're mad.'

– 'thinks just now that she can't please you unless she keeps her thoughts to herself, limits herself to the precise letter of what she's been told to do, and operates in so narrow a field that she offers nothing of what made her a decent cop in the first place: her doggedness and her willingness to risk a bit of creativity, if you will. She needs to be able to take the bit in her mouth and prove to herself and to you that she can do two things at once: be a fine cop and *still* obey an order when she hears it. You know this, guv. I know you know it because you're a fine cop yourself.'

'She can't obey orders when she doesn't hear them in the first place,' Isabelle snapped.

'That's been the issue,' he agreed. 'You'll get no argument from me on that. But I'd like to see—'

'It's not your place to see anything. You're becoming as bad as she is, and I'm not having *any* officer under my command—'

'I was out of order,' he said. 'Guv, I know that. If you want to have me up before CIB2, I quite understand and I'll take the medicine.'

'Oh please. Don't give me noblesse oblige on top of everything else. I'll sick up on my desk top.'

He gazed at her. She glared at him. He finally said, 'What would you have me do?'

'I'd have you set an example,' she told him. 'I'd have you listen. I'd have you display just a modicum of the respect that . . .' She turned from him to the windows, more a whirl of movement than a deliberate pivot away from him. Her hands both clenched. He knew what this meant. She wanted a drink. She'd have it in her bag or in her desk drawer: two or three airline bottles of vodka or gin or God only knew what and he'd driven her to it.

He said, 'Isabelle. Forgive me.'

She lowered her head and shook it. She took a moment. He said nothing else.

Finally, she turned back to him. 'I'm putting you in charge of all this, and don't even think about arguing. I want no corners cut. The instant she talks to a single member of the press—'

'She won't.'

'Get out of here, then. Leave me, Tommy.'

'Isabelle . . .'

'Guv,' she said wearily. 'Guv.'

'You won't—'

'Regret it?' She arched an eyebrow. 'Is that what you were going to say?'

It wasn't and they both knew that. *You won't drink, will you* was in the air between them.

'I apologise,' he told her. 'And I *will* dog every move she makes.'

'See that you do or face the consequences.'

'Accepted,' he said.

'Dismissed,' she told him.

He related all of this to Daidre, ending with, 'Praise God she didn't know the dog was with me.'

'You were very naughty, Tommy. I do see her point.'

'That's the devil of it,' he admitted. 'I see it as well.'

'As to the dog . . . ?'

Arlo had found a pile of dust sheets in the sitting room and had fluffed them and sorted them. With a mighty sigh, he'd deposited his furry body for a snooze. It had been a long and trying day at the Met: having walkies and snacks and being generally coddled.

'Ah yes, the dog,' the Lynley said. 'Arlo, he's called. I couldn't face taking him anywhere but with me. I've not the first clue what sort of dog he is, but he's extremely well trained. More like one's shadow than a dog.'

Daidre went to squat in front of him. Arlo cocked his head and blinked at her. She extended her fingers. He sniffed them and lowered his head to his paws. He still looked up at her, though. He was, Lynley thought, very difficult to resist.

Daidre did not even make the attempt. She said, 'Of course, Tommy.'

'What?'

'I'll keep him till his owner is able to have him back. As he's trained, he can come to work with me. What's one more animal when one works at a zoo? He can ride in the basket on the bike, I daresay. It'll be a bit of a squeeze for him, but I expect he'll manage.' She caressed the little dog's head. 'What kind of dog are you?' she asked him. 'We'll have to sort that out.'

'He's not a mongrel?' Lynley asked.

Daidre covered the dog's ears and glanced over her shoulder at Lynley. 'Please!' she said. 'Do not insult him.' And then to the dog, 'He didn't mean it, Arlo. Men are sometimes . . . How can I put it? . . . They can be so terribly ignorant when it comes to one's breeding.'

Lynley said, 'I like to think I'm not that sort.'

Daidre stood. She examined him with a gentle smile. 'Truth to be told?' she said. 'You're not that sort at all.'

# 16 October

For Barbara Havers, it was beggars and choosers. She'd wanted to be on the case. She was on the case. She'd wanted an opportunity to prove herself fully capable of working an investigation without recourse to the sort of colouring outside the lines that had got her into the position she was in with regard to a less-than-sunny future in Berwick-upon-Tweed. She had that opportunity. But her imagination had taken flight over the prospect that the case she might be able to work on – the death of Clare Abbott and the poisoning of Rory Statham – would be hers alone, part individual path to redemption and glory, part gauntlet thrown down by Detective Superintendent Ardery. To discover that she'd been out-manoeuvred and was thus going to be merely a cog in a machine operated by DI Lynley was not the fulfilment of her girlish dreams. To discover that she'd been partnered with her fellow detective sergeant Winston Nkata made her position worse.

Barbara knew why Winston had been assigned to work with her. Lynley wanted Nkata to keep her on the straight and narrow, and he wanted a report beamed in his direction the very nanosecond she got creative. It was humiliating. It was unfair. It was not right.

To her 'But, Inspector . . .' Lynley had levelled a steady gaze over the top of his reading specs. She knew better than to say another word. The rumour mill had been grinding energetically with the tale of Lynley's row with the detective superintendent.

Ardery, as reported by that fount of information Dorothea Harriman, had even gone so far as to throw something at him. 'Shouting like a binge-drinking uni student out on the street at two a.m.' was how Harriman put it. 'Really, Detective Sergeant Havers, I thought I might have to intervene.'

So further argument with DI Lynley was out of the question. Barbara accepted the facts as they were: her current lot in life was to be watched over by a six foot four inch former street fighter from the Brixton Warriors. There were, she reckoned, worse fates.

She and Nkata thus began the day together, with Nkata behind the wheel of his new and exceptionally pristine Prius, and with Barbara suggesting that he drop her at Chelsea and Westminster Hospital to check on Rory Statham while he himself went on to that woman's flat. She hoped to have a word with Rory if she'd regained consciousness, she explained to Nkata. If they divided their time and their efforts, they could accomplish more and—

'I'll stick with you, Barb,' was his reply.

She locked eyeballs with him. She said, 'Winnie . . .' to which he shrugged and replied, 'It's not like I'm chuffed with th' 'rangement, innit,' a remark that told her it was pointless to argue.

They found Dr Bigelow in the vicinity of the isolation ward, but a few words with her told them that talking to Rory Statham wasn't going to be on the day's agenda. The patient, as Dr Bigelow explained it, was holding her own, but they were not to take this as necessarily a good sign. With this kind of poisoning, people had been known to rally for a day or two and then to relapse and die. That could happen here and, no, she would not allow them to look in on Rory who was not conscious anyway.

They went on to Rory's flat and found that three blokes from SO7 were waiting in their van and none too happy to be hanging about anticipating the arrival of someone who would give them access to the scene. They clambered into their boiler suits, gloves, and booties, handed over the same to Barbara, eyed Winston with the obvious concern that they might not have something large enough to house him, and did their best to suit him up as well. Here at Rory's building, Barbara was relieved to see that Nkata was going to be reasonable with respect to a slight division of labour. He would begin with checking the rest of the flats in the building to see whether Rory had had any known visitors on the day or night of her poisoning. Barbara in the meantime would take the SO7 team into Rory's flat where they would begin collecting everything that could possibly contain sodium azide.

Just outside the door, the forensics team put on additional protective gear. Since they'd not brought any for Barbara, they advised her not to go into the flat at all although the fact that they'd given her the boiler suit suggested that they knew already she'd ignore their advice, which she did. She told them that she'd already been inside the place galumphing about and was still alive to tell the tale, so she reckoned she was safe enough to have another go. But she did put up the hood of her boiler suit and she did put on gloves in a bow to procedure. When they entered, the forensics blokes spread out to do their bit while Barbara went to Rory's desk, which sat beneath a nicely framed poster of some French birds doing the can-can.

She was about to sit down and have a go when one of the SO7 team popped his head round the kitchen door and told Barbara that the answer machine's light was blinking. She went to it, clocked the work of the officer who was removing everything from the fridge, and sorted out how to make the messages play. In short order she heard four. The first was some woman ringing to say that Professor Okerlund had had another think about the advance and, while he wasn't thrilled to bits with the offer, he did not wish to end his otherwise fine partnership with Rory's publishing company although he still had very high hopes that his proposal about the little princes was both timely and meaningful and he trusted that book sales would prove him correct. Barbara hadn't the first clue what that was all about, aside from some book deal, but the second message was easier to decipher: 'Rory, it's Heather again. Dad thinks Mum isn't going to want a party. He says she'll be cross if we have one and taking her out to dinner is a better bet. Ring me, OK? I did try your mobile. Why aren't you answering?' Then came Barbara's own voice, telling Rory Statham that she would be by soon with the second autopsy report. And the final one was clearly from her assistant at the publishing house: 'Rory, are you taking the day off? Did you forget you have an appointment with Mr Hodder this afternoon?'

Barbara made notes of all this and then went in search of Rory's mobile, which she found charging on a table next to the sofa. It would have to be looked at, gone through, and dealt with. The perfect job for Winston when he finished harassing the rest of the occupants of the building, as Winston was skilled at technology while Barbara was hopeless with anything more difficult than a telly remote, and even then it was a case of touch and go.

She went to the desk and a two-drawer wooden filing cabinet next to it. She opened this latter and discovered a collection of manila folders each with a different woman's name printed neatly upon it. The folders' contents turned out to consist of a plethora of printed material: from the internet, from magazines, from good old-fashioned gum-shoeing round a library or a news clipping morgue. Barbara began to go through them and saw that they appeared to be topics for future books, possibly suggestions that Rory was making to the relevant writer whose name was featured on each folder's tab. The first dealt with child beauty contests in the United States, featuring five- and six year olds dressed up, made up, and coiffed to resemble unsettling miniature facsimiles of adults. The second contained gruesome material about female circumcision in Africa. The next dealt with the prevalence of 'accidental' burnings in the kitchens of young married women in India whose families were not able to come up with additional dowry money after the fact. This was followed by information on rape in that same country, and hard upon the heels of this uplifting data came the stoning of women accused of adultery in several Islamic fundamentalist countries after which came the discarding of female infants in China. Barbara sought Clare Abbott's name on one of the folders' tabs. She did not find it.

Winston returned. 'Nuffin',' was how he put it. 'Only there's a bird downstairs? She had some words 'bout a "dishevelled creature" who came banging on her door 'bout Rory couple days ago. Her words, not mine, Barb. Sorry. But tha's it. Other'n that, no one knows a thing. Seems she kept mostly to herself. What've you got?'

'Reasons to swear off men forever,' Barbara told him.

'Say what?'

'Some research Rory seems to have done. Can you check the bedroom and see what's what there?'

As he went to do so, Barbara opened the second drawer. More files, these for what seemed to be book proposals. She fingered through them to see once again if Clare's name appeared. This time it did.

*Anonymous Adultery – Clare Abbott* was on the folder's tab. Inside the full title swept across a cover sheet. *The Power of Anonymous Adultery: Internet Encounters and the Dissolution of Family*. For this Clare appeared to have created an introduction, a table of contents, and an explanation of her intentions for a book. Barbara reckoned that she was looking at Clare's proposal. To her, it seemed a winner if the subtitle could be lost. *Anonymous Adultery*? That was a real attention grabber. It probably wouldn't have been as hot as *Looking for Mr Darcy* was proving to be, but it would have sold.

The first of the SOCO boys was leaving the flat with what looked like every item from Rory's bathroom when Nkata came out of the bedroom with a stack of photos in one hand and a stack of letters in the other. Both stacks were contained by elastic bands. He said, 'Bedside table. This looks like it, Barb,' and he joined her briefly at the desk. ''Cept a stack of books by the bed, unpacked suitcase heavy on funeral togs, an' her clothes in the cupboard and a chest of drawers.'

The photos, Barbara saw, were oriented towards Rory's personal life: herself and a younger woman on holiday somewhere. The letters were all in the same handwriting with the name *Abbott* in the corner. Barbara flipped through these but opened none. They'd have to be gone through, but that could wait.

She found a laptop computer inside the shallow drawer above the desk's kneehole, and she handed this over to Winston for carting back to Victoria Street along with Rory's mobile. In advance of SOCO scooping up the suitcase, which would put it out of their hands for days, she decided to have a quick look inside while Winnie took a moment with Rory's phone.

The suitcase lay next to a chest of drawers in Rory's bedroom, and a brief inspection told Barbara that it might well not belong to Rory Statham at all, although Winston would not have known this from a look at it. Nor would she have done, in fact, had she not recognised the garment carelessly folded on the top of an equally carelessly folded stack of other clothing. It was a black linen blouse with a stripe of white descending from the shoulder to the hem, and when Barbara lifted it out, she recalled at once the sight of Clare Abbott at the front of the gathering in Bishopsgate, striding back and forth on the dais with a microphone clutched in her hand as she fielded questions from her audience on the night that Barbara had bought a copy of *Looking for Mr Darcy*.

Either Clare Abbott had borrowed the blouse from Rory Statham for her appearance at Bishopsgate Institute that evening or everything in the suitcase belonged to Clare.

*River House Hotel*
*Cambridge*

Despite the rain, which was bucketing down from a tarnished sky, Lynley arrived in Cambridge in an uplifted mood. An

Oxford man, he knew it was wildly disloyal to find Cambridge appealing, but it was also impossible to ignore its beauty. Even in a downpour, the backs offered an unmatchable view of the stunning architecture of the colleges across an expanse of lawns from which autumn-decked trees erupted, and the colleges themselves rose splendidly beyond the river from these lawns with the town spread out behind them. Everywhere university students biked, walked, jogged, and roller-bladed among professors engaged – he liked to think – in deep discussions of the critical issues of their times. It made him very nearly wish for the intellectual life and he would have believed all of this was the cause of his fine frame of mind had he been a less honest man.

He'd rung Daidre prior to leaving Victoria Street. His excuse had been the dog. He was merely checking to see that all was well with Arlo, he'd told her.

She'd laughed. 'Are you actually ringing a veterinarian to ask about the wellbeing of a dog put into her care?'

'I see your point,' he admitted.

'You're very silly, but Arlo is fine. He's far more partial to lions than to elephants, I've discovered.'

'It must be a feline/canine thing.'

'It could well be. Listen, I must dash, darling. I've a meeting to get to. May we speak later?'

Of course they could.

It was the *darling*. It comprised a first time moment, and that first time moment was the sort of thing a young woman of the eighteenth century might have made note of in her nightly entry into a journal. He knew how ridiculous he was being in his decision to find *darling* somehow fraught with meaning, but the fact was that Daidre did not as a rule toss about *darling* – or any endearment – without attaching a sentiment to it. What that sentiment was . . . ? He wasn't sure. But he liked to think it signalled a subtle shift between them.

Inside the River House Hotel, he showed his warrant card and asked for the manager. It had now been just over two weeks since Clare Abbott's death, and the first order of business was

to speak with the employees who had been on duty on the
night she'd ingested the sodium azide. An identification from
the Metropolitan Police gained him quick access to a Mr Louis
Fryer: grey-haired, dapperly dressed in a pinstriped suit, and
wearing a carnation buttonhole. As it happened, Detective Chief
Superintendent Sheehan had brought Fryer a bit more fully
into the picture about Clare Abbott's death than he'd been on
the morning that her body had been discovered in one of the
rooms of his hotel. While the River House's manager did not
know the exact cause of death, he did know it had been found
unnatural. His primary concern, not unreasonably, was the
reputation of the hotel since one didn't like to see one's residents
carted off to the morgue after a night therein.

With a display of disturbingly white teeth, Mr Fryer ushered
Lynley into his office. There, the words *murder or suicide* made
the man cooperation incarnate. It became a small matter to
unearth the duty schedule for the night of Clare Abbott's
passing. These individuals, Mr Fryer pointed out as he handed
it over, were not on duty at present as, obviously, they comprised
part of the night staff and would not be in until much later.
He could, of course, ring them all and ask them to come in
and he'd be happy to do so. In advance, however, if he and
the inspector could have a word about adverse publicity . . . ?

Lynley told him that he could not promise anything when
it came to publicity, but he'd do what he could to keep any
word of the hotel's involvement out of the papers. 'The best
course,' he said, 'is to bring your employees in today as smoothly
as possible so I can speak to them and be gone. I'd like to see
the room as well, which I assume I might be able to do while
I'm waiting.'

Fryer flashed his teeth another time and said, 'The room?'

'Where Clare Abbott died,' Lynley said.

'But surely, Inspector, you wouldn't be looking for evidence.
A drinking glass had been overturned, but I assure you that was
the only thing amiss when the poor woman's body was found.
And now, two weeks after the fact . . . ? As the cleaning staff

have been in and out a number of times since then, you can't hope to find . . . What does one look for? Fingerprints and such?'

Lynley told the man wryly that he hadn't brought his finger-printing kit with him nor did he have his magnifying glass. It merely helped him, he said, to see where events occurred. He wanted to add that he hardly expected to find anyone lurking behind the arras at this late date, but he reckoned the allusion might fall upon unknowing ears.

Fryer took himself off to fetch the key to the room and to ask his assistant to start ringing the night duty staff. 'I'll arrange for coffee and cakes,' he told Lynley, as if some form of bribery were going to be necessary to get them to the hotel on their off hours.

Considering her reputation, it was no surprise to Lynley that both the hotel manager and the staff at the reception desk during the day remembered Clare Abbott as the woman who'd died. They also remembered Clare Abbott's assistant who'd apparently caused a scene in the hotel's garden that had required the intervention of first a waiter and then Mr Fryer. As to what had been behind the scene, no one could say. But two men had been there as well as another woman and her dog.

In the room Clare Abbott had occupied, Lynley found that a balcony overlooked the garden and the backs, and the Cam was well in view, flowing placidly not far from the garden's low wall, its surface pockmarked with rain. He tested the lock on the balcony door and, while it wasn't as substantial as it ought to have been, he saw that additional security had been provided by means of a rod that could be inserted into the track upon which the door slid.

The furniture and other trappings were standard hotel fare, although this particular room adjoined the one next door by means of two doors, either of which could be locked from the inside to prevent intrusion. The second door was locked at the moment, but Lynley assumed the room it sheltered was iden-tical to this one: a desk built into a wall's alcove, a flat screen television on the wall, a table and chairs set in front of the balcony doors, a bed with stands and lights on either side. Historic scenes of university life done in watercolours decorated the walls, heavily given to the bygone days in which students wore black gowns to their lectures.

He tested the lock on the connecting door inside what had been Clare Abbott's room, and he found it worked smoothly. He went next to the alcove desk, where lay the usual notebook of hotel information.

The room service menu was what he was looking for, and there it was, along with the hours that meals could be ordered. This was at any time of day, he found, with a limited menu after eleven at night. So a cook or a chef would have been on duty, he reckoned.

By the time the first of the night staff had arrived, Mr Fryer had sorted a conference room for Lynley to use, the daytime kitchen staff had come up with refreshments for their nighttime counterparts, and Lynley had spoken to the waiter who'd put him into the picture as to the identity of the men who'd been in the garden with Clare Abbott's assistant during the teatime row. Her husband and her son, he said. They'd come to fetch her home to Dorset as she'd been in no condition to get there on her own.

Late at night, he learned, the kitchen staff comprised a single individual, orders for food being taken by whoever was manning the reception desk and these being sent along to the kitchen in due course. The night chef turned out to be a female pensioner from Queen's College kitchen who'd returned to the workforce once she'd discovered that being alone with her husband on a twenty-four/seven basis was not contributing to their connubial bliss. He'd done the same, she confided, and now he worked part time days and she worked full time nights and in this manner they reckoned they could sail on towards their golden anniversary without killing each other.

Her time at Queen's had developed her skill at remembering people, their faces, and their quirks. The fact that she worked nights alone in the kitchen had developed her propensity for chat as she had none at all most evenings and spent her time reading the complete works of Shakespeare – 'seven down and bloody big pile to go,' she told him – as she waited to be called upon by one resident or another of the hotel. Thus despite being awakened from sleep and asked to come to the hotel for a chinwag with the cops, as she put it, she was dead happy to be there and to be of help. Being served coffee and cakes made the event all the more special.

She'd come into the conference room prepared for a lengthy interview. 'Something to tell the grandkids,' she confided to Lynley as she settled herself and adjusted the cardigan of the twinset she wore. She'd never been spoken to by the police before, she said. And to have her first conversation with a policeman be with a detective from New Scotland Yard . . . ? Made her feel like a suspect on a television drama, it did. He was to give her a right proper grilling, she told him. 'You have a real go at me, darling,' she concluded. *Darling*, Lynley thought, and his spirits sank. Perhaps he shouldn't have been quite so taken with Daidre's use of the word.

He hated to disappoint the night cook, but as time was of the essence, he had little choice. He complimented her on having come well prepared and seeing that she'd brought a record book with her, could she tell him if any orders for food had gone to the room occupied by Clare Abbott on the night of her death?

Indeed, a late night order had been made up for her. Two identical meals, as it happened. They were for tomato bisque soup 'my speciality, and I had it put on the menu straightaway when I came to work here, don't you know' – followed by a nice crab salad, fresh rolls, and creamery butter. Two glasses of water. Two glasses of white wine. And she was pleased to report that plates and bowls had returned to the kitchen empty.

To this information, the night porter – in charge of delivering meals – was able to add that two women were waiting for the food in Clare Abbott's room. He remembered this quite well because one of the two women had made much of the fact that each of the two waters had ice in it as she'd been quite specific, she informed him, that one of the glasses was to contain no ice. 'She went on a bit about it,' he told Lynley. 'Th'other woman told her to stop being a ninny – those were her words – and to "bloody drink your wine and mine as well if that's what it'll take for you to ease up, for God's sake."'

'Rather odd that you recall it,' Lynley pointed out, 'as you must make room service deliveries frequently.'

Oh aye, that was the case all right, the night porter admitted. But he remembered it well because one of the two women had died and because when he went back to the room much later to fetch the trolley, which had been rolled into the corridor, he heard both of the women shouting.

'Shouting?' Lynley asked, as it seemed extreme given that Clare Abbott and her assistant would have known they were in a hotel surrounded by other guests.

'Well, p'rhaps not shouting but talking angry and loud,' the porter told him. He'd reported this to the local police when he'd been questioned along with the rest of the night staff post the death of the occupant of the room to which the delivery of food had been made. Because of this, he remembered what he'd overheard.

'And this was?' Lynley asked him.

'First one said "We're finished, you and I." Then th'other said "Not with what I know 'bout you. We'll never be finished." Or words like that. And dead angry, they both were when they was talking,' the porter said. 'A door crashed shut directly the second one spoke.'

*Victoria*
*London*

''Course, it could've been someone else,' Barbara pointed out to Lynley. She'd brought him the photos and letters from Rory

Statham's flat. They'd looked through the first. Lynley had set the second aside for the moment. They were in his office in the late afternoon as the rain beat steadily against its single window. It felt a bit like old times to Barbara and despite being saddled with a watchdog in Winnie, she found herself feeling rather nostalgic as she sat there with Lynley looking thoughtful and – as she knew by his expression – poised to disagree with her.

'It could have been,' he said, 'but the night receptionist reported that no one who was not a guest in the hotel came through reception while he was on duty, so it was probably Mrs Goldacre the porter heard. He also had something of a run-in with her. The night receptionist, that is.'

Caroline Goldacre had rung the reception desk around one in the morning, Lynley told her. She'd requested a traveller's kit be brought up to her room. 'You know the sort of thing, I expect,' Lynley said. 'Guests forget something or their luggage gets lost in transit and the hotel can supply them with simple needs.'

According to the night receptionist, however, there were no traveller's kits available. They'd run out, they'd been reordered, they'd not yet been received. He'd explained this to Mrs Goldacre, who then asked if their sundries shop was open. When he told her it wasn't, she became quite angry. 'She wanted to know what sort of hotel didn't have emergency kits,' Lynley concluded, 'and she demanded that someone go to the chemist's for her.'

'At one in the morning?'

'Hmm. Yes. He said that he was incredulous someone would think a chemist's would actually be open and he told her – politely, he stressed when he reported it to me, so I suppose we can assume he was running out of patience at this point – that really there was nothing to be done but could he possibly assist her with something else.'

'And?'

'She hung up on him. You've met her, haven't you?'

'Just in passing. She had a bit of a go at me when I bought Clare Abbott's book, but that was it.' Barbara related the story of Caroline Goldacre, Clare's business card, and Rory Statham.

'A point of interest only, but why did Clare Abbott give you her card?' Lynley asked.

'She was a fan.'

'Of?'

'You won't approve.'

'Of?' he persisted.

'My T-shirt. I was wearing the one about bacon. And don't give me one of your looks, sir, as I hadn't worn it to work.'

'Ah. And was Mrs Goldacre perhaps attempting to prevent Ms Abbott from adopting your sartorial style?'

'More like Mrs Goldacre was attempting to prevent me from contacting Ms Abbott.'

'And the T-shirt?'

'Oh, I sent it along. It was clotted cream, though. Not bacon.'

'I'm somehow relieved.'

'More wholesome food group?'

'I wouldn't go that far.' Lynley shifted a few of the manila folders on his desk and brought out the autopsy report. All things considered, it appeared that the sodium azide had been in the food that Clare Abbott had eaten or, perhaps more likely, in the wine.

'Or,' Barbara said, 'there was that bit about the ice water. One glass with ice and one without would've made them easy to tell apart, eh?'

'There's that as well,' Lynley said. 'And a glass was also left overturned in the room, although I'm not sure that's relevant.'

'Why?'

'If it had contained the sodium azide, someone else would have been exposed to it. The fact that no one else in Cambridge fell ill in the aftermath of Clare Abbott's death suggests that she ingested all of it.' Lynley looked up from the report as Winston Nkata entered the office. He was carrying Rory's mobile with him.

'Messages and texts all seem on the up and up,' he said. 'She's got pictures's well. Last eleven 'f them got the Abbott woman in them and a boiling lot of people hanging about some garden having a champagne an' tea, looks like.'

He handed the mobile over to Lynley who glanced at the pictures before handing it on to Barbara. 'You've met some of this lot. Recognise anyone?' he asked her.

Barbara looked at pictures. They'd been taken, she saw, at a kind of ceremony, which appeared to be happening at a hillside water course in view of an expanse of countryside. She said, 'It's Dorset, I expect. One of Clare Abbott's addresses was in Shaftesbury. That's where I posted the T-shirt.'

In the photos a woman in the getup of a town mayor was speaking, then Clare Abbott was speaking, then a big stone was being revealed by Clare to Caroline Goldacre, then Caroline Goldacre was hugging Clare, followed by being embraced by an unattractive bloke with a pot belly, thinning hair, and gold-rimmed specs. There was a close shot of the stone as well, with a bronze plaque on it. A memorial, she saw.

*William Goldacre* was written upon it, along with what appeared to be a poem and the dates of his birth and death. She did the maths. Twenty-six years old when he'd died.

Got to be the son, she said to herself, and then she identified Caroline Goldacre for Lynley as the only person aside from Clare whom she recognised. Someone had also been given Rory's phone to snap a few shots of Rory and Clare together, she saw. This was in another garden – Clare's own possibly? – where the tea and champagne spoken about by Nkata were being served along with sandwiches. Barbara identified Rory and then said to Lynley, 'Looks like summer in the photos, sir. Dedication of a memorial stone?'

'And as the stone is apparently for Mrs Goldacre's son, she must live nearby.'

'They got her in common,' Nkata said. He was leaning against the door jamb, arms crossed in his habitual manner.

'Rory probably saw her the day before I found her in her

flat,' Barbara added. 'She left me a message here. I'd rung her about the autopsy and asked to meet with her, and she was ringing back. She said – this was in her message – that she'd only just got back from Clare's funeral where, I expect, she saw Caroline Goldacre as well.'

'Two women seeing Caroline Goldacre and getting themselves poisoned d'rectly,' Nkata said.

'Let's keep the horse where it belongs,' Lynley noted drily. 'A motive would be a very fine thing before we start pointing fingers at someone.'

'Shall I track her down?' Barbara asked.

'Begin with a phone call,' Lynley said. 'If she's in Shaftesbury, both of you go.'

'But sir, wouldn't it make more sense for Winnie—'

Lynley gave her what Barbara was coming to think of as The Look.

She scowled. 'I'll make the phone call,' she groused. 'Pack your jammies, Winnie. I expect we're having a holiday in Dorset.'

*Shaftesbury*
*Dorset*

Because Alastair MacKerron had to sleep in two shifts in order to see to the early-morning baking, he'd only just finished his afternoon kip and shower when his wife burst in upon him. He was in the midst of examining himself in the full length mirror on the back of the bathroom door and not particularly liking what he was seeing. He'd gone to seed. He'd never been much to look at in his youth, but in his London days at least he'd kept fit on his bicycle and in his kayak on the Thames. All of that had passed with the advent of Caroline and her boys into his life and for a very long time their presence had been more important to him than seeing to the daily upkeep of his body. In the ensuing years since they'd met, he'd let vanity go in the cause of taking care of those three escapees from an unhappy marriage, and the only bit of pride of appearance he'd held onto was connected to keeping his thin, curly hair from greying. A monthly application of dye had taken care of this, and he liked to think of it as his little secret. So when Caroline burst into the bathroom, he was caught out because the box in which the dye had been sold was still sitting on the bathroom vanity unit.

She didn't see it. She almost didn't notice that he was starkers, either, which he supposed was just as well since his pot belly had nearly become more than he could suck in and even Sharon's kind 'Don't worry about it so, Alastair,' had not made him feel better about his girth. Sharon said she liked him just as he was and she proved it to him with what was quite a surprising creativity in bed. Beneath that retiring exterior of hers, she was wonderfully imaginative. But truth was, she explained to him, she was just in love. 'Love makes one want to please the other,' was how she put it. 'Are you not used to being pleased?'

That was the question, all right. He knew the answer before Sharon even finished speaking. For Caroline had been bent on pleasing him once and he her. That had gone by the wayside, and although they'd carried on for a time with each other on a weekly and then a monthly basis for a few years, mostly their focus had been on the boys. And between the boys mostly they'd concentrated their efforts on Will.

'It's Will. I'm so worried about Will,' became passion's death knell. These things happen, was what Alastair had told himself. Doesn't mean the end of love.

But with Sharon things were different. Just thinking of her could get him going. And, miracle of miracles, Caroline had come round with regard to Sharon. While she'd earlier demanded that he 'sack the pathetic grey-faced little cow', she'd decided soon after that Sharon's importance to the business could not be discounted. She'd admitted 'having let things go, having let *myself* go, Alastair, and no wonder you don't want me any longer,' and had determined to alter the state of their relationship, a state that had – she declared – driven him into the arms of another woman. Three times she'd come to him during his period of rest from the bakery, and she'd slipped into his bed and offered herself to him, reaching down to arouse him, lifting one of her huge bosoms to his lips and caressing them with her nipple.

Nothing, though. Not only could he not perform, he didn't *want* to perform. It felt like a sin against Sharon. Caroline wept. She declared that it was her body that no longer aroused him. It was the weight she'd gained from the food she'd eaten to comfort herself after her son's suicide, it was the strength of her need for him – for Alastair – which made her less appealing because there was no *chase* to it and he was a man who liked to pursue. Pursuit and capture and she's done this for you, hasn't she? So he'd comforted her and he'd said, 'Caro, don't worry so,' when he wanted to say 'She's not like you, she makes me her world,' only it wasn't quite that, was it? It was just that she was Sharon.

Now, he grabbed his towel and wrapped it round his waist, and in the same movement he swept the empty hair dye box into the rubbish. Caroline said to him, 'The police have rung. Alastair, the *police* and I don't know what to think except . . .' She tapped her fist against her teeth in that way she had when she was trying to calm herself.

He said, 'What's happened?'

'They want to speak with me. The London police. It's someone from Scotland Yard. A woman. She's rung and said she's coming to speak with me about Clare's death. Do they think I did something to her?'

Alastair reached for his glasses, which were on the top of the toilet cistern, and he said again, 'What's happened, then, luv?'

She said, 'I just *told* you—'

'Right. But I mean, d'they suspect you of something?'

'Of *course* they do. Why else would they phone? Why would they be on their way at all? She said she'd be here in late afternoon to speak with me and if I want to have a solicitor present . . . Alastair, she talked to me like . . . It's as if I was a criminal. Do they think I harmed Clare? *Why* would I do that?'

'You wouldn't.'

'You must stay with me. I can't be on my own today Especially in front of the police. I can't have them looking at me and thinking whatever they're going to think. They've decided I must be guilty of something or why else would they be coming from London when the only thing—'

'Course I'll stay,' he cut in. There was, really, nothing else he could do. 'But I expect they're just sorting through everything related to Clare and Cambridge and as you were there—'

'Oh God, I packed her bag. Clare's bag. She hadn't the time so I packed her bag for Cambridge. Do I have to tell them that? Do they need to know that? I can't tell them that. I won't. God knows *what* they'll think.'

'If they ask, you tell the truth, Caro. That's always the best way. But don't worry so.'

'How can I help it? With Clare dead and Will dead and my life spinning out of control and . . .'

'Hush, now.' He put his arms round her. 'You let me get dressed and we'll have ourselves a cuppa 'fore they get here.'

Her voice altered, a softness coming into to it. 'How you always calm me. Thank you, darling.' She lifted her face to his and she kissed him, adding, 'I've been terrible for such a long time. It was down to Will. His troubles, everything that ate at him and made his life such a trial and you were always there for me. You know what you mean to me, don't you?'

'Aye,' he said and his heart felt heavy. 'That I do.'

She kissed him again, in the old way. She felt for him in the old way as well. But again and completely unlike the old way, his body didn't respond. He hung there flaccid and knowing this would set her off, he took a step away and gazed at her and made his expression as loving as he could.

He said, 'Better now?'

'Always better with you.'

'So let me get dressed and I'll make us some tea.'

She nodded and turned to go. Then she said at the doorway, 'They asked me . . . Alastair, the woman who rang? She asked me about Rory Statham. When was the last time I saw Rory, she wanted to know. Why would she ask me that?' She drew her eyebrows together thoughtfully and then said, 'That day in her office when Clare and I went in to sign all those copies of her book . . . That was the same day we went to Cambridge. And then Clare died that night. Could Rory have . . . Could she have done something? Messed Clare about in some way?'

Alastair shrugged and gave her what he hoped was a fond look. 'It'll sort itself out, pet. These things always do.'

*Shaftesbury*
*Dorset*

They were slowed considerably by the rain, which had not let up since early morning. When Barbara and Winston Nkata finally arrived in Shaftesbury in his Prius, it was just after six in the evening, and the wind had come up in athletic gusts so fierce that the rain was lashing the town horizontally.

Caroline Goldacre lived outside the town, at the base of a hill where the landscape altered from narrow streets lined with grey or whitewashed limestone buildings to a valley in which the yellow and umber of autumn trees interrupted a placid panorama of rolling emerald hills. In these the occasional set of farm buildings scattered into the distance, where slopes offered woodlands and outcroppings of stone.

Caroline Goldacre's home had at one time been part of one of the farms. It was situated in a horseshoe of buildings similar to it, a large stone house just off the road with a waist-high boxwood hedge in front and a driveway leading past an artful sign that read MACKERRON BAKED GOODS. The bakery appeared to be purpose built. It sat opposite the house on one arm of the horseshoe and between the two buildings a fanciful sunken garden offered a limestone terrace, a fire pit, outdoor seating, a bubbling fountain, and colourful plantings in both urns and pots as well as borders that mixed exotic looking grasses of varying heights with hydrangeas, holly, and heather.

The area for cars was to one side of the bakery, and here Nkata parked near a window that looked into a room with enormous cast iron ovens and spotless working surfaces of stainless steel. Barbara and he got out into the rain, and they bent against a wind that fairly fought to keep them away from the house. On their way, they passed another rain-streaked window. A quick look inside showed them a storeroom of sacks, containers, and boxes. Beyond this, they could see mixers the size of old Volkswagens and baking sheets as big as camp beds. It appeared to be a place where everything was made by hand.

Barbara led the way to the house, which took them past the bakery and through the garden. Closer to it, the building appeared to be cob faced in stone. It was freshly whitewashed with a grey slate roof where moss filigreed between the tiles. An oak door was set into a porch from whose peaked roof rainwater was falling in great sheets. Nkata did the honours at the door. A bell rang somewhere deep within the place.

Caroline Goldacre opened the door, but she wasn't alone. The unattractive bloke from the pictures on Rory Statham's smartphone stood just behind her, and he put one hand on her shoulder as Barbara dug out her warrant card and simultaneously Caroline Goldacre said to her, 'You,' in the sort of tone that implies recognition. She added, 'From the book signing. The T-shirt,' to which Barbara replied, 'For my sins.' She introduced Winston, and Caroline Goldacre did the same for the man who stood behind her. This was Alastair MacKerron, they were told, Caroline's husband. He was giving Nkata the eye, his expression asking who the bloody hell would've wanted to get into a knife fight with this bloke – let alone with a cop – and Barbara didn't shed light on the facial scar having come from the black man's misspent youth.

Caroline led them from the stone-floored entry into a sitting room to the right of the front door. Barbara took the place in and thought that if half of its contents were carted off by the dustmen, it would still be packed with so much clobber that sudden movements without overturning a table or breaking one of the two billion Toby jugs would probably still be well nigh impossible.

Alastair cleared his throat roughly. He offered them tea. Barbara demurred but Winston indicated that a cuppa might be the very thing, with thanks. Alastair hastened off to see to this while Barbara took in the rest of the room. Along with everything else, it contained a plethora of photographs of, presumably, Caroline Goldacre's deceased son along with another young man who had to be his brother. They were featured in various stages of childhood-to-manhood. She picked up one as Caroline said, 'Those are my two boys. Charlie and Will,' and she added oddly as if wishing them to know how things stood familially, 'Alastair's not their father, although he's been more of a father to them than their real father ever was.'

'Passed on, has he?' Nkata asked.

'No. Francis is very much alive. Francis Goldacre. He's a surgeon. In London.'

'What sort?' Barbara asked idly as she studied the picture. One of the two young men was somewhat odd looking. He wore the long hair of the Beatles' generation, and his full Cupid lips would have been potentially luscious on a female but served to make him appear pouty and difficult to please.

'Plastic,' Caroline Goldacre said. 'Ladies' facelifts mostly. Breast enhancements. So much money to be made in the industry of youth and beauty, is what he used to say.' After a pause, she added, 'It's unfortunate that he never wanted to use his talents on our Will.'

Barbara set the photo down and glanced at Nkata to see if

he had clocked the strangeness of that remark. Caroline Goldacre seemed to read the glance that passed between them because she went on to explain that Will had been afflicted with a birth defect, a misshapen and nearly missing ear that Francis Goldacre had refused to put right. 'His boys were never his priority,' she concluded.

Alastair returned. He carried a tray with a mug, a spoon, and two packets of sugar. 'Milk's gone off,' he said to Nkata. 'Sorry. We've not been to the shops.'

Caroline still hadn't asked them to sit, but Barbara decided not to stand on ceremony. She sought the only chair that bore fewer than three decorative pillows, and into it she plopped. There was little for it but for Alastair and Caroline to do the same. Nkata remained standing although he moved to the fireplace and set his tea mug on the mantel.

'Can you tell me about Cambridge, Mrs Goldacre?' Barbara switched on a lamp with a 'D'you mind? Bit dark in here, is all.'

'What about Cambridge?' Caroline had taken a spot on the love seat that faced the fireplace. Alastair sat with her. She lifted his hand and linked her hand to it.

'What you were doing there and why you were with Clare Abbott. Let's start with that.'

'I'd rather hoped you might tell me why you're here.'

'Procedure,' Barbara said with a dismissive wave. 'Dot the t's and cross the i's.'

Caroline did not smile. 'How did Clare die? The only thing I know is from the papers afterwards. They said her heart . . .'

'A seizure that happened when her heart misfired,' Barbara said. 'Then a second autopsy carried things a bit further. So the heart thing and the seizure bit? They were . . . how do I put this? . . . well, *caused*.'

'What's that mean?' It was Alastair who spoke.

Barbara ignored the questions and repeated her own. As to Cambridge and why Mrs Goldacre was there . . . ?

Caroline told her briefly about a debate and a book signing.

She added a radio broadcast and a lecture meant for the
following day. She included an editorial comment about Clare
Abbott's tendency to humiliate people in public forums and
indicated that this was what she'd done to the woman priest
with whom she'd debated. No one could rein Clare in when
she got going, Caroline added. One tried to advise her, one
tried to suggest that less sarcasm might make the medicine go
down more easily, but Clare tended go her own way.

'What was your position in her life?' Barbara said. 'Sort of
a dogsbody were you?'

Alastair seemed to find it necessary to intervene at this. 'Far
sight more 'n that. Clare wouldn't've known night from day
if Caroline wasn't there to switch on the lamps.'

'It's all right, darling,' Caroline said. And then to Barbara
she went on to explain that she and Clare had met at the
Women's League in Shaftesbury when Clare had come to
speak shortly after moving to the town. They'd struck up a
conversation, it had come out that Clare needed a cleaner, and
Caroline was up for the job as she quite liked the woman and
reckoned mere housework could lead to something far more
suited to her talents. The cleaning quickly extended to the
cooking and the weekly shop as well. At that point, Caroline
had offered to sort out Clare's home as organising was not
one of Clare's . . . well, let's say it wasn't one of her special-
ities, Caroline explained.

'She'd never got round to it when she bought her house,
so I sorted out her kitchen, pantry, linen cupboard . . . that
sort of thing. Clare asked could I do the same for her office,
and things went on from there. We got on quite well, she asked
me to stay on and over time I took on more responsibility. I
was happy to do it although she could be rather prickly at
moments.'

'Got a bit prickly in Cambridge, I hear,' Barbara said.

Caroline cocked her head, a puzzled expression on her face.
'What d'you mean?'

'You two had a row the night she died. What was that about?'

Caroline stirred on the love seat. She loosened her hand from Alastair's. 'Who told you that?' she asked, not unreasonably. 'It's Rory, isn't it? You may as well know that Rory very much dislikes me. She always has done. She wanted Clare to give me the sack. She thinks I don't know that, but there're scores of things I know that she's unaware of and that's just one of them. Clare and I didn't argue.'

'Bloke at the hotel overheard you.' Nkata took a sip of tea. He sounded casual enough, just a comment in passing.

Barbara added, 'Seems he was collecting your room service trolley and you two were going at it.'

'Really? I certainly don't remember . . .' Caroline drew her eyebrows together. They were drawn-on-her-face eyebrows, but nicely done in perfect arches. After a moment of reflection she said, 'Ah. I expect it was about my wages. We had words about that. For all her success, Clare was tight with her money. I put it down to how she grew up. On a sheep farm in the Shetlands, this was. So when it came to paying me . . . ?' She shrugged. 'Even in her will and despite my having worked for her for two years . . . Well, it's water under the bridge. I wasn't happy about it, but there you have it. There wasn't much I could do about it, after all.'

'In'eresting, that.' Nkata flipped back a few pages and read out the words that Lynley had reported to them from his interviews in Cambridge with the hotel's employees. '"We're finished, you an' I." An' then "Not with what I know about you. We'll never be finished." Doesn't sound like wages to me, innit.'

'I don't recall having said that. Or Clare having said it either. Neither one of us would have had a reason.'

'Did you know the terms of her will?' Barbara asked.

'See here,' Alastair MacKerron said hotly. 'What sort 'f question—'

'Alastair, it's fine,' Caroline said.

Barbara added, 'She'd have needed a witness to it. Was that you?'

'I was always signing this or that for her,' Caroline said. 'But truthfully? I didn't know Clare even had a will till Rory started waving it about directly after the funeral, telling me to clear out of the house as it was now hers.'

'How well d'you know her?' Nkata asked.

'Rory? Not well. Mostly, I know *about* her.' Caroline was silent for a moment as if waiting for either Barbara or Nkata to take the bait. When neither of them did, she went on. 'She's Clare's editor. She's also a lesbian. Not that I have the least problem with that but the point is that she was in love with Clare. She tried to hide it but who can hide that sort of thing successfully? Clare, by the way, was heterosexual. Non-practising heterosexual, was how she put it. Not the case, of course, but that's hardly important.'

'Which part?' Nkata took more tea, always managing to imply that his questions were casual.

'What?' Caroline said.

'"Not the case,"' Nkata quoted. 'Which part? The hetero or the non-practising?'

'The latter. Clare had her lovers, but I doubt she told Rory about them. I daresay she didn't want to hurt her feelings.'

'Sounds out of character, that,' Barbara commented. 'Seems like she was fairly direct. When did you last see her? Rory, this is.'

'At the service for Clare. Five days ago, wasn't it, darling?' She turned to her husband. He nodded and reminded her that afterwards – next day, pet – she'd gone to the house as well. That would be when Rory wouldn't give her enough time to collect all her things, mind you.

Caroline said, 'I think she assumed I'd come to steal the silver. I do have to ask this, Sergeant . . . Havers, yes?' And when Barbara nodded, 'You're not intending to imply that Rory . . . ? Rory was disappointed in love, but we all are occasionally, aren't we? And we don't . . . well, cause our love objects to somehow have heart problems and seizures.'

'It's just the opposite,' Barbara said. 'Rory's in hospital.'

'Someone tried to give her the chop,' Nkata added.

There was a silence at that. During it, the wind whipped a frenzy of rain against the window panes, and Caroline started at the sudden sound. It was chilly in the room and a coal fire was laid in the grate, which would have been pleasant had someone made a move to light it, but no one did. Caroline finally said, 'Are you saying that someone tried to *kill* Rory? How is this even possible? And why?'

'That's the question, all right,' Barbara agreed.

*Shaftesbury*
*Dorset*

They decided on a drink afterwards, so they repaired back up to the town where in its centre they found the Mitre. When they'd taken their ale (Barbara) and their lemonade (Winston) to a table, Nkata was the one to point out what they both had been thinking from the moment they'd left Caroline Goldacre and her husband.

'Poison's a woman's weapon, Barb.'

'There's definitely that,' she agreed. She glanced at her watch. She fished her mobile from her shoulder bag, saying, 'Let's see what the inspector's got.'

Most of what Lynley had referred to Rory Statham personally, as he had not yet heard anything from SO7 about the source of the sodium azide in her flat. Nor had the technicians sorting through her mobile phone records and her laptop reported back. But as far as Rory herself went, Lynley had spoken at length to her sister and had learned from her that Rory had lost her longtime lover Fiona Rhys to murder some years earlier: a crime along the Costa Brava. Fiona had died of multiple stab wounds and internal injuries.

'They'd taken a small villa for a summer holiday,' Lynley

explained. 'It was, apparently, just isolated enough for someone to target them.'

'Was the someone caught?' Barbara asked.

'A bloke was tried, convicted, and sentenced. After it all, according to Rory's sister, she remained at Clare Abbott's home in Shaftesbury for several months.'

'Caroline Goldacre claims Rory was in love with her.'

'The sister gave no indication of that. *Grateful* and *close friends* were the words she used.'

'So is there a connection among all this?' Barbara said, more to herself than to Lynley.

'One has to wonder,' Lynley replied.

17 October

Bleary-eyed, Barbara staggered down the stairs at Clare Abbott's house at half past seven. As they had the keys to the place and it was no crime scene, they'd reckoned that using it as their accommodation would simplify matters when it came to going through Clare's belongings to assemble usable information in their quest for her killer. So Barbara had taken one of the house's spare rooms while Winston had settled across the corridor in another, and they'd said their goodnights sometime after one a.m., having made an initial recce of Clare's office. Barbara had intended to rise earlier but the bed had been so comfortable and the sound of the rain so soothing that she'd lost consciousness entirely and had slept without dreams.

She descended the stairs into the scent of bacon and coffee. She found Nkata in the kitchen, standing before the cooker in running clothes: silky shorts, a hooded sweatshirt, trainers, and a towelling band round his head. She noted he had quite lovely legs before she said, 'Bloody hell, Winnie. You run, on top of everything else?'

'What's everything else?' he asked, turning from the cooker, on whose hob bacon was crisping.

'You don't drink. You don't smoke. You're moderately capable of defending yourself with a flick knife. And now I find that you cook.'

'Not so capable with the knife.' He fingered his scar.

'You lived through it, and that's what counts. Plus whoever

he was, he missed your eye. Good dodging on your part, so you're quick on your feet as well. But what I want to know is what the bloody world's come to when people begin thinking that "staying in shape" – whatever that's actually s'posed to mean – trumps what's truly important in life.' She looked round the kitchen, at the neat worktops on which four grocery bags had been unloaded and were now neatly folded. Good God, the man had done the shop as well although God knew where he'd found a supermarket open so early in the morning. 'You didn't happen to sort me out some Pop Tarts?' she said.

He shot her a look but said nothing.

'Do not bloody tell me the inspector ordered you to feed me properly, Winston. You're supposed to keep me on the professional straight and narrow. My diet's in my own hands. And where're my fags?' She pointed to the worktop. 'I left them right here last night.'

'I binned them,' he said.

'You *what*?'

'Table's laid in the dining room, Barb. Coffee's ready. Let's tuck in.'

She excavated for her Players first. True to his word, Nkata had tossed them in the rubbish, where they lay under five eggshells. She rubbed egg ooze from the packet on the hem of her sleeping T-shirt – *I'll wake up when the dachshund is housetrained: Sleeping Beauty* – and she followed Nkata into the dining room.

He'd cooked them a proper English breakfast, probably the sort of meal his mum made for him every day: eggs, rashers of bacon, sausage, grilled tomatoes, mushrooms, toast, and jam. 'Sets you up proper,' was how he explained it. She didn't offer the argument that Pop Tarts and a fag did much the same.

Not only had he been out running and to the supermarket, Barbara found, but he'd also been once again into Clare's office. On the table along with their plates and cutlery, he'd placed a laptop, a mobile phone, and Clare's diary. This latter he handed over to Barbara. He himself took the mobile and switched it on. Like Rory's, it was a smartphone, so there would be a history of calls, text messages, and potentially photos as well. Meantime, Barbara flipped open the diary and worked her way back through the dates to see what Clare's appointments had been.

She quickly discovered that, unsurprisingly, the writer had led a full and busy life, but she had not, unfortunately, spelled it out exactly in her daily planning. Instead, over several months preceding her death, she used either names or initials next to the times of her appointments. Most of these appeared to be with women: Hermione, Wallis, and Linne were recent engagements. In addition to these, Barbara found a Radley, a Globus, and a Jenkins as well as three appointments with Rory and eighteen different appointments indicated by Wookey Hole, Lloyds, Gresham and Yarn Market over a period of five months. The most recent engagements were indicated by initials only. Clare had apparently spent time with MG, FG, and LF.

'Bloody hell,' was Barbara's reaction. From the looks of the diary, it seemed to her that she and Winston might well be spending any number of weeks in Shaftesbury.

She read out the list to Nkata and, pausing in his perusal of the mobile phone, he asked the logical question. 'What d'you make 'f the way she listed 'em?'

'Using Christian names, place names, surnames, or initials?' And when he nodded, Barbara thought about the matter. 'I expect she knew the Christian named people well. Mates of hers, p'rhaps? Fellow writers? Other feminists? She sees "Hermione" in her diary and she knows it's Hermione Whosit. Last names: people she knew less well or p'rhaps not at all? Could be people she meant to interview?'

'Wha' about the places . . . What was it? Wookey Hole?'

'Meeting places? Or could be spots she was giving lectures, I reckon.'

'Wha' about the initials?'

Barbara looked at these again. 'Those're interesting, eh? Seems like when someone uses initials like that, she knows she's going to remember who the appointment is with. She wasn't about to jot a few initials next to times in her diary and risk looking at it a week later and wondering who the bloody hell FG is. So . . . could be the names're familiar to her but too long to write out.'

'Could be she was in a hurry so she just jotted them down as initials.'

'Or could be she didn't want someone with access to this diary – someone besides herself – to know exactly who she was meeting.'

*Shaftesbury*
*Dorset*

Caroline awakened him at half past seven, less than thirty minutes after he'd dropped into bed, the day's baking completed and the vans filled and on their way to the shops. He'd only just started to dream when his wife came into the room and said his name in a low voice that suggested she was merely testing the waters of his slumber in an effort to see how deep they were. Not deep enough, especially as she made sure this was the case by also touching his shoulder. He was dead spent, as the visit from the police on the previous late afternoon had put paid to his usual evening's kip prior to having to go to work. Now all he wanted was a few hours' sleep. But when she said his name a second time as she touched his shoulder, Alastair opened his eyes.

Caroline always took care with her appearance, but now she looked as if she hadn't slept all night. Her face was puffier than usual, and she had a bruised look about the eyes. She was wearing her mack and carrying her handbag, and he thought irritably that she'd awakened him merely to let him know she was going out when a bloody note would have done the job just as well. But her expression said she had information to impart and as he took note that drops of water hung upon her mack, he realised that she was returning to the house from wherever she'd been earlier that morning.

She said, 'You've not gone to sleep. Thank God. Darling, I hate to ask, but I need you. I can't cope with doing this alone.'

He tried to process this information. 'What's happened, pet?'

She sat on the edge of the bed. 'They're at Clare's. I drove by her house and there was a car in the driveway in addition to Clare's Jetta, and it must be theirs. They can't have finished up, here in Dorset. They'll be at her house, and . . . I must go there to collect the rest of my belongings, but I can't face them alone, Alastair. The police. I know I'm being impossible, but after having them here questioning me as if I might have actually done something . . . as if it were truly possible . . . Will you take me there?'

'If I c'n have just a few hours' kip . . . ?'

Her face altered, a wound coming upon it although he couldn't have named the source of it until she spoke. 'Is it that . . . You aren't thinking that I would have . . . that I could ever have . . . But you *are* starting to doubt me, aren't you. The police coming all this way from London, with me the person they wish to talk to . . .' She rose from the bed.

He said, 'Caro, I think nothing like nothing. I jus' need an hour or two's kip and they're not going anywhere if they're at Clare's house, eh? At least not for a while. You got her card, yes? She gave it you, yes? You just ring her and let her know we'll be by to collect your clobber and you tell her she's meant to wait there till—'

'You'd do it for her,' she said abruptly. 'I understand. Funny thing is, I don't really blame you. I won't ask again.' And she left him watching the door that she'd closed behind her.

He lay there staring at the door's white panels for a good half hour after that, knowing that what Caroline said was true. He would have risen had Sharon been making the request of him. And as things developed, he could have risen for Caroline and accompanied her up to Clare's house since once she left him he wasn't able to return to sleep.

What was keeping him awake was more than just the disruption from his wife, though. It was the wondering. His mind was going at fifty miles per, and it headed in one direction, and then another like a vehicle he was trying to control but one that was already self-determined. No matter where it headed and why it headed there, it had a destination called Sharon Halsey.

'I feel trapped,' was how he'd explained it to her, speaking gruffly into her soft hair. 'It's that I don't know *how* I'm ever to—'

She'd shushed him mildly. 'Alastair, nothing has to be decided just now. Or even next week or next month. At the moment, just to have this new thing between us, isn't it enough?'

No, he thought. So he reached for his mobile on the bedside table and he rang her.

She was on her way to the shop in Bridport, she told him. She'd pulled into a lay-by to take his call. The sound of her voice brought a groan to his lips, rising from his groin and escaping him before he could stop it. She asked him what was wrong.

'I'm wanting you,' he replied. 'Very blokey of me but there you have it.' He felt the blood coursing down his body, felt the throb of it, tried to stop himself from groaning again.

'You have me,' she said. 'There's no one else I'm seeing. To be honest, I've not had a man in that way in a good many years. I'd thought I lost the touch. I've not felt beautiful in so long a time, and feeling beautiful makes a woman want to do . . . to please . . .' She laughed. 'Good heavens, I can't believe I'm speaking this way.'

'You, not beautiful?' was his reply. 'Look at me if you want to see someone who's no great shakes in the looks department. There's a gulf between us, Shar, and you made a bridge right across it.' He slid his hand down to feel his hardness. He closed his fingers, tightened the grip, felt the throbbing. He said, 'I want to be free for you.'

'Let's not talk of that,' she said. 'I'm not going to find someone else. I don't want someone else. No worries, all right? I'll never hold things over your head.'

'"Things"?'

'I'll never say that I'm finished with you 'less you do something to . . . *you* know. I do want us to be together, though. But I c'n see how difficult everything is for you just now. Really, Alastair. I don't like to say more than that.'

'You're my angel,' he whispered.

She chuckled. 'Hardly that. I just don't want us chipping away at each other by comparing what we have to anything else. Do you understand what I mean?'

He didn't, really, because he couldn't see how one *wouldn't* compare in his situation. For there was where he was, with whom he was, and how they were together. And then there was the promise of what could be. How could one ever not put those two situations into the balance scale and evaluate them?

He said to her, 'I love your voice, Shar.'

'That's a silly thing to say, but it's for you, all the same.'

'C'n you talk to me to sleep, then? I can't have you here, but I c'n have your voice. C'n you talk to me till I drift off? I'd drive to Bridport directly, you know, just to put eyes on you. Just to look at you like I did in the moonlight that night. But now . . . could you talk me to sleep?'

''Course I can,' Sharon told him.

*Shaftesbury*
*Dorset*

'Got a Hermione here, Barb,' Nkata said. 'Tha's one of the names in the diary, innit?'

The washing up finished, they were back at the dining table, comparing the text messages on Clare Abbott's phone to her diary. Barbara confirmed that Hermione was one of the names listed and Nkata read the messages aloud.

From Hermione to Clare: *Need to talk. Another bit from tea with L yesterday. You'll be interested.*

From Clare in return: *Wine 2nite?*

From Hermione back: *Mitre. 8:00?* to which Clare agreed.

Barbara noted that the time was different from the time listed for Hermione in her diary, as was the date as things turned out. So Clare had spoken to the woman more than once. *Another bit* and *you'll be interested* suggested that Hermione had information for her. Gossip, perhaps? Something more significant?

Barbara went to Clare's office to get on with things as Nkata continued with the many texts contained on the feminist's smartphone. They'd agreed not yet to ring anyone whose name they came across. They'd track everyone down physically when the time came as some of them had to be local; the rest they'd hand over to Lynley to see about in London. No sense in giving them advance warning that the police wished to speak with them, they reckoned.

Barbara sat at Clare's desk. In its centre drawer, she found the kinds of office supplies she expected: pens, pencils, Post-it pads, a stapler, a ruler, a package of Blu Tack. She also found something that was unexpected: ten packets of condoms. One had been opened and lay spread out inside the drawer as if for some kind of inspection.

She set these to one side and went on to the side drawers of the desk. There were three: two shallow and one deep, of the type suitable for filing folders. The shallow drawers held stationery, business cards, a dead-as-a-doornail digital recorder, wax tapers, a torch, a calculator, a cheque book, a calendar from the National Trust, a box of staples, another of paperclips, and the previous year's diary. The deeper drawer was locked.

Barbara muttered, looked in the three unlocked drawers for a key, found nothing, and went in search of the keys to Clare's house, which they'd used to admit themselves into the place on the previous evening. She found them next to the grocery bags where Winston had left them, and aside from two Banham keys – one of which was for the house she was standing in – and a key to Clare's car, still in the driveway, there was another much smaller key, which Barbara hoped would fit into the desk drawer's lock.

It did. She slid the drawer open to see within a neat collection of manila folders, arranged in sets within green hanging files. The first set had tabs that named their contents as life insurance, car insurance, house insurance, bank statements, investments, all fairly standard stuff. Behind these were a group pertaining to Caroline Goldacre's employment, and Barbara removed these from the drawer and gave them a look.

They comprised records of the woman's mileage for which she was paid, along with tax documents related to her employment. They also comprised what appeared to be a set of demands with which she'd presented Clare Abbott at the end of her first and then her second year of employment. Increased pay, increased holiday time, private medical insurance, two personal emergency days every month, additional pay for what she referred to as 'going beyond the call of duty' but otherwise left undefined. Next to most of these demands, someone – presumably Clare – had written either *OK* or *Rubbish*. Next to 'going beyond the call of duty', she had applied a heavy black exclamation point and the sketch of a stick figure sicking up into a toilet.

Barbara placed these folders on the corner of the desk and dug back into the drawer to find a set bearing on their tabs the Christian names of two men followed by what she reckoned was the initial of their surnames: Bob T and John S. Inside these two folders were three sheets of paper apiece, appearing to comprise a questionnaire, and the handwriting on each was the same as the writing on the folders' tabs, which Barbara again assumed to be Clare's. So Clare had . . . interviewed them? Barbara wondered. She read through the questions, and the penny dropped. These were two anonymous internet adultery blokes whom Clare had somehow unearthed.

At the farthest reach of the drawer, a final hanging folder bore no identification. Barbara gave a look inside and found no documents. Rather a very small manila envelope comprised the sole contents, and she removed this. It was unsealed, merely paperclipped closed, so she removed the paperclip and upended the envelope into her palm. A small key fell out.

Barbara flipped the key back and forth, considering the possibilities. The fact that the key had been locked away suggested that the contents of whatever the key unlocked had to be important. She wondered if banks still had safe deposit boxes, but she abandoned this wondering when she realised that the key had no identifying number engraved upon it and surely a safe deposit box would have a number, wouldn't it?

There were four filing cabinets in the room, and she considered these, only to note that none of them had locks, so they were nonstarters. She thought about a gym locker somewhere in town or a padlocked chest in the loft or cellar. Either was a possibility and as she was in Clare Abbott's house, she would have a look round for something safely locked. At least that was a place to start.

She was on her way to the stairs to see if the house even had a loft when Nkata called to her from the dining room. He was still beavering away at Clare's mobile and he said to her, 'The FG in her diary, Barb?' as he looked up. She saw that he was still wearing his running clothes, but he'd removed the hooded sweatshirt to reveal a blindingly white T-shirt beneath it, which did not even have the courtesy to be marred by the sweat of his earlier run.

'Yeah?'

'I reckon it's Francis Goldacre.' He held up the phone. 'She's got him in here: name, address, mobile. She's also got five calls going to and coming from him.' He rose, going into the kitchen from where Barbara heard him say, 'Now why d'you expect she talked to Francis Goldacre?'

'That's a bloody good question,' Barbara replied.

Lynley was surprised at the humble nature of Francis Goldacre's home. He knew that Goldacre did an impressive amount of charity work as a surgeon. Prior to leaving Victoria Street to speak with the man, he'd done his homework. But he'd also assumed that in addition to charity work, the surgeon would have an income that rose from the kind of elective surgeries upon women always delicately referred to as 'having a bit of work done'. So he'd had it in mind that a plastic surgeon would be likely to showcase his successful career through the purchase of a pricey London property.

This was not the case. Instead of a mansion in Hampstead, Highgate, or Holland Park, he lived in an ordinary semi-detached in a street of similar residences. It was tree-lined and at this time of year the leaves were glorious, but that was the extent of its beauties.

Barbara Havers had rung Lynley shortly after his arrival in Victoria Street. She'd been hot on the topic of Francis Goldacre and some conversations that she believed Clare Abbott had had with him. Someone needed to speak with the man, she declared. As she and Nkata were in Shaftesbury and as Lynley and Francis Goldacre – one assumed – were in London, could he . . . ?

Lynley felt cautious. Barbara sounded excited and he well knew that her enthusiasm sometimes got the better of her common sense. But as this represented the very first time since her unauthorised trip to Italy that she'd actually offered an idea that wasn't carefully laundered in advance, he agreed to make the journey to Brondesbury Park where – according to Winston's research on the internet – he would find Francis Goldacre's home. His surgery was in central London in Hinde Street, not far from Manchester Square, if that was helpful, Nkata had said.

Lynley had rung Goldacre in advance. The surgeon, he

discovered, was preparing for a working trip to India on the following day, so he was at home. He voiced surprise that a Scotland Yard detective wished to speak with him, but as he would be at his residence for the entire day, Lynley was welcome to come along if he wished to do so. Thus Lynley found himself ringing the front bell at ten forty-five that morning.

Goldacre answered, a beaky-faced man in his fifties whose seriously cratered face indicated a score of skin cancers having been removed, leaving his complexion a collection of divots. Lynley's first thought as they introduced themselves to each other was that as a plastic surgeon Goldacre would have had many resources to improve his appearance. He had to wonder why the surgeon had not done so.

Goldacre appeared to read his mind because he shrugged in an affable fashion. He ran his hand back over his skull to smooth thin hair of a faded straw colour that suggested it had once been ginger and he said, 'I suppose I could ask you as well.'

'What?' Lynley stepped into the house's entry, a small square anteroom ambitiously tiled on floor and halfway up the walls by a Victorian craftsman who knew his trade. One side of this contained a battered coat rack with a collection of similarly battered umbrellas and wellies placed beneath it.

'Why you haven't had that scar on your upper lip seen to,' Goldacre said. 'It wouldn't be difficult whereas for me . . .' He gestured to his face. 'It would take some doing, and I don't have the time or the inclination.'

'Ah,' Lynley said. In reference to his scar, he went on with, 'It reminds me of what an idiot I was at sixteen. If I had some sort of repair, I might forget.'

'Interesting point. Do come in, Inspector.'

Through the entry and into the body of the house, a sitting room lay to the left and a stairway climbed to a second floor directly in front of them. Goldacre indicated the sitting room, and once inside offered food and drink. Lynley accepted a coffee and Goldacre was about to leave him in order to sort this out when an exotically beautiful Asian woman came into the room to tell the surgeon she was heading out to work. She was dressed as a medical person, and Goldacre kissed her fondly in farewell before introducing her as his wife, Sumalee.

She was many years younger than the plastic surgeon, and she comprised what Lynley wryly thought of as every white woman's nightmare: some five feet four inches tall, shapely where she needed to be shapely, glossy hair falling to her waist, perfect olive skin, large dark almond eyes, lovely white teeth, and full unpainted lips. It happened that she was a surgical nurse, he discovered, and Francis Goldacre had met her in Phuket when he'd gone there on one of his charity missions.

Although she was heading out for the hospital, she wouldn't be assisting in the operating theatre today. Her arm was in a cast although a certain griminess suggested she'd worn it for some weeks. 'Three days more,' she told Lynley when she caught him glancing at the arm. 'I had a rather bad fall.'

'You were pushed,' her husband said. And then to Lynley, 'We had an unfortunate run-in with my elder son at a memorial service for his brother. We'd been invited by William's partner – a girl called Lily Foster – but we'd no clue the invitation was a trick played on my former wife. So we turned up and got into it with Charlie and this –' he touched the cast on Sumalee's arm – 'was the unfortunate result.'

'Charlie didn't intend to hurt me,' Sumalee said mildly to her husband. 'He wanted to get me out of the way of what was going on.'

Goldacre said to Lynley, 'What was going on was a brawl. Our appearance at the memorial did not go down well.'

'That's in the past now,' Sumalee said. 'And the arm is healing.' Then, 'I must be off, Francis. Have you finished your packing? Do you have everything?'

'I'll be getting to it all. Don't be a mother hen.'

She smiled, raised her eyebrows at Lynley, and said, 'He'll forget his passport if I don't check.'

They made their farewells to each other, which seemed

authentically fond on both their parts and not the perfunctory peck of an indifferent couple. When Sumalee then left them, Lynley asked the logical question. Had they been married long?

'Twelve years,' Goldacre told him.

'Have you children?'

'She isn't able, I'm afraid.'

'Ah. I'm sorry.'

Goldacre went to a photo on a table next to the room's small fireplace. He handed it over to Lynley. It depicted a very large Thai family group: paterfamilias, mother, and eleven children. Lynley saw a much younger Sumalee among them, perhaps seventeen years old and as beautiful then as she was now. Goldacre said, 'She fell pregnant twice when she was a teenager – once at fifteen and once at seventeen. This was at the hands of the same man each time, her uncle. She wouldn't name him, so her father required her to have abortions. The second one was accompanied by a tubal ligation. Botched, unfortunately, and irreversible.'

Lynley handed the photo back to Goldacre. 'I'm terribly sorry.'

'What savagery men do,' was Goldacre's only comment.

'Is that why Clare Abbott had an appointment with you? She interviewed you, didn't she? As a feminist, I expect she would have been outraged by your wife's story.'

'I hope anyone would be outraged by it,' Francis declared. 'But Sumalee never came up between us. Clare wanted to speak about my first wife.'

'Caroline.'

'Yes.' He studied Lynley for a moment during which he appeared to be evaluating for the first time the various reasons a detective had shown up on his doorstep. He said, 'Let me get you that coffee, Inspector Lynley,' and he went off to do so.

Lynley took the time to look at the other photos in the room, some on the fireplace mantle, others on tables. Among them he saw pictures of Francis with two young boys – and then young men – who were, presumably, his sons. One was fair like Francis and the other dark. The fair one had Goldacre's height and his aquiline features. The other was short, with hair always worn long no matter his age or the style at the time. It was fashioned in a pageboy vaguely reminiscent of Richard the Third's portrait, a cut that achieved nothing to enhance his features. The hairstyle and the contrast between the brothers put Lynley in mind of that winter of discontent and of the difference between those two Plantagenets.

When Goldacre returned, he carried a plastic tray holding a cafetière, two mugs, sugar, and milk. He indicated a sagging sofa in front of which a narrow table held newspapers in various stages of being read, along with magazines, and unopened post. Without ceremony Goldacre set the tray on top of it all. He sat and Lynley joined him. They faced an unlit fire.

'Did Clare Abbott give you a reason for wanting to talk to you about your former wife?' Lynley asked.

Goldacre stirred the brew he'd concocted, pushed the plunger on the cafetière, poured them both a cup. He didn't answer the question, rather saying, 'I saw in the paper that she passed away unexpectedly. Does this –' he indicated Lynley's presence in his house with a gesture that took in both Lynley and the room itself – 'have anything to do with her death?'

'You ask that because . . . ?'

'Because after your saying that you'd come to see me about Caroline, I can come up with no other reason for this interview.'

'Clare Abbott was murdered,' Lynley told him.

Goldacre had been in the process of adding milk to his coffee, but he stopped with the jug in midair and the single remark of, 'Good Lord.' Then he set the jug down and went on with, 'I'd no idea. In the papers, there was no mention of anything . . .'

'A second autopsy was performed. The first didn't catch the cause of death accurately. It's become necessary to sort the matter out. Do you know that your former wife was with her?'

'When she died? I didn't know. You aren't assuming Caroline harmed her, I hope.' Goldacre went back at this point to ministering to his coffee, and he seemed deeply thoughtful. He finished up with the milk and sugar and said, 'Inspector, sometimes the woman's mad as a hatter. I can't lie and say I wasn't thoroughly delighted to see the last of her – as much as anyone can ever see the last of a woman with whom one has had children – but even so, it doesn't seem remotely possible that she could be a murderer.'

'We're not assuming anything at the moment,' Lynley told him. 'While Caroline was in the next room when Clare Abbott died and while she discovered the body the following morning, that's all we know. Since Clare was her employer and since Caroline didn't apparently benefit from her death, it's difficult to see why she might have killed her. But once your name came up as someone Clare had spoken to in advance of her death . . . you can see our interest, I expect.'

'I hope you're not thinking I might have had something to do with her murder.'

Lynley smiled thinly and took up his own coffee. 'Tell me about her visit to you.'

Goldacre looked reflective, coffee mug in hand. 'At first I thought she wanted a consultation about surgery. I reckoned she knew I was a plastic surgeon and was perhaps thinking of having some work done. I don't do that sort of thing, but she wouldn't have known that, so when she rang me, I gave her my specifics to set her straight. She had quite a laugh at the idea that she would have surgery. Since she was a feminist writer, I then thought she was creating a piece about the kinds of surgeries women expose themselves to, trying to look youthful into their eighties. That seemed right up her alley. But she told me it was on another matter altogether and would I agree to meet her?'

'She didn't tell you the purpose of the meeting?'

'She didn't.' He took a sip of coffee and put the mug down on a magazine whose cover featured before and after photos of children with cleft palates. 'What she did tell me – and I thought this rather odd – was that she wanted to meet me on "neutral ground".'

'What did she mean by that?'

'Exactly what I asked her. She merely told me she didn't want anything to influence her, my home or my surgery might colour her conclusions. I asked her then what this was all about, and she told me it was part of a study she was engaging in as she sorted out what kind of book she intended to write next.'

'You remember that quite well.'

He shrugged. 'It's to do with how things turned out. I agreed to meet her and we had lunch at the Wallace Collection. It's not far from my surgery and it seemed quite neutral enough.'

'And your conversation?'

'She wanted to talk about my marriage to Caroline. Frankly, I was more than a little irritated by this, and I told her so. I reckoned she'd got me to lunch on false pretences and I wasn't happy about that. As it happened, the conversation was a bit of he said/she said although I didn't know at first. Clare told me afterwards.'

'Your story of the marriage differed from your former wife's?'

'Evidently, over time, Caroline had done some talking to Clare about our marriage. The problem is that she's always had trouble with the truth.'

All things about Clare Abbott's death considered, Lynley thought, this was a rather telling point. He said, 'In what way?'

Goldacre took up his coffee again. 'I don't mean to speak ill of her, but marriage to Caroline was rather like a sojourn in a circle of the Inferno, and apparently she'd told Clare a lorryful of rubbish about it all: myself caught between untreated clinical depression – God knows where she came up with that – and what she referred to as "sexual inertia", by which I reckon she meant I didn't perform as often as she liked; herself heroically coping with my periods of depressed inactivity, with my lack of interest in her and the boys . . . But the truth was rather different, as I explained to Clare.'

'What was it, exactly?'

'That even on a good day, Caroline could drive any man directly into a monastery, Inspector. Essentially, she was very unhappy that my career took the turn that it did.'

'I'm not sure I understand.'

'We married shortly after I completed my training. She'd assumed that I'd be bringing in buckets of cash doing elective surgeries. She'd no clue that I'd never intended to use my skills operating upon celebrities, trophy wives, and wealthy widows. Once I qualified, I chose to work with birth defects, burn victims, terrorist victims, wounded soldiers, that sort of thing. I spent – and still do – a considerable amount of time away from home in other countries, and that didn't help the marriage, as you can imagine. And then, of course, there was the matter of William. Clare asked especially about him because of his suicide and Caroline's apparent belief that it was down to me that he killed himself.'

'Why?' It was, Lynley thought, a most complicated picture of a marriage and family. Tolstoy, he decided and not for the first time, had been right.

Goldacre rose and went to a table beneath the room's bay window. From the plethora of photos arranged there, he selected one far at the back. He handed it to Lynley, who saw that the picture depicted the darker of his two sons with his Richard the Third haircut. While Lynley gazed at this and wondered what he was meant to be seeing, Goldacre rustled in the table's centre drawer and after a moment found another photo, this one a snapshot taken of an infant's head, his face turned in profile to the camera as he rested on his mother's shoulder. The baby, Lynley saw, had no ear, just a hole and a miserly flap of skin.

Goldacre said, 'Caroline wanted surgery for him directly. Days after he was born. She simply could not come to grips with the fact that it had to wait. Giving him surgery as an infant would require an infant sized ear and, as he grew, another ear after that, and another after that. I tried to explain this to her, but she wouldn't have my explanation and she carted the poor child all over London to other surgeons who told her the same thing. It was better to wait. This, unfortunately, made her so overprotective of the poor boy that she ended up making more of the deformity than he ever would have made of it himself. It became a case of constantly telling him he was fine, he was beautiful, he was talented, he was clever, he was whatever came into her mind. And of course, the boy knew that at least some of this wasn't true.'

'This led to your divorce?'

'Alastair MacKerron led to that. She left me for him, although she apparently told Clare that I left *her* for Sumalee. Truth told, I've always been grateful to poor Alastair for having taken Caroline off my hands. I did miss the boys. But over time, Caroline made it so difficult to see them and as I've always travelled so much for my work . . . Frankly, I allowed Alastair to take up the reins of fatherhood. I'm not proud of that. It's led to all sorts of difficulties with the boys. Well, with Charlie now that William is gone. We're not close. And he despises Sumalee.'

Lynley considered all this. A phone rang somewhere in the house, but Goldacre made no move to answer. After six double rings, a disembodied voice that was Sumalee's asked the caller to leave a message. No one did.

Lynley said, 'So all of this is what Clare wanted to talk to you about?'

'That and what she referred to as Caroline's "relationship with the truth". Evidently, she'd caught her out in a number of lies.'

'Was her job in jeopardy?'

'I suppose it could be argued that having a liar working for one is disconcerting, so Clare may have been looking for a way to sack her, but she didn't indicate that. Just that she wanted to talk about Caroline and her relationship with the truth as she'd told Clare some . . .' He smiled as he looked for the word he wanted. 'What do children say? Whoppers?'

'Beyond your marriage, you mean?'

'It seems over time she gave Clare quite an earful about her entire life, but in the way of pathological liars, she began to contradict herself. Clare wanted to check with someone to learn if there was any truth in what Caroline was claiming.'

'You could have lied to Clare as well,' Lynley pointed out.

'Indeed I could have done. So I suggested she speak with Caroline's mum and with other people – women in particular – who've had the experience of knowing her.'

'But not with men?'

Goldacre laughed ruefully. 'Inspector, Caroline has always been perfectly capable of charming the trousers off any man. I can attest to that and I expect Alastair MacKerron can as well.'

*Shaftesbury*
*Dorset*

'So he suggested that Clare arrange to speak with a woman called Mercedes Garza.' Lynley's voice broke up for a moment. He was on his mobile, Barbara reckoned. He said, 'Hang on, I've got to . . .' And then after a moment, 'Sorry. I was wrestling with my car keys. Mercedes Garza is Caroline Goldacre's mother. Have you any indication that Clare Abbott interviewed her?'

MG, Barbara thought. The initials were there in Clare's diary. She told him this.

The front bell rang assertively, three times in quick succession. Barbara walked to the window and looked out on a rainy day. On the front step stood Caroline Goldacre.

'She's here,' she told Lynley.

'Caroline Goldacre?'

'Large as life with a cardboard box on her hip.'

'Bringing you something of Clare Abbott's?'

'Haven't a clue. What're you onto next?'

'Mercedes Garza.'

'Anything from SO7 yet?'

'Not a whisper.'

Outside, Barbara saw that Caroline Goldacre had clocked her through the window. Her eyes narrowed and she gestured to the cardboard box. She rang the bell another time, more insistently, and she turned to the door as Winston opened it. Barbara listened to the ensuing conversation with one ear as Lynley spoke into her other ear.

''Fraid not, Missus Goldacre,' came from Winston.

'Whyever not?' from Caroline Goldacre. 'Look here, Sergeant . . . What was your name? This is ridiculous.'

Her voice grew louder and from the window Barbara saw her elbow her way into the house as Nkata said, 'A police investigation means—'

'Really, my personal effects have *no* bearing on a police investigation. Do step out of my way.'

'Can't do that.'

'Am I going to have to ring your . . . your superiors or whatever they are?'

'. . . about Lily Foster,' Lynley was saying.

'Say what, sir?' Barbara asked him. 'C'n you hang on? Something's going on with Winnie and the Goldacre woman.'

Mobile in hand, Barbara left Clare's office and went out into the entry area of the house where Winston had managed to block Caroline Goldacre's access. They were doing a bizarre dance together, consisting of you-step-one-way and I-follow your lead. Winnie obviously did not want to put his hands on the woman.

Barbara said, 'You can't be here, Ms Goldacre.'

'I've come for my property,' Caroline said. 'I have no intention of stealing one of Clare's baubles if that's what you're

worried about. This . . . this *policeman* here is preventing me
from—'

'Like he's supposed to do,' Barbara said.

'I want to speak with whoever is in charge,' Caroline said.

Barbara extended her mobile to the woman. 'Have a go,
then. He's called DI Lynley.'

She turned on her heel and went back to the office. Lily
Foster, she was thinking. Lynley said something about a Lily
Foster. She looked at Clare's diary and there it was not long
before Clare's trip to Cambridge: LF and a date and a time.

While Caroline was speaking to Lynley – who, Barbara
could only pray, was using the Voice upon her – Barbara went
back to the files displaying the Christian names and the surname
initials of the two men. It was time to take a deeper look at
these, and she opened the first of them to the questionnaire.
She began to read as Caroline Goldacre's arguing voice came
from the other room.

In short order, Barbara understood that Clare Abbott had
indeed been speaking to married men about assignations they'd
been having with women met over the internet, and for their
part, the men appeared to have been quite frank. The how,
when, where, and why of it all revealed that for Bob T, it was
'for laughs', 'for a bit of fun', and 'to get away from the ball
and chain', and for John S it was 'because the wife won't do
what these birds're willing to' and 'because I'm not getting
enough at home' and 'because how many bloody headaches can
one woman have in a month.' Both men indicated that having
kids had put paid to romance, and for these reasons they had
logged onto two different web sites on which married individuals
sought out other married individuals for no-questions-asked sex
in hotels, in the open air, in the back of cars, in the ladies' toilet
of a Dorchester pub, in a relative's house, in a garden shed, in
a holiday caravan and – in one case – in a pew at St Peter's
Church here in Shaftesbury.

Caroline Goldacre came into the room. Stiffly, she handed
the mobile to Barbara. She said, 'I could have come earlier.

I could have come directly Clare died and cleared out my belongings.'

'And you didn't because . . . ?' Barbara said.

'I assumed that I would be needed to continue my work here till everything regarding Clare's career and her death was handled.'

Barbara nodded. 'Good of you, that.' And then into the mobile, 'Sir?'

Lynley's smooth baritone replied with, 'I suggested a court order although I cautioned her that it's not likely she'd be granted one in the midst of a police investigation inside the very premises she wishes to invade.'

'Used that lingo, did we?' Barbara asked. 'That lovely sentence structure of yours and all the rest?'

'I do what I can. As to this Lily Foster . . .' He went on to explain that this individual had played a trick upon Caroline concerning a memorial service dedicated to her dead son William. 'You might want to inquire about that,' he said.

They rang off and Barbara turned to Caroline Goldacre, saying, 'One Lily Foster, Ms Goldacre. Can you enlighten me about her?'

*Heston*
*Middlesex*

Mercedes Garza lived not far from the magnificent neoclassical mansion of Osterley Park which had once, during the time that Robert Adam transformed it from a redbrick Tudor dwelling of the sixteenth century to the grand palace it became, rested deep in the countryside. Now it lay in the flight path of Heathrow Airport, and around its spacious grounds the suburbs of London consumed the once open land. The Garza home was in one of these suburbs not far from the park. It sat across the street from a collection of allotments in a state of autumnal disrepair.

From her home, Lynley had discovered, Mercedes Garza ran a quite successful house cleaning business. Calling it The Cleaning Queens, she had over the years built her clientele to such an extent that she now employed fifty-seven individuals to do the work.

When Lynley arrived, he found Mercedes doing the monthly billing. With fifty-seven people working two or three to a house, some of them doing two houses a day . . . There was a lot of maths to contend with. But Mercedes appeared up to the challenge, he discovered, as she sat at her computer with a cigarette hanging out of her mouth and a plume of its smoke snaking into the air.

She put her work aside after a member of her cleaning team answered the door and led him into her sitting room/office. They had to dodge a bucket and mop that stood in the corridor leading to the back of the house. The same cleaner who'd come to the door was seeing to the place's weekly scrubbing, it appeared.

Mercedes slapped her hands on her desk and rose to greet him. Lynley knew from speaking to Francis that the woman was from Colombia and sixty-eight years old, but although he might have guessed the former – or at least somewhere in South or Central America – he wouldn't have known the latter. It wasn't so much that she didn't look her age, but rather it was her overall devil-may-care appearance. She dressed in an aggressively ageless manner out of line with her years: an orange cowl-necked tunic hung over purple leggings and on her feet were beautifully polished knee-high brown boots of the type worn by officers during World War One. Her spectacles frames were lime green and the headscarf holding back black-coffee hair threaded with grey was bright yellow. Somehow, it all worked upon her. Lynley reckoned it was the woman's confidence, which she appeared to have by the bucketful.

She shook his hand firmly. She talked past the cigarette bobbing between her lips. 'Francis, he rings me when you leave.' She spoke rough English with a heavy accent. 'You don't to think that means nothing. Just courtesy on his part. You want coffee? Tea? Water?' She smiled. 'Or you like whisky?' She blew cigarette smoke into the air. She stubbed the cigarette out in the perfect saucer of a Georgian pattern that Lynley recognised from his Cornwall home. He thought of his fore-bears spinning in their graves at such a misuse of fine china.

He demurred on all offers of refreshment as Mercedes lit another cigarette. She told him to sit and he took a place in the bay window. Then, she did not sit herself, and he felt an immediate discomfort associated with his meticulous upbringing. When he started to rise, she said, 'Stay. I sit all day and my piles act up. I give them a break.' She laughed at his expression. 'Didn't expect me to say that, *sí*? People need to be real. *Ahora.* What do I do for you, Inspector? Not wanting your house cleaned, I expect. Since you see Francis and now you come here, it's probably about Carolina, I think. She's the only thing we have in common, me and Francis.'

'There're problems between you?'

'Me and Francis? Not a whit, as you Brits say.' She took off her glasses and went to the desk, where she excavated for a cleaning rag. She used this upon the lenses vigorously. '*Verdad*? I couldn't work out why he married her. 'Course, when she tells me she is two months pregnant, it all gets clear.'

'Did you speak to Clare Abbott about her by any chance?'

Mercedes nodded. She flicked ash into the room's small fireplace, took another deep drag and spoke through the smoke. 'We don't see each other in years, so at first I can't understand why this woman wants to talk to me. We were . . . Carolina and me . . . oh, I forget the word sometimes . . . can you help? We are not talking to each other?'

'You were estranged?' Lynley asked,

'Yes, is it. We don't see each other p'rhaps . . . ten years? No, more. Back then, I ask her . . . no, I tell her . . . I am at my limit with her. I have other children, see, and I ask her to stay away from all of us till she can control what she says.'

'To the other children? About the other children?'

Mercedes used one hand to massage the small of her back and then made an adjustment to her yellow headscarf. 'I get tired of being accused of . . . how do you say this word? . . . *mal*-something. Bad behaviours, this is.'

'Malefactions.'

'These are acts of cruelty she says I have to done to her life. I bring her to London, you see, when she has two years and what she wants to believe is that back in Colombia she would be happy with my mother.' Mercedes chuckled past her cigarette. 'My mother? She does a nice thing for Carolina one time. She gives her a kitten. And 'course, we can't bring this animal to England when we come. The rabies, you know. And the aeroplane. But Carolina, she dwells on this and makes it something big in her mind. It's all very stupid because – this I tell you in honesty – I would be happy to leave Carolina with my mother if it was possible. To be free and twenty-one years in London? How nice that would be, eh? But my mama tells me that Carolina is my "little consequence" and daily I must be reminded of my sin.' Mercedes made an adjustment to an ornament on the fireplace mantel, a figurine of a woman in a bathing costume of the 1930s. There was a collection of them, all in different costumes and in various poses. She admired them for a moment. 'Catholics,' she said, more to herself than to him. 'Purgatory, hell, heaven, and so on. We live in the past. To stay in present, this is impossible. You are a Catholic, Inspector?'

'I'm not.'

'You are lucky. Me, I still try to recover from being Catholic. My sins, you see.'

'Having a child at nineteen? That was the sin?'

'I was not married to the papa.' Mercedes seemed to gauge him for a reaction to this, but as women having children outside of marriage was the rule and not the exception these days, there was hardly a point to his having one. 'This is a grave sin to my mother,' she said, 'and I pay for it those first two years with Carolina at home in Bogotá. Then I come here and I work and I am not afraid of hard work, ever. I clean other people's houses and because I have a head for business, I make a big success. Carolina has pretty dresses, she has a special toy now and then, she eats well, she sleeps in her own bedroom, she goes to school. This is not a bad life, I think.'

'I take it she thought otherwise?'

'I marry when she is sixteen, *si*? This she doesn't expect. I have three more children. This she also does not expect.' From her desk next to the computer she'd been working on when he'd entered the room, Mercedes fetched a framed photo. Twin boys, by the look of them, along with a girl. It was an older picture, the children in it long since grown. Mercedes proudly told him that one boy was a hedge fund manager, the other a solicitor, while the girl was a graduate student in nuclear physics. She was understandably delighted with their success. Carolina, she informed, was not.

'And your husband?' he asked her.

'A locksmith,' she told him. Like her, he had his own company. Like her, he'd begun with nothing. 'Not even an education,' she said. 'Neither of us. But we know how to work. I try to build this in Carolina . . . with determination you can achieve much, eh? But here, I fail.'

Mercedes went on, unbidden, to confirm much of what Francis Goldacre had told Lynley about how he and Caroline Garza had met, about their marriage, about her disappointment in her husband's choices regarding his career. She finished with, 'She decides to stay at home and raise their boys – Guillermo and Carlos – and this should work, no? But Guillermo is born with this . . . this bad ear and Carolina makes so much of it.' Mercedes shook her head. 'She is like . . . she swarms him. Like bees.'

'Is this why Clare Abbott wanted to speak with you? Was it about William?' Lynley told her of the memorial that Clare had arranged for Caroline Goldacre's son.

Mercedes said that, no, Clare Abbott wanted to talk only

about Carolina. She had a notepad with her, Mercedes revealed, along with a recording she'd made on her smartphone. This she played for Mercedes, and it bore the sound of Carolina talking about her childhood. Clare Abbott had explained to her that she'd made the recording on the sly. She'd said she didn't want Carolina to know she was recording her because she didn't want the fact of a recording 'to influence' what Carolina had to say. It seemed, from listening to it, that they were in a restaurant or perhaps just having a meal together because the sound of cutlery was clear.

'Did she tell you why she wanted you to hear the tape?' Lynley asked.

Having finished her cigarette, Mercedes lit another. She had a way of drawing in on the tobacco that put Lynley in mind of a young Lauren Bacall although there the similarity ended. She rested against the fireplace mantel and went on to explain. 'There is story Carolina is telling on the recording and Clare wishes me to hear it so that I make comments. And this story . . .' For the first time, Mercedes seemed affected by the tale she was telling. Her eyes grew cloudy. She was silent for a moment as out in the corridor the cleaner began to slosh water on the floor.

Lynley gave her a moment. When still she said nothing, he prompted her with, 'Anything regarding Clare Abbott might be helpful. Did Francis tell you she was murdered?'

She nodded. When she went on, her voice was altered. A heaviness had replaced the prior frankness. 'What she says on this recording . . . There are lies I know Carolina has said in the past about Torin, my husband. How he breaks her nose in a rage one night when she comes home late; how he only allows her clothes from Oxfam till she has money to buy her own; how he will have no holidays in this house . . . No Christmas, no Easter. These things I hear before, from what my other children tell me that Carolina has said.'

'But on this recording there's something else? Is that what you're saying?'

She went on in a lower tone, and Lynley had to lean forward to hear her. 'She has said things to Clare about what I am as a mother. I have many men during her childhood, she has said, and this is true. I admit. I have a liking for men and till I found Torin, I had them. But I do not leave her for a week with one of the cleaners each time I meet a new man so that he and I can . . . you know, in bed. But this is what she tells Clare. And she says I awaken her in the middle of the night to accuse her of this and of that . . . and I allow Torin . . . when I am heavy with the babies . . . to do what he wishes on her. This is what she has said.'

'On the recording,' Lynley clarified.

She shook her head. 'No, no,' she said. 'All of this she has reported over time to Clare Abbott but this recording, it is something more. And for me to say it . . .' Her eyes filled with tears. She coughed mightily. She did not appear to be a woman who allowed herself the luxury of weeping about things over which she had no power.

Lynley said to encourage her, 'Francis told me that Caroline sometimes has trouble with the truth.'

Mercedes gave a broken laugh. 'She tells Clare that in the dark of night when she is small I come into her room. I force her to . . . I use a Coca Cola bottle on her. This is what she says. She says she tells her teacher about this and then it is very bad for me.'

'This is on the recording Clare played for you?'

'It is on the recording. She is placed in care, she says, and there is an investigation. I am held in gaol for a time, but no one is willing to believe her story, she says, because she can't remember enough of the details, and they change – these details – this way and that. Because of this, I am released and she is returned to me and I seek my revenge when I am able.'

'How old did she say she was she when this occurred?'

'She has eight years, she says.'

'And are you saying that none of what she said to Clare was true?'

'I say this, *si*. None of it is true. I did nothing and she did not ever accuse me of nothing and there was no investigation and none of this happened. Everything, this is her fantasy. Clare Abbott, she has suspected this and that is why she has come to have me listen to the recording. She tells me she has already checked many records from the police so she has decided the story isn't true but what she wants to know is why.'

'Why she told the story in the first place?'

'And why she lies. And this is something I do not know, Inspector. Me, I would think it was an evil she had inherited if I did not have other children. But I do have other children and they are not liars. I would think, too, it was because I bring her to London and tear her from the granny who loved her, but this granny did not wish her to remain behind and made this very clear. So I have no real reason to offer and this is what I tell Clare Abbott. And what I think when we are finished together – Clare Abbott and me – is that she wants to have a collection of reasons to sack her and maybe lying is one of the reasons.'

Mercedes pulled some tissues from a pocket of her tunic and used them beneath her eyes. She stubbed her cigarette out and blew her nose as Lynley considered everything she had said. She was right, of course. Had she been accused of child abuse, questioned, and held in gaol for a period of time during an investigation, there would be records of this and they wouldn't be difficult to track down. One wondered, though, why Clare Abbott had gone to such trouble.

He said, 'You mentioned something about seeking revenge. You said Caroline reported that you got your revenge when you were able to do so, after she made her accusations.'

'She would think my revenge was the child.'

'What child?'

At fourteen, Mercedes said, Carolina had fallen pregnant. Her mother had insisted that the child – delivered when the girl was just fifteen – be placed for adoption, for what fifteen-year-old girl should be allowed to raise a child? 'I could have raised her on my own—'

'It was a daughter?'

'*Si*. And I could have raised it, but I was not willing and this is, I think, the sin she holds against me. This, I think, is what she means when she says I got my revenge.'

'The father? Who was it?'

Mercedes laughed shortly. 'She says it is a man I was seeing, but this turns out not to be the case. Then she says it is the father of one of her school friends. But as she lied before, I do not know if this is the man. Then I find a bank book, with much money put in, and this bank book, it is in her name.'

'The father was paying to support a child she no longer had?'

'No. She tells me very openly when I ask her: she is making him pay so that she does not tell his wife.'

'Blackmail,' Lynley said.

'She does not think of it that way. She says it is what she is owed for letting him do what he wanted on her. This I must stop, so I go to speak to this man. He denies everything – baby, blackmail, all of it – and I do not know what the truth really is, so what can I do ? There are tests, *si*, and I can force him to have them but the baby, she is with a new family, and Carolina cannot be trusted to hold to the same story from one day to the next. I think it is best to put it all behind us.'

'D'you know what happened to the baby?'

'The child is gone, the adoption is finished, and I pray she grows up well and is not afflicted like her mother with this lying thing.' Mercedes smiled, an infinitely sad expression. She said, 'I tell you this, Inspector. Had I not three other children to prove to myself I am not so evil a mother to have produced such a child as Carolina, I would have long ago strangled myself in my own bed.'

Caroline's child, Lynley learned, had gone to a Catholic charity for placement, and the records had been sealed. But many aspects of adoption had been altered by law, so it was no longer impossible to find one's biological parents or one's lost offspring. He wondered if Caroline Goldacre had done so or if the lost child had done so and if either was the case, what that might have to do – if anything – with Clare Abbott's death.

What remained was the name of the putative father of Caroline Goldacre's lost child. Mercedes was reluctant to give it and, as the man had denied everything anyway, there wasn't much point to having it unless the child herself could be found and the appropriate DNA tests could be given. And even then . . . Lynley simply wasn't sure what a man's identity and the whereabouts of an adult daughter had to do with anything, unless, of course, Caroline Goldacre was now interacting with them both or with one of them for some reason. So while Mercedes finally gave him the name of the putative father of the child – one Adam Sheridan – Lynley put him low on the list of people to speak with.

Outside, the grey sky had cleared and a milky blue had taken its place. Work was going on in the allotments across the street: several gardeners trundled wheelbarrows down the rows of autumn vegetables, collecting the heaped up and rotting remains of the summer harvest.

His mobile rang. He answered with his name, as usual.

A voice he did not recognise said, 'Inspector? Got something for you here.'

SO7, as things turned out, was reporting in at last.

*Shaftesbury*
*Dorset*

Despite her displeasure about being denied access to whatever of her belongings were squirrelled away in Clare Abbott's house, Caroline Goldacre seemed only too happy to give Barbara chapter and verse on Lily Foster. In very short order, Barbara learned that Lily Foster was not only the erstwhile partner of Caroline's deceased son Will, but she was also a resident of Shaftesbury who'd come to live there after Will's death, according to Caroline, in order to make the life of the young man's mother hell. The truth of this lay in the ASBO that was now attached to Lily Foster's presence in the town. The police – and Barbara did not need Caroline to inform her of this although the woman did so at some tedious length – did not hand out ASBOs unless there was a very good reason for them to do so. In the case of Lily Foster, there were apparently a half a score of reasons having to do with the young woman's persistent tormenting of Will Goldacre's mother. What lay beneath these behaviours was her apparent belief that Caroline was responsible for the young man's death.

On the other hand, Caroline declared Lily the responsible party since she'd called an end to her relationship with Will, casting him into a black depression from which only a removal from London and several months under the care of his mother and stepfather had saved him. 'But then back she came like a yearly visitation of influenza,' Caroline asserted. 'And then Will . . . He couldn't get over her. He *wouldn't* get over her. He was loyal and true while she . . .' She clenched her fist at her side, either to do metaphorical violence or to keep herself under control. Then she added, 'I did tell you what happened to my son.'

'Clare knew all this, did she?'

'What does Clare have to do with it?'

'Don't know, especially,' Barbara told her. 'But when someone dies unnaturally . . .' She let the rest hang there.

'Are you saying *Lily* might have . . . ? Why won't you tell me what actually *happened* to give Clare this heart thing, for the love of God?'

'Sorry but I've not been authorised.' Barbara brought forth Clare's engagement diary and asked Caroline to have a look at it. Could she identify anyone with whom Clare had an appointment? They had first names, initials, place names, and

surnames on various dates. Anything she could tell them would
be extremely helpful.

Barbara was at Clare's desk, and she slid the engagement
diary across it. Caroline, as Barbara had hoped, made short
work of the matter. Radley was Clare's dentist, she told her.
He was here in town and . . . She paused and an expression
of startled understanding flickered on her face. Did Sergeant
Havers think that perhaps a tooth filling had been cleverly
designed to hold something until, after a time of chewing, it
finally broke through to a substance that caused the victim
to have a heart attack? Very imaginative was what Barbara
thought. What she said was that everything was being looked
into. After all, when people were done away with by poisonous
injection through means of an umbrella in the streets of
London, anything could happen, eh? As to the rest of the
names . . . ?

Jenkins was her GP in London, Caroline revealed. Hermione,
Linne and Wallis were all power brokers in the Women's League
in Shaftesbury, a group who met and listened to guest speakers
and took up good causes and mentored young girls in need
of positive role models and raised money for charities. The
Women's League was, in fact, how Caroline and Clare had
met not long after William's death when Clare came to the
group as a speaker.

'I can't think why she had appointments with them,' Caroline
said in reference to Hermione, Linne, and Wallis. 'Perhaps
they'd taken up the task of persuading her to join, as she lived
here in town. She wouldn't have done, of course. Clare wasn't
a joiner. But to have her in the league would have meant a big
fish to that lot –' with a nod at the diary – 'and ready money
for them as well.'

'As individuals?'

'I'm not sure I understand what you mean.'

'I mean her money. Would they have been after that for
themselves or for the group?'

'I expect you'll have to ask them. But when someone has

money, don't you find that someone else is generally intent upon having some of it?'

That, Barbara thought, was an intriguing point with possibilities pointing to Caroline herself if it came down to it. She asked her about the entries in the diary that were indicated by initials only: MG, LF, FG. Did Caroline have any idea what these were about? She watched the other woman closely. Caroline surprised her with, 'Oddly enough, M and G are my mum's initials. L and F . . . Well, she did know about Lily Foster as I'd told her when Lily made her occasional nasty appearances in my life. This would be before the ASBO. But why Clare would want to meet with her . . . unless it was to have herself tattooed . . . ? As to the other . . . It's odd that she used only initials, isn't it? Could it be she was in a rush? Or . . . well, I expect she must've known these people well else she would have completely forgotten what she was meant to do with them or where she was meant to go.'

Barbara didn't miss the fact that FG – obviously the initials of her former husband – had been avoided or dismissed by the other woman. She said to her, 'What about the name Globus? Any clue there?'

'None whatsoever, I'm afraid.'

'And the place names?'

'Same thing. Sorry.'

Barbara studied her. Aside from the FG matter, she did seem to be forthright. Perhaps she was utterly clueless as to Clare Abbott's incursions into her personal world. But she also seemed like someone who could be an excellent liar, just as her former husband had told Lynley.

Considering what she'd seen in Rory Statham's flat as well as the questionnaires for Bob T and John S, Barbara asked Caroline about Clare's current writing project. Had she herself met either of the blokes whom Clare had interviewed for her next book?

'Next book? There was no book,' Caroline replied. 'Clare was working on nothing.'

'Anonymous adultery?' Barbara tried.

'I beg your pardon?'

'Knee tremblers between consenting adults with no questions asked and no strings attached? Sound familiar? She appears to have been interviewing blokes on this topic and there was what looked like a book proposal for it in Rory Statham's desk.'

Caroline shrugged. 'There may have been a proposal but I know nothing of that. And there's certainly no book. But if there *was* a proposal, it explains why Rory and I disagreed.'

Barbara frowned. 'Disagreed?'

'I tried to tell her there was no book being written. She'd brought up hiring someone to finish what Clare had started and I advised her not to bother as Clare wasn't writing anything. For all I know, Clare was reporting herself slaving away at a massive project she'd agreed to write, but if she was . . .' Caroline gestured round the room. 'Have a look round and see if you can find it.'

'So was Clare lying to Rory? Why?'

'I'm not sure. I do know she was under contract. I know she'd taken an advance for the next book. Perhaps she just didn't want to return the money. Would you?'

'Barb . . .' It was Winston at the door to Clare's study, her laptop in his hands. Caroline bristled at the sight of him and her expression said that she hadn't forgotten his attempts to keep her out of the house. 'Found summat in'eresting here,' he went on. 'Could be you need to have a look.'

*Fulham*
*London*

The elderly woman said, 'You've had a terrible time of it, darling, but you're on the mend,' and her voice was kind. There was a tenderness to it that suggested Rory ought to know her but the difficulty was that Rory did not. Nor did she know where she was or why she was in this place. There was a word for it – this place where she lay in bed with small tubes shooting what seemed to be oxygen into her nostrils and a clip on her index finger that was connected to a flex of some sort that itself led to a blipping monitor to one side of the bed – but Rory could not come up with that word.

The woman bent over her and smoothed her hair from her forehead with a shaking hand. Palsy? Rory wondered. Fear? Parkinson's? She said, 'You gave us a terrible fright. When the police came round . . . We thought at first that one of the neighbours had complained about our music, about that African drumming, especially. But they told us that you'd been brought to hospital and then—'

That was the word, Rory thought. Hospital. She was in hospital. Her chest was heavy and sore, her throat was so dry that she couldn't swallow, her vision was slightly blurred. Were these the reasons she'd been brought to this place?

'Here, Rory.' Another woman came into Rory's field of vision. She was younger, perhaps somewhere in her forties?, and in her hand was a plastic lidded tumbler with a straw emerging from it. She held it to Rory's lips which, Rory could feel, were badly chapped and ached as if in places they had entirely split open. 'Have some water,' the younger woman said. 'You must still be parched.'

*Still* suggested to Rory that she'd been conscious before this moment although she had no memory of it. Indeed, she had no memory of anything at all after arriving home from Shaftesbury and taking Arlo for his nightly stroll round the neighbourhood in order to—

Arlo! Rory heard nothing more. If she was here in this hospital bed, where was Arlo?

She struggled and failed to sit up. She said, 'Arlo!' although the word was little more than a croak as she tried to throw the thin blanket off her body.

The older woman said, 'Rory, you mustn't . . . She wants

the dog, Heather. We must find out what happened to the dog.'

Heather. Rory had a sister called Heather and this younger woman was she. Which meant that the older woman . . . 'Mum,' she said. 'Mummy. Arlo.'

A third woman entered the room. Her clothing identified her as a nurse. Heather said to her, 'She's wanting her dog. What's happened to her dog?'

'We don't allow dogs in here,' the nurse said sharply and then to Rory, 'Ms Statham, you must settle. You're quite ill and we can't have you—'

'I understand you can't have dogs here,' Heather cut in. 'But he's an assistance dog. She has paperwork for him. He's . . . Mum, can you remember his breed? Cuban? Cubanese? That can't be right.'

'Havana,' Rory murmured.

'What's she going on about?' This from the nurse.

'Havanese,' Heather said. 'He's a Havanese. He would have been brought in with her. He's been trained not to leave her, so he'll be in some distress. Please, can you ask someone about him at once? She's not going to settle if—'

'I certainly cannot. A dog would have been sent immediately to Battersea.'

Rory began to gasp. She made an attempt to swing her legs out of the bed. The nurse said something about ringing for the doctor, about Rory's mother and sister needing to leave the room at once, about many other things that Rory didn't catch because it was all coming back to her now. Clare was dead. She herself had fallen ill. She'd been dizzy and then not able to breathe and then nauseous and stumbling stumbling stumbling and Arlo was barking—

The door opened. It was not a white-coated doctor who came in, but a tall blond man in the company of Rory's returning mother, with her sister Heather following close on their heels.

The nurse snapped, 'Get that man out of here. You as well. I've *told* you to leave.'

'He knows about the dog,' Rory's mother said. 'And if you think she's going to settle without knowing what happened to her dog, you're wrong.'

The man came to the bedside and spoke quietly, his hand on Rory's shoulder as he said, 'Arlo's fine, Ms Statham. You've no cause to worry. I've taken him to a friend of mine. She's a vet, and she'll take quite good care of him until you're well. Fact is, she's taking him to work with her. At London Zoo. She tells me he fancies the lions.' He smiled. He had a bit of a crooked smile and a small scar above his lip. He was otherwise quite handsome and it came to her that his looks might well put people off. He said, 'I'm Thomas Lynley. I'm a colleague of Barbara Havers at New Scotland Yard.'

His presence had the oddest effect. His voice soothed her, and Rory felt her body ease.

'Barbara was the one who found you,' he said. 'I'm afraid she broke a window to get into your flat when she heard the dog. You had an appointment with her. Do you remember?'

This sounded familiar, but Rory wasn't sure. She knew it should be crystal clear – along with everything else that had happened to her – but it was not.

The door opened again. A white-coated woman strode into the room. She said, 'Thank you, Sister,' to the nurse and then to the rest of then, 'You're disturbing the patient, and there should be no more than one of you in this room anyway. Please leave at once.' She came to the bed and looked at the blipping machine which Rory took for a heart monitor. She was on a drip as well, and the woman – she would be the doctor, Rory reckoned – checked the bag hanging from its pole.

When no one stirred at her order, she said sharply, 'Do you lot not speak English? How did you get in here in the first place?'

Rory murmured, 'No. Mum . . .' and her mother came forward.

She said, 'Right here, darling. Heather is here as well. Heather . . . can you?'

Heather came forward and took Rory's hand. At her touch, more of what had happened to her came back to Rory. Heather's voice had been on her answer machine that night she'd arrived home from Shaftesbury. She'd walked Arlo. She'd got a few things from her car and gone up to her flat. She'd fed Arlo. She'd heated some soup and made some toast with butter and jam and she'd been so awfully tired. So she'd had a bath and gone directly to bed but she'd begun to feel so terribly ill: dizzy, nauseated, with pounding head and pounding heart . . .

Thomas Lynley was speaking to the white-coated woman. She was holding his identification in her hand and she was saying to him, 'Police? You're the last person we need in here. The mother may stay, but you two . . . ? Leave at once or I'll ring security.'

But Rory realised that the man had just said something to her about Barbara Havers and she said, 'Please,' although it took more strength that she would have expected. She forced out more words. 'What happened?'

'You were correct,' Thomas Lynley said to her, ignoring the doctor's protestation. 'Something caused Clare's heart attack and seizure. Neither was natural and the same thing – they think – happened to you.'

'You're going to have to leave,' the doctor said. 'That's quite enough for now.'

'I want . . . him . . . ,' Rory murmured. 'Stay.'

'You're not the person to be deciding that,' the doctor said.

'If you'll give me ten minutes with her, I'll be gone,' Lynley said. He appeared to be trying to read her name tag, but it looked to Rory as if he needed specs to do so. 'She's going to have some valuable information and it's going to pertain to whatever happened to her as well as someone else. Ten minutes,' he repeated. 'Doctor . . . ?'

'Bigelow,' she said, 'and I'll give you five.'

'Seven,' he said.

'This isn't a bloody negotiation.'

'Five, then.' He looked at Rory's mother and sister and added, 'If I might speak with her alone?'

They left with promises that they would be just outside of the room. The doctor left as well with her own promise that there would be hell to pay should Lynley take more than his allotted five minutes with the patient.

He drew a chair up to the bed, saying to Rory, 'Clare was poisoned with something called sodium azide. We believe you were as well. You were in Shaftesbury prior to returning to London, weren't you?' And when Rory nodded, 'Did anyone give you anything before you left? Something that you brought back with you?'

Rory thought about this, but she shook her head. No one had given her a thing.

'Could someone have got access to your flat while you were gone, then? Does anyone have an extra key? *Are* there extra keys?'

Rory thought about this. 'My desk . . . at work,' she said. 'But no mark on it. No one would know.' Her mind was largely on the idea of poison as she spoke, She raised her hand – God, it took an almighty effort – and laid it on her chest, saying, 'How?'

'It was in your toothpaste, Ms Statham. As most people do, I expect you cleaned your teeth before you went to bed, yes?' And when she nodded, 'There you have it. Since both of you were targeted, we're looking for connections, and there appear to be two of them. The first is Clare Abbott's recent book. You're her editor, aren't you?'

Rory nodded and murmured, 'But . . . a book? Only a book.'

'I don't disagree,' he said. 'Which takes us to the other connection, Caroline Goldacre. You were staying in Shaftesbury, weren't you? One or two nights, perhaps? In connection with a memorial service for Clare? Could Caroline Goldacre have got access to your belongings while you were there? To your toothpaste, specifically?'

Rory thought about this as best she could. But so little was available to her. Yet Caroline Goldacre had indeed hung about, maddeningly so and far more than was completely necessary. But why would she seek to harm Clare and then to harm Rory afterwards?

*Prevention* came into Rory's mind. But she had no idea where to apply it.

*Shaftesbury*
*Dorset*

Barbara saw in short order that Winston had found a website Clare Abbott had ostensibly accessed, and it was directly in line with the questionnaires in her desk. It was also in line with the book proposal that Barbara had found in Rory Statham's flat. This seemed to negate what Caroline was asserting about the absence of a new Clare Abbott project.

The website in question was called Just4Fun, and unsurprisingly one used it to find married adults willing to meet for extracurricular sex with no strings attached. It was a simple matter to find someone in your immediate vicinity with whom you might have a decent go, apparently, as the site was set up by region and within the region one could even choose the desired city or town, possibly with the wish to engage in the sexual act with a fellow supporter of one's football team, Barbara reckoned.

Pictures were not included, she saw, and for obvious reasons. One would hardly wish to advertise one's infidelity to a curious public who might stumble on the site for a bit of ooh-la-la. The chances of an associate or – worse – one's life partner *also* stumbling upon the site were far too great, she reckoned. One would wish to be at least moderately clever. She assumed no one used his or her real name, either.

Winston was standing in the doorway as she looked the site

over. He was casually blocking Caroline Goldacre's access route to liberty should she decide to seek it. She didn't seem bent on going anywhere, however. Instead she said, 'What's going on? Whose laptop is that? Clare's? What've you got onto? Her email? How did you do it?'

'She had it set so it 'members all her passwords to ever'thing,' Nkata told her. 'Dead thick to do that but people get lazy with their own PCs. Anyone with access could see wherever she'd been.'

Barbara looked up, as the penny certainly dropped with that remark. She was about to speak when Caroline said, 'Are you accusing *me* . . . ? What is it exactly that you're accusing me of, Sergeant?'

Barbara continued to click through the website, looking at the various adverts regarding who wanted what from whom and where and how. Some of them were bloody imaginative, she thought. It was sodding incredible what people could manage to do with their body parts and a decent amount of flexibility.

'. . . having sex round Dorset, Hampshire, and Somerset,' Nkata was saying to Caroline. 'How much 'bout this d' you know?'

Caroline appeared to be taking this in at some considerable length. She stared at Nkata, and, for that matter, so did Barbara as she realised what Nkata was declaring, having apparently done his homework with regard to Clare's use of the site. A vein beat energetically in Caroline's temple. She said, 'You seem to be telling me that Clare Abbott was meeting strangers for sex.'

'I'm telling you *someone* was trolling for men and meeting 'em,' Nkata corrected her. 'Clare Abbott? P'rhaps. But could be someone else was using this laptop to do it. 'Cause like I said 'bout her laptop . . . ? Passwords were on it so anyone could've spent some time having a look at summat she was 'xploring and then deciding . . .' He shrugged.

'What the sergeant is saying,' Barbara added, 'is that it

could've been Clare or it could've been Mother Goose on this site. Or . . . I s'pose it could even have been you looking for a friendly anonymous poke.'

'Me? Using Clare's computer to troll for men? Oh, that's very rich. You do know I'm married, don't you?'

'So's everyone else on the site,' Nkata pointed out.

'Or they're people *pretending* to be married,' Caroline said tartly, 'as I doubt they ask each other to bring proof of marriage with them for their little encounters. For all you know, that . . . that *thing* you've got there on her computer is merely a filthy place to meet and have it off with a nameless someone without any strings. Someone merely *pretends* to be attached by marriage so that no one has any expectations of him.'

'Or her,' Barbara said. 'Sounds good to me in either case. Playing a bit of anonymous mattress poker in the afternoon. Sound good to you, Winnie? Whoops. Never mind. I forget about that moral streak you have.'

'Hmm,' he said. 'My mum find out I do summat like that and she beat me with a broomstick, Barb.'

'Child abuse. Terrible. And at your age.'

'Very amusing.' Caroline had dropped her shoulder bag on a chair near the door, and she made a move towards it, prefatory to leaving them. She said, 'I can see that—'

But Nkata broke in. 'Blokes responding?' he said, with a nod at the laptop. 'Here's summat in'eresting. They're writing to someone called Caro, not Clare. Caro.'

Caroline stopped in her progress to the door.

'Now that *is* an intriguing bit,' Barbara said. 'Would that be you, Mrs Goldacre? Caro short for Caroline?'

'Of *course* it's not me. These individuals don't *use* their real names. She's obviously . . . God, all her rubbish about feminism . . . And using *my* name . . . she didn't even know them. She didn't bother to discover if they were criminals or . . . or diseased . . . or rapists . . . or . . . or wife beaters . . . or *God* only knows because they're probably all psychopaths anyway and there she is trotting round the country, spouting all this rot about women being their own masters and putting themselves into the picture about romance being utter nonsense intended to trick them into marriages where they can only be miserable for the rest of their lives while all the time she's running round making damn sure those women are *going* to be miserable once they uncover what they're husbands are up to . . .' She laughed, but it wasn't amusement. It sounded to Barbara like something very close to triumph.

'The men seem to've liked her, though,' Nkata said. 'Looking at their reactions in the afters . . . ?' He nodded at the computer. 'You see that, Barb?'

Barbara had indeed seen. 'She was picking and choosing after a while,' she said. 'Second go, third go. Lots of energy for a bird her age.'

'Wasn't exactly a looker either, eh?' This Nkata directed to Caroline Goldacre.

'What does *that* mean?'

'Means, like I said, they're calling her Caro.'

'And *I've* already said she's used my name. And don't you bloody dare *begin* to think . . . If you believe that I was so madly stupid as to use Clare's laptop to seek whatever sort of loathsome males are advertising themselves for whatever sort of disgusting encounters they have in mind, then what I suggest is that you meet with them. Meet with each one of them. Take along my photo. Take a photo of Clare. They'll have a look and tell you at once that the bloody filthy whore they've been fucking—' She stopped herself. She'd begun to perspire lightly on the forehead and her skin showed this in the light from the lamp on Clare's desk.

Barbara and Nkata said nothing. Barbara's mobile rang and she gave it a glance. Lynley, she saw. She would ring him back.

Caroline said to them, 'You've upset me.'

'Happen a lot?' Nkata asked.

'What?'

'You getting upset like that. You get pushed too far and what happens next?'

'Nothing we need discuss,' she told them.

She made for the door. Nkata stepped aside and allowed her to go.

*Shaftesbury*
*Dorset*

Alastair found that he was having difficulty actually hearing what Sharon was saying. He was listening well enough. That wasn't a problem. But remembering from one moment to the next the details of their bi-monthly meeting was a challenge. He looked down at his notes. They needed to hire a few more shop assistants: Dorchester, Bridport, and Wareham were doing so well that a single person behind the counter was no longer sufficient. Then, there was something not quite right about the building being worked on for the new shop in Swanage, he saw. Sharon was recommending that she spend half a day there soon to look things over and to have a meeting with the contractor doing the renovation.

He nodded and nodded, said yes and yes, and he became aware of how well taken care of he was by Sharon. He also felt completely calm with her, and it was a strange and not unwelcome sensation to be with someone who was so tranquil and confident. His experience of so many years with Caroline had given him an entirely different view of women, as if he'd forgotten that they could be any way other than needing him and sucking upon his essence in order to drain it from him until there was nothing left.

'You're a miracle.' He heard himself say it to Sharon. He hadn't intended to as she was in the midst of telling him something, with a sharpened pencil in her hand and its point directed to the bottom of a column of figures that represented . . . He did not know.

She sat back in her chair, surprised. 'What're you on about, Alastair?'

'A widow,' he said. 'Two children. Tiny bit of government pension. And look at you. You provided for yourself and your kids without needing anyone to help you work out how to do it. I know the history of it all, Shar. It was Yeovil where you started, working in the shop. And from there you came to be where you are, managing all the bakeries and the whole enterprise. You walk out on me, and I'm done for.'

'I'm not walking out on you.' She smiled at him. She had on her specs – perched on the end of her nose, they were, and she looked like a schoolteacher when she wore her specs like that – 'Is that what you want to know?'

'You've not asked me to leave her,' he said. 'Why? We meet over and over, you and me. And you've not asked me. You've not even told me to move her somewhere else so you and I c'n be what we want to be to each other.'

'What is it we want to be to each other, then?' She set down the pencil and laid her hand over his, fingers curling through his that were splayed, her palm soft on the back of his hand. He felt a stirring at this gesture, so tiny and insignificant.

He said, 'You know what we want to be.'

Her fingers tightened. 'Alastair, listen. We don't have to be so traditional. We needn't be husband and wife, with you making an honest woman of me. Times have changed and we're happy, aren't we? Just like we are?'

'Do I look happy here, Shar?' He gestured round the office in which they sat but he knew she would understand that he meant his life with Caroline.

Her face altered to concern. Seeing this, Alastair thought how there was nothing at all sly about Sharon's face. She was an open book.

She got up from her chair and went to look out of the window of the little bakery office. She gazed beyond the glass to what could be seen, which was Will's garden and then the house. He wanted to tell her that Caroline wasn't in at the moment if that was what she feared, but before he could say this, she turned back to him.

She said, 'Things're rough for you just now. But could be this is only an uneven patch you're in.'

'You,' he said.

'Are you saying I'm the uneven patch?'

'I'm saying you're all I think about. You're in my blood. It's like you *became* me, Shar, and I became you and now we're inside each other's body. And don't tell me it's not like that for you cos if you tell me it's nothing but a laugh, I don't know what I'll do.' At the end of saying this, he understood for the first time all the ways in which men are driven to act by what some might call their baser natures but what he knew very well was a desire to be joined to another's existence in such a way that nothing could ever rend the fabric of what they created between them.

Sharon's eyes widened behind her specs, which she took off and cleaned on the edge of the skirt she was wearing, 'Romantic, that's what you are. I wouldn't've thought it.'

'What would you've thought?'

'Rough and tumble bloke with lots of flour about him,' she said.

He felt immediately crestfallen, and he understood that he must have looked it as well, for Sharon said, 'Alastair, don't look like that. It's the same for me, how I feel I mean. Only things're difficult for you and let's not make them worse.'

'How can they be worse?' His voice was low, as he was speaking mostly to himself.

She answered nonetheless. 'By wishing for what can't be just now. You and me know you're caught by her for the moment, but let's not talk of it.'

'How c'n I do that when I can't even *think* 'less I'm . . . It's like I'm not even alive if I'm not with you and what's *that* about? It was never like that with—'

'Don't say that!' she declared. '*Don't* make an issue of she's like this and you're like that and it'll kill me if I don't rid myself of this bloody millstone round my neck. That'll send you mad and *then* what'll you do, Alastair? Let things just be for now.

I'm not going anywhere. I haven't been going anywhere for years and I'm not about to go anywhere now.'

'Bet your kids tell you to move along.'

'My kids know nothing 'bout you. No one does. This is a me and you thing, and it's fine that way.'

But how *could* it be? he wondered. It was bloody unnatural to call everything fine.

He gazed at her. His heart, he found, was pounding like a heart that's had a scare. He could feel it in the tips of his fingers. He could feel it in his throat and under his arms and most of all, 'I want to touch you. I want to kiss you. I'm hard as a limb and you know it, don't you?'

'Hush about that, or we'll not get our work done,' she said. 'And if *that* happens, then—'

Caroline walked in. She was clearly agitated, and without thinking Alastair jumped to his feet. He saw her gaze drop to the bulge in his trousers. She looked from him to Sharon and he frantically tried to think how to divert her, but she was the one to speak.

'They're trying to trap me. They want me to say things when I don't even know what *happened* to her. Just that she died of some heart thing. And then they look at me like . . . *Why* won't they tell me exactly what happened? I needed you to be there with me so that you could tell them I'm not the sort of woman they apparently think I am. I needed you to take my part. Do you know how that feels? To need someone so desperately by your side while you listen to strangers – to the police, my God – and all the time to know that the reason the person you so passionately need will not attend you is . . . I just can't.'

That said, she turned from them and left. The outer door opened and then banged shut and he went to the window and saw her hurrying across the garden, Will's lovely garden that had been intended to make her so happy.

Behind him, Alastair heard Sharon say, 'I'm that sorry, Alastair. I do wish I could make things different for you.'

*Spitalfields*
*London*

India loved what rainfall did to the streets in the waning daylight of autumn, causing the traffic signals to shine in slick pools of rainwater, making the headlamps of passing cars seem to flicker like hesitant beacons. She also liked the odd scents that the sodden air trapped along the thoroughfares: the diesel fumes that she knew would always remind her of London no matter where she might in the future smell them on the wet air of a different environment, the cigarette smoke from those who were forced to see to their habit out on the pavements, the cooking odours from restaurant kitchens she came to as she approached her former home. She could see that the lights were on in the flat. Charlie was waiting for her.

'Mum's rung me in a real state,' he'd said. 'I know this is asking a lot, India, but could you come over here after work? I do need to talk to you. I'd come to you but I've only an hour between the afternoon and the evening clients. What about you? Have you anything on?'

She did. She told him frankly and she used Nat's name because she wanted to hear how Charlie would take it. While she and Nat had not set out a definite time for it, they'd agreed to meet at a corner restaurant not far from St Paul's. Whitebait was fried there and Nat loved whitebait and he wanted to demonstrate for India the culinary delight of dipping into a bowl of tiny fish served with great lashings of tartare sauce. So she hadn't a lot of time. When she explained this to Charlie, he was perfectly reasonable about it.

'I see,' he said. 'Damn. Well, I'm a big boy and I suppose I can cope.'

'What's happened?' she asked. 'Are Alastair and that woman still . . . Charlie, I'm so sorry but I've forgotten her name.'

'Sharon Halsey. No, it's not to do with her.'

'Did he sack her?'

'He didn't. Apparently, Mum came to realise that Sharon's

essential to the business, considering how long she's been employed there. So she's still working for the bakery and if they're carrying on together, I haven't a clue. No, this is to do with the London police. They're in Shaftesbury.'

When India asked him what on earth the London police were doing in Shaftesbury, she learned the truth about Clare Abbott's death: while it *was* a heart attack, it wasn't natural. The police weren't declaring exactly what had occurred, but a second autopsy had revealed details other than those originally named. And now, Clare's editor Rory Statham was in hospital as well.

'Good heavens. What's going on?'

'Haven't a clue. But the crux of the matter is that Mum pointed out to me at considerable length that she has a connection to both of them – to Clare and Rory – and because of this, she's got it into her head that the police actually suspect her of something. As she hasn't the first idea why Rory's in hospital – the poor woman might have had an emergency appendectomy for all she knows – this looks like another Mum drama to me. And, India, I'm almost loath to tell you this part: she's on her way here.'

'Your mum? To London?'

'Hmmm. Yes. So I need to come up with a plan to deal with her. I'd thought you might help. What I mean is that I had a feeling I'd be much more able to contend with her if I've had a conversation with you.'

So she said she'd come to him at the flat, and she arranged a time to meet Nat for whitebait afterwards. Now she unlocked the building's door, and she went up the stairs. She could hear music playing from within, but when she knocked upon the door, it was shut off and footsteps came down the corridor towards her.

'Here you are,' Charlie said when he opened the door. 'Thank you for coming.'

India saw he looked good. More and more his appearance was like the Charlie of old. She found she quite liked the look of him: tall and rangy in blue jeans, with an air about him of casual ease. He wore a jacket she'd not seen before and a new pair of shoes as well. He coloured a little as she smiled at him, his cheeks matching the ginger of his hair. 'Come in,' he said. 'Why've you not used your key?'

It hadn't seemed right to her, but India had no wish to tell him that. She said instead, 'I thought you might still be with a client,' as he beckoned her inside. 'And as to the keys, Charlie . . .' But oddly, she couldn't say what she'd thought she'd be able to say so easily, which was, 'Here are the keys to the building and to the flat because the truth of the matter is that you and I actually *do* know the truth of the matter at this point.'

Nat, of course, was wondering why she'd not yet said exactly that to Charlie. 'When?' he'd whispered only last night as he'd drawn her against him damp and spent and on the edge of dreaming. He'd pushed her hair from her neck and kissed her skin and his hand cupped her breast, which lay within his palm as if it had been created to rest only there, just there. 'Because you know what this is,' he'd murmured, 'what we have. You do know.'

That, however, was just the point. She didn't know. She only understood that what she had with Nat was very much different from what she'd had with Charlie. But different didn't mean rare. It was only dressed like rarity, a costume worn by a breathlessly exciting new experience that could wear itself out through repetition.

Charlie said pleasantly, 'As to the keys . . . ?' in that way he had of seeing that something needed to be said and he was the one meant to receive the words.

She frowned and lied. 'The keys . . . It's quite slipped my mind. How odd. Now tell me everything about your mum.'

'Will you have something to drink? I've laid out . . . well, it's just in here.' He led her into the sitting room where he'd set everything up for martinis. The Bombay Sapphire stood on a tray, its blue bottle freshly sweating from the deep freeze where he liked to keep it. There was a bottle of good vermouth as well, and she knew how he'd use it, just a few drops to coat the side of the martini glass. There were also olives in a dish, along with a bowl of salted almonds.

India felt a little stab, for she recognised all of it, as she was no doubt intended to do. It was their welcome-to-the-evening ritual, although the evening in question had always been a Friday when it wouldn't matter if one martini slid into two and they went to bed pissed.

She looked at Charlie. She had dinner with Nat. She'd told him as much. But really, what would it hurt not to disappoint him? He'd gone to trouble and she could see beyond him into the kitchen where the whiteboard on the wall told her from its neat printing that Charlie was back to volunteering as well, another step in his recovery. Even from here, she could read the headings: Samaritans, Battersea Dogs, among other listings.

She said, 'I did say I can't be here very long.'

'You did,' Charlie said. 'There's Nat and dinner. And I'm grateful you've come. But I reckoned one drink . . . Or I can make tea. We can talk in the kitchen if that's better for you. I hadn't intended . . . Well, that's not quite true. Everything I do at this point is intended. *However*,' and this came with his old Charlie smile, 'I'm delighted to amaze you with a resurgence of my former, admirable flexibility. Tea, then? I've Earl Grey and Assam.'

She decided that one martini wasn't going to put her under the table, so she said, 'I'll do the gin instead. But a small one.'

'I've a client later. That's best for me as well.'

He set about making the drinks and she glanced round the sitting room. She saw that he'd made some changes. Although the summertime picture of them was still prominently displayed, there were new books of all types and sizes on the bookshelves. He'd also brought in a few pieces of Chinese art: five chops displayed on a purpose-built stand, two sculptures, a long-handled calligraphy brush for painting Chinese characters. There was a new canvas on the wall, a market scene with piles of fruits and a group of Chinese men playing cards. When she'd lived with him, he'd wanted to make these sorts of purchases, but she'd argued against it. Practising medicine from the Orient was enough for her, she'd said. She didn't want to come home to the Orient. But Charlie had been right when he'd said that art and artefacts from the Orient would work beautifully in an Art Deco flat. They did. Which made her wonder what else her husband had been right about but had allowed himself to be talked out of.

They were too alike, she and Charlie. Both of them had been too accommodating to others.

As he mixed the martinis and she watched him do it, India thought about how one comes to know another's movements. Charlie's had always been precise: just so much vermouth to swirl in the glass, just so much gin, two olives speared on a pewter toothpick.

She said to him, 'The clients are keeping you busy?' just to say something.

He glanced her way. 'I wish I'd taken your advice on board from the first. I did need to go into therapy myself during the grieving process. I've thought about why I wasn't able to do it, probably more than you could imagine, and the only explanation I have is the obvious one: Will's death gutted me because I knew I should have been able to prevent it. I failed him, and having to face that asked me to take a look at myself and I didn't want to do it. I still don't, to be honest. God. I miss him, India.'

'Of course you do.'

'I've had to consider what missing him is going to feel like to the end of my life and how missing him is going to colour my world if I choose to allow it.'

'I've said this before, Charlie: You've always been too hard on yourself.'

He looked at her earnestly, seemed to hesitate, but then plunged on with, 'India, I want you to know that nothing's changed for me. Well, that's not true, is it? I mean everything's changed but nothing's changed.'

'What's the everything?'

'You know, I daresay. Will and what that did to me. The loss of you and what that did to me. Going through it all and coming back from it. That's the everything. You already know the nothing. But in case you don't . . .'

'I do,' she said before he could tell her that his love for her was unchanged and was – perhaps surprising to them both – unaffected by the intrusion of another man into her life. Charlie knew that they were lovers, she and Nat. But the fact that he somehow was actually coping with this knowledge . . . India had to admire his determined resilience at the same time as she also knew that had she not walked out on him, he might well still be lying on the sofa in their flat and upon him a coverlet largely made of despair.

'Well,' he said, 'Let me be wise and dismiss that for now. The point is: the London police have completely taken over Clare Abbott's digs in Shaftesbury. From what I was able to get out of Mum when she rang me, they've found a website on Clare's computer having to do with meeting married blokes for sex. The police have spoken to Mum about it.'

'Why?'

'Apparently, Clare had been messing about with the site – and with these blokes – but using Mum's name to do it. To meet married men for sex, I mean.'

India took this in with her lips parted and her martini raised. She'd had the intention of having some of it, but she set it down instead on the glass top of the coffee table. She was about to ask what on earth was going on when Charlie went on, saying, 'Mum thinks the police are looking at this as a motive for her harming Clare.'

'But how on earth was she supposed to have given Clare a heart attack?'

Charlie set down his martini as well. India was sitting opposite him, in a low chair across from the sofa. He reached for some almonds and held them in his palm, saying, 'After she rang me, I had a look at the statistics on this sort of thing, the kind of research the police might do? My guess is *if* they're truly looking at Mum – always open to doubt, let's face it, Mum being Mum – there must be a poison involved.'

'I don't understand.'

'A poison that gives someone a heart attack. Or one that makes it *seem* someone had a heart attack.'

'How on earth would your mum ever know about something like that? And even if she did know or found out or whatever . . . Why would she kill Clare? For using her name with married men? I see that doing that sort of thing is . . . well, it's extraordinary, isn't it? But did your mum even know this was going on? That Clare was using her name?'

'She says she hadn't the first clue. She told the police that.'

'Do you . . . I hate to say this, but do you believe her?'

'Admittedly, she's been known to lie. But there's this situation with Rory Statham – Clare's editor? – being in hospital here in town.'

'But where does that fit in?'

'Aside from everything else going on in her head, Mum seems to think she's set up to be next because she worked for Clare and because Rory was Clare's editor. But to be completely honest with you, India, she was going off in every possible direction when I spoke to her: she's next in line because of Clare's book. She's next in line because someone discovered that Clare – under Mum's name – was having it off with a cartload of adultery-seeking blokes and one of their wives discovered this or one of the blokes decided to kill her because . . . I don't know . . . because she was threatening him? Blackmailing him? What makes it all worse is that Mum says she doesn't feel safe around Alastair either. She thinks everything that's happened could be down to Sharon Halsey trying to kill her in order to get her hands on Alastair. Or it could be Alastair trying to kill her to get his hands on Sharon.'

'Doesn't that beg the question: why target Clare?'

'Of course it does. But you know Mum. When she gets going, there's a terrible gap between here –' he pointed to his head, meaning his brain, naturally – 'and here.' He pointed to his lips. 'She apparently rang the local police about all of this, but they're in the dark or they're merely saying they're in the dark as it's a Scotland Yard case. Could be they know very well what's going on and are trying to fend her off. I just don't know.' He took a deep breath and blew it out. 'It was the devil trying to sort out everything that she was throwing at me over the phone. But the long and short of it is that she's on her way and . . .' He paused, sipped his martini, looking over the rim of the glass at her.

In his hesitation, India knew exactly why he'd asked her stop by, why he hadn't wanted to talk on the phone about his mother. He was going to request that she take Caroline in, and he wanted to make the request in person. He could hardly take her in himself as he met his clients here in the flat. India said, 'Charlie . . .'

'I swear, it will only be for two days at the most, till I can sort things out.'

'*What* things?'

'Mum and Alastair for one. This murder business for another. For all we know, could be she's got the wrong end of the stick on everything and is just confused.'

'I don't see how I can manage it, Charlie. Can't she go to a hotel?'

'Believe me, she's in no state to be alone in a hotel. I know it's a lot to ask of you. I know it's too *much* to ask of you. If I didn't have the new clients, I'd take her in myself. Or if the flat was larger. But as it isn't and as I do have clients . . .'

India knew at least part of his present problem was down to her, as she'd been the one to insist upon the Art Deco flat when she'd seen it. He had consented because he'd wanted to please her since she'd gone to such lengths to make herself pleasing for his mother. They were both caught by Caroline, India thought with resignation. It always seemed to come down to that.

India realised that she could actually do this for Charlie

without unspeakable trouble to herself. She was working long hours at the clinic anyway; she was seeing Nat most evenings after work as well, which she could easily arrange to occur away from her home. She could give Caroline her bedroom and herself use the sofa in her office. For two days only, she could do this. How difficult could it actually be?

She said, 'Two days? You promise?'

He held up his hand. 'Had I a Bible. I can offer this as well: I'll keep her here tonight and bring her to Camberwell in the morning. If you'll leave me a key, you don't even have to be there. If it helps, I also swear that I won't look through your knickers drawer . . . although I can't promise Mum won't. You've not got anything you mind if she sees?'

Her birth control, India thought. She would have to remove the pills and put them somewhere away from potential snooping by her mother-in-law, although it was something of a pleasant jolt to realise that she no longer regularly thought of Caroline as her mother-in-law at all. Other than that, there was nothing for Caroline to find and nothing that she could conclude about India or her life.

'Very well, Charlie,' India told him. 'If you'll promise . . .'

'I do,' he told her.

18 October

Lynley parked the Healey Elliott in Chalcot Crescent and walked the short distance from there to Primrose Hill. He'd offered to go directly to the zoo just inside Regent's Park – which actually would have been easier for both of them, considering the weather – but Daidre had said that, as it was time for Arlo's midday walk and as this walk generally involved a saunter across Prince Albert Road and up to the top of Primrose Hill, she would meet him there.

The rain had lessened. What had earlier been something of a downpour was now merely a heavy mist creating a tenebrous shroud over most of the city but hardly enough to warrant an umbrella. So Lynley left his on the floor of the car, and he turned up the collar of his coat instead. By the time he reached the top of Primrose Hill, he regretted this but reckoned he'd survive.

Daidre was not yet there. Considering the nature of the day, no one else should have been either, but the carpet of rising lawn that comprised the hill was dotted with people nonetheless, both on the grass and on the paved paths that triangulated the slope. Nannies with pushchairs and prams strolled together, exposing their charges to whatever fresh air managed to reach them beneath the plastic tenting that kept the drizzle away, three optimistic young men kicked a football among themselves, an elderly couple studied what could be seen of the view and compared it to the engraved cityscape that stood on a pedestal at the top of the hill and faced in the general direction of St Paul's Cathedral, and a middle-aged woman sat on one of the benches a short distance from this engraving, moodily smoking beneath a golf umbrella.

Under the glowering sky, Lynley took a position close to the engraving and looked at the route Daidre would take from the zoo. She was not yet on it. He glanced at his watch and from there to the trees that bordered Regent's Canal on the north side of the park. Their seasonal colours were dulled by the day's lack of sunlight. Soon enough their leaves would be gone altogether, heralding months of gloom, extremely short days, rain, and, as was becoming more common, snow.

He felt grim. He'd spent the morning at his desk, having finally carved out enough time to read the letters and to go through the photographs that Havers and Nkata had found in Rory Statham's flat. The photographs appeared to document the holiday that Rory and her partner Fiona Rhys had taken to Spain, which had ended in Fiona's death. There they were on the strand, with the surf coming in behind them, as they stood arms-round-each-other and grinned happily at the camera. They sat at a bar with tall lagers and a shared plate of fried fish. They shopped at colourful markets where the Mediterranean fruits and vegetables gleamed in the dappled sunlight. All they had wanted – like so many British before them – was a bit of sun. It certainly hadn't been a lot to ask.

They looked happy, Lynley had thought. They looked in the photos like a longtime couple who knew each other's rhythms and who accepted how these individual rhythms contributed to the ebb and flow of a human relationship. But the collection of letters that Nkata and Havers had given to him showed something else.

They were all from Clare Abbott. They formed a revealing arc of emotion, which began as one professional to another, evolved to friends in correspondence over life, deepened to a form of intimacy in which serious issues were explored, and then dropped with a sudden thud to a firmness whose genesis was not in question. Since Clare was the only writer involved – Rory's letters to her being either somewhere in one of Clare's houses or, perhaps, tossed away when answered – there were gaps in what they revealed. They spanned a number of years, but in them Lynley learned that the paradise of passion and devotion which one would hope for in a relationship with another human was not quite what it seemed on the surface when it came to Rory and Fiona.

Children were the crux of their problem. Fiona's desire came into conflict with Rory's caution, with the reason for Rory's caution going unspoken to Fiona. Anorexia nervosa had evidently been the dead elephant whose rotting corpse was fouling the air of the women's partnership. Fiona was the sufferer; Rory was the anxious witness. In and out of treatment for repeated bouts with it, Fiona was not – Rory thought – material for parenthood. She had shared this and other concerns with Clare who lectured her on 'the value of honesty for the love of God, Rory', to no avail. Instead, Rory watched Fiona's eating or lack thereof with a growing obsession that undermined their commitment to each other, breaking them apart for a period of time, which estrangement had resulted in Rory's leaning upon Clare for emotional succour. This had been given freely and then withdrawn when it became apparent to Clare that Rory was misinterpreting the buttressing of a friend in time of need for something that did not interest Clare at all.

Fiona's murder had thus been followed by an understandable amount of guilt: the guilt of a survivor of a terrible crime, the guilt of a lover who knew that passion was dead and the sustaining influence of devotion had been beaten over time like a harvest of rice, the guilt of a fugitive whose escape had come at enormous cost to another. Through this, Clare Abbott had been at Rory's side both physically and metaphorically, but at the end of the day, she'd had to be frank: 'I miss you as well, Rory, but it's not the same for me as it is for you, and you and I both know that life must go on.'

Or must it? Lynley asked himself. Murder-suicide came to

his mind. He sorted back through what he knew of the days leading up to Clare Abbott's death and in his notes he found what he'd sought: Clare had been in London on the morning of the night she died, signing books at her London publishing house, in the company of Caroline Goldacre but, perhaps more tellingly, also in the company of Rory Statham.

He was considering everything this might signify when his mobile rang. He assumed it was Daidre letting him know that she was either held up at the zoo or on her way, but he saw it was Barbara Havers, and in short order the detective sergeant brought him into the picture of a website that Winston Nkata had turned up on Clare's computer on which someone calling herself Caro24k ('As in twenty-four carat gold, as in *Goldacre*, Inspector,' Havers added in case he hadn't twigged the reference) had ostensibly looked for extramarital sexual encounters.

'Caroline's claimed Clare was using her name while she slunk round Dorset and regions beyond in order to do the deed with married blokes. She threw down the gauntlet and told us to take her picture and Clare's round to these blokes if we didn't believe her.'

'And?' Lynley asked.

'Winnie's onto that. He's still sorting these blokes' real names and their phone numbers or their addresses. You know Winnie. He'll wring it from the wireless universe eventually. And he reckons once he has what he needs, the magic words *New Scotland Yard* and *murder inquiry* are going to be the open sesame with these blokes.'

'What's your thinking on it, Sergeant?'

'Clare's got some interview sheets filled out for a couple of blokes,' Havers said. 'And there *was* what looked like a book proposal in Rory's desk in London –' here Havers paused as she apparently rustled through her notebook for information – '*The Power of Anonymous Adultery: Internet Encounters and the Dissolution of the Family.* But Caroline says there was no book being written and I got to tell you, she might be right.'

'Meaning?'

'This proposal? It's all about sex and the internet and married geezers and birds looking for love in all the wrong places. But I can't find any evidence of a book at all. Winnie and I are thinking it's possible something else was going on.'

'Which is?'

'*Caroline* and these blokes having sex.'

'But doesn't that fly in the face of Caroline suggesting that you show her photo and Clare's to these blokes? And what about the interview sheets you mentioned?'

'Could be Clare worked out what Caroline was up to and interviewed these blokes in the afters. As to the picture bit, could be she's bluffing. She doesn't expect we'll be able to find the blokes in question. She also doesn't expect that they'll talk to us even if we manage to find them. But, like I said, you know Winnie. This is nothing for him. Meantime, I'm trying to sort out a key I found in a drawer in Clare's desk. A locked drawer, matter 'f fact. First I thought it was a locker key of some sort, but when I brought it into town just now—'

'Hang on,' Lynley said. 'Is Winston with you?'

'Like I said, he's sorting Clare's computer.'

Lynley knew where this could lead. He felt his jaw tightening. He said, 'Barbara, weren't your orders to remain with Winston at all times? Weren't Winston's orders to remain with you?'

There was a little silence. On her end of the call, he heard a man calling out 'You missed a bit here, Patrick,' presumably someone on the Shaftesbury pavement along with Havers. She finally said, 'I didn't reckon we were supposed to be joined at the hip, Inspector.'

'I want you working together. You were expressly *told* to work together.'

'We *are* bloody working together. You never said we were meant to be in lockstep. What're we s'posed to be, like those bathing beauties in a pool swimming about underwater with their legs scissoring round in the air? What're they called anyway?'

'Don't let's get off the topic, Sergeant. This is precisely the way it begins with you and you know it.'

'*What* begins?'

'An interpretation of orders. Which quickly becomes a slight bending of them. Which then transforms into sidestepping police regulations. Which *then* finds you creating your rules as you go along. Have you any idea at all how seriously Isabelle looks at—'

'Have you any idea at all that *you* sound like an hysterical . . . I don't even *know* what. C'n I point out that *Isabelle* didn't exactly give us a murder squad to sort this out? We got me and Winnie in Shaftesbury and you in London and mountains of clobber to sort through without a scrum of promotion-hungry DCs to help out anywhere. Winnie 'n' me have got to be able to divide up actions. Now I can hang over his shoulder like a devoted bride to please you and *Isabelle* or I can get on with things, one of which is working out what this bloody key that Clare had squirrelled away in her desk was used for.'

The repetition of Superintendent Ardery's first name was, he knew, meant to derail him, but he didn't intend to go there. Instead he considered what the sergeant was saying. There was actually some truth to it.

She went on, obviously recognising the advantage when she had it. 'That key opens something. I need to find it. I'm onto some sort of locker in town. I've had a look through Clare's house and up in her loft, but there's no joy there. I don't know *what* the hell she has inside whatever this key opens, but you and I know we got to see it. So are you willing to help me out here or should I just come back to London and return to pulling my forelock in Ardery's direction? Has she had you in her office for a report about me yet? If not, she will. And when she does, you can tell her whatever you want, but for the moment Winnie and I are going at this best we can with limited manpower and limited resources and—'

'For God's sake, cease,' Lynley cut in. 'Carry on as you are.' He saw Daidre at last, crossing Prince Albert Road, Arlo in his assistance dog vest and on the lead trotting along at her side. He raised his arm to wave, but she didn't take note. She and the dog made for Primrose Hill and soon left the paved path to cross the lawn for a shortcut.

'Ta, sir,' Havers said at her end. 'What're you onto, then?'

'I'm going back to the hospital to talk to Rory. There's more to her relationship with Clare Abbott than meets the eye. And Clare and Caroline *were* in Rory's office in Marylebone prior to leaving for Cambridge, weren't they?'

Havers confirmed this and asked what was up.

'Rory may have been in love with her.'

'Bloody hell,' Barbara said. 'That's more or less what Caroline Goldacre's claimed. I hate to think that nasty cow was right.'

They rang off, and Lynley watched Daidre coming towards him along the rise of the land. He reflected on the entire idea of love and how kindness, pity, compassion, or simple generosity of spirit could be mistaken by someone in extremis for devotion leading to commitment. In that moment of observing Daidre and the little dog, he couldn't help wondering if injudicious thinking on his part was at the bottom of how he interpreted Daidre's behaviour, unable to distinguish love from what was only the kindness of a compassionate woman directed towards a man who'd had his life torn asunder.

When she reached him, no umbrella sheltering her, he said, 'I would have come directly to your office, you know. And now I've no umbrella to offer you.'

'It *is* a bit odd,' she said, gazing round their surroundings. 'Looking out of the window, I thought there was no rain. But the mist is more daunting than I expected.' She looked back at him and smiled at him fondly although he couldn't tell how much of him she could actually see since her glasses were covered with a watery down that also beaded her sandy hair and his own. 'At any rate, Arlo needed his walk and as I've been spending my lunch hours walking him, this is fine. And it's lovely to see you. My heart quite leapt at the sight of you up here. I felt rather like a Victorian heroine. Tommy, that raincoat looks ancient. Wherever did you get it?'

'My father's,' he told her. 'And I have a feeling it was his father's before him. I'm not sure it's effective at repelling rain any longer, but I like the look of it.'

'It's rather MI6-ish,' she said.

'And I've always longed to be a secret agent. Does it impress you?'

'It does. I find I rather like you more or less . . . well . . . crumpled.'

'As I was in Cornwall.'

'But with rather less dirt and mud hanging on your person. How's it all going?'

He knew she didn't mean his life and how it had altered since they'd met in Cornwall. He said, 'I'm not sure. I feel a bit odd, delving into the lives of this particular group of people.'

'Isn't that part of the job?'

'It is. But this time, it's all rather sadder than usual: love, loss, confusion, misunderstanding.'

She examined him in that way she had that told him she was following beneath the superficial meaning of what he'd said. 'Do you think you're getting to the bottom of everything?'

'Truth to tell, I'm not at all certain.'

'Ah. Mankind's condition.' She extended Arlo's lead to him, saying, 'I'm finding I quite like having this little fellow round me. I've never had a dog, at least not as an adult, which I realise is quite a strange admission from a vet. They do so wriggle their way into one's heart, don't they?'

'They do. Perhaps that's why you've never had one.'

She didn't avoid his eyes when she replied. Instead she looked at him directly and said, 'Yes. Perhaps. I do guard my heart.'

'So I've noticed,' he said.

They might have said more, but his mobile rang. When he saw that it was SO7, he told her that he had to take the call. She said on her part that she had to get back to work. She added, 'Take care of our little friend, won't you?' and he told her that he would do so.

'This is Lynley,' he said into the phone once she'd kissed

him lightly in farewell and turned to go on her way back to the zoo.

At the other end, someone said, 'We've finally got the fingerprints, Inspector. Sorry it took so bloody long.'

*Cerne Abbas*
*Dorset*

Upon Barbara's return from her sojourn into the centre of town, she did not find it a shocking revelation to learn that Caro24K's Just4Fun companions were reluctant to speak to anyone about their use of that website. As Winston told it over a tuna and sweetcorn sandwich at the dining room table – he knew his way round a jar of mayonnaise, Barbara thought as she tucked in – the blokes had concocted a variety of excuses: from a mother-in-law rushed to hospital with severe angina to I don't believe I have to talk to *anyone* about a perfectly legal arrangement between consenting adults. However, when the full facts concerning the various methods of tracing the physical location of an internet user were revealed to each of them, their cooperation had been garnered. The last thing any of them apparently wanted was to have New Scotland Yard showing up on their doorsteps to question them about their use of an internet assignation site.

Nkata hadn't illuminated them with regard to the death of Clare Abbott. All in good time, he told Barbara. They had an appointment at the Royal Oak in Cerne Abbas to meet the lot of them round half past two.

'Do these blokes know it's a group meet?' Barbara asked the other DS.

Winston shook his head. 'Surprise,' he said. 'It's a good thing, innit?'

When they'd consumed their sandwiches, they set off for

Cerne Abbas, with Winston at the wheel of the Prius once he'd checked it over from bow to stern to quell whatever anxiety he was feeling over having allowed Barbara to drive it from Clare Abbott's home to a car park in the centre of town. She waited for him patiently although she did allow herself to shoot him a look when he at last was willing to take them on their way. He shrugged and said, 'Jus' checkin, Barb,' to which she said, 'Bloody hell. I'll use Clare's motor next time. I swear, Win, some people take less care of their children than you take of this thing.'

She'd never been to Cerne Abbas just as, prior to Clare Abbott's death, she'd never been to Shaftesbury. As the crow flew, it wasn't an enormous distance, but as this was the countryside, there was no direct route. Winston's chosen direction took them first towards Sherborne and then through the middle of Blackmore Vale, where the grassy covering atop the natural clayland created a pleasing green and rolling carpet that ultimately climbed to a limestone ridge bisecting the valley north to south. On the valley floor and lower hillsides, cows grazed in lush pastures defined by hedgerows while small farms were sheltered by whatever trees could find a foothold in soils that ran the gamut from unbreathable clay to soaking marsh.

Cerne Abbas was a bit beyond Blackmore Vale, a village of ponds, rivulets, and antique houses that appeared to span more than four hundred years. It was a small enough place that time and the creation of the A352 just beyond its boundaries had not managed to spoil. The remains of an abbey graced it, as did a row of half-timbered houses whose narrow front doors, uneven rooflines, and sagging beams declared them to be the real thing and not some coy replica of buildings from a bygone age, complete with mod cons and WiFi access. Across from them stood the village church and in front of this, the village stocks still occupied a position from which disgraced citizens might while away a few hours being humiliated for one infraction or another.

The Royal Oak rested at the intersection of Abbey Street

and Long Street, two of the very few lanes that defined the
village. It was a steeply gabled structure with a single moss-
speckled picnic table before its front door and a sign above
its slate-roofed porch declaring the building's genesis as 1540.
Vines covered it, newly brilliant with rain-washed autumn hues,
and as Barbara and Winston Nkata approached the place, the
sun appeared for the first time that day, shining its particular
beams on the pub's freshly created sign: a nobleman bearing
only a slight resemblance to Charles the First, his position of
hiding in the branches of the eponymous tree doing what it
could to confirm his identity.

Nkata had to duck to get in the door of the pub, and once
inside Barbara saw that two men stood chatting at the bar,
one with a half pint of Guinness and the other with a virtuous
Coke in which two pieces of ice and a slice of lemon floated.
Otherwise, aside from the barman, the place was empty.

In the way of all pub goers, both the barman and the drinkers
turned for a look as Barbara and Nkata entered. If these were
the blokes who'd used the Just4Fun site, Barbara reckoned,
they did not twig instantly that she and Winston were the
expected rozzers.

She took out her warrant card. Winston did likewise. That
was all it took. One of the men said, 'So I'm here, all right?
I'll give you ten minutes' as the other said, 'You didn't say
there'd be two of you,' at which point they looked at each other
and said, 'You as well?' simultaneously.

The barman looked immediately interested. He was a young
individual of rather ovine appearance suggestive of too much
inbreeding among people with excessively curly hair and faces
of a triangular shape in which the apex was upended to form
a chin. Business was slow at this hour and his curiosity was
piqued. It grew even more so when the door opened another
time and a fifth stranger to Cerne Abbas entered and clocked
the others who were – at Nkata's suggestion – removing themselves to a table as far as possible from the bar.

Introductions followed, with the interviewees insisting upon

Christian names and surname initials only. Barbara waited for Nkata to tell them that it didn't matter, his expertise with the internet being what it was, but he didn't bother. He shrugged and the men identified themselves as Dan V, Bob T, and Al C.

Bob T spoke first once the social niceties were gone through. He wanted assurance that this meeting was private, that no record was going to be made of it, that whatever information he provided was going to be considered background only, and that when he left, he would so in advance of the others. Barbara wondered why he reckoned he had any clout when it came to negotiating terms with the police. She was about to tell him this when Nkata said that, as far as he was concerned, what they needed to know was limited at the moment to an identification of the woman they'd met for sex after connecting with her on the internet.

Bob T surprised them then. He said, 'I didn't have sex with her,' to which one of the other men guffawed as the third rolled his eyes. Thus Bob T declared himself ready to tell all in order, it seemed, to prove his chastity, and he launched into the tale of his acquaintance with 'this bloody mad women's libber, she was' who showed up at an establishment called the Wookey Hole Motel in Somerset.

Barbara recognised the name from Clare's diary. One of the two other men snickered at it, but when Bob T fired a look at him, the man produced a clearly spurious sneeze and said, 'Sorry. Allergies, mate.'

Winston provided a photograph of Clare Abbott at this point, taking out a publicity shot that he'd apparently unearthed from the writer's study. Bob T gave it a glance and said 'That's the slag, all right, and not too sodding glad *I* was when it turned out she wanted to interview me and nothing else. Case of thank God for small favours cos I had no clue how I was goin' to get it up for her once I had a look at her face. You say she's dead?' he then asked Winston.

'Said it was a murder inquiry is all,' Nkata told him pleasantly.

'Well, who else would be dead if not her?' Bob T asked.

'Hell, if she was tricking men into meeting her and they thought it was for a good shag and she turned up with her forms and her pens . . . She was taking her life in her hands, you ask me. When she got there, she told me it was about a book she was writing and I bloody well told *her* I didn't want to be in a book. I just wanted to get it off because the wife . . . Christ, women, you know? Hot and cold and on and off they are. Makes me want to become a Catholic priest.'

'Altar boys being what they are,' Barbara noted.

'Hey, I don't do—'

'What about you?' Nkata said to the other men. 'This the woman?' And when they both nodded, 'Sex or interview?'

They looked at each other as if trying to decide upon truth or falsehood and which of these choices would make them look less like louts. Dan V finally took the plunge with, 'Sex,' and Al C nodded. 'Same,' he said.

'So what was different with you?' Barbara asked. 'Did she not have her interview forms with her? Or did something happen?'

'Like what?' Dan V asked.

'Like force,' Barbara said. 'That comes to mind.'

Dan V said hotly, 'Are you accusing *me* of . . . Let me tell you, that's bloody well not on. No one had to force anyone to do anything, and I've never forced a woman in m'life.'

'Goes as well for me,' said Al C. 'She might've had forms or whatnot with her, but I never seen them, did I. We met for a drink—'

'Where was this?' Barbara asked him as Winston took out his leather notebook and mechanical pencil to memorialise the details.

'Over Bournemouth. At Travelodge.'

'What, she wore a bag on her head?' Bob T asked. Dan V guffawed.

'Didn't need to,' Al C said frankly. 'My thing is melted chocolate and women's private parts and you c'n figure out the rest on your own. All's I'll say is I keep the chocolate warm.

She liked what I was giving her just fine. She was the one – not me, mind you – who wanted a few more goes after the first one. So we met – me and her – maybe five times? I dunno for sure. Then that was enough for us both and off we went to find someone new, no apologies and no regrets. I mean, that's what it's about, eh? Someone new.'

Barbara glanced at Winston who was managing to keep his face impassive although God only knew what he was thinking. Despite his past street gang affiliation, she knew he was a virtual innocent when it came to some of the seamier ways of the world. She said to Dan V, 'Anything you want to add about your own proclivities?'

'Say what?' he said.

'The where, the when, and the how,' she clarified.

'Best Western,' he said. 'Ilminster.'

'You lot are real romantics, eh?' Barbara commented. 'Travelodge, Best Western. I have to wonder where things go from here.'

''S not about romance, is it,' Dan V protested. ''S about sex. No questions and no expectations. Condoms required. We have a few drinks and we decide. It's yes or no, split the cost of the room, have some fun, and off you go. Easy as anything since everyone wants it or they don't use the website in the first place.' He shrugged. He glanced at the other two men. They glanced back. Everyone looked away.

There was a silence. In it Barbara wondered what had happened to the fourth bloke who was meant to show up. They'd have to make an effort to track him down at this point, and she was considering how much a waste of time the entire line of inquiry was turning out to be – aside from its marginally dispiriting amusement value – when Dan V said to Al C, 'She get back to you, then?' in a casual tone but with an expression on his face that belied his indifference.

Barbara felt the hair stir on the back of her neck. Winston, she saw, looked up from his note taking. She waited to see how Al C would reply and for a moment he didn't, although he moved in his chair and glanced towards the window before looking back at Dan V and giving a single head jerk as a nod.

'What's this, then?' Barbara asked them.

Bob T was the one to answer. He said to the other two men, 'She went after you, didn't she? She tried it with me: "I expect you'd like it if the wife and kiddies didn't know what you were up to, eh?" Email. 'Bout two weeks after I met the slag.'

Winston and Barbara exchanged a look. Winston said, 'What'd she want, then? Money?'

'Aye.' Dan V was the one to answer. Al C confirmed with a nod and then a headshake of what seemed to be disgust: directed at himself, the woman, or the entire idea of meeting for anonymous sex and expecting no fallout? It was difficult to tell.

'Blackmail,' Barbara added. 'So how'd you play it?'

Bob T said, 'I told her I didn't bloody care what the wife knew about me giving an interview to a women's libber. I reckoned she'd like it just fine and I told the bloody cow as much. As f'r the kids, I got twins in nappies and I don't expect they'd care what their dad was up to.'

'And you?' Barbara said to Dan V and Al C.

Dan V, it turned out, had paid. The other two men groaned when he admitted to this. He explained that he had a lot to lose in a divorce if the wife had decided to go that way upon a revelation of his extracurricular activities with willing women. 'Eight hundred quid this was,' he said.

'Oh, mate,' Al C groaned sympathetically while Bob T said, 'Dead mad, you are.'

'How'd it go and where'd it go?' Barbara asked, hoping for a bank transfer or the like but fairly sure she wasn't going to get one.

'Cash,' he said.

'Posted or dropped somewhere?'

'Posted. An address in Shaftesbury.

'D'you happen to remember it?'

'Just the street, Bimport, this was. I went up and had a drive

by in the afters. Fancy big stone house. Nice garden out front.
She wasn't hurting for it.'

'What about you?' Barbara asked Al C. 'Cash as well?'

'Didn't pay, did I,' Al C said. 'That message she sent? The
wouldn't-wifey-like-to-know? Didn't sound like the same
woman wrote it, you ask me. I teach composition, see. English
and the like at the local comprehensive and I'm not saying
where so don't even ask. Kids. You know what they're like
when it comes to writing. Plagiarists one and all. There's a site
you c'n use on the web to work out whether the kids've done
their own writing or "borrowed" someone else's. I ran the all
the emails came from Caro24K through it. Programme said
the last one . . . ? The one asking for eight hundred quid . . .?
Wasn't from her. You ask me, someone was on to what this
woman –' with a nod at Clare's picture which lay on the table
looking up at them all – 'was doing on the website. Someone
either knew her passwords—'

'Or had access to the same computer Clare Abbott had
used, where her passwords were all stored in memory,' Barbara
finished. 'Did you let Clare know?'

'Rang her mobile and left a message,' he said.

'Did she ring you back? Ask any questions? Get in touch
in any way?'

He shook his head. They all sat there for an additional thirty
seconds during which time an elderly couple and their three
West Highland terriers came into the pub. They were followed
in a moment by a family of four, who joined them at the bar
where a noisy examination of the menu began, accompanied
by 'Granny, I want the steak pie!' and 'Fish fingers for you
and no argument' from Dad and 'I'm paying, Ian,' from
Granddad, 'so let the boy have what he wants?'

That was it in a nutshell, Barbara thought wryly as the
family continued their discussion over food. Wasn't it always
down to a case of letting the boy have what he wants?

*Fulham*
*London*

Rory Statham knew she was nearly back to normal when the expression on her mother's face caused her to smile. She was being quite heroic, her mum, having brought from Rory's flat a recording of a piece of music she'd been composing in her free time for the last several months. Rory had very little occasion to use her Cambridge first in geopolitics in the course of her work as a non-fiction editor. But her other first in music theory she still dabbled with in her limited free time. She'd done so from the first when she'd graduated. She'd let it go for many of the years with Fiona. But she'd ultimately returned to composing purely for her own enjoyment. And if she had nothing published, professionally recorded, or produced for the public by one or another of London's orchestras, it was no matter. She enjoyed the process.

'My,' her mum said with her customary gracious smile when Rory showed mercy at the end of the first movement by switching the music off. 'That's all quite . . . different, isn't it?'

Rory could tell she meant that the composition sounded like a tailback on the Hammersmith Flyover at rush hour, with countless taxis heading to Heathrow carrying anxiety-ridden passengers in fear of missing their flights. There was an accident up ahead. The fire brigade was involved as were two ambulances. Lorries were jockeying with buses and SUVs. Nerves were unstrung. Tempers were flaring. Rory wanted to tell her mother that she was completely spot-on in her understanding of the piece.

But instead she said to her, 'We don't have to listen to this. It was good of you to bring it, but . . . well, obviously it needs work.'

'Nonsense, darling,' her mother said. 'It's lovely. Quite lovely.'

Rory laughed. 'Bet it reminds you of *Swan Lake*, Mum.'

Her mother chuckled. 'All right, then. I'll never understand these things. Did I tell you Eddie and David have been phoning twice a day to see how you are? They were going to come up to town straightaway, but it seemed to me that as you're on the mend and what with having a four-year-old and a seven-year-old to contend with . . . I told them best to wait till the holidays. I hope that was right.'

Rory felt the flicker of an expression cross her face at the mention of her brother, his husband, and their children. Her mind went to Fiona and what things might have been like had Rory only agreed to a baby. But no, she thought. How much more horrible would everything have been to have had a child with them on holiday, a child who would have been at least ten years old when Fiona was murdered. She said to her mother, 'You did exactly right. I'd rather see them all at Christmas anyway.'

The room's door opened, and all regret was swept away when Rory saw that Detective Inspector Lynley had come again to the hospital, only this time he had Arlo with him. The dog wore the vest that declared him an assistance animal, and when his eyes lit upon Rory in the hospital bed, his tail became a blur of joy.

Lynley said, 'I managed to convince everyone below that Arlo is indeed an assistance dog. What with my police credentials, his winsome ways, and my own limited ability to be affable, we have a quarter hour to visit.'

'Do lift him onto the bed, Inspector,' Rory said and when Lynley did so, Arlo writhed ecstatically among the linens before placing himself at Rory's legs with his chin on her thighs and his eyes fixed lovingly on her face. Rory said, 'He's giving me love eyes. Hello, darling boy. Have you a dog, Inspector?'

'I don't,' he said. 'But my mother has three who generally spend their time arranging themselves artfully in front of the fireplace in her home. Completely addicted to a roaring blaze, they are.'

'Where does she live that she's even allowed a roaring blaze?' Rory asked.

'Cornwall.'

'You don't sound like a Cornishman,' Rory's mother said. 'Did you not grow up there?'

'I did,' Lynley told her. 'But my schooldays – and my father – made certain the accent didn't stick.' And then to Rory, 'I've had a call from our forensics people. They'd been backlogged when it came to fingerprints but now they've managed to sort everything out. It's a bit curious, what they've found. Your toothpaste has not only your fingerprints on it but two other sets as well.'

Rory frowned, wondering what this meant. Lynley clarified with, 'One of the sets is unidentified as yet. The other belongs to Clare Abbott.'

'*Clare's* fingerprints?' Rory's mother said. 'And someone else's? On Rory's toothpaste?'

'It could mean any number of things to have more than one set of prints,' Lynley said. 'But to have Clare's prints on Rory's toothpaste in circumstances in which Clare herself has been poisoned, the most reasonable—'

'Wait!' Rory cried. Arlo sprang to his feet. Rory said to him quickly, 'Arlo. Stay. I'm fine.' And then she said to Lynley because everything had suddenly become quite clear to her, 'Oh God. Here's what it is, Inspector. We had words.'

'You and Clare?'

'Caroline Goldacre. Before I left Shaftesbury. She was quite angry. She'd been banging on about Clare and her next book and there not being a book at all, and we got into a bit of unpleasantness about it. I ended up telling her that she wouldn't be needed any longer because – obviously – she wouldn't be. She wanted to collect her things but I said that wasn't going to be possible just then as I had to go through everything in the house. I allowed her to take a few articles from the office, but that was it.'

Rory's mother said, 'But darling, surely the woman wouldn't poison you because—'

'It's not that at all,' Rory cut in. 'I don't like to argue with people. You know that, Mum. All I wanted to do was to get back to London at that point. So when she'd left, I gathered up Arlo's things in a hurry and off we went. It was only when we got to London and I gave him his walk that I realised I'd left my suitcase back in Shaftesbury. I'd nothing with me at home—'

'Nothing?' Lynley asked.

'I mean one-off items. What one puts in a sponge bag. I'd none of those things, so I used Clare's. I had her overnight case, you see,' she said to Lynley. 'From Cambridge. From the night she was there.'

'Of course,' Lynley said. 'Because when her death was initially declared to be heart-related, you were sent her belongings, I expect.'

'I'd not even unpacked them,' Rory told him. 'There was no reason. But when I realised I'd left my own things in Shaftesbury—'

'You used her toothpaste. Who would have packed her bag for the Cambridge trip?'

'Clare herself. Possibly Caroline.'

'And they had adjoining rooms in Cambridge,' Lynley said.

They all took a moment. Rory saw what the implications were. She said, 'She would have known what kind of toothpaste Clare used. She always did the shop for her. She could have substituted . . . But, Inspector, she had no reason to murder Clare. It would have been biting the hand, and why on earth would she have done that?'

It was a good question, Lynley acknowledged. But at this juncture motives or the lack thereof were details that could be mooted forever. The real issue was getting to the bottom of the third set of fingerprints next. If they weren't Caroline Goldacre's, then they were someone else's, and that person would have had to have access to Clare Abbott's possessions in order to slip the poison into those items she had taken with her to Cambridge.

'So we've had a chat with three of the four blokes,' Barbara Havers said, 'with the fourth declaring his motor conked out on the way so that's why he didn't show. *Which*, at this point, I believe like I also believe I can swim to France. But he's declaring we can come to him if we want to check his story. He says he's in a lay-by off the A352 waiting for a tow.'

Lynley leaned against the wing of the Healey Elliott. Traffic crawled by him on Fulham Road. He'd rung the sergeant to get her onto Caroline Goldacre's fingerprints, but they hadn't got there yet. Havers was recounting the group interrogation that she and Winston Nkata had conducted with three men who'd met Clare Abbott for, as Havers put it in her inimitable fashion, a bit of pound-and-dash. Two of them had gone through with it once they'd met her in the flesh, Havers was saying. The third was someone Clare had merely interviewed about using the adultery website in the first place.

'Way I'm starting to see things,' Havers was saying in conclusion, 'the reason we can't find any internet adultery book could be that Clare Abbott was doing nothing more 'n' catting round with men she'd picked up off the internet. At first she *meant* to write that book. P'rhaps she even started it. But she ended up liking what she found when she got to man number two – this is the bloke who smears chocolate on the ladies and then licks it off – and decided the whole meet-greet-eat-and-beat of Just4Fun chuffed her a hell of a lot more than writing about it did. But what's really interesting is what happened next.'

'There's actually something more interesting than licking chocolate off a woman one's just met?' Lynley enquired pleasantly.

'Too right there is,' Havers told him. ''Cause every one of the men we talked to heard from her afterwards.'

Havers told him about emails from Caro24K, then, directed to the men with whom Clare had had assignations. She touched on demands that were made for eight hundred pounds, as well as which of the men caved in to the blackmail and which of them didn't. 'One 'f them reckoned the blackmail message hadn't come from the same person at all and he had some sort of computer programme or access to a website or something like to work out he was right. Now, what's your guess on who that person is?'

'If that's the case and it proves true,' Lynley said, 'doesn't it make more sense that Caroline Goldacre was the target for a murder and not Clare Abbott?'

'I see that,' she said. 'Me and Winnie? We talked about it as well.'

So when they'd returned to Clare's house, she said, they'd had a look at Clare's bank statements and her chequebook and, as things turned out, 'Those blokes weren't the only ones hearing from someone who wanted money after they'd met up with Clare. There was cheques written to Caroline Goldacre as well. Not pay cheques, these, but cheques for varying amounts. Twenty-five quid here, fifty quid there. One hundred once. What d'you reckon that's about? You ask me, she was blackmailing her.'

'That doesn't sound like blackmail, Sergeant. Twenty-five pounds? Fifty? Even one hundred? It well could be that the Goldacre woman was merely being repaid for something she'd bought with her own funds. Food, wine, office supplies, God knows what. If she was blackmailing Clare, doesn't it seem more likely that she'd want cash? Have you checked Clare's other accounts? There and in London?'

'Not yet. But bank accounts aside, the situation *also* could be Caroline casually dropping the word that "Clare, luv, I'm running short this week. What d'you think about giving me fifty quid?"'

'Not direct blackmail but implied?'

'Right.'

'It's possible, but that takes us back to Caroline Goldacre as the target for murder,' he reminded her.

This led them directly to the fingerprints on the toothpaste tube and to Lynley's request that Havers get Caroline Goldacre's prints as soon as possible. The local police would, he reckoned, be able to assist her with a mobile fingerprinting device and at this point, SO7 would have put the unidentified fingerprints from the toothpaste into the system.

Havers acquiesced to this but added, 'If Caroline Goldacre's dabs're the ones on that tube of toothpaste, something's rotten, and it's not in Copenhagen, Inspector.'

Lynley smiled. 'You impress me. To be rather more accurate, however: Elsinore.'

'What?'

'Elsinore,' he repeated. 'It's in Denmark.'

'So's Copenhagen, 'less they moved it.'

'Never mind,' he told her. 'Carry on, Sergeant.'

*Camberwell*
*South London*

India wished lying to Nat hadn't been necessary. She'd already created an excuse to cancel her last three clients of the day and while telling them that there was a family emergency she had to deal with hadn't actually constituted a lie, she still didn't like having to let them down. But to Nat, she couldn't use the excuse of a family emergency since he would ask with justifiable concern what the emergency was and could he do something to help her. So instead she'd asked him if he'd mind her cancelling their after-work wine date. Her last three clients had all changed their scheduled appointments, she told him, and that being the case, she'd like to go home early and do the pile of laundry that had been growing exponentially for the past two weeks.

'You wouldn't be desperately unhappy if I just went home?' was how she put it.

He'd said, 'Of course I'll be desperately unhappy, darling. You were going to be the antidote to the day I've had.'

He'd been meeting at some length with an architect chosen to design the plans that would preserve an enclave of tiny cottages in Tower Hamlets, which comprised his new project. Facing each other across front gardens with a single pavement bisecting the minuscule neighbourhood, they were just the sort of accommodation that could go under the wrecking ball in order to make way for a block of modern flats if someone didn't fight for their historical significance, which Nat and his battalion of twinset wearing warriors had done for the past two years. They'd won the day but now there was the matter of getting to the work of preservation, and in this cause the firm of architects with whom Nat generally worked had decided that this particular project would be perfect for their twenty-three-year-old intern.

'Limited experience and thick as yesterday's porridge,' Nat told India with a sigh. 'I need a diversion. I was intent upon your being it.'

'I'm so sorry.'

'Not to worry. Just tell me I've made an impression upon your guarded heart.'

'You know you have. And my heart has hardly been guarded in your case.'

'Christmas, then,' he said. 'In Shropshire. Say that you'll come. Dad dressed as Father Christmas for the grandkids. A neighbour's four alpacas done up as reindeer. A wheelbarrow badly disguised as a sleigh. Hats, crackers, poppers, and the Speech after lunch. Really, darling, you don't want to miss it.'

She laughed. 'It's only October. You might not be able to bear me by Christmas.'

'Try me,' he said.

'I shall think about it.'

'And I shall be thinking of you the rest of the day. You and your laundry.' So he'd accepted her excuse as given and as she *did* have laundry to do, India had not needed to mention that she was hosting her mother-in-law for what she earnestly hoped was going to be less than forty-eight hours.

Caroline had been in Camberwell since the morning. Charlie, as promised, had taken her to India's house and had secured the spare key from where she'd left it just inside the rim of the porch light. He'd phoned India once he'd establish his mother within. With thanks that India knew were sincere, he told her that Caroline was far calmer on this morning than she'd been the night before. 'It was a grim evening all round,' he said, 'so it's just as well that I kept her even though it meant sleeping on the sofa. Me, not her. What were we thinking when we bought that piece of furniture, India? It's like sleeping rough in a shop doorway. At any rate, she shouldn't give you any trouble. She was completely on board with staying with you in Camberwell. Far less obvious a place, she says, for a killer to come looking for her.'

'You haven't been able to talk her out of seeing herself as the third victim?' India asked.

'I learned long ago that one can't talk my mother out of anything. I don't expect this will be any longer than a day or two, by the way. She doesn't want Alastair on his own for long. I think she's afraid he'll get used to her absence and start seeing its benefits.'

India was depending on that repeated promise of brevity. She also knew that Caroline's chameleon moods could make that promise a reality as well. She might have left Dorset in a state about Alastair, about his inamorata, about her treatment at the hands of the police who had come calling upon her, about the likelihood of someone out there having her – Caroline – in his or her sights as a murder victim, but all of that could turn on a knife's edge and have her trotting back to Shaftesbury on a moment's notice.

Finally back at home, India looked the house over before she entered the front gate. The curtains were drawn over the sitting room window, the window of the upstairs bedroom that India used as her office/sitting room was also curtained, and

when she put her key in the lock, she found that the door was
bolted against her.

She rang the bell. Once, twice, three times, although she
had to admit herself unsurprised when nothing happened to
give her entrance to her own house. Finally, she rooted her
mobile out of her bag and punched in her home number.
When the answer machine came on, she said, 'Caroline?
Caroline?' And then when Caroline did not answer, she went
on sharply with, 'Mum, open the door at once. I can't get in.'

At this, finally, Caroline's voice came into India's ear. She
said inanely, 'Who is this? Please identify yourself.'

To which India snapped, 'Honestly, who do you think it is?
Open the door at once.'

'I've no idea who you are without your identifying yourself,'
Caroline told her.

'Oh for heaven's sake. Whoever I say I am, I might be lying,
so I suggest you come to the sitting room window, have a look,
and then open the goddamn door.'

There was silence at this. India reckoned that Caroline was
trying to come to terms with the alteration in her previously
compliant daughter-in-law who was now tartly ordering her
about. After a moment, movement at the bay window attracted
India's attention, and she saw her mother-in-law peering
through the glass at her, hand grasping one melon breast as
if to still her pounding heart. India gestured at the front door,
saying loud enough to be heard within the house, 'Unbolt it
at once. This is absurd.'

Caroline disappeared. Then came the sound of the bolt
being released. The door opened. Caroline stepped back from
it and said, 'It was the way you were speaking to me. I'd no
idea you . . . Well, never mind, then. I'm so glad to see you,
darling India. Thank you so very much for allowing me . . .'
She gestured round the small entry and beyond as India stepped
past her. When the door was closed and once again bolted,
Caroline went on. 'I've been in the kitchen and the bedroom
most of the day, just watching the telly and trying to distract

myself from . . . I don't know what to call it, India. From
whatever is going to happen next, I suppose. First Clare and
then Rory and then Scotland Yard detectives showing up on
my doorstep with their questions and their peering at me like
some kind of specimen, as if I might have actually had a hand
in what's happened. And there was Alastair being no support
whatsoever because of that . . . that . . . I don't want to call
her what she deserves to be called.'

India moved past her. There was little enough room to do
so, both because of Caroline's girth and because of the size
of the entry. She scooped up the post on her way and carried
it into the kitchen, Caroline following her and continuing to
speak. 'Forgive me, India. I'm at the point of I don't know
what. If it hadn't been for Charlie and his willingness to take
me in – and your own willingness, of course, my dear – I
wouldn't have known where to turn. And I do understand why
Charlie needed me out of his hair. He can't have his mum
lurking round while he's doing whatever it is he does with his
clients.'

India had been thinking about tea, but she switched to the
idea of wine. She had a bottle of Orvieto in the fridge, and
she brought it out. Caroline, she saw, had already uncorked
it.

'I would have cooked us something for dinner,' Caroline
told her, 'But I didn't know and Charlie didn't say what time
you'd be home. And I have so little appetite myself. But can
I get you something, dear? You must be exhausted. On your
feet all day. Poking people with needles and having to listen
to their stories of their aches and pains. I don't know how you
do it.'

As she poured herself some wine, India saw that the answer
machine was blinking. She went to it. She said over her shoulder,
'I'll make us some pasta in a while. Do have some wine, Caroline.
Some more wine, that is.'

'Oh my dear, I hope it was all right that I opened it? I
thought . . . My nerves . . . I've been on the brink, India. That's

your dad on the phone, by the way. I didn't pick up, of course, but I heard the message. And the young man you were supposed to see after work? He's phoned as well. Nat, he's called, isn't he? Charlie told me his name.'

India set her jaw. She entertained a very clear image of Caroline rushing into the kitchen when the phone rang in order to hear the message being left. Determinedly, she pushed the button to her father's voice saying, 'Your mum has told me about this new bloke, India. Well done. You listen to your old dad when it comes to this. Only a fool decides to fold when there's a chance of a royal flush if he takes another card.'

The message from Nat followed, with him declaring, 'Darling, it's me. We've only just rung off, but I want this message waiting for you when you get home. I'm completely serious about Christmas. And I forgot to mention the soot. Dad does himself up with soot in the beard as well. So far the grandkids haven't noticed that the fire is gas and the chimney wouldn't accommodate a gnome. They might this year, though. You don't want to miss that. We'll speak later, I hope. Happy laundering, by the way.'

India took a large gulp of the Orvieto before she turned to face Caroline. Caroline was sipping her own wine, but her eyes were fixed on India's face, taking in the colour that India could feel in her cheeks. She had no reason to be embarrassed or guilty or ashamed, India told herself. But she still felt . . . something. And this rankled her. She turned back to the worktop, where she'd deposited the post. She began to look through it.

Behind her, Caroline said, 'After Will's suicide, do you really want to do this to Charlie? You're breaking his heart.'

India said nothing. She divided the post into bills, useless adverts, and a greeting card sized envelope with handwriting that she recognised as Nat's. The bills she opened: phone bill, council tax. The adverts she binned. Nat's card she slipped into her shoulder bag for opening later, once Caroline and she weren't occupying the same room.

She decided that now was the moment to make that happen, so she took her things and went upstairs to the second bedroom where what went for her office occupied a space in a corner opposite to that which was devoted to a small television, a sound system, and a DVD player. She saw that Caroline had been on the computer. She realised at once how easy it would have been for her mother-in-law to delve into her personal life. Her computer was set to remember nearly all of her passwords. More the fool I, she said to herself.

Behind her once again, Caroline spoke, having followed her up the stairs. She said, 'You didn't answer me, dear.'

'I'm going to change out of my work clothes,' was what India settled on saying to Caroline. 'I'll meet you back downstairs and then we can talk. But I won't talk about Charlie, so you're going to have to pick a different topic.'

Caroline regarded her, head cocked to one side. It was an evaluative look: the sort one gives to a recalcitrant child while one decides upon the best mode of disciplining her. She said nothing more, but merely turned and, wine glass in hand, went back down the stairs. Ten minutes later – which was as much as India could stretch out her changing from workday clothes to leggings, ballet flats, and a tunic-sized sweater – India found her at the kitchen table, pouring herself another glass of wine. When Caroline opened her mouth to speak, India saw at once what her mistake had been. She'd said she wouldn't speak about Charlie. She hadn't said as much about Nat.

Caroline flicked her fingers in the direction of the phone. 'I suppose he had an idyllic childhood, complete with a loving father present every day. Just as you had, which makes you right for each other to your way of thinking, doesn't it? You've decided that he's solid and reliable, that he comes from an excellent family with no skeletons emerging from cupboards at inopportune times. And certainly no skeletons of the type—'

'I've told you, Caroline,' India cut in. 'I'm not going to talk about Charlie or anything relating to Charlie.'

'But tell me, please . . .' And here Caroline's tone altered.

It was no longer arch as it had been, but instead pained, presumably with a mother's love which, if she had to be honest with herself, India did not doubt Caroline possessed. 'What is it that went wrong for you? Because there has to be a way to mend this. He *wants* to mend it, India. He'll do nearly anything to have you back. He understands that, from the first, he should have . . . I don't know . . . asserted himself more. And I'm at fault here. I'm intrusive. I always wanted the best for my boys in their childhood because God knows their father provided them with less than nothing in the way of nurturing and because of this, I hovered too much. And then I found it impossible to stop the hovering because I'd become so used to it and because no one told me just to *stop*. Someone should have said that to me. No one did. But now . . . India, if you give him another chance, you'll see—'

'What part of my not being willing to talk about Charlie do you not understand?' India demanded. As she spoke, she set her wine glass on the worktop with a *click* against the tiles that was so forceful she was surprised the stem of the glass didn't snap in two. 'Do you not listen when someone speaks to you or do you just disregard what they have to say?'

Caroline appeared to consider this, and for a moment India thought she'd got through to her mother-in-law. When she next spoke, however, Caroline's tone of supplication had altered, but not to apology or to acquiescence. She said tartly, 'You've changed entirely. It's not just your appearance. It's the heart of you. It's gone, isn't it? Or is it just that the heart of you was never even there?'

'I don't know what you're talking about.'

'I expect you've convinced yourself that you're in love with this whoever he is, with his Christmas and his chimneys and his soot in the beard and all the adorable grandkids. You've told yourself that this – *whatever* it is that you're feeling, India, if you can feel at all – is what real love is like when you don't know the first thing about love. Love isn't a momentary obsession with some bloke you may have met in a bar. Love is devotion. It's being willing to stand at the side of someone when he's at his worst and support him, keep him in one piece, do what it takes to make his life a beautiful thing, be his lover, his confidante, his friend, his life's companion, his—'

'Is that what you do for Alastair?' India could feel her heart pounding all the way to her toes and she could feel her face burning as if it had been branded. 'Would that be why he's taken a lover, Caroline? Because you've made his life such a beautiful thing?'

Caroline gulped and clapped a hand over her mouth. She said from behind her fingers, 'You're a monster . . . You're utterly selfish. This . . . It's all about you, isn't it? This . . . this thing with Mr Christmas that you've got. This rejection of my son whose *only* sin was to fall apart when his brother . . . when Will . . .'

She pushed away from the table and got to her feet. She swung round, sank for a moment against the door jamb, righted herself, and left the room. India heard her climbing the stairs and she expected the next sound to be the slamming of her bedroom door, door to the room she'd given up so that her mother-in-law could sleep in comfort. But no slam came. Instead, India heard the quiet closing of the door, following by the *snick* of the lock being turned to bar anyone from entrance.

Thank God for small favours, was what India thought.

*Shaftesbury*
*Dorset*

It was the third ringing of the doorbell that awakened Alastair MacKerron from his kip. He'd dimly heard the first two rings, but he'd assimilated them into the dream he'd been having, which involved trying to find a way out of what seemed to be a medieval castle of the type that lay in ruins round the country. Only this castle wasn't a ruin at all, but the real thing: dark and dreary and cold within as he tried one corridor and then another, all the time knowing that he was looking anxiously for someone whom he could not find. It *seemed* to be Sharon, but it could have been his wife. She was always just out of reach so that the longing he felt to see her grew and yet remained unresolved.

He woke with a start and a sense of sorrow. He reckoned it had indeed been Sharon whom he was seeking because, alone and with Caroline fled to London, he wanted to do what was impossible just now: to move Sharon into the house so that they might begin their life together.

The bell went a fourth time, and on this occasion someone leaned upon it. Alastair groaned and rolled out of bed in his underpants. It hadn't been his regular time for kipping, not this late in the day, but he hadn't slept a wink the previous night, what with worrying what to make of Caroline's decamping to London, so when he'd had the chance for a lie down, he'd taken it, only to fall deeply asleep and now to stand groggily at his bedside, wondering what event would occur next to shatter his life.

At the window, he saw that next event at the same moment as the infernal ringing ceased. It comprised the woman who'd come earlier with the black detective from New Scotland Yard. The black wasn't in sight, and the woman herself had stepped off the porch and was now gazing at the front of the house. She clocked Alastair at the window and she beckoned him down.

He held up one finger to indicate he would need a moment. He struggled into his jeans and his pullover, but he didn't bother with socks or shoes. Nor did he comb his hair. Better she should see she'd disrupted his sleep, he reckoned.

He couldn't remember her name. He told her this when he opened the door. She walked inside, unbeckoned to do so, and said she was DS Havers. Was the wife about? she wanted to know.

'What's this, then?' he asked her. She was making her way

to the sitting room, tugging a ragged bag off her shoulder and depositing it on the sofa, where she also deposited herself. She opened the thing and began to root through it.

'Official bit of work needing to be taken care of,' she told him. 'Orders from London.'

'What's that mean?'

'Fingerprints,' she told him. 'I need your beloved's dabs, Mr MacKerron.' She brought out some sort of device and set it on the coffee table among the magazines, the teacups, and the remains of a cheese and pickle sandwich that he should have binned the previous afternoon.

He felt groggy still. 'You're wanting Caro's fingerprints? Is she s'posed to have committed a crime?'

DS Havers shot him a look, friendly as the dickens. She said pleasantly, 'Well, two crimes've been committed, haven't they? Thinking of it, I need your dabs as well. What this is here . . . ?' She indicated her device. 'It'll run your prints through the system to see if we've got ourselves the match we're looking for. It'll do the same for your wife, fast as anything. No more pouring over whirls and spaces and the like, this is. Amazing what technology can do, eh?'

He looked past her to the garden, which he could see from the sitting room window. He could think of nothing else to say other than, 'Where's the other one, the African.'

'I expect you're talking about DS Nkata,' was her reply. 'He's 'bout as African as I am, but let's not make that matter. You and your wife didn't run him off back to London, if that's what you're asking. He's carrying on with another line of inquiry. So . . . as to the wife . . . ? You want to fetch her for me or should I just start yodelling and hope she hears?'

Alastair said, 'Might be I need to ring a solicitor.'

'Could do, 'course,' DS Havers said cheerfully. 'But all I want is your wife's dabs and yours to clear you of suspicion and as that'll take us something less than five minutes while it'll take your solicitor an age to get here, I expect you'd rather I was out of your hair than making myself a home in it.'

'Suspicion of what?' he asked.

'Murder and attempted murder. Mr MacKerron, I could go at this with a trip to the local magistrate and a warrant, which they're going to grant as easy as my buying myself a pork pie for dinner. But it'd be quicker – not to mention a hell of lot more efficient – if you'll give me your dabs and then fetch your wife so I can take hers.'

'She's not here,' he said. 'You c'n have my prints for all the good it'll do you, but Caro's gone up to London.'

DS Havers didn't look surprised at this, but she did look like someone considering her options. She seemed to reach a fairly quick conclusion about her next move because she then said, 'Sorry to hear that. If you can give me the details on where she is – an address would be nice, phone number as well – then we c'n send someone over to collect her dabs. As for yours . . . Why don't you step right up and let me show you some magic. I expect you don't get to see this sort of thing every day.' She tapped on the device, and said exactly what the coppers always said: If he'd done nothing, he had nothing to fear.

Alastair had his doubts about that.

*Victoria*
*London*

'I thought we had reached an understanding about that animal, Inspector.'

Lynley winced. The doors to the lift had only just opened upon his return from having taken Arlo for his late afternoon walkies. Lynley had expected it to be a simple matter of spiriting the dog down to Reception and then outside and across the street to the smallish green on the corner, followed by a quick jaunt back to work and a depositing of him beneath his desk. But it had taken Arlo longer than Lynley had anticipated to do his business, accompanied as it was by much olfactory examining of the environment. And while Isabelle Ardery had been safely out of the way at a meeting in Tower Block when he'd gone on his way, now here she was, carrying a black, institutional three-ring notebook that told him her meeting had just now ended.

She moved to the side of the corridor to allow others to exit her lift. Lynley did the same. She said to him, 'Had we not reached a friendly, mutual accord?'

'We had,' he said to the superintendent, joining her and ignoring two civilian secretaries who cried, 'A dog!' and 'What a sweetheart!' and wished to give Arlo attention, which would, he knew, cause the guv's own hackles to rise. He went on with, 'This is only a temporary measure, guv. I'd taken him to hospital—'

'Please don't tell me now he's got ill,' Isabelle said wearily.

'He's completely fit. I took him to see his owner. Or his mistress. Or his person. Or whatever is the politically correct expression for someone living with an animal these days. I can't quite keep up with all of the linguistic changes that seem to come up yearly.'

'Don't be amusing. I want him gone. And what sort of hospital allows visiting hours for animals?'

'He wore his vest. That's what he's got on, by the way. It explains he's an assistance dog so—'

'All right, all right.' Isabelle shifted the black notebook, holding it more like a shield than a container for a sheaf of papers.

'I thought it might help her to see him,' Lynley said. 'And it did. She recalled how she came to have in her possession toothpaste that contained the same substance that killed her friend.'

Isabelle cast an eye down on Arlo, who was looking at her in his most appealing fashion. She said, 'And how was this?'

Lynley explained how it had come about: the sight of Arlo

triggering Rory's memory of her hasty leave-taking from Shaftesbury without being in possession of the suitcase which contained her things, toothpaste included. Isabelle listened, her eyes narrowed, her gazed fixed on the dog. When Lynley had completed the tale, she said, 'Why's he doing that? What does he want?'

Lynley glanced down. Arlo was sitting obediently next to him, his tale sweeping the floor like a toppled metronome, his gaze on the superintendent. 'He's a dog, Isabelle,' Lynley explained. 'He wants you to love him. Or at least to act as if you don't wish to hurl him from the nearest window.'

She rolled her eyes. 'The twins,' she said. 'They were absolutely mad for a dog.'

'And . . . ?' he asked.

'Bob wanted one as well. I was the "bad guy", as they say. Of course now he and Sandra have two dogs, four cats, and God only knows what else. Ferrets, I think, Guinea pigs? It could even be rats. I've no idea. Just that they're everywhere. I think they all sleep together in some bizarre version of the family bed. It's all gone overboard and Bob's become quite smug about it. "Another hedgehog to add to the crew," he says like a martyred saint when the truth is he's as mad as she is and even if he weren't, it's such a joy for him to rub my face in . . . in the piles of excrement they no doubt leave round the house. This is the animals, I mean. Not Bob, Sandra, or the boys. I assume all of them are housebroken.'

Lynley smiled. She caught him doing so. She said, 'Why are you smirking? I don't like you smirking, Inspector Lynley.'

'Because,' he told her, 'you're not very good at hiding who you really are. He'd like you to pat his head, by the way. Arlo, not Bob.'

'I'm sure he would. I don't want to see him here tomorrow. Are we on the same page?'

'We are.' His mobile rang. He looked at it, said, 'It's Havers,' and Isabelle said, 'You've not given me a report about her yet. That's not escaped my notice.'

Into the phone he said, 'Hang on, Barbara,' and then to Isabelle, 'It's all going quite well at her end.'

'That's hardly a report. Sergeant Nkata is filling you in daily, I hope?'

'Not enough time has passed for him to fill me in on anything. They're taking the necessary actions and—'

'Don't avoid, Inspector. By tomorrow morning, I'd like to be up to speed. And don't give me that look of yours.'

'I wasn't aware I had a "look".'

'Oh, I'm sure of that. It's your Isabelle-you're-micromanaging look. But allow me to remind you that if anyone round here needs micromanaging, we both know who that person is.' She set off in the direction of her office at that. Arlo gave a little yip as she departed. She waved over her shoulder in acknowledgement and her parting shot was, 'Tomorrow morning, Inspector. Either on my desk or in my email.'

'That was Ardery, wasn't it?' were Havers's first words. 'The air temperature dropped straight through my mobile.'

'She's concerned about how things are progressing at your end,' Lynley told her. 'And as she's *rightfully* concerned, let's not discuss it. I've managed to avoid letting her know that you've set off without Winston, by the way, so whatever you've got to tell me, it had better be indicative of the wisdom of my agreeing to your working on your own instead of doing what I should have done, which is to blow the whistle on you at once.'

'She's done a runner,' Havers said.

'Who?'

'Caroline Goldacre. She's gone up to town. I went round to get her dabs, but her husband told me she's scarpered.'

'Have we any idea where we might find her?'

'With the son. Charlie.' Havers recited an address and, Arlo's lead looped over his wrist, Lynley took it down as the dog waited patiently for whatever was going to happen next.

'Can we assume that the husband will be phoning her with warning?' Lynley asked. 'He can't have been pleased to learn we're after her fingerprints.'

'I don't think we c'n assume anything, sir. He didn't seem broken up by the fact that she's gone, you ask me, but then I'm not a romantic so my antennae aren't attuned to the finer indications of anguish when separated from one's beloved.'

'Frankly, I doubt that,' Lynley told her. 'But I'll sort out the fingerprinting at this end, then. You carry on in Dorset.'

Sorting out the fingerprinting meant coming up with the sort of mobile fingerprinting unit that constables in the street used, which wasn't a problem. Once that had been taken care of, Lynley fetched Arlo, and checked the *A to Z* for the location of Leyden Street and Charlie Goldacre's digs.

A broken water main courtesy of London's Victorian plumbing made traffic its usual horror, but at least Spitalfields was close to the city and not tucked away somewhere in the far reaches of the suburbs. When Lynley arrived there and found a place to deposit the Healey Elliott where it would be safest from the vicissitudes of life in a megalopolis, he attached Arlo to his lead once again, and they walked a few streets back to a curve-fronted Art Deco building where Charlie Goldacre had his flat. As an elderly woman with a drag-along shopping trolley was just setting out of the place, he didn't need to ring Caroline Goldacre's son to ask admittance. He merely held the door open for the woman, graciously accepted her cooing over Arlo – the dog was becoming quite an effective tool, he found – and then stepped inside the vestibule and headed for the stairs. On his way up, he passed a red-eyed woman who was pressing a handful of crumpled tissues to her face and then a sour-faced man a few paces behind her who looked to be the cause of her distress. When he rang the bell at Charlie Goldacre's flat, tucked into a corner of the first floor of the building, he concluded that these two individuals had been seeing Charlie for some reason, for the young man opened the door, saying, 'Did you forget . . .' with his words drifting off when he saw Lynley standing there.

Strangely enough, what he then said was, 'I know this dog,' with a nod at Arlo.

'I'm afraid I'm far too soft-hearted to leave him in the car,' Lynley told him. 'Charlie Goldacre?' And when Charlie nodded, Lynley reached in his jacket for his identification and said, 'Thomas Lynley. New Scotland Yard.'

Charlie looked somewhat taken aback and took half a step into the corridor for a look round, as if expecting someone else to be lurking there. He said, 'I thought you were two of my clients. They'd only just left.'

'I believe I saw them on the stairs. Weeping woman and irritated man?'

'Sounds about right. Marriage counselling.'

'Ah. I need a word with your mother, as it happens. I understand she's come up to town.'

'She's not here. What's this about? You must be part of this Clare Abbott situation. Are you? Mum said she'd spoken to Scotland Yard detectives, but this was in Dorset. Are you one of them? Come in.'

He appeared nervous as he stepped back and held the door open wide, but it seemed to Lynley that it could be merely the nervousness of surprise. He reckoned that the psychotherapist – for such Charlie Goldacre was, apparently – did not open his door to detectives from the Metropolitan Police on a regular basis.

'Two of my colleagues are still in Shaftesbury,' Lynley told him. 'One of them went to speak to your mother a second time, only to learn from her husband that she'd come to you in London.'

'It's yes and no,' Charlie told him. He led the way down a short corridor and into a sitting room. Here the Art Deco period of the building showed itself in decorative crown mouldings, in the fireplace surround, in the bookshelves, and in the style of the windows. The place was decorated to suit the period as well. Someone, Lynley thought, had exceptional taste. Arlo certainly seemed to think so. He looked round, sighed, and curled comfortably beneath a glass-topped side table next to the sofa. 'Mum did come to me, and she was here last night, but I'm afraid I've passed her on to my wife.'

Lynley glanced round the room. There was, he saw, no real indication of a wifely presence. The place was neat, Chinese in its style, and devoid of what he liked to think of as feminine touches although – put to the rack – he wouldn't have been able to say what those feminine touches were supposed to be. There *was* an attractive photograph of Charlie Goldacre and a woman, presumably the wife. Smallish, it stood on the table at one end of a pale green sofa.

Charlie Goldacre seemed to read Lynley's confusion. He said, 'I should say my estranged wife. She's across the river. In Camberwell.' He went on to explain that as he met his clients here in the flat, he'd asked his wife if she'd take in his mother for the duration of her stay in London which, he reckoned, would not be long. 'I think she's come to escape Alastair – that's Mum's husband, my stepfather – rather than hide from the police.'

'Really? How does he fit in?' Lynley asked.

'It's rather a mess between them.' Charlie went on with a charming but – considering his listener – curious honesty. 'Alastair's taken a lover, a woman who works for him. Mum found out some time ago and you can probably work out the rest. I've tried to make peace between them, but I'm afraid I haven't got very far. Alastair gave Sharon up once, but according to Mum, they're back at it, with things having apparently gone too far for the giving up Sharon business. I'm sorry for Mum's sake, but to be honest, she has a way about her . . . I don't know how to describe it.' He shrugged. 'I was about to make myself a martini. Will you join me?'

Lynley said that he would. 'A twist, if you have it,' he told Charlie. 'Rather than olives.'

Charlie said, 'In a tick. Do sit,' and he took himself through a small dining area and into the kitchen, where the sound of refrigerator and cupboards opening commenced.

Lynley didn't sit at once, but rather looked round the room as Arlo raised his head momentarily – perhaps with the hope of dinner – and gazed at him with trusting eyes. Lynley said,

'Later,' and went first to the photo on the table, putting on his specs for a better look. A younger Charlie, a smiling wife, love in bloom. He felt a stab of the occasional sadness that continued to pierce him these seventeen months since Helen's murder. She came to him as she sometimes did and probably always would, and he knew if he concentrated he would hear her voice – *Tommy darling, it's not been a very good day for you, has it? Do tell me, won't you?* – and even feel the touch of her fingers as she smoothed back his hair.

He set the photo onto the table and went to the bookshelves that rose to the ceiling gracefully on either side of the fireplace. They contained art books and works of non-fiction of a type that told the tale of men and women overcoming disasters. Interspersed here and there were the occasional novel as well as *objets d'art* in keeping with the Chinese theme. And on the lowest shelves, books related to Charlie's work and indicative of his background in psychology. Some of these were quite tattered and with their titles missing from their spines; some of them looked like well-thumbed old journals. Everything, however, was neatly arranged. Not a speck of dust rested anywhere.

He turned back to the sofa as Charlie came from the kitchen bearing a tray with their drinks, along with a plate of cheese straws. He set this on a coffee table in front of the sofa with a 'Here we are, then,' and removed a stack of manila folders, a box of tissues, a carafe of water and three glasses. These he put on the dining table, returning to switch on a table lamp and switch off the overhead lights. The room transformed to a home and not a professional meeting place for client and psychotherapist.

While in the kitchen, he'd written an address and two phone numbers on the back of a card. He handed this to Lynley. It was his own card – Charles Goldacre: marriage, family, and individual counselling – and as he gave it to Lynley, he said, 'My wife's details.'

Lynley tucked the card into the breast pocket of his jacket

along with his glasses, saying, 'I'm surprised your mother's husband didn't ring you to tell you the police had come by to speak with her again. It's actually her fingerprints we're after. We've two sets identified on something of Clare's , but we've also a third that's gone unidentified.'

'You're thinking the third set are Mum's?'

'We need to rule her out. It's all procedure unless, of course, she had a reason to do away with Clare Abbott. She was poisoned, if you haven't been told. The fingerprints are on the vehicle that delivered the poison.'

'I see.' He was quiet for a moment. Then, 'You said there are two other sets of prints.'

'One belonging to Clare and the other to Rory Statham.'

Charlie took a sip of his martini. Lynley did likewise. It was very cold and very good. 'You're not suggesting that Rory did something.'

'We're working every angle at the moment,' Lynley told him, 'both here and in Shaftesbury.'

'Still and all, they'd worked together for years, hadn't they? Clare and Rory?'

'They had. What about your mother?'

'Admittedly, she's a handful and God knows she had her issues with Clare – frankly, she has her issues with just about everyone – but I don't think it's likely . . . I know her, probably better than most sons know their mums.'

'You're quite close to her then'

'We both are. Were. My brother Will as well, although he was probably closer to her than I am as he lived with her longer. She was shattered when he died. It changed her. But not into a killer, Inspector.'

'Changed her how?'

Charlie looked regretful for an instant, perhaps feeling a twinge of conscience at having spoken disloyally. But he said, 'She's eaten herself into borderline obesity, although she wouldn't admit that. She'd be far likelier to call it . . . I don't know . . . a sudden problem with her metabolism? A thyroid malfunction? She's on edge a fair amount of the time as well. Close to snapping, experiencing anxiety. Distrustful of people whom she at one time trusted. I expect part of it is down to Alastair, though. His affair and all of that.'

'The name Lily Foster has come up several times,' Lynley told him.

'Are you taking Lily's fingerprints as well?'

'Should we?'

Charlie set his martini on the coffee table, maintaining his position of leaning towards Lynley but looking at the rim of the glass. He'd drunk a fair amount in the few moments that they'd been speaking. His face was flushed. 'Lily was my brother's partner,' he said. 'She was present when . . . Do you know about Will?' He glanced at Lynley as if wishing him to complete the sentence about Lily, and when Lynley did not do so, he explained, adding further details to what Lynley had already gathered. He spoke of Lily's presence when Will Goldacre jumped to his death, her disappearance from the lives of everyone associated with Will, her subsequent reappearance some time later in Shaftesbury, her haunting of Caroline Goldacre's home and the bakery in which Alastair MacKerron made the goods for his many Dorset shops. Charlie concluded with, 'I presume she's still in Shaftesbury. She was when Will's memorial was dedicated. Clare did that for Mum, by the way. She arranged for the memorial. That would be another reason – if you're looking for one – that it's not likely Mum would want her dead. She was touched by it all. She was very grateful.'

'As for Lily Foster?'

'She had no relationship to Clare at all, as far as I know,' Charlie told him. 'I saw her lurking about at the dedication for my brother's memorial. I spoke to her as well. But I think she's gone too far round the bend to plan something like a killing. She blames Mum for Will's death and Mum blames her but, frankly, I see them as mutually harmless.' Charlie finished off his martini and placed the glass on one of the cocktail napkins he'd provided for both of them. He said,

'Mum's a bit . . . Look, you must talk to her yourself. She's always been dramatic about things, overwrought and all that, but I honestly don't see her ever lifting a finger to hurt anyone.'

Lynley said, 'I've spoken to your father, by the way.'

Charlie's face was, for a moment, motionless. Then he said with what seemed like a deliberate lack of concern, 'I expect that's part of what you have to do.' Interestingly, he didn't ask why Lynley had met with Francis.

'I've spoken to your grandmother as well.'

'Have you indeed? What're you after?'

'Clare Abbott went to see them both shortly before her death. We're after why.'

'May I ask if you found an answer?'

'Not exactly. They both did indicate that your mother is something of a pathological liar, however, and Clare appears to have been on the trail of that for some reason we can't work out. Do you experience your mother that way?'

'I experience her as over-the-top when it comes to personal drama. I experience her as frequently manipulative as well. She's sometimes delusional and rather grandiose, but as far as I know she's never been an out-and-out liar.'

'What about someone who lies by omission?'

'Have you an example of that?'

'According to your grandmother, your mother had a child out of wedlock at fifteen years of age. Has she told you this?'

'Gran told me. And before you point out that this is a very good example of a lie of omission, I have to say that Mum never told me about it because there was actually no reason to do so and that when Gran told me, it was owing to some sort of row she and Mum had had. Gran likes to take her revenge when she can and the revelation about Mum's adolescent pregnancy . . . ? That was the way. The baby she had – and by the way, I know it was a daughter – wasn't part of our lives. She wasn't posing as a cousin or a friend of the family. There was no reason for Mum to bring her up and she probably wanted to forget about ever having her anyway. It was years ago. She was very young. It wasn't our business, and there's an end to it.'

Barbara felt rather proud of what she'd managed to accomplish while waiting for Winston to return from his out-and-about. While she'd gone in Clare's car for Caroline Goldacre's fingerprints, he'd headed out in search of Hermione, Linne, and Wallis: the women whose names had been in Clare Abbott's diary. Since Barbara had finished up first, she'd decided she owed Nkata a meal. He, after all, had been doing the honours with breakfast and lunch. Applying herself to dinner didn't seem like something that would tax her knowledge.

There was a supermarket in the centre of Shaftesbury, where she stopped before returning to Clare Abbott's house. She grabbed a shopping trolley and sauntered in the direction of whatever was tinned. There was a limit, admittedly, to her culinary skills.

Of course, Winston didn't need to *know* that tins were involved. How difficult could it actually be to pull the wool over his eyes? All she needed to do was get back to the house in advance of his arrival. She could heat up whatever she happened to come upon that looked decent in the market and she could also hide the tins. A quick trip up and down four aisles did the trick. She grabbed tinned beef goulash and tinned beetroot, and then went in search of something that would do for a starter. She settled on savoury biscuits with orange marmalade accompanied by tuna and mayo paste, and she then made her selection of pudding by scoring a frozen toffee pecan Dream Pie. After that, all she needed was drink, which was simplicity itself. Three cans of white wine would do for her and three bottles of Fanta Lemon would satisfy Winston. It was time he broadened his horizons anyway. One could not possibly stay hydrated over a lifetime on skim milk and water alone.

She had the goulash bubbling away on the cooker and everything else – save the toffee pecan pie – on a neatly laid table when the sound of the front door opening heralded Nkata's return. She'd burned the pie a bit, but she'd knocked the blackened bits into the rubbish, where she'd also placed the tins and the jars from which her sumptuous repast had come. These she'd covered with the plastic carrier bags from the market and, for good measure, she'd also crumpled up two old newspapers and smashed them down to hide the bags whose Co-op logos were something of a giveaway, she had to admit.

Nkata paused in the kitchen doorway. He observed her at the cooker, wooden spoon in her hand and steam rising from a copper-bottomed pot. He said, 'You doing dinner, Barb?' and he held up a shopping bag himself, adding, 'Guess I di'n't need to bother. I was goin' to do us beef, mushroom and lager pie. Sprouts with bacon, shallots, 'n' hazelnuts, 's well.'

'Shallots, eh?' Barbara wondered what the hell they were. 'I did us a goulash,' she said. 'Can yours wait for tomorrow?'

'Can,' he said, and he began to unload his carrier bag, whose contents proclaimed his intention actually to make the beef, mushroom, and lager pie from scratch. From *scratch*, she thought. She felt her mouth water. Beef, mushrooms, lager, a delicious gravy, flaky crust, sprouts, bacon, nuts, and . . . whatever they were . . . oh yes, shallots. But she got a grip and turned determinedly back to the cooker where she lifted the lid of her pot and let its aroma waft into the air.

Admittedly, it smelled a bit burnt. She scraped the bottom of the pan energetically to mix the burnt bits more thoroughly into the rest of the goulash. She said, 'Have a seat and I'll bring this out. There's a starter on the table. Drinks 's well.'

'Will do,' he said, balling up his carrier bag. 'I'll just toss—'

'No!' Wooden spoon in hand, she leaped towards him so frantically that he started. He looked from her to the rubbish bin. He said her name in what she recognised as a what-am-I-about-to-discover-here tone. And then he strode to the rubbish, lifted its lid, lifted the crumpled newspapers, and shot her a look once he'd clocked the tins. 'Barb,' he said in a voice that spoke largely of his concern. Not for her, of course, but for his body. God knew he'd probably never sullied it with something factory-made before now.

'You'll survive,' she said. 'It'll be a new experience. It might change your whole world. Live a little. Spread your wings.'

He considered her, then the discarded tins and jars, then her again. He chuckled and said, 'Should've guessed when I saw you at the cooker. I almost passed out. The shock an' all that. Least it's a good thing you're not smoking over the pot, innit.' He gazed at her earnestly. He sniffed the air. 'You *didn't* smoke while you were heatin it, Barb? Get some ashes in it and stir 'em up?'

'Me? No. What d'you think I am? Bloody hell, Winston, go sit down.' She slid her jar-top ashtray out of sight to the side of a stainless steel canister. When he'd obediently left her for the dining room, she flung the jar top and its contents of five dog ends into the rubbish, where a nice stirring mixed it all in with the rest of the evidence of her sins.

Nkata was at the table, cooperatively tucking into the tuna and mayo paste. He spread some on a biscuit and topped it with marmalade. Had his mother been dead, Barbara reckoned, she would have spinning. As it was, when he smiled and nodded his approval at her, she said, 'Your every secret will be safe with me.'

She dished up the goulash. She handed over the beetroot. She sat and dug in. A little over-cooked, a little burnt, the beetroot a little soggy, but what the hell. She dolloped tuna and mayo paste on top, tried it out with the goulash, and decided it wasn't half bad. She said, 'Got toffee pecan pie for our pudding,' as she popped open her can of white wine.

'Jus' don't tell my mum.'

'Like I said,' she agreed.

It wasn't until they'd finished their meal that they got down to business. Her part of the telling was brief: Caroline Goldacre was in London but Alastair MacKerron had cooperated and she'd taken his prints. Nkata's part was lengthier and far more interesting. He'd tracked down both Hermione and Linne – 'Seems this bird Wallis's gone off to Canada to see the first grandkid' – and they'd been happy to give him everything they knew when it came to Clare Abbott and Caroline Goldacre.

'First off,' he said as he forked up some goulash and inspected it carefully, 'seems she's not quite right in the head when it comes to lookin' at herself in the mirror.'

'Which one of them? Caroline?'

'Caroline, yeah. 'Cording to Hermione and Linne, she sees herself as a real fem'nist but she's been supported by one man or th'other since she was summat like . . .' He held his fork suspended while he examined his leather notebook . . . 'eighteen years old. Tha's when she had her first kid. Been involved in the Women's League round here since she an' Alastair got the bakery and first she tried to take over the thing—'

'The Women's League?'

'Right, 'cos she saw herself as the most comp'tent person to run it. Which these two ladies – Hermione and Linne? – reckoned was the funniest thing this side of a comedy show on the telly. Also . . .' He finally deposited the goulash into his mouth and chewed thoughtfully as Barbara watched to see his assessment. He grabbed his glass and took a hearty gulp of Fanta Lemon before saying politely, 'Not half bad, Barb. My mum, she doesn't ever make goulash. It's got a . . . an in'erestin' flavour, eh?'

'That would be the burnt bit,' Barbara told him. 'I probably shouldn't have scraped the bottom of the pot.'

'Oh. Makes the clean up easier, that,' he said. 'No worries.'

'The tuna paste might make it go down easier.'

''Spect it would, but I like it how it is.' He went back to his notebook. 'Also,' he continued on the topic of Hermione and Linne, 'Seems that she wasn't 'xactly happy working for Clare. Seems she felt—' He ran his long finger down the notebook page to find something and then said, 'Ill-used. She thought her wages were too low by half, 'specially 'cos she was the one doin' the heavy lifting, she said.'

'Meaning?'

'This Hermione? She says Caroline claimed she was doing most of the writing of Clare's books 'n' articles while Clare was takin all the glory.'

Barbara drew her eyebrows together as she thought this one over, comparing the information to the various cheques that had been written by Clare to the woman.

Winston continued. 'Said she could take over Clare's work in a minute and Clare was nothing if *she* wasn't round to see to it pages got sent in regular to her editor. 'Cording to Hermione, this is. Plus, she says, af'er the service for Clare at St Peter's? Tha's the church in town here. She was banging on 'bout Clare taking advantage of her for the whole time she worked for her.'

'What about the other woman? Linne? How's she fit in?'

That, Nkata told her, was a more interesting tale. It seemed that Linne and Caroline Goldacre had once been friends. 'Real besties,' was how Winston put it. But they had a falling out about a building that Linne and her husband owned in a part of Shaftesbury called Swan's Yard. 'Some sort 'f artsy place with a few galleries and such.' The building that Linne and her husband owned comprised a shop below and a small flat above, and they had let both the flat and the shop to a tattoo artist. As it turned out, the tattoo artist was Lily Foster, and Caroline wanted Linne and her husband to evict her.

'She wouldn't do,' Winston finished. 'Said the girl had a lease she'd signed, she'd put a fat deposit on the place, she wasn't trouble, and Linne had no cause to evict her. Caroline wants her to *make* a cause to evict her, more 'r less. Linne says no.' He flipped his notebook closed and Barbara was gratified to see him spear up some more goulash, although he did take it on with a load of beets as well. 'So tha' was it 'tween them as friends. It all happened 'bout a year after the son killed himself. Which, 'cording to Hermione, is something Caroline keeps picking at like it's a scab she doesn't want to heal over. Turns out neither of these ladies had a heart for Caroline, but they liked Clare. Weren't thick with her, nothing like that. But they admired her. Said they couldn't ever sort out why she kept Caroline working for her 'less Caroline was blackmailing Clare or summat. They had a good laugh on that one, Barb. Said they couldn't 'magine what secrets Clare might've had that Caroline knew enough 'bout to blackmail her over. In'erestin', that, I thought, specially considering Clare's chequebook, the blokes she met up with for sex, an' the black-mail someone tried with them.'

'I can't see Clare wanting her meetings with those blokes to get out,' Barbara agreed. 'But when I told the inspector, he banged on about the amount of money involved in the cheques we looked at: hardly looked like blackmail money is what he said and wouldn't Caroline have wanted cash anyway? I'm more or less on board with him, Winnie, when it comes to that. She wanted eight hundred quid from the blokes. Why go for so little from Clare? We need to look into all of her accounts – she's got to have some in London – but . . . I don't know if money is the way to go.'

'Maybe her job was the blackmail, Barb. Cos when Clare talked to those ladies Hermione and Linne . . . ? They reckoned, at the end of the conversation, it might've been cos she was trying to come up with some way to sack her. "She needed sacking" was how one 'f them put it. But no way was Caroline ever going down without a fight.'

'"We're finished." That's what one of them said in Cambridge, eh?' Barbara reminded him.

'"Not with what I know 'bout you. We'll never be finished,"' Nkata countered with a nod.

India was doing the washing up when the doorbell rang. Behind her at the kitchen table, Caroline drew in a sharp breath and said, 'You *mustn't* answer that, India. It could be anyone, especially round here and after dark' and it was the evaluation of her neighbourhood more than anything else that made India determined to slide the bolt back and throw the door open.

They'd just finished dinner and Caroline had just helped herself to another bottle of wine. Sangiovese, this one was. India had been saving it for a dinner with Nat that she'd planned for next week, but true to character, Caroline had simply helped herself.

When the doorbell went a second time, India dried her hands, called out, 'Coming,' and strode towards the entry. Caroline, irritatingly, followed her, saying, 'Look through the curtains at least. Please.'

India sighed and went to the bay window in the house's sitting room. She flicked back the curtains an inch to see Nat standing there, the recognisable shape of him illuminated by the street lamp just beyond him on the pavement. Behind her, Caroline said, 'Ah. That's the new man, isn't it?'

India said nothing. She tried to decide what to do – to ignore the bell or to open the door – and what might be the consequence of either action. She'd told Nat she'd be at home, so anything else would encourage him to think her a liar. Thus, it didn't seem she had much choice. She headed for the door as Caroline added, 'I suppose I can celebrate that you've not yet given him your house key.'

Ignoring this jibe, India unbolted and opened the door, switching on the porch light first. It wasn't like Nat simply to turn up like this, and while the last thing she wanted was for him to meet Charlie's mother, she knew that asking Caroline to give them some privacy was not going to move her from what was clearly her intention: to be introduced to India's lover. Her mother-in-law made this apparent by standing directly behind India, although out of sight, which was a very small blessing as things turned out.

Nat said, 'Ah. There you are. I went to the church first,' which reminded India that this was one of her rehearsal nights with the choir, and she'd forgotten. 'When I saw you weren't there, I was . . . well, not so much concerned as selfishly intent to give this to you. I was thinking it might convince you.'

*This* was a photograph, which he handed over. She saw that it was of a toddler on the back of an alpaca 'reindeer' with cloth antlers attached to its head. Nat as an adolescent wore elfin clothing and an expression of forbearance as he held the reins of the animal. A light dusting of snow was on the ground.

He said, 'It was all true, as you can see. I think I was about . . . Let me see. I must have been seventeen when I realised that the alpacas *weren't* actually reindeer and that my dad was certainly not Father Christmas. I ought to have drawn the conclusion earlier . . . say at sixteen? . . . but I was rather thick.'

She laughed. 'You're very persistent, Nathaniel Thompson.'

'I've a good reason to be.'

At that, Caroline stepped out from behind the door and said, 'I'd so like to be introduced to your friend, India.'

Nat looked surprised. 'Oh. Sorry. I'd no idea you had company.'

Caroline responded with, 'You must come in. We're doing the washing up. There's wine left, and I expect you'd like a glass. You're Nat, aren't you?'

India felt frozen to the spot. The last thing she wanted was Caroline's presence polluting her nascent relationship with Nat. She merely wasn't sure how to avoid it.

Nat said, 'I . . .' and clearly tried to read the situation, which was admittedly a confusing one for him.

Caroline reached past India's blocking of the doorway and plucked the photograph out of her hands. She carried it towards the kitchen where the light was better. She called back over her shoulder, 'Don't be a stranger out there, Nat. Do come in. Is this you, then? Ah. Yes. I can see that it is. You were quite a handsome adolescent, weren't you? And you've become quite a handsome man. I can see the attraction, India.'

There was no choice at that point. India stepped back from the doorway, holding it open for Nat. She said, 'Sorry,' in a low voice. 'There was so little I could do.'

Caroline was busying herself with the wine: fetching another glass for Nat, pouring him a nice dose, doing the same for herself and for India, ever the bustling hostess. When they joined her, she said brightly, 'I'm Caroline Goldacre, Charlie's mum. Have you met Charlie?'

'He has,' India told her.

'How very civilised.' Caroline handed round the wine. India had no intention of drinking hers, but Nat was willing. He took a sip and studied the wine as if to admire the ruby colour. He was, India reckoned, probably trying to sort out what to make of all this. Caroline went on. 'You seem to have a lovely family Christmas every year, Nat, if your telephone message is anything to go by. I happened to hear it earlier. That and one from India's father. It was about you. You'll be happy to know that the Honourable Martin Elliott is encouraging his daughter on your behalf. I can't say that I'm doing the same. Charlie is, after all, my surviving son.' She took a swig of her wine.

India said, 'Caroline . . . Mum . . .'

Caroline held up her hand. 'I've said too much. I always do. Let me make myself scarce so the two of you can do whatever it is that you wish to do. I ought to check in with Charlie anyway. He'll want to know how I'm coping.' She sent a fond glance in India's direction. 'It was good of India to take me in. Charlie asked her to do it, you know.'

She left them at that, taking her wine and the bottle with her. India knew that her face was colouring, for she felt the heat rising from her chest. She started to say, 'I'm so—'

Simultaneously Nat said, '*Did* they cancel?'

She looked at him blankly. He was gazing at her, both of

his hands cupping his wine glass now. He seemed to realise he was still holding it without wanting to hold it, for he set it on the table as she tried to work out what he meant. She said, 'Did who cancel?'

'I see. Listen, I'm not bothered by your lying to me, India, considering the circumstances. But I *am* bothered by the fact that you thought you had to.'

Then she twigged: the clients who she claimed had cancelled their appointments. She said, 'I'm sorry. I didn't know what you'd think. I could hardly say no to Charlie when he asked me. He meets his clients in our flat. He couldn't have them and his mum there at the same time. It would have been impossible.'

His gaze was level, his dark eyes serious. 'Our flat,' he said.
'What?'

'You just said "He meets his clients in our flat".'

'It's a turn of phrase. It doesn't mean anything. Just that I owe him at least the amount of kindness that it takes to give his mother a place to stay for a night or two.'

'And are you sure that's all?'

'I can't think it'll be longer. She's going to want to get back to Dorset. Her husband's there – Charlie's stepfather—'

'I meant the kindness bit, not how long his mum will be staying.'

She sighed. 'Oh, Nat. Really . . .' She turned from him and went back to the sink where the washing up had been interrupted. But she didn't do more than merely stand there and look through the night-blackened window to the tangled mess of a garden that she couldn't see.

Behind her, he said, 'Never mind. That was . . .' He paused as if seeking a way to describe what he was feeling, and he settled on saying, 'All of a sudden I felt myself doing a werewolf thing. Only there's no full moon and I don't suppose I mean a werewolf anyway.'

She turned from the window. 'Whatever are you talking about?' she asked with a smile.

'Sorry. I think I meant caveman. I grab you by the hair and drag you into my lair. I don't think werewolves do that.'

'Did cavemen have lairs?'

'They had to have something else they wouldn't be called cavemen. It's quite odd, though, isn't it? The primitive is always there, just beneath the surface of our civility, all those carefully cultivated social mores. One still wants to lay claim, and the claim comes down to possession. My fire, my hearth, my . . . whatever.'

'My woman,' she finished for him. 'But I don't want to be anyone's woman.'

'I understand. And the truth is that I wouldn't want you to want to be someone's woman, even mine. It's just that moments come when what I really want is to make definite something that can never *be* definite. Because, of course, nothing ever is.'

She returned the gaze he was directing at her. She felt such a swelling within her, a real movement towards him although she wasn't herself moving at all. She wondered at it, asking herself if this particular sort of feeling was what she'd always been meant to experience with and for a man. But she didn't know because she had to admit to herself that part of what she felt was the desire for Nat to sweep into her life and make all of her decisions for her.

Nat roused himself. With a nod at the photo, which Caroline had deposited on the table, he said, 'This is what you'd have to look forward to, by the way. I'll go on to tempt you with the menu for Christmas lunch later. It's always spectacular. And of course the great gathering of the clan to hear the Speech in the afternoon. That's always accompanied by plum pudding with massive amounts of cream.'

She returned to him and to the table, where she picked up the photo and looked at his achingly young adolescent face. She said, 'May I keep this? Somehow, the sight of your teenage self – complete with a few spots, I see – makes you seem . . . I don't know the word.'

'Less like a caveman? Although a caveman would have had hair, not spots, I expect.'

She looked from the picture to him. 'You've a lovely history behind you, don't you? Family, love, traditions, security.'

'For my sins,' he admitted. 'I'm embarrassed to tell you that I allow my brothers' and sisters' children to crawl all over me. There are – God forbid – ten of them now. And counting as my youngest sister is pregnant again.'

'That's very compelling.'

'Her pregnancy?'

'All of it.' She put the picture down and slid her arms up and around his neck. When they kissed, she let go of everything else that was eating at her mind: Caroline, Charlie, loyalty, love, guilt, and fear. Instead she allowed herself the pull of her desire for him. His arms encircled her and drew her close and she saw his desire was a match for her own.

The doorbell rang. As if with guilt, they jumped apart. They stared at each other and India knew they shared the same thought: Charlie.

Caroline was down the stairs in an instant, before India could make a move. She scurried into the sitting room where she did her bit with the curtains, calling back to them, '*Another* man? Goodness, aren't you the sly one, India.'

*Camberwell*
*South London*

Lynley had left Arlo in the car this time. It had been a long and invigorating day for the dog – at least that was how Lynley liked to think about it – and he was happy to snooze in the passenger seat of the Healey Elliott, which Lynley left just outside the house where Charlie Goldacre's wife India apparently now lived.

When he rang the bell, he had to do so twice. He was surprised when it was opened not by a woman who might have been married to Charlie Goldacre but rather by a man. He was tall and dark of hair, eyes, and eyebrows, and his skin suggested the need to shave more than once a day. He was wearing a suit that fitted him very well in the manner of something not off the peg, and his shirt was white and crisp, even with his tie removed and his collar unbuttoned. Physically, he was completely different from Charlie Goldacre.

His expression was somewhere between wary and confused. Behind him stood a young woman whom Lynley recognised from the photo in her estranged husband's flat. Behind *her* and just emerging from what was apparently a sitting room to the left of the entry was an older woman: far too heavy, double-chinned, a great deal of spectacular eyeshadow, showy gold earrings, two necklaces, swirls of brightly designed silk fashioned into some sort of garment meant to disguise her body's shortcomings. Presumably, this was Charlie's mother.

Lynley removed his police identification from his jacket. He introduced himself. He saw Caroline Goldacre fall back, as if with the hope of going unnoticed, which was hardly likely. He said he was there to speak with her. 'I understand from Charlie that you're in town for a few days,' he said. 'If you might give me five or ten minutes?'

Caroline said, 'What's this about?' as India said, 'Of course. Come in, Inspector. I'm India Elliott. This is Nathaniel Thompson.'

Thompson said to her, 'Shall I . . .' and indicated the street outside with an inclination of his head.

'No. Please stay,' India said.

He stepped back from the door, admitting Lynley to the house as Caroline Goldacre protested with, 'I've already spoken to the police. I don't see what more I can possibly have to say to anyone.'

Lynley made no reply to this. Inside the house, he saw that the sitting room wasn't actually a sitting room, but rather something of a medical suite. It contained an examining table of sorts, along with a blocked fireplace, a cabinet, and shelving being used to store equipment and filing folders. He'd seen the sign on the front window advertising acupuncture. This, then, must be where India met her patients.

She said to him, 'I'm afraid we'll have to go to the kitchen if you don't mind. Would you like a coffee?'

Caroline said sharply, 'India,' in a way that suggested how unacceptable to her was the other woman's hospitality. India ignored this and led the way to the kitchen. Everyone followed.

Lynley saw that the washing up from dinner was in progress, some crockery languishing on the draining board and some pots piled in the sink with a washing-up brush tilted down among them. It wasn't a large room, and four people crowded it. India offered to leave him with her mother-in-law but Caroline protested. She wanted a witness, she insisted.

Lynley wondered what she thought was going to happen, but he let it go. He had the mobile fingerprinting kit with him, and he set this on the table, saying that India's presence or absence from the scene was no matter as he wouldn't be there long. He told Caroline Goldacre that he'd been in Spitalfields at her son's flat in order to—

'How did you know I'd gone to Charlie?' Caroline demanded.

'My colleague, Barbara Havers,' he said. 'She went to speak to you another time in Dorset, only to be told by your husband that you'd come up to town.'

'Why did she want to speak to me?' Caroline had not sat at the table. Neither had anyone else. India stood near the sink and the unwashed pots, Thompson leaned against the fridge, and Caroline herself remained in the doorway, ready to fly at the least provocation, Lynley reckoned. She continued when he didn't immediately answer, 'I told you. I've already spoken to her. More than once. And with you as well. That *was* you on the phone, wasn't it?'

'It was.'

'I'd only gone to Clare's to fetch the rest of what's mine,

you know,' she said. 'I tried to tell her that. I don't understand why you lot need to have my personal belongings. They are, after all, mine. A letter opener, an antique toast rack that I used for the post, a Sellotape dispenser that I bought because Clare couldn't be bothered, my coffee mug, a lunch kit I'd forgotten was there. None of this can be relevant.'

'It's all procedure,' Lynley told her pleasantly. 'Another way of clearing the deck of suspects.'

He saw India and Thompson exchange a glance as Caroline's voice rose on, 'And *what* am I a suspect of?'

'It's awkward, of course,' Lynley said, 'considering you were the last person to be with Clare Abbott before she died.'

'Aside from whoever killed her,' Caroline pointed out. '*If* she was murdered at all because this whole business of something supposedly *causing* her heart attack . . . Your sergeant told me, by the way. And what, may I ask you, is meant to do that?'

She spoke, Lynley thought, as if it was a personal affront to her that Clare had died. He said, 'That's why I've come, actually. I'm going to need your fingerprints to rule you out as a suspect. The source of the substance that caused Clare Abbott's heart arrhythmia, seizure, and death had three sets of fingerprints on it. We're in the process of identifying all of them.'

'And you believe one set of them is mine.'

'This is all normal procedure, Ms Goldacre,' Lynley told her another time.

'Oh please. Of *course* that's what you'd say. But do you actually believe I had a reason to kill *anyone*?'

'The substance in question – the poison – was found in toothpaste. We've learned only today that this toothpaste belonged to Clare. Since you were travelling with her when she died—'

It was Caroline's expression that stopped him. From pinched and annoyed, her face had altered to unmistakable shock or a very good imitation of it. He said, 'What is it?'

'Mine.' Her tone of alarm seemed genuine enough.

'The toothpaste?'

'Yes. Oh God.' She swayed. India moved to her. She drew out a chair from the table and told her to 'Sit, Mum. Here.'

Caroline did so. She spoke with her eyes fixed on the mobile fingerprinting device on the table. 'Clare had forgotten hers. We had words. Yes, I *admit* we did have words because I was exhausted and she'd sworn to me that the evening wouldn't go on past ten, but it had. Earlier, before we argued, she'd realised she'd forgotten to bring her toothpaste along to Cambridge, so I gave her mine. To borrow, not to keep. But we had a . . . a discussion and things got heated, and I left her. I locked the door between our rooms as I didn't want to have anything more to do with her that night. She could be so overbearing and full of herself and . . . You do see what happened, don't you? I realised later that I had no toothpaste, so I phoned down to reception for a resident's kit or whatever they're called. But there wasn't one, so I went without.' She placed her hand over her ample left breast as if to pledge to the truth of what she was saying, but instead of making that pledge she said, 'I feel unwell. India, dear . . . Is there water?'

India brought her a glass of mineral water that she took from the fridge. Before drinking, Caroline examined the glass's contents and then India's face as if with suspicion that her daughter-in-law was about to do her in directly in front of New Scotland Yard. But she drank and said, 'My heart is absolutely *pounding*. Give me a moment please.'

They all watched her. Whatever she was feeling, her expression was of a woman considering the ramifications of having in her possession and then giving to another what had apparently been the means of that other's death. She said, 'You do see what happened, don't you? I'm the only person who was ever meant to die.'

19 October

A lastair reached Sharon's house at seven forty, when the sun was just beginning to strike the outlying fields so that their heavy-topped grasses coruscated like diamonds as the dew that bent them was hit by the daylight. For the very first time he'd left the job of loading up the bakery's delivery vans to his assistant and to the three drivers who'd then deliver fresh goods to his shops. But despite this, he was suffering from not a single moment of guilt. Instead his arrival at the farmhouse tucked so neatly among the terraces and cottages in Church Road felt completely natural.

He allowed himself a mad fantasy as he approached the front door. He was a husband coming home to a wife who was waiting for him with breakfast cooking. She was a wife who'd risen at half past six to lay his place at table and who was now, even as he inserted his key in the lock, anticipating his footsteps coming along the stone floor.

He'd phoned the moment Caroline had stormed off from Shaftesbury. He'd told her that Caroline had gone to London and he tried not to sound anticipatory, hopeful, or anything else that might make her think he presumed. She'd said, 'Has something happened, Alastair? Are you at odds with Caroline?'

'When are we not at odds?' he said. 'She's gone to Charlie. For protection is what she said.'

'Are you not her protection?'

'Doesn't seem that way.'

'What are you meant to do now?'

'I'm meant to be with you.'

She'd not said anything at first, and Alastair thought he'd gone too far. In his hours alone he'd dwelt too much on a future he was daily more determined to have with her.

Finally, she said, 'But surely, she's not gone off forever. This is just a bump in the road.'

'I'm sick and tired of bumps in the road,' he told her.

'I do wish I could smooth them for you, my dear.'

He let the *my dear* reach into him. He could feel it touch the heart of who he was truly meant to be.

She said, 'Would you like to come to dinner, Alastair?'

'I would.' So he'd gone to her and after they'd eaten, they went to bed. He'd risen at half past one in order to get to the bakery by two, and he was bleary-eyed because he'd slept so little because he had not wanted to sleep.

She'd not slept either, not more than two hours. She'd come to the door with him and had sent him off with a flask of hot coffee to get him going. And now here he was, back in Thornford, where she was no doubt in bed trying to catch up on a few hours' kip.

He couldn't help himself. He yearned – that was indeed the word for it – to feel her hand on the back of his neck, the lightest caress as he sat at table waiting for the breakfast she would cook him. Or just the touch, the touch itself, no breakfast at all because it was, truthfully, only the touch that he wanted.

He entered the house. At once, he smelled coffee. He went to the kitchen, and there he saw that two places were laid on the table with a shaft of sunlight falling upon them. At each place a half of a grapefruit glistened, and these were joined by a box of cornflakes, a jug of milk, a bowl of sugar. On the worktop across from the table, two slices of his bakery's wholemeal bread were upright in the toaster, and a bowl in front of this held four eggs, companions to the half dozen or more rashers of bacon that lay neatly in a pan on the hob.

It was like an advert for marital bliss. The blessed woman meant to cook him breakfast, but he decided he would set about it himself and surprise her with a tray brought to her bedside.

He broke the eggs into the bowl and went for the rubbish to toss the shells. That was when he saw her through the window, up and about already and fully dressed for the day. She was sitting beneath the laburnum tree in one of the two colourful deck chairs. It was leafless now – that elegant tree, so long safely unplanted till her children were older – and it wept its thin and deadly brown pods onto the rectangle of lawn beneath it. Sharon was fingering one of these pods as she looked beyond her garden and out into the fields of the farm behind it where the sheep were grazing.

He was surprised to see her at repose like this, so clearly thoughtful and dwelling on something that he could only hope was himself. In the times they'd been together, she'd always been at work: sewing a button onto his shirt, ironing table napkins worn thin with age, folding laundry, cutting spent flowers from the herbaceous border that fringed the lawn and formed an undulating motley against the house. She still wrote letters, and when her chores were done, she sat at a narrow secretaire in the sitting room and penned them in her neat handwriting to her children. No email for her, she told him. A letter lasts, she explained. A letter could be saved, collected, and bound with a ribbon to send onward to the next generation. An email could not. True, one had to *wait* for a letter, but she was a patient woman, and she'd taught her two children to be likewise. One has to learn to wait for what's important, she explained.

Perhaps, he thought now, that was what she was doing outside in the morning light. Not thinking or dwelling at all. Merely waiting for what was coming.

Since she did not know he was in her house, he continued to watch her. He was taken with how the morning sunlight struck her hair. Caroline called it mousy, he recalled. Thin and baby fine and straight and 'You can hardly call it hair at all,' she'd scoffed, but he could see in this light that blonde worked its way through it in strands so subtle that you wouldn't notice them if you were not looking.

She seemed to realise that she was being observed, for she turned in her chair and at that point he knocked upon the window. She didn't look at all surprised to see him, but her expression did seem pleased. She got to her feet and came across the lawn in his direction, tossing the laburnum pod to one side and running her fingers back through her hair as if to neaten it. She wore her gardening clogs, he saw, the bright red of them a pleasing contrast to the equally bright green of the lawn. He heard them hit the back step with a *thunk* as she removed them, and then the door opened and she was with him.

He'd turned the burner on beneath the bacon and he'd lowered the bread into the toaster. She saw this and said, 'I'm meant to be doing that for you,' to which he replied, 'How'd you know I'd be back?'

'I didn't.' She'd paused at the door to put on her indoor shoes. She didn't come farther into the kitchen but instead observed him for a moment, saying, 'But I hoped.'

He had started whipping the eggs with a fork, but the way she'd said that final word made him pause. It had seemed to come from within her chest, like something deeply felt but only reluctantly spoken. The tone of it prompted him to ask her, 'And if I'd not come . . . ?'

'My life would go on. Life has a way of doing that.'

He could feel his face alter despite his attempt to keep it from doing so. It hadn't been the answer he'd hoped for. She apparently saw this change in him, for she came to him and said, 'Alastair, have I hurt you?'

He shook his head. 'Bloody stupid is all.'

She brushed her fingers against his thinning curls. Her look was fond. 'Are you caught up in wanting what you already have? I'm yours, my dear. I'm no one else's, and I've no intention of things changing. Now, do step aside and let me cook. I love cooking for you and looking over my shoulder and seeing you with that way you have of watching me. Like what you really want is not related to food at all.'

Christ but he started to harden at that. What *was* it about her? He said, 'There's the truth of it.' He took her hand and pressed it to his groin.

'Naughty,' she said. But her fingers squeezed and released, and made him catch his breath. She gently pushed him out of the way, though, and she went on with, 'I'm due this morning at the Swanage site. I've just time for breakfast and then I must be off. Will you sleep here? Once we've eaten, I mean. You must be dead on your feet. Did you sleep at all last night?'

'Enough,' he lied. 'But it's no matter as it wasn't sleep I wanted.'

She adjusted the flame beneath the bacon. She took over whipping up the eggs and added some milk to them, some salt, some freshly ground pepper. She said to him, 'That'll fade, you know. You best be prepared for that, or you'll be very disappointed. It always fades.'

'What's that, then?'

She gestured between them with her whipping fork. 'This hunger we have for each other. It doesn't stay the same. It can't. What you want just now – this you and me thing of it with nothing else on our minds but climbing the stairs or me just taking my knickers off here in the kitchen – it doesn't last.'

'I know what I want,' he told her huskily. 'This's way bigger than lust between you and me.' And when she shot him a look of sceptical amusement, 'I don't deny the lust is there. You feel it, as well, and you got to say it.'

She smiled. 'Your hands in my knickers would tell you the truth of it, *but*' – as he approached her – 'I c'n only attend to the one hunger just now. We can't let things fall apart in our lives. You've a business to run and—'

'Curse me if I care about the business.'

'You *must* care. You've built it up—'

''Cause of you.'

'Rubbish. I've only suggested this and that. So let's not forget what's truly important cos no one lives on . . . well . . .' He could see her blushing and he loved this about her. 'What you 'n' me've been up to? No one lives on that. Now be a good lad and sit at table and wait for me to cook you this meal. Have some cornflakes. Eat your grapefruit. I reckon both of us need to keep up our strength.'

*Shaftesbury*
*Dorset*

When Lynley finally rang her, Barbara was mightily cheesed off. She'd been waiting for him to give her the word about his interview with Caroline Goldacre and when he'd not rung her by nine o'clock on the previous evening, she'd begun to ring him. If the prints on that tube of doctored toothpaste were Caroline's, it had seemed to Barbara that matters should have been to give the bloody cow her rights and cart her off to the nick. But ringing Lynley from nine until midnight had got her no information, so she'd finally dropped into bed with a 'Where the bloody hell are you and what the bloody hell is happening?' and seethed for a good three more hours before she'd finally fallen asleep. His phone call awakened her at seven, and she punched the mobile in answer and barked, 'Why the hell didn't you ring me back when you knew I was waiting for word?'

'Good God. Are you always this cheerful in the morning?' he asked pleasantly. 'Have you not had your coffee?'

'*Why* didn't you ring me? What did you expect we were going to do without word from you?'

'I expected you'd have dinner and make an early night of it. I had to take Arlo back to Daidre, Sergeant. I didn't leave Camberwell to do that till nearly ten.'

'You could've rung me on the way to north London.'

'And violate the law regarding driving and using one's mobile? Hardly.'

'Then at Daidre's. You could've rung me then. Oh, I get she was probably mad for you, ripping off your kit directly you stepped inside the place, eh? But seems to me you could've fought her off long enough to—'

'It's your leisure reading, Sergeant,' Lynley said. 'Time to elevate it, I think. Although . . . Aren't the men doing the clothes-ripping in romances? No. Don't answer that. As it was, Daidre was asleep.'

'And you didn't tiptoe to her bedside – shoes in hand – to lower yourself gently onto her comfortable mattress and breathe seductively onto the back of her neck?'

'Alas. It's a sleeping bag on a camp bed. She likes to rough it.'

'Oh, I bet she does.'

'Amusing,' he said.

'Where are you now?'

'Walking to the car. In Belgravia, by the way. Having spent the night on my own extremely comfortable mattress breathing onto my pillow's neck, should pillows have necks. Now that we've established all that, shall we get down to business?'

In short order, he brought her into the picture, and it was a game changer, if Caroline Goldacre was to be believed. The killing tube of toothpaste was hers, and according to Lynley's questioning of her, she hadn't packed Clare's suitcase for the trip to Cambridge so she didn't plant the toothpaste within it.

'Clare forgot hers, and Caroline handed her own over,' Lynley said.

'So she *says*. She could've packed Clare's bag and conveniently "forgot" the toothpaste. No one's ever going to know the truth of that one.'

'I'm not blind to that.' Needing some toothpaste later on in the evening and after their argument, Lynley went on, Caroline had rung down to reception in an attempt to acquire a tube so that she wouldn't have to speak to Clare again. 'All of this was mentioned earlier by the night receptionist, by the way,' Lynley said. 'She wasn't pleasant to him when there was no toothpaste to be had.'

'*That's* convenient,' Barbara noted.

'The unpleasantness making her phone call memorable?' Lynley enquired. 'Certainly. I see how all of this conveniently underscores Caroline's declaration of herself as the true target, Sergeant. On the other hand, a motive for her actually *wanting* to kill her employer would be welcome. As to the third set of fingerprints on the tube? They were hers, so that rather supports her story. She's not a fool, after all. If she poisoned the toothpaste, she'd hardly have left her prints on the tube.'

'But that works both ways, sir, the motive bit. Who would have had a motive to kill *her*? Oh. Never mind. I've met the minge bag and made a note of her predilection for blackmail.'

'Piquant as always,' Lynley said. 'But it turns out that the present husband has been having a relationship with a woman who works for him, someone called Sharon. The son told me this. And they've been an item for a few months now, according to Caroline. So that wants looking into.'

''Spose there's that ASBO as well,' Barbara said, filling him in on what she knew at the moment about Lily Foster, much of which she discovered he'd already learned from Caroline Goldacre's son. 'We'll be getting onto Lily Foster today.'

They rang off. She made quick work of getting herself ready for the day, aware that Winston had probably been up and about and doing his duty for two hours. She descended the stairs to find him in the dining room – fast becoming their incident room – making some sort of appointment with someone via his mobile. He gave her a nod and indicated the kitchen doorway. She took this to mean there was something edible therein, and she took herself to find out what it was.

Within the oven was a baking tray covered neatly by aluminium foil. It contained a plate of toast and another of poached eggs, grilled tomatoes, and bacon, all of which were accompanied by the miracle of Heinz baked beans. The coffee maker held a half-filled pot, so she poured herself a cup and carried the carafe out to the dining room, saying to Winston, 'May I top you up, sir?' with a waitressly smile.

He'd just ended his call. 'Psychiatrist,' he told her, nodding at the mobile.

'Am I sending you round the bend?'

'Too right,' he acknowledged. 'But tha' was Clare's, not mine. Bird called Karen Globus. Remember the name? In her diary? Linne recognised it as she belongs to the Women's League 's well. Got an appointment to talk with her this af'ernoon in Sherborne. "Don't know how helpful I c'n be to your inquiry" and all that, she says.'

Barbara went for her breakfast, returned with it, and brought him up to the minute on her call from Lynley. Nkata, she saw, didn't look surprised at the information about the fingerprints, the toothpaste's ownership, and Clare Abbott's lack of the same inside her suitcase. He said what Barbara herself had been forced to admit: if Caroline was telling the truth about Clare packing her own suitcase, then the recipient of the ASBO wanted looking into. On the other hand, if she was lying, they had a different situation entirely.

When she'd eaten and got herself in order, they set off. What additional information they had on Lily Foster had been supplied by Linne Stephens during Winston's conversation with her on the previous day. This largely amounted to where Lily was: in a flat above her tattooing business in Swan's Yard.

This business, they discovered, was called Needle Brush and when they arrived, the proprietor was just opening for the day. As they crossed the courtyard from the High Street she was setting up a sandwich board outside her door. She looked like one's fantasy of a tattoo artist, Barbara thought. She was dressed in black from her boots to her unevenly hemmed skirt to her unseasonable tank top; black of hair which was clearly dyed; arms sleeved with colourful designs that would prove upon closer inspection to be dazzling in their pornographic intricacy. Her limbs were Gomorrahic in their depiction of intercourse in a variety of athletic positions. In all of them, curiously, the man was blindfolded. Barbara was awestruck at the detail involved but she wondered how Lily was going to feel about her colourful skin when she hit fifty years of age.

Winston was the one to say, 'Lily Foster?' as they followed the young woman into her shop.

She glanced over her shoulder with a, 'Yeah, me,' and continued on her way to a desk that sat behind a shop counter. The walls round her displayed photographs of completed work along with myriad designs from which a potential client could choose. These ran the gamut: a real A to Z of animals to signs of the zodiac and all points in between. None were like Lily's, but Barbara reckoned there was a limited clientele for bodily painted perversity.

While Winston pulled out his police identification, Lily scooted a rolling stool from beneath the desk. A bright light was illuminating a design she was working upon, rendered on some sort of tissue paper. She sat, studied it for a moment, and made an erasure before turning back to them. Barbara saw her clock Winston's warrant card, but she made a point of not reacting. Instead, she asked if they were wanting tattoos.

'Got a thing about needles,' Barbara told her. 'And Winston here? He's got a thing about not disappointing his mum who, I suspect, wouldn't go in big for body art. Would she, Win?'

'Might go f'r her name in a heart, but tha's about it,'Winston acknowledged. 'Lily Foster, right? We need a word.'

Lily rolled back from the desk. The way the light hit her face, Barbara could see that she could have been quite pretty had she possessed fewer body piercings – the thick half-hoop through her septum was particularly gruesome – had her hair colour been whatever nature had given her, had her choice of clothing been less funereal, and had the body art not created such a disturbing diversion. She had an extraordinarily beau-tiful complexion of creamy white with an appealing dash of freckles on her nose and a mouth so perfectly formed that it looked like something created by a plastic surgeon. She had practically no eyebrows or eyelashes but this made her look exotic rather than odd. All the strange accoutrements of her appearance aside, Barbara could see what her appeal had been.

Lily said, 'If they've told you I've been hanging about, they're lying. And even if I *was* walking by – which I wasn't – it's a public roadway and even the cops agree with that. So if I want to take a walk, I'll take a walk. And if I want to stop to catch my breath, I'll stop to catch my breath. And that, by the way, is all I've *ever* done.'

'You're talking about the ASBO, eh?' Barbara waggled her warrant card before the young woman. 'You don't really expect New Scotland Yard to come round because you've violated an ASBO, do you?'

'I *haven't* violated the ASBO,' Lily said. 'I live in this town as well. I can't help it if I occasionally see her.'

'There's that to be talked about,' Barbara admitted.

'What?'

'Why you're living here,' Winston put in.

'I can live where I want,' Lily said. 'Last time I looked that wasn't against any laws.'

'Still and all,' Barbara pointed out, 'I wouldn't think tattoos would go down a treat in this part of the world.'

'You'd be surprised,' Lily told her. 'There's no artist within fifty miles of here. I checked before I moved house. So business is fine.'

'Yourself being an advert for what body painting can do to enhance an individual's appearance,' Barbara said.

Lily flushed – she had the sort of skin that was going to do that easily – but she said nothing. She also did nothing to cover her tattoos. There was a loose cardigan – black, of course – hanging on the back of her chair, which she could have donned. She didn't give it a glance.

'You were Will Goldacre's partner, right?'

Lily turned back to her work, which appeared to be a compli-cated design incorporating a bull, a monkey, and a horse within it. She took up a pencil and as she did so, Barbara went on with, 'Will's mum told us a bit about you. Like how you were there when he went over the cliff. You hold her responsible. Why's that?'

Lily tossed her pencil onto the desk. 'She reduced him to a shell of a person who could barely function if she wasn't round. And she hovered over him like she was put on earth to shepherd him through life and cure him and solve his every problem and—'

'Cure him of what?' Nkata asked, reaching into his jacket pocket where he habitually kept his notebook. 'He sick or summat?'

'He had this thing with words that he couldn't control,' Lily said. 'They came out of his mouth when he got upset. They were nonsense words and foul words and . . . Oh, *what* does it matter now he's dead?' Her eyes had grown brighter as she was speaking. She surged from her chair and began rather desperately working among the shelves behind the counter, reorganising what seemed to be art books, collections of magazines, bottles and vials of liquids, and various volumes. When neither Barbara not Winston said anything, she finally continued, her voice sharp. 'She wanted to make him normal and perfect. She wanted to *be* him if she could possibly arrange it. He'd got away from her when he came to London, but he couldn't manage it permanently.'

'That's where you met him?' Barbara asked.

'He was doing a garden near my parents' house. I stopped by to look at it. We talked. I liked him. I asked him did he want to go for a drink and we got on. After a bit, we started to live together. Only, of course, his mother couldn't have that, could she? Lord, he might become happy. He might actually function like a normal person and *then* what would she do? But there was no chance of that, was there, so he came back here and she got her claws into him and yes, she's who drove him to his death. No one who really knows her thinks anything else, but I'm the only one who'll say it.'

She'd been speaking in nearly a stream-of-consciousness fashion – every cop's wet dream, Barbara thought – but now she seemed to clock Winston writing rapidly in his notebook. Yet rather than put a plug in her gob to stop herself, she went on. 'So did I hate her? Yes. Do I still hate her? Yes. She drove William over that cliff as well as if she'd been chasing him. He'd been doing well in London. We'd been doing well together. But she couldn't leave him alone any more than she can leave Charlie alone. She's always there and when she's not there, she's *still* there: this constant *presence* of her and yes, all right, the only cure for that would be for her to die.'

Winston looked up at this. Barbara glanced his way. Lily laughed. She moved from the shop counter and held out her wrists. 'Got the silver bracelets on you? Or don't you lot use them any longer? Is it those pathetic plastic fasteners everyone uses now? I s'pose they're more efficient.' She dropped her hands. Across from them a padded table appeared to be the spot for individuals to lie as their bodies were seen to with needles and inks. She went to this and began dressing it for the day in spotless linen – high end tattoo shop, Barbara thought – which she tucked in firmly beneath the padding. She said, 'Didn't expect me to say all that, did you? So why don't you tell me why you're really here.'

'You know that Clare Abbott – Caroline Goldacre's employer – died in Cambridge?' Barbara said.

''Course I know it. You can't live in Shaftesbury and not know it.'

'She was poisoned,' Nkata said. 'So was her editor, few days later. Woman called Rory Statham.'

Lily stopped her tucking and adjusting and said, 'What does that have to do with me?'

'Their poisonings?' Barbara said. 'Nothing, prob'ly, as it relates to Clare. Only . . . now it looks like Caroline Goldacre might've been the target. And let's be honest. That looks like something having a hell of a lot to do with you.'

Lily snorted. 'So how am I s'posed to have poisoned Clare

Abbott and her editor? While all the time intending to poison William's loathsome mother?'

Barbara smiled. 'Well, bloody hell, Lily, that would be telling,' she said pleasantly. 'But with a gun in yours ribs, I expect you can see that this . . . What d'we call it, Winnie? Animosity?'

'Sounds 'bout right to me,' Winston said.

'OK, then. I expect you can see that this animosity you have towards Mrs Goldacre—'

'I'm probably one of two dozen people who wouldn't mourn her passing,' Lily said. 'Turn over a rock round here and you'll find someone who wouldn't've said no to putting arsenic in her porridge.'

'That could be the case,' Barbara acknowledged. 'I've met the woman and she's not at the top of my must-be-mates-with list. On the other hand, what you've said about her puts you in a dead bad light. And with an ASBO hanging over your head because you've not been able to keep away from her . . . Motives for murder have a way of piling up. So does circumstantial evidence.'

Lily laughed. Barbara wanted to think it was the wild laugh of a half-crazed woman with a canister of sodium azide hidden in her knickers, but she sounded genuinely amused. She went back behind the counter and sat at the desk where she once again took up her pencil and examined the drawing she was creating. She said, 'You've got the wrong end of the stick on this one. If I'd decided to kill that bloody woman, believe me, I wouldn't've used poison. I'd have strangled her with my bare hands 'cause not much else would've given me satisfaction.'

'What about Clare Abbott?' Winston asked this, and he made it sound like a point of curiosity.

'What about her?'

'We been looking through her clobber, and she's got a diary with 'pointments in it. She did some names and she did some initials and LF are 'mong the initials. That be you?'

'I never talked to Clare Abbott,' Lily said.

'She never looked you up, rung you up, tracked you down?'

'She would've known who you are,' Barbara added. 'Can't think Caroline would've been mum on the ASBO business once it got filed.'

Lily considered all this, and it seemed as if she was weighing not only her words but how much information to include in them when she next spoke. She finally made up her mind, saying, 'She rang me. She wanted to talk. We set up a time. I cancelled.'

'Why?'

'Because she wouldn't tell me what she wanted to see me about and I bloody well reckoned it wasn't a tattoo.'

'Why'd you want to miss a chance to bad-mouth Caroline?' Barbara asked. 'No matter what she wanted to talk about, that was your chance to run her over hot coals with her employer.'

'Like she'd believe me?' Lily scoffed. 'Not bloody likely. And Caroline would've given her sixteen earfuls about me in advance. And even if that wasn't the case, I like people to work out what Caroline's like on their own. It's far more amusing that way.' She gave them a tight little smile and concluded with, 'I've got to get to work now. I've someone coming in this morning to start the year of the bull, the year of the horse, and the year of the monkey. Those're his kids' birth years. Lovely how some people celebrate their children.'

That said, she turned from them and took up her pencil. She couldn't have made it clearer that, unless they intended to arrest her for some infraction of the law or set themselves up for tattoos, their interview was finished.

*Victoria*
*London*

'Wouldn't mind seeing her guts on a spit and she's nothing if not straight about that. Says Caroline was the ruin of the kid who offed himself – there was something bats about him as it turns out – and 'cording to Lily, she might 's well've been there to give him the shove that sent him over the cliff.'

'"Bats"?' Lynley was on his way to Isabelle's office, having been summoned via phone message from Dorothea Harriman, but he paused in the corridor to complete his conversation with Havers before he met with the superintendent. 'Curious. I've seen his picture and his father's pointed out a badly deformed ear – did that come up by the way? – but as to there being something else wrong with him . . . Did Lily Foster mention his ear?'

'Not a whisper. But she told us about this speech problem he had. It was this thing like blathering that took him over when he was pissing blood about this or that. Talked all kinds of rubbish and most of it rude. Some made up language and some words you wouldn't want said at your funeral, if you know what I mean. Lily puts it all down to his mum, but then she puts everything down to his mum. I don't see her as a killer, though, leastways not like it happened.'

'Why?' Lynley nodded at Harriman, who'd apparently come personally to fetch him. She pointed at her wristwatch and then adopted a stance with arms akimbo. It was a fairly good imitation of Isabelle in impatience mode. She even had the expression spot on. He held up a finger. She shrugged and went back towards Isabelle's domain.

'I've had a think,' Barbara was saying in answer, 'and I can't come up with how she's s'posed to have put her mitts on the poison, first of all, then put it into the brand of toothpaste Caroline uses, then get it into the house, then assume Caroline's going to use it and not the husband. Just too much chance of something going wrong or of her getting caught. It's not like they didn't have their eyes open to watch for her since she'd been lurking round so much.'

'Alastair and Caroline, you mean.'

'Right. An' she's forthright enough about how happy she'd be if someone gave the woman the chop, which 'f course I know *could* be her just saying something that we'll think makes her look *less* like a killer cause what killer's going to come out 'n' say she'd be chuffed if the supposed victim went belly up, eh? Sort of a reverse psychology thing, if you know what I mean.'

'One can overthink these situations, Sergeant,' Lynley told her mildly. 'Any luck with the key you found in Clare's desk drawer?'

'Since there's no bank vaults for the peasantry these days, apparently there's now safe companies taking up the slack. But the nearest is in Yeovil and why'd she want to trek all that way?'

'What are you onto next? Where's Winston, by the way?'

'Right here. We went hand-in-hand to speak to Lily Foster. We're virtually conjoined twins, aren't we, Win?'

Lynley heard no reply to this as a rumble of traffic on Havers's end sounded like the dust men were collecting Shaftesbury's rubbish. Havers said, 'We've got Alastair MacKerron, this Sharon who works for him, and a psychiatrist on the agenda here. What about you?'

'Superintendent Ardery's preempted everyone else. She wants a report. I'm on my way to her as we speak.'

'Sir, when's the bloody woman going to stop—'

'You know what she's looking for, Barbara. Make sure you continue to give it to me to give to her.'

They rang off then. He went on to Isabelle's office, where Dorothea indicated he was to go in at once. He said to the superintendent, 'Sorry. I had to take a call from Sergeant Havers.'

Isabelle was at the battered credenza, where a vintage coffee maker of her predecessor's was groaning through its cycle. She apparently had been watching it in her usual fashion – impatiently – because she said, 'Oh bloody hell,' and poured herself a cup as the hesitant stream of coffee continued to burble out, onto the hot plate now instead of into the pot. She asked if he wanted a cup. He demurred.

She said, 'Where's the dog?'

He said, 'Back with his minder. Why? Are you becoming fond?'

'Really, Tommy. Do I look like someone becoming fond?'

'Admittedly, no.'

She carried her coffee to her desk. She gestured for him to sit but he wasn't going to be caught, so he waited and when she herself sat, he did likewise. She said, 'It's missing. I searched high and low and I even had a word with Dorothea about where she might have hidden it – this would be to keep it safe from prying eyes – but to my consternation, it has apparently not been delivered. This is your report to which I am referring, by the way. We were in agreement when last we spoke that you would have something in writing on my desk or in my email this morning.'

He glanced at his watch meaningfully.

'Amusing. I'm fully aware that morning hasn't yet ended, but let's not split hairs.'

He said, 'The report's coming. I had a late night, owing to the dog among other things. I've only just—'

She held up a hand. 'The details of your life don't interest me. A report on the investigation does. What's Sergeant Havers up to, Tommy? Can I hope she's still managing to follow your orders?'

'To the letter,' Lynley said. Mentioning the fact that on the previous day Barbara and Winston had split up briefly would not, he thought, be a good idea. He brought the superintendent up to date on all matters concerning the death of Clare Abbott and the attempted poisoning of Rory Statham. She listened in her habitual fashion, with her penetrating attention indicating a mind at work. When he was finished with his report, she gave a sharp nod.

'To the sergeant's credit,' she said in reference to Barbara, 'there has been nothing about this matter in any of the tabloids so far, and believe me, I've been checking. No follow-up after the first two days of reportage on the death, I'm happy to say:

no accusations of police foot-dragging, and no whisper of malfeasance on anyone's part.'

'Barbara's learned her lesson, guv.'

'*But,*' Isabelle went on, 'I expect that's so far due to the story's lack of sex appeal, and frankly I don't put it past Sergeant Havers to murmur the word *murder* into some reporter's silken ear if that will help her position.'

'She's not stupid,' Lynley said. 'Impetuous, yes. Bloody-minded, yes. But she isn't stupid and she's not a fool. She understands what's on the line for her. For all its charms, I daresay that Berwick-upon-Tweed doesn't hold much appeal in her case. It was, if I might say, a rather inspired choice.'

Isabelle picked up a pencil. She tapped it on the top of her desk. She smiled. 'I can't think someone didn't use it before now,' she admitted. 'I don't mean Berwick necessarily but the transfer papers.'

'She's not stepped so far out of order before.'

'I suppose there's that. At any rate, it's quite a nice change to have her under control. Do see that she stays that way.' She turned to her computer's keyboard and with a few clicks, she opened a file that from his position Lynley couldn't see. She said over her shoulder to him, 'I'd like to hear from you tomorrow morning, Tommy. *Without* having to summon you.'

He didn't rise. Nor did he allow himself to be offended at her implied dismissal of him. He said instead, 'Isabelle, in the past, I was never required to bring the superintendent into the picture on a daily basis.'

'I expect that's the case,' she agreed. 'But I assume that, in the past, you also didn't go against your superior's express orders by involving an outside police force in order to manipulate matters to your satisfaction. Let's not forget Detective Chief Superintendent Sheehan. Now, I've work to get to, I assume you do as well, and tomorrow morning's report is –' here she glanced at her watch – 'a mere twenty-one hours away.'

He considered asking her for another officer to assist in the gathering of information. It would be helpful to have someone at the Met digging into everyone connected to Caroline Goldacre, to Clare Abbott, and to Rory Statham. It would tick a few items off the list if the whereabouts of all the associates of these women could be established for the days leading up to Clare Abbott's death. But he knew how unlikely it was that Isabelle was going to approve the movement of so much as a civilian secretary onto his team, so he let the matter go unsaid and returned to his office.

Caroline Goldacre as intended victim, he thought. That was a wrinkle in the blanket that could not be discounted. Assuming there was more here than met the eye, he reckoned that she was the direction in which they ought to be heading. Considering her actions in the past, he also reckoned that some delving in that area would not be a waste of his time.

*Wareham*
*Dorset*

Barbara told herself that it wasn't *such* a lie. She *had* been with Winston that morning. They *had* gone together to call upon Lily Foster. It was merely the fact that at the conclusion of their confab with Lily, they'd made a decision to separate for a while. *Which,* she asserted mentally, was what any other team of investigators would have done at that point.

It had to be said that Winnie had not exactly embraced the idea. But he had to get himself to Sherborne to speak with the psychiatrist with whom Clare Abbott had had an appointment. Since it would save them time for Barbara herself to take on grilling both Alastair MacKerron and his lover, he acquiesced to an afternoon apart although she could tell he didn't like it any more than he'd liked their previous parting.

'Think of it like absence, the heart, and growing fonder,' she advised him.

'Best I think of it like being out of order,' had been his response.

'The inspector isn't going to know unless you tell him, Winnie, 'cause I sure as hell won't be wagging my tongue on the topic.'

Reluctantly, then, Winston had agreed, especially when Barbara pointed out to him that Clare's Jetta was sitting in her driveway waiting to be used and because of this Barbara would not require the keys to her fellow sergeant's hallowed Prius a second time. He went on his way to Sherborne after dropping Barbara back at Clare's house in Bimport Street.

Barbara tossed round the various scenarios available to her in the Alastair-and-Sharon department. She made a few phone calls. She decided there was more grist in having a chinwag with the mistress than with the betraying husband. While he had a lot to lose should things come to a divorce between himself and Caroline Goldacre, this Sharon had a massive amount to gain if Caroline Goldacre conveniently choked it.

Barbara got the woman's surname from one of the bakeries. No problem since Sharon Halsey turned out to be a big player in Alastair's business. So she wasn't tough to locate since her name was in the directory. Ultimately, Barbara tracked her down across the county. She phoned her house first and from her answer machine got her mobile number. Sharon reported herself in Swanage checking on the progress of a new MacKerron Baked Goods under development there. She'd be going on to Wareham, where she could meet Sergeant Havers at one o'clock. She sounded perfectly pleasant, Barbara thought. Butter wouldn't melt and all the rest. She either knew there was no way that sodium azide could be tracked to her doorstep or she was completely innocent in all matters. Yet she didn't even ask why a Scotland Yard detective wanted to have a chat with her. Interesting, that.

Barbara scored Clare's keys from the kitchen worktop. The Jetta was old, but it started without any trouble, and the drive to Wareham thereafter was a pleasant one. It took her through the dips and curves of the grassy chalk downs of Cranbourne Chase, coursing south in the direction of the Isle of Purbeck's great limestone plateau. There was no direct route, so she twisted and turned through valleys and hillsides dotted with farms and broad with meadows till she reached the River Frome.

They'd decided to meet at the town's war memorial, where Sharon Halsey said she would be having a sandwich. She'd told Barbara that it was her habit always to visit the war memorial wherever she was, and there she would often eat her lunch.

The memorial in Wareham wasn't difficult to find. It stood along North Street near an ancient church. It was conveniently close to where Sharon Halsey had told Barbara she'd be spending her afternoon: across the street in MacKerron Baked Goods, one of the bakeries that sold what Sharon's lover concocted.

Barbara would never have taken the demure little woman who was sitting among the poppy wreaths as a home wrecker. One thought of home wreckers as brassy blondes with serious physical goods on offer to tempt a bloke away from his marital vows. One thought of home wreckers as women offering decided competition to a haggard wife. But in this case, the advantage was all Caroline Goldacre's, Barbara thought. Despite Caroline's heft – which was, admittedly, considerable – she still had mounds of glossy hair, gorgeous skin, great dark eyes, shapely hands, and a serious bosom whereas Sharon Halsey wouldn't have garnered a second glance on a desert island were she the only woman among a tribe of desperate men.

So her looks weren't what was dragging Alastair MacKerron away from hearth and home, Barbara concluded. The woman was either lit dynamite in bed or she'd forged a Great Spiritual Connection with her employer.

It began to rain the moment Barbara approached Sharon Halsey. Warrant card in hand, she was about to introduce herself when the heavens opened. Sharon said, 'Oh dear,' and rose from the poppy wreaths. She said, 'You're the police-

woman?' to Barbara, and she advised that they decamp to the
church. It would be open, she said. It was Saxon and of historical note, and people did like to have a look at Lawrence.

Barbara hadn't a clue what she meant, but she followed
Sharon Halsey. The church was quite small and plain with a
single aisle only and its north side was dominated by the
Lawrence mentioned, who turned out to be of Arabia fame.
An impressive marble effigy of him lying in state atop a tomb
and garbed in an unmistakably Arabian kit asked to be admired.
He wasn't actually buried in this place, Sharon Halsey told
her in a quiet voice, but merely remembered, much like the
names on the war memorial outside.

'Thought he'd be taller,' Barbara commented as she took
in the supine figure in his robes, dagger clutched on his chest.

'That would be 'cause of the film, I expect,' Sharon told
her.

'They don't make 'em like they used to,' Barbara said.
'It's all car crashes and shootouts now, isn't it?'

'Like films are all made for twelve-year-old boys.'

'They probably are.' Sharon turned from the monument
and gazed at Barbara with peaceful looking eyes. 'What d' you
want to talk to me about?' she asked directly. 'I phoned Alastair
to ask him, 'cause the only thing I could think of was that this
has to have something to do with Clare Abbott's death.'

'And with Caroline Goldacre's life,' Barbara told her. 'We
have it from her son Charlie that you and the husband are
making the big nasty.'

'Oh.' Sharon coloured deeply.

'You can lie about it, 'course,' Barbara said, 'but neighbours
have a way of forgetting to turn a blind eye, and when they
see things like blokes coming and going or coming and staying
and when this goes on for a bit of time—'

'I'm not trying to hide it,' Sharon told her. 'It's only . . . It's
the way you put it. The big nasty. You make it sound dirty.
But it's not.'

'I 'spect not. Fraught with emotion. Hearts and flowers.

P'rhaps a fag shared between you in the afters as you stare up at the ceiling and wonder where it's all going to go if one of you doesn't make the necessary move. You know what I mean.'

Sharon frowned, seeming not so much offended as puzzled. 'Are you always so rude?'

'When it comes to murder.'

Sharon moved to one of the pews. It stood before a small side chapel where the faint remains of a painting done onto the wall of the church suggested the building's Saxon origins. She sat here. She still had her sandwich in hand, but it seemed that her appetite had left. She rustled in her capacious handbag and brought out the sandwich's wrapping. She used it carefully, tucking the cling film round the bread as if she were seeing to the nighttime ritual of a beloved child. Barbara joined her in the pew although Sharon didn't look particularly welcoming when it came to sharing the space with her.

She said, 'If all this's about Clare Abbott's death, we didn't have a thing to do with that, me or Alastair. He told me the police came round to talk to him and Caroline and it's true like you said that he told me "in the afters". But I didn't know Clare Abbott and 'f Alastair knew her, it was 'cause Caroline worked for her. Course she arranged that memorial for Will and I met her then 'cause I was invited to the dedication ceremony just like everyone else from the shops. But that was the whole of it.'

'The whole of Clare but not of Caroline,' Barbara pointed out.

'I already told you the truth about that. Me and Alastair . . . It's not dirty no matter how you try to make it look.'

'Right. Making a note in my brain. It's not dirty. Man, woman, true love, meant-to-be, bigger-than-both-of-us, and all the rest. Got it. But why I'm here? It's not about all that. Or I guess I should say it's only part about that. The other part is murder, with Caroline and not Clare Abbott being the target.'

Sharon's lips – colourless like the rest of her – parted then closed. After a moment she said carefully, 'What're you on about, then?'

'Poison. It started out in Caroline's kit, not in Clare's. Caroline handed it over to Clare and—'

'Then *Caroline's* the one who—'

'Clare used it. Presto she's dead. But, see, no one has a reason to knock her, far as we c'n tell. Whereas looking at Caroline as potential victim . . . I got to admit I didn't care much for her in the limited time we shared the same airspace, and I *also* got to admit I'm learning why someone might want to wave her the permanent bye-byes. And I reckon you can see how you and the husband would top the list. Doing the big nasty . . .? Whoops, pardon. There's that term again. Sorry.' Barbara paused for a moment to reach for another more suitable euphemism. She went on with 'Playing sink the pole in such a way that only taking an advert out in the local newspaper would make it more apparent . . . ? That doesn't look good for you or the husband either. Makes him or you or both of you look nice to set up a killing, Mrs Halsey. That whole we-must-be-together-beloved? In my experience, that scores high, alongside I've-never-felt-like-this-before when it comes to motives for murder.'

To her credit, Barbara thought, Sharon Halsey maintained a look of complete dignity. She smoothed her hand down the front of her plaid skirt – Barbara wondered where she'd unearthed the thing as she hadn't seen plaid on anyone save a schoolgirl or a Scot since before her tenth birthday – and she tucked it round her legs. She said, 'You c'n call it what you like, I s'pose, what me and Alastair have together. I can't stop you, can I? I c'n even see how it looks to you, like we're sneaking round the countryside looking for a place to meet with no one the wiser.'

'No, I expect you've done it openly, Mrs Halsey, else why would Caroline know? 'Less she caught you at it. *Did* she catch you? Did she threaten you? Or him p'rhaps? Did she take the first step to sort you out proper?'

'Like how?'

'Not sure, but I expect running our Alastair through the juicer to squeeze what she could get out of him in a divorce settlement before she drops him into the dustbin . . . ? That would work a real treat.'

'So what you're thinking is this's all 'bout what Alastair has and the business he's built and how I'm set on his keeping it safe from her no matter what. But what you can't work out is that I don't need Alastair to leave her. We know what we are to each other, me and Alastair, and whether he's with Caroline or with me, the truth of what we are isn't about to change.' She stood at that as if with the intention of departing.

Barbara did likewise, in order to block her. She said, 'Now, that makes you one bloody *extraordinary* bird, Mrs Halsey.'

'What's that mean, then?'

'You're saying that whether he leaves his wife to come to you or stays with her and uses you couple times a week as the mash for his banger . . . it makes no difference to you? You don't give a toss? Is that what you actually want me to believe?'

'Believe what you want with your talk of bangers and poles and the big nasty and such. You never loved anyone, I 'spect. If you did, you'd talk different about it all.'

That said, she started to push past Barbara. For Barbara it was a case of let her go or do some sort of chest dance with her to keep her inside the pew. But she reckoned enough had been said between them. She now had one of two choices: either to believe the woman's assertions about the great and tender love between her and Caroline Goldacre's husband along with her completely unlikely lack of interest in having him become a permanent fixture in her life or to uncover a different truth entirely. That one would point to her or to her lover putting eager mitts upon some sodium azide and planting it in Caroline's belongings. No matter the case, Barbara wasn't going to achieve anything by arguing the finer points of love with Sharon Halsey. So she let her go. It was time, she decided, to pay a call on Alastair in order to have a prowl round the bakery where tucking away a deadly poison would probably be child's play, considering everything she'd seen inside the place from a simple glance through the windows when she'd been there earlier with Nkata.

So Alastair MacKerron it was, she decided.

She returned to Clare's car, dodging raindrops. She'd left it along North Street, in front of a café whose menu suggested a chip butty was in order, especially as Nkata wasn't with her to offer his frown of dismay when he heard her order it.

She was about to duck inside the place when her gaze fell upon the Jetta's left front tyre. It was, maddeningly, flat as fried bread. She stared at it. She cursed. She considered waiting for an alteration in the weather while building up her strength to change the tyre by downing two chip butties instead of one because the sodding inconvenience of a sodding flat tyre meant she was owed, didn't it? But in the end, she gave in to duty and she dug Clare's keys out of her bag and headed for the car's boot and the spare tyre within it.

There wasn't one. There was a space for it, of course, in a well just beneath a sturdy cover that made the floor of the boot usable for storage. But inside this tyre-sized hollow was not what she needed. Instead what rested within the well for the spare tyre was what appeared to be a strong box of the sort one stored valuable papers in to protect them in case of a fire. Barbara felt her pulse increase as she took in the sight of the box and she clocked the lock upon it. She cast all thought of chip butties and flat tyres aside as she lifted the thing out of its hiding place. She couldn't open it, of course, because of the lock. But inside her shoulder bag and inside a small manila envelope that she'd been carrying round, she had a key.

Unceremoniously and in the rain, she dumped her shoulder bag's contents onto the wet pavement. A quick paw through everything from fags to Wrigley's spearmint to two small calculators gifted her by her bank and she'd disinterred the small manila envelope from the dog-eared pages of her chequebook where it had become lodged. She shook the key into her palm and inserted it into the lock on the strong box. Bingo, she thought as it turned like a dream.

She opened the thing a fraction only because of the rain. Inside she glimpsed a veritable bonanza of filing folders. No one needed to carry round their personal papers in the boot of a car in a strong box, Barbara reckoned. A box such as this would protect them well enough if left inside one's house. The way she looked at it, what Clare Abbott had been carrying round in the car was something she didn't want the prying eyes of her assistant ever to see. In other words, she – Barbara Havers – had hit the jackpot.

*Wareham*
*Dorset*

The café wasn't making a killing on this particular day and from the look of the place Barbara reckoned it wasn't making a killing on any other day either. Everything was worn: from the lino on the floor to a crusty-looking fan on the ceiling. The tables were of a vintage and an unmatched variety suggesting rescue from skips, and the chairs looked like a furniture version of the United Nations. In short, it was perfect for her needs. She could sift through the contents of the strong box unbothered and unless they tossed her out onto the pavement, she could take as long as she needed to read whatever she came across.

She ordered enough food to keep everyone happy: the previously decided upon chip butty to which she added a cheddar toastie, a ham salad, and a slice of pineapple upside down cake. The waitress looked like someone's ageing mother and she seemed ready to comment about Barbara's selection and the likelihood of its contributing to her overall health. But it appeared that tired feet got the better of her, for after saying,

'*And* the cake 's well?' she merely staggered off to put in the order.

Barbara had selected the largest table since there was no one else in the place. She placed the strong box at one end and began to empty it of its neatly and blessedly labelled filing folders. In short order she found herself looking at the transcript of an interview with Francis Goldacre, the transcript of an interview with Mercedes Garza, nicely typed notes from conversations with Hermione Barnett, Linne Stephens, and Wallis Howard, and a very thick manila folder that contained printed and highlighted copies of received emails. These were all from Caroline Goldacre to Clare Abbott. Barbara felt her arms come out in goose bumps when she saw them.

She wanted to begin with the emails, but they comprised such a massive collection that she decided having a look at the interviews might be more efficient. So as she waited for her food to arrive, she began with the transcript inside the folder marked with Francis Goldacre's name. She skimmed it first, dipping in and out of the information.

It appeared to comprise a history of the relationship between Francis and Caroline, told in Francis's own words and beginning with how he had met his wife, a circumstance that he claimed he remembered vividly from his first look at her in a wine bar: *She was gorgeous and my God so voluptuous that I couldn't take my eyes off her breasts. She was making the most of them in some sort of peasant blouse displaying deep cleavage. Perfect, actually, for working at a wine bar since having a look at her was enough to encourage repeat custom. I thought she was foreign at first. She looked foreign. She drew me out about my studies and as I was just completing them, I was more than ready to be drawn. I went back three or four times before we got together . . . sorry, euphemism . . . before we were sexual, and I felt bloody lucky that she'd chosen me. I mean, everyone wanted her, but she kept her distance. She was always friendly to the drinkers, but you knew where the line was with her. So I felt quite flattered when she wanted me. Ego and all that. She was very young. She said she was twenty-one, but it turned out she was only just eighteen and that nearly put me off because of the difference in our ages – more than ten years. But to tell the truth she made so much of me and I wanted to be made much of. What man doesn't?*

What then followed was a detailed description of the budding relationship as it was remembered by the man being interviewed. Barbara skimmed this till the words *attempted suicide* leaped out at her. She homed in on them and on *directly she told me she was pregnant. I didn't feel caught, as you might conclude. Rather, I felt needed. After she recovered from the attempt, she offered to abort but I could see she didn't really want that and neither did I. What I thought at the time was that I'd always intended to marry and I'd been thinking more and more of asking her and we did get on so well in bed . . . not that one ought to base a marriage on that, but when the blood is boiling, it does take a while to cool off and common sense goes out the window. So marriage seemed right and I asked her. She was hesitant at first. I had to talk her into it. We did the registry office thing and set up house. That was it. But then as the pregnancy continued, it seemed to bring out the worst in her. I thought it was hormones and I told myself this change in her it would fade in time and she'd go back to being herself after the baby was born, but that wasn't the case.*

Then on the top of the third page Barbara saw *actually drove the car into a tree and even today I couldn't tell you why. But by then I knew I was dealing with something troubling. She said Yes of course she'd driven the car into a tree because she'd been angry with me for ringing to tell her I'd be missing dinner. Not for forgetting to ring her, mind you, but for ringing in the first place. She'd already started to prepare it, it was something special, and she was beside herself when I wouldn't be there to eat it. So she went outside, got into the car, drove it at speed straight into a tree on the lawn, and left it there for me to find. After that, to tell the truth, I didn't cope well in dealing with her. Withdrawing seemed best. Being silent and watchful, as I wasn't at all sure what she might be capable of.*

Barbara closed the folder and tapped her fingers thoughtfully on it. She had to admit that, despite the fact that the tale was being told by Francis Goldacre about his former wife, which alone might have been intriguing to Clare, the story itself was also the antithesis of romantic love. So she was forced to consider something less sinister than Clare Abbott wearing her brothel creepers as she slithered round Caroline Goldacre's past for something juicy. She could have been merely engaged in gathering information for a future sequel to *Looking for Mr Darcy*, providing herself with more facts for her thesis.

Barbara opened the Mercedes Garza folder and gave its contents a glance. Its documents began with *Caroline's mum is sixty-eight years old. My request for an interview with her was met with surprise but no reluctance once we got through the reason for my subterfuge in arranging the meeting, which she said didn't surprise her at all. She came to me in Spitalfields.*

There followed a history of the mother–child relationship between Mercedes and Caroline, and the fact of it being a mother-and-child exploration made Barbara consider that previous folder had no real connection to *Looking for Mr Darcy* at all. For as far as she knew, the Darcy book didn't deal with mothers and their children. So was this a stab at yet another topic for a book? she wondered. Or was it something else?

The first of Barbara's food arrived: the chip butty and the cheese toastie nesting together on a plastic plate decorated along its edges with munching bunnies enjoying their veggies and perhaps attempting to encourage diners to do the same. Barbara ignored them and made a request for brown sauce, ketchup, and malt vinegar on the theory that one never knew which was going to take the chip butty directly over the top into gourmet dining. She tucked in and went next to the thick folder containing the emails.

It would, she knew, take hours to read through them all, so she decided to begin with a selection. She doused her chip butty with brown sauce, took a hefty bite, evaluated the level of gastronomical delectation it provided her, added some ketchup, and dipped into the emails, making an arbitrary selection of several from the beginning, several from the middle, and several from the end. Thus she was able to see the alteration in both tone and content although further delving also demonstrated that the alteration in tone illustrated not a consistent change but rather one that, like a rollercoaster, rose and fell in what appeared to be an indiscriminate fashion.

The emails began in the polite manner of one woman writing to another to whom she has only been recently introduced. These dealt largely with Caroline Goldacre's admiration for Clare Abbott as a writer, lecturer, and feminist. Clare had apparently handed over her email address following a talk she'd given in Shaftesbury – mention was made of the Women's League and the date on the email was just over two years earlier – and Caroline declared herself surprised that Clare would respond to her. This was along the lines of 'when I think about all you've achieved and compare it to what I've done with my own life, which isn't much' accompanied by a fair amount of social grovelling that made Barbara squirm. However, it soon appeared from the ensuing emails that – chatty and friendly though she was in them – Caroline was angling for employment and while what Barbara herself had learned about Clare – as well as what she'd witnessed when she'd met her – didn't indicate that the feminist would actually fall for Caroline's obvious manouevring, she reckoned that it had seemed to Clare Abbott at first that an affable and much needed house cleaner had fallen into her lap.

So Caroline Goldacre hadn't been lying when she'd claimed that she'd begun as an 'umble charwoman, Barbara thought. This was a mark in her favour, although it went no distance to explain why Clare had printed her emails and kept them locked away in the boot of her car.

Skipping ahead, Barbara found the first alteration in tone, some ten months later. Something was amiss in the housecleaning: a question about damage to the hob was met with a tart offer to 'turn in my keys if my work is so lacking in what you're looking for, Clare.' Clare had apparently responded in some unacceptable way not present in the collection Barbara was looking through, for what followed was a missive of the are-you-accusing-me-of-LYING variety, which was then followed by an excruciatingly long 3.30 a.m. document in which Caroline – had she been drunk? drugged? hysterical? channelling Henry James? – banged on for three pages about her former husband, the suicide of her troubled son, the marriage of her older son and his 'disgusting wife India', and then back to her former husband for a revelation of his 'failures as a man'. She wound herself up and launched from there into a comparison of herself to Clare Abbott with all her 'bloody privileges and Oxford education and have you any idea how you intimidate people or do you just like to play with them as you've been playing with me' and on and on till Barbara's head was swimming. This particular email had been highlighted here and there with yellow marking pen, and on its edge were written *Timms 164* and *Ferguson 610*.

If Clare had made any answer at all to this, there was no record. Indeed, thumbing through the emails, Barbara saw that answers – if there had been any – were not included. In the case of this particular email, what followed was something written less than twenty-four hours later by Caroline, apologising for having unceremoniously dumped her anxieties upon Clare. She'd been out of order in her previous email, she wrote, and her outburst had been stimulated not one whit by Clare's reasonable question about the hob but rather by a phone call from 'the perverse India' regarding Charlie, Caroline's surviving son. India had declared her concerns about Charlie's low spirits and his refusal to seek help for a depression that India believed might lead him to take his life as his brother had done. 'It broke me. I'd only just spoken to her when I wrote to you,' Caroline explained to Clare. 'Forgive me, please. Working for you has given me a way of not thinking about Will for a few hours each day, and I'm desperate for that.'

Barbara looked back at the earlier email sent at 3.30 in the morning. Caroline had just spoken to India by phone? At 3.30 in the morning? That hardly seemed credible.

Whether Clare had considered this fact, it was of no account, for within two emails Caroline was back to normal again. Oddly, although they saw each other nearly every day, Caroline wrote as if they were miles apart and playing at penpals. She wrote to Clare daily, and the next fifty or so emails seemed to be innocuous until something set her off again. Caroline was, at this point, advancing in her employment. She'd gone from charwoman to housekeeper and cook, and a little delving indicated that Clare had transgressed by questioning a meal that Caroline had prepared. 'The fish seemed a bit off' had apparently been what launched Caroline into two pages of 'Let's just have a look at how you use me, Clare, and at how you use other people as well because that's really who you are isn't it you're just a user and haven't I learned THAT and MORE about you.'

She'd been afire with indignation, creating a document in which she listed Clare Abbott's sins, the mightiest of which appeared to be Clare's relationship with a brother who'd turned to her for financial help but 'oh you won't help him will you because you can't forgive him can you because you're the ONLY one on the planet who was ever made to suffer aren't you Clare. You act like you're the FIRST person EVER to have a brother who CLIMBED INTO YOUR BED so let me ask you if you have any idea what it's like to be RAPED by your own father because you don't have any idea do you when your brother didn't rape you but just stuck his FINGERS up into you and there you are like this is the worst thing that could ever happen to someone oh please.' She'd been subjected to repeated attacks by her own father, Caroline declared, and when she had gone to her mother 'do you know what it's like when your OWN mother doesn't believe you no I expect you don't. So I make a mistake with some BLOODY fish and it's all about you isn't it Clare because you are such a narcissist only I didn't know that and if I did I wouldn't have ever come to work for you you selfish cow.'

*Narcissist* had been circled in black and another name and number had been scrawled in the margin *Cowley 242*. If Clare had made a reply to this rambling discourse, it, once again, was not in the folder. As before, however, a day later had come the apology. This one was along the lines of 'I misunderstood what you meant when you said the fish was off. I'd bought it fresh and I thought you were saying to me that I didn't know what fresh fish should be like while you knew better. I can't explain why this got to me but I think it had to do with Francis and all of his refusals to help Will when it would only have taken a simple surgery. God, I can't go there and write about Will. I think I'm going mad.'

At the conclusion of this one, Barbara blew out a breath slowly, considering not only the emails but also the notations in the margins. She could only imagine what her own future might have been like with the Met had she – in addition to her numerous transgressions – fired off a volley of provocative missives to her superior officers. She found it curious that Clare Abbott had not sacked the woman at some point but had instead not only kept her on but also increased her responsibilities and her access to the feminist's life. The only inference Barbara could draw at the moment was that Caroline had the Just4Fun goods on Clare, which she threatened to reveal if she was ever sacked.

She flipped to the final few emails. She'd finished her chip butty and cheese toastie, and her ham salad had long since arrived. She requested tea and when it appeared with surprising alacrity, she doctored it with milk and sugar, asked if she could have the ham salad wrapped up for takeaway, downed a couple of gulps of tea, tucked into her pineapple upside down cake, and read on. Alastair MacKerron, Caroline reported to Clare, was having an affair with 'that slag Halsey who probably sucks his dick for a fiver because believe me he wouldn't pay more for it' and despite Caroline's having caught them at it after hours on the bakery floor 'with her on her knees and he's leaning back just smiling and smiling because he's USING her just like he used me in the days before I caught him with our CHILDMINDER for God's sàke nineteen years old she was and there was Will all alone in the kitchen and them in the larder and you do not even want to KNOW what my little boy told me he'd seen them up to in the past and him barely eight years old! I do not know why I don't walk out on him because believe me NO ONE would ever want him, not permanently like I have the yob,' plus her husband had declared that he would 'no more give up the BLOODY COW than would he have a limb removed. He said his arm but we know he meant his best friend which is his DICK.'

This section was once again heavily highlighted and annotated with names and numbers. Added now were pencilled notes in, presumably, Clare Abbott's hand. They were heavily dependent on some sort of short hand abbreviations: *del.*, *abandon*, *grand*, *s.o.s*, and because of these and the annotated names and numbers, for the first time, Barbara wondered if Clare had been actually encouraging Caroline to write to her, perhaps telling her to unburden herself. If nothing else from Caroline's continuing emails, it did not seem that Clare had asked her to cease and desist.

'He's drinking now, every night this is, Clare,' began the final email that Barbara looked at, 'and how he's also managing to get up and do the baking without ruining everything he puts into the oven is a mystery to me because I assure you that I am NOT lending him a hand and I won't till he gets RID of the cunt. Which of course he has no intention of ever doing. She's expecting him to leave me for her but he knows I'll have him for EVERYTHING if he even tries it. I've given him my LIFE and this is how he says thank you which is how he's always been by the way not two years into our marriage and there he was having girls to his SHOP in Whitecross Street and I discover this don't I when I stop by with a lunch I've picked up for him specially and he's locked the door and

I know he's there so I break it I smash the glass with my fist and you can bet he felt rotten after that with his trousers round his ankles and this little tart doing the business on him and his own WIFE spurting blood all over his precious floor. Told a real tale to the paramedics, he did. Made it She's upset and she cut herself and could be she needs watching for a few days. During which time, naturally, he had the CHILDMINDER constantly. I can't even remember her damn name but anyway she was in and out or hahaha it would be better to say that he was in and out wouldn't it and when I got home and found the two of them doing it like dogs and with Will and Charlie actually WATCHING like this is something on the telly—'

Barbara stopped reading. She felt as if her eyeballs were on the verge of bleeding. The why of it all was ricocheting round her mind like the remaining ball in a pin ball game. What prompted someone to blather on for pages like this, vomiting forth either personal details or a doctored version of them? And perhaps more important, considering what had ultimately happened, what prompted another person to receive these details in an endless stream without putting a halt to it all?

She could feel an answer developing to these questions as she started to put the files back into the strong box. For beneath them all lay a memory stick, and Barbara knew enough about computers to understand its import at once. For the memory stick could be used to back up existing files that one was working upon on a computer. But it could also be used to *contain* the files in the first place, hiding them from the sight of someone with access to the computer upon which they might have otherwise been left once they were created.

She needed to get back to Shaftesbury. She needed to see what it was that was so important to Clare that she couldn't risk leaving it in her house, just like the documents in these locked-away manila filing folders she'd just been reading.

India was touched that Nat wanted her to see the site of his new project, so when he asked her if she had time to meet him there in the late afternoon, she said at once that she did. Her last client was at half past three. She had paperwork to do, but she decided to leave it for the next day as the fading daylight at this time of year meant that she needed to get over to the location of Nat's terrace of cottages before five.

Getting there presented no difficulty as his directions were as straightforward as the man himself. She went by taxi as far as Shoreditch tube station and from there she walked to Hunton Street where the two terraces of cottages faced each other across a narrow path, with the northern half of them abutting a schoolyard. There, the sounds of children's excited voices mingling with those of adults calling out to them indicated the end of a day of lessons.

The cottages were, she saw, ancient, tiny, and in sad disrepair: ramshackle from lack of care. They were formed from London brick which had gone unwashed for so many decades that the uniform colour of the place was sludge grey, and India could see why a developer might look upon them and decide that buying the lot of them and clearing the site for a tower block would be far more profitable than rehabilitating the little residences, no matter their historical significance. With their dismal and nearly useless front gardens and their paintless front doors, with their roofs looking little better than sieves, it was difficult to imagine that anyone would ever want to live in the places.

Nat was standing in one of the front gardens in the company of a young woman. They both wore hard hats in a bow to what was essentially a construction site, although there didn't seem to be any construction going on, at least not upon the exterior of the residences. Some of these appeared to be occupied still, for as India set off along the path between the cottages, a *shalwar kameez* clad woman attempted to manoeuvre a pram through one of the front doors. Nat went to help her.

In doing so, he saw India approaching. He cocked his head with a smile and finished his business first with the pram and then with the young woman whom he introduced as the architectural intern Victoria Price. She was very pretty, India thought, quite tall and very athletic looking. She also seemed rather more than a little attracted to Nat, if the looks and smiles she was directing towards him were anything to go by. They briefly conversed about their next meeting before Victoria removed her hard hat, released masses of glorious, sun-streaked hair that fell well below her shoulders, and took out her smartphone to make note of her follow-up appointment with Nat. She would, she told him, have the new drawings ready by then and in the meantime should she bring on the garden designer? He would prefer to wait on that, Nat told her. He smiled, she beamed, she went on her way. She wore, India thought, completely unsuitable shoes for a worksite: very high heels that would no doubt cripple her before she was forty. In the meantime, they made her legs look long and toothsome.

'She's very pretty,' India told Nat when Victoria was out of earshot.

'She is,' he agreed. 'I only wish she was the total package.'

India shot him a questioning look.

He said, 'The creativity isn't quite as good as the body. But she's very nice all the same and she's eager to do well, so I can't complain as much as I'd like to.'

'Which, I expect, isn't all that much.' She said it in a teasing fashion, but he didn't react as she thought he might, with a dismissive chuckle.

Instead he said, 'Let me show you round,' which he did much as he might have shown a newspaper reporter or a casual acquaintance. This was disquieting, but India reckoned he might merely be in work mode still. She herself would have probably shown him round the Wren Clinic in much the same manner.

Inside one of the abandoned cottages, however, Nat made

it clear why he had actually asked her to come to the site. He escorted her round the gutted place and explained how it would look when its interior was completed, but when he was finished with what was a tour of five minutes' length only, instead of returning to the exterior, he paused at the front door and said to her, 'You've probably worked out that I've more than one reason for asking you to trek over here.'

She played it as an innocent, saying, 'The only thing I'd worked out about why you've asked me here is that you want to share what you're doing.'

'I do,' he said. 'But there's a bit more.'

'Victoria Price?'

He actually looked confused, which was gratifying. He took a moment and then said, 'Oh. You mean as a love interest? God no. She's not my type.'

'I'd think she was any man's type.'

'Not mine.'

'I'm glad to hear it.'

He didn't smile. She felt a corresponding chill come over her. It seemed to settle between them. He still didn't open the door of the cottage but rather leaned against it – hips and shoulders with hands in his trouser pockets – and he said, 'The thing is, India . . . I'm not sure how to say this so I'm just going to say it.'

She felt more chill and said, 'Is something wrong?'

'Well, yes and no. But the thing is . . . I'd prefer not to have my heart broken. I've had a long think about everything, and I've decided it's best if we cool things off between us for now.'

India frowned. The rug felt pulled out from beneath her of a sudden, and it didn't take a great deal of thought for her to understand who was jerking the fringe. She said, 'It's Caroline. The fact that she was – that she is – staying with me.'

'That's part of it, of course.'

'Nat, it's not as if I want her there. It's not as if I invited her. I'm only having her stay because Charlie—'

'That's just it,' he pointed out. 'Charlie. I *know* you're doing it for Charlie's sake and it's you and Charlie and everything involved with you and Charlie that's forced me to come to terms with how things really are. Look, darling, it's fairly clear that you're not ready for what I'm offering you, and I don't want to rush you into anything.'

'I don't think you're rushing me. Is this about Christmas? Asking me to come to Shropshire with you? The fact that I haven't yet said yes?'

'It's more than that.' He glanced away, to the window of the cottage which was covered with some sort of filmy material to protect it from what was going on inside the building. He gave a mighty sigh. 'I'm in love with you, India, but the way isn't clear. And if we keep on as we've been going, as things stand now it's a good bet that I'm going to end up fairly devastated. Which, to be honest, I'd like to avoid.'

'What things?'

'Hmm?'

'You said if we keep going, as things stand now. What things?'

'You know what things.'

'Charlie. And his mum.' She crossed the room to him. It was so small she was able to do it in two steps. Directly in front of him, she put her hands on his shoulders and gazed into his face. She said, 'This is a favour I'm doing for Charlie. It's something I'd do for any friend. Charlie's flat is small and he meets his clients there and—'

'You've told me. But I can't see that it makes any difference at the end of the day.'

'*And* please take note that without even thinking, darling Nat, I said "Charlie's flat" and not "our flat" because there is no "our" between me and Charlie. I'm not going to return to him. But after all that's happened in the last few years with his brother dying and him falling apart and . . . Heavens, Nat, you've *met* his mother. She'd love it if Charlie was never able to stand on his own two feet again. That would give her such power, and I see that in ways I couldn't see when he and I were together. I see how she *always* wanted him to fail as a brother, which he did. And she always wanted him to fail as a husband, which he also did. And now she'd love it if he failed in his career as well. He'd be forced, then, to return to Dorset just like his brother. And there she'd get her claws into him once and for all.'

'He's an adult. It can't be that bad.'

'It can and it is. If you knew what she reduced me to when he and I were married . . .'

'You *are* married.'

'Just for now.'

'Right. So I suppose what I'm trying to say is that when things change for you, India—'

'No! You're not hearing me and I insist that you hear me. If taking Caroline in for a few days helps Charlie stay the course, I can't say no to that. But it doesn't mean . . . I don't want you ever to think it means . . .' She felt the heat of tears at the back of her eyes, but she was determined not to cry. How humiliating, she thought. Like being a schoolgirl whose boyfriend is attempting to rid himself of her. What did he really want her to say? she asked herself. What sort of promise did he need her to make him? She finally settled on, 'I can't bear your walking out of my life, not when it seems I've only just found you.'

He closed his eyes briefly. He opened them. He lifted his hand and his fingers passed so gently over her hair that she could barely feel his touch. He said, 'I want you to be that fixed point I'm heading towards.'

'I *am*,' she said. 'I'm as much yours as anything can make me in the present moment and nothing will change that. I'm whole with you, I'm alive with you, I'm the woman I want to be with you and only with you.'

He pulled her to him. He kissed her and she matched his passion with her own. 'Yes,' he murmured against her mouth. 'It's the same for me.'

Had they been in some other location, she would have undressed him, so badly did she want to prove to him that she was his. But here in this filthy place it seemed that love-making of the kind she had in mind would be a form of sacrilege that she couldn't admit into what she shared with Nat. But then his hands moved across her body, relieving her of buttons and enclosures and lifting her skirt even as she reached blindly for him and the zipper to his trousers for suddenly the *where* of it didn't matter at all.

Unexpected footsteps outside hurried along the path between the two sets of cottages. And then, 'India? Are you here?'

She and Nat were simultaneously motionless.

'India?'

God in heaven, she thought. Charlie. But how . . . ? And in an instant she not only knew but actually saw it all play out in her mind's eye: herself in the shower and Caroline using those moments to tiptoe into the second bedroom where India had been sleeping on the sofa that defined the space as a sitting room and office; Caroline quickly going through India's mobile phone to check for messages and make note of anything and everything she could use to do damage; Caroline reading the text from Nat and learning from it and from India's answer where she would be and at what time; Caroline reporting it all to Charlie but in such a way that he felt he had to dash over from Leyden Street in order to . . . what? Who knew? India only knew that he was there, just outside, striding down the pavement with worry in his voice.

Nat said, 'What the *hell* . . . ?' and released her. Quickly he sorted out his clothing. She wanted to say, 'No, don't. We must move forward,' as if lovemaking in a derelict cottage under renovation would mean some sort of commitment to him that Charlie's presence couldn't obviate.

'India? Are you here?'

She held her breath. Surely he wouldn't rattle the door handles or try to enter any of the cottages. She hadn't come in her car, so all they needed to do was to wait in silence until he departed.

But Nat wasn't having any of that. He said, 'Your clothes . . .'

in a way that indicated to her she was meant to straighten them as he had done to his, and ever the obedient child when ordered to be one, she did as he asked. She buttoned and tucked and soon enough Nat opened the cottage door and went outside and what could she do but follow him?

Charlie was at the far end of the row of cottages and he'd just turned to retrace his steps when India, on Nat's tail, stepped into the unkempt front garden of the dwelling Nat had showed her. Charlie stopped at once. His face altered, and in its alteration India knew at once that he had been his mother's dupe. She wanted to call out, 'What did she actually tell you, Charlie?' but she reckoned she could work it out well enough. Darling, India's gone into a worrying area this afternoon and I'm terribly concerned about the nature of this place. Don't even ask me why she's doing it, but apparently she's paying a call on someone in a neighbourhood worse than where Will and that wretched Lily lived. I think it's so *very* unwise of her and I've tried to tell her that alone at the time of day she intends to visit . . . Anything could happen to her. You see that, don't you?

He had seen that and here he'd come, ending up being confronted not only by India but also by her lover. Or her erstwhile lover. Or whatever he was because Nat was saying to her quietly, 'We must speak later,' and before she could tell him to stay or insist that he remain at her side or use some sort of wily female act at which she was so miserable anyway . . . He was gone. He said nothing to Charlie and did not acknowledge him with so much as a nod. He strode in the direction of Hunton Street where earlier she had seen his car.

'What did she tell you?' India asked Charlie. 'And did she mention that she went through my mobile? Because that's the only way she would have known where I was. And let me ask you this: do you think that's even remotely acceptable?'

Charlie came to her and she could see from his face that he felt no triumph at his successful interruption of her time with Nat, but only misery. He knew very well that his mother had manoeuvred him into this jaunt, and he hated this fact as much as did India. Still, he said, 'I can't be angry with her.'

India ran her hands back through her hair, felt its tangles from Nat's caresses. She said, 'Oh, for God's sake. What's it going to take?'

'How can I be angry when she wants what she assumes is the best for me?'

'So it's appropriate for her to lie to you? For her to invade my privacy in order to manufacture something designed to move you? This is all fine?'

'Of course it's not fine.' Charlie indicated that she was to join him on the path and when she'd done so automatically, he began to walk in the direction Nat had taken. She followed him as the only course of action available at this point. He said, 'I'm offended that she lied to me but I'm not offended at her intentions because they're the same as mine. I want my wife back. I want my *life* back. Mum knows this and she wants to help me make that happen. Her approach is clumsy and stupid. This entire situation is clumsy and stupid. D'you think I actually wanted to stumble on you and him? To interrupt . . . whatever it was.'

'*She* wanted you to stumble upon us. She knew I was meeting him. God knows what she thought was going to happen between us in a building site but whatever she thought, she wanted you to be here to witness it. That's cruel, Charlie, and if you don't see that, I don't know *what* will ever make you understand that your mother—'

'I understand,' he said sharply. 'All right? I understand. Her. You. Nat. This entire bloody situation. What you two were up to when I came on the scene just now. I understand that. Perfectly.'

India felt like a balloon with the air released in one fell swoop. She so much longed for Nat to be there, for the taste of him and the touch of him and the blessedly wonderful *normal* of him. She said to her husband, 'I can't do this. I'm bringing her back to you tonight.' She looked at her watch and evaluated how long it all would take: the trip to Camberwell, packing up Caroline, returning her to Charlie. She reckoned she could have her at the flat by eight o'clock and that was what she told her husband.

He said, 'India, you know I have obligations.'

She said, 'Then put her up at a hotel. You should have done that from the first. I should have insisted. I'm finished with this business.'

'Give me till tomorrow. I'll get on the phone with Alastair and convince him to come to—'

'This is all *about* Alastair when it's not about you,' India argued. 'She's run off from him in a ploy to get him away from Sharon *and* to get herself into London where she can mix herself into *our* lives. Which she's doing quite well. I want her gone. I don't care how you manage it but I want it to happen. Tonight.'

'I've the suicide hotline tonight, India.'

'Skip it.'

'You *know* that I can't.'

'What time do you finish, then? I'll have her packed and waiting by the front door. I'll ring a taxi. I'll hire a car and driver. Whatever it takes because I've reached my limit.'

He rubbed his brow, fingers so hard against his flesh that his nails turned pure white, speckled with small, angry blotches of red. 'I'm on till two a.m., India. What would you have me do? Shall I come for her then?' He waited for her to see the impossibility of what she was demanding. After a moment, he went on. 'Let me drive you home. Let's find some takeaway and have a meal with her before I go to the hotline. I have time for that. I'll have a word with her. Then tomorrow, I'll arrange for her to return to Shaftesbury. I'll phone Alastair, I'll put her on a train, or I'll drive her down myself. You have my promise. If you'll just keep her with you one more night.'

'I don't *want*—'

'I know. And after this —' he gestured at the line of cottages — 'I quite understand. I'm sorry for what happened. I should have suspected or at least wondered, but I didn't. And believe me, I intend to speak with her at some length about what she's manufactured here between us.'

India wondered about that. It seemed to her that one could speak and speak and speak to Caroline, and never did it make the slightest difference in whatever her intentions were. But she had Charlie's promise and it was only for a night and he would make certain his mother knew how deep his displeasure ran when it came to what she'd done to him this day.

She said, 'All right, then. But she's gone tomorrow.'

He nodded. 'Thank you,' he said. And then casually, 'You've entirely misbuttoned your blouse, by the way. And I'm afraid you've somehow lost an earring as well.'

*Victoria*
*London*

'Do you know what the hell *time* it is, whoever you are?' told Lynley that he'd probably awakened the man from sleep. He hadn't a clue what time it was in Wellington, New Zealand, and having tracked Adam Sheridan down in the antipodes after spending considerable effort on the task, he'd rung the B & B that Sheridan and his wife operated in that town without dwelling upon the time change at all.

He said, 'I beg your pardon, Mr Sheridan. This *is* Adam Sheridan, isn't it?'

'And who the hell am I speaking to?'

Lynley thought it was a strange way for the owner of a B & B to talk, no matter the hour of the day, since he could have been a potential customer ringing with an enquiry about a lengthy stay at Bay View Lodge. Nonetheless, he identified himself mildly to the man, who then said, 'Scotland Yard? At . . . five in the morning . . .' And in the background a woman's voice spoke, to which the man said in reply, 'I don't bloody know, do I?' and then into the phone to Lynley, 'What's this about?'

'A woman called Caroline Goldacre,' Lynley told him, 'although you would have known her as Caroline Garza.'

There was a silence. Lynley could picture the man sorting through this bit of information as he swung himself to the side of the bed where his slippers lay with his dressing gown in a jumble on the floor. He would put them on – the dressing gown as well – and he would leave the bedroom to take their conversation elsewhere. He wouldn't want his wife to hear what he had to say, Lynley reckoned. It wasn't going to be a pretty story.

He said, 'Are you still there, Mr Sheridan?'

'Yeah. Hang on.'

A bit more silence, although this time it was broken by breathing whose stertorous nature suggested a life of heavy smoking or asthma or both. When after thirty seconds, Sheridan still hadn't spoken again, Lynley said again, 'Mr Sheridan? Are you still there?'

'Yeah, yeah. Right. I c'n talk now. Shit. Raining. Wait. Let me . . .'

Finally the man situated himself both out of earshot and out of the rain. He said, 'That's a name I never expected to hear again. What's this about then? What's she done?'

Lynley wasn't entirely surprised by the question since a phone call from New Scotland Yard at five in the morning did suggest that something untoward had occurred. But it was interesting that the man asked what Caroline Garza had *done* and not what might have happened to her.

Lynley told him that he was ringing to confirm the history that Sheridan shared with Caroline, one revealed to him by Mercedes Garza. He went directly to the heart of the matter: pregnancy, childbirth, adoption, and blackmail. Interestingly and contrary to what Mercedes Garza had told him about her confrontation with the man all those years ago, Sheridan did not deny any of it.

'A childminder. That's what she was, more or less. She was a mate of our Rosie and what the wife and I thought was that while Rosie was a bit too immature to mind the younger ones when the wife and I went out, she and Caroline together might do quite well and save us money at the same time.'

His wife had thought at first that both of the girls were too young, Sheridan explained, but as Caroline seemed mature for her age in comparison to Rosie, they decided to give the plan a go. They liked their date nights – 'Important to the relationship was how the wife put it,' Sheridan said, 'and I was happy to go along with it because we had four kids, and most days and nights we hadn't the time or energy to say a word to each other' – and this looked a good way to have those nights more regularly than they would have been able to do had they been forced to pay an adult minder.

Caroline would generally spend the night with Rosie but occasionally – 'early morning dance lessons or something . . . can't remember and don't want to, frankly' – Sheridan would drive the girl home. It was on one of the drives that things heated up between them.

'She'd been giving me messages all along that I should've ignored,' Sheridan said. 'But instead, like the bloody fool I was – in my thirties, this was, and overrun with testosterone – I crossed a line with her.'

'Perhaps more than one line,' Lynley noted.

'Yeah. Right. I admit to that. I was the adult. I was the responsible party. But I swear to you by all that's holy and on my dead mother's grave that she was . . . It was like she was in season. Look, I don't really want to talk about this. It's in the past and I paid.'

'You've served time? Her mother indicated that—'

Sheridan barked a laugh. 'That would've been easier, believe me. No. I wasn't stitched up for anything, was I? No word given to the coppers and all that. I denied everything when the girl's mum confronted me and she let it all go for some reason. But I lost my wife and I lost my kids and to this day the kids'll have nothing to do with me. Won't even answer a Christmas card from me and their stepmum, will they. They've never met her. And all this despite the fact that I paid that little tart—'

'I understand she was fourteen years old, Mr Sheridan,' Lynley cut in.

'That gash was never fourteen years old, Inspector. So yes, we had relations, her and me, with all the while her telling me she's on the pill. Then she comes up pregnant. I start paying her to hold her tongue about who got her that way – I'm not proud of any of this, it sickens me to tell you, you understand? – and her mum somehow uncovers it all. She puts a stop to my paying the girl but the girl herself . . . ? She goes ahead and tells my wife. And I don't blame her a bit for walking out on me and taking the kids with her because I deserved it. And to this day, Inspector, I don't know if there was a baby at all or if the girl was lying to get money off me.'

'There was a baby,' Lynley told him. 'She's long gone and the adoption was sealed.'

'So there's an end to it. But you've not answered me. What's she done? Why're you ringing me about her?'

'Caroline? We think someone may have tried to kill her.'

Adam Sheridan said, 'Tried? You mean without success?'

'That's correct.'

'Bloody too bad, that. And what? You're thinking it might've been me? Trotting up there from Wellington with blood on my mind?'

'We're following every possible lead.'

'You can cross me off the list, then. I haven't left New Zealand for fifteen years. Check if you like. I expect you lot can do that easy enough these days.'

Lynley believed the man. If he'd travelled anywhere out of the country of his present residence, Sheridan was correct in assuming that there would be records aplenty to show it.

He finished his phone call. It was, he decided, simply something that had needed crossing off his list. Another motive to have attempted to kill Caroline Goldacre, to be sure, but it was a nearly impossible feat for Adam Sheridan.

That was just the point, Lynley thought. The near impossibility of *anyone's* being able to manage what had been managed to get the doctored toothpaste into the woman's possession. There were motives aplenty. Turn over a stone and another one popped up. But with so few people with both access and opportunity . . . Were they – the police – being played for fools by Caroline Goldacre? For truly, what better way to eliminate someone was there than to do it in such a manner that the killer herself looked like the intended victim? But then they were back to the question of why Caroline might have wanted to kill Clare Abbott. Because she'd discovered that Clare had interviewed both her mother and her former husband? Because Clare had used a form of her name when meeting married men for sex? Where in that was the desperation that drove one person to kill another?

His mobile rang as he was pondering all this. He saw it was Havers. He took the call. She sounded lit up with excitement when she said his name. Then, 'Everything was in the boot of her car. In Clare's *car*, Inspector,' told him what her excitement was all about.

*Fulham*
*London*

Rory had just bade farewell to her sister Heather and to her own assistant from the publishing house when DI Lynley arrived. Her assistant had come bearing flowers, cards, a stuffed animal, and well-wishes from everyone, beginning with the managing director and ending with the interns who sorted the post. Her sister had come bearing fresh pyjamas, shampoo, and lotions. Together, the two women had got Rory out of bed for the first time and over to the window to look out at a blustery autumn day. And now she was longing to wash her hair and to have a shower, which she assumed was a good indication that she was fully mended, with no touch-and-go about it any longer. She also wanted Arlo, and she asked the inspector about him straightaway.

Lynley declared Arlo well and awaiting her. He reported the dog's adventures at London Zoo, and he pulled a chair up next to her bed, crossed one well-trousered leg over the other. He spoke frankly, all the time with his gaze fastened on her face in a manner that told her he would be reading her every reaction. This belied the friendliness of his tone and put her on her guard at once.

He began by telling her that one of the two detective sergeants he'd sent to Shaftesbury had discovered a mass of data in the boot of Clare's car. It had been hidden in the well for the spare tyre, he explained, and locked carefully into a strong box to protect it. The box's contents turned out to be transcripts of interviews with individuals associated with Caroline Goldacre as well as several hundred emails to Clare from the woman herself and a memory stick that suggested additional material might be contained upon it.

'I'm hoping that, as her editor, you might make something of all this,' he said.

DI Lynley waited for her response and asked no questions as Rory tried to take in the information he'd given her. She told him that she wasn't sure what any of it meant. Nor could she claim, she said, that what had been found in the boot of Clare's car had anything to do with the world of publishing. Clare had been hard at work on a book about adultery. So this business of transcripts and emails from Caroline Goldacre . . . ? Rory didn't know what to tell him.

'We've not come across a book on adultery,' Lynley told her. 'So I'm wondering . . . Could this material from Caroline and about Caroline comprise data for a different book or another book Clare wanted to write? Perhaps a future book?'

'Emails? If she was planning to develop a book from emails, I couldn't guess what it was, Inspector.'

Lynley appeared to think about this before going on. He sounded reluctant when next he spoke, but Rory wasn't sure if his reluctance was real or manufactured. She reminded herself that, despite his pleasant manners, he was still a cop. He said, 'There's something else,' and her told her it had also come out that Clare had made contact with a number of men who looked for sex online.

'That would be for the follow-up to the Darcy book,' Rory reminded him. 'Adultery. She was interviewing the men.'

'I understand that was her intention,' Lynley said. 'But upon questioning them, we've learned that Clare had been meeting these men for more than interviews.'

Rory looked at him in silence as the implication became clear. She wondered if she could somehow avoid it, but she knew at heart that she couldn't. She said, 'You're saying that Clare was . . . what? Sexual? With these men?'

'It does appear that she was. Two of them she interviewed. But then even with one of those two and then with the others—'

'I see.' Rory smoothed her hand along the rumpled hospital sheets upon her bed. 'Caroline kept claiming that there was no book, that there *is* no book, that Clare wasn't writing a thing. I daresay . . .' She chuckled weakly. 'I do hate to think she was right, Inspector.'

'She may not have been. Clare's "research" may merely have gone too far. There might well be a book that we've not yet uncovered.'

'How can you suggest that, really?' Rory found that the question – lightly spoken – worked a fist tightly round her heart.

Lynley's face, she realised, was far too compassionate for a policeman. They were never compassionate on television dramas. They hadn't the time, and they'd seen far too much anyway. He said, 'Perhaps getting these chaps to speak to her honestly was more difficult than Clare thought it would be, since she was apparently corralling them in the first place by making it seem that she was interested in sex. But then, once she met them . . . It could be the temptation was too much for her. Sex with no commitment and no questions asked, without even a surname attached to the partner? For some people, that would be a powerful draw.'

'For you?' she asked him.

'I'm far too romantic for my own good,' he said with a shrug. Then he added, 'According to my sergeant, Caroline Goldacre could easily have worked out that Clare was meeting these men. She could easily have got access to her email. And it seems Clare was using a version of Caroline's name as a sort of *nomme de coucher*: Caro24k in email, then Caro in person.' He paused for a moment as if to let her digest this, then added, 'And Caroline's done a bit of blackmail in her time, we've discovered.'

'Has she? I'm not surprised.'

'Why?'

'Just a feeling about her. Honestly? I don't like her much.'

'Here's what I'm wondering, Ms Statham. If Caroline knew about these men – as it could be she did – and if she attempted to blackmail them, could she also have been blackmailing Clare? Not for money but perhaps for something else?'

'What else, for heaven's sake?'

'We've no clear idea yet. But as you knew Clare Abbott . . .' His pause suggested that Rory think about the matter, so think she did.

'It would certainly explain why Clare kept her on despite her being rather unpleasant at times and not a particularly talented employee,' Rory said. 'I did ask Clare about that. Repeatedly.'

'What did she tell you?'

'Everything from "she needs the work" to "she's not a bad sort when you get to know her". Frankly, I never believed her. I just felt something was wrong, something was going on, but I never knew what. Now I do, I suppose.'

'If the case is that Caroline was blackmailing her with regard to these internet men in order to keep her job, might Clare on her part have been gathering information to prevent Caroline from revealing what she knew? In the event, let's suppose, that Clare did sack her?'

'Possibly. But what was Caroline supposed to *do* with her information about Clare and these men, such as it was?'

Lynley seemed to think about this for a moment before he said, 'Let's consider the country's foremost feminist arranging online to meet married men for anonymous sex. If that got out, wouldn't it have been a rather serious blow to her reputation? The tabloids alone would have had a field day. And Caroline certainly had enough information to interest a tabloid.'

'God, yes.' Rory recognised how weary she sounded. 'Yes. God, yes. And with Clare under contract for the adultery book, with a deadline for it looming . . . No wonder you can't find evidence of a book being written. How could anyone write a single word with that hanging over her head? God. How I *bloody* wish that she'd just told me what Caroline was up to. Certainly, we could have done something.'

'Perhaps Clare thought she couldn't tell you, for some reason,' Lynley said.

Rory kept her eyes deliberately on his. She waited for him to ask *why* Clare hadn't revealed what she'd been going through. Rory was, after all, not only her editor but also her longtime friend. So what was it that had kept Clare from speaking? Concentrating on coming up with an answer for these two unasked questions, Rory wasn't prepared for what the inspector said to her next.

'We had to go through your flat once you were poisoned, Ms Statham. The source of the poison was crucial, as was a motive for poisoning you. The forensic team took everything that could have contained the poison. The detectives took everything that could have pointed to a motive.'

Rory felt her heart beating more rapidly than before. The pulse of it was in her fingertips. 'I'm not sure where you're heading.'

'I've read Clare's letters to you. Forgive me, but it's part of my job. So is evaluating the evidence to reach a conclusion about murder, suicide, or accidental poisoning.'

Rory said nothing. But her mind went back over the letters from Clare and she wondered whether hers to Clare were among Clare's belongings and perhaps hidden away. She would have liked to think that this was the case, but she was forced to look squarely at the facts. If Clare had binned them – God, so pathetically fraught with love the later ones had been – then she herself had more information than she really wanted and certainly more than she could bear to face just now.

Lynley said, 'I suspect you were in love with her.'

Rory nodded. If he'd read Clare's letters, he knew the truth of it, so what did it really matter?

'But on her part . . . ?'

'She didn't lead me on, Inspector. I wouldn't have you think she ever led me on because she wasn't like that.'

'Were you lovers at some point?'

'Briefly. While I stayed with her. After Fiona . . . You know about Fiona, of course.' And when Lynley nodded as she'd reckoned he would do since he was, after all, a detective, 'Clare eventually told me she just wasn't easy with sex with a woman. I told her I could make her easy. I could see who she really was, I said, and everything she wrote and believed pointed to who she really was. She said that I was trying to replace Fiona, that I would see it eventually and anyway, this thing about sex . . . She said none of it actually interested her. Women and women, men and men, men and women. She said she'd never liked sex much – the closeness, the intimacy, the flesh-on-flesh of it. She said it was good at first but soon enough she didn't want any of it. "I just like to get *on* with things," was how she put it, "and sex bloody well gets in the way."' Rory cleared her throat, which was close to shutting off her windpipe. She added, 'Of course, I see now that she was merely trying to let me down gently. She didn't want to wound me after what I'd been through when Fiona died.'

Lynley took this in and once again she was forced to meet his deeply dark eyes. He gave the impression that he knew exactly what she was talking about: love and desire and disappointment and loss and the agonising pain of being human. But how could he? For unless one experienced the magnitude of love at its fullest, with all its blessings and all its curses and its untimely end, how could anyone really know what it was like to live with its loss?

He said, 'Actually, her involvement with these internet men rather suggests she was telling the truth. If you think about it, with these encounters she'd have had an outlet for whatever sexual needs she had. They'd be taken care of in some hotel, with no commitment, no requirements, no questions, and no future. It probably made perfect sense to her.'

Rory nodded although she felt so heavy with the knowledge he'd given her that all she wanted to do was to curl on her side and sleep for days. She said, 'And Caroline knew all of this. The internet business. The men Clare arranged to meet.'

'She declares not, but that doesn't seem likely.'

'And you agree that Caroline was probably using all this to keep her job?'

'That part's trickier, isn't it? We just don't know. But the fact that Clare was doing some sort of investigating of Caroline suggests things were becoming insupportable for her. So what we need to discover now is whether there's something Clare uncovered that made things just as insupportable for Caroline.'

*Belsize Park*
*London*

Sitting in his car a short distance from Daidre's flat, Lynley suddenly felt the loss of Helen more acutely than he had in weeks. He certainly hadn't expected this to be the result of his conversation with Rory Statham. Blackmail, internet sex, delving into the private life of one's employer . . . Certainly none of this could have triggered the overwhelming ache within him, having the absence of his wife as its throbbing centre. So he knew that it was something more, and he came up with it when he considered the relationship between Rory Statham and Clare Abbott. At its heart had been what Rory had wanted and what Rory had been denied.

He himself had had it all with Helen: the connection, the commitment, the future unfolding. It had been ripped from him in an instant that he could not have anticipated no matter how he'd looked into the years that had lain ahead of them. He wanted it all back. He was, he admitted, quite terribly desperate to have it all back. Now. Today. This night. Whatever. He couldn't keep going, he thought, if he didn't know it was out there somehow, a goal he was within yards of reaching.

He sighed. He looked up the street to the conversion in which Daidre lived. He examined his brief history with her in an attempt to see whether in reality all he was doing was running from the void. He simply didn't know. He couldn't decide. He felt at once immobilised and frantic for action, as if everything in what comprised his life had to be determined in the next quarter hour.

He understood exactly why he wanted to see Daidre: to move her forward, to move *them* forward. What he didn't know was what was compelling him to this action. Was it her obvious reluctance to dip into his world more deeply than she had acquiesced to so far? Or was it a real connection he felt to her, a sense that combined profound belonging and emancipated homecoming that, without Helen, he now shared with no one else?

He'd grown up knowing that he owed a great deal to more than two hundred and fifty years of his family's history on a great estate in Cornwall. He'd grown up knowing that part of what he was intended to do as the eldest son was to produce the child who would inherit this land and pass it along to another child. He'd managed a life away from that responsibility for a good many years, but there was a limit to how long he could stretch that time before the demands of his birth and his position told him it was necessary to get on with things as they'd been got on with for generations. He asked himself how much that knowledge also influenced his behaviour. He had no answer to that any more than he had an answer to what he was doing at this moment in Belsize Park asking himself questions in the first place when any other man would have bounded up the steps, banged on Daidre's door, and taken her to bed without a second thought. Or taken her to camp bed, he thought wryly. She was being rather clever about not having a real bed.

He rather hated himself for being so caught up in his thoughts. It was owing to his conversation with Rory, he reckoned, and watching the dawning understanding break over her face as she came to terms with who the woman she loved might actually have been. It was also owing to his exhaustion, though. He ought to go home, he told himself. If nothing else, he could manage a good night's sleep.

But he wanted none of that. He wanted to see Daidre. Even if he could not explain why he wanted to see her, he wanted to see her.

He got out of the Healey Elliott. Climbing the short flight of stairs to her front door, he was still telling himself that he could turn round, make the drive down to Belgravia, unlock his front door, go through the day's post, and take himself to bed, with or without a meal because he still had not had his dinner. Ringing the buzzer to her flat, he continued to question himself about the rightness of what he was doing with Daidre. But when he heard her voice – a simple 'Yes? Who is it?' – nothing of what he'd been considering seemed to matter.

He said, 'I've sworn to Rory Statham that I'd check on Arlo. Is he in?'

'He is. Would you like to see him or would speaking to him be enough?'

'Seeing him is preferable.'

She released the lock. When he went inside, she'd already opened her door and she stood with Arlo at her feet, his tail happily flicking the air. Woman and dog were backlit by a floor lamp in the sitting room. Its shade had been removed so that stark shadows were cast upon the walls, and the colour of the walls themselves was in the process of being altered, with Daidre wielding a roller on which a soft grey paint dripped onto one of several dust sheets spread across the floor.

She was wearing what looked like a man's second-hand boiler suit. The name *Jackson* was embroidered across the left breast of it, and the various colours that speckled it at once brought Pollock to mind. Arlo wore some of the paint himself, Lynley saw. One of his eyebrows was grey and it appeared that his left front paw had done some exploration in the tray that held Daidre's paint.

'He wanted to help,' Daidre explained, seeing the direction of Lynley's gaze. 'We had words about it and he's been in the kitchen ever since.' And to the dog, 'Bed, Arlo. After you say hello to Inspector Lynley.'

Lynley patted the dog's head, and Arlo obediently trotted to the kitchen where Daidre had placed a folded blanket within viewing distance of the sitting room and the work going on there. Lynley inspected this. She'd had the walls re-plastered or – knowing Daidre – she'd done the plastering herself. She'd also repaired and sanded the woodwork of the room, which was now taped off against the pearl grey that was going up on the walls. He saw that she'd also broken through the postwar walling of the Victorian fireplace. It would need the replacement of some of its decorative tiles, but he had no doubt she was the woman for the job, as well as the job of refinishing the dreadfully painted lavender floor that lay beneath the dust sheets.

He said, 'You've made good progress.'

'What d'you think of the colour?'

'On the walls, fine. In your hair, perhaps not.'

'Oh God, have I got it in my hair?'

'On your cheek as well. And there's a rather beguiling spot of it on your chin.'

'I've never been terribly good with paint,' she told him regretfully.

'On the contrary, you wield a brush like . . . well, like a real housepainter. I didn't think to find you embroiled in the project at this hour, though. Do you know the time?'

'I expect I've missed dinner. What about you?'

'The same.'

She set down her roller and moved the tray to the top of a ladder, where she carefully balanced it. 'Are you hungry?' she asked him. 'We could easily forage in the fridge. I'm afraid it would be an every-man-for-himself sort of meal, though. I'd love to whip up something spectacular for you from the remains of whatever's in the kitchen, but when it comes to that sort of whipping, I'm completely out of my league.'

'I don't want to ask what the other sort of whipping is,' Lynley said. 'Let me see what you have while you . . . I expect you don't want to eat in the boiler suit.'

'And you'd be correct,' she told him. 'Only . . .'

He paused. He'd been on his way to the kitchen, and he turned to see her watching him. Her glasses, he saw, were also speckled with paint, as were her feet which, curiously, were bare. He raised an eyebrow. 'Only . . . ?' he said.

'Only I have nothing on beneath this,' she told him. 'Well, not quite true. Knickers and a sports bra. But nothing else. I could put on jeans. A T-shirt or pullover, perhaps. But, to be honest, it seems rather like a waste. Unless, of course, you're famished. In which case, I completely understand.'

'You seem to be suggesting something other than foraging in the fridge,' he told her.

'Right. Well. How hungry are you?'

20 October

*Shaftesbury*
*Dorset*

They'd been up till half past three, so Barbara at least had an excuse for her lie in the following morning. Together she and Winston had read every one of the emails that Caroline Goldacre had written to Clare Abbott. There were hundreds and they had run the gamut, covering everything from her personal history – with heavy emphasis on Caroline's relationships with her mother and with her first husband – to her friendships and affiliations with other women in Shaftesbury during the years of her habitation in the town. She wrote of her sons often, particularly of Will and his suicide and her refusal to look upon his ruined body after his leap from a Dorset cliff. This soul-crushing inability had, she explained at great and repetitive length, robbed her of a final look upon her son even in his coffin when all the damage had been repaired by an undertaker who'd come down from London as a personal favour to Francis and wasn't *that* the only time that Francis Goldacre had so much as lifted a finger to help his son . . . when he was dead . . . because God knew he wouldn't do a thing to help the boy when he was alive, no matter how she begged or what she did or what Will himself did to illustrate the depth of his self-loathing. This was, it developed, a favourite theme that Caroline had pursued in her emails, closely followed by her many examinations of her son Charlie's marriage to the 'loathsome India' who was 'plain as a pikestaff and doing nothing at all to make herself otherwise. It's as if she wants to be as unattractive as possible and what woman would do that unless it's to torment Charlie because I swear to you she wasn't like that when he met her, she was quite lovely, but she has COMPLETELY let herself go.'

On the theme of India, Caroline wound herself up tightly and let fly. In most cases, her epistolary creation was a rambling diatribe as one thought seemed to trigger the next. India wanted to make herself undesirable to Charlie, went one explication, because she had never liked sex in the first place and, 'believe me, she was the one who insisted on marriage and she wouldn't let up till she had him, and now she has him supporting her because what in God's name can she expect to make as an acupuncturist I ask you? Now that he's out there working like a dog for her, you watch, she isn't going to bother with him sexually any longer. And I didn't want him to marry her, you know. They were too young, and now what if India wants to have a baby which I wouldn't put past her for a moment. That's what's probably behind everything she does. And if she does get pregnant – God forbid – what then? I'll tell you: he'll be caught for good.'

It did not appear to dawn on Caroline that she continually contradicted herself, sometimes within a single email. It was as if, once she began writing, something was unleashed inside her and she was unable to control what she said. But the real question that Barbara and Winston asked each other throughout the long night and into the early morning hours of their reading was why Clare Abbott had kept all the emails, had gone so far as to print them, had highlighted bits and pieces of them, and had made references to unknown names and numbers in the margins, as well as obscure abbreviations. But these were questions they could not answer as the night wore on. They were too exhausted, drained from all the reading and from their attempts at interpreting the motives of both women – Caroline and Clare – in writing to each other in the first place.

Prior to sitting at the dining table with their respective stack of emails, Winston had reported to Barbara the details of his time in Sherborne with Dr Karen Globus, the psychiatrist whose name Clare had written in her diary. At first – and as they both had expected she might do – Dr Globus had given Winston an outright refusal even to verify that Clare Abbott had come to her office, no matter his warrant card. But a revelation of the details of Clare's death went a very long distance to loosening Dr Globus's tongue, her memory, and her files. It turned out that Clare had not gone to see the psychiatrist as a patient. 'Or so she said at first,' Dr Globus added.

'Meaning what, 'xactly?' Winston had enquired.

'Meaning that she presented as someone merely seeking background information for a book she intended to write. In her case, what she wanted to talk about was child abuse. In fact she requested a series of interviews about the long term effects of the sexual abuse of a child,' Dr Globus explained. 'But it became clear during the course of our conversations that the child in question was herself.'

This piqued Barbara's interest as Winston told the tale of his conversation with Globus who, it had turned out, was not only a psychiatrist but also a fellow feminist whose paper on female genital mutilation within the UK had gathered a great deal of attention at the time of its publication. So Clare Abbott had known who Dr Globus was and because of her reputation, Dr Globus was also quite familiar with Clare Abbott's work.

'Sometimes,' she had told Nkata, 'a person of Clare's celebrity needs to approach a disturbing subject indirectly, and I think her "information gathering" was a way she was beginning to deal with some deeply troubling aspects of her own past.'

'Her brother, Barb,' Winston said. 'He did the job on her when they were kids.'

'That was in one of the emails, as well,' Barbara said. 'One of Caroline's. She made a deal of it.'

Clare claimed, the doctor said, that she'd put the issue to rest when she'd been up at Oxford as a student. 'Talked it all over with a head shrink then. But 'cause she wanted to talk 'bout *late adult* man'festations of child abuse, the doctor thinks she was trying to cope with summat in her present life.'

They never quite got round to dealing with that, though, because over twelve sessions, Dr Globus revealed, she and Clare had engaged in a wide ranging series of discussions instead of more intimate ones, and it proved impossible to draw Clare out any further than she wished to go. While these discussions began with conversations about child sexual abuse and its ramifications in adulthood, they went on to touch upon chronic anxiety, bipolar disorder, borderline personality disorder, dependent personality disorder, sociopathy, the roots of passive-aggression, narcissistic personality disorder, obsessive compulsive personality disorder. Clare had taken extensive notes and had asked good questions, a great many of them.

'No surprise there,' Dr Globus had concluded. 'She was not only a writer but also a highly intelligent woman.'

During their reading of Caroline's emails, then, Barbara and Winston had gone back and forth and round the mulberry bush on the *why* of it all. Not only on the *why* of a series of revealing emails from Caroline to her employer but also on the why of Clare's appointments with Dr Globus. It seemed to them at the end of a gruelling evening of reading and evaluating and discussing that – given the circumstances of Caroline's being employed by Clare, the email collection, and the range of conversations with the psychiatrist – either Clare was attempting to understand the other woman in an effort to help her in some way or, more probably, they themselves had further evidence that she was looking for a way to get Caroline Goldacre out of her life with as few consequences to herself as possible. The overheard conversation – 'We're finished, you and I' – seemed to confirm this.

'Not so easy to bring off when someone's barking, I expect,' Barbara put it, and Winston did not disagree.

When she finally dragged herself out of bed, Barbara found that Winston was getting on with Clare's computer as well as with the memory stick that she had found in the locked box in the boot of Clare's car. To 'Why the computer, Winnie? I thought you were finished with it,' Winston replied that 'Far as I know, there's got to be some sort of answers from Clare to Caroline in deleted emails. Else why'd Caroline keep writing to her?'

'Because, like we agreed, she's barking?'

'Maybe yes, maybe no,' was his reply. He rubbed the back of his neck and looked thoughtful. When Barbara asked him what was on his mind, he said, 'Could use some help with all this, Barb.'

'I've told the inspector we could use help here, but it's not a goer, Winnie. You can try, though. He might believe you better 'n me. But I expect there're too many blots in my copybook for the superintendent to go along with sending someone down to assist or ringing the local nick for the loan of a couple of DCs. She's hoping for a major cock- up on my part so she can pack me up north.'

Barbara fetched her breakfast from the oven – once again carefully wrapped in aluminium foil – and she took this along with her coffee into Clare's office. There, she'd placed the pile of emails, and she leafed through them hoping for an aha! moment while she gobbled down eggs scrambled with cheese and flavourful bits of green that appeared to be some sort of vegetation. With a final piece of wholemeal toast in her hand, she had a wander along Clare's bookshelves and saw what she expected to see in the home office of a noted feminist: *The Feminine Mystique*; *Against Our Will: Men, Women, and Rape*; *The Fountain of Age*; *The Female Eunuch*, among other volumes of that ilk. She clocked the names of the authors, large in the feminist pantheon: Steinem, Greer, Friedan and others. They were, of course, familiar to her. Then she came to another, familiar also but for an entirely different reason.

Geoffrey Timms. She paused when she saw it. Timms, she thought, and she took the book back to Clare's desk. She found the reference among the emails written by Caroline Goldacre. It was scrawled in the margin of one of them: *Timms 164*.

The book itself was called *Frantic: Manifestation of Borderline*

*Personality Disorder*. Barbara opened it to page 164 and saw that two passages had been bracketed off in pencil. Neither was long. She read the first: "The abandonment fears are real. They relate directly to an intolerance of solitude. They hearken to an inability to be on one's own in life and a chronic need to be cared for by another.' And then she dropped her gaze to the second, which declared that 'This tendency towards unstable and inappropriately intense relationships can be characterised by an inundation of the object necessary for need fulfilment. It can also be seen in the sharing of intimate details early in a relationship.' She considered the quotes in light of Caroline's emails – *inundation* was the word, all right, she reckoned – and then she quickly leafed through them to find another annotated with *Ferguson 610*. This turned out to be a reference to one Jacqueline Ferguson whose book *The Psychopathology of Emotional Vulnerability* stood on the same shelf that held the Timms volume. On page 610, Barbara found what she expected to see, more bracketed material: 'It is when emotions repeatedly reignite or when their extended duration cannot be explained by the circumstances arousing them that a closer examination is in order.' And like the Timms volume, a second passage was marked, this one in yellow highlighting pen: 'This dysphoria is generally characterised by extreme emotions, destructiveness or self-destructiveness, lack of strong identity, and feelings of victimisation, particularly at the hands of those previously trusted. This last often arises out of what other people might see as inconsequential but what the patient sees as of paramount importance, such as a cancelled lunch date or the lack of timely response to a telephone message.'

Barbara frowned, put the volume back onto the shelf and quickly found the next name in the margin of one of the printed emails. This was Cowley and on page 242 of Howard Cowley's book *Obtaining Nurturance in a Hostile World* she saw that 'perhaps the most common misconception is that the impact of pathological behaviour upon others is the intention of the person with the disorder. The opposite is the case. The normal ability to manage painful emotions and interpersonal challenges has been impaired.' And further down the page 'Frequent expressions of intense pain, self-harming, suicidal behaviour, and even violence directed towards others may instead represent either a method of regulating mood or an escape from a situation that feels unbearable.' On the facing page, a final quotation declared that 'It should not be assumed that the patient bears no responsibility for his actions, however. Nor should it be assumed that the harmful nature of these actions should be allowed to continue. While it's helpful for those involved with the patient to understand what drives the behaviour, the development of firm boundaries must be encouraged in those who deal with the person.'

Barbara tapped her fingers on the page with this quotation. It seemed to her that things relating to Caroline and Clare were becoming clear. While Clare's possession of these volumes, her visits to a Sherborne psychiatrist, and her annotating of Caroline Goldacre's emails – not to mention her maintaining them among her records in the first place – might have indicated an attempt to understand Caroline, the fact that Clare had been going to such extreme lengths to gather information pointed in another direction altogether. With the emails and Clare's own research declaring that something could be seriously wrong with Caroline Goldacre, that Clare had not eliminated her from her life suggested one of three things: there was indeed some significant blackmail going on, or Clare needed desperately to keep Caroline close to her for some reason, or Clare was afraid. If the last were true, perhaps she'd come to realise that only by dabbling into Caroline's psyche could she possibly hope to—

'Barb?'

Winston, she saw, was in the doorway. He held Clare Abbott's laptop computer in the broad palm of his hand. 'Got summat you need to look at,' he said.

'Is it going to help sort all this out?'

'Think so,' he replied.

*Camberwell*
*South London*

The fact that she'd already had to cancel her first two appointments of the day made India predisposed to be furious. She rang off on the telephone call from Charlie, and the first thing she wanted to do was throw a very heavy book through a very large window. Unfortunately, there was neither a large enough window nor a heavy enough book in her house, so she was left with nothing else to do but cancel her next two appointments as well.

She told herself it wasn't Charlie's fault. He'd arrived in the vicinity of Tower Bridge only to discover it was up in order to accommodate 'some bloody huge ship, India, I swear it must an RN destroyer' and the ensuing tailback took ages to clear. Then a downed cyclist on the Old Kent Road caused further difficulties for him, and it was on this second apologetic phone call that she'd just rung off. He *was* on his way, he promised her. He was sorry this situation was turning out to be such a nightmare.

That was one way to put it, India thought. The other way was to point out to herself – for the thousandth time – that such were the spoils of being spineless.

To his credit, Charlie *had* told her to go on to work. He was on his way, he'd be there as soon as he could, she should be free to go about her day and not worry whether he was going to show up to collect his mother because he *was* going to do so just as he'd promised. But India wasn't willing to leave the premises, for her fear was that Caroline – left alone with Charlie when he came to fetch her – would talk him into letting her remain in India's house. Worse, while she waited for her son to arrive, she would no doubt delve into India's computer again since she'd already made mention of India's planned trip to the Broads with Nat, which she only could have known about by invading her email. India had changed her password on the previous night, altering things so that her laptop did not remember it. But she had great faith in Caroline's abilities in this area, and even if she had not, she just wanted the woman gone.

When Charlie had driven India home from her meeting with Nat at the building site, Caroline had been all aflutter with delight to see them together. Her poorly concealed triumph at what she'd managed to bring off seemed to quell her previous terrors of being the intended victim of a poisoner. Prior to the moment of seeing her success at bringing Charlie and India together, Caroline had purported herself to be a wreck once the Scotland Yard detective had come for her fingerprints and the truth about Caroline's toothpaste and Clare's use of it had come out. She'd been up most of that night, wandering the house, watching the television, oblivious to the fact that she was keeping India from sleeping as well. She'd talked, she'd wept, she'd dived into the fridge for wine, she'd drunk, she'd eaten. At the end of it all, she'd drugged herself into sleep, and India had found herself left awake and anxiety ridden.

She had to get out of her marriage. She knew that now. She was in love with Nat, she wanted Nat, she wanted the normal sort of life that loving and being with Nat promised. She was not going to get it if she allowed Caroline Goldacre to remain anywhere near her. She should have seen that from the first time she'd met Caroline, but she hadn't, so charmed had she been by the woman's declarations of delight over having a daughter at long last. India knew now that all of that had merely been the machinations of a mother who wished to control her son's marriage, and India had gone along with it all because, ever the diplomat's daughter, she'd been taught not to make waves in delicate political situations.

Enough, she thought now. She'd really had quite enough. And she'd arranged for Nat to come over that evening just to make certain she held true to her decisions regarding Charlie and his mother.

Upon Charlie's first phone call, India had tried to get Caroline up for the day. But she'd apparently taken some sort of sleeping pill – she definitely would have gone in for laudanum in a very big way in its heyday, India thought – and India had not been able to rouse her. But now she had to, for Charlie would probably suggest that he fetch his mother in the evening if India wasn't able to get her up and ready to go. So she went to the bedroom a second time, determined to drag her mother-in-law from sleep.

Caroline was curled foetally. India glanced at her and went to the window, where she opened the curtains first and the window second. The room smelled like a brothel. Caroline's perfume permeated everything. India knew she'd have to launder the counterpane and blankets in addition to the sheets upon Caroline's departure, and she might have to take down the curtains and see to them as well.

She went to the bed. She said, 'Mum,' and then '*Caroline*,' to very little avail. Caroline's eyelids fluttered but it was with the movement of her eyeballs in sleep. India grasped the covers and whipped them back, saying, 'Charlie's on his way. Time to get up.'

For a moment, Caroline didn't stir and India wondered if she'd taken an overdose of something. It wouldn't be the first time she'd attempted to harm herself, at least according to what Charlie had told her. He'd declared these attempts a pathetic cry for help – very kind of him, India thought, since her first try at suicide had been when she was pregnant with Charlie himself – and with that kind of history, he went on, she needed to be watched more carefully.

India bent over her. Caroline was definitely breathing, so India grasped her shoulder, shook it, and said her name again. At this, Caroline stirred, but she didn't waken, so India considered the water glass that stood on the bedside table. She would have dashed its contents into Caroline's face, but she didn't want to wet the pillow. Thus she found herself slapping Caroline lightly on the cheeks and enjoying the sensation perhaps a bit more than she ought to have done.

She said sharply, 'Caroline. Mum. Wake up,' and at this her

mother-in-law opened her eyes at last. 'Charlie's on his way,' India told her.

'Charlie?' Caroline murmured. 'Has something happened?'

What had happened, India thought, was that her own head had become remarkably clear in the last twenty-four hours. She said, 'Nothing's happened. Charlie's just coming to fetch you.'

'But where am I supposed to go? It's safe for me here.' Caroline reached for India's arm but missed. 'I know I've been trouble, dear. I wasn't my best with you and Nat. But when I think of Charlie and what he's been through—'

'Up,' India grasped Caroline's elbow and gave a heave.

Caroline resisted, stiffening, saying, 'This is what mothers do. You'll understand when you have your own children. India, you're hurting my arm.'

'Are you getting up?'

'Of course I'm getting up. What on earth are you thinking?' Caroline sat up, swayed a little, but determinedly put her feet onto the floor as if intent to assure India that she meant what she said. 'Listen to me please. When I saw you with Charlie last night . . . When he brought you home from wherever you'd been—'

'You know very well where I'd been since you told him yourself. And you only knew that by invading my privacy, which, frankly, I don't appreciate.'

– 'and we sat round the kitchen table having that lovely curry, what else could I think other than this is what was meant to be?'

India had gone to sort out Caroline's clothing, which she tossed onto the bed. She left her to see to the shower in the bathroom. Apparently, Caroline heard this latter for when India returned, she said, 'I prefer a bath.'

'Today it's going to be a shower. You can take one alone or I can get in with you to make sure you're quick. Which is it to be?'

Caroline's dark eyes narrowed. She pushed a bit of her

curling hair back from her face in that gesture she had: sort of an Elizabeth Taylor doing Tennessee Williams. She said, 'You've become quite hard. Does Nat like you that way?' She chuckled before India could answer and went on with, 'No, I expect it's just the opposite. You were always a dark horse when it came to sex. I could see that straightaway. When you and I met, I tried to tell Charlie, but what boy wants to hear from his mum on the subject of sex?'

'You've not said about the shower,' India told her. 'What's it to be? Alone or with me?'

Caroline indicated her preference by making her way to the bathroom, where she closed and locked the door. India expected to hear an alteration indicating she'd switched the water to fill the tub, but that didn't occur. It seemed that her mother-in-law was conceding the battle. India didn't expect her to concede the war, however.

She went below to fix Caroline a breakfast tray. It would be simple and quick, consumable within five minutes of semi-concentrated eating. By the time she had it assembled – tea, butter, jam, a croissant, a sectioned orange – Caroline was actually out of the shower, back in the bedroom, and putting on her make-up. She glanced at the tray India carried, said, 'How continental of you, my dear,' and went back to her face. She'd always worn too much make-up, India thought.

The doorbell rang, announcing Charlie's arrival. India went to let him in. He was all apologies about the lateness of the hour, but he didn't ask if his mother was packed up and ready to go. India steeled herself at once, and she wasn't surprised when Charlie next spoke, saying, 'Look here, India. I'm not sure taking her back to Shaftesbury is the best idea. How's she coping?'

'Why?'

Charlie knew she wasn't asking about the coping. He said, 'Obviously. Alastair. This business with Sharon. Then there's Lily Foster as well.'

'Are you truly thinking that one of them tried to poison her?'

'They're the people with motives. And isn't that the point: who has a motive to kill whom? I can't see anyone has a motive to kill Clare. And now with this toothpaste being Mum's . . . She rang me, you know. She told me.'

India shook her head. 'Really, Charlie, I can't believe you're even considering what she tells you at this point. But if you're going to do that, then you have to look at something no one's been willing to look at so far.'

'Which is what?'

'Your mum.'

'Suicide? No one's going to kill themselves that way.'

'I'm not talking about *actual* suicide.' India glanced at the stairway. She could hear Caroline still moving round up above, so she drew her husband into the kitchen. There, she leaned against the work top. He did the same against the fridge, his arms crossed. He said, 'What then? You can't *possibly* think Mum wanted to kill Clare. They may have had their difficulties—'

'I've been thinking about this most of the night,' India said quickly. She wanted to get it all said before Caroline joined them. 'She kept me up, by the way, so it wasn't exactly difficult to find the time to think.'

He scowled, said, 'Sorry, darling. Really.'

'Never mind that. Just listen, please. A suicide attempt – just enough to make her very ill but not to kill her – would have been in character for your mum. She's done it before. And with Will dead and Alastair carrying on with Sharon—'

'And with our marriage breaking up . . .' Charlie said meditatively.

India didn't want to head there, so she hastened on to say, 'Another suicide attempt would galvanise people.'

'Then why in God's name give the toothpaste to Clare?'

'If it was after they argued—'

'They had an argument?'

'Evidently, yes. So when that happened, perhaps your mum handed the toothpaste over, thinking it would make Clare

good and ill and put a real spanner into her book promotion
and she bloody well deserved it. But when she saw what
happened . . .' India warmed to her explanation. 'Charlie, let's
assume she found Clare dead far earlier than she indicated
to the police. Let's assume she found her that night instead
of the next morning. If that's the case, she could have manufactured everything else. She said she phoned down to
Reception, but what if she did that *after* she'd discovered
Clare's body, quite late, to establish that she had no toothpaste.
Don't you see that—'

'You wouldn't make a very good detective, India,' Caroline
said as she entered the kitchen. She was carrying the breakfast
tray, which she set on the table before turning to eye India
head to toe. 'Or perhaps,' she continued, 'it's just that you've
not been watching enough police dramas on the television
because you'd know that your personal feelings for your suspect
can't be allowed to get in the way. Should I take it that only
my eventual murder is going to convince you of my innocence?'

'Mum . . .' Charlie spoke in a way that told India he intended
to placate her.

She found she didn't want Caroline placated. She said to
her mother-in-law, 'Frankly? I've begun to think that just about
anything's possible with you.'

'Have you indeed? And I've been wondering these past two
days why the police haven't looked more closely at you.'

'Mum, let's be off,' Charlie said. 'This kind of conversation—'

'Oh, I'm altogether ready to be off,' Caroline told him. 'Have
you told your stepfather I'm coming? I'd like to make sure he
has plenty of time to rid the house of the evidence.'

'You aren't thinking that Alastair—'

'I'm not speaking of evidence of his intention to murder
me. I'm speaking of evidence of his filthy piece of tail being
in my house while I've been gone. I have no hope that he's
given her up. Both of them have too much to gain. So did you
phone him, Charlie? Does he know I'm coming? Ah. Never
mind. I can see it on your face.'

'She wasn't there, Mum,' Charlie told her. 'She hasn't been there at all.'

Caroline patted his cheek with a marked lack of affection. 'You've always been extremely credulous,' she said. 'That's not a very good quality in a psychotherapist.'

*Shaftesbury*
*Dorset*

Barbara followed Winston back into the dining room, where there was space for them both to sit with the laptop computer opened in front of them. She could see that he'd been deep into following the trail of Clare's deleted emails. He'd been intrigued, he told Barbara, that Clare had printed up Caroline's messages only. At first he'd reckoned she had never responded to her but that didn't make sense ''cause seems to me Caroline would've stopped writing to her eventually, eh?'

Barbara complimented him on his psychological analysis of the situation. 'Plenty more of that in her library if you want to have a go,' she told him.

He tapped a few keys on the laptop, then, and told Barbara to have a look. What she saw proved Winston's point. Clare had indeed replied and she'd done so consistently although what she'd had to say had been brief, just a few sentences at most in response to emails that went on for pages. Sometimes she wrote only a single line. Barbara read through her replies as Winston brought them up:

*Good for you to get things off your chest. It's healthy to blow off steam now and then.*

*Don't apologise. No hard feelings. You must have a go at me when I'm out of order.*

*Alastair sounds like a perfect monster. How do you manage to put up with him?*

*I'm utterly amazed you remained married to Francis as long as you did.*

*But what happened after that?*

Barbara looked up at Winston who said, 'An' there's more, Barb. Practic'ly every time, she says something more or less supporting her, an' she never points out that one time Caroline said this and the next time she said that and the third time she said something diff'rent. It's like . . .' He rubbed the back of his neck and looked, if anything, regretful.

Barbara finished his thought. 'It's like she was encouraging her to keep writing. Only thing is . . . why?'

'Well, there's this to consider,' Winston told her. 'It was what was on the memory stick, Barb.'

He moved the laptop to sit in front of him, and he accessed a folder that Barbara saw was named *Internet/Adultery*. It contained a list of documents. Nkata opened the first of them and turned the computer to face Barbara fully. Across the top of the screen in bold she saw *The Power of Anonymous Adultery*. Beneath this, Barbara read a few lines. She recognised at once that she was looking at the same introduction she'd seen in the folder in Rory Statham's desk.

She went from this introduction to the table of contents, from there to the chapters themselves. She saw that indeed there was and had always been a book that Clare Abbott was writing, and it looked as if she had been well into it at the time of her death. She'd completed twelve chapters. She'd begun the thirteenth. From what Barbara could tell, they were strongly but simply written, perfectly accessible to the ordinary reader. But the fact of them on a memory stick only and the fact of that memory stick's being hidden away in the boot of Clare's car insisted upon a question being asked: why the secrecy?

'Has to be she di'n't want Caroline to know,' Winston said without hearing the question. 'She print up chapters or she leave the chapters on the desktop PC, Caroline sees them. And Clare di'n't want that.'

'But if that's the case, *what* the bloody hell was going on between them?'

'We been thinking financial blackmail,' Nkata said, 'an' even job blackmail, but what if we're lookin at summat else here, Barb? Here's Clare goin round havin it off with married blokes while all the times she's spoutin all her feminist beliefs. What if Caroline jus' couldn't cope with th' whole hypocrisy thing? That'd be how she saw it, innit?'

Barbara thought about this. 'So Clare's being celebrated right, left, and centre for the Darcy book,' she said slowly. 'Feminist of the century, a sisterhood with women, and all the trimmings. She has in the works another book to add to her reputation. More celebration set to come in the future. More champers by the bootful. More hoohah all round. She's already done the proposal for it. Her publisher wants it. She's probably signed some kind of contract. She's sitting pretty.'

'Meantime, she's also catting around Dorset and Somerset,' Nkata added, 'bonking married blokes every which way to Sunday.'

'She's betraying her sisters and all the rest. And now she's going to write a book about this internet adultery thing . . .'

'But no bloody way is she *about* to mention she'd removed her knickers as part of her research.'

Barbara nodded. 'I can see how it would work, Win. Caroline can't abide the whole two-faced part of it all. She tells her that if she publishes that book, the word goes out about her and her "fact-finding" missions at the Wookey Hole Motel. Clare's burnt toast if that happens. Great publicity on one hand. A ruined reputation as a feminist on the other.'

'So Caroline's got all the power now. Over her writing. Over her reputation. Over everything, Barb. Who wouldn't like that, in her position, eh?'

Barbara sighed and shook her head. 'But bloody hell, Win. That puts *Clare* in the spotlight as the killer, not Caroline. Caroline's got her job into eternity. She's got Clare Abbott under her thumb. Why kill her, then?'

'Could be we got the answer in those interviews of her husband and her mum, Barb. Clare's looking for something to unlock Caroline's grip on her. You ask me, she found it. We work out what it is—'

'We've got our motive. That has to be it. Clare needed something more explosive on Caroline than Caroline had on her.'

'She must've found it.'

'So she had to die before she let loose with what it was.'

*Victoria*
*London*

Lynley didn't allow himself to feel irritated at Isabelle's requiring a daily report from him. He'd gone round her in acquiring this case for Barbara to work upon, and had he been in the superintendent's position, he would have probably been as outraged as Isabelle herself had been. So rather than exacerbate matters by sending her the previous day's details by impersonal email – which he would have frankly preferred as a time-saving manoeuvre – he went to her office. He reported what there was to report, making a point of going on at some length about the carefully hidden set of documents that DS Havers had managed to unearth, which were, even as he spoke, being carefully assessed by the sergeant herself and DS Nkata in Dorset.

Isabelle asked him what Winston Nkata had reported to him about Sergeant Havers's behaviour in Shaftesbury. This surprised him. He said to her, 'I don't make that requirement of any officer, guv. If Barbara goes wrong, we'll know of it eventually.'

'It's the eventually that I worry about,' was her reply. 'Do get on with it, then. We'll speak tomorrow.'

The abrupt dismissal told him she had things on her mind. He wanted to ask her what they were – pressure from above as to how she was using her manpower was always an issue – but he let the matter go. He had things on his mind as well, although very few of them had to do with the case in hand.

He hadn't parted from Daidre as he would have liked on the night before. He'd found, for once, that a sleeping bag on the floor of her bedroom – there was hardly room for both of them on the camp bed and it was far too unstable anyway – had lacked both physical comfort and romantic appeal. So afterwards, lying side by side with a thin blanket of questionable provenance thrown over their lightly perspiring bodies, he'd asked a question he knew she wouldn't like. When, he wondered, was she going to get round to completing the bedroom?

She chose to misunderstand him, which should have told him at once that this was territory best avoided. The flat had two bedrooms – this one and a very small one that she intended for a home office – and she spoke about having to make some sort of decision about keeping or removing a plate rail that indicated its long ago use as a dining room. Thus he knew she was avoiding the real issue: this bedroom in which they were forced to use the floor for their lovemaking if they didn't wish engage in a knee trembler.

Because he was tired, he said, 'Daidre, you know which bedroom I'm talking about.'

She rose on one elbow. Her glasses were a few feet from where they lay, and she reached for them and put them on, the better to see him clearly. She said, 'I suppose I do.'

He could tell from her voice that she was tired as well. More reason for postponing their conversation. But he didn't want to and whether this was selfish of him or not, he found that he didn't at the moment care. He said, 'Should we talk about why you're avoiding it? I ask because it seems logical to me that one would have provided adequate sleeping arrangements first when taking on a project of this size. Sleeping and bathing. The rest can wait.'

'I hadn't thought much about it.' She rose to a sitting position, her arms around her legs and her cheek resting upon her knees. There was virtually no light in the room due to the window that had been painted an unappealing shade of blue by some previous owner without the means to purchase curtains for the place. Thus he could barely see her, which he didn't like. He wanted to read her face. She said, 'What I have at the moment is adequate and it seemed to me that the larger question is—'

'One of avoidance,' he finished for her.

There was a silence. In it, they both could hear Arlo lightly snoring from the next room. Dimly in the distance, too, the sound of a bus passing along Haverstock Hill came through the single pane of glass. She said, 'What do you think I'm avoiding, exactly?'

'I think you're avoiding me.'

'Does the last hour look like I'm avoiding you, Tommy?'

He touched her bare back. Her skin was cool and he wanted to put the blanket round her shoulders but he stopped himself. The gesture would be too fond, and he didn't want fondness at the moment. He said, 'On the surface, no. But there's a sort of . . . I don't know what to call it . . . an intimacy, I suppose, that you find frightening, perhaps? Not physical intimacy, but the other. Something deeper that can exist between a man and a woman. And I think it's represented by this bedroom.'

She was silent and he knew that she was pondering this, for that was exactly who she was and why he had been drawn to her from the first, even when he'd met her in Cornwall as broken as he had been at the time. She said, 'I think it's the guise of permanency that I'm avoiding.'

'Nothing is permanent, Daidre.'

'I know that. I did say *guise*. And then, of course, there's the rest of it. Which is always there and always will be.'

At this, he lifted himself to a sitting position as well. He was suddenly aware of *feeling* naked, which was so much different than merely being naked. He reached for his shirt.

He began to put it on. Oddly, it was a bit of a struggle and he put this down to the lack of lighting. He said, 'Christ, Daidre. You can't be thinking of . . . what shall I call it? An antiquated social gulf between us? We're not living in the nineteenth century.'

She moved her head in a way that told him she would have cocked it had she not still been resting it upon her upraised knees. She said, 'As it happens, I'm not thinking of that, the social thing. I'm thinking of the growing up thing and how that "thing" moulds us from infancy to be who we are – standing here . . . or rather sitting here – as adults. We think we leave the past behind us, but it follows us round like a hungry dog.'

'So it *is* the social gulf thing,' he said, 'at the bottom of it all.'

At this, she rose. In the corner of the room she had a chest of drawers and across this lay her dressing gown, which she donned. It was – like everything about her – practical, a serviceable garment of towelling material completely unlike something Helen would have worn. She said to him, 'I think sometimes that you'll never come close to understanding me.'

'That's unfair,' he said. For he believed he did know the nature of her struggle and what forces within her held the world at bay. Taken away at thirteen years of age from the ramshackle caravan in which she lived with her parents with her teeth loose and her hair falling out, she'd not even had the culture and traditions of a travelling community to provide her with a handhold in any world. Rather, her father had been a solitary tin streamer, and the decrepit caravan the family called home had been positioned in various locations near riverbeds and creeks throughout Cornwall while he plied his marginal trade and his children – there were three – went largely ignored. They'd lacked the essentials – decent food, shelter and clothing – but they'd also lacked the intangibles that form an infant into a child and a child into an adolescent becoming ready to step well rounded into the world. Her adoptive family had been loving, but in

Daidre's case the die had been cast and it was against the long ago throw of it that she continued to struggle. Lynley understood this intellectually. It was emotionally that he had difficulty with it.

He too rose. He began putting on the rest of his clothing. He said, 'No one can dive back into the past and make things different. That's stating the obvious, I know. But my point is that to allow the past to become a rampart against the future—'

'That's not what I'm doing,' she interrupted. 'It's not a case of doing at all. It's a case of being. Tommy, it's who I am. And there *is* a gulf. And it *isn't* social. But it's so deeply ingrained in each of us that there may well be no way to breach it.'

'I don't want to think that.' He'd been holding his shoes. He set them on the floor.

'I know,' she said. 'I think that's why you keep coming round.'

'You could stop me. A word from you would do it. Well, a sentence, rather. I wouldn't like it. I'd feel it deeply. But a single sentence could settle matters between us.'

She put her hands on the chest of drawers, as if she wished to keep herself across the room from him when her inclination was to come to him as he wished her to do, to stand before him so that he could do what he also wished, which was to take her into his arms. She said, 'I've known that for a few months now. But the truth is, I've not been able to say it, that sentence.'

'I *am* in love with you, Daidre. You do know that,' he told her.

'Oh, I wish you weren't. Or at least that you hadn't said. You're still much too vulnerable after Helen and—'

'That's not the case.'

She rubbed her eyebrows. She pushed her glasses into a better position. She pressed her lips together and he could hear her swallow. In this as well she was so unlike Helen. As guarded as she was, there were moments when Daidre let her feelings escape, and this was one of them. She said, 'There's such equanimity in stasis, Tommy,' and he could tell from her voice that a tightness had come into her throat. It was one that he recognised, for he felt it as well, if for an entirely different reason.

'For you, perhaps,' he said in answer. 'But not for me.'

Despite their conversation, they had not parted badly. At her door, they'd stepped easily into each other's arms and wished each other a good night's sleep. But he was still thinking of what had passed between them when he returned to his desk after his conversation with Isabelle. And when his phone rang, he did hope it was Daidre although the words, 'We've worked it out, sir. We've found the book. She was writing it; Caroline was trying to put a screw in it. Clare was looking for something to free herself of Caroline, and she found it,' told him otherwise.

Havers went on, words tumbling one over the other as she sought to explain what she and Nkata had discovered, how they had interpreted it, and what it all had to mean about the death of Clare Abbott. Their conclusions were remarkably similar to those he himself had reached with Rory Statham during their conversation on the previous day. And she had something powerful with which to back them up: the book on adultery, kept only on a memory stick and nowhere else, carefully hidden from Caroline Goldacre.

Still, Lynley said at the end of Havers' recitation, 'But why give the Goldacre woman such moral support all along? If, as you said, Clare was trying to find something compelling to hold over her head . . .'

'She wouldn't want her to know that till she had it, sir. She *had* to hide from her that she was delving into her life, at the same time she had to make it look like she was cooperating with everything Caroline wanted. If Caroline dropped a few hints about needing fifty quid or – say – wanting a nice bloody memorial for her son, Clare knew better than to ignore them. Caroline had complete control over Clare's life once she knew about the Just4Fun blokes. Clare had to get that control back somehow. She found a way and it was huge and, because of that, she had to die. Believe me, it's the only explanation for

Clare encouraging the crazy-arse messages she was getting
from the woman on her email practically every day. She needed
some significant goods on her and she was trying to get them
any way she could.'

'And the goods are . . .'

'We don't know.'

Lynley blew out a frustrated breath. 'Christ, Barbara. Then
where are we? Precisely nowhere, wouldn't you agree? Or at
least back where we were yesterday.'

'I'm on it, sir. I'm going to find them. The goods. Whatever.
There's something. It's here. It's somewhere. Just look at what
was going on. Caroline's completely barking. She sends email
after email to a woman she sees every day and Clare keeps
replying with "tell me more, darling" and never with "put a
sock in it" which any other person – believe me – would have
done in a tick. And Caroline? She never notices this. Not once.
Clare could've said, "Hang on, you're contradicting yourself
here because last time you said Alastair is a giraffe and now
you're saying the man's a mongoose." Because that's what's in
Caroline's emails, sir. She says this, she forgets, then she says
that. She rants, she raves, she wails, she whines. And all Clare
ever says in return is along the lines of "Oh me, oh my, do
tell." Because she's *looking* for something and by God she
bloody found it. So what I want to know is, can we get a search
warrant because if there's sodium azide anywhere, you ask me,
it's going to be at Caroline's house.'

'We're not at the point of a search warrant,' Lynley told
her. 'Not with this. Not in any sense.'

'We are. We have to be.'

Lynley could hear the desperation in her voice, and he knew
very well where that might take her. He said, 'Barbara, get
control of yourself. Even if everything you're conjecturing is
true, doesn't it stand to reason that Caroline would be rid of
whatever sodium azide was left over once she had the toothpaste tube loaded with it?'

'She would do if Clare was the only person in her life she

wanted to off. But think of what else is going on: her hubby's bonking a woman who works for him. She stands to lose a bundle if they divorce. D'you think she'd let that go when the poisoning bit worked so well the first time round?'

'But it didn't, Sergeant. It was found out.'

'Right. But she didn't know that would be the case. And it wasn't found out at first and wouldn't have been had Rory Statham not made an issue of it. Look, the stuff might not be there. I'll give you that. It's prob'ly not. But we need that warrant because her house and that bakery . . . ? They're a *t* that wants crossing and with me and Winnie trying to work out all this alone—'

'Barbara, it's just not on. There's not enough.'

'There bloody well *has* to be.'

'Calm down and you'll see that there isn't. What I suggest – if you're intent on pursuing this – is that you use one of your many charms upon Mr MacKerron. He might well let you have a look round the premises without a warrant. And – perhaps this is even more important – while you're there you can question him about the contents of some of Caroline's emails to Clare. I mean the facts of them. Her former husband and her mother have both suggested she's quite a liar. You might well get something from Alastair that confirms it.'

'What good's that going to do? It's his word, her word. And their words, her word. We've got enough of that. We need the evidence that—'

'I have no argument there. But I know you'll agree that where there's this much smoke—'

'It's time to circle the wagons,' she finished. 'Yeah. I see it.'

'Not to mix a metaphor, but yes. Frankly? I doubt you'll get more than mere conversation with the man. I can't see a canister of sodium azide left lying around by *anyone* for future use. And there's the question of how she could have come by it in the first place. But I admit that everything must be checked out.'

'Well, thank God for small blessings,' Barbara said. 'Ta, sir. As to the warrant, will you—'

'No. Go to the house another time. But *when* you go there, for God's sake be careful. Go by the book. Because *if* we need a warrant later—'

'Can you at least *start* the paperwork on that? It'll help if me and Winnie don't have to come up with it.'

What would it hurt to do that much? Lynley asked himself. He said, 'I will,' and when they rang off, he decided to set about it. But he'd not even begun when his mobile rang. Assuming it was Havers, he answered with, 'Sergeant, if this is —' only to be cut off by a soft voice.

It was Sumalee Goldacre, to his surprise. Francis, she said, had not told her at first why someone from New Scotland Yard had come to call upon him. But while he had been speaking to her on the previous evening via Skype from the work he was doing in India, they'd got onto the subject of Lynley's visit and he'd explained. That, she said, was why she was ringing Lynley now.

'Is there something you'd like to add to what your husband told me?' Lynley asked her.

There was, she said. She would have a break in an hour at St Charles Hospital. Could he come up to her there? They were about to scrub for surgery at the moment, but it was due to be quick and afterwards she'd be free.

Lynley looked at his watch. North Kensington, he thought, nearly to Kensal Rise. He intended to keep his promise to Havers, but this sounded important. He would be there, he told her.

*North Kensington*
*London*

There was a small car park stretching the length of the hospital's several buildings, but it was full. So he did a bit of a drive-around and found a space among the residents' parking in St Charles Square between a skip being used for a home renovation and a pile of three rusting bicycles that looked rather like a piece of modern art. He left the Healey Elliott here and walked back to the hospital, a complex of purpose-built London brick structures divided by a leafy central lane, becoming bright with yellow and burnt umber. It looked more like a city university than a hospital, and it was sheltered from street noise by its position some distance from the main artery, Ladbroke Grove.

His mood wasn't the best. Prior to departing Victoria Street, he'd made a request of Isabelle that she'd denied. He'd argued with her. She'd argued back. 'This is down to you, Tommy, and I won't be moved,' was her final word on the topic.

She was, he decided, a woman who knew how to hold a grudge, and he didn't need her to intone the words *Detective Chief Superintendent Daniel Sheehan* for him to be very clear what the grudge was. But given that all he'd asked was the use of a civilian typist to do the paperwork for the search warrant that DS Havers needed, the fact that Isabelle had denied him this in order to prove a point was maddening.

So he'd gone round her, even though he knew it was on the border of professional suicide to do so. He'd spoken at some length to Dorothea Harriman who, given enough information, could manage what he needed while at the same time appear to be doing something else. Would she? he'd asked her *sotto voce* after leaving Isabelle's office. Leave it to me, had been her quiet reply.

He and Sumalee Goldacre had settled on meeting in the hospital's restaurant. He found this in the basement of the main hospital building. The air inside was redolent of malt vinegar, and the speckled grey floors and faux ash tables were reassuringly spotless.

There were comfortable sofas, chairs, and coffee tables along two of the walls, and Sumalee was at one of these with a plain lunch bag resting unopened before her and her small feet flat on the floor. She stood when she saw him. When he crossed to her, she suggested they head out of doors. Despite the cool breeze outside, the day was sunny and in the garden just beyond the restaurant, there were tables, chairs, and benches where she and he might have a private word.

The privacy of it seemed to be important to Sumalee, so Lynley followed her to the far end of the restaurant where a fire door stood open to allow fresh autumn air into the building. Outside he saw that there was plenty of seating and few people were using it at present. Her choice was a quirky bench set on the edge of an area planted with rhododendrons and youthful limes. The bench's back had been fashioned fancifully from a halved wagon wheel. The wheel's size made the bench more of a settee and put them in close proximity to each other which would, he knew, make it easy for her to speak in a low voice. This appeared to be her preference.

The sunlight dappled her dark hair and her smooth olive skin. She was, he thought another time, very lovely. And the contrast between her exotic beauty and her professional uniform only added to her appeal. He waited for her to explain why she'd asked him to make the journey from Victoria. She did not hesitate or even begin with social niceties. She merely opened her lunch bag, told him that she would have to eat as they spoke, and removed a triangle of homemade egg salad sandwich from a small plastic bag.

'I'd thought at first that you'd come to speak to Francis about Will,' was how she began. 'Perhaps because something had come to light regarding his suicide. It was more than three years ago, but it seemed to me that information might have fallen into your hands and you wanted Francis to know about it.'

'Were there lingering questions about his death?' Lynley asked.

She held the sandwich triangle in her two small hands, the way a priest might hold the Host in the moments before the consecration. 'It was definitely suicide,' she said. 'His partner was present, and more than one person saw her running after

Will before he jumped from the cliff. But still . . . One never knows about these things. Not entirely.' She took a bite of her sandwich, chewed thoughtfully. She brought out a small container of grapes, and she offered him some. He shook his head. She went on. 'I didn't like to ask Francis about your call on him because . . . You know that there are sometimes matters that don't bear bringing up in a marriage. Are you married, Inspector?'

'I was. My wife died nearly eighteen months ago.'

'I'm so sorry. I hope yours was a happy union?'

'Very much so. Which makes the loss, of course . . .' He raised his fingers, lowered them. Enough said, the gesture told Sumalee.

'I expect you know, then, that often there are subjects that one doesn't touch upon with a partner, sometimes to respect his privacy and sometimes merely to keep the peace. In our case – Francis's and mine – he has always been hesitant when it comes to talking about his first family, and I've learned to respect this. So it was only last night that he told me you'd come to speak to him about an interview he'd had with Clare Abbott.'

'That's right,' Lynley said. 'Did you know he'd been interviewed by Clare?'

'I did,' she said. 'But Francis didn't know that I knew.'

'Ah,' Lynley said.

She looked at him warily. 'It's not, perhaps, what you are thinking. I didn't . . .' She frowned as if searching for the proper word. 'I didn't *delve* to discover this. I knew he'd had an interview with Clare because Clare told me. When she interviewed me.'

At this, Lynley altered his position on the bench, swinging slightly to face her profile. Her expression was as serene as it had been from the first. 'When was this?' he asked her.

'Perhaps ten days after she interviewed Francis.'

'And did she tell you why she'd interviewed him and why she wanted to interview you?'

'About Will,' Sumalee said. 'She wanted to know if I'd had a relationship of my own with him. As he was my stepson, I told her that of course I had.'

'What was she after?' Lynley asked.

Sumalee glanced his way another time, saying, 'This is difficult for me as a second wife. I understand how it might appear: that a second wife wishes to cause trouble for this first wife by passing along gossip. Only, it isn't actually gossip and anyway, it is not my intention to cause difficulties for Caroline, nor was it ever. Indeed, I have no way of knowing if what I might tell you now is even important to Clare Abbott's death.'

'I see the problem,' Lynley told her. 'But as we're attempting to sort out a great deal of information regarding Caroline and Clare's relationship, whatever you tell us might be helpful.'

'I understand. I just don't know if I can live with myself if it's harmful to Caroline.'

Lynley waited. He wasn't in a position to reassure her. He reckoned it wasn't likely she possessed details that would lead them along a path of culpability whose destination was Caroline Goldacre, but one never knew.

Across from them, a group of nurses came out of the restaurant's fire door and trooped over to one of the picnic tables squarely in the sun. As most Londoners would do, they positioned themselves to get the sunlight onto their faces. One of them unbuttoned her shirt to expose her chest.

Sumalee watched them, smiling faintly, before she went on. Her voice was lower than ever as she said, 'She wanted to speak to me about Caroline's treatment of Will, Inspector. She wanted to know if Caroline abused him.'

'Caroline? Not Francis?' And when she nodded, 'What kind of abuse? Physical? Emotional?'

'Any kind of abuse.'

'What did you tell her?'

Sumalee's appetite seemed to leave her. She replaced what remained of her triangle of sandwich into its bag. She took four grapes and rested them in her smooth, small palm. She said, 'I told her that Will had always been troubled, from the time I have known Francis and – according to Francis – from long before that time. He would come to us on occasion, along with Charlie, and it seemed to me that he could never separate from Caroline completely although he did seem to try. But she didn't want a separation from him.'

'What about from Charlie?'

'It was different with Charlie. He managed to get some distance from her. But Will . . . ? No. The way most young men want to be off on their own, establishing themselves and their own identity? Will couldn't quite be talked into it until he met Lily Foster. Perhaps he was afraid to venture forth before that, but the feeling I had was that there was something else at the heart of his relationship with his mother. It made me uneasy.'

Her eyes were lowered, but Lynley could see that her gaze moved to take in his proximity to her. He could see a faint pulse in her temple. His thought was that she wanted to say more but was hesitant to do so.

He said, 'Mrs Goldacre, if you know something that might help us get to the bottom of Clare Abbott's death, if this is somehow related . . . Let me put it this way. Did you tell her anything that might have come out later in a conversation she had with Caroline? Something that, when spoken, could have set Caroline on a path to harm her?' Or, Lynley added to himself, something that, when written and later discovered by Caroline, could have done the same thing.

Sumalee was quiet for a moment, as if considering this. Then, barely perceptible, came the nod. 'I've never told Francis,' she said. 'I could see no point and it did seem that it would only make matters worse if I said anything. I told Clare, though. I probably should not have and had Will not already been dead, I would have held my tongue.'

'So it was about Will?'

'For a time I told myself that he might have been lying to me. Indeed, I even told myself that it could be something among you English that I don't understand. Every culture has its own . . . rituals, I suppose.'

A burst of laughter came from the women at the picnic table, along with 'He didn't!' and 'He bloody well did!' Sumalee gazed at them. She took a moment, it seemed, to gather her thoughts before going on.

'Will was visiting us as he sometimes did. He was perhaps fourteen years old. I came upon him in his bedroom. I had some laundry – T-shirts and jeans of his – to put away and I opened the door, not knowing he was there. He was . . . well, he was standing at the side of his bed with his trousers lowered and there were pictures of women . . . ? From magazines, these were, the sorts of pictures . . . nude and some of them quite explicit. He was seeing to himself, just staring at them and it was the moment of his orgasm that I entered. The spray of it across the bed and on the pictures and it all happened so quickly that I gasped. It was the surprise and I suppose the shock, and I left the room quickly.' She didn't look at him as she spoke and had she been of a different complexion, he reckoned that she might have been blushing but perhaps not. She didn't tell the tale as if she was embarrassed but rather as if she felt some regret.

She went on. 'Afterwards, I thought he might feel embarrassed or, perhaps, he would act as if nothing had happened. Or perhaps he would say something about my not telling his father what I had seen although Francis would not have been shocked, I think. I apologised to him for entering his room without knocking upon the door and what he said . . . He said, "No matter, Suma. I'm used to being watched."'

Lynley felt a chill go through him. 'Did he elaborate?'

Sumalee glanced at him, her fine eyebrows drawn together as she said, 'He told me she taught him, Inspector.'

Lynley's thought was that a boy hardly needed to be taught, so he wondered at this and the wonder must have shown on his face because Sumalee said, 'What I mean is that when he was ten years old, she did this – she taught him to do it – to control the words. He had an affliction with language. Did you know this?'

'My sergeant has told me something about the problem.'

'It was something he couldn't control. It didn't happen often, but when it did . . . He told me that when the words came on badly, this was something he could do to stop them. Of course, he also said that often he just did it because he enjoyed it. But there were times, he said, when she watched to make sure he did it . . . I suppose *properly* is the word.'

'How long did this go on? Do you know?'

She shook her head. 'When he grew older, I don't know what might have happened between them, but when he fell apart in London and had to leave to stay with her and his stepfather in Dorset . . . ? He was in a very bad way and not coping well at all and I suppose anything, really, is possible. But at that point – in his twenties – what young man would ever admit to his mother watching while he gives himself pleasure? If, of course, this happened at all.'

'This is what you told Clare Abbott?' Lynley asked.

Sumalee nodded. 'She wanted to record me, but I would not allow that. Nor would I allow her to take notes. I didn't know what she was going to do with the information she was gathering but since she was gathering it, I wanted her to have the truth.'

'Will could have been lying to you because you'd walked in on him,' Lynley pointed out. 'The admission that he was used to being watched . . . that his mother taught him to masturbate? Could he have said that merely to shock you?'

'Certainly. And yet, what young man would lie about such a thing, Inspector? His mother teaching him . . . watching him . . . I do not think he was lying.'

'Would he have told anyone else?'

She smiled thinly. 'Inspector, would you?' She smoothed the front of her trousers. Finally she took one of the grapes she held and she ate it, chewing thoughtfully. He asked her if she knew what Clare had intended to do with the information she had given her, and Sumalee said that she did not. Clare had been, however, clearly fascinated by what Sumalee had revealed to her. There had been no mistaking that.

Lynley nodded. He reckoned, however, that far more than mere fascination had been involved. He couldn't believe that, given this explosive information, Clare Abbott wouldn't have made immediate note of it somehow. She had to have written about her interview with Sumalee. And whatever she'd written and wherever she'd hidden the information, Caroline Goldacre must have found it.

*Shaftesbury*
*Dorset*

Alastair found himself wielding the mop with more energy than usual. His assistant had long departed, having cleaned the machinery and used the antiseptic spray on all of the surfaces where the dough was shaped into cobs and bloomers and cottage loaves and where the confections were made. Caro had been after him for years to employ a cleaning crew to see to the bakery when the breads and the cakes had been loaded into the delivery vans, but Alastair liked to do most of it himself. That way, he reckoned, the job would be seen to properly. Had he the time, he would have done the antiseptic part of the cleaning as well. As it was, he was the broom and mop man.

Today, he found, the employment suited him more than usual, especially the requirements involved in the physical part of it. Indeed, he was building up something of a sweat with all the scrubbing he was doing. Good, he thought. Perhaps he could rid himself of the thoughts that were tormenting him.

Charlie had phoned to tell him that Caro was returning home and that he himself was driving her to Dorset. Of course, Alastair had known at heart that she would return eventually.

But he'd allowed himself a nonsensical fantasy in which she somehow conveniently disappeared off the face of the earth.

He'd spent the last two days with Sharon. He'd asked her to come to him, to be in the house with him, even though he expected that she would refuse, which of course she had. She also confessed that finally she'd broken down and told her daughter about him, and she said she'd got quite a lecture from her Jenny about 'mixing it up with a married man, Mummy. What're you *thinking*? Not that he's going to leave his wife for you. They never do.'

She hadn't told her daughter who the man was because, knowing Jenny, she'd've rung Alastair straightaway and she'd've given him a piece of her mind. As it was, Sharon confessed to him, Jenny had rung her brother instead, and hadn't *he* then rung his mum to tell her she was worth more than 'sneaking round the county with a married bloke who's going to drop you the first time his wife says the word *divorce*. Just you wait and see.'

Sharon laughed gently, telling Alastair that they wanted her to start internet dating, didn't they, for there were piles of sites where she could look for a mate, they said. And hadn't Jenny emailed her a dozen sites just to prove this to her. Then over the phone from San Francisco, hadn't she walked her mother through how to access a site and how to mount her picture on it, and what to say about herself? And hadn't Jenny refused to ring off till she'd made certain her mum had done as she was told? Not that she would *ever* consent to meeting a man that way should one actually contact her, Sharon assured him, but there was no saying no to Jenny when she got her dander up about something. Children have their ways of being insistent about these things, haven't they, and sometimes wasn't it easier just to go along with them?

Alastair had nodded. What else could he do? He said to her, 'But Shar . . . the thought of you and some bloke off the internet . . . Let me ring your kids. I'll make 'em understand that you an' me have a real future if I c'n only . . .'

She'd looked alarmed. 'See here, ' she said, 'you're not to think I'll abandon you. I'm *yours*. Don't let your mind go anywhere else.'

But Alastair knew he could not hold her to that. The temptation of men wanting to meet her was going to be far too strong for Sharon to resist. And this was what he was thinking as he furiously mopped the floor right up to the shadow that fell across the cement from the open doorway. He looked up. It was the policewoman who'd been there before.

'That floor's wet there,' he told her. 'Mind you don't—'

'I don't,' she said. 'Mind, that is.' And the maddening woman stepped right inside.

For the second bloody time, he couldn't remember her name. This irritated him as much as her tramping on his clean floor. He said, 'I just told you, didn't I, that the floor was wet. I expect you c'n see I'm working at cleaning and I'd be that grateful if you didn't muck round leaving dirt everywhere.'

'Oh.' She laughed. 'Thought you were worried I'd slip and break my head. Sorry. Look, can I have a word?' She looked round the mixing room, which was where he and she were at present. She'd come in quietly from the out-of-doors, and he'd been so deep into his thoughts that he'd not heard her car. He knew he had to pull himself together because if she'd come to call upon him, it couldn't be a good thing.

He said, 'What sort 'f word? You got my fingerprints off me. What more d'you want? And Caro's not here any more 'n she was here last time you called.'

The woman – God, what was her bloody name? – dropped her shoulder bag on one of his newly and antiseptically cleaned work surfaces. She opened it up and rustled through it, shoving her bits and bobs round till she finally excavated a tattered notebook. She brought this forth along with a stub of a pencil that didn't look good for anything, much less for writing. She flipped the notebook open and she flashed him a smile.

He was startled. Odd, he thought, how someone so plain – not to mention so unappealing of body – could be transformed by a smile. It was the same for Sharon but then in her case it was also the soul of her that shone through like sun through sheer curtains. She became an angel when she smiled, did Sharon, whereas this woman merely became just a little less like a barrel on legs with porcupine hair.

When she had the notebook in hand, she said, 'Turns out your dabs weren't necessary after all, Mr MacKerron. But your wife's? That's another matter.'

He put his mop into the bucket and rested its handle against the spotless wall. The policewoman – Havers, that was it! Sergeant Havers. Odd how things dropped into one's mind like that – looked round with a bright and interested expression on her face. She said, 'This is where the magic happens, eh?' and she set about having a look at this and at that: thrusting her head into the adjoining rooms and having a go with the mixing machines as if she expected a finished loaf to appear at the bottom of one of the enormous vats. 'I always reckoned bread grew inside plastic packages in the grocery.' She returned to where he was and she fingered a row of utensils hanging from the wall. 'How d'you keep the unwanted creepy crawlies out of your ingredients? I expect that's a chore. Weevils and all that. They're dead mad for flour, aren't they?'

He said to her, 'Every bag of flour opened gets used up each day. Same for the salt and sugar and yeast. Nothing left loose for them to get into.'

'Mind showing me round?'

He narrowed his eyes. 'Why? And you been looking round already, far as I c'n see. Can't tell me you've come to learn how to bake bread. And wha's this 'bout Caro anyway?'

'What's what?' She leaned her bulk against one of the work-tables where the clean baking trays were stacked, waiting for tomorrow's work. She cocked her head and looked at him pleasantly, but he didn't miss the fact that her gaze was darting all over the bakery, like the woman expected a plague-carrying rat to come running across the large sacks of flour stacked on pallets in the room beyond where he and she were standing.

'Caro,' he said. 'You said her prints were another matter.'

'Oh, that. My colleague went to fetch her dabs up in London and hit a bull's eye with them. We were looking for a third set and there they were, sitting at the end of her fingers. So what it means is that there's a very strong possibility that she whacked Clare Abbott. 'Course, there're other ways to look at the matter, but just now we're liking Caroline for the job.' The sergeant paused. She pushed herself off the worktable and said, 'D'you mind if I have a peek through here?' She didn't wait for his reply. 'Are these the ovens? Always on, are they? Sort of a Hansel and Gretel thing you've got going on? Should I have brought breadcrumbs? Bloody hell, they're huge, they are.'

She was peering at the temperature gauge in the upper of the old cast iron ovens. It was true what she said: they were always on. It was less costly to keep them fired up than it was to heat them again every morning. She sauntered from the baking room into the storage area beyond it where the wood pellets were fed into the heating unit for the ovens. He had already topped up the bin through which they slowly slid into the burner, and she fingered these meditatively as she took in the pellet sacks in their neat ranks waiting to do their job of keeping his business running.

He said, 'What d'you mean? You saying you think *Caro* meant Clare harm?'

The sergeant shrugged. 'Could be someone else, I s'pose. Someone who had access to your wife's bits and bobs and clobber and togs. I reckon that's you. And your lady friend, 'course. She comes round here, right? She works for you, after all.'

'Sharon's got *naught* to do with Clare Abbott!' Alastair said hotly. 'You even once think she'd lift a finger to harm so much as a . . . a . . . a butterfly or . . .' He found himself sputtering.

'I expect the butterflies are safe,' Sergeant Havers said. She waggled her hand and added, 'As to everyone else . . . maybe yes, maybe no.'

He followed her. She was popping her head into the big

refrigerator, having her way with butter, eggs, milk, cream, and the like. She said, 'I'd no idea so much stuff was used in baking. You lot have an official taster or someone like? You don't want all this going bad, eh? Make the customers sick up over their morning toast and there goes your business down the toilet. Where d'you keep your salt, by the way? And that other business for baking. Powder, soda, what's it called?'

'Like I said. It gets used up. Every day.'

'So you . . . what? Run to the market and buy more? Bloody inefficient, that, I'd think.'

'It comes by the crate and gets stacked in the storeroom with everything else. What're you looking for? Cause I'm not thick and I c'n see you're looking.'

'Whoops. That obvious, eh? Might as well tell you we're setting things up for a search warrant, Mr MacKerron.'

'What the bloody hell for? What're you thinking? Caro did something? Me? Who?' He felt a heat in his gut and he didn't know what to name it. Anger? Fear? Nerves? He said to her, 'You look where you want 'f you think someone round here did something to someone and then . . . what? Hid evidence? Like what? A knife dripping blood?'

'Worked for Shakespeare, that,' she said. 'Only, I s'pose it wasn't hidden, was it?'

'What?'

She paused. She'd come full circle round the premises and was standing in front of his office door. She nodded at it, said, 'C'n I . . .' and walked inside. He followed her and saw her take in the desktop computer, the printer, the stacks of paperwork, the folders, old newspapers, a few magazines, and a pile of unfolded laundry. She placed her hand flat on the top of the old computer monitor as if testing its warmth and then she said, 'Did you know your wife was penpals with Clare Abbott? Wrote to her every day, she did. Great long email missives these were and Clare kept 'em all. Even printed 'em.'

Alastair knew nothing of emails. He told the sergeant this, and she informed him that these were early-in-the-morning emails – three in the morning as often as not – and would Caroline have written them here in this room or was there another computer in the house.

'Her own laptop,' he said. 'She took it back and forth from Clare's. Why?' he demanded. 'What's emails got to do with anything?'

'They tell interesting tales, is all,' Sergeant Havers said. 'C'n I park it, by the way?' She indicated a chair. He shrugged. She sat. She beckoned him to do the same. He did so with great reluctance, thinking how he should ring a solicitor or at least ring Sharon 'cause it came to him that if this cop was here on her own to question him, the other might well be on his way to bother Sharon. But then he thought how it would look, him ringing Sharon. It would look like they had something to hide.

'Has Caroline mentioned Clare's next project?' Sergeant Havers asked.

'Caro didn't talk to me about work.'

'No? Never "What a bloody day I've had." No "Rub my feet darling, there's a dear"?' When he said nothing in reply to this, the sergeant asked him – of all mad things – about an affair he was supposed to have had with a childminder when they all lived up in London!

He gaped at her before he asked the obvious which was, '*What* childminder? I don't know naught about any childminder.'

'The one Caroline says she caught you with? The one she says Will saw you with?'

'Will? Me with some childminder? And what? You talking about sex or summat?'

'Caroline told Clare all about it. It was part of her emails.'
'When? Where?'

'In the early morning, like I said.'

'I mean where'm I s'posed to have sex with the childminder and Will watching?'

The sergeant scratched her ear with her pencil and said, 'As I recall, it was sex in the kitchen. Or was it the larder?'

Alastair laughed. He couldn't help it although he could hear the edge of wildness his laughter had. It was, actually, more like a bark than a laugh. He said, 'Bloody stupid. Do I *look* like someone a childminder would have it off with?'

'My experience, Mr MacKerron?' the sergeant said. 'Looks don't have much to do with anything. When it comes to the this-ing and that-ing below the waist, pretty much anything goes. F'r all I know? Could be you slipped her an extra bob or two on the side. But Caroline waxed more or less eloquent on the topic.'

'Then she's lying.'

'Does that often?'

'Didn't say that, did I?'

'Admittedly, no. What about the girl she caught you with in your shop? I think that one was a trousers-round-the-ankles job. That'd be you and not the bird. She – I expect – is on her knees or spread out on the shop counter. Not sure about which. But the end of it all was your wife putting her hand through the window when you won't unlock the door for her.'

'The window,' Alastair said, 'that part's true,' but he couldn't get his mind round how Caroline had altered the facts of it. She'd come to his shop, but she'd come inside and she'd locked the door because she wanted to have it out with him. She'd found the bakery advertised for sale in Dorset some months earlier; she'd wanted him to buy it; he was dragging his feet. He'd been trying to work out how to say no to the woman in a way she'd understand. For he wasn't a baker, he didn't want to leave London, he loved his little business, and it was growing. But saying that had got him nowhere with Caroline who argued that he was, at the end of the day, just like all men, wasn't he? All about himself, he was, without a thought of her and her boys and especially Will who so *obviously* needed to be *away* from London but that didn't matter to him, did it, when *he* could be here with his *stupid* repurposed items that no one wanted and no one would buy when people buy bread every day of their lives, Alastair, are you listening to me? Oh no, that would be too much trouble, wouldn't it why should you listen to me when all I do is keep your house and launder your clothes and cook your meals and open my legs for you no matter do I want it or not and why, eh?, so that you can do whatever is it you do because I don't for a moment believe you come here day after day and sit here and wait for someone to come in off the street to purchase this . . . this ludicrous rubbish . . .

She'd run off, or at least she'd tried to, but she forgot she'd locked the door behind her upon entering and when it wouldn't open, she pounded on the glass till it broke into shards.

He told the sergeant this – the relevant bits – and she pointed out that it would take a hell of a lot of strength to put one's hand through the glass of a shop door, wouldn't it? He agreed. But Caro, he told her, had a hell of a lot of strength and a temper to match it. And when she got unreasonable, it was double temper and double strength.

'That why you took up with Sharon Halsey?' Sergeant Havers asked. 'We know all about her, by the way.'

'I'm not speaking to you 'bout Sharon.'

The sergeant shrugged. 'No real matter as Sharon was happy to speak about you.'

He felt a little roll of his stomach at that. He wondered what Sharon had said, but he told himself that she was true and never mind anything else.

The sergeant went on. 'You see how it looks, I expect. You and your employee doing some horizontal trampoline jumping on the closest mattress?'

'Eh?' he said.

'Dip the banger,' she clarified. 'Send in the probe. Whatever you'd like to call it.'

'I call it lovemaking,' he said in something of a rising temper, 'and don't you try to make it what it's not.'

'Which is what?'

'Something unclean. That woman's an angel and if I had the chance – a single chance like one thing in the entire world that I could do tomorrow – then I'd bloody do it and not look back and—' He stopped himself. Fool, he thought. He'd walked directly into the sergeant's plans for him to run his mouth like an open tap. Even now she was listening, those bright eyes of hers locked on his, her expression saying *Gotcha* or whatever police types thought when they reckoned they were one step away from giving the caution. He said, 'I don't deny anything 'bout Sharon, but I won't have you making it look like what it's not. How it looks is how it looks. I know what it *is*.'

'In the regular way of things, I s'pose you're right,' the sergeant said. 'But in the middle of a murder inquiry . . . ? With something deadly tucked into your wife's belongings? Looks count, and I reckon you see it.'

'Something deadly? Caro's belongings? You telling me *Caro* was the one meant to die?'

'Maybe yes, maybe no. We're not sure yet. But the long and short of it is that with you and Sharon giving true love a go . . . ? Makes me think someone wouldn't mind seeing Caroline's coffin heading into the oven for a proper baking.'

'You think that, then you look round,' he told her. 'You see *anything* suggests I tried to hurt Caro, you take me in. And don't you bother Sharon over this 'cause the last thing that woman wants is having anything go wrong in my life, her life, or anyone's life. She's a decent woman, she is. She's the only reason . . .' He couldn't go on. It wasn't that he sensed a trap in his words; it was merely that Sharon was the heart of the matter, the clean and precious soul of the matter, and bringing her anywhere close to this vile business was something he couldn't allow himself to do.

But the copper didn't know that, did she, so when he paused, she jumped in with, 'Yeah? She's the reason . . .'

'The reason I keep going,' he said. 'Here. In this. With this. With her.'

'You mean with your wife? And what? You saying Sharon wants it that way? You and Caro tight as squirrels in the winter with Sharon doing what? Just waiting? That doesn't make sense to me, Mr MacKerron.'

'It's not meant to make sense to you,' he said. 'The woman's a saint.'

'Is she that?' the sergeant said. 'In my experience, Mr MacKerron? No one's a saint when it comes to what you two have been up to together.'

*Fulham*
*London*

Rory was moving along carefully, pushing her drip pole as she went, with Dr Bigelow assessing her progress. A word from the doctor and Rory would be released back into her life, her recovery deemed complete with no chance of a sudden onslaught of symptoms that would suggest the poison had not completely washed out of her system. She was just about to make the turn to head back towards her room when Inspector Lynley came off the lift at the very end of the corridor. He was carrying a few manila folders under his arm.

He walked up to her, saying, 'You're looking fit.'

She said, with a nod at Dr Bigelow, 'I'm hoping to impress.'

'And is she?' he asked the doctor.

'She'll do,' Dr Bigelow said. 'Back to your room now,' she added to Rory. 'Let's check your vitals.'

Rory made the turn, Lynley at her side. She told him she was very close to being released. Her sister Heather had promised the doctor that she would remain with Rory at her flat for four more days to make certain all was well, and if she – Rory – got back to her room without having to grasp onto the railing that ran along the corridor's wall, she believed she'd be able to go home in the morning.

'Arlo,' Lynley said, 'will be delighted.'

'He's still with the vet?'

'He was attempting to help her paint her sitting room last evening. He's a very clever dog.'

'He is.' She arrived at her room, where Dr Bigelow took her vitals: heart beat, blood pressure, listening to her lungs. At the end of this, Rory said, 'Well . . . ?'

'Tomorrow morning,' Dr Bigelow said. 'Be careful what you ingest henceforth.' With a nod at them both, she left the room.

Rory didn't return to the bed but rather to the two chairs by the window. She sat in one and said to Lynley with reference to the folders he was carrying, 'Have you brought me something?'

'I have.' He placed the folders on a small table between the chairs and he sat as well, once she'd asked him to do so. Where on earth, she thought, had he got such good manners? 'One of my two sergeants in Shaftesbury has been going through Clare's computer: her documents, her emails, internet searches, correspondence . . . whatever he's been able to find. He's forwarded all the relevant items to me. It's been quite a project.'

'I imagine it has.'

'Among other things, we've learned that Clare didn't keep everything she was working on in sight,' he went on. 'Or even conveniently accessible. I mentioned that my sergeant had come across a memory stick in the boot of Clare's car . . . ?' When Rory nodded, he rested his hand on the top of the folders and told her that his sergeant had made certain that the documents on the memory stick had been among what was forwarded to London. The folders he'd brought contained these materials, and he said he'd much appreciate Rory's looking at everything.

She did so, and here it was before her at last: proof positive that Clare had indeed been as good as her word. She had been hard at work upon her next book and, from the look of it, had also been determined to meet her deadline. Rory skimmed the proposal she'd seen before, went on to the table of contents, and dipped into a few chapters. It was very good, she thought. She looked at Lynley.

'You said it was on her memory stick but nowhere else?'

'It was,' he said.

'That's extraordinary. Not at all like her. She always had copies, hard and electronic. Just to have one . . . She'd have considered that tempting fate.'

'And yet that's what she did,' he said. 'We're thinking that she wanted – and needed actually – to keep Caroline Goldacre from knowing she was at work on the project.'

'Because Caroline may have threatened her, you mean. To reveal Clare's involvement with men from that site.'

He nodded. 'As you and I have agreed, the information was explosive. It would have revealed her to be . . . a rather whited sepulchre.'

'An empty vessel,' Rory agreed. 'She could have overcome that in time. Perhaps she could even have talked her way out of it. But the damage would have been significant. She was in a dreadful position. I wish she'd explained it all to me. This book was such a strong idea. It's the logical next step in what Clare was working on. It proved her thesis about romantic love and marriage: that it's all stuff and nonsense and she had the proof, courtesy of internet adultery.' Rory sighed. She looked out of the window. There was little to see: just Fulham Road, traffic, and a crocodile of children heading somewhere with a chaperone fore and a chaperone aft.

'Do you really believe all that?' Lynley asked her suddenly.

Rory turned back to him. He looked very earnest. 'What?' she asked.

'Romantic love and marriage. Are you a believer in Clare's thesis?'

She examined him. He was, she realised, still quite young, somewhere in his thirties. Clare would have said that he had a few good years left before he put away romantic dreams forever. Rory said, 'You're in love, aren't you?'

He smiled ruefully. 'I'm afraid I am.'

She cocked her head and thought about everything he'd said up to this moment. 'I suspect it's the veterinarian.'

'It is. And it's early days, so it may come to nothing as she's not . . .' He shrugged.

'Romantically inclined? The marrying kind? Or merely not falling into your arms?'

'Not precisely in the way I would like. But one has hopes.'

'There's nothing wrong with that, is there. One has to take a risk now and then. Even Clare would approve of that.'

'Actually,' he said, 'that's what we think may have led to her death. She took a risk. She'd been interviewing members of Caroline's family.'

'Who? Alastair? The son?'

'Her mother. And Francis Goldacre. And then Francis's current wife. She'd also spoken to a Sherborne psychiatrist about various aberrations in personality. We think that somewhere along the line, she came across something serious enough to stop Caroline in her tracks.'

'And revealed it to her?'

'We've not yet found evidence that she did. Did Clare give you any indication . . . We do know they were arguing in Cambridge the night Clare died.'

'Clare did tell me they'd had words. But she said they'd been about the length of her debate that night.'

'That's doubtful, considering what was overheard. One of them saying "We're finished" and the other "Not with what I know about you. We'll never be finished."' He was quiet a moment. Then 'Let me ask you,' with a gesture at the folder. 'How committed was Clare to her written work?'

'What do you mean?'

'I mean how far do you think she would have gone to free herself of someone's hold on her in order to complete her writing?'

Rory thought for a moment. 'She would have hated what Caroline was doing to her,' she said slowly. 'She would have done anything to rid herself of her. But she wouldn't have killed herself, Inspector, if that's what you're wondering. Nor – if this is where you're heading – would she have killed Caroline.

She would have absolutely hated herself for getting into the position she was in with the internet adultery business, but the fact that she was writing her book secretly tells me that she had no intention of letting Caroline win whatever game she was playing.'

Lynley looked out of the window when she said this. Rory could tell that he was considering something. He finally said, 'You knew her well. If she had managed to uncover something, an unexpected detail that – revealed – would render Caroline completely powerless, would she have used it, no matter what it was?'

'To safeguard herself and her work?' Rory asked. And when he nodded, 'Absolutely, Inspector.'

*Victoria*
*London*

With all of this information in hand, Lynley rang Havers from the Healey Elliott. He brought her into the picture of Sumalee's story first, and at the conclusion of this, he heard her low whistle and then, 'That's *it*, Inspector, exactly what we've been looking for. God, but it's sick. I never heard anything like it. Gives me the bleeding creeps. What sort of mum makes sure her boy knows how to wank off properly, then watches to see the show? And wouldn't you reckon he would've worked that out on his own anyway? I mean how to wank off.'

'One would assume,' Lynley agreed. 'But apparently, masturbating was a device that stopped him from carrying on verbally. God knows how they came up with it, but apparently – at least according to what Sumalee tells me that Will told her – it settled him.'

'And Sumalee passed the story to Clare?'

'She claims she did.'

'There *have* to be notes somewhere, then. She's kept notes on *everything* else. No way would she have let that one go without jotting down the A to Z on the whole bloody mess.'

'My thinking as well.'

'But where are they? We've gone high and low. We've been in every nook and cranny. I swear to you, sir. Unless they're in London . . . They could be in London. She's got a house there. If you could arrange . . . God, this is impossible. It's taking forever. How much more time d'you reckon the super-intendent—'

'I don't want to begin a guess on that, Barbara. But if there *are* notes that Caroline saw, you've got to find them,' Lynley said.

They rang off. It seemed to Lynley that – this new information about Caroline Goldacre notwithstanding – a crucial question needed resolving and that was where the sodium azide had come from. No matter who was its intended victim, someone had to have access to the deadly poison. When he returned to Victoria Street and sat at his desk, he flipped through all the notes he'd made. He began with the various uses of the substance, and he compared these uses to what they knew about everyone associated with the case.

Oddly enough, he quickly discovered that aside from its use as a reagent, sodium azide was also employed in automobile airbags. No matter the chemical's toxicity, it was instrumental in saving lives . . . as long as it remained within the airbag itself, merely assisting in the bag's inflation within an instant. For someone to have put hands upon sodium azide through means of an automobile, however, that person would have had to open the airbag without detonating it while simultaneously wearing a hazmat suit so as to keep from being affected by the poison. That seemed improbable, but it was either that or having employment in an airbag factory, which was not the case of anyone involved in Clare Abbott's life.

Dismissing the entire idea of airbags took Lynley to the use of sodium azide in detonators and other explosives, with much the same result, so he moved to its use in agriculture for pest control. That appeared to bring under the microscope everyone who lived in the area of Shaftesbury, where there would be farms. As far as he knew, no one's abode was on a farm or near a farm, but he made a note to ask Havers and Nkata to delve into this as a possibility.

Also in need of checking out was the use of sodium azide as a chemical preservative in hospitals and labs. Both Francis Goldacre and his wife Sumalee worked in and round hospitals, and he wondered if India Elliott somehow had access through her employment. He recalled the sign in her sitting room window that said she offered acupuncture at the weekends in her home. But the rest of the week . . . ? She had to work somewhere and he made a note to suss out where and whether that place would have sodium azide on the premises.

In all of these cases, however, the strongest suggestion was that Caroline Goldacre had – as she had claimed – been the target of the killer. But that could have been what Caroline had wished them to believe from the first: that this had all been a deadly mistake, with the wrong woman falling victim to the poison. They had only Caroline's word that Clare had packed her own bag and forgotten her toothpaste, and it was clear that Caroline was nobody's fool. If she wanted to make certain that there was no way her secrets would ever come to light, what better way than to kill Clare while making herself look like the intended victim? She knew that she herself was disliked and hated, even. There appeared to be more than one person who would be happy to see her dead. All she had to do was to make it look as if one of them had attempted to kill her, with Clare being collateral damage.

It was a clever plan, and it hadn't been difficult to carry off considering how often she was with Clare Abbott. The only question was: how could Caroline Goldacre have put her hands on sodium azide?

Lynley turned to the internet. He accessed a search engine and into it he typed *sodium azide* as a starting point. He followed a link, and to his surprise, he saw that the toxic compound was accessible directly from suppliers via the internet. His heart pounded hard a few times as he took in this information and what it meant to the case. No expertise was needed to purchase it, no guarantee for the legitimacy of its use, no affidavit as to the identity of the purchaser, either. There wasn't a single control on its sale. Anyone could have bought it.

*Thornford*
*Dorset*

Alastair had come on the run. He'd been driven to Sharon's home by Caroline's return, and he understood as he shut off his car's engine that his wife's anger, accusations, and insults had probably been intended by her to prompt this flight to Sharon from the moment she'd stepped out of Charlie's car.

Charlie's bringing her back to Shaftesbury had taken much longer than it should have done. She'd been sicking up along the way, forcing Charlie to call a halt to their trip time after time until she felt well enough to travel again. With each incident of Caroline's sicking up, her recovery had taken longer. Between vomiting and giving in to anxiety attacks that apparently provoked not only claustrophobia but also the ultimate need to leave the motorway and to remain off it lest she fall victim to a full blown panic attack, the drive ate up over six hours. To get her home, Charlie had had to cancel his every appointment for that day, straight into the evening.

Alastair would have felt sorry for the lad had the purpose of this excursion with his mum not been to return Caroline to her home. The boy looked completely done in when they arrived, and Alastair wouldn't have blamed him had he merely escorted Caroline to the front door of the house and then turned on his heel and left her there. But instead, he seemed to feel compelled to repair things between his mother and stepfather.

Alastair was in Will's garden when they arrived. He'd been sitting on one of Will's benches, doing nothing more than gazing at the flagstones at his feet and wondering idly how the lad had managed to get anything to grow in the sandy soil that surrounded each heavy stone. Tiny hedges of unnameable greenery grew in many of these cracks now. They formed a pleasant patchwork effect, and Will must have known that they would although he'd not lived to see it.

The detective sergeant had taken Alastair up on his invitation to look round the place. Indeed, Alastair had finally realised to his chagrin that that had been her intention all along. He wondered how he'd ended up such a perfect fool when it came to the ways of women. He seemed to lose all sense of self-preservation when faced with a female, caving in to whatever wiles she might use to position him to do whatever she desired. He began to feel ever the complete idiot as the policewoman had inspected each nook and cranny of the bakery. The last thing he now wanted to do upon Caroline's arrival was to admit that he'd stupidly played into that bloody cop's hands.

She'd found nothing, of course, the detective sergeant. He'd known she wouldn't. But she didn't seem put off by the lack of evidence. She'd pointed out that there was more than one way to skin a cat and more than one cat that wanted skinning and from that he'd taken that she meant Sharon. So the moment the detective left, he'd phoned her. Sharon had not been at home – obviously, she was still at work – and as she was also not answering her mobile, he'd stammered a message about the police, a search of his home and business, Caroline, poison, Clare, and perhaps the coppers coming to you now, Shar, and you don't have to let them in or even speak to them. That message given, he'd spent ages waiting for her to ring him back, but she hadn't done. He was left in a state of nerves unlike anything he'd ever experienced.

His life felt like something reduced to tatters, with him

trying vainly to piece those tatters back together into some sort of fabric. He thought that there had to be a way to bring all of this to an end. But he didn't know what that way was, he couldn't even define what 'this' was in the first place, and here was Caroline returning to Dorset and God God God *how* could he bear that?

When Charlie arrived with Caroline, Alastair rose heavily from the bench, discovering that he felt quite stiff from the time he'd spent sitting and attempting to devise a plan. He walked across Will's terrace of stones, and he waited for his wife to come round the side of the house, where Charlie parked his car.

'So you're still here,' were the first words Caroline said to him. She didn't look as he expected her to look after a day of sicking up along the side of various roads from London to Dorset. She looked quite fit. But he wasn't surprised. He'd reckoned the sicking up had been a ruse, as had the claustrophobia and everything else she'd tried on Charlie that long day. Either that or she'd forced him to pull onto a lay-by so that she could see to her appearance before descending upon Alastair once again.

She said to him, 'It was among my things, but you know that, you and your little bit of skirt, don't you? What you didn't expect was that I'd hand it over to Clare. And what you *also* didn't expect is that someone along the line wouldn't believe Clare's heart gave out. So nothing's worked out the way you planned it. But that really shouldn't surprise any of us. In the brains department, you were always rather wanting.'

'Mum,' Charlie said wearily, 'you need to get inside the house, have a cup of tea, sit down, relax, and—'

'What I need,' she cut in sharply, 'is to have some words with your stepfather. You can listen to them or you can leave us. The choice is yours.'

Charlie was carrying his mum's overnight bag, and he passed her to set this on the front step. He opened the door and said to her, 'Whatever you want to say can be said inside.'

He was showing good sense, Alastair thought. There was

no reason to remain outside, and the fact that Caroline wanted to do so prompted him to follow Charlie into the house. If she was after words with him, she would come along. She did.

She went into the sitting room and he had half a mind not to join her there. Charlie took himself to the kitchen, where the sound of cupboards opening and closing and water running told Alastair he was making the tea he'd spoken about. As he was considering joining Charlie, Caroline turned to him. She said she wanted a word 'before you do whatever you intend to do next', and while he had no plan to do anything at all at that juncture, it did come into his mind that they were fast approaching a point of no return when he was going to have to take an action.

In the sitting room, she went to the fireplace and there she stood. She said, 'You should have thought everything out more thoroughly. The toothpaste wasn't a good idea. Not everyone would have had access to it, just the three of us, and I'd hardly want to poison myself.'

He stared at her, trying to work out what in the name of God she was talking about.

Her expression altered, losing its sharpness but not its exasperation. She said, 'The poison, Alastair? The police did trace it to the toothpaste, you know. It wasn't difficult to put in, naturally, since these new tubes of the stuff bounce right back into shape when you squeeze a bit out. So all that was needed was squeezing, allowing the tube to reshape, putting the poison inside the hollow bit, and mixing it with what remained. I've had most of the day to think how it was done. Access to my toothpaste was the key, which makes it all a bit of a giveaway.'

He said to her, 'What're you on about?'

'I'm *on* about the police looking for a motive for someone wanting to kill *me*, not Clare. They want motive, means, and opportunity. And what exactly are you and little Miss Roundheels going to do about that since the two of you happen to have all three?'

'Police were here,' he told her. 'Least she was, the woman sergeant. She talked about you and me. I told her if she thought

I had a single reason on earth to hurt you, she could look round the place for whatever it was she was after 'cause she wasn't going to find it and she didn't.'

'Played directly into her hands, eh? How bloody like you, Alastair. D'you know how to put your socks on if I'm not here to say "they go on your feet, darling"?' She left the fireplace and walked to the window. A table sat beneath it, on it an open fan of the magazines she spent hours perusing: celebrity tales with their marriages and their partnerships and their dozens of children, long articles about European millionaires, house decoration, women's beauty, high end travel, living the good life. It came to him that she read these as if expecting that it was all out there for her, just within her reach if she could only put together the proper circumstances to make it happen as she wished it would. She said to him, 'You do know, don't you, Alastair, that you're the simplest man to manipulate who ever lived? This policewoman tricked you into telling her she'd be welcome to look round the place without bothering to get a search warrant. All she had to do was position you to invite her to overturn my drawers or whatever she did. Have a nice look round for whatever you want, you told her. Well, you can bet that your little piece of skirt won't be so stupid, so I hope the two of you hid the poison at her place.'

'This is nothing to do with Sharon, so you best keep her out of it, Caro.'

Her expression was arch. 'You've actually become a bigger fool than you were when I married you and I hardly think that's even possible.'

'Mum.' Charlie was coming into the sitting room from the kitchen. He bore a tray with three mugs, teapot, and the rest. He'd excavated some chocolate biscuits, with which he'd circled the edges of a plate the centre of which held a sectioned apple. He set this on the coffee table in front of the sofa and said to his mother, 'That's not exactly helpful just now.' And then to Alastair, 'Have you phoned a solicitor?'

'What need have I for a solicitor?' Alastair asked. Charlie was being mother with the tea and the mugs. He drew over the smallest of three stacking tables, putting a mug upon it and administering milk and sugar. This, he indicated, was for his mother, and he placed the table next to an armchair at a distance from the sofa as if with the intention of keeping her and Alastair apart. 'I've not done nothing,' Alastair said. 'So what's the point of ringing up someone and telling him . . . what? That I've done nothing but the coppers are here and what should I do next?'

'It's always best . . .' Charlie handed a mug to Alastair and indicated that he was to sit on the sofa. It came to Alastair that his stepson was in therapist mode, but he knew it was going to take more skills than Charlie possessed to smooth the wrinkles in this marriage. Charlie said to him, 'Look . . . You mustn't talk to the police again. Really. I know you want to help and that's quite admirable—'

'He wants to help me to my grave,' Caroline said. 'And so does she, Miss Butter Wouldn't Melt. God, I ought to divorce you *just* so you can see what she's really been after all along, Alastair, which isn't you. It's this.' She flung her arm in a wide gesture that took in the room. 'It's this place, this business. It's the money the business brings in, how we've built it from barely nothing and now she's too happy, isn't she, to step in and enjoy the results of our work?'

Alastair gaped at her, so incredulous was he. Charlie began to say something, but Alastair interrupted. 'You're a bloody mad cow, that's what. You've done nothing. It's Sharon an' me built this business. Oh, you were good for two months of work, weren't you, but then it was the boys, always the boys, and how they kept you too busy and "Alastair, I can't be everything to everyone," when you and I together . . . That was the deal and you well know it.'

'The *deal*? What are you saying, that marriage is some kind of *deal*?'

'Mum . . . Alastair . . . This isn't going anywhere useful,' Charlie said mildly. 'If both of you will take a moment to—'

'I'm saying,' Alastair cut in, 'that we agreed if we brought the boys to Dorset, if I sold up *everything* in London – my shop, my work, my house – that we would work together to build a life here, only I was doing all the work along with Sharon. You understand that? With Sharon and her never saying a word about anything but never a word especially about you and your television programmes and your magazines and your women's meetings and your takeaway food in place of proper meals because you were far too busy, weren't you, with your "boys". And that was it, wasn't it, Caro? They were always *your* boys, no matter I was a proper father to them.'

'Be quiet, both of you!' Charlie raised his voice to get their attention, then went on more quietly with, 'Everyone's nerves are raw. When people are in this state, they say regrettable things that have far too much weight. You need to let your passions cool because in this kind of state, there's absolutely nothing to be gained that—'

'So just go to Sharon. Go!' Caroline's voice rose above her son's. 'I do *not* care any longer. It's always been about you at the heart of things. It's always been what Alastair wants, what Alastair needs, and never a single thought for anyone else. Oh you pretended to be a proper father to them. And you pretended you were reluctant to leave London because there was so much you "loved" about your stupid work. And all along we both knew the truth is that I lifted you out of a real tip, and it was only because of my divorce from Francis and the money I got off him that we were even able . . . Oh you and your *ridiculous* business. Some pathetic shopfront in a part of town that no one would ever think about visiting when anyone with any sense at all would have a stall in a market—'

'Listen to yourselves,' Charlie said. His was the voice of reason. 'This is exactly what people do in this kind of state. It's a case of slash, burn, and take no prisoners. Mum, stop it. Alastair, stop it. You're both worn out. You're both frightened.'

'I'm not feared of nothing,' Alastair said. 'The coppers want to look round this place? Let 'em, I say. They want a search warrant for a deeper look? Even better.'

'Because it's gone, what you used, isn't it?' Caroline said. 'No. It's not gone. Sharon has it.'

'Don't you say her name another time,' Alastair warned her. 'I swear to you, Caro, if you start accusing that decent, loving, God fearing—'

'Cocksucking,' she snapped. 'Can I add that to the list?'

He lunged towards her. Charlie leaped between him and Caroline, upsetting the small table that held Caroline's tea. She cried out, 'Do you see what you've made me come home to? Don't you know what will happen if you leave me here, with the two of them planning and scheming against me?'

'Christ, Mum,' Charlie said. 'You don't know that. You don't know anything. Nobody does. Just that someone somehow managed to put something into your toothpaste and that's the limit of what we—'

'You'd like it as well!' she hissed. She rose, advancing on him. 'That would be *exactly* your style.'

Charlie took a step back from her. 'Jesus.' he said. 'What are you saying?'

'Me,' she said. 'Dead. Out of your life so that you can scurry over to India's pathetic little house and reduce yourself to whatever that little cunt wants you to be in order to get her to return to you. And you can't do it yet, can you, because as things stand I'll fling myself in front of a train before I let you lower yourself to beg and grovel and be less than a man because that's what she wants, don't you understand that? And I won't allow that, I will never allow that, I won't have you end up like Will, with me standing by and seeing India do to you what Lily Foster did to your brother.'

She finally took a breath, her chest heaving. The silence among them was shattering because in it her words took on a power that was fuelled to ever greater heights by everything that had passed before she spoke them.

Charlie was the one to speak. 'Lily made my brother happy,' he said with some dignity.

Caroline gave a short laugh. 'Oh for God's sake. You're as

big a fool as your stepfather. God in heaven, why am I surrounded by such pathetic men?'

Which was when Charlie left them. He said only, 'I'm not discussing India with you, Mum. And clearly, there's nothing I can do here,' and he was gone.

Years of living with her had told Alastair what to expect next: the on-the-edge-of-a-knife alteration in Caroline that was soon in coming. Where one might consider a further rampage as a distinct possibility – launching an attack upon the nearest person, overturning tables, crushing the glass of photographs beneath her feet – he knew that this would not be her way. She stumbled back to the chair that Charlie had arranged for her. She sat there, looking stunned at his departure, as if someone had slapped her hard across both cheeks. Her eyes filled.

'Why do I hurt the people I love?' she said. When Alastair did not reply – for what, indeed, was there to say in answer to such a question – she began to weep. 'What's wrong with me? I didn't intend things to turn out like this. I didn't want my *life* to turn out like this. Oh, I *wish* I'd been the one to use that toothpaste. I wish I'd shoved the entire mess of it down my throat. The world would be a better place now if I'd done that. That's what you think, isn't it, Alastair?'

He said, 'I don't think anything, Caro.'

'Ah, well . . . Yes. That's exactly what I'd expect of you.'

So he left her. He'd made this drive to Thornford. He had to cleanse himself of all that had gone on with his wife and his stepson.

He entered Sharon's house. He'd seen her car, so he knew that, at last, she was at home. There was music playing from the kitchen where she kept a radio tucked towards the back of one of the worktops. He followed the sound of it, and there she was. He merely watched her for a moment.

She was cleaning her cupboards. Everything had been removed from them and was now arrayed before her. Wisely, she was turning each package and tin to examine its best by date. As he stood there, she tossed into the nearby rubbish bin a small half-filled bag of coconut.

He said her name.

She shrieked, turned. She clutched her throat. 'Such a fright!' she said. 'I didn't hear you come in. And you've caught me in the midst of *such* a mess.'

'Autumn clean up?' he asked her.

'That's exactly what,' she said. 'Has something happened, Alastair? Because how you look . . .'

'You've not had my messages about the coppers?'

'Oh yes, I did get the message.'

'And you know not to let them inside. You've no need to. They'll make you think there's a need, and they'll make you think it's owed them. But you've not got to do a single thing.'

Sharon's face softened. She tied the strings of the rubbish bag, and she carried it to the door, placing it in the dust bin outside. She turned back to him and her expression was as fond as it had ever been. She said to him, 'It's how you care for me.'

'What is?'

'Why I'm yours and no one else's.'

He felt completely unburdened when he heard those words. He crossed to where the radio was, and he turned the knob to shut it off. In the silence it seemed to him that he could hear not only his own heart but hers as well, and it seemed to him that they beat in unison.

He said to her, 'That, my girl, is the only music I ever need to hear.'

# 21 October

For the first time, Alastair hadn't left her. Instead, he'd thrown duty directly out of the window. He'd put the morning's baking into the hands of his assistant, and he'd remained with Sharon the whole blessed night.

He felt no guilt. Nor did he feel even a twinge of concern that the bakery's goods might not be quite up to the mark as a result of his failure either to oversee or to have a hand in their creation. There were too many other emotions to be feeling, and supreme among them was what he could name only as triumph. This involved a rightness to everything that was now going on between Sharon and him.

Caro he'd left to her own devices, whatever they were going to be in the aftermath of her return from London. Sharon he would leave no more.

They'd walked out into the garden in the fading daylight upon his arrival, and there they'd watched the farmer in the fields behind them. They'd listened to him whistling to direct his border collie in the gathering of the sheep and the herding of them. They'd commented on the skill and the partnership of man and dog.

After that, they'd had a simple supper: chops and a salad. Alastair realised then that he should have stopped somewhere along the way to purchase a bottle of wine, but he hadn't done as he'd been in so much of a rush to get to Sharon. She declared it was of little matter.

Then to bed together, during which time he began to understand that Sharon brought out the best in him in all ways but especially in this. And he knew it was the same for her because she'd whispered, 'It's never *ever* been like this,' and he'd declared that this was how it would always be with them. She'd chuckled at that and he'd said, 'I swear it.'

She wondered when he did not rise at two in order to get back to the bakery for the early morning's work. He told her that he wasn't leaving, that he wanted to be with her for the rest of the night.

He hadn't expected to sleep so well. It had been so many years during which his sleep was a broken thing, interrupted by the baking, interrupted by Caro, interrupted by his own restlessness. He'd supposed he would sleep only fitfully and spend most of the night merely enjoying the sensation of Sharon's warm body next to his. But instead he'd fallen deeply and almost immediately to sleep, and he'd stayed asleep.

He awakened just after five. For a moment he panicked, forgetting both where he was and what his intention had been: to allow his assistant to man the ovens. His heart slammed him into purpose, and he was about to leap from the bed when in the mirror opposite he caught sight of Sharon. That was all it took to calm him.

She slept the sleep of the innocent, curled on her side, her fists tucked beneath her chin. On her face a faint smile reflected whatever dream she was dreaming.

He eased from the bed and reached for his clothing, careful not to awaken her. He realised he needed to bring more of his belongings here so that he would be comfortable until such time he was entirely free of Caro. A dressing gown would be nice, he thought, a pair of slippers as well. A cardigan for the autumn evenings.

He descended to the kitchen, where he could see the sky above the farm's fields was beginning to lighten. He saw movement at a distance from the house, a light bobbing in the direction of the great stone barn as the farmer began his day.

He decided he would do the same: begin his day. And it would start with an extraordinary breakfast for Sharon, no typical English breakfast this but something memorable that used his skill. He'd make her a batch of succulent breakfast muffins, he thought. He'd accompany them with an omelette of cheese and mushrooms, he'd include a fruit salad and fresh squeezed orange juice, and if she rose before he managed to finish his work, he'd insist she sit at table and talk to him while he worked.

He chuckled at himself as he set about on his search for everything he would need. Of course, he was *assuming* and well he knew it. Did she have cheese? Did she have mushrooms? Was there fruit for a salad or oranges for juice?

He heated the oven and browsed till he found her electric mixer, a bowl for his muffin ingredients, a baking pan to hold them. Well and good, he thought, and he went from there to assemble the rest of what he would require. Lemon and poppy seed muffins, he reckoned, melting onto the tongue along with creamery butter.

He fetched eggs and butter from the fridge. He rustled through the neat cupboards and brought out the flour, the sugar, and the salt. But then he couldn't find baking powder and he muttered in frustration over this as he gazed out of the window, saw the steady light shining from the farmer's barn, and tried to work out what he could bake without baking powder to help the concoction rise.

His gaze fell on the dust bin just outside to the right of the steps that led to the garden. Seeing this, he recalled Sharon upon his arrival, cleaning her cupboards industriously and tossing items that had passed their best-by and use-by dates. Perhaps, he considered, there was baking powder among them. If the best-by date wasn't too far in the past, the powder would probably do just fine.

He flipped on the light above the door and went outside. Within the dust bin was the rubbish bag into which Sharon had been discarding items from her cupboards. He unfastened this and began to riffle through what was within. He was in luck because a container of baking powder was upended – but not spilled out – inside an open bag of rock-hard brown sugar. He rescued it, holding it up under the light to see the date upon it. To his surprise, it was one month away. Excellent luck, he thought. Shar had made a mistake.

He heard a rustling nearby and he looked up quickly to see that one of the farmer's sheep had wandered close to Sharon's garden and was nibbling upon the longer grass that grew at the base of one of the fence poles. The animal was just beyond the fence, but the light of the day had now increased and in it the laburnum tree showed off its long brown pods. A trick of shadows made it difficult to tell how close the laburnum tree was to the fence, and Alastair wondered about its proximity to the sheep and whether its pods were dangerous to them and he considered how he should speak to Sharon about this as it wouldn't do to have one of the farmer's animals poisoned as the ill-will involved would hardly be worth the tree's brief beauty in the spring.

And then. No crash of thunder, no rise of dramatic music playing, no bolt of lightning. He simply knew.

He'd rung her. He'd left a message: both on her mobile and on her landline. He'd told her the coppers were on the trail of a poison and they'd been at his house to talk about it. He'd advised her, hadn't he, not to let them into her house because she didn't *have* to let them into her house, and they certainly could not search the place without a warrant. He'd told her this.

She'd had no idea from that that he would come to her in Thornford. *He* hadn't known he would come to her. It was Caro's madness that had driven him to Sharon last evening, and when he'd arrived it was to find her . . . He tried to call into his mind the images of what he'd seen upon his arrival, and it was an easy thing to do because it seemed that every image he had of Sharon in the last few months was branded into his memory and consequently simple to bring forth. Last evening's image was especially simple: Shar in the kitchen and what she'd been doing.

As he saw this image, Alastair tried to make the cleaning of her cupboards a completely innocent thing. But there was no getting away from what he had in his hand just as there was no getting away from the laburnum tree, which she hadn't planted until her children were old enough to understand the deadly nature of the tree's long pods. And those pods hung from it now. Announcing themselves, they were.

Alastair carried the baking powder container into the house, a sickness coming over him. He set the container on the table, sat, and considered what to do.

She'd done it for him and for their future. Because of this, he could no more turn her over to the coppers than could he climb to the farmhouse's rooftop and take to the air. But there had to be truth in all things between them, and especially there had to be truth in this. What had occurred could not remain lying like a dead dog between them, for it would eventually pollute what they had together, and he wasn't about to allow that to happen. Everything would be in the open, he thought. It was the only way if they were to go forward.

When Sharon came into the kitchen, then, he was ready. He'd started the coffee and she'd smelled it upstairs. Like a siren's call, it had brought her down to him and she wandered sleepily into the room, wearing a dressing gown that was fraying at the cuffs and slippers that were tattered.

She said with a smile as she stretched her arms above her head, 'What're you about then, my fine man?' She took in the items on the worktop that he'd not yet returned to the cupboards, and she said, 'What's to do?' And then she seemed to take in the baking powder sitting alone on the kitchen table and she frowned at this, picked it up, examined it, and said, 'Didn't I toss this in the rubbish?'

He said, 'Aye. That you did. But we best be rid of it in a better way. Leaving it in the rubbish like that . . . It makes no sense asking for trouble, Shar.'

'What're you on about?' She asked this with a perplexed little laugh, and it was the laugh that made him certain.

He took the container from her and he tucked it into his trouser pocket. He said, 'I'm taking this . . .' And then he paused for he hadn't thought it all through. He looked at the time – just after six, now – and he said, 'To Sherborne. There's the supermarket, and they'll have wheelie bins behind it. We got to get this far away and at this hour no one's likely to see me.'

'But Alastair, why are—'

'It's the best-by date, Shar. Everything else out there . . . ?' with a nod towards the back door and the bin outside of it, 'Its best-by date and use-by date . . . they're passed. But this –' here he tapped on his pocket where the powder was tucked – 'we're not close to the date.'

'So put it back into the cupboard,' she said.

'We can't have it there,' he told her. 'No matter the date. Cops aren't going to concern themselves with dates.'

She was silent, and he could see her thinking. He could imagine her calculating and worrying, with anxiety driving her into a state of nerves. He couldn't have this. What she'd done . . . It was for them, it was for their future, it was for their life together. He said, 'You're not to worry. I'm taking care of it, and then I'm taking care of you. Now and always. I know you've meant well towards me since the day we met. It's down to God that you're in my life and you *are* my life and the point is I don't even care. What I'm saying is I know what this is.' Again he tapped his pocket. 'And what I'm saying is I'm taking it away. And from the moment I walk out of the door, we won't talk about it ever again. Only just now . . . It's that I can't have a lie between us, not after last night and what it meant that I stayed and Caro knows I stayed. I'm saying I don't want there to be something not said, something not quite right, something others might see as evil but I never will cos like I said, I know what you did you did for me and for us.'

She licked her lips. He could see that they were dry as a twig. She said, 'Alastair . . . What're you saying?'

'Them laburnum pods. There, I've said it. But no worries cos I swear on everything that's ever been holy that nothing you do can part me from you.'

She rose in a movement so slow it was as if her bones had aged her to ninety years. 'You think there's poison in that container?' She extended her hand. 'Give it to me, then. I'll show you the truth.'

'I'm thinking only that nothing matters, just you and me. I'm thinking that everything's out in the open now and everything there is begins with this: I love you. I'm telling you that I got not a single regret, and no one is parting us. That's what you thought would happen, isn't it? That she would part us. And I c'n see why because of everything that's involved in ridding myself of her. Only it doesn't matter what I lose in a divorce, cos the only thing that matters is you.'

'I'm not a poisoner,' she said.

He said, 'Shar, I rang you. I told you the cops—'

'I was cleaning my cupboards. I always do. Twice each year I do it.'

'The best-by date, Shar.'

'Give it to me then. *Give* it to me.'

He began to walk out. He knew they would go round and round about this unless he rid them of the poison. He knew he needed to get it to Sherborne, to put it into the bins behind the supermarket there, and to walk away. It was only in this manner that they could put the past behind them and make their way into a future together.

She cried, 'Alastair! You mustn't! Don't leave me. Please.'

He understood how worried she was that he would be caught doing what needed to be done. But he had no intention of being caught. His only intention was to return to her.

*Shaftesbury*
*Dorset*

DI Lynley had been as good as his word. He'd managed the paperwork, laying out the facts and circumstances in such a way as, Barbara hoped, to persuade a magistrate to grant them a warrant to search Caroline Goldacre's house and the bakery that stood near it. But tracking down a magistrate hadn't been as simple as it might have been. Once Barbara Havers and Winston Nkata had everything in hand for a search warrant – with a compulsive attention to detail and language suggestive of Dorothea Harriman's competent involvement – they rang the local nick for the magistrate's location. As the hour was early, they'd gone to his home only to discover that the bloke was on holiday in Croatia. So they had to dig deeper to find a judicial official who could authorise a warrant. This involved a trek down to Dorchester, where they'd cooled their heels for an hour in the institutional reception area of the magistrate's court while Sylvia Parker-Humphries finished up business in another part of the building.

Barbara had received an early morning call from a Shaftesbury solicitor called Ravita Khan who'd briskly announced that any further dealings with her new clients – Mr MacKerron and Ms Goldacre – would have to go through her, so Barbara knew from that phone call forward, everything would have to be on the up and up. Still, she was in a lather to get back to MacKerron Baked Goods and the house that faced it. She could well imagine what was going on there inside those buildings while she and Winston waited to be escorted into the presence of Sylvia Parker-Humphries: a team of removal men doing their bit to empty the house of all its contents followed by massive cleaning and scouring during which anything having to do with Clare Abbott's demise was carefully and thoroughly removed or destroyed. She told Winston this in a hushed tone. He advised her to step outside and 'Have a fag, Barb. It'll settle your nerves.'

She did so, but didn't feel much better afterwards. He suggested next that she spend the time getting Dorset Constabulary on board. He was fully confident that they'd have the warrant in hand soon enough and they were going to need more than just themselves to sort through everything at the bakery and in the house. This seemed a productive plan, so Barbara stepped outside to make contact with the county's chief constable. He'd have the manpower they needed. What remained to be seen was whether he would lend them out for a romp in Shaftesbury.

By the time this was all in hand, they'd made it into the office of Sylvia Parker-Humphries whose fresh face made her look far too young to be a magistrate but who also knew her way round a search warrant request. A Q & A followed. Barbara could have done without this – as well as without the magistrate's scrutiny of her leopard print high tops, Barbara's bow to dressing for the occasion – but Winston was as ever imperturbable, and his good-mannered confidence seemed to assuage whatever concerns the magistrate had.

They arrived back in Shaftesbury late in the morning to find four Dorset constables hanging about in the parking area. They quickly discovered that Alastair MacKerron was at present in parts unknown but suspected – by Caroline Goldacre – to be, as recounted by one of the constables, 'in Sharon Halsey's undoubtedly unwashed bed because *I* haven't seen him' – while Ms Goldacre was now locked into the house with a Mrs Khan advising her not to open the door.

'Not even to let Stan here use the loo,' the other constable said, indicating a beefy red-faced police brother who had apparently been forced to do his business down the road and behind yew and hawthorn hedge, no bathroom roll provided. He'd had to use leaves, such and as they were. Ouch, Barbara thought.

Having heard all this and acknowledged their grievances, Barbara and Winston went to the door and rapped smartly. A stunning Indian woman opened it – Ravita Khan herself, Barbara supposed – and held out her hand wordlessly. Into it,

Barbara laid the warrant. 'House and bakery as well,' she said.

The solicitor closed the door and bolted it. One of the constables said, 'Hang on there,' but Barbara told him that reading the warrant was in order. It would take a few minutes. She and Winston had even been the recipients of a compliment from Sylvia Parker-Humphries on the depth of its detailed explanations. Barbara reckoned she owed Dorothea Harriman a pint for having done such a fine job of ensuring their entrance into Caroline Goldacre's digs.

The door opened again. Ravita Khan nodded. 'Search as you will,' she told them. 'But keep your distance from my client as she's not – I assume – under arrest.'

'Cross my heart,' Barbara told her. 'You, Winnie?'

'Hope to die,' he finished cooperatively.

The solicitor did not look amused. Nonetheless, she stepped back from the door.

They used a division of labour: with Barbara and two of the Dorset constables taking the house and Winston taking the bakery with the other two constables. Before they began their search, though, Barbara brought the Dorset team into the picture of what they were looking for and its inherent danger to their health. Anything remaining sealed by the manufacturer they weren't to bother with at this juncture, she told them. Anything whose seal was broken they were not to open at all. Bag it, mark it, document it for analysis at the lab, she said. And be aware: this was a nooks and crannies job. What they were after could be in plain sight and merely disguised as something else – 'It's crystalline, so think salt or sugar' she told them – but it could also be hidden away: under floorboards, in the garret, in a hollow behind a picture on the wall, tied in place to the sofa springs, buried in a mattress . . . God only knew. What she didn't add was that it might also be entirely gone at this point, carefully spread along a country roadside in the dead of night over a period of miles so that it dissipated into the wind. Who knew what was actually possible?

Caroline Goldacre was nowhere to be seen, for which Barbara

thanked her stars as she and the constables ducked into the house. Ravita Khan informed her that her client was above stairs and there she would stay until the search reached that part of the house, at which point she would retreat elsewhere.

Barbara doubted that Caroline would manage this feat of keeping herself away from what was happening, and this proved to be the case. Once one of the constables set to work in the kitchen, another in the sitting room, and Barbara herself in the laundry room, pantry, and what appeared to be a home office, Caroline's footsteps sounded in the upstairs corridor and quickly afterwards they came down the stairs.

'Ms Goldacre,' spoken by Ravita Khan went completely unheeded.

'I want to see what they're doing to my house' was her sharp reply.

'Please be advised,' the solicitor said.

'Oh I have no bloody intention of saying a word to them, but if they're taking *anything* out of my home, I intend to watch them do it and you'd do the same.'

'I'm here to monitor—'

'You're here because my husband's a fool. I am not. And as he's not present at the moment, you've little enough to do, so don't block the stairway or I'm afraid I'll have to elbow past you.'

The silence that followed might have indicated anything from Ravita attempting to control her temper to a bout of arm wrestling between solicitor and client. As things turned out, it indicated that Ravita had stepped away, giving Caroline access to the officers who were conducting their search.

Her commentary followed: 'Oh you can't be thinking I'd be so stupid as to put something there . . . Hang that picture back properly . . . If you break a single plate from that collection . . . They're pre-World War One and they're extremely valuable and . . . Really, would *anyone* hide something up a chimney?. . . Do *not* overturn that sofa! . . . A hollowed-out book? This is unbelievable . . . What on earth could be hidden in a fireplace poker?'

Barbara reckoned that the constable was thinking what to

do with the poker, not what was hidden in it. She popped into the sitting room. She said, 'You can bang on as much as you like, Ms Goldacre, but you're slowing the process which is only going to result in our being here hours longer than this would've taken if you kept your distance.'

Caroline, she saw, was stylishly dressed for going out in tea length skirt, soft-looking leather boots, a large pullover worn to hide her girth, and a handsome scarf to tie everything together. Dorothea Harriman couldn't have managed it better, but Barbara wondered what the message was supposed to be: a busy woman whose day has been interrupted by the local rozzers or a visual distraction intended to throw the coppers off their game.

'What is it exactly that you're looking for? And do you think I'm so stupid – if I did *anything*, which I did not – as to keep evidence lying round this place? I'll tell you this much, if you'd care to listen, if you stumble across—'

'Ms Goldacre.' Ravita Khan made an heroic attempt to gain control of the situation. 'You have to understand that in the presence of the police, anything you say—'

'They haven't cautioned me,' Caroline argued. 'I watch the telly. I know my rights. I can say anything I please in my own home, which I intend to do.'

Barbara wanted to get on with things, but this was too interesting to walk away from. She leaned against the doorway as one of the two constables made for the stairs to begin above. She said, 'Go on.'

'Ms Goldacre,' the solicitor said, and then to Barbara, 'You're being warned not to encourage this.'

'Why do I think she doesn't need encouragement?'

'I'm asking you to get about your search and get off this property immediately afterwards,' Ravita Khan said.

'I have something to say,' Caroline told her, 'and I won't be stopped by you or anyone.' When the solicitor did not reply, she shot Barbara a look that seemed triumphant. She went on with, 'There's *nothing* here. Do you understand that? Neither of them would be so idiotic as to hang onto whatever it is they used in the first place and even if they were both of them completely mentally incompetent, they'd at least be wise enough to keep this . . . this *stuff* at her house, which is where you ought to be conducting your search.'

Barbara nodded. 'I'll take that on board.'

'You've got a warrant for that, don't you?' Caroline persisted. 'Because if you've come here without the intention of going there next, you're more stupid than—'

The front door opened. Winston came in and gave Barbara a head jerk indicating a word was in order. She excused herself to Caroline, asked the second constable to finish up in the sitting room and head into the kitchen to take up where she'd left off, and joined Winston in the garden.

He said to her, 'Didn't take long, Barb. There's not much. Most is sealed up proper back where it came from. We got everything from the fridge, we emptied the pellets from the heating unit, we bagged whatever was left unsealed.'

'Loose floorboards, a garret, chimneys, a safe, cupboards too shallow to be reasonable?'

He shook his head. 'Nuffin. An' I got to say: way I see it, not likely anyone'd hang on summat so dangerous.'

'*If* they knew exactly how dangerous it was.'

'They got to or they'd be dead themselves, innit. This's the wrong tree, Barb, you ask me. We c'n bag stuff and cart it off and have the lab do its bit, but I say the proof of who did what is goin to come from where everything else's come from in this case.'

'Which is?'

'Words. What got written, what got read, what got said, what got recorded, what got heard. Tha's what it's been from the first. You ask me, the answer's at Clare's digs where it's always been.'

'That's what the inspector thinks as well. Sumalee's words, in his case.'

'Well?' Winston said.

Barbara didn't disagree, but once again they were caught in a t's and i's spot. So she thought about words from every direction, and she considered where they were with the case because of words. Ultimately, she could see that aside from checking every inch of the property for a sign that sodium azide had ever rested upon it, there was another route to go and they had the search warrant to go it.

She said, 'Pack up every computer, then. There's at least one in the bakery's office. There's probably others in the house as well. An' she's got a laptop. If it's words we're after, we might as well go straight to the source and see where else they lead us besides her nibs's emails.'

He nodded. 'Will do, then,' he said.

'It'll take bloody hours,' she warned him. 'Christ, Winnie. It could take days.'

'Not like we have much choice,' he said. 'I know you got the super hanging over your head, wanting a result and all that. But . . . What else we got, Barb?'

'Like you say, nothing. Pray we get lucky with the computers, then.'

*Fulham*
*London*

Lynley arrived at Rory Statham's flat round half past one in the afternoon, making the drive over from London Zoo with Arlo in the passenger seat. He hadn't seen Daidre, but he hadn't expected to see her. When he'd rung her to tell her Arlo's mistress was being released from hospital, she'd reported that a beastly day was in store for her – 'pardon the pun,' she'd added with a laugh – since one of the giraffes was in labour as was one of the zebras. But she would make certain that all of Arlo's belongings were packed up and ready in her office. Her assistant would hand the dog over. 'We'll all miss him, Tommy. He's been a delight,' she said. 'Again, he makes me think I ought to have a dog. Or something.' Lynley didn't ask what the *or something* was. He hated to think that *or something* might mean that he was being compared to a dog.

In Fulham, once he turned into the street in which Rory had her flat, Arlo's floppy ears lifted, elephant-like, in the universal sign of dog expectation. His feathery tail began a rapid beat. When Lynley parked and came round the side of the car for the animal, the dog shot out, made a dash for the proper building, and hurtled up the steps.

Lynley followed, carrying the dog's belongings, along with what he had of Rory's. He used his elbow on the bell, and Arlo's happy yipping was all the identifcation required for Rory or her sister to release the lock on the door. The dog was inside before Lynley had the door open more than twelve inches, and he was up the stairs before Lynley had the door closed behind him.

The sounds of greeting between dog and mistress floated down the stairs: Rory laughing, Arlo barking joyfully, Rory's sister saying, 'Come inside, you two.' When Lynley got to the flat, the door stood open. Rory was supine and giggling on the floor as Arlo sniffed her, licked her face, ran in tight circles, and licked her face again.

Around the sitting room stood the boxes of materials that had been removed earlier by SO7. Heather was in midst of returning items to the kitchen, the bathroom, and the bedroom and instructing her sister to occupy the sofa and rest. This Rory was clearly reluctant to do, as prior to Lynley's arrival she'd apparently been at her desk, involved in dealing with the accumulated post and in putting things back in order. She returned to it as Lynley entered.

The sitting room's French window had been repaired, Lynley saw, and all other evidence of Barbara Havers's unceremonious entrance into Rory's flat had been removed. The curtains were open to let in the sunlight, and once he was finished making certain Rory was absolutely Rory, Arlo went to a shaft of this light that lay upon the carpet. He made four circles, fluffed up the area to his satisfaction, and lowered himself to bask in the sun's warmth, giving a gusty sigh.

Lynley set the dog's belongings on the floor and closed the door. From among Arlo's possessions, he removed the two of Rory's that he'd brought from his office: her letters from Clare and the stack of photos of her final holiday with her partner Fiona. He went to Rory at her desk and handed these over. She looked down at them, then up at him.

There was a stool nearby, and he drew it closer. Heather emerged from the kitchen, asked if he wanted a cup of tea, apparently clocked the letters and photos, and from these understood that he would have a word with her sister. She nodded, disappeared back to the kitchen, and from there called out that she would be boiling eggs for sandwiches but they needed mayo and bread – 'not to mention lettuce and tomato, which would be nice as well' – so she was going to pop out to the shops for a bit if no one minded and if Lynley would remain with Rory until her return . . . ?

When her sister left, Rory looked through the pictures. Lynley had already inspected them several times so he knew what she was seeing: the photographs of her final days with Fiona. She slowly turned them one at a time face down on her desk, and he waited. Ultimately, she set them next to the letters from Clare, and she observed both stacks as if comparing what each of them revealed about her and her relationship to both of the other women.

She looked at him frankly. 'I did love Fiona, Inspector. The relationship was difficult, but I did love her.'

'I hadn't thought otherwise,' Lynley told her. 'I find that people aren't all one thing. One rather wishes they were for simplicity's sake, but isn't the truth that people are good and bad, simple and complicated, happy and sad, frightened and courageous? It's all a mix. We learn to take in everything about a person as disparate parts to the whole, and it's the whole that we love, even at moments when the other isn't who we wish her to be.'

She gazed at him. 'You're quite unusual for a policeman. I expect you've been told that before.'

'Know lots of cops, do you?' he asked with a smile.

She chuckled. 'There is that.' She fingered the edges of the envelopes that held Clare's letters, just the corners of them, and from the looks of the corners, it seemed that this action was something she'd done often, perhaps as she considered what the contents of the letters were really saying to her. She said, 'We'd separated for a few months, Fiona and I. It wasn't for the first time. We'd been off and on for a good long while. We'd gone to Spain to see if we could patch things up one more time. We were . . . In those last days we were quite happy.' Her expression was one of a woman seeing where she'd been, not where she was. She dropped her gaze to the surface of her desk. She was silent for a moment before she said, 'I saved myself instead of her. I don't think I'll ever get past that if I'd not jumped from the window, she'd be alive.'

Lynley thought about everything he'd read and heard about the case. What Rory was saying, he decided, was a natural reaction to the violence she'd been caught in. It was also an unreasonable judgement upon herself. He said to her, 'In a moment like that, you can't have expectations of how you're meant to behave. It's not as if your life experience gives you training in what's proper when someone appears out of the night at your bedside to attack you. There *is* no proper in such a situation. There is only the instinct for survival.'

'You know that's not true,' she said, shifting her gaze to his. 'Soldiers in battle disprove that every time there's a war.'

'Indeed,' he said. 'Soldiers do just that, every day and all over the world. But those soldiers are also trained. You weren't.'

Again, she was quiet, her face looking weighted down with profound sadness. She said, 'I've told myself for years that I was going for help when I jumped from the window. I said that afterwards, in court as well. But, you see, there was no help because the cottage was so far removed, which was why we'd chosen it. Privacy, the view, the sun, the beach. No phone to bother us, no internet, not even coverage for a mobile near the house. There was no one in miles to help and I certainly knew it when I leaped from the window. I stumbled round in the dark – in that perfect away-from-humanity darkness – and there was a drop that wasn't quite a cliff some yards from the cottage and I fell down it. So he couldn't find me afterwards, not in the dark and he'd lost his torch in the chaos. So that's how it was. For want of a torch, one woman lived. Who should not have.'

Lynley leaned forward. 'You're leaving out part of the story. As I recall it, you were bleeding from multiple knife wounds. You'd been raped. You'd been beaten. You can't leave out that part *because* it's part. The fact that you made it to the window and leaped out saved your life, it's true. But it also preserved you not only as a victim but also as an eyewitness so that for him there was no escape. Not with you still alive and with DNA evidence and with what would be made of both at the trial. You did the right thing, Ms Statham. You did the only thing.'

She turned the photos face up again. She began to go through them till she found the one she wanted. She didn't switch its position so that he could look at it right side up, but he could see it was a picture of the little villa itself, an Englishman's holiday dream destination with crimson bougainvillea tumbling over a wall, with flowerbeds brightly planted with Mediterranean blooms. A woman he recognised as Fiona Rhys lounged in the sun, dressed in crisp blue and white linen with a sunhat shading her face and her slim feet in sandals. She had a glass of white wine in her hand and with it she saluted the camera.

Rory said, 'The night was quite warm. We'd kept the windows open. Without a sound he came in and there he was.' She flipped through more pictures, interior shots taken of the villa's charms: the decorative tiles, the perfect white walls, the casual furniture, the vases of flowers brought inside to make it a home away from home. 'At first,' she said quietly, 'you think what you've been taught to think, what so many women are taught to think: if I just do nothing to rile him . . . if I just submit . . . if I don't make things worse . . . But then you think of all the women who did just that and died anyway and something gets right inside you and you decide you won't be one of them. I think that's what happened to Fiona. It wasn't in her to submit. I told her not to fight him. I said to her, "Fiona, don't just don't," but he had a knife at my throat and he'd managed to tie one of my arms to the bedpost and she . . .' Rory was silent for a moment, as if thinking about what she'd just said. 'No,' she went on. 'My arm wasn't tied. He used a belt, something thin that they sold in the markets to tourists, something a woman would use with her trousers or a skirt and he'd punched more holes so he could get it quite tight and God he must have had so much practice. He said, "I mean business," in English, so he knew we were English and he'd been stalking us and waiting and we'd even been nude in the sun on the terrace and walking round the villa naked because we thought there was no one nearby.'

Across the room from them, Arlo seemed to sense Rory's distress. He rose and came to her. He stood on hind legs, his paws on her knees, and she bent to him and rested her cheek against his head. She said, 'He said, "I will cut her," to Fiona, and he did. Not with the tip of the knife but a slash across the front of me and there was blood . . . so much . . . and you would think that would stop him from what he really wanted to do to me but it didn't, of course. Fiona made a run for the bedroom door, probably for a weapon to match his, but he was on her. He didn't cut her at first. He beat her and I could hear the sound – the grunting, the fists pounding into flesh and bone, the thrashing round – and then, of course, when she was whimpering from the pain and he'd broken her collar-bone and her nose and three of her ribs – then he raped her. He beat her more and he raped her again and then I could hear the sound of the knife clattering on the floor and they struggled for it and God how she fought him but she couldn't manage to . . . He got the knife and I could hear what he was doing to her and then he left her there on the floor. I thought she was dead. I thought, "Nothing matters now." And then he came for me.'

'I am so profoundly sorry,' Lynley said. 'But hear me well. You are not to blame for anything that happened that night.'

'He raped me . . . I don't know. Four times? Five? It doesn't matter and it didn't matter because Fiona was dead. Only . . . she wasn't, you see. God knows how she managed but she did. She got up from the floor, she *threw* herself on him – *how* did she do it? – because he was slashing at me and he was going to use the knife to . . . he was going to . . . the knife inside me . . .'

Lynley left the stool then. He had never felt so deeply ashamed merely to be a man.

Rory had begun to weep although she didn't seem to be conscious that she was doing so. Lynley went round the desk to stand next to her chair and then he knelt and took both of her hands in his. He wanted to remove her pain. More than that, he wanted to remove the memories that would doubtless haunt her straight to the grave. He could do neither, and so he did the only thing he could do, which was to listen to the rest of the story.

'She was so weak by then. She'd lost so much blood. But she threw herself on him anyway and he flailed at her with the knife and it was this . . . this moment and its ferocity that cut the belt that was holding me to the bedpost. He lost the knife then. Fiona got to it but she had virtually no strength while he . . . he was *driven* to do what he'd intended to do and it was as if something coursed through him and made him superhuman, completely able to subdue two women who should have been able—'

'*No*,' Lynley said.

'He set on her again. He got the knife from her. He threw her down. And I could hear the sound of the knife hacking into her body – I still can hear that, Inspector, the . . . the horrible *meatiness* of the sound – and that was when I leaped from the window. I left her to him. I told myself I was going for help but I don't know if that's the truth of the matter and I'll never know. So while he beat her and murdered her, I hid from him and I have to live with that. With that and with the fact that Fiona tried to save me while I couldn't do the same for her.'

Lynley got to his feet and drew Rory to hers. He wanted to get her away from the desk, away from the photographs, away from anything that connected her mind to that night. He knew that the act of walking her over to the French windows and opening them and leading her outside to stand on the tiny balcony overlooking this simple London street was not going to achieve this end, but it was something and he needed to do something. He said to her, 'Ms Statham . . . Rory . . . People will have doubtless told you that you did the best you could that night. Indeed, you did the only thing you could. I expect Clare Abbott said that to you repeatedly.'

'She did.' Rory's voice was low.

'So I want you to believe me now because I'm a cop and I know what I'm saying in this matter. Will you listen to me?' And when she nodded, 'People . . . Clare . . . everyone . . . They will have been right.'

She used her arm to wipe her eyes. It was a childlike gesture that felt like a grip on Lynley's heart. He wanted to say that she was loved by so many people, that those same people would have done what she had done, that her life had continued as a consequence and *that* was the important bit, but he knew that, despite the years that had passed since Fiona's murder, Rory had so many miles to walk before she could forgive herself for the simple act of being human.

'You think you're going to be able to vanquish this thing that's happening to you,' she said. 'You're going to do it by taking him down, by killing him if you must. There are two of you and one of him and even now people look at me and I see it in their eyes. Why were two of you not able to gain control over the situation? And I have no answer for that.'

'No one would have an answer for that.'

'I tell myself that I was in shock. I tell myself I *was* going for help. I tell myself I was out of my mind with terror. I tell myself anything and everything. But the truth is still the truth.

I left him to kill her, to finish her off like she was . . . not even a dog, Inspector. I wouldn't even have allowed that to be done to a dog.'

He had no response to this other than to say, 'Please. You mustn't . . .' but he knew what it was to lose someone to violence and to feel the weight of responsibility and the equal weight of guilt to be left among the living. In Rory's case everything was so much more complicated by the difficulties inherent in her relationship with Fiona, while in his own case, he'd lost a beloved wife who'd known, even in the last moments of consciousness as she lay bleeding into her own chest on the front step of their home, exactly how beloved she was. There was a form of consolation in this, something onto which he'd been able to grasp in his deepest moments of despair. Rory did not have that in her relationship with Fiona. And he could not give it to her.

She turned to him. She smiled, it seemed, as best she could. She said, 'So you see, Inspector. Clare saw as well. In her eyes – as in yours – I was a victim. In my own? That's something I never shall know. I came to believe that if *she* wanted me, if I could make her mine—'

'Clare?'

'Yes. If I could – call it what you will – turn her somehow, then it would mean forgiveness.'

'But wasn't that like attempting to take your definition of self from the unlikely? Or even worse, the impossible?'

'It was,' she admitted. 'But there you have it all the same.'

*Shaftesbury*
*Dorset*

Barbara was feeling a feverish sort of restlessness – anxiety running up and down her arms – and she knew she could interpret this one of two ways. Either her body was demanding nicotine or they were closing in on Caroline Goldacre. She tested the first possibility by stepping outside Clare Abbott's house and into the brisk north-east wind that was tossing the shrubbery in the back garden. She lit up two Players at once, double-smoked them with far more satisfaction than Winston Nkata would have deemed even remotely acceptable had he been there, and when she still felt no different, she knew that she could safely assume that her instincts were alerting her that the track they were on was the track that would end with Caroline Goldacre in the nick. *If*, Barbara knew, they could nail down everything in such a way as to please the Crown prosecutors. For the police could make an arrest and haul her away, but if they didn't have something quite solid for the CPS, the woman would be back home within twenty-four hours and the coppers would be wearing an unbecoming amount of egg on their faces.

That, of course, was going to be the problem: what evidence they had so far was circumstantial. Unless they were able to come up with someone who'd witnessed Caroline topping up a tube of toothpaste with sodium azide and someone else who'd seen her packing Clare's overnight case and conveniently forgetting to include her toothpaste within it, nothing they had was going to put Caroline away.

Killers had been convicted by means of circumstantial evidence before, of course. But when that occurred, the circumstantial evidence was overwhelming. The way Barbara saw the investigation, there were five essential elements to building a compelling circumstantial case against Caroline Goldacre: proving she had access to sodium azide; finding evidence that she knew about Clare's conversation with Sumalee; nailing down something within that conversation that was sufficiently eyebrow singeing to set Caroline off on the path to kill Clare lest she reveal it; forging a link between Caroline and the sodium azide; and making the discovery of the sodium azide itself, preferably on Caroline's property.

Honesty required Barbara to admit that coming up with that last bit of evidence was looking remote. She had to acknowledge how unlikely was the possibility that the poison would turn up among the substances they'd taken from the house and the bakery. So they were left with locating evidence by means of the written word, just as she and Winston had decided after searching the house and the bakery.

Towards this end, Winston had gone with the computers to Dorset police headquarters, where two techs there would assist him with the monumental task of delving into the electronics from Caroline's house and from Alastair's bakery. Towards this end, also, Barbara had returned to Clare's house. When her mobile rang, she'd just completed a second search of the locked drawer of Clare's desk to see if she'd overlooked anything the first time through.

It was Lynley ringing. He wanted to know their progress. Managing to acquire the search warrant was going to impress him, but Barbara knew that what little they had as a result of that warrant was not. So she tried to put on it the best face possible.

'We've carted off everything that could be hiding a load of sodium azide,' she told him, 'and it's on its way to forensics. But Winnie and I have started to think that may well be a non-starter, sir.'

'That's hardly good news,' Lynley said. 'What're you on to next?'

'A convincing trail running *from* Caroline *to* the sodium azide, one that's going to be enough to cook her once we come up with the goods telling us that Caroline knew Clare had uncovered lightning.' What Barbara didn't add just then was that how odd it seemed that Caroline might have found this evidence and not written an email about it to Clare since she'd written emails about everything else. On the other hand, it did make sense that there was no email on this topic if Caroline had decided that her only recourse was to eliminate the author before she could reveal what she'd discovered.

'Winnie's taken all the computers to police headquarters,' she said and added hastily, 'so yes, we've split up again but—'

'I've no problem with that at this point,' Lynley interrupted, surprisingly. He went on with, 'Sodium azide can be ordered straight from the internet—'

'Bloody hell.'

– 'so Winston needs to be looking for that connection as well. In the meantime, I've had a word with Rory Statham.' He explained what Rory had claimed about Clare's willingness to reveal *any* detail – no matter how damaging to Caroline – to spare her own work and allow her to continue it.

Barbara considered this. She said, 'That whole business about Caroline watching Will play with himself . . . ? Looks good to me as a detail damaging to Caroline, Inspector.'

'I don't see how,' Lynley said.

'The creep factor alone—'

'What I mean is it's completely inadmissible in court. It gives us nothing. It's hearsay of hearsay, actually. So using it to get an arrest—'

'But Caroline wouldn't know that, would she?'

'That it's inadmissible? Possibly not. But believe me, her legal counsel would. Besides that, the information passed along by Sumalee about Caroline and the son isn't enough to declare Caroline a killer. We have the second wife accusing the first wife of something with absolutely no proof and, for all we know, a world of animosity between them. That closes no gaps, no matter how you look at it. You need to find something that will. And I can't say how much more time you have to do it. I'm painting things as well as I can with Isabelle—'

*Isabelle*, she thought. It's always Isabelle.

– 'but I can only bang on for just so long about how well things are going in Dorset without her wanting to know when an arrest is going to be made. What would you have me tell her?'

'Tell her Winnie 'n' me can close this.'

'You know she's going to ask how long that will take.'

'Right. Well. OK. I get that. Tell her twenty-four hours.' It was an utter lie, but what else could she do?

'I'll tell her that, then. See that you do it.'

They rang off. Barbara muttered an oath. It was absolute murder to be desperate for something without knowing what that something was.

She turned back to Clare's desk. If it or Clare's office contained what they needed to put the cuffs on Caroline Goldacre, Barbara knew she had to begin seeing everything in the room not as a cop would see it but as Clare Abbott's assistant would see it: as a reason to be rid of her employer.

Barbara completed her examination of the contents of Clare's locked drawer, but once again she came up dry. She shoved the drawer closed and went to the bookshelves. She began removing volumes and uselessly shaking them, not sure what was going to fall out but hoping that if anything did, it was going to be gold. There was nothing, though. Aside from the marked off sections of the individual books that Barbara had found earlier – which were going to prove exactly nothing to the CPS – Clare Abbott had been a reader who left her books in pristine condition.

Her filing cabinet offered no sizzling details, either. Nor were there any smoking-gun messages on her answer machine, and although a list of phone calls on Clare's mobile to and from Francis Goldacre's home *could* have been seen by Caroline, what was supposed to be concluded from these calls in the mind of the woman remained supposition only.

At the end of her search, Barbara threw herself into Clare's desk chair and stared and thought and further stared. A set of in and out trays stood upon the desk's surface, with the in tray empty and the out tray waiting to be dealt with. Moodily, she grabbed the contents of this latter. She saw they consisted of letters that had been answered and posted, as a copy of the reply to them was stapled to each, preparatory, she reckoned, to the letter's being filed somewhere.

She looked at the letters and the responses: requests for

interviews, offers of temporary postings at various universities, requests for personal appearances, invitations to conferences, propositions about joining this and that board of trustees. She read through three or four of them as well as Clare's replies before she twigged to how the latter had come about. At the bottom of each, below the signature, were two sets of initials: CA/cg. Clare Abbott and Caroline Goldacre, she realised. The letters had been composed by Clare but typed by Caroline.

Well and good, she thought. Caroline took dictation. This seemed reasonable of an assistant . . . Only Caroline hadn't begun her employment as an assistant so did she take dictation or had there been another way the contents of the letters had been communicated from Clare to her?

Barbara opened the unlocked desk drawers and saw the answer to her question in the top one where the dead-as-road-kill digital recorder lay among the other contents. She searched through the desk for batteries, but found none. She carried on in the kitchen looking through the drawers there. Everyone had a junk drawer somewhere. She could only hope that Clare's held batteries.

It did. A package of triple A batteries lay among a jumble of small household goods.

She took these back to Clare's office, and in short order she had the digital recorder operational. Pushing the play switch gave her Clare's voice at once, with its unmistakable gravelly nature:

'A letter for University of East Anglia, Caroline,' Clare's voice said. 'Damn . . . where is it? Ah. No. Sorry. It's some-where on my desk. Will you search it out? It's a Dear Professor Whatever, I've received and all the et ceteras and blah blah blah. Tell her that while I'm complimented by the invitation to whatever groups she's asking me to appear before, the calls upon my time just now prevent me . . . and you know the rest. Add a few lines about the possibility of doing this for her next spring. With regards blah blah blah.'

Barbara frowned. Disappointing, to say the least. She looked

at the recorder and could see from its tiny screen that more
was contained on it, so she hit play another time.

It was Clare again, dictating in the same off-hand fashion
as the first letter, but this missive going to America, to someone
in Austin, Texas, where a conference was going to deal with
the insidious encroachment of the American legal system into
women's right to self-determination. Directly up Clare's alley,
Barbara thought. She'd agreed to this along the lines of 'Have
them get in touch with my speaker's bureau, Caroline. Very
interested and all the polite et ceteras.'

A third letter was in the same vein, and there was no fourth.
Barbara sighed, muttered, and reached to switch the damn
thing off. She hit the wrong button, however, an easy thing to
do, considering its size. On the display screen, then, she saw
that there were two more tracks on the recorder. She'd been
listening only to the A track. She switched to B. Nothing was
there. But when she switched to the C track, the screen showed
that there was something was on it.

Again, Clare's voice. No letter this time but rather some
sort of musing that began with, 'I've just left Sumalee Goldacre.
I want to get all of this down before I forget any of the details
so I can transcribe it all later. Not at my best when I can't
take notes or record, but that's how she wanted it so I had to
go along. Right. Here it is. I'll need to speak to Karen Globus
again and more frankly this time, obviously.'

What followed, then, was Clare Abbott's recounting of her
conversation with Sumalee Goldacre in precise detail, beginning
with Sumalee's phone call to her, continuing with her insistence
that Clare not record or make a single note of what she said,
and going on from there to document the same tale that Sumalee
had told Lynley about Will Goldacre. To this tale, however,
Sumalee had apparently added two points that she'd not
mentioned to Lynley. 'This next bit rather beggars belief but
anything's possible, I suppose. Will apparently told her that
sometimes Caroline *helped* him although God knows what that
actually means because, heavens, does a boy need to be helped

to wank off? Isn't it more or less second nature? Two year olds stick their hands down their trousers for a feel, after all. But she said he was something like ten or eleven years old when Caroline first showed him what he was meant to do and helped him do it and this was apparently something to deal with his language problem. So all right, p'rhaps she'd come up with this somehow or been advised or whatever by a doctor. But the chilling thing is that she watched him and, according to him, she also *enjoyed* watching him *and* helped him, which suggests rather a bit more than a mum's concern for her boy's well-being. Sumalee said he was quite casual about it all. A bit shifty-eyed as she remembered it, but not embarrassed. More like . . . There was an undercurrent, she said. She said it felt like defiance, a sort of hitting her in the face with something to see what she would do about it, but she didn't *know* what to do about it and she reckoned it was best not mentioned again. She said he was fourteen or fifteen at the time when he told her. Could he have been lying? Yes. I suppose. Nonetheless, *enjoys* is the operative word. Or *likes*. "She likes watching." And *helps*, of course. Not past tense. Present tense and Sumalee was certain about that. She just didn't know how to interpret it. Sometimes boys like to be sensational, don't they? So do girls. A case of, Let me see how much I can shock you. But this whole extended grief of hers with no end in sight, experienced now at the very same level as the day he died . . . tears and wailing and gnashing of teeth whenever his name is brought up? What *are* we looking at here? Reaction-formation? Note to myself: check Ferguson again. Additional note to myself: I must speak to Charlie. The boys were close. Doesn't it stand to reason that Will might have said something to him if his mum was into his trousers? Or that Charlie might have suspected there was something seriously *off* between Will and his mum? I'll need to speak with him. Can't go at this directly, ask for his number or anything because she'll twig something's up. But I can get it off her mobile easily. She always leaves it—'

Barbara switched the digital recorder off. Her entire body was tingling. Charlie, she thought. The other brother. Clare had intended to speak to him. She had intended to unveil for him the nature of the relationship between his mother and brother. The information was a nuclear warhead that detonated directly in the centre of how Caroline Goldacre depicted herself, not only to the world but also to her remaining child.

This, Barbara thought, was the evidence they were looking for, and what rang out for her in that moment were the words overheard by the night porter in Cambridge. One woman saying 'We're finished, you and I,' and the other declaring 'Not with what I know about you. We'll never be finished.' Caroline had to have spoken the first, having come across Clare's mental musings, having understood from them that the power had shifted. Clare had responded. She had the goods on Caroline, and she could easily use them. As long as she held the threat of speaking to Charlie over Caroline's head, she could write her book and proceed on her way to further glory. Unless, of course, Caroline killed her.

*Shaftesbury*
*Dorset*

Alastair parked in his regular spot at the far end of the bakery. He stared through the windscreen at the building's brick-clad exterior and shifted his gaze to the window to take in what he could see of the pristine shelves. Acknowledging that his assistant had got on quite well with the work in his absence, he felt largely numb.

He wondered how he could possibly have got so many things wrong in his life. He wanted to put it down to a badly set broken leg long ago and what that leg had done not only to obliterate his soldiering dreams but also to foster within him the sense of desperate unworthiness that had driven most of the decisions he'd made.

What nearly slew him was the whole concept of *intentions*. No matter what he'd decided or what actions he'd taken, he'd always intended the best. From that first embrace of Caro in the street straight on to sitting on a cold wet bench in Pageant Gardens earlier that day, he'd meant to hurt no one, he'd intended only to express his love.

Despite Sharon's protests that morning, Alastair had adhered to the belief that he knew the ways of the world far better than she did. So once he'd removed the damning container of baking powder from her house, he'd driven off to Sherborne to be rid of it. Their conversation had delayed him, though, as had looking into Sharon's stricken eyes. That last had prompted him to tell her not to worry. He'd said 'Let me do this for you,' and she'd let him be on his way.

When he arrived in Sherborne, jouncing over the railway tracks and making the turn into Sainsbury's car park, he did it in the company of two articulated lorries, there to make their morning's delivery to the supermarket. One lorry bore baked goods – there was an irony, he thought – and one bore paper products, and the presence of them pulling up to the great delivery doors at the back of the building necessitated his coming up with Plan B to be rid of the container he'd taken with him from Sharon's house.

Nearest to Sainsbury's was the railway station, so he scooted there. But people were already gathering for the morning train, and he couldn't afford to be seen disposing of anything in their presence, which called for Plan C.

He left his vehicle near the station, in the car park, and considered his options. From where he was, he could see the autumn leaved trees in Pageant Gardens across the street from the station, and this seemed to him to be what he was looking for. But it had to seem natural, just in case.

He went first into the station where he bought a newspaper and a takeaway coffee. Then he carried these across to the garden, where he strolled along the macadam path and paused as if to admire the bandstand in the garden's centre. There were others in the garden, despite the hour, but they were hurrying across to the railway station and he knew they wouldn't remember him, just a bloke on his way home with the morning paper and a cup of coffee. Bit young to be a pensioner, of course, but who really knew these days anyway?

Benches stood at intervals along the path, and Alastair was about to stroll to one when a uniformed policewoman came striding into the gardens and set off in his direction. He had a heart slamming moment as he did his best not to note her progress while noting her progress. He was fully expecting her to stop to have a word – just as he was fully preparing some sort of excuse to give her about why he was there – when she strode past with a brisk nod and a 'good morning' and went through a gate at the top of the gardens. He followed her a bit to make certain she wasn't going to linger, and that was when he saw the proximity of the police station to where he was. He nearly gave it up then.

But he pulled himself together and decided his plan was still a good one, for how likely were the coppers to come through the gardens and riffle through the rubbish? He went to a bench, frowned at its sheen of morning dew, and reckoned there was nothing for it but to sit or to walk on to look for another rubbish bin, which he was loath to do.

So he sat. He opened his paper with a crack. The heir to the throne and spouse, surrounded by minority schoolgirls in headscarves, a very large cake with dripping candles, everyone smiling toothily. He saw the photo without seeing it. He read the accompanying story without reading it. One bloke passed him on the way to the train and a young woman floated by on a scooter. Two dog walkers said hello. And then, finally, there was no one.

Alastair slid the container of baking powder out of his pocket in the same movement as he rose from the bench. His trousers were wet in the back – he should have had the sense to sit on part of the paper, he thought – but his jacket fell far enough to cover the damp, so all he had to worry about was the discomfort and not someone catching sight of a pathetic bloke who looked like he'd pissed himself.

He headed in the direction of the railway station and the car park. Directly on his route was a rubbish bin. As he passed it, he slipped the container into its depths. On top, he placed the paper he'd bought. It was all completed in less than three seconds.

He went on his way and decided that it only made sense for him to stop inside Sainsbury's. He needed to buy Sharon a replacement for the baking powder, for she had to have that stored among her baking ingredients. When the coppers showed up to have a go with her house, it would be something of a giveaway, wouldn't it, if she had everything else but not a crucial leavening substance without which no decent cake would rise.

He had to wait a bit for the supermarket to open and when it did, he thought it would be wise to purchase a few things that he was accustomed to eating, things she didn't have like the granola he favoured, the type of honey he liked to use, a lemon curd that she didn't have in her stock. It would do for him to have shaving gear as well, he thought, and while he was at it, he picked out a bouquet of flowers because what woman didn't like flowers brought to her, eh?

Thus encumbered with offerings among which was the new baking powder, he returned to Thornford. He called Sharon's name as he entered the house, and he found her sitting at the kitchen table. She was dressed for work, which called to his mind that it *was* a workday for her, and although he wanted to tell her to forget about going to work today, he knew that it wouldn't do for her to behave any different from normal.

He presented her with the bouquet, saying, 'Flowers for the flower of my heart. That's you, girl,' and kissing the top of her head. He set the rest of his purchases on the worktop and he told her he'd 'got rid of that business. I'm not telling you where, am I. Just know that it's safely gone and just to make certain no one's the wiser . . .' He rustled through the carrier bag for the baking powder. This he handed over to her. 'Wouldn't do for you not to have this,' he said.

She said nothing in reply. She'd set the bouquet on the table and now she held the baking powder in her hands. It was a circular container and she rolled it between her palms. Finally, she got to her feet and went out of the room.

He followed her. She was, he thought, behaving oddly. She looked . . . He wasn't quite sure what to call it. Just that she walked like someone in a dream. She went to a cupboard in the corridor between the kitchen and the sitting room. This she opened and from within, she brought out a container of baking powder, which she handed to him.

He said, 'What's this then?'

She said, 'Like I told you, Alastair. I do my cupboards twice each year. This's the replacement for the other. If something's use-by date is close enough, I toss it. Like I *told* you, Alastair.'

He wasn't sure what he was meant to think, let alone what he was meant to say. So he said nothing. He merely stood there – a mute – and he couldn't bring himself to raise his gaze from the baking powder. As she had done, he turned it in his palms. Unlike her, however, he upended it to see its best-by date. He saw what he expected to see: the date was, of course, for the future.

She said quietly, 'We don't know each other 's well 's I hoped. Else you wouldn't've thought . . . What was it you were thinking? That I was trying to poison . . . who? Caroline? You? Why? 'Cos I'm after the bakery myself or something? Why'd you think that?'

He felt something clutching at his throat. He saw a door closing, and he knew he had to rush through it before he was locked out forever, but he didn't know how to get himself going. He said, 'That tree out back. It clouded my mind. It's due to living with Caro that I can't think straight and besides there's that tree and how easy it would be . . . But I believed you. Every word, Shar.'

'Not the words that counted,' she told him.

'I couldn't let something happen to you. You're . . . it's everything I have, you are. And . . .' He set the baking powder on the shelf from which she'd taken it. 'We c'n laugh 'bout this later, can't we? Me rushin' off to Sherborne whiles all along you got this powder here to use and I would've found it had I only looked, eh?'

She was quiet for a moment, her gaze on the container: where he'd put it and what it meant. She said at last, 'You would've found more'n that if you'd only looked. I wish you'd done that.'

Now, Alastair forced himself to open the door of his van. Because he couldn't face coming home to Caro after what had passed between Sharon and him, he'd spent hours driving round Dorset instead. He'd visited his bakeries. Might as well see how well his assistant had done, he'd reckoned. So he went to five of the shops and while he felt like a block of ice in every single one of them, he could see that business was brisk and that his assistant could do very well without him. As, he was concluding, could everyone else.

He approached the house. It looked unoccupied, but he had little hope that this was the case. Caro's car was in its usual spot and as she wasn't given to walking, she was probably within.

She met him at the door. 'They've taken everything,' she told him. 'They've been here, they've torn the house apart, it's taken me the rest of the day to put it together. But you're not to worry about that because the important bit is that you had your night with your piece of tail.'

He pushed past her into the body of the house. 'Her name is Sharon. Call her that or keep still.'

'I'll keep still when I'm dead,' she said behind him. 'Of course, that's what you were hoping for, isn't it? The two of you with your Very Big Plans. Well, they're about to come to nothing, Alastair. The police have your computer and mine and everything else that can possibly link you and her . . . And they'll go there next. Don't think they won't. So if there's nothing to find among your things – because there's certainly nothing to find among mine – then off they'll go to that bloody little cunt—'

'I damn well *told* you, Caro.' He heard his voice in an entirely new way, as the instrument of violence it had never been before.

– 'once they work out that whatever they think *I* might have done was actually done by someone with a hell of a lot more to gain.'

'You listen to me,' he said, and he grabbed her wrist for emphasis. 'Shar wanted nothing.'

'Oh please,' she scoffed.

'You don't understand cos you're not like that. You want everything. You want to suck a man dry. I should've seen that when you went on and on about Francis like you did, when you did everything you could to keep your fingers on Will and Charlie and not let them, not *ever* let them—'

'You don't know what you're talking about. And let go of my arm. You're hurting me.'

He found he quite liked that idea of hurting Caro. He gave her wrist a sharp twist. He said, 'God but I was mad for you. Course, you knew that. That was part of it. Men always go a bit mad for you and you use that, don't you?'

She tried to jerk away from him. He held her fast. 'Let *go* of me!' Her voice rose. He liked that as well: the sound of fear in it. But then she regrouped as she would always do. She tossed her head and said, 'Let me understand this. Sharon didn't use you but I did. Sharon offered you *nothing* to get you exactly where she wanted you, but I did. I'm some sort of . . . What am I? A schemer? A demon? While she is what? What is she, Alastair?'

'Decent and good,' he said. 'Only for ten minutes maybe I forgot that: the decentness and goodness that would've stopped her. I saw that tree outside and I remembered what she said and I thought she . . . But she wouldn't've, 'course, and I see that now. Because she was telling the truth from the first, just like from the first you never knew what the truth even was.' He released her then and threw her arm to one side and was intensely gratified to see the harsh redness of her wrist and to know that it was going to bruise.

She said, 'You're mad.'

'Prob'ly,' he told her. 'But for the first time what I feel is sane.'

*Shaftesbury*
*Dorset*

Lynley wasn't impressed. It was an intriguing detail, he told Barbara, but it wouldn't serve their purpose because there was – and she knew it – no way to prove that Caroline Goldacre had ever listened to what Clare Abbott had dictated onto another track of the digital recorder. Yes, yes, it stood to reason that just as Barbara had discovered there were two more tracks, so Caroline could have done had she, too, pressed the wrong button on the recorder. And unlike Barbara, Caroline might have assumed that what was on the third track was another letter she was meant to type so she had reason to listen to it just to make certain. But Barbara *knew* this was supposition and declaring it proof of anything, no matter how it helped fill in the picture of what had happened, would get them tossed out of the CPS office on their collective ear. It would also serve as yet another element to convince Isabelle—

*Isabelle*, Barbara thought sourly. Bloody sodding Isabelle.

– that this entire venture was a waste of the Met's valuable resources. Then, of course, there was the question of why it was still on the digital recorder at all.

'Because she hadn't yet transcribed it,' Barbara said.

'Still and all,' Lynley began.

She cut him off with, 'Look, sir. You *know* how unlikely it is that there's going to be hard evidence. But when we link things up – and we're going to do that – that recording's going to make the chain unbreakable.'

'*When* you link things up,' Lynley told her.

He also told her he'd made his dutiful report to the superintendent who'd agreed on another twenty-four hours. But that was it, she'd told him. If Sergeants Havers and Nkata had nothing sewn up by that time, they were to hand over what they had to the Dorset police and be on the road back to London before she had to enquire as to their whereabouts.

Thus Barbara was more than a little worried. She'd thought the recording was going to be their smoking gun, and she didn't like learning that Lynley considered it a water pistol. She continued her search through Clare's office. She was still searching to absolutely no avail when Nkata rang from Dorset police headquarters with an announcement that immediately cheered her:

'Got it,' he said. 'Trail of breadcrumbs, Barb. We got a search for poison, we got a zeroing in on four of 'em and sodium azide's one, and we got an order for it. All been deleted, 'course, but tha's nothing for these blokes at headquarters.'

'Yes!' was Barbara's reaction and she wanted to ring Lynley immediately. The hour was growing late, the twenty-four hour clock was ticking, and they had to move. 'We need to bring her in,' she told Nkata. She brought him up to the minute on the recording she'd found and said, 'That's motive in a sandwich, you ask me. I'll fetch her from the house and take her to the nick. If you c'n meet me there in, say, an hour, we c'n—'

'Little problem,' he told her.

God, she thought. What? *What?* She said, 'What sort of problem, then?'

'It's both computers.'

'What's both computers?'

'What we found. It's Alastair's computer and Caroline's been used. And there's something more. It's 'bout Lily Foster.

Look, I'm heading back there now. I'll 'xplain when I get there.'

She wanted to demand that he explain *now*. But she needed time to regroup. Both computers? Lily Foster as well? Barbara had a very bad feeling about it all.

So she smoked and paced and smoked again. She did her pacing round Clare's house: kitchen to sitting room to sun room. She did her smoking in the front garden away from the wind. Nkata was coming from south Dorset and, like every route to any place in the county, there was no direct way to make the journey from there to Shaftesbury unless one sprouted wings. So while she waited, she had plenty of time to examine not only what they had on Caroline Goldacre but also her own predilection for pinning guilt upon the woman.

It wasn't pleasant to consider she might be blindly stumbling towards disaster merely because she disliked Clare's assistant. Caroline had declared herself the actual target of a killer, and wasn't the reality that it could still be the truth?

When Winston finally arrived, Barbara had smoked so much that her eyeballs felt raw. She also, she reckoned, smelled like an afternoon in Wigan circa 1860 if Winston's expression was anything to go by. His comment of, 'D'you *ever* give it a rest, Barb?' sent her up the stairs to search out some mouthwash but at that point, it did little good as the rest of her – hair, clothing, and probably skin – was permeated with smoke.

She made coffee and toast while Winston did them some scrambled eggs. They'd neither of them had dinner, so a quick after-hours high tea was going to have to do. As they cooked and then ate, Winston went over the details. Barbara had to admit that it was going to be difficult to massage them into anything impressive in the guilt department.

Winston referred to his notebook. First, Alastair's computer, he said. It contained the search for the poison. Phenmetrazine hydrochloride had been choice number one: it caused, among other things, tachycardia—

'There's the heart,' Barbara pointed out.

– circulatory collapse, and coma. Possibly rejected by the killer as death wasn't a certainty. Next was chloral hydrate, which depressed the central nervous system. Probably rejected because it took too long for the victim to succumb to all the respiratory problems it caused. Then came amitriptyline which could bring on heart attack. Rejected, no doubt, because of the difficulty involved in putting one's hand on it as it was a prescription medication. And then, at last, sodium azide. Quick, effective, and available over the internet.

'The inspector told me to let you know about that internet bit,' Barbara said. 'Sorry. I forgot.'

No matter, he told her, because the order for sodium azide hadn't been difficult to find. It was on Caroline's laptop. Deleted, of course, buried as well as it could be buried without taking the hard drive out, smashing it to pieces, and having the laptop rebuilt with another hard drive in it. The order appeared to use her credit card number as well.

'So Bob's your uncle.' Barbara breathed in relief.

'Tha's where things get dodgy,' Nkata said.

For although the delivery address was indeed the address of the bakery and the home of Caroline Goldacre, the person whose name had been given as the recipient was Lily Foster.

'Bloody hell,' Barbara said. 'Can I count the ways that doesn't make sense?'

'She has motive, Barb,' Nkata pointed out. 'Has done from the first, innit?'

'Christ, but how is she supposed to have done it? Sneaked into the house in the dead of night? Sneaked into the bakery as well? Used Alastair's computer to lay a trail there and then the same on Caroline's? And how'd she put her mitts on Caroline's credit card? Better yet, how did she manage it all without getting caught? That beggars belief. Makes more sense to me that Caroline's the one who's laying false trails left, right, and centre. Does the search on Alastair's computer to sink him once she declares herself the intended victim: "He meant to kill me 'cause of his lady love" and all that. And she hates

Lily as much as Lily hates her, so if she could make it seem that Lily was after her just in case the Alastair bit didn't work . . . Win, it *does* start to make sense if you look at it that way. Caroline wants Clare gone because Clare was going to talk to Charlie about what she'd done to Will. She wants Lily gone because she blames her for Will's death. And on the chance we *don't* work it all out the way she intends, if we settle on Alastair as our boy, she takes care of him and his affair. No matter how it worked out, it's a win for her.'

'If tha's how it happened.' Nkata's voice was slow, though, so Barbara knew he was thinking. When he next spoke, he made his thinking clear. 'Charlie,' he said.

'What about him?'

'He could've done it all, Barb. He comes down from London to see them, yeah? That gives him opportunity to mess about with the computers much 's he wants. When Alastair's having a kip middle of the day, he uses his. When Caroline's asleep dead of night, he uses hers. He c'n put his hands on her credit card easy, too. He'd've had a good idea where she keeps it.'

'Charlie? Why? And why the Lily Foster bit? Why have the poison sent to Caroline's digs but in Lily's name?'

Nkata admitted that that was where things got tricky. With an ASBO hanging over her, Lily couldn't exactly linger round the bakery and the house to receive a package sent to her there. There was far too much risk involved. Yet if she hadn't been there to receive it and if it had fallen into the hands of either Alastair or Caroline, what would they have made of a package sent to their address but to Lily's name?

'They'd've taken it d'rec'ly to the police,' Nkata said slowly. ''Less, of course, they were meant to open it. They open it, have a whiff, and you know the rest.'

'Which they'd never have done. Not with what had happened already between them and her. They'd have been dead mad to do that.'

'So it's all back on again,' Nkata said.

'Let's ring the inspector,' Barbara suggested. She told him

about the limit of twenty-four hours, and then she said, 'We need more time, and I think the computer trail's going to give it to us.'

That, however, did not turn out to be the case. When Barbara had Lynley on his mobile, she put hers on speaker and let Nkata do the honours. He went through the information he'd just given to Barbara: Alastair's computer, Caroline's computer, the bakery's address, Lily Foster's name as recipient of the sodium azide. Barbara added her bit about the manner in which the information could be interpreted: with the logical conclusion that the person who could have managed all this with the most ease being Caroline Goldacre.

Lynley sounded deeply unimpressed. More, Lynley sounded exasperated. He said, 'This is ice so thin we're all about to fall through it, Barbara.'

'By itself, yeah. I see that, sir. But when you put it with everything else we've got—'

'You know as well as I that we can't hand over a mountain of supposition to the CPS.'

Barbara rolled her eyes and exchanged a look with Nkata as Lynley went on. She could practically see the inspector ticking the list off on his fingers.

'A conversation overheard in Cambridge, a hidden book being written, an internet adultery site being used, score of emails printed up and—'

'Hundreds of *her* emails, Inspector.'

– 'annotated with references to various psychology books. Interviews with people significant in her life that she *might* have heard or whose transcriptions she *might* have read. An overnight case that she *might* have packed. Toothpaste that she *might* have doctored. Without a single witness, without definitive evidence of some sort that actually *is* definitive evidence and not something we conveniently *declare* definitive evidence . . . We've got sod all unless you manage to wrest a confession out of the Goldacre woman.'

Barbara looked at Winston. His expression was regretful. It seemed to be saying, along with Lynley, that the time had come for them to pack their bags. But returning to London without something to show the superintendent for the time she'd allowed Barbara to spend in Dorset was not an option. So Barbara said, 'So that's what it'll be, Inspector.'

Winston frowned. Barbara had little doubt that up in London Lynley was frowning as well. He said, 'What?'

'Caroline Goldacre's going to confess. And she's going to confess to me. It'll be on tape. It'll be transcribed. It'll be initialled on every page. And it'll be signed.'

'That's not very likely, is it?' Lynley asked.

'You said twenty-four hours, didn't you? Twenty-two now, to be exact. That's plenty of time for me to question her. She's going to confess. Depend on it.'

She rang off. She knew there was very little chance that she could persuade Lynley into believing she could get a confession out of Caroline Goldacre. Truth was, there was very little chance that she could persuade herself into believing it. But given the options of producing a confession or returning to London in defeat, she didn't see any other choice.

*Shaftesbury*
*Dorset*

Alastair knew he should have been abed at least two hours earlier. He'd made the attempt but, finding he couldn't sleep, he'd given it up. He hadn't heard from Sharon. He'd rung her, both her house and her mobile, and he'd attempted to explain himself . . . only, he hadn't known quite what to say. He hadn't *really* believed that Sharon could have harmed anyone, and that was how he began his message at first. The problem was that he *had* believed in Sharon's guilt, no matter that there were indications to the contrary and the biggest indication was Sharon herself. She'd been as consistent as the rising and setting sun,

straight from the day he'd met her. Yet he'd actually thought . . .
and that was the point, wasn't it? What he'd thought was the
whole bloody point. He'd thought she was someone who could
poison another person for what was truly an ill-defined gain. It
was little wonder that she wanted nothing more to do with him.

He lectured himself as he tossed in his bed. He tried out
various means of earning Sharon's forgiveness. He had mental
conversations with her and more mental conversations with
Caro. He stared at the dark ceiling of his room; he stared at
the shadows thrown by the wardrobe against the wall; he stared
at the closed bedroom door.

Through it he could hear the blare of Caro's television. It
was so loud that he could even tell what she was watching,
some kind of mad programme on plastic surgery, a bloody
stupid bloke who'd decided he needed to have his willy made
larger and had gone to a hack in South America to have it
done. Disaster with accompanying photos. Pause for a commercial even louder than the programme itself.

She was watching the telly in her retreat, and the thought
of this retreat that he'd fashioned for her put Alastair in mind
of everything else he'd done to this house they lived in, all of
it at Caro's request, accomplished because he'd sought to please
her. A new kitchen, new bathrooms, an extra bedroom so that
each of the boys could have his own room as they'd had in
London. The house had had enough bedrooms when they'd
purchased it but one of them, she'd decided, was meant to be
her personal retreat. This was, she'd told him, essential to her
peace of mind. But the reality was that there was no peace of
mind for Caro, and a personal retreat had not provided it for
her. In time, she'd altered it to her bedroom. 'We keep *such*
different hours,' had been her excuse. 'You do want me to be
able to sleep, don't you? I need my sleep. It's not unreasonable.
And really, Alastair, it's for the boys, after all.'

Stupidly, he'd thought it would change when the boys left
home. She'd be more of a wife to him then, he reckoned.

He rose from his bed. As he did so, he considered how

many nights he'd only slept fitfully because of the noise from Caro's telly programmes. He realised he'd never once asked her to turn the sound lower, instead merely pointing out to her that 'It's a bit loud for me to be able to sleep, love,' a veiled request that she blithely ignored. Sharon, he told himself, would not have done this. Indeed, Sharon wouldn't have been watching the telly into the wee hours of the morning at all. She'd've been in his bed, having adapted her hours to his hours so that they could be together, going to bed at eight and rising not at two in her case but perhaps at four because she, too, had a full day of work ahead of her and it wouldn't do for her to be driving round the county without having had a decent night's sleep. But Caro? It hadn't been like that. Nothing with Caro had been the way life might've been with Sharon.

He could list the differences: how Caro hadn't wanted more children despite his longing for just one child of his own; how she hadn't taken his name because she'd wanted to keep the last name of 'her boys'; how they were always 'her boys' and never 'our boys' no matter the father he was to them; how, most of all, they'd begun their relationship on a lie and one lie or another had carried them through all these years till he'd finally had enough.

He fumbled for the light on the bedside table and just as he was about to switch it on, he heard the sound of a car outside. He saw the headlamps beam through his bedroom window. Then the lights were extinguished, two doors opened and slammed smartly shut, and that was when he went to see what was going on.

A full moon was shining silver everywhere, and in its light he could see the police: the woman detective and the black again. They paused at the entrance to Will's garden and exchanged a few words. Then they came across and rang the bell.

With her telly roaring, Caroline wouldn't hear it, Alastair reckoned. He idly thought about ignoring the whole thing. What could they do if he didn't answer? Ram the door down? He didn't think so and he was so bloody miserably tired and—

Caroline's telly went off. The bell rang again. This time it was held down, so there was no real pretending that the noise it made wasn't enough to wake one from sleep. And even if it hadn't been loud enough to alert the fire brigade, Caroline came out of her room. She didn't descend the stairs, however. Instead she opened his door and said, 'Probably for you, don't you think? Little miss hot pants coming to claim her man. Ah. I see you're ready to leave with her. Up and dressed and all the rest, hmmm?'

He said, 'It's the cops.'

Her expression altered. She entered his bedroom and went to the window. The ringing continued. She said, 'I have no intention in the middle of the goddamn night . . .' and then she left him. He could hear her pound down the stairs. In a moment, he could hear their voices: the cops' quiet, Caro's loud and outraged. Her sleep disrupted. Did they know what time . . . ? What they hell did they . . . ? Her solicitor at once. And all the rest.

He went to the stairs, and he could hear her more clearly. He descended slowly and listened to his wife.

'Do you *know* how many hours it took me to put my house back together once you lot had your way with it? And I do *not* appreciate it that you've taken personal effects of mine with you. D'you want me to believe you actually *need* my face powder? What for, unless *this* one intends to improve her appearance which, let me tell you, could do with improvement.'

Alastair reached the bottom of the stairs. The two detectives saw him. The woman cop said, 'Mr MacKerron. Sorry to disturb. We need a word.'

'Call the Khan woman,' Caroline said over her shoulder.

'Can do,' the black detective said. 'But you might want to have a listen first, innit.'

'A listen? To what?'

Here the female – Sergeant Havers, Alastair reminded himself – brought something out of her pocket, which without his specs he could not quite make out. Caroline assisted with,

'You intend to record me, do you? Then I'll want my solicitor. Now.'

'Happens it's Clare Abbott's,' the black said.

'What's she done, then? Recorded the name of her imaginary killer?'

The two detectives shared a look. 'Matter of fact,' said the black.

'Like I said. You might want to have a listen,' this from Sergeant Havers. 'Before you make any decisions about the solicitor. Course, it's up to you and I can see why you might not want to take my advice. On the other hand, no skin off your nose to have a listen first.'

'Oh fine,' Caroline snapped. 'I can tell you're not about to be gone until I hear whatever nonsense you've come up with.'

She stepped back from the door and admitted them into the house. They knew where the sitting room was, of course, and they took themselves to it. Caroline followed but she did not sit. Alastair brought up the rear.

'Just let me make sure you understand that I am *well* aware that I have no obligation to speak to you,' Caroline said.

'Winnie,' Sergeant Havers said to the black.

Astoundingly, he gave Caroline what Alastair – from years of television viewing at the side of his wife when those years had been good ones – knew was the caution: she didn't have to speak but what she said could be held against her and all the rest. Caroline's reaction to hearing this was, 'You're joking. This is absolute rubbish. You've taken virtually everything from my house. You can't tell me you've found something because there's nothing to find. So *what* am I supposed to have done now?'

'We've got a nice trail of research into poisons off one of your computers, Mrs Goldacre,' Sergeant Havers said. 'We've got a website where one poison in particular can be ordered. Sodium azide, it's called. *And* we've got an order for it sent to this address.'

'You're lying,' she said. 'You're trying to trick me by—'

'Winston here and some very talented blokes at police

headquarters found everything. The whole A to Z of it. More than one computer was used, which was quite a nice touch, but everything's there.'

'And *I'm* supposed to have ordered it? *I'm* supposed to have wanted Clare dead? Let me ask you this. When are you going to come round to the fact that I had no reason to want her dead whereas it's fairly clear that there's someone standing right here in this room who, along with his pathetic bit of skirt, would've been only too happy to see *me* gone for good?'

Alastair took all of this in: not only what Caroline was announcing, which he considered par for the course at this point, but also what the cops were saying about the computers and what had been found on them. He could see that Caro's colour had gone high, two bright streaks in particular shooting up her face from her neck.

'As to someone wanting someone else dead . . .' Sergeant Havers said, 'well, let's all sit and get at it straightaway.' She did so, and she placed the recorder on the coffee table in front of her. Alastair sat opposite, the other detective sat next to the sergeant on the sofa, but Caroline remained standing. The sergeant shrugged and said, 'Batteries were dead in this thing and I didn't twig at first. Thought it didn't work. Silly me. I put batteries in and had a listen and . . . well, you'll be able to sort out the rest.'

Alastair watched as the detective sergeant switched the recorder on and Clare Abbott's voice – it was unmistakable, more like a man's than a woman's, he reckoned – came into the room. He saw Caroline flinch. He reckoned the cops saw this as well.

Clare was speaking to Caroline on the thing. He could tell it was a letter. But he couldn't work out how it could be important since all it had to do with was Clare's response to an invitation to speak somewhere.

Caroline's response to this was, 'What on earth is this supposed to prove?' which she made with an angry gesture in the direction of the recorder. 'She was too lazy to write her own letters. I wrote them for her. So what?'

'I had a listen just like you,' Sergeant Havers said. 'Then I saw that if you hit another button on this thing, it switches to another track. I skipped to it – just like we're about to do – and I heard this.'

She picked up the recorder, did whatever one had to do to switch to another track, hit play and there was Clare's voice another time, saying, 'I've just left Sumalee Goldacre, and I want to get this down before I forget any of the details.'

At this, Caroline approached the coffee table. The black man stood and positioned himself between her and the recorder. As Clare continued speaking, he left Caro no alternative but to sit. She couldn't get past him.

'. . . walked in on him and caught him masturbating over some pornographic pictures of women. She backed out of the room fast as she could, she said, but not before he saw her which also happened to be the same moment he ejaculated. So here's the first question: is she telling the truth and, if not, has she reason to lie?'

'What is this thing?' Caroline's voice was less assured than it had been.

'I expect you know,' Sergeant Havers said as the recording continued to play.

'I have *no* idea. Who is she talking about?'

The black said, 'Pretty obvious, innit?'

The tape had gone on. '. . . all sorts of ways in which this crosses the line but can it be called abuse or just an appalling lack of boundaries and an equally appalling invasion of privacy? It *seems* abusive to me, but is this just my natural aversion to what went on? *If* it went on and if Will *wasn't* lying to her, then—'

'Will?' Caroline cried.

Alastair looked in her direction. He swallowed and his throat was dry as cold toast. He felt distinctly as if something very big and very ugly was hanging above their heads, about to crash upon the room and envelop them all.

Clare was saying – '*was* telling the truth, where does it fit in? Evidently, Will showed no embarrassment when he told her about it, just said that his mother had helped him and that she enjoyed watching him do it. Except it was in the present tense. She *enjoys*, he said.'

'What is this twaddle?' Alastair said, having managed to swallow and to find his voice.

'It's about the Wording,' Caroline said to him, speaking over the recording. Her tone was anxious. Sentences began to tumble from her. 'It was how he learned to control it. To stop it before it became unstoppable. He'd begin to word . . . one of his seizures . . . and if he . . . if he *did* this to himself, it redirected him. That's what he was talking about.'

Alastair said, 'How'd you know that, then? He said you watched. He said you helped him. *Helped* him? Bloody hell, Caro, he said you *enjoyed*—'

'He was lying. What else was he going to do? There she was interrupting him in the midst of something clearly private and . . . Why would I watch him? I didn't watch him. I wouldn't have watched him. He's saying that—'

'. . . said it felt like defiance on his part, a sort of hitting her in the face with something to see what she could do about it.' They turned back to the coffee table. Sergeant Havers had increased the volume and Clare's voice was relentless among them although from that point forward Alastair picked up only the occasional word or phrase, so loudly was the blood rushing through his head and pounding like a snare drum inside his ears. '. . . best not mentioned again . . . fourteen or fifteen at the time . . . present tense and she was certain about that . . . this whole extended grief of hers with no end in sight . . . whenever his name is brought up? . . . check Ferguson again . . .'

And then like the trumpets at Jericho, '. . . Additional note to myself: I must speak to Charlie about all this. The boys were close. Doesn't it stand to reason that Will might have said something to him if his mum was into his trousers? If Charlie—'

Caroline leaped. The black detective was quick, and he grabbed her arm. Caroline cried, 'Make it stop!'

Sergeant Havers did so, saying, 'We call this a motive, Mrs Goldacre. I expect you didn't much want Charlie to hear the tale, did you? Mum watching his little brother, making sure it was all done right and proper, eh? Mum helping his little brother 's well when he was . . . what? Maybe ten years old? And doing what . . . hmmm? What *did* she do? Try something new when he was in the middle of his problem with words, p'rhaps? Get him to lower his trousers? No. Can't be that. He'd be into his words so he wouldn't take note of what she said, so she would've had to lower them herself, those trousers. She'd've had to take his hand . . . or p'rhaps she used her own. Or p'rhaps not her hand at all but something more effective that would show him what a little *proper* stimulation—'

'Stop it! You're filthy! You're—'

'If Caroline came to believe,' Clare's voice now said as Sergeant Havers played more of the tape, 'that a sexual distraction would alleviate Will's vocalising of obscenities, which was proving embarrassing both to him and to anyone he was around when it happened, does it follow that she brought on board the pornography as well? What I mean is that as the obscenities heightened in offensiveness – assuming they did – would he need to be exposed to something that also heightened in offensiveness? And would he have reached a point where the pictures weren't enough for him, like a drug addict needing more and more of the drug? Obviously, this means that if he was fixating verbally on something particular when his words went off . . . say . . . fellatio or cunnilingus—'

Caroline surged past the black detective who tried and failed to stop her this time. She got to the recorder and smashed her fist upon it as if to break it. Sergeant Havers got it away from her and silenced Clare's relentless voice.

'Here's how you did it,' the sergeant said. 'You did your research on your husband's computer. You did your ordering on your computer. You used Lily Foster's name as the recipient for the same reasons you used your husband's computer for the research: if things didn't work out – which of course they didn't – you had a very nice trail leading away from you and reason to declare yourself the victim. The only problem was having to use a credit card to buy the stuff. You couldn't put your hands on Lily's – if she even has one – and I expect Alastair's on the same account as you. But that works anyway, doesn't it, because it'll still lead to him. And you had to use your own toothpaste, didn't you, because just in case someone worked out that Clare *didn't* have a heart attack but just got bloody ill, *you* needed to look like the intended victim.'

And then – just then – Alastair heard her words as she had said them to him when the Scotland Yard police had first come to town: *I packed her bag.* Yet he could not say them, even now. He could not betray her.

Caroline was silent, but she was breathing in short gasps. She stared at the recorder in the detective's hand. Then she raised her eyes to look upon the ceiling as if an answer would appear above her. 'Charlie,' she said.

'Your motive in a nutshell,' Sergeant Havers noted. 'Clare was going to talk to Charlie to see what he knew about you and Will. But you couldn't have that. You couldn't have him learning what you'd done to his brother. Did you know Clare was writing her adultery book despite your attempts to prevent her, by the way? She was damn well sure you'd hold your tongue about her countryside flings long 's she promised that she'd hold hers.'

'I want my son,' was Caroline's reply to this as she began to weep. 'I want Charlie. I want my son.'

*Camberwell*
*South London*

India's mobile rang at half past three. At first she thought it was the alarm but when she woke into absolute darkness, she knew otherwise. She grabbed it and quickly silenced it. She glanced at Nat. He hadn't stirred.

It was Charlie who'd rung, she saw. What she felt was annoyance, which was quickly replaced by consternation. What she did not need upon this first occasion of Nat remaining the night with her was Charlie injecting himself once again – no matter the reason – into their relationship. It was tenuous enough.

She eased herself from the bed. Her mobile showed no message left, and that was odd as Charlie usually left a message if he couldn't reach her. But then the landline began to ring in her study and in the kitchen below. That she couldn't ignore. If she did, the answer machine would take the call and that was guaranteed to awaken her lover.

She hurried to the study and picked up the phone before the third double ring. She said, 'Charlie?' and expected him to ask why she hadn't answered her mobile.

But instead he said, 'Thank God. Alastair's phoned me. India, my mum . . .'

'Has something happened to her? Is she ill? Have she and Alastair . . . ? Did he leave her for Sharon?' Because if he had done . . . India didn't want to think of how the subsequent care of his mother would fall upon Charlie's head.

'She's been charged with Clare's murder,' Charlie said. 'India, it's worse. She's confessed.'

India opened her mouth, which went dry so quickly so felt as if someone had scoured it. All she could manage to say was, 'My God. *Why?*'

'Alastair says they have a recording. The police. Clare had worked it out in her head that . . . Oh my God, India.'

'What? *What?*'

'She . . . Mum . . . She did things to him.'

'To Alastair? What on *earth*—'

'To Will.'

India pulled the desk chair out and sank upon it. 'She did things to Will? What's that even mean?'

'Sexual things. To Will. Alastair said he reckons it was going on for years and . . . Clare discovered . . . Will told Sumalee. I don't know when. I don't know anything else. Just that Sumalee told Clare and then there was some kind of recording and Mum fell apart when she heard it and they arrested her and something like an hour ago she confessed to everything or they wrote it up an hour ago and she signed . . . I don't *know.*'

'But how is that even possible?' India asked. '*Surely* someone would have known. Will would have told . . . Did he not tell you?'

'God, no. He *never* . . .' Charlie's voice broke.

India's heart opened. But just as quickly as it had done so, she snapped it shut. What she felt was absolute fury at the whole boiling lot of them.

Charlie was struggling to speak. 'Alastair said . . . He's beyond distraught. He says he sees so many things now . . . They're clear to him and they were right in front of him all the time . . . how she lost interest . . . how she had to have this . . . this special retreat . . . and there I was and here I am, and India, you know that I failed—'

'You did *not* fail him,' she cried. 'Don't you say that, Charlie. If she did something to Will, you couldn't have known unless Will told you, so do not bloody go there. Do you hear me? Do *not* go there!'

'She always swooped in. She always rescued him. But what she was doing all the time . . . and I did nothing.' He began to weep. The sound was horrible.

'Stop,' she said. 'Don't do this to yourself.'

'Can't,' he said. 'Nothing. Just . . .'

'Charlie. *Charlie.*' And when he did not reply, she said, 'I'm coming over there straightaway. Do you hear me, Charlie. I'm coming over at once.'

She rang off and stood. She replaced the phone.

She saw Nat standing in the doorway.

# 22 October

*Victoria*
*London*

'It's always been a circumstantial case,' Lynley said. 'But despite that, she's achieved a remarkable result.'

'You must admit we can hardly send up celebratory flares for a circumstantial case, Tommy.' He and Isabelle were meeting in her office. He'd come to her as soon as Dee Harriman had given him the word that the superintendent was in at last.

'But we can do for a full confession. It's been written up and signed and the Goldacre woman's been remanded into custody. I spoke to Barbara round six this morning, guv. It happened – the confession – round half past two.'

'Solicitor present?'

'She didn't want one. Offered repeatedly but she kept refusing, so they brought in a duty solicitor, but she instructed him to observe and say nothing. All of it's documented.'

Behind her desk with the rain-streaked window glass distorting the view of St James's Park and its wealth of glorious trees, the superintendent nodded slowly. She sucked in both of her cheeks and then released them. She was, he knew, considering his announcement and everything that his announcement implied about Barbara Havers and her ability to do the job as required and – in this particular case – with constraints that might have held another cop back.

'I'm glad to hear it,' Isabelle settled on saying as she shifted a folder to the middle of her desk. She opened it and looked down at its contents before adding, 'I take it that Sergeant Nkata was of assistance to her.'

'He was. As Barbara tells it, they worked well together.' Lynley decided not to mention the fact that Havers had gone off on her own more than once. It mattered little at the end of the day since the investigation had concluded with what Isabelle was looking for and what Barbara was desperate to have: a good result.

'How does Sergeant Nkata tell it?'

'I've not spoken to him.'

'Have you not?' The question was arch. 'Please see that you do. I'd not want to have to speak to him myself. Nor, I think, would you or Sergeant Havers want me to.'

Lynley got the implication well enough. He said, 'Barbara could easily have managed this on her own with one or two DCs to direct. You do know that.'

Isabelle glanced at him. She did a half turn of her head, one smooth cheek exposed and a jade green earring brushing against her skin. It was a movement and an accompanying look that implied there were subjects best left untouched at the moment and what Sergeant Havers could or could not manage on her own was one of them.

'You're not a believer yet,' he said, despite the look, 'and I won't deny you've a score of reasons to doubt her.'

'That's very good of you,' she said.

'But if I could point out . . . ?'

'Do I appear to be someone who needs something pointed out to her, Tommy?'

'Admittedly, no. But, Isabelle . . . guv, I think some leeway is called for after this.'

'Do you indeed? No need to reply. Let me say this: I'm delighted that the situation in Shaftesbury has been cleared up successfully by Sergeant Havers and Sergeant Nkata. And I fully agree that more leeway is called for.'

Lynley was no fool. He knew there was more coming and come it did.

'Given enough rope, Tommy, I have no doubt that Barbara Havers will hang herself eventually. So giving her more leeway from now? I've not a single difficulty with that.'

She went back to considering the work on her desk. He wanted to say more, but there was little point. Isabelle, he knew, was going to go her own way in matters regarding Barbara. She would take note of Barbara's success in Shaftesbury, she would even make it a mark in her favour, but she wouldn't dismiss her intention to be rid of Havers when and if she could.

He wanted to argue a bit, but it seemed useless to do so. More to the point seemed to be Barbara herself and the necessity of making Superintendent Ardery a believer in the long run. That wasn't going to happen overnight. He could only pray it would happen eventually.

He left Isabelle to her work and set off to see to his own. In the corridor, he caught sight of Dorothea Harriman coming towards him. She gave a slight inclination of her head when she reached the door that led to the stairway. Apparently, a word was in order.

Lynley followed her. She said, 'Well . . . ?'

He raised an eyebrow, awaiting clarification.

'I mean, was it good enough for her? You went to talk to her about Detective Sergeant Havers, didn't you?'

'While I'm curious as to your method of concluding that—'

'Oh really, Detective Inspector Lynley, I'm not an idiot. You arrived an hour early today. You've recently polished your shoes and there's . . . what do I want to call it? . . . a vaguely festive air to your walk. Is that a new aftershave as well?'

'Holmes, you amaze me,' Lynley said.

'Well . . . ?' she repeated.

'Barbara's wrapped matters up with a complete confession.'

'Has she indeed? That's brilliant. Now. Onward, wouldn't you agree? Would you like me to get back to it?'

'To . . . ?' Lynley prompted. He had an uneasy feeling about where Dee was heading.

'To normalising her, for want of a better word. I've had a think, you see. I've been wrestling with this whole matter for quite a bit. I *do* see that I pushed her rather too hard. I suppose I overwhelmed her. Too much information? Heading in too many directions at once? Forcing her into that terrible speed dating situation? After that, to be frank, I'd fairly well concluded that she prefers women – *not* that I have a problem with that – but upon reflection I realised there's never been a woman in her life either. Has there?'

'Not that I know of. But she's rather discreet in personal matters. As you've no doubt discovered.' Lynley added this last bit in the hope that Dee would take Barbara's personal life and its mysteries as a knot too tightly tied for her to unravel.

Such was not the case. 'Obviously, I was expecting her to . . . I don't know . . . unburden herself to me? And really, how can one expect it on so brief an acquaintance?'

'Saving the fact that you've known her for years,' Lynley pointed out.

'Of course. But knowing her isn't the same as *knowing* her, if you take my meaning.'

'It's not Biblical is it?'

'What?'

'Your meaning. The knowing bit. Adam knowing Eve? Noah knowing . . . whoever it was.' He was joking, of course, but he could see Dee's confusion. Obviously, she was not a reader of the Bible.

'What I mean,' she plunged on, Bible or not, 'is that I have to spend more time with her. We have to build some sort of friendship. One can't possibly hope to have an effect upon someone if there's no history between them. One can't hope to make someone think differently from how they've always thought merely on the strength of a shopping excursion or the like. So what I'm saying is that I'm ready to tackle the project again but *this* time—' She'd hurried this last bit as Lynley opened his mouth to protest the entire idea of putting Barbara Havers once more into Dee Harriman's efficient hands. That, he thought, was a kite that was never going to fly. 'I'll take it more slowly. She hasn't exactly said *no* to the dancing lessons, Detective Inspector. She's reluctant but I think I can make it work. You see, I'd thought of dancing with partners, which would, naturally, put her into the arms of a man. But what if it was dancing merely as exercise? Let me ask you this: what do you think she'd say to ballet?'

The very thought of Havers in a leotard – the instant image he had of her – caused Lynley to cough back a laugh. He said, 'Dee, I tend to think—'

'Yes, yes, you're right, of course,' she cut in. 'What about tap, then? Brilliant for exercise, requiring less costuming . . . ? How does it sound?'

It sounded as absurd as ballet to Lynley, but he could tell when Dee had her mind made up. He would have to leave Barbara to her own devices on this one, he thought. And really, who knew? She might like tap dancing. It certainly wouldn't hurt her.

'It sounds quite a brilliant plan,' he told Dee. She smiled brightly. He hastened to add, 'But if I might make one small request?'

'Of course.'

'For God's sake, don't tell her I said so.'

*Shaftesbury*
*Dorset*

For the second night running, Alastair's assistant had taken up the reins of MacKerron Baked Goods, producing what he thought best to produce. Alastair hadn't even thought to ring him in order to let him know he would be absent for another day. He hadn't thought about the baking at all. But when he'd arrived at home after hours upon hours sitting in reception at the local nick, it was to see that the vans were being loaded for the day, and things were ticking along quite well without him.

This did nothing to lift his spirits. He thought about being grateful that the young man had taken the initiative. It revealed much about him and all of it good. He gave his thanks and trudged to the house. He caught a look flash across his assistant's face and he reckoned the young man had concluded where he'd been on the previous night: in Sharon Halsey's bed. Alastair had not bothered much with discretion when it came to Sharon, had he?

She'd rung, he found. He'd silenced his mobile at the police station and while he'd turned it on briefly to make the one tortured call to Charlie, he'd switched it off again, not having the heart to speak to anyone after that. He was still reeling from Caro's confession. He was still trying to come to terms with how badly wrong he'd been about Sharon. How had he *ever* thought that Sharon Halsey might harm another being? he asked himself again and again. It was as if he'd lost whatever limited ability he'd ever had in the first place to reach a conclusion about who a woman was. Well, Caro proved that well enough, didn't she? Years of being married to the woman, and he'd been utterly in the dark.

When he got into the house, he plodded into the kitchen. Weary but feeling hollowed out inside, he emptied his pockets onto the worktop. He set the kettle to boil and then picked up his mobile. He switched it on, and he saw the messages that had come in on the thing: his assistant, Sharon, India, Sharon, Sharon again.

The only one he wanted to listen to was Sharon, so that was what he did. She wasn't coming into work today. Then, she'd had a think and would like some time off. Then, Did you get my messages, Alastair? Has something happened? I've heard you've not been at the bakery.

Although the last message could be interpreted as Sharon wanting a phone call in return, he didn't have the heart to make it. He was monumentally tired, more exhausted than he'd ever been in his life. He made for the stairs, but reckoned he would find it impossible to fall asleep.

That didn't prove to be the case. It was as if he slipped into unconsciousness, to a place where at long last there were no more dreams to torment or delight him. Ultimately, it was the landline that awakened him. He grabbed it, heart hoping for some kind of reprieve from what it was going through. But on the other end of the line, Ravita Khan identified herself.

She got directly to the point. 'Why didn't you ring me at once?'

He blinked and tried to shake the sleep out of his brain. It seemed to take longer than it should have done. He wondered how the solicitor had discovered whatever it was that she'd discovered. She'd finally been phoned by the custody sergeant, she told him. It was irregular but she knew the man. Obviously once Caroline had been remanded, she was going to need a very good solicitor to bring on board a very good barrister and somehow the custody sergeant had known . . . What did it matter how he knew? Caroline might well have finally made the request she should have made at the start of this mess, Ravita Khan said.

He said, 'She didn't want a solicitor. The cops asked her. They told her—'

'Oh, don't be absurd. They would've been *thrilled* I wasn't there to advise her.'

'They brought in the duty solicitor.'

'Some grossly incompetent has-been jurist who hasn't a clue what he ought to do.'

Alastair didn't think that was the case. Fact was that the duty solicitor had nothing *to* do once Caroline made it clear that she wished to confess. He told the Ravita Khan this much.

She went on with, 'You should have rung me the moment those detectives showed up at your house. Why *didn't* you?'

'Like I said—'

'People think that when the police show up they're meant

to give them access, but they aren't. The police rely on your knowing nothing about your rights. They rely on the element of surprise, on just about anything but your understanding what your rights actually are. *Why* did she confess? Did they coerce her? Did they threaten? Did they disclose that there was something they'd found in the house? God. Never mind. How would you know? You weren't in the interview room either.'

He told her what he did know from having been in his own sitting room when the police had first spoken to Caro the previous night. 'There was poisons researched,' he said. 'She ordered it off the internet. There was a trail.'

'They told her this? My God, anyone could have ordered it. And a good barrister would have brought that up at trial.'

'She packed Clare's bag,' he went on. 'She told me herself. All she had to do was leave out Clare's toothpaste. Clare was meant to borrow hers and that's what she did. The poison was in it.'

'But my God, is there supposed to be a motive in all this?' Ravita Khan demanded.

And at this point, Alastair had to lie. He couldn't bring himself to tell the solicitor or anyone else about what Caroline had done to Will. So what he said was, 'If there's something behind it, Caro's got to tell you.'

'She won't see me. I've already tried. That's why I'm ringing. Will you try to talk some sense into her? We'll retract the confession. All of their evidence is circumstantial from what you've told me. Beyond that, she had no solicitor present.'

'Like I said, the duty solicitor—'

'They threatened her into accepting his presence. She was bullied into it.'

He sighed. 'Don't think that happened, is what,' he said. 'It was like . . . The cops told her what they had on her and she confessed. It was like she'd been waiting for them to work it all out and when they did, she just gave it up. It was like . . . I think she was tired of fighting and pretending.'

'What on earth do you mean?'

'I don't know, 'xactly.'

And that was the truth. He didn't know a thing. Whatever Caroline had done to Will, he'd been completely, utterly, and stupidly in the dark. That she'd kept things that way was no excuse, he thought. And the *why* of everything she'd done to the boy asked to be defined with the term 'for his own good', but Alastair couldn't make himself believe that.

He saw her insistence that Will return to them in Dorset after his London breakdown in an entirely new light. He saw her dislike of Lily Foster in a new light as well. He understood how people convinced themselves of all sorts of mad things to excuse the horrors they inflicted on others. What he simply could not come to terms with was how he had missed every single sign.

*Leave us alone, Alastair.*

*I'll see to this.*

*He needs his mother just now.*

And all the rest. He'd gone along because he thought that a mother's love dictated what was best for her child. More fool him.

It was afternoon when he finally left the house. He wasn't sure where he intended to go but he needed to be out in some air, he decided. He had little enough energy for the act, but he walked the distance back towards the town, up between the hedgerows the length of Foyle Hill, making the turn at last into Breach Lane. He came upon Will's memorial without understanding that all along he'd been heading to it.

He saw that, as Caro had described it, people had been hanging slips of pink and blue ribbons from the shrubbery that had been planted near the spring. On the slips names were printed, some fading, some bleeding into the fabric after being hit by the rain, some new, some old. He lifted a few and read what was written, name after name of the dead and buried.

There were candles as well that had been brought to the spot, lit and left to burn down to stubs or to be extinguished

by the Dorset wind. As it was a windless afternoon, he relit
those that still had wicks. Those that had burned to the ground,
he removed, beginning to stack the stubs on one of the limestone benches.

When he was finished with this little job, he sat next to the
candle stubs he'd gathered and he gazed upon the boulder and
its memorial plaque. He felt the need to say something to the
young man who was remembered here, but all there was to
voice was his profound sorrow.

'I didn't know, Will,' he told him. But, he thought, had he
been more of a man, more certain of himself, believing himself
to be the equal of anyone and especially the equal of his own
wife, he would have known, seen, understood, and acted. But
he hadn't ever once felt her equal. Instead he'd felt so stupidly
grateful that a woman such as Caroline Goldacre would look
upon him favourably. He'd seen himself a toad to her princess.
But when she'd kissed him, he'd remained a toad.

A car stopped on the lane behind him, but he didn't stir.
Someone coming to visit the spring, to light a candle, to hang
another ribbon . . . this was a good thing, he thought. Somehow
it made Will's suicide less of a horrible senseless heart-crushing
event.

'I expect you'll be wanting a rubbish bag for that.' Behind
him, Sharon's voice was low. He swung round, but he said
nothing. She touched his shoulder. 'I'll fetch one for you,' she
said.

He watched her walk back to her car. From the back seat's
floor she brought out a Sainsbury's carrier bag. When she had
the stubs of the candles cleared from the bench, she tied off
the bag neatly and sat. Together they looked out beyond the
spring to the land falling away to the valley beyond, Blackmore
Vale, where even from this distance the familiar Jersey cows
could be seen placidly grazing in hedge-defined fields as their
ancestors had done for more than two hundred years.

'Peaceful, this spot,' Sharon said.

'It is.' Alastair found he had nothing else to say. An apology was needed, and he knew that, of course. But how to apologise for something such as he had done: adhering to an outrageous belief that she was a killer despite her attempt to tell him otherwise. He didn't have the words.

'You didn't ring me back,' she said. 'I was worried. I went to the bakery, finally.'

He felt her looking at him, but he kept his eyes straight ahead and his gaze as far as his gaze would take him, which was the gentle sweep of Melbury Hill across the great chalk downs – favoured by grassland – that formed the valley.

'No one was there,' she said. 'But nothing was locked up, which didn't seem right what with the trouble and Lily Foster's ASBO and all of that. I didn't go inside the house, but I tried the door. Something seems a bit off, Alastair.'

He realised, then, that she didn't know, but then how would she? Not even twelve hours had passed since Caro had signed what the police had placed before her, and there was no real reason for the word to be out yet. It would go out, naturally. One didn't murder someone like Clare Abbott and hope one's arrest, charging, and confession might pass by unnoticed.

So he told her. He was brief. He did it as he'd so far done the rest of it: his gaze fixed in the distance. 'It's Caro,' he said.

'Has something happened to her?'

'It's down to her,' he clarified. 'The police have been. She told them everything. She's the one, Shar.'

Sharon changed her position then. She got off the bench and knelt in front of him so that he couldn't avoid looking at her. Her face, he saw, was all sympathy. There was no triumph in it, no I-told-you-so. She wasn't that sort of woman.

She said, 'She told them what?'

'Clare Abbott,' he said. 'It was down to Caro. They had evidence, 'course, but it might've not been enough. But then they played this recording they also'd come up with . . . Clare talking about Will and Caro and what Caro did to him . . .' He bit down hard on his lip. He wanted to feel the pain of it, now. Not only the pain of having hurt this woman before him but also the pain of having failed his stepson.

Sharon leaned forward – still on her knees, she was – and she put her arms round his waist. She said, 'I'm mightily sorry.' Any other woman, he thought, might have asked for the details, displaying an unattractive interest in another's misfortune. Sharon asked to know nothing else. She merely repeated, 'I'm very sorry.' And then, 'How are you, Alastair?'

'Dead sorry as well,' he replied.

''*Course* you are,' she said. 'It's not like you wanted a single bad thing to hang over her head, did you? And now . . . like this . . . poor woman. What will become of her? What happens when someone talks to the police? Where is she? Has a solicitor—'

It came to him that she'd misunderstood his words of sorry, thinking he was echoing her own when that was not the matter at all. He said, 'I mean for what happened, between you and me. For thinking what I thought. That laburnum tree and its pods and all the rest when you tried to tell me . . . when you even asked to eat the sodding baking powder in front of me . . . as if you had to prove or wanted to prove . . . I'm so bloody sorry.'

'Ah. That.' She got to her feet. She walked to where the slope began to fall away, where the Shaftesbury plateau, so exposed to wind and to weather, gave onto the farmland spread out below. She studied it for what seemed an eternity and finally said, 'I'd come to speak to you about all that. It did change things between us.'

'I only wish I'd listened to you. You were trying to explain and there I was all kinds of a fool because . . . Here's the worst. It didn't matter to me because I wanted you one way or the other and what's that say about me? I don't even know. I just couldn't face you not being in my life. And if that meant you wanted Caro dead and gone and out of our way, so be it. That's how it was for me.'

'And how is it for you now?' She turned back to him. The

light struck her face, and he could see that she, too, was exhausted. She'd probably not slept since he'd devastated her and what under heaven was to be done about that?

He gave a weary wave of dismissal in the direction of the bakery and his home. 'I'm finished with this. I was never a baker. I took this on for her and the boys. It was what she wanted and what she said they needed. While all the time . . .' He couldn't put into words the pictures he had in his head of what Caroline had been up to with poor Will, so he said, 'While all the time what I wanted was to do what I did in London, the work I used to do. I loved it, I did.'

She nodded. She tilted her head, as if this would allow her to observe him better. She said, 'What I'm wondering . . .'

'What?' he asked her.

'Whether you could do that work in Thornford. See, I'm a country girl, lived here forever, and it's all I know.'

He said, 'What're you . . . Sharon . . .' He was too afraid to finish his question.

She said, 'I was bloody damn angry after what you thought. I couldn't believe you saw me as someone who could murder *anyone*, no matter the reason.'

'I know. And I'm so . . . sorry's not even enough to say, Shar.'

'Then I started to think how we all say mad things and do mad things from time to time. We all reach conclusions that we sometimes regret. But this . . . Between you and me? There's nothing *bad* here, is there? Aren't we just a man and a woman who found each other, stumbled round badly, and then righted themselves? Oh, I was furious with you at first. Make no mistake. I wanted you gone from my life. But then I had a day to think things out – like who you are and what's gone so badly wrong for you since Caroline's boy died – and I came to see that I c'n go on from here, but I don't know about you. After what's happened.'

He said, 'You're saying you'd have me? After all my thinking and accusing and everything else?'

She said, 'I told you from the first the only thing that matters is you and me, Alastair. P'rhaps it's time you begin to believe me.'

*Spitalfields*
*London*

India didn't know what to name what was going on inside of her. She knew part of it was profound sadness based on profound loss. The other part felt like the frustration of being unable to persuade another person to one's way of thinking but, then again, that frustration seemed to be bleeding directly into the anguish of being set adrift without oars or rudder on an ocean whose current was both unmanageable and unknowable. There had to be, she thought, a single word for what she was feeling, but she was so done in from a nearly sleepless night that she couldn't grasp it. So she stood at the window of Charlie's flat, and she looked down at the takeaway chicken shop on the corner where still the customers came and went despite the lunch hour being long since past. She willed herself to feel nothing, but failed in that endeavour.

She'd been with Charlie since one hour after he'd rung her with the news about his mother. Nat had driven her from Camberwell. She could have driven herself, but he'd said no, let him do this for her because she was clearly upset and more than a little frantic. It wouldn't do to have her out in the street driving round in this condition, no matter the hour. And besides, they could talk on the way, he said, and she could tell him what had happened that Charlie had rung her in the middle of the night.

To her 'Charlie didn't know you were with me,' Nat replied, 'Of course. I know that,' which she allowed to soothe her. He would see that it hadn't been Charlie's intention to disrupt the first full night that she and Nat had spent together in her home.

On the way to Spitalfields, she'd told him everything. She'd been calmer then, and she was able to lay the facts out in a way that asked Nat to understand her need to offer Charlie her comfort and support. He nodded, looked gravely concerned, and appeared to find this reasonable. It was only when he'd stopped his car at the glass doors to the building in Leyden Street that his words told her something different.

Her hand was on the door handle when he said, 'India, it's best we break things off.'

She looked at him, at how the light from a street lamp struck the plane of his cheek and put his eyes in shadow. But she didn't need that light to display his eyes in order to show her their pain because she heard it in his voice. She said, 'Please, Nat. No. At least not now. If nothing else, it's not fair of you to—'

'I know it seems like that: unfair, bad timing, and all the rest.'

'Nat, his mum's just confessed to murder. His brother's committed suicide.'

'How many years ago, darling?'

'Don't. It's not been easy for him. He's made enormous strides, but this is a setback and it's not as if he's asked me to come to him. I just can't abandon him at the moment. Not with his mum . . . Please. Try to understand. I'm only trying to be his friend.'

'I understand that. But I also understand that he's got a hold upon you that he's not going to release and that you're not going to break.'

'For God's sake. His mother—'

'First his brother, then you leaving him, then his mum. It's all been devastating and I'm on board with all that. But it's always going to be something in Charlie's life, isn't it? His mother's trial, her imprisonment, his distress at seeing her imprisoned, his further distress upon visiting her in prison. It will go on forever.'

'I'm swearing to you: that's not going to happen.'

He smiled at her, his expression fond but sad. 'I know that's what you think: the possibility of walking away and not looking back, but it isn't who you are and I suppose that's one of the reasons I love you. But sometimes a woman's tie to a man is just too strong, and this is one of those times.'

She swallowed. How she wanted to argue. How she desired to lay out the facts yet another time, to call him unreasonable, and to maintain that compassion was the better half of all types of human intercourse. But she could only come up with, 'But your tie to me isn't strong enough to see this through?'

He did think about this. She could see that. At least it seemed he was considering her words but, at the end, perhaps it was only his response that he considered, for he said, 'That's not entirely fair of you, India, but I'll play along. I suppose it's not.'

He leaned towards her then and kissed her goodbye.

'Nat . . .'

'Go to him,' were his final words.

She'd done so. She would never know if Charlie had been waiting for her at the window overlooking the street, but he was so quick to the door at her knock that she reckoned he must have been watching. He would have seen the brevity of her conversation with Nat. He would have seen the kiss. But the rest he would not know, and she did not intend to tell him.

He'd been in bed when Alastair had phoned him, but there was little enough sleep left for him or for her that night. She insisted he at least attempt sleep, though, and she went to the bedroom with him and made certain he tried. She'd lain next to him, not under the covers but on top of them and completely clothed. She did this, she told herself, so that Charlie would understand that she'd come to him only as a friend would come, to see another friend through a terrible moment. She did this although she knew it was a futile gesture, most especially as far as Nat was concerned. There had, she understood, been a great deal of truth in what he'd said to her. Always, there would be Charlie on the periphery of her life.

She wouldn't let Charlie speak although she knew he wanted to. When he tried, she'd whispered, 'Later. Try to relax for now,' and she'd caressed his head. The reality was there wasn't a great deal to say. He would, at this point, have only limited knowledge of what was going on in Dorset. It was far better to wait till they had more details before they began to try to understand them.

He'd finally fallen asleep round half past six. She'd eased herself off the bed at that point. She'd left him and had gone into the sitting room. She'd lowered her body to the sofa and recalled Charlie's words about its discomfort for sleeping. He was right. It was boardlike. But even if that had not been the case, she admitted to herself that sleep would have eluded her. She spent several hours attempting it, though. Ultimately, she'd given up the effort and swung her legs to the floor.

She'd remembered to phone the Wren Clinic and to leave a message that she would not be at work that day and probably not the following day either. Family emergency was what she'd called it. If they would please reschedule her appointments . . . ? She'd probably have to go out of town, but she'd be in touch as soon as she was able.

That going-out-of-town business was something she actually didn't know, but she reckoned Charlie would insist upon going down to Dorset. He would want to see Alastair in person for the details of what had occurred; he would want to talk to his mum and make what sense he could of her confession; he would want to be of help in making whatever arrangements one made in that confession's aftermath. Would there be a trial, as Nat had suggested? Would there merely be an appearance in court where sentence was passed? What occurred when someone confessed and why didn't she know this? India asked herself.

Her head had felt cloudy and incapable of coming up with

answers, which was how she'd ended up at the window over-looking Leyden Street. Perhaps, she'd thought, the view of something other than the interior of the flat would give her different facts and possibilities to consider. When it hadn't done that, she decided that having a coffee was in order. So finally she went to the kitchen to make one.

There was only instant coffee powder, but that would have to do. She set the kettle to boil, and opened the fridge for milk. She wasn't at all hungry but she gave thought to eating as well. And Charlie would need to eat, when he finally rose. He was probably operating on nerves alone at this point, but he'd end up collapsing if she didn't force some food upon him.

There was little to eat in the fridge. An opened package of Stilton, one egg in a six-pack carton, sausage rolls, condiments, limp broccoli, even limper celery, carrots, an unopened package of romaine lettuce going bad, and a half-used container of artificial butter.

In the freezer, things were little better. Frozen kedgeree, waffles, ice, and a package of chicken breasts bearded with frost.

The cupboards held baked beans, Pot Noodle, a loaf of bread, an unopened package of rice crackers. There were oils and vinegars and a rack of spices, but that was it.

Making a shopping list was a good plan, she decided. She fixed herself the coffee when the water boiled, added milk and sugar, and carried this out to the dining room table. In her bag, she had a pen but no paper, so she returned to the kitchen for a search. The back of an envelope would do, a piece of junk received in the post or a handout from the street. But Charlie was neat as a pin, so there was nothing to use. She went back to the sitting room.

She settled on one of the dog-eared notebooks that were held upright on the shelf along with the art books that Charlie had purchased since the time of her leaving him. There were four, and arbitrarily she chose the one nearest the book end holding everything in position. Surely it would have a blank page she could rip out, she thought. She opened it and saw that indeed it did.

To make certain this wasn't a document essential to Charlie's work as a therapist, though, she flipped quickly to the front. That was when she realised that she wasn't looking at Charlie's possession at all. The sketches of gardens plans and garden features along with the notes declared that the notebook belonged to Will.

She riffled the pages a little sadly and saw how lovely Will's drawings had been. He'd had great talent for this occupation. It was one of fate's finer cruelties, she thought, that his afflictions had prevented him from using that talent to its fullest.

Less than midway through the notebook, though, she saw that the drawings had ceased and that writing had begun. She read the first of it and understood from this that at some point Will had begun using his notebook as a journal of sorts. There was no date accompanying the entries he made, but the alteration in inks suggested he'd made them over time. They were interspersed with still more drawings of garden features. There were perhaps two dozen of both in gradually worsening cursive. She began to read.

*Should have listened to Lily. The blabs are worse here than anywhere and I want to leave but I can't. Can't, Will? Isn't won't the truth? But if that's the case, what's the why of it, man?*

India frowned. The fact that Will was declaring that Lily was right suggested that his decamping to Dorset from London was his subject. India knew that Lily had been opposed to that. But if the Wording had been worse there, as he said . . . She read on.

*That day in London when she and Alastair came is when I should have known. The blabs coming on that damn day and nothing stopping them and it was all no good till she saw to me herself and right then in that second I could see what would happen if I came back but I let her and I can't declare I was too far gone to stop her because I don't believe that I'm not a six year old am I? She says don't worry about it if it works to help you I want to*

*help you because mothers are meant to help their children. But I
don't want it and I don't even find it pleasurable but—*

A large section was scribbled over, making it illegible. The
word *pleasurable* made India pause, though, as did *she saw to
me herself*. The combination of the two caused her skin to
prickle with warning.

She flipped forward a few pages till she saw *when she blows
me*, and it seemed in that instant time utterly stopped.

*Jesus make her leave me alone when I don't want her to leave
me alone and I want to cut the brain from my head. It's working
and you can see it's working when was the last time you had a
seizure is what she says and I know it's the truth. It stops them
and if there isn't another way because that's the worst I've started
wanting—*

More scribbling over, half a page torn out, a thick-stubbed
pencil trying to write in a script that was most illegible save
for:

*I must have known it would be like this*

And further down the page:

*I knew we'd go back to it. I lock the door but then a seizure at
dinner and I ran but it got bad and she was saying Don't do this
to yourself when I can help you let me help you I do this only out
of love for you that's all it is and it was like London that day and
I tried to say what does it matter that she's your mum if it works
and it's always worked only now she tells me she says I have to
confess forgive me darling boy but I love it the feel of you inside*

India froze. She felt as if her gaze had become fixed on the
word *inside*, in such a way that she'd not be able to move her
eyes away from it. But move they did, of their own accord, to
allow her to see:

*me and the truth is terrible but I want you to because it means
we have this time together and let me confess that I love you in so
many different ways And the worst. I like it. I hate it. I like it.
And I'm useless and I've always been unless I can get away from
her from this*

India found she'd actually begun to crumple the pages as

she read. Her stomach was churning and she swallowed convulsively in reaction to the bile that rose in her throat. She made herself continue and was reading *Found a place in Yetminster I mean to take it It'll be a fresh start and I swear the rest is done with* when she heard the words 'Oh God' come at her on a breath from across the sitting room, and there was Charlie watching her and on his face she saw a dawning horror that told her more clearly than a confession could have done what she should have known all along, from the very first time they'd attempted to make love.

She said, 'Oh no. Oh Charlie.' She thought he might turn, perhaps run to the bathroom and lock himself inside like an adolescent girl whose most carefully guarded secret has just been exposed by a parent. But he didn't do that. He merely sank against the wall – one shoulder against it to hold him up – and his gaze fixed on hers with such anguish that she knew the rest of his story as if he'd recited it. Which was what he did, in a voice so low she had to strain to hear him.

'Dad would go off to do his surgeries. All round the world. A month or two, this was. Sometimes three. She said she was frightened. In the house alone. Of course she wasn't alone – Will and I were there – but what were we? Kids. Inadequate protection at best.' He licked his lips. She could see that his tongue was nearly colourless. 'We'd search the house first, she and I. I'd go into the rooms ahead of her to make sure there were no intruders. Every room, this was. Upstairs, downstairs, in the basement as well. We'd make the search with a torch because she said it was important intruders didn't know we were looking. This didn't make sense but then nothing made sense. We did her bedroom last.'

'Charlie,' she said in a rush, 'you don't need to tell me.'

'I must, I think. What do they say? What do I say to my own clients?' He laughed weakly. '"You're only as sick as your secrets." Well, God knows isn't that the truth about me? And haven't I been as sick as my secrets since the dawn of my life.'

'Please. Don't.'

'She'd stay outside the room while I went in,' he plunged on. 'I'd look under the bed and behind the curtains and into the cupboards and all the time I thought I'd piss my pants because I was so scared but I couldn't tell her this when she was calling me her big brave man. "You're the man of the house, my darling," she would say. "You're my big brave man." And what six-year-old doesn't want to be—'

'You were six? *Six?*'

'But she was too frightened to sleep alone when Dad wasn't there, no matter that we'd searched the house together top to bottom and made certain the windows and doors were all locked. Sleep with your mummy while Dad's off saving the world with his surgeries was how she put it. Mum needs to be held to feel quite safe, she said. That's how it began. "Hold me, Charlie. Give me a cuddle. D'you know how to spoon, darling boy? Tuck your legs behind mine, just so. Put your arms round me nice and snug. It's nicest when you hold Mummy's breast as well, just the way you did when you were small. There. Cup it nicely darling. Just like this. Hold the nipple between your fingers. Squeeze if you like. Isn't that lovely? I can sleep now, Charlie. So peaceful, darling." And all the rest.'

'How long did she . . . do this?' she asked.

'Long enough,' he said. 'When she left Dad for Alastair, it ended. I thought . . . Well, I can put this behind me. What happened, happened. And really, what was it? Not much, actually. And it didn't *mean* anything. She just needed someone to take care of her and Dad wasn't there to do it. And now, I told myself, she's got Alastair and he's always round so she won't be frightened. What I didn't know . . .' He gestured to the notebook she held on her lap.

'She'd moved on to Will.'

'She never stopped. She got worse. But I didn't know. I swear to God, I didn't know. Till Lily gave me that journal.'

'*Lily?* How did she come to have it? When did she give it to you? How long have you known?'

His gaze was level as he apparently let her think it through. He moved into the sitting room and he sat in his therapist's chair and he just waited, wordless.

She said, 'Charlie?'

He said, 'You know, India. You don't want to, but you know.'

'Truly, I don't. Except . . . it would have to be after Will died that Lily got this somehow because he wouldn't have wanted her to know or anyone, really, to know . . .' And then she did see it play out in her mind's eyes and she said, 'The envelope. The dedication of Will's memorial and Lily was in the street nearby, watching and . . . Oh my God, Charlie, *I* gave this to you. Oh *God*, why didn't I leave it lying there in the weeds? But you said the police. You swore the police. You were taking it to them. You swore to that.'

'I took it to them,' he affirmed. 'But when they saw what it was, they handed it back. It wasn't a bomb. It wasn't anthrax. To them it was just a notebook of drawings and some random scribblings that they didn't bother to read because all of it meant nothing as far as the ASBO went.'

'You read it straightaway?'

'There in the station, sitting in Reception, because I couldn't work out why Lily wanted me to have it. And then I saw. And I knew . . . You see, I had to make amends to him, India. I suppose I had to make amends to myself as well when you come to it. That was the only thing left as far as I could tell. I'd not seen that the Wording had been about her all along, the only way he could tell me what she was doing to him, and I had to make amends.'

India stared at her husband. She drew a breath, and it caught in her chest like a sudden occlusion. She said, 'Amends,' as the only thing she *could* say. She willed herself out of this place and away from him. But she'd already set out on this journey with Charlie, and she knew that it was waiting to be completed.

'I never meant to harm Clare,' Charlie said. 'God save me. I didn't. And when she died . . . and then the police . . . I can't even think how she ended up with Mum's toothpaste.'

'Oh my God, Charlie.'

'So it's all down to me. Do you see? That decent woman dead, at *my* hand, India, and—'

'Please.' India spoke faintly. She wished him to stop. And then after a moment because it was part of the journey after all, 'How did you manage it?'

'I was down there to make peace between her and Alastair after the dedication of Will's memorial. Four times. Maybe five. Because of Sharon Halsey and his affair with her. It was easy. I'd done the research here in London, an internet café and a search engine and that was all it took. I just needed to leave a research path on their computers in Dorset. And not everything on the same day, of course. Which is why I went there more than once.'

'And Lily . . . Does she know?'

'Not everything. She came on board directly I ordered it. I knew from the site what day it would be delivered. All she had to do was hang about the bakery to receive the package. That was a risk but even if she missed the delivery, had Mum seen her name on the package, she wouldn't've opened it. She would've rung the police. That would've been bad for Lily if the cops then opened the package, but I reckoned she'd take real care to hang about the bakery well out of sight once she knew the delivery was intended to see justice done for Will. And that's what happened. She sent the package on to me. She never knew what was inside.' He gazed at the floor where his bare feet looked as defenceless as he himself had been as a six year old in his mother's hands. 'I *never* meant . . . I still don't know . . . Clare.' And then without apology but with heavy grief, 'God how I wish it had been Mum.'

'But why did she confess? Charlie, did she actually confess? Is that the truth?'

'I expect it is,' he said. 'She'd've worked it out. Alastair says the cops played out what they had against her, including something Clare had put on tape, something she'd learned from Sumalee. I don't know what. But if that's true – and I have no reason to doubt poor Alastair – Mum would've known that I was the only one who could have managed it all from start to finish.'

'But why would she . . . ? That still doesn't explain why.'

'Alastair told me the last thing she said to him before they remanded her,' Charlie said. '"Tell Charlie what's happened" is what she told him. "Ring Charlie," she said. I think she wants to make amends for everything and this is how she's doing it.'

India said nothing to this, for it seemed there was nothing left to say. Charlie was putting himself into her hands. The way she saw it, in those hands, too, she held the journal that could destroy him. But as it turned out, Charlie saw something more that needed to be said between them, and he was the one who spoke once more.

'So you see,' he said.

She roused herself at this. 'What?'

'Why I was . . . how I failed you . . . and why. The why of it most of all. It's useless to say sorry, but that's how it is. Some things are past forgetting. I knew this all along, India, which makes my sin against you all the worse. I'm bloody well trained to know that one doesn't run or try to hide or simply never get round to mentioning . . . The past, India. It does that Shakespeare thing. It shakes its gory locks at one no matter how one tries to avoid it. I married you knowing that I was next to useless as a man. There was no help for me—'

'Don't say that, Charlie.'

– 'but I hoped for the best. Still do, in fact, and isn't that a bloody good laugh? I don't blame you for a single decision you've taken. In your place, I hope I would have done the same.'

'Nat and I,' she said.

'It's all right,' he told her. 'It doesn't matter actually.' He looked thoughtful, as if he was considering the words he'd just said. 'Christ, I hope that's a good thing, India. I mean that nothing quite matters as it once did.'

'What I was going to say is that we've ended our relationship, Charlie,' India said. 'What I was going on to say is that I want to come home.'

'You can't mean that,' he told her. 'It's good of you to think it. I appreciate – even – what it implies about what you intend to do.'

'What's that mean?'

'It means you know it all now and you can do with me and with the information what you wish.'

'I know that, Charlie. And what I wish is to come home.'

'That's mad.'

'I don't say it isn't. But I want to be with you. I want to try. I want to see if there's any way – with what I know now and what you know now – that we can go on.'

'You and I,' he said as if he needed still to clarify. 'I, the killer of Clare Abbott. I, the poisoner of her friend.'

'No. You the man who failed his brother once and couldn't bear to fail him another time.'

# 23 October

*Marylebone*
*London*

When she arrived in Marylebone High Street – not a
destination that had ever been high on her bucket list
– Barbara Havers reckoned it was just the sort of place that
Dorothea Harriman would aspire to make a regular haunt, if
she wasn't haunting it already. It featured a plethora of boutiques
interspersed among trendy coffee houses, upmarket restaurants,
vintage clothing shops, and high end retailers selling everything
from must-have kitchenware to designer handbags the approx-
imate size of dog kennels. A narrow thoroughfare, the street
was reflective of the days when hansom cabs tilted along cobble-
stones – long since paved over by tarmac – to deposit well-
dressed ladies and gentlemen in the vicinity of Regents Park.
Now and at this late hour of the day, its pavements were
teeming with the after work crowd. They made for the wine
bars, the restaurants, and the pubs, texting as they blindly
walked, seeming oblivious to the commercial delights that
surrounded them.

Barbara had not come to be part of this mix. Rather she
had an appointment with Rory Statham who'd suggested they
meet at a shop that, to Barbara's chagrin, turned out to be a
lingerie boutique. She had to pick something up after work,
Rory told her, and as the shop was generally not crowded
there was little chance they'd miss each other in the mass of
pretty young things seeking other pretty young things for casual
hookups in the area. Since she'd only given Barbara the name

of the place. Barbara had no idea what she was in for when she shouldered her way through the door into an embarrassing display of bustiers, suspender belts, corsets, suggestive albeit tasteful nightwear, and knickers of a design clearly meant to bring to life some bloke's panting wet dream. Had Barbara not seen Rory at the shop counter paying for something being placed into a coy little bag with lots of tissue sprouting from it, she would have turned tail at once. She had, after all, her reputation to consider.

As it was, she sauntered to the back to join the other woman. Rory was signing a credit card receipt while the bustier-clad shop assistant at the till appeared to be doing her best to look welcoming of Barbara who was clearly not the sort of woman who frequented this sort of fancy-knickers establishment. She said brightly, 'Be right with you, madam,' which caused Rory to look in Barbara's direction. She smiled and said, 'Ah. You've found me. Let me just finish this up and we can be off.'

The finishing up took very little time. Barbara spent it looking at a pair of knickers with matching brassiere and suspender belt – Did one actually *wear* a suspender belt if one did not truly have to? she wondered – while doing her best not to gape at the astronomical cost of these bits of fabric. As a woman who bought her undergarments only at Marks and Spencer and only if the elastic on what she was wearing was irreversibly done for, Barbara found it impossible to embrace the idea that someone would quite happily pay any more than five pounds (and that was in a sale) for – at least at M & S – an entire packet of knickers. But such appeared to be the case. She idly wondered if Dorothea Harriman knew about this shop and she made a mental note to tell her the next time they met up in one corridor or the other.

They'd done so, however briefly, upon her return from Dorset late that very morning. Barbara had only just undergone receiving what went for congratulations from Superintendent Ardery at the end of a job, as Ardery had put it, 'adequately done, Sergeant Havers'. Along with, 'I'm happy to know you and Sergeant Nkata got on well together,' she'd added, 'And I hope I see more of this kind of work from you in the future,' as her parting shot. She'd offered no warm fuzzies, and she hadn't ceremoniously ripped up Barbara's transfer request. But Barbara hadn't expected her to do so. Since that signed request – no matter how reluctantly she'd signed it – was guaranteed to keep Barbara on the very straight and the exceedingly narrow, Ardery would know pure madness lay in the direction of destroying the document. She still had Barbara where she wanted her. Pending a very unlikely miracle, she would keep her there.

Dorothea had seemed to understand this as Barbara had approached her along the corridor. Perhaps, Barbara thought, it was in her walk. She tried to look jaunty to avoid becoming corn in the rumour mill at the Met.

Coming abreast of her, Dorothea said, 'I've heard you had a good result, Detective Sergeant Havers.' And to Barbara's nod, she went on to say, 'Onward. I do have to say this. I'm *completely* sorry.'

That, Barbara thought, seemed rather harsh: that Dorothea Harriman had wished failure upon her. She was about to make a remark destined for the regret-it-later pile heaping in the background of her life, when Dorothea made matters clear by going on.

'Speed dating? It was a terrible idea. I shouldn't have put you through it. I didn't meet anyone that evening either although I did think at first there were several possibilities.' She shifted her weight to one hip, always a preparatory move on her part, signalling a proper natter was called for. 'It's the blokes who show up,' she went on. 'It's the fact that they lie about their ages and expect it won't make a difference to a woman.'

'No worries,' Barbara told her. 'Just another experience to spice up my autobiography when I finally write it, eh? Got to have 'em or the reading's dull. That's always been my motto. Or at least it is now.'

Havermann smiled. She looked, in fact, far too cheered upon hearing Dorothea's declaration. She said, 'I'm so pleased because I've had a think about things. I've come up with tap dancing. What d'you say?'

'About tap dancing?' Barbara wondered if they were free associating. Matches/fire, cowboys/Indians, gun/shoot. That sort of thing. She went with, 'Fred Astaire comes to mind. I mean, obviously, there'll be recent blokes as well, but somehow . . . Gene Kelly and that film about the rain? No. Fred Astaire. It's definitely tap dancing/Fred Astaire.'

Dorothea frowned. 'Actually, I meant in place of ballroom dancing. No partner needed. Not that you wouldn't have a partner if you wanted one, of course. I don't mean to imply that. But it seemed a good way to ease into a new activity since one can, obviously, tap dance alone.' She considered this. 'Come to think, one *must* tap dance alone, yes? Your legs and feet would be all tangled up otherwise. Course, that doesn't mean you can't tap dance at someone's side, naturally. But that comes later. At first, it's alone.'

Barbara narrowed her eyes. 'What's this all about, Dee?'

'Our next venture into the greater world, of course. Now, don't say no. I can see you want to, and I understand. The shopping didn't work out well and speed dating was a *complete* disaster. But consider the dual benefit of tap dancing before you say no: one meets an entirely new group of people and one exercises at the same time.'

A steadying breath was called for. Barbara took one and said, 'Do you actually *see* me with tap shoes on, Dee?'

'No more than I see myself,' she admitted. 'But considering that autobiography, Detective Sergeant . . .'

'For God's sake, I was joking.'

'So am I. What I mean is that one's whole *life* is an autobiography, don't you agree? Whether it gets written or not doesn't make a difference. What goes *into* it, though? That's what counts.'

'I never saw you as a philosopher, Dee.'

'It's just occurred to me,' she admitted. 'I think there's a point that I've been missing and . . . well, I have to say it. I think you might've been missing it as well. It's an *auto*biography because we write it ourselves. I don't write yours and you don't write mine. So what I'm saying is that *my* autobiography is due to include tap dancing and I'm wondering if you'd like yours to do the same.'

'Can you *see* me tap dancing?' Barbara repeated.

'More to the point,' Dee countered, 'can you see yourself? Or better said, do you *want* to see yourself with tap shoes on? Which is, let's face it, another way of saying D'you want to see yourself as different from who you are now? No, no,' she added as Barbara opened her mouth to reply. 'Don't answer me yet. Have a think about it. You can tell me tomorrow.'

She fluttered her fingers and tapped in her stilettos in the direction of her desk. Barbara shook her head but it was, she admitted, in admiration and not dismissal.

Now as Rory turned to her with her purchase, Barbara said, 'What d'you think of tap dancing?'

'Excellent exercise,' she replied at once. 'Are you considering it?'

'I hadn't thought to.'

'Let me know if you decide to give it a go. I may want to join you. Now,' with a nod of her head at the door and the street beyond, 'shall we decamp to somewhere less . . .' She lowered her voice, 'less inclined to make one run screaming for the Darcy book? It's all male fantasy, this. I've bought something for my mum. Her birthday and Dad plans to take her to Italy. I thought a bit of whimsy –' she lifted the bag – 'might be in order. Although the thought of my mum in a leather bustier . . .' She laughed. 'Some things don't bear imagining.'

'Well, it's for your dad anyway, isn't it?' Barbara asked.

'I suppose it is.'

They went back into the street, where a short jaunt took

them to a restaurant in the modern minimalist style where
the menu prices kept the taint at heart at bay. Rory told
Barbara that she liked the bar here. It was on the top floor
in the open air. As the evening was fine, they could have
drinks and Barbara could tell her what she didn't want to tell
her over the phone.

This didn't take long, and it had to be said that Rory Statham
was not surprised by the revelation of Caroline Goldacre's
guilt. Nor was she surprised by the motive behind what the
woman had confessed to doing. She had, Rory said, always
thought there was something not right in Caroline's excessive
grieving over her younger son. It wasn't that the grief was
unceasing. One didn't expect a mother to walk away easily or
even at all from the suicide of her child. But it was the undif-
fering nature of Caroline's grief that had caused Rory's suspi-
cions about the woman. And despite her words to the contrary,
Rory went on, Clare must always have suspected that there
was more at work behind that grief than Caroline's reaction
to a dreadful loss.

'Clare was setting Caroline up for . . . I s'pose we could
call it double blackmail,' Barbara finished. 'We think it went
like this: "You decide to reveal anything about my catting round
with married blokes, you even *think* about trying to stop me
from writing a book my publisher's waiting for, I ruin your
life by letting it be known that you drove your son Will into
flinging himself off a cliff." We're fairly certain that's what
Clare intended. And once Caroline heard about Clare's plans
to speak to Charlie in order to check out Sumalee's story, she
had to go.'

'So Clare hadn't yet spoken to Charlie?'

'Not a whisper of it anywhere. But she intended to. She'd
already been trying to get something worthy from Francis,
from Caroline's mum, from women who knew her in town.
But nothing they had was useful or good enough when it
came to stopping Caroline in her tracks. It was only when
Sumalee told her about Will that Clare saw she finally had

what she needed to wrest control of her life away from Caroline.'

'I wish she'd told me everything,' Rory said. 'We could have . . . I don't know . . . done something?'

'What? The UK's leading feminist was making the big nasty in hotels with married blokes she met on the internet?' Barbara asked. 'What were you lot supposed to make with that?'

'Declare it research for her book?' Rory seemed to ask herself the question rather than Barbara.

'Not bloody likely to go down a treat when it had to do with betraying her fellow females, eh?'

'There is that.' Rory sounded ineffably sad.

It came to Barbara then that there was no sign of Arlo, and she wondered about this. She'd never seen the other woman without her assistance dog. She asked what it meant that he was not at her side. 'Nothing wrong with him, is there?' Barbara asked. 'He's quite a nice little bloke, that Arlo.'

No, no, there was nothing wrong with him, Rory said. He was, in fact, at present waiting for her in her car back at the publishing house. Rather anxious to see her walk off by herself, but he was adjusting to the idea. 'I've been trying a bit each day to get along without him,' Rory told her. 'I can't depend on a dog forever just to be able to leave my flat. At some point I'm going to need to get on with life without assistance any longer.'

There was good sense in this, and Barbara saw that immediately. Seeing it, she was forced to wonder how Rory's words applied to herself.

It wasn't till half past nine that she reached Chalk Farm. She managed to find the miracle of a parking space in front of the church at the bottom of Eton Villas, and she paused for a moment on the pavement to listen to the music from a concert going on inside the building. It came to her that in addition to church services, these concerts had been taking place for all the time that she'd lived in the area. She wondered why she'd never bothered to attend one. She wondered if the moment had come when she ought to see what they were all about.

The music ended. It was followed by applause. The applause went on and someone inside called out, 'Encore! Encore!', a cry taken up by more than one person until the music began again. Barbara hadn't a clue what was being played. If it wasn't Buddy Holly, she had to admit that she was hopeless.

She headed up the street. Lights were on in the flats contained within the Edwardian villa behind which sat her tiny dwelling, all save within the ground floor flat where darkness prevailed as it had done for months. The little path along the side of the building was lit, as always, by motion detecting lights. They flashed on the moment Barbara headed in the direction of her hobbit-sized home. There was no additional light above her door since the bulb had long since burned out and she had long since failed to replace it, but she was used to wrangling with her keys and the door lock, so it was no difficult matter to get inside.

She was fairly knackered. She was also hungry but decidedly unwilling to cook something up. So she went for the cupboard where she stored her Pop Tarts and rustled through the various boxes for a new flavour she'd found that had sounded intriguing: cupcake. With no one there to cast a disapproving eye upon her choice – namely Winston Nkata – she opened the package, scored two of the tarts, and deposited them within the toaster. She set the kettle to boil, dug the last sachet of PG Tips from its box, and gave a desultory look to the post that had been collected by her neighbour – the always turbaned Mrs Silver – while she'd been gone.

It consisted of the usual collection of bills – she gave idle thought to not paying her television licence and then dismissed it since she was, after all, supposed to be a law-abiding member of society – along with three credit card offers, one recommendation that she buy private medical insurance post haste so as to avoid putting herself in the hands of the NHS, and a greeting card with unfamiliar handwriting upon it. She opened this.

A panda sitting under an umbrella was its cover. A note was inside: *Ciao, Barbara. I ask from Thomas Lynley your address. He gives it to me. You stay well, I hope. Also I. I come to London with Marco and Bianca four days when is Christmas. We practise English together. Bianca talks it well. I not much. If is enough time we would see you. Also Thomas we see and the sights of London. You write to me if you want to meet with us? You see here I learn English some since you are in Lucca.*

It was signed only *Salvatore*. Lo Bianco was the rest of his name. Marco and Bianca were his children. She'd met them all during her folly-driven trip to Tuscany in the spring. It was largely down to Salvatore Lo Bianco that her friend Taymullah Azhar and his daughter Hadiyyah – former occupants of the darkened ground floor flat at the front of the building behind which Barbara lived – had been able to make their escape to Pakistan. Whether they needed to remain there . . . ? Perhaps Salvatore Lo Bianco could tell her that.

She would definitely welcome the Italian and his children to London, she decided. She'd liked the bloke.

She wandered – newly toasted Pop Tart in hand – to her answer machine, which was blinking to alert her to a message.

'Told Mum about that goulash you made me,' was the first. 'When she finally stopped laughing she said you're meant to come over here for some proper lessons in cooking, innit. Ring me, eh? She's dead serious, Barb.'

And then, 'I know, I know.' It was Dorothea's voice. 'I *said* have a think and then let me know but I *did* want to tell you that I've found a tap class. It's in Southall of all places, so it's a bit of a slog, but consider the multicultural experiences we'll have if we decide to take it on. Plus curry. God knows there'll be masses of curry. *Guiltless* curry as well because we'll have all that massive exercise before we sit down and tuck in. There. I've said enough. Think about it. The auto-biography and all.'

Barbara shook her head with a chuckle. It was odd, she thought, how one could look at this particular form of human contact: an intrusion or an introduction. It was up to her to decide what to call it.

She was about to launch herself onto the day bed to pick up where she'd recently left off in her latest romance novel when she caught sight of the carrier bag that she'd unceremoniously stuffed beneath it upon the conclusion of her sojourn into Middlesex Street with Dorothea. It seemed ages ago and she'd nearly – but not quite – forgotten the experience. What she *had* forgotten was what Dorothea had purchased for her: those trousers, their accompanying jacket, that shirt.

She reached for the bag and dumped its contents onto the day bed. She had to admit that none of it was half bad. Not what she'd have chosen for herself, but perhaps that had been the point. And it wouldn't hurt to try everything on. She didn't have to wear it in public.

All pieces fitted, she discovered once she'd shed her old clothes and shimmied into the new ones. Odd, that, as she hadn't told Dorothea her sizes. But the departmental secretary apparently had an unerring eye when it came to clothing.

She had to stand on the seat of the loo to see herself completely, and when she did this, Barbara found that the colour of the trousers and the jacket was right. So was the cut. It was rather amazing.

She *could*, she reckoned, wear this sort of clobber to work. Of course, a few of her colleagues would take the mickey, but that was only to be expected. It wasn't the worst thing in the world to amuse one's fellows in the workplace. It also wasn't the worst thing in the world to cooperate with her superiors when it came to her manner of dress. She would have vastly preferred to go her own way in this, but she could chalk it up to a new experience, as Dorothea would have put it. There was the autobiography to consider, after all.

Aside from speaking to her on the phone once, Lynley hadn't had contact with Daidre in four days. Even then, their contact had been simple: had he mentioned that Daidre now lived quite near his colleague Barbara Havers? had been the excuse he'd used for ringing her, and the subsequent conversation they'd had after that introductory remark had kept them safely away from any issue more personal than the pressures each of them faced at work: Daidre was ethically opposed to breeding programmes whose intentions were to produce more animals for captivity and this was putting her into conflict with several powerful members of the zoo's board of directors. For his part, Lynley reported on the successful conclusion of the case in Dorset. Admittedly, he was still walking carefully round Superintendent Ardery after using the Cambridge police to orchestrate Barbara's involvement in the investigation. But at least Havers and Nkata had produced a result on the final day they'd been given to produce one prior to being recalled to town. Et cetera et cetera went the conversation. Lynley knew they were skirting round what needed to be said. He reckoned Daidre knew it as well.

*I'm in love with you* hung between them.

He'd had dinner at home in Belgravia on this evening, but he found that there was no pleasure in solitude at the end of the day. He had the morning's newspapers to finish reading, the day's post to go through, a phone call from his sister to return, and an invitation to dinner with Simon and Deborah St James – 'I swear I won't do the cooking, Tommy, and we do long to meet Daidre, you know,' Deborah had said – to consider. All of these activities could have occupied him once he'd eaten his meal. Still, the only activity he wished to pursue was seeing Daidre.

He rang her. He made no excuse. He didn't lie. 'I think we've gone off course,' he said. 'May I come to see you?'

It was late for a call upon anyone, but Daidre said that she would welcome a visit. 'I've been missing you,' she added. 'Work's been deadly – when isn't it, actually? – and you could be the antidote for my anxiety about having taken on this bloody job in the first place.'

'Politics at the zoo?' he said.

'Politics at the zoo. Anyway, do come. Are you nearby?'

'Belgravia, I'm afraid.'

'Well, that can't be helped, can it? If you don't mind the trek, I'd love to see you.'

And so he went. He'd had four days to think things over: what he'd meant about being in love with her and how being in love with her – or with anyone – led to having expectations that, frankly, he'd preferred to ignore. Supreme among those expectations were those that had their roots in Daidre's background and in what she'd tried time and again to communicate to him about that background and its effect on who she was and who she was likely to remain.

When he rang the bell, her voice said, 'Shall I assume it's you?'

'You shall,' he replied and when she admitted him, he pushed open the building's door to find her waiting in a shaft of light from her sitting room. She was, he saw, attired for bed and it came to him that, exhausted from her day of zoological politicking as she probably was, she might vastly prefer simply to sleep. He said to her, 'Perhaps I shouldn't have come. Did I awaken you with the call?'

'You did. But you take priority over sleep.'

She closed the door and shot the bolt home. She'd opened a bottle of wine, he saw. Along with two glasses and a plate of grapes, it was on the old window cum table that they'd been using for ages. She'd not got beyond painting the walls of the sitting room. This dispirited him for all it implied. Lack of progress on the place suggested that she was calling a halt – or at least a hiatus – to them as well. He couldn't actually blame her, he decided. He'd been pushing her, and she wasn't the sort of woman who was going to like that.

She poured them each a glass of the wine. It was very good. When he told her this, she said with a smile, 'I've found that buying wine based strictly on the appearance of the label leads to all sorts of completely delicious surprises.'

'I'll adopt the practice tomorrow,' he promised.

'Of course, I choose only Italian wines, so there is that,' she admitted. She lifted her glass to him and said, 'Congratulations on a case concluded and at least part of your reputation redeemed. Was Superintendent Ardery pleased?'

'She'd have vastly preferred we all go down with the ship.'

'She hasn't forgiven you yet?'

'She's a woman who knows how to hold a grudge.'

'Ah.' She reached for some grapes. She said, 'Well. Hello, Tommy. Do sit. You have an expression that suggests you've something to say.'

He sat. They were thus opposite each other with the old window between them, much as they'd been when consuming the endless pizzas that had been their meals over the past few months. He'd have preferred to be closer to her – all the better to touch her hand as he spoke – but his preferences were what had brought them to this pass, and he was finally able to recognise that.

He said, 'I've put us in a difficult place. I'd like to alter that, if you'll allow it.'

She frowned. 'I'm not sure what you mean.'

'I'll explain if you'll listen.'

'Of course I'll listen.'

'I've had to think it through, what it means that you're so fiercely independent, what it means that you're – truly, Daidre – the most self-reliant woman I've ever met.'

'I did try to tell you that, Tommy. From the very first or at least from the moment I considered coming to London.'

'You did. But, of course, ego told me that was all mere talk. I'm attracted to her, I want what I want, she'll fall into line eventually.'

She nodded and looked regretful, hearing this. 'I never do,

you know. It *is* my curse. I'm fairly certain I told you that as well. There's a point beyond which I simply don't go or can't be known or . . . call it what you will. It's been the death of every relationship I've had.'

'I remember. You told me. Either that or something very like. But what I want to say to you is that I believe I understand what's behind it and you and everything. I've been expecting you to put aside your past when your past is what created you in the first place. It seems obvious, of course.'

'It *is* an anchor, though. Or perhaps better said, a ball and chain. You do see that, don't you?'

'I do. But more important is that I expected you somehow just to shed it. But how does one ever put aside one's past? I've never been able to put mine aside, and yet I'd persuaded myself to believe you could manage to put aside yours and not allow it to affect how you might come to feel about me.'

'It does stand between us. It always will, you know.'

'I do. Now. I do know that.'

'And?' she said. 'Or is it *but*?'

He took a sip of wine. He gave a tired chuckle. 'I'm not sure. I know that I want you in my life, Daidre. And I want to say that you are free to define us – whatever we're to be to each other – as you will. You can define us in any way that works for you or gives you comfort or allows you the space or freedom or whatever it is that you need.'

She considered this, her gaze on her wine which was ruby in colour, deeply so, reflective of the Tuscan vineyards where its grapes had grown. 'Want,' she said.

'Hmmm?'

'You said you *want* to say all that. But something stops you.'

'Of course. I'm a man who likes his hatches battened, and being with you requires leaving them . . . well, unbattened. God knows for how long, but possibly forever. That, my darling, is not going to be easy for me.'

'You seem to be saying you're willing to try.'

'I seem to be saying I'm determined to try. I can't promise

you I'll be successful. But I can promise you my very best effort.'

He saw her swallow. She looked away from him although there was nothing to see through the bay window since the shrubbery there was so overgrown that it acted virtually as a wall. She wasn't at all a woman who cried, but he fancied he saw the glitter of tears in her hazel eyes.

'You're a very good person,' she said quietly. 'That's always made everything difficult, Tommy.'

'Difficult but not impossible?' he said.

'That's something I simply don't know.'

He was silent. There was, he reckoned, nothing else to be said. He'd done his best to explain himself to her and to make some sort of declaration that might soothe her. The rest was completely up to her. He felt a heavy thudding his chest. It was wretched, he realised, to allow the future to be defined in any way by someone else. He saw that as well and at last, he realised. He wanted to tell her, but he suspected he'd said enough.

She stood finally. She placed her glass on their makeshift table. She said to him, 'I've something to show you,' and she extended her hand.

He allowed himself to be drawn to his feet, setting his own glass down, and feeling her fingers twine with his. She led him from the sitting room, past her finished bathroom, and into the bedroom. The walls were still not painted, he saw, the floor was still not refinished or sanded, and the window had yet to be replaced. But where the camp bed had sufficed for her to sleep inside her sleeping bag, a real and blessedly normal bed stood. A floor lamp stood next to it, and a box served as a temporary bedside table with a clock and a glass of water upon it. But the only point was the bed itself, and it was large, not king sized but more than enough for two people to sleep quite comfortably in it. Together.

She said, 'I'll have to work round it when I finally get to this part of the flat, but it did seem to me that it was time.

It's not a perfect situation, of course. But really, when you think about it, what actually is?'

'Very little, I find,' he admitted.

'So will it do for now, Tommy?'

'Daidre . . .' He took a steadying breath. 'Yes. It certainly will.'

# Acknowledgements

I owe a great many thanks to Dr Doug Lyle, who first suggested sodium azide to me as an efficient poison and who also revealed to me how astoundingly easy it is to purchase. He fielded questions once I had dispatched my victim, and he was infinitely patient about providing me with all sorts of information. My fellow writer Patricia Smiley put me on to Doug, and I thank her for this, as I thank my fellow writers Nancy Horan, Jane Hamilton, Gail Tsukiyama, and Karen Joy Fowler for moral support when I needed it. My additional gratitude goes to Dr Gayl Hartell, who provided much insight into aberrant personality types.

My cheerful assistant Charlene Coe did research for me, never inquiring why she was delving into everything from the various uses of baking powder to the dates of the Industrial Revolution. During the time of my creation of this novel, she also did laundry, shopped for groceries, fetched the mail, walked the dog, taught the cat to walk on a leash, acted as sous chef, watered plants, arranged flowers, saw to the upkeep of my car, and helped run the Elizabeth George Foundation.

My husband Tom McCabe graciously accepted my trips to England as well as the lengthy disappearances into my office required to bring this novel to life. He also heroically managed to rid our property of marauding deer, giving me one less thing to worry about.

My longtime cold reader, Susan Berner, asked merciless questions and made merciless comments on the draft of the manuscript, and these were indisputably helpful in my wrestling a complicated story to the mat.

My editor in the US, Brian Tart, was wonderful, generous, and completely supportive about my getting the manuscript in to him 'when it's completed' and not necessarily when the deadline called for it to be completed. His editorial comments – along with those of my UK editor Nick Sayers – proved critical to the completion of the story.

And as always, I must thank my literary agent, Robert Gottlieb, for his endless endeavors on my behalf.

In the UK, I turned often to the indefatigable and always resourceful Swati Gamble, of Hodder & Stoughton, who has for so long graciously tracked down individuals whom I need to interview or facts that I need to check.

My UK publicist Karen Geary suggested both Spitalfields and Camberwell to me as potential London locations, and she was spot-on with what they had to provide me in the way of settings. She also kept me amused during the time of this writing by making sure I had the latest thrilling details on Prince George and his parents.

Oxfords Bakery in Dorset became a central location for the novel, and its owner was good to show me around, to allow me to take photographs of odd objects, and to answer my questions.

The topographical gumshoeing I did in London and in Dorset provided me with all the locations for this book, and while I have attempted to be accurate in all things, the acute reader will occasionally notice that something may have been moved slightly to accommodate the needs of the story. But most things are as I saw them during the time of my research, including the amazing find of the Wren Clinic, where India Elliott plies her trade as an acupuncturist.

Mistakes herein are mine alone.

In the best books, the ending often comes as a shock.
Not just because of that one last twist in the tale,
but because you have been so absorbed in their world,
that coming back to the harsh light of reality is a jolt.

If that describes you now, then perhaps you should track down
some new leads, and find new suspense in other worlds.

Join us at www.hodder.co.uk, or follow us on
Twitter @hodderbooks, and you can tap in to a
community of fellow thrill-seekers.

Whether you want to find out more about this book,
or a particular author, watch trailers and interviews, have
the chance to win early limited editions, or simply browse
our expert readers' selection of the very best books,
we think you'll find what you're looking for.

And if you don't, that's the place to tell us what's missing.

**We love what we do, and we'd love you to be part of it.**

www.hodder.co.uk

@hodderbooks

HodderBooks

HodderBooks